I0787971

UNSILENCED

AUNG SAN SUU KYI

Conversations *from a* Myanmar Prison

—

A Work of Fiction *by* Alan Clements

Disclaimer

This is a work of fiction inspired by real events and figures. All dialogues and narrative scenarios are products of the author's imagination, created to challenge authoritarianism and advocate for justice. While historical events, public figures, and documented facts are referenced throughout, their portrayal within this fictional narrative is artistic and not intended as a literal or factual representation. Characters may embody real individuals, including living persons, but their words and actions in this context are dramatized for literary and ethical exploration. Any resemblance to specific private interactions or undocumented events is purely coincidental.

Published in 2025 by World Dharma Publications

Library of Congress Cataloging-in-Publication Data
Clements, Alan 1951 —

UNSILENCED
Aung San Suu Kyi:
Conversations *from a* Myanmar Prison
A Work of Fiction *by* Alan Clements

p. cm. **ISBN** 978-1-953508-35-5
1. Myanmar—Politics and government—2021–present
2. Military dictatorship—Psychological aspects
3. Human rights—Myanmar
4. Resistance movements—Myanmar
5. Freedom—Political and philosophical perspectives
6. Authoritarianism—Global impact
7. Aung San Suu Kyi—Political imprisonment
8. Revolution—Nonviolent and armed resistance
9. Consciousness—Political and ethical dimensions
10. Global justice—Political and environmental activism
11. Social movements—Democracy and human rights
First printing, September 19, 2025
ISBN 978-1-953508-35-5

WORLD DHARMA PUBLICATIONS
www.WorldDharma.com

UNSILENCED

AUNG SAN SUU KYI
Conversations *from a* Myanmar Prison

A Work of Fiction *by* Alan Clements

"Freedom and Democracy Are Dreams You Never Give Up."
—AUNG SAN SUU KYI, Myanmar's Imprisoned Nobel Peace Laureate

WORLD DHARMA PUBLICATIONS

To the people of Myanmar—
the dissidents and the dreamers,
the fearless and the fallen,
the ones who rise with nothing but dignity
and refuse to kneel.
To the voices silenced,
the lives stolen,
the names erased from history—
you are not forgotten.
You are not lost.
You live in memory,
in resistance,
in the marrow of those who carry your courage forward.
    To those crushed beneath the weight of terror,
who still find a way to sing, to write, to speak truth.
To the prisoners who remain defiant behind bars.
To the monks, the mothers, the students,
the rebels with empty hands and unbreakable spirits.
    To the exiles who carry their homeland in their bones.

To the journalists and the artists,
the teachers and the truth-tellers—unbowed, unbroken.
To the fighters who fight with conscience.
To the lovers who love with justice.
    And to all who stand against tyranny—
across borders, across generations, across time—
who risk everything
not only for a nation's liberation,
but for the deeper freedom:
the right to think, to speak, to imagine,
to live with dignity.
    This book is for you.
This book is because of you.
And one day—
beyond barbed wire,
beyond propaganda,
beyond silence—
freedom will rise.
And when it does,
you will be remembered not as victims—
but as the authors of a revolution.

If you could leave the world
with one message, what would it be?

Daw Suu:
Freedom is not given.
It is earned—
moment by moment,
act by act,
by those who refuse to give up.

Even here, in this cell,
I am free.

Free because my mind,
my heart,
my soul
remain unbroken.

That is the freedom
no dictator
can take away.

And to the people of Myanmar,
to those around the world
who still believe
in the power of truth:

Do not give up.

The path is long,
but the destination
is worth
every step.

The quintessential revolution is that of the spirit, born of an intellectual conviction of the need for change in those mental attitudes and values which shape the course of a nation's development. A revolution which aims merely at changing official policies and institutions with a view to an improvement in material conditions has little chance of genuine success. Without a revolution of the spirit, the forces which produced the iniquities of the old order would continue to be operative, posing a constant threat to the process of reform and regeneration.

Gandhi, that great apostle of non-violence, and Aung San, the founder of a national army, were very different personalities, but as there is an inevitable sameness about the challenges of authoritarian rule anywhere at any time, so there is a similarity in the intrinsic qualities of those who rise up to meet the challenge.

It is man's vision of a world fit for rational, civilized humanity which leads him to dare and to suffer to build societies free from want and fear. Concepts such as truth, justice and compassion cannot be dismissed as trite when these are often the only bulwarks which stand against ruthless power.

Aung San Suu Kyi,
from Sakharov Prize
for Freedom of Thought
Acceptance Speech,
Strasbourg,
October 22, 2013

TABLE OF CONTENTS

———— ◆ ————

FOREWORD

———◆———

The human spirit, under the weight of tyranny, does not falter—it burns brighter. *Unsilenced* stands as a testament to that unquenchable flame: a literary revolt unveiling the soul of resistance and casting light upon the shadow of oppression.

Transcending Myanmar's borders, it probes the architecture of dictatorship, the rhythm of revolution, and the moral ferocity of nonviolence—offering a prismatic lens on the universal quest for freedom and dignity against the forces of dehumanization.

This is not solely the story of one woman—though Aung San Suu Kyi, Myanmar's Nobel Peace Laureate, now 80, in her fifth year of solitary confinement, her fate uncertain—radiates a clarity so enduring it defies both and walls. It is a mirror for our era, reflecting the courage of millions who confront the machinery of tyranny through the sacred alchemy of conscience: the transformative act of forging defiance from suffering, and song from silence.

In these pages, I weave dialogues distilled from decades of heeding voices broken yet unbowed, drawing on Aung San Suu Kyi's moral clarity and the courage of countless others. *Unsilenced* is no mere record; it is a confrontation—with the mindset of power that demands submission, the surge of revolution that rejects it, and the leadership that heals while it resists.

Here, dictatorship is revealed not merely as a regime, but as a pathology: a relentless will to dominate, stretching from Moscow's halls to Beijing's surveillance networks, to the algorithmic chains of digital autocracy.

Revolution is recast—not as disorder, but as the alchemy of awakened conscience, forging freedom through sacrifice. Nelson Mandela did, enduring twenty-seven years of captivity to transform apartheid into a vision of reconciliation. Nonviolence emerges not as passivity, but as a force fiercer than fear—a resolute will wielded by those who shape history with truth, as Mahatma Gandhi did with a handful of salt and Martin Luther King Jr. with the moral force of his dream.

Myanmar's citizens' revolution, blazing since the 2021 coup, is a crucible for this alchemy of steadfast conviction. Over 10,000 lives lost, 3.5 million displaced, 22,000 imprisoned—yet the junta, a criminal syndicate trafficking in fentanyl and terror, cannot quell the spirit of resistance.

This is no isolated tragedy; it resounds in the global call for liberation—from Sudan's blood-soaked streets to Ukraine's unbowed trenches, from Soweto's defiant cries of decades past to Tiananmen's stifled whispers of 1989, from Chile's marches against Pinochet in the 1970s to Belarus's ongoing protests against autocracy, from the courage of Kabul's schoolgirls today to the resolve of Hong Kong's umbrella-wielding youth in recent years. *Unsilenced* captures this shared rhythm, revealing how ordinary people—students, monks, mothers, poets— become architects of destiny, their defiance a blueprint for humanity's renewal.

As one who has witnessed Myanmar's enduring struggle for freedom, I hold this truth: history bends not through domination, but through the steadfast power of moral courage. *Unsilenced* is my pledge to amplify that power—not as a chronicler of events, but as a steward of the unseen: the dignity that resists, the truth that outlasts exile and imprisonment.

These dialogues illuminate a leadership born not of power, but in perseverance—forged in hunger strikes, whispered prayers, smuggled letters, and the resolute choice to speak when silence would be safer.

This volume is a charge—to readers, critics, and visionaries: immerse yourselves in its truths. Let them awaken your voice, your pen, your platform. In an age of rising authoritarianism, *Unsilenced* is not merely a book—it is a summons to conscience, a revolution in language, a radiant act of defiance. It declares that freedom must be safeguarded, not assumed—that silence, unchallenged, becomes complicity.

Join this cause. Let *Unsilenced* ignite your resolve, as it has mine, to confront tyranny, uphold dignity, and build a world where freedom is not a privilege, but a birthright. The hour is now.

—Alan Clements
SEPTEMBER 1, 2025

"In the end, we will remember not the words of our enemies,
but the silence of our friends."
MARTIN LUTHER KING JR.

PREFACE

———◆———

In a hidden corner of Naypyidaw—Myanmar's fortress capital, engineered by paranoid generals to enshrine their illusion of permanence—I imagine a conversation the world was never meant to hear. A dialogue with Aung San Suu Kyi—Myanmar's unlawfully imprisoned, democratically elected State Counsellor—woven in silence, memory, and exile. A communion beneath history's veil, where fiction becomes a crucible for truths too vital to be silenced.

This book is that imagined encounter: a clandestine exchange between two voices—hers, silenced yet resonant; mine, listening across decades with reverence, resolve, and a journalist's unrelenting gaze. Two souls—one in solitary confinement, one free—bound by a shared vow to summon truth, accountability, and vision into a space of moral imagination. It is a work of fiction, yes. But more profoundly, it is an act of remembrance, of conscience—a literary defiance against erasure.

To conjure that voice today, I return to the moment it first entered my life—with the clarity of memory and the urgency of truths yet to be spoken.

I first met Aung San Suu Kyi at her home in Rangoon in 1995, shortly after her release from six years of house arrest. She was already a global icon, having won the Nobel Peace Prize in 1991 for her nonviolent resistance to Myanmar's military regime. Her name was a beacon—of courage, defiance, and hope. Yet in Myanmar, hope was still nascent. The generals had not only confined her—they sought to erase her from the nation's soul.

My journey with Myanmar began in the late 1970s as a Buddhist monk at Mahasi Thathana Yeiktha in Rangoon, guided by the Venerable Mahasi Sayadaw and, after his passing in 1982, the Venerable Sayadaw U Pandita. They taught me that mindfulness was not a mere practice, but a way of being: an unceasing engagement with awareness in every moment. It demanded not only precision, but a deeper wisdom—one that navigates complexity without yielding to judgment, summoning moral courage in a world aflame.

I learned, too, from the laypeople who filled the monastery—a culture vibrant with reverence, curiosity, and boundless generosity. Yet beneath this vitality lay a grim reality: we lived not in tranquility, but under dictatorship. Surveilled and fearful, silence was not serenity—it was survival.

After disrobing in 1984, I returned often, traversing Myanmar's remote villages, ancient ruins, cave temples, and teahouses. I wandered through cultural splendor, hardship, and the oppressive hush of tyranny. The *Dhamma* of my monastic years gained new resonance: awakening is not confined to meditation halls, but is a sacred act of presence—caring for others as kin amid suffering.

On August 8, 1988, silence shattered. The *8888 Uprising* erupted as students in Rangoon sparked a nationwide rebellion. What began in classrooms surged into streets, uniting monks, doctors, children, students, housewives, and farmers—hundreds of thousands demanding freedom. For a fleeting moment, the nation's conscience stirred awake.

Then came the reckoning. On September 18, the military seized power in a savage coup. Soldiers fired on crowds, stormed hospitals, and left bodies strewn in the streets. Thousands perished, with eyewitnesses reporting mass graves where the living were burned alongside the dead. Sacred pagodas bore the blood of unarmed protesters.

In this crucible, Aung San Suu Kyi returned from England to care for her dying mother, only to step into a nation on the brink of transformation. Amid collapse and carnage, she emerged—quietly, almost reluctantly—as the voice of a silenced people. Within months, she became the revolution's beacon: principled, unarmed, resolute.

Soon after, I ventured into the war-torn jungles of northern Myanmar, where thousands of student leaders—the heartbeat of the *8888 Uprising*—had fled to survive and resist. Sheltered by ethnic armed organizations, they forged fragile alliances, trained for battle, and clung to hope. The regime's response was merciless: villages incinerated, forests strafed, rice fields reduced to ash—a landscape turned deliberate killing field.

There, I became one of the first foreign witnesses to document the systematic persecution of Myanmar's ethnic minorities. The atrocities

I recorded—villages razed, civilians executed, cultures besieged—formed the foundation of my first book, *Burma: The Next Killing Fields?* published with a foreword by His Holiness the Dalai Lama.

Among young revolutionaries—once students, some former monks and nuns, now wielding rifles with trembling hands and steadfast hearts—I confronted the limits of nonviolence. I patrolled with them, often under fire, in silences heavy as prayer. Around jungle campfires, their stories—of loss, righteous fury, and unyielding justice—kindled a sacred clarity. Their moral outrage—not mere emotion, but clarity forged in pain—was a sobering necessity.

Could nonviolence prevail where bullets ruled, where mercy met slaughter? These were not abstract queries, but the pulse of a moral reckoning. They drove me deeper—to listen, to learn, to seek voices like Aung San Suu Kyi's, who dared to believe nonviolence could be a force more powerful than fear.

From those firelit nights, a new calling emerged—not of combat, but of conscience. It drew me to the woman whose clarity embodied its soul: Daw Aung San Suu Kyi.

When I sat with Daw Suu, I met not a politician, but a presence—still, precise, fierce. She embodied the *Dhamma* with singular humility, her gaze—steady as candlelight in still air—bearing the weight of generations who suffered yet stood unbowed. She saw no divide between inner and outer freedom, fusing universal principles of awakening with revolutionary action. Our conversations, held in her lakeside Rangoon home under constant surveillance, spanned politics, meditation, mortality, literature, and the moral limits of compromise.

For five months, we recorded dialogues that became *The Voice of Hope*—smuggled out of Myanmar, translated into numerous languages, and hailed by The London Observer as "a possible future for politics itself." Her words—vows of justice and inner freedom, democracy and mindfulness—were not mere opinions, but sacred commitments.

Those transcripts revealed a society scarred by tyranny, yet radiant with resilience. They illuminated a philosophy of freedom grounded in courage, compassion, and resolute truth. Daw Suu introduced me to her colleagues, mentors, and family, each voice deepening my reverence for their vision: a free Myanmar built on justice, reconciliation, and radical inclusivity.

This work continued in *Burma's Revolution of the Spirit*, co-authored with Leslie Kean, a photographic tribute to Myanmar's nonviolent struggle, featuring a foreword by the Dalai Lama and essays by eight Nobel Peace laureates. I also contributed as script revisionist and principal adviser for *Beyond Rangoon*, a feature film portraying Myanmar's fight for freedom.

In 2012, I reunited with Daw Suu in San Francisco, where she received the Václav Havel Award for Creative Dissent, after Myanmar's former General Thein Sein lifted a 17-year ban on my return. Her counsel inspired me to persist, connecting me with revolutionaries whose voices shaped *Burma's Voices of Freedom*, co-authored with Fergus Harlow—a four-volume oral history probing dictatorship, resistance, and the moral fortitude of prisoners of conscience.

Since the February 1, 2021 coup, Aung San Suu Kyi has been abducted by the junta and held incommunicado—no letters, no statements, no proof of life. As of September 2025, her fate remains shrouded, her survival unconfirmed. Yet, her presence endures—vivid

in the hearts of millions rising in resistance, her name—Ma Suu—
etched in whispers in bombed-out villages, daubed on protest walls,
and carried in the dreams of a generation.

Myanmar's catastrophe echoes global tragedies: China's stifling of
dissent, Sudan's genocidal wars, Yemen's humanitarian ruin, Ukraine
and Russia's mass graves and staggering death toll, Tibet's silent
suffocation, Gaza's unthinkable horror—all testaments to humanity's
capacity for cruelty and the urgent need for conscience unbound by
borders.

But Myanmar's crisis is a full-scale civil war—regions ablaze,
the military unleashing fire from the skies, while revolutionary
forces—students, artists, farmers, monks—fight with resolve forged
in sacred fury.

A dream of a free, federal democracy persists, unyielding, echoing
South Africa's moral triumph, Romania's liberation, or Havel's Velvet
Revolution. Aung San Suu Kyi's "revolution of the spirit" burns in
millions.

Hope persists—not as blind optimism, but as conscience's steady
flame: quiet, defiant, inextinguishable. At Myanmar's heart burns
a metaphor: a candle piercing the totalitarian dark, its fragile flicker
At Myanmar's heart burns a metaphor: a single candle piercing the
totalitarian dark, its fragile flicker bearing the spark that could ignite a
global awakening. It invites us to stand with Myanmar, to honor Aung
San Suu Kyi, and to embody the truth that freedom matters—dared and
shared, it becomes unstoppable.

This summons us to one of the modern era's most courageous
struggles for liberation, a rebellion radiant with spiritual resilience.
Daw Suu wrote, "Feel always free… Nobody can detain [your] mind…
master your mind [and] nobody can abuse you." Her call rises from a
nation at war, urging us to act when freedom bleeds and hope treads
through fire.

My years in Myanmar revealed what emerges when conscience
stirs—when people act for a purpose beyond self. From the 2007 Saffron
Revolution to the 2020s' fierce youth, Myanmar's struggle intertwines
with the world's quest to end tyranny. Since 2021, the people have
risen—across mountains, deltas, monasteries, and jungle camps—in a

revolution blending rifles with reverence, strategy with soul, yet rooted in Aung San Suu Kyi's moral clarity.

This is no mere rebellion—it is a vision for a federal democratic union, grounded in equality and the sovereign will of the people, a defiance of dehumanization born of spirit. Aung San Suu Kyi's life reminds us: true change begins within, and every lasting revolution is fueled by conscience.

I envision a liberated Myanmar—a nation reborn ethically and spiritually, a democracy with a human face, guided by compassion over cruelty. This revolution is a moral compass for the world, a summons to decency against the machinery of oppression, resounding across borders and histories.

How do we claim this revolution? By answering with hope's insistent voice, conscience's steady sound, and the courage to act before silence rewrites history. *Unsilenced* is that testament—a refusal to forget, to be silent.

Though fictional in form, *Unsilenced* is rooted in truth—drawn from nearly five decades of engagement with Myanmar, thousands of hours listening to its people, and, most intimately, Aung San Suu Kyi's voice. Not a mythologized icon, but a woman—scarred, resolute, radiant with loving-kindness—*metta*. These reconstructed dialogues, crafted with scrupulous care, distill over half a million words drawn from her speeches, statements, and interviews—meticulously transcribed by Fergus Harlow—and enriched by our many private conversations, as well as those with her closest colleagues, mentors, and teachers.

They are further shaped by an ongoing, intuitive communion with Daw Suu during her solitary confinement—a form of meditative attunement rooted in the contemplative practices we both received from our shared *Dhamma* teacher, the late Venerable Sayadaw U Pandita.

Aung San Suu Kyi said in her 2012 Nobel Lecture, "The fate of prisoners of conscience anywhere has become the concern of peoples everywhere—an age when democracy and human rights are widely accepted as the birthright of all."

I write as a witness and ally, shaped by Myanmar's monasteries, temples, and graves—as monk, journalist, and friend. *Unsilenced* breaks her silence—a literary rebellion, a vow in the dark.

Myanmar's crisis ranks among the world's gravest humanitarian tragedies:

- Over 22,000 political prisoners endure torture, rape, or starvation. More than 10,000 civilians have been killed, including children and monks.
- 3.5 million are displaced, villages erased by airstrikes and scorched-earth campaigns.
- The junta funds its war, in part, through fentanyl, heroin, and methamphetamine trafficking, enabled by China, Russia, and global inaction.
- On March 28, 2025, a 7.7-magnitude earthquake killed over 3,600, razed thousands of monasteries and schools, and left Mandalay and Naypyidaw reeling. The junta weaponizes even disaster, hoarding aid while villages suffer.

This is not governance, but a military-run criminal syndicate—trafficking in death and fear, masquerading as a government. A relentless slow-motion-genocide unfolds in real time, while the world turns away.

Yet, the people rise—across ethnicities and faiths, united in resistance, fighting for dignity and a future worthy of their children. *Unsilenced* stands with them—unapologetic, unbowed, refusing to seek permission to speak. It is a rebellion in language, channeling what Aung San Suu Kyi might proclaim today: truths, questions, a vision for a Myanmar reborn in justice.

These pages unfold as imagined conversations—spanning time, borders, and silence—not as transcripts, but as reconstructions shaped by lived encounters. What Aung San Suu Kyi cannot say from confinement lives here—her conscience, her clarity, her *Dhamma*—radiant with *metta*, steadfast in dignity, ablaze with truth.

May this book spur us to speak when silence tempts, to resist not with hatred, but with truth, forging a free Myanmar rooted in dialogue and unshakable compassion.

Václav Havel wrote, "I stopped waiting for the world to improve and exercised my right to intervene… or at least to express my opinion about it." *Unsilenced* is such an intervention—a refusal to wait, a vow to bear witness, a declaration that silence is complicity.

I call upon world leaders—from President Trump to democratic heads of state and architects of justice everywhere:

- Demand the immediate release of Aung San Suu Kyi and all political prisoners.
- Designate the Myanmar junta a terrorist organization.
- Freeze their assets, sever financial lifelines, and enforce diplomatic isolation.
- Expose the complicity of China, Russia, and others in the junta's war crimes.
- Support Myanmar's people in building a federal democracy rooted in justice, equality, and spiritual resilience.

This is a moral emergency—a test of our shared humanity. Howard Zinn reminds us, "The most effective political acts are often the human voice's simple sound." Mahatma Gandhi wrote, "When I despair, I remember that… tyrants and murderers may seem invincible for a time—but in the end, they always fall. Always."

Aung San Suu Kyi is not a relic—she is the beating heart of a nation that refuses to surrender. A leader. A warrior. A guide. In an age of rising authoritarianism—from Moscow to Manila, from digital shadows to unseen tyrannies—her life declares: freedom is not inherited. It is lived, chosen, defended daily.

Even in silence, she speaks—an unextinguished flame, a vow undimmed, a conscience that will not fade. *Unsilenced* weaves a bridge to the future she foresaw: "The ultimate answer to injustice lies in awakening a shared humanity—a revolution not of vengeance, but of values."

Free Aung San Suu Kyi. Free Myanmar. Do not wait. The time is now.

—*Alan Clements*
September 19, 2025

THE COMPASS OF FREEDOM

———

Author's Prelude

In 1988, Aung San Suu Kyi returned to Myanmar not as a revolutionary, but as a daughter, compelled by duty to care for her ailing mother. This personal act of devotion, devoid of political intent, became the unlikely catalyst for a national awakening. Her presence in Yangon coincided with a nation simmering under decades of authoritarian rule, and her quiet resolve ignited a movement that would reshape Myanmar's struggle for democracy.

This chapter explores the origins of that movement, not as the story of a singular figure, but as the convergence of individual conscience and collective aspiration. Aung San Suu Kyi's return marked a turning point—not because she sought leadership, but because her unwavering commitment to truth resonated with a people long silenced. Her moral clarity, rooted in empathy rather than ideology, became a beacon for a nation yearning for dignity and self-determination.

Drawing on her writings, speeches, and the accounts of those who rallied beside her, our dialogue examines how one woman's fidelity to principle galvanized a broader uprising. It traces the ripple effects of her stand against oppression, from the streets of Yangon to the rural heartlands, where ordinary citizens found their own courage mirrored in hers. It also situates her within Myanmar's broader historical context, as the daughter of independence hero Aung San, whose unfinished vision for a free nation animated her resolve and inspired others.

This is not a hagiography. It is a rigorous inquiry into the dynamics of moral courage and collective action. Through meticulous analysis, the chapter unpacks how Aung San Suu Kyi's personal integrity—forged in solitude, tested by surveillance and house arrest—became a touchstone for a movement. It invites readers to consider the power of principled defiance in the face of systemic injustice and to reflect on the universal question of what it means to act on one's deepest convictions, even at great personal cost.

◆ ◆ ◆

Alan Clements: Daw Suu, over the years you have spoken about the profound importance of "following one's inner truth"—what you call a "revolution of the spirit"—an unwavering inner compass guiding us to live with dignity, conscience, and moral courage, while confronting the ancient forces of *lobha* (greed), *dosa* (hatred), and *moha* (delusion).

That inner compass, so firmly rooted in your sense of duty and integrity, brought you back to Burma in 1988, when your mother, Daw Khin Kyi, suffered a severe stroke. What began as a deeply personal journey—a daughter answering the call to care for her ailing mother—quickly became revolutionary in scope.

At the same time, Burma was erupting in political unrest, with the *"8888 Uprising"* unleashing a nationwide cry for freedom and democracy. You once said, *"I could not, as my father's daughter, remain indifferent to all that was unfolding."*

That decision, born of both duty and intuition, set you on a path of extraordinary sacrifice—a lifetime dedicated to nonviolent revolution, reconciliation, and the enduring hope of your people.

Now, decades later, imprisoned once again, your life continues to inspire a nation—and far beyond its borders.

Daw Suu, what does it truly mean to live by an inner compass so unwavering, especially when the cost is so profound? In the depths of this dark chapter, how does that sacred wellspring of truth and courage sustain you—not only as a leader, but as a human being?

Aung San Suu Kyi: Alan, the decision to return to Burma in 1988 was not a calculated one. It was immediate and deeply personal. My mother, Daw Khin Kyi, needed me—her call was sacred, clear, and undeniable.

Yet when I arrived, I found myself stepping into a nation ablaze with hope and turmoil. *The 8888 Uprising* had unleashed a collective roar for freedom. The streets were filled with people risking everything to demand democracy. I felt an undeniable pull—*an inner compass*, as you describe it—that pointed me toward a path I could neither deny nor abandon.

"When I said, 'I could not, as my father's daughter, remain indifferent to all that was going on,' during my speech at the Shwedagon Pagoda on August 26, 1988, it was not rhetoric—it was a truth spoken from the marrow of my being.

My father, General Aung San, gave his life for Burma's independence. But his vision reached far beyond the end of colonial rule. He dreamed of a free, secure, and just society—where every person in our country, regardless of ethnicity, could realize their full potential. He believed in the oneness of humanity, and in the moral courage needed to bring that vision to life. To witness my country crying out for those ideals, and to remain silent, would have been a betrayal—not only of him, but of the very principles I had been raised to uphold.

Returning to Burma was, in many ways, a convergence of personal and national duty. Caring for my mother was inseparable from caring for my country. Her resilience, even in vulnerability, mirrored the strength of our people. She became my anchor, grounding me as I stepped into a role I had not sought but could not refuse. It was her quiet dignity—her unwavering sense of responsibility—that gave me the courage to face what lay ahead.

In accepting the Nobel Peace Prize years later, I reflected on these intertwined truths. The Nobel Committee's recognition was not of me alone, but of the oppressed and isolated people of Burma.

As I said in Oslo, *"They were recognizing the oneness of humanity... The prize we were working for was a free, secure, and just society where our people might be able to realize their full potential."* That vision—my father's vision—still guides me, even through the darkness of this chapter.

Now, as I sit confined once more, my conscience remains unchanged though the weight it bears feels heavier. Solitude forces reflection, and I have often turned to the *Dhamma*—the liberating teachings of the Buddha—for clarity and strength. *It teaches that even in the face of greed, hatred, and delusion, there remains a path of truth and courage we can follow. My conscience is my compass. It is not a tool of convenience; it is a moral imperative that reminds me who I am, and where I belong.*

Today, as Myanmar convulses with revolution and my fellow citizens endure unspeakable suffering—even in the wake of a devastating earthquake—I hold steadfast to that same inner compass. It is not merely a guide, but a profound reminder: *freedom is not a gift bestowed by the powerful—it is a birthright, one that must be claimed, nurtured, and fiercely defended.* The journey is arduous, but it is one we undertake together—as individuals, as a nation, and as part of the collective human family.

I remain, as I was in 1988, Burma's daughter. In that identity, I draw the strength to continue walking this path, no matter the cost— even here, in prison. *Nothing will stop me. Nothing will stop the people.*

Nothing will stop the revolution until we achieve the freedom and justice we have long fought for.

Alan Clements: Daw Suu, that moment back in '88 seems like the convergence of so many profound forces—personal duty, the legacy of your father, the swelling tide of revolution, and a sense of spiritual inevitability. It was, as if history itself, called you to step into a role that few could bear. Yet that path has demanded extraordinary sacrifices—not just from you, but from millions across your country.

Now, as you endure solitary confinement under torturous conditions—alongside 22,000 other political prisoners—and as a nation convulses with revolution and mass trauma, I can't help but ask: how have you reconciled the cost?

When intuition demands a path so fraught with suffering—for yourself, and for an entire country—how do you embrace it without being consumed by the immense pain and loss it entails?

Aung San Suu Kyi: Alan, instinctual integrity is not a refuge of solace. It rarely brings ease, comfort, or certainty—especially when it confronts the crushing forces of external oppression. What it offers—and insists upon—is truth. *Not some perfect idea, but the choice to keep seeing clearly, even when it hurts—and to speak from that clarity, even when it costs everything. Because more often than not, truth carries an unbearable weight.*

The sacrifices I have made—my family, my freedom, and the quiet dignity of an ordinary life—are immense. But they have never been mine to bear alone.

Every Burmese family carries an unimaginable burden. Parents watch their children fall to the regime's bullets. Entire villages are razed to the ground, leaving nothing but ashes and memories. Displacement has become a way of life for millions. My solitary confinement, while isolating, pales in comparison to the horrors endured by so many of my fellow countrymen. The torture cells of Insein Prison, the relentless airstrikes on civilian communities, the lives lost in secret—these are wounds that scar the very soul of our nation.

In the face of such suffering, it is impossible not to question the cost of our struggle. *Yet intuition has a way of quieting doubt.* It reminds me that this is not a burden I carry for myself, nor a battle I fight alone.

My imprisonment is tied to the freedom of my people. My isolation is a reflection of their resilience. My role, however small or flawed, is part of a collective struggle for something far greater than any one life.

Still, intuition is not infallible. It calls for integrity, but it does not shield us from mistakes. And I have made mistakes, Alan. To lead through such complexity is to accept that no decision will ever be entirely free of error. I have misjudged, faltered, and struggled. But the choices I made were always guided by a conviction that we must act, even when the path forward is shrouded in uncertainty.

When I think of the thousands of political prisoners suffering in isolation, the young revolutionaries risking everything in the jungles, and the millions displaced and grieving in silence, I do not see this as a question of reconciling sacrifice. I see it as a collective act of moral courage. None of us walk this path alone, and none of us do so without doubt. But we walk it because to turn away would be to abandon the truth—to abandon our humanity.

Even now, in the confines of this cell, I feel the presence of the people who have kept this revolution alive through their sacrifices. It is their courage—their defiance—that sustains me. My suffering is but one thread in the vast fabric of their resilience. And for that, Alan, I feel only gratitude, not regret.

Alan Clements: Daw Suu, you've spoken before about the profound weight of carrying your father's legacy. In '88, as you said, "I could not, as my father's daughter, remain indifferent to all that was unfolding." Now, with decades of reflection behind you—and as you endure this current chapter of solitary confinement—how do you perceive his influence on your choices and your leadership?

Aung San Suu Kyi: Alan, my father's influence is a paradox. It is shaped as much by his absence as by his ideals. He was taken from us when I was just two years old, so I never knew him as a father in the traditional sense. Yet his presence was never absent from our home. His vision for Burma—a nation free from tyranny, united in its diversity, and upheld by the principles of justice—was woven into the fabric of my upbringing.

His beliefs were not theoretical; they were lived truths, born of sacrifice and an unshakable conviction in the dignity of all people. He believed in the transformative power of dialogue, the strength that comes from moral courage, and the necessity of humility in leadership. These ideals were not just words in my childhood—they were the foundation of my ethical compass.

When I returned in 1988, I saw the military—his creation—wielded as an instrument of oppression. It was a profound betrayal of everything he had envisioned. The very institution he had hoped would safeguard the people was now being used to crush them. That realization pierced me deeply. How could I, as his daughter—and, more importantly, as a Myanmar citizen—stand aside when his legacy was being so distorted?

I have often imagined what he might say to me today, if he could speak to the daughter he barely knew and see the Burma of now. I believe he would recognize the enormity of the struggle we face, but I also believe he would challenge me. My father was both a pragmatist and an idealist, and he would not hesitate to point out where I could do better, where I might have failed to live up to his principles or my own.

Would he agree with my unwavering commitment to nonviolence as the only path to genuine freedom? I believe he would. But I also think he would remind me that nonviolence requires not just courage, but creativity, persistence, and the willingness to engage even with those who oppose you. He would urge me to look forward, to learn from past mistakes, and to strive toward a future that is more inclusive and compassionate—not just for the majority, but for every person who calls Myanmar home.

Alan Clements: Daw Suu, your reflection on your father's paradoxical influence is profoundly moving. The way his ideals continue to shape your moral compass, even through the lens of their complexities, is a testament to the enduring power of his legacy.

In these moments of isolation, as you bear the extraordinary sacrifices demanded of you, I wonder: does his vision for Burma offer you solace—a sense of continuity and purpose? Or does it sometimes feel like an even greater weight pressing upon your shoulders, a reminder of the enormity of what remains undone?

If I may, building on that: how do you reconcile the burden of your father's ideals with your own evolving vision for Burma's future?

Does the interplay between legacy and personal evolution inform how you imagine freedom for your people today?

Aung San Suu Kyi: It does both, Alan. My father's vision is a light that sustains me—a source of hope and purpose that cuts through even the darkest moments. But it is also a constant reminder of the unfinished work, of the immense responsibility I bear as his daughter and as a leader.

When I sit in this cell, I reflect not only on his sacrifices but also on his unyielding faith in the people of Burma. He believed deeply that our nation's strength lay in its people—their resilience, their capacity for empathy, and their commitment to justice. That belief sustains me, even now.

At the same time, the weight of his legacy can feel overwhelming. To be Aung San's daughter is both an honor and a burden. There are moments when I find myself questioning whether I have done enough to live up to his ideals. Have my choices honored his vision? Or might some of them have disappointed him?

But I also know that leadership is not about achieving perfection. It is about continuing to strive, even when the path is fraught with uncertainty, sacrifice, and the inevitability of failure.

What comforts me most is knowing that my father's legacy does not rest on my shoulders alone. It belongs to the people of Burma. Every act of defiance, every sacrifice made by our citizens, is a continuation of the struggle he began. I am but one part of a much larger story—a story written by the courage and determination of millions. It is in that collective effort that I find solace, and it is through their resilience that I find the strength to continue.

Alan Clements: Daw Suu, as you sit here in your prison cell—still guiding the spirit of a nation convulsing with revolution and enduring unrelenting suffering—I have to ask: How does that compass—the one that led you back to Burma thirty-seven years ago—continue to guide you today, in these conditions of isolation, in a country torn between hope and despair?

Aung San Suu Kyi: Alan, the compass remains steady, though the landscape it navigates has become harsher, more fragmented, and more uncertain. In this solitude, I have had no choice but to rely on the inner guide that has always directed me—to turn inward and deepen my understanding of leadership, sacrifice, and the enduring power of hope.

The Dhamma has been my unwavering companion. It teaches that even in the depths of darkness, light can still be found—not in our circumstances, but within ourselves.

Meditation has been both a sanctuary and a tool of resilience. Each breath connects me to the millions of my fellow countrymen and women who resist oppression daily—not only with weapons or protests, but through the quiet, indomitable acts of survival.

I think of the mothers rebuilding their homes after airstrikes, the monks still praying for peace, the children who dare to dream of a future they've never seen.

Even here, in confinement, I send *metta*—loving-kindness— not only to those who suffer, but also to my captors. This is not an act of surrender, nor is it born of naivety. Compassion-fused love is the greatest strength we possess—it dismantles hatred from within. If we are to overcome tyranny, it will not be through hatred, but through the transformative power of understanding and forgiveness. This is not weakness. It is the root of true strength.

Alan Clements: That vision, Daw Suu, clearly comes from the heart. But the path forward for Burma—stating the obvious—is fraught with immense challenges. The junta's grip remains ironclad, propped up by unwavering support from China and Russia, who continue to flood the regime with high-tech weaponry: jets, missiles, attack helicopters, drones, fuel, training, and more.

Meanwhile, the nation's wounds—ethnic, political, generational— run deep.

What do you see as the way forward?

How does a fractured nation move toward unity, justice, and reconciliation?

Aung San Suu Kyi: The path forward for Burma is not an easy one, Alan—but it is one we must walk with unwavering determination. It requires three essential elements: unity, reconciliation, and justice.

These are not abstract ideals. They are deeply practical necessities for a nation as diverse and wounded as ours.

Unity begins with acknowledging the shared humanity of every citizen of Myanmar—every faith, every ethnicity, every voice long silenced or denied.

For decades, the military has sought to divide us—pitting communities against one another, sowing fear, mistrust, and resentment. But I see signs of hope in the alliances forming today—among ethnic armed organizations, young revolutionaries, and citizens of every background who are bridging divides that once seemed unbridgeable. This is where we begin—on common ground, with humility, and a deep openness to dialogue.

Reconciliation is equally vital, and it begins with truth. But not only historical truth—we must also confront the truths we've buried within ourselves.

Generations have lived under authoritarian rule, and many of its patterns—fear, self-censorship, blind obedience—have been internalized. We must learn to recognize how dictatorship seeps into the psyche, how self-slavery and degrading compliance are passed on like inheritance. *We must unlearn what we were taught to accept.*

True reconciliation requires this inner revolution—an awakening from *moha*, the delusions that masquerade as truth. Not only the lies of propaganda, but the deeper distortions of identity and worth that come from decades of subjugation. This awakening is not a luxury—it is essential. We cannot build a just society if we are still chained by the invisible bars of our own conditioning.

And justice—true justice—is not vengeance. It is the restoration of dignity. It is ensuring that no one is above the law, and that the structures which have enabled oppression are dismantled—root and branch.

The military as an institution must be reimagined—not as a force of domination, but as one of protection and service to the people. This will be a long and difficult process. But without it, democracy cannot survive.

Alan Clements: Daw Suu, your ability to speak of hope and compassion, even from this confinement, is deeply moving. And allow me to ask: how do you sustain hope in the face of such overwhelming suffering? The crackdowns, the airstrikes, the imprisonment of over 22,000 political prisoners—how do you continue to believe in the possibility of freedom?

Aung San Suu Kyi: Hope, Alan, is not something that simply exists—it is something we cultivate. It is an act of defiance against despair. I hold on to hope because I have seen, time and again, the extraordinary resilience of the Burmese people. They endure unimaginable hardships, yet they refuse to be broken.

I think of the prisoners I have met—those who have endured torture, deprivation, and isolation, yet emerge with their spirits intact. I think of the young people across the country, fighting not only with weapons, but with vision—with dreams of a Burma rooted in dignity and freedom. And I think of the ethnic groups—many of whom have suffered for generations—now reaching toward one another across the chasms of history. These acts of solidarity, however fragile, are signs of awakening.

But we must not romanticize the path. The wounds run deep. The mistrust between groups is not only historical—it is human. We all carry scars. We all carry egoic fears and pride that cloud our ability to truly listen and trust. The path to unity is not only political—it is spiritual. It asks each of us, every party, every movement, to confront our own inner obstacles, our inherited biases, our need to be right. It asks us to *choose conscience over ego*.

I hope—and I pray—that all parties, especially the leaders, will have the courage to turn inward, to challenge the reflexes of division, and to do everything and more to find common ground. Not for appearances, but for the birth of a new vision—a shared future luminous with trust, mutuality, and generosity.

This is the promise of federal democracy—not as an abstract model, but as a living ethic. A system governed by conscience, shaped by dignity, and animated by *mindful mutuality*. It will not be easy. But if we succeed in rooting our democracy in these principles, Myanmar can become not only free—but profoundly whole.

Alan Clements: And when that day comes, Daw Suu, what do you hope the people of Burma will carry from your life, your sacrifices, and your vision?

Aung San Suu Kyi: I don't hope to be remembered as a symbol, Alan. Symbols fade, and I've never been interested in being admired. What matters is whether we've moved, even slightly, toward a deeper understanding of what it means to be free.

Freedom isn't just surviving tyranny—it's learning to live with dignity. To speak honestly, to listen without fear, to disagree without hatred. It's the courage to let others live fully in their truth, even when it challenges our own.

My life is just one path among many. If it's remembered at all, I hope it's as a life lived in service—not to perfection, but to possibility.

And when people look back on this time, I don't want them to see a single figure on a stage. I want them to see the whole landscape—the mothers who kept going after everything fell apart, the farmers who planted through war, the children who dreamed in the rubble, and the elders who remembered a gentler time. I want them to see the quiet revolutions—of kindness, of conscience, of courage in the smallest acts.

What I long for—what I still believe in—is a future where we recognize each other as necessary. Where no region, no culture, no language, no faith is seen as a threat, but as part of the whole. Not a melting pot, but a living mosaic—interdependent, imperfect, and alive.

If we are to build a new democracy, let it be one that breathes. One rooted in trust and shaped by mutual care. Not just governed by law, but guided by conscience. Where leadership is measured not by power, but by presence, humility, and the willingness to listen. If we can begin to move in that direction—even now—then nothing has been in vain.

Alan Clements: And for whatever reason, should we be unable to continue this conversation, Daw Suu, if there one final message you would wish to share with the world, what would it be?

Aung San Suu Kyi: Alan, if I were to leave a single message, it would be this: Freedom is not a gift to be bestowed by the powerful, nor is it a fleeting privilege granted by circumstance. It is an intrinsic truth—a birthright that resides within every human heart.

But truth alone is not enough; freedom must be claimed, nurtured, and fiercely protected. It is not a destination to be reached and left behind, but a way of being—a daily commitment to live with dignity, compassion, and integrity, no matter the challenges.

This freedom transcends the boundaries of oppression—whether in the chambers of government, the jungles of resistance, or the silence of a prison cell.

True freedom is the ability to hold fast to one's principles, even when the cost is unimaginable. It is in the courage of those who rebuild after their homes are burned, in the steadfast resolve of a farmer sowing seeds in scorched soil, and in the whispered prayers of a mother cradling her child amidst the chaos of war. It is in the unyielding will of a nation that refuses to surrender its soul, no matter how heavy the chains.

If there is one lesson I have learned in this long journey, it is that freedom is not an individual endeavor. It belongs to the collective—it is forged in solidarity, in shared sacrifice, and in the recognition that our humanity is bound to one another. None of us can truly be free until all of us are free.

This is my hope for Burma—a country that has endured so much suffering yet remains unshaken in its spirit. And it is my hope for the world—a world too often divided by fear and greed, by the illusion of "otherness." Freedom must be nurtured not just in revolution, but in reconciliation; not just in resistance, but in understanding. It demands that we see beyond our differences to the common dignity that unites us.

Finally, I would ask this of humanity: Let us not define freedom by what we fight against, but by what we fight for—a world where every child can grow up without fear, where no one is silenced because of their beliefs or their identity, where love and justice are not lofty ideals but lived realities.

This is what we owe to those who came before us, to those who walk beside us, and to those who will inherit the world we leave behind. Freedom is not something we can hold in our hands—it is something we must plant, water, and grow, so that it may bloom across the generations.

And yes, Alan, this truth—whether it is realized in the chambers of government, in the silence of prison, or in the quiet acts of daily life—is always worth fighting for. *Always.*

32

THE UNYIELDING SPIRIT: FREEDOM AMIDST OPPRESSION

Author's Prelude

In this conversation, Aung San Suu Kyi does not simply speak—she bears witness. Through her voice flows the unbroken lineage of spirit carried by those who turned captivity into grace.

Her longtime colleagues in the NLD (National League for Democracy) stand among them: Dr. Zaw Myint Maung, who gave his life after more than two decades as a political prisoner; Saya U Win Tin, the fearless journalist who endured twenty years in solitary confinement; Saya U Tin Oo, the former general who became a moral force for democracy; Saya U Kyi Maung, the satirist and quiet architect of the party's early vision; and Saya U Win Htein—her principal advisor, beloved friend, and tireless colleague—now in his fourth incarceration, with a total of twenty-three years spent behind bars.

Their voices live in hers—and in truth, in every woman and man who has ever dared to dream of a free Burma.

Here, resilience is not romanticized. It is forged in solitude, in silence, in unspeakable loss. It is found in the act of sending *metta—loving-kindness*—even to the architects of one's torment. This is not the kind of strength that can be taught. It must be lived—and lived again—until it carves the shape of the future.

◆ ◆ ◆

Alan Clements: Daw Suu, I know I am recounting what you know far more intimately than I ever could, as I reflect on the immense loss of your dear friend and colleague, Dr. Zaw Myint Maung. His passing in junta custody—after more than 22 years in prison, and after being denied medical treatment for his cancer—is a profound tragedy, not just for those who knew and loved him, but for the entire democratic movement. As a lifelong champion of Burma's freedom, a four-time elected lawmaker, and your close ally, he embodied radical courage, resilience, and an unyielding dedication to the people of Burma. A true revolutionary freedom fighter in every sense.

I'm also reminded of a conversation I had with him—one that you graciously arranged back in 2012—where he spoke of the *Dhamma*, the teachings of the Buddha, and the practice of compassion as the foundation of his resilience during his many years of imprisonment.

In the humblest manner, he shared: *"Meditation means practicing birth and death in daily life, every hour, all the time. It also means practicing compassion, even for our oppressors, who, like all of us, are conditioned beings bound by suffering."*

Daw Suu, this profound philosophy of compassion and resilience—which you and so many others have embodied through decades of unimaginable struggle—feels especially urgent in this moment of nationwide revolution and reflection.

As we honor Dr. Zaw Myint Maung's legacy, along with the more than 2,000 political prisoners who have died or been killed in detention since General Min Aung Hlaing's military coup in February 2021, I humbly ask: How do you carry forward not just his spirit, but the spirit of so many other leaders—including your mentors and co-founders of the NLD, Saya U Tin Oo, Uncle U Kyi Maung, Saya U Win Tin—and the countless women and men whose sacrifices have shaped the fight for Burma's freedom? What does it mean to embody unyielding hope and compassion in the face of such tremendous injustice?

And if there is one lesson from your decades of struggle, one piece of enduring wisdom, what would you impart to future generations of freedom fighters who look to you and these remarkable figures as guiding lights?

Aung San Suu Kyi: Alan, when I think of Dr. Zaw Myint Maung, I see not just a dear friend and colleague, but a man who *embodied* the deepest truths of our long struggle for freedom. His life was a reflection of the values that define our movement: courage tempered by compassion, strength rooted in humility, and an unwavering commitment to justice. His loss is profound, but his legacy—*like the legacy of so many others*—is a source of strength that will continue to inspire us.

You ask how we carry forward his spirit, and the answer lies in remembering that this struggle has never been about any one individual. It has been built by countless women and men whose sacrifices and courage have shaped our path.

I am particularly indebted to Saya U Tin Oo, Uncle U Kyi Maung, and Saya U Win Tin—all pillars of the movement. Uncle U Tin Oo's unwavering dignity, Uncle U Kyi Maung's wisdom, and Saya U Win Tin's relentless dedication to truth—especially after twenty years of solitary confinement—were gifts to us all. I also hold in deep respect Saya U Win Htein—my trusted advisor and dear friend—whose strength and loyalty remain a quiet light, even through the trials of his continued imprisonment.

And how can we forget the women whose strength has been the backbone of this struggle? Daw Aung Shin, Ma Thanegi, Ma Phyu Phyu Thin, and so many others—they carried the torch forward with extraordinary grace and resilience. Alongside the men, they have shown us that the fight for freedom is not bound by gender, but by the shared humanity of all who yearn for justice.

Their lives remind us that freedom is not granted—it is earned, through sacrifice, courage, and an unshakable belief in the dignity of all people. It is a lesson I have carried with me throughout my life: *that the struggle for democracy is not just about political change but about preserving the humanity of everyone involved, even those who oppose us.*

To future generations of freedom fighters, I would say this: learn from those who came before you. Study their lives, their sacrifices, and their wisdom. Let their example guide you, but also find your own path, rooted in your unique strengths and convictions.

And remember, as Dr. Zaw Myint Maung and so many others taught us, that true resilience comes from within. It comes from aligning yourself with the truths of the *Dhamma*—recognizing impermanence, cultivating compassion, and staying mindfully grounded in the present moment. These are the tools that will help you endure loss without losing hope, and face injustice without losing your humanity.

The path to freedom is long and often filled with suffering, but it is also where our greatest humanity is revealed. Let us honor the lives of Dr. Zaw Myint Maung, Saya U Tin Oo, Uncle U Kyi Maung, Saya U Win Tin, and so many others by carrying forward their vision for Burma—a vision of freedom, dignity, and peace for all.

Their sacrifices remind us that no act of courage is ever in vain. Every step forward, no matter how small, brings us closer to the day when their dream becomes a reality. Let us walk that path together, with the light of their lives guiding us forward.

Alan Clements: Daw Suu, the world has long been inspired by your unyielding spirit. But I know, as you have said, that it is not about you—it is about the people, your colleagues, and the shared struggle for justice and dignity. Still, I must ask, as someone who has been a prisoner of conscience for over two decades, how do you endure? How do you maintain your clarity, strength, and spirit amid such unrelenting adversity?

Aung San Suu Kyi: Alan, thank you. But truly—my suffering is not unique. It is not greater than that of so many others. I am neither stronger nor more significant than my people, or than the many prisoners of conscience who endure far from any spotlight. The pain of my colleagues, my friends, my fellow citizens—it is our shared burden, our collective grief, and our common strength.

If I endure, it is because of them. My spirit is carried by those who came before me—the mentors I've spoken of, yes, but also the unnamed—the villagers, the monks, the students—who gave everything for a dream greater than themselves. Their courage is my inheritance. Their quiet defiance is the rhythm of my breath.

Even here, in this cell, life offers moments of renewal. Silence teaches. *The Dhamma remains with me—like a friend who never leaves.* In meditation, I find a refuge—not to escape—but to remain steady. To meet sorrow with wisdom. To greet fear with equanimity.

Freedom, as I've come to understand it, is not the lifting of a lock or the opening of a gate. It is the refusal to betray yourself. It is staying true—even when the world turns from you. Even when the darkness lingers. And that is what keeps me whole.

Alan Clements: Your ability to transcend personal suffering and focus on the collective struggle is remarkable, Daw Suu. But I imagine there must be moments when doubt or despair arise. How do you navigate those emotions?

Aung San Suu Kyi: Doubt and despair are natural, Alan—but they are transient, like clouds passing through the open sky. *What matters is not that these emotions arise, but how we meet them.*

The *Dhamma* teaches us to observe these mind states without clinging, without judgment. In meditation, I allow grief, anger, longing to arise—not to suppress them, but to witness them with clarity, knowing that none of them can ultimately define me. Beneath these passing storms lies a deeper truth: *the impermanence of all things.*

I often think of Saya U Win Tin, whom you mentioned—a courageous man who spent nearly twenty years in prison, much of it in solitary confinement. He once told me he survived by composing and recomposing articles in his mind—imagining himself as a journalist still serving the people. His creativity was not an escape; it was an act of freedom, a quiet rebellion that kept his spirit alive.

Similarly, Uncle U Kyi Maung, with his profound wisdom and steady strength, often reminded us that *patience is not passive—it is the quietest form of resistance.* He would say, *"We do not simply wait for freedom; we cultivate it in our hearts, every day."*

Their examples teach me that doubt and despair, like hardship, are part of the journey. But *endurance is not simply surviving—it is choosing, again and again, to align ourselves with hope.* By enduring with dignity, we honor the sacrifices of those who came before us, and we strengthen the path for those who will come after.

Alan Clements: Over the many years of our conversations, you've often spoken of *metta*—loving-kindness—as a foundational practice. In such a hostile and brutal environment, how do you cultivate *metta even for your captors?* Does it ever feel, in itself, like an act of resistance?

Aung San Suu Kyi: *Metta* is indeed an act of resistance, Alan. It is a refusal to allow hatred to take root in the heart. When I extend *metta* to my captors, it is not an acceptance of their actions, but an acknowledgment of their humanity. *They too are victims of their own conditioning—trapped in systems of fear and greed.*

There is a story about Daw Aung Shin, a remarkable woman who faced relentless interrogation and imprisonment. Despite her suffering, she would silently send *metta* to her interrogators, visualizing them as innocent children, untainted by hatred. She believed that this practice not only protected her spirit, but also softened the hearts of her captors—even if only momentarily.

Metta reminds us that loving-kindness is not a weakness, but a profound strength. It disarms hatred and creates space for transformation. In the context of revolution, it ensures that we do not become what we oppose. It keeps us anchored in our humanity, even as we confront inhumanity.

Alan Clements: The resilience of the Myanmar people is extraordinary, Daw Suu. Yet, given the escalating brutality—and the military's increasing use of advanced weaponry against villages, even monasteries—sacred spaces that should be untouchable—how do you not fear for the toll it is taking on the spirit of the nation? In your isolation, how do you stay connected to the heartbeat of your people, who continue to suffer and resist with such courage?

Aung San Suu Kyi: Alan, the spirit of the Myanmar people is like a river—sometimes it encounters obstacles, but it finds ways to flow around them, carving new paths even through the hardest stone.

It is true that the toll is immense. Entire families have been torn apart, villages razed, and monasteries—once sanctuaries of peace—reduced to rubble. The violence inflicted on defenseless communities, often with advanced weaponry, is staggering.

Yet even in the face of such horror, I see resilience shining through. *Resistance does not mean the absence of suffering; it means finding renewal even amidst the ashes of despair.* Every act of defiance—whether it is a protest, an underground newspaper, or simply the refusal to bow to fear—is a reaffirmation of our collective strength.

The Myanmar people remind me daily that *courage is not the absence of fear, but the determination to act despite it.*

Even in isolation, I feel deeply connected to them. This connection is not dependent on communication or news; it is something much deeper—a shared understanding, a bond forged through decades of struggle.

I sense their courage, their love for this land, and their unyielding hope for a better future. It is as if the collective spirit of our nation breathes through me, sustaining me even when the darkness feels overwhelming.

I also think of younger women like Ma Phyu Phyu Thin, whose tireless work with those affected by HIV/AIDS exemplifies the resilience and compassion of our activist-politicians. Despite the constant threat of violence, she continued her mission with unwavering dedication. Her courage reminds me that hope does not merely survive hardship—it is strengthened because of it.

And then there are the women who lead community movements in the face of military violence. Many are mothers who have seen their children taken or killed, yet rise each day to care for their neighbors, organize resistance efforts, and rebuild what has been destroyed. They are not simply survivors; *they are the living embodiment of Myanmar's indomitable spirit.*

Alan Clements: You mentioned the youth and women who are integral to the struggle for freedom, Daw Suu. In light of Myanmar's current reality—a nationwide civil war against the regime—how do you see their role evolving? With so many young people taking up arms alongside the underground resistance, *what does this transformation mean for the future of the country?*

Aung San Suu Kyi: Alan, the youth and women of Myanmar are no longer just the vanguard of our revolution—they are its lifeblood. In this nationwide struggle against a brutal dictatorship, they have risen with extraordinary bravery and resolve. *They are not merely shaping the future; they are fighting for its very survival.*

I think of the young men and women who, seeing no other path to freedom, have joined the armed resistance. These are not warriors by choice; they are teachers, students, artists, and farmers who have been forced to take up arms in defense of their families, their villages, and their dreams of a just and democratic Myanmar. Their decision to fight is born not of hatred, but of love—for their people, and for the enduring principles of justice and dignity.

At the same time, women continue to play an indispensable role in *every dimension* of this struggle. They organize humanitarian aid and serve as *critical figures within* the underground networks *sustaining* the resistance. Women like Ma Thanegi, who endured imprisonment with such grace, and countless others who now risk their lives *each day* to keep the movement alive, are shaping a future that will be more inclusive, *more equitable, and more compassionate* because of their sacrifices.

The youth bring a vitality, creativity, and fearlessness that inspire us all. Their actions remind us that this is not merely a continuation of past struggles, but a revolution with its own distinct character and energy. They have seized the tools available to them—whether social media, community organizing, or global advocacy—and turned them into powerful instruments of resistance.

Alan Clements: With so much at stake, and the rising tide of armed resistance, how do you see the movement maintaining its core values of justice and compassion?

Aung San Suu Kyi: This is one of the greatest challenges we face, Alan. To take up arms is an extraordinary step for a people long committed to nonviolence. Yet I believe it is possible to resist oppression without losing our humanity.

The heart of this revolution must remain anchored in compassion, even as we fight for survival. Many of the young people who have joined the resistance carry with them a deep understanding of what they are fighting for—not just the end of tyranny, but the creation of a society rooted in justice, dignity, and equality.

The stories I hear reflect this balance of strength and compassion. There are soldiers within the People's Defense Forces (PDF) who, even in battle, make efforts to protect civilians and treat captured opponents humanely. These are not acts of weakness; they are acts of profound strength—rooted in the belief that our fight must not replicate the very injustices we seek to dismantle.

This is where the role of women and youth is especially vital. Their courage is matched by their vision—a vision not merely of victory, but of the kind of nation we want to build. They remind us that while the means of resistance may evolve, our values must remain unwavering.

Alan Clements: Do you believe the spirit of the revolution can hold strong amidst the violence and loss?

Aung San Suu Kyi: The spirit of the revolution is unbreakable, Alan. We have been battered, yes—but not bowed. The people of Myanmar have faced unimaginable violence—families ripped apart by airstrikes, villages burned to the ground, entire communities turned to smoke and silence. Schools reduced to rubble. Monasteries flattened. Children orphaned. Mothers disappeared. Lifelines severed.

Yet even in the face of such suffering, the will of the people remains steadfast.

The youth and women leading this movement inspire me profoundly. They rise from the wreckage and find ways to rebuild—not just shelters, but meaning. They organize, educate, heal, resist. Their courage reminds us that the revolution is not merely about dismantling a regime—it is about creating a future where every citizen can live with dignity and freedom.

This revolution is not born of hatred—it is born of love. Love for truth. Love for justice. Love for one another.

This spirit is what will sustain us. It is a spirit of resilience, compassion, and unwavering hope. Even in exile, it marches. Even in prison, it breathes. Even in silence, it sings. As long as it lives in the hearts of the people, no regime—no gun, no prison, no propaganda— can extinguish our dream of a free Myanmar.

Alan Clements: Daw Suu, if you could speak directly to those who oppose you—the military generals, the architects of oppression, particularly General Min Aung Hlaing himself—what would you say to them?

Aung San Suu Kyi: Alan, if I had the opportunity to speak directly to those who wield power through fear—especially to General Min Aung Hlaing—I would begin simply: Stop. Stop the killing. Stop the destruction of our nation. Stop before the weight of these actions buries not only the lives of the innocent, but your own humanity.

General, you must see that power built on the blood of the people is not power at all—it is a fragile illusion, destined to crumble. The fear you instill in others will one day consume you. The history of tyrants is clear: *no regime built on oppression, cruelty, and lies has ever endured.*

Look to the *Dhamma*—the same truths that underpin our shared culture and traditions. *The Dhamma teaches that hatred cannot be overcome by hatred; it can only be overcome by love.* Your actions not only defy this principle; they deepen the suffering of all—including yourself.

Reflect on the story of India's Emperor *Ashoka*. After witnessing the devastation of the Kalinga War, he chose to renounce violence and embrace the path of the *Dhamma*. That decision did not diminish his power—it elevated him, transforming him into one of history's most revered leaders. His legacy endures not because of the wars he waged, but because of the peace he chose to build.

You, General, stand now at a similar crossroads. The suffering you have unleashed upon Myanmar—the villages burned, the children killed, the families torn apart—need not define your legacy. You have the power to stop this. Use it. *Release the political prisoners. End the violence. Begin a dialogue rooted in reconciliation and justice.*

This is not a plea born of weakness, but of strength. *True leadership is not measured by the fear you inspire, but by the lives you uplift.* Imagine being remembered not as a destroyer, but as a redeemer—someone who had the courage to change course, to listen to the voice of conscience, and to choose humanity over tyranny.

It is not too late. The *Dhamma* teaches us that redemption is always possible. But it requires action. The choice is yours, General. *Stop the killing. Set the political prisoners free. Begin the process of healing our nation.*

Alan Clements: And to the freedom fighters, the political prisoners, and those who continue to resist this regime—what would you say to them?

Aung San Suu Kyi: To those who fight for justice, I say this: Hold fast to your principles. The road is long, and the suffering is great, but your courage is not in vain. Every act of defiance, every moment of compassion, every sacrifice builds the foundation of a freer, more just Myanmar.

Freedom is not simply the absence of oppression; it is the presence of dignity, love, and truth. Even in the darkest moments, remember: the light of truth cannot be extinguished. Your resilience, your humanity, and your hope are the greatest weapons against tyranny.

To my fellow prisoners of conscience: You are not alone. We are bound by a shared vision, and our collective spirit cannot be broken. Together, we will continue walking the path toward justice, no matter how long the journey.

And to the youth and women leading this movement with extraordinary bravery: Know that you are not only the present—you are the architects of our future. Your actions today ensure that the sacrifices of the past were not in vain, and that the dreams of tomorrow will one day be realized.

This is our time. Our struggle. Our shared destiny. Let us honor it with the full measure of our humanity. And let us never forget: Freedom will come—because it is rooted in the deepest truths of our shared existence. No force can suppress it forever.

A REVOLUTION OF THE SPIRIT

Author's Prelude

There are moments when a nation stands not merely on the edge of political upheaval, but at the brink of moral awakening. This chapter belongs to such a moment. It is not simply a meditation on resistance—it is a reckoning with the soul's defiance under siege.

In these pages, Aung San Suu Kyi speaks not only as a political prisoner or national leader, but as a courageous witness to something more enduring: the sacred flame of inner freedom—fierce, quiet, inextinguishable.

In a world unraveling beneath the weight of its own violence—where the engines of war drown out the prayers of the innocent—what follows is not merely a conversation. It is a spiritual act of resistance. A luminous refusal to let brutality define the boundaries of what it means to be human.

A call to remember: revolutions do not begin with armies or slogans. They begin in the hush between heartbeats—in the untamed tenderness of a conscience that refuses to be conquered. This is the terrain of Daw Suu's voice—raw, resolute, luminous with inner discipline.

She reminds us: the most enduring revolution is not fought with weapons, but with presence. Not declared—but lived. Not shouted—but whispered into the silence that power cannot touch.

◆ ◆ ◆

Alan Clements: Daw Suu, as I sit with you now, I am drawn back to our conversations three decades ago, when you spoke with such clarity and conviction about a "revolution of the spirit." Even then, it struck me as the essence of your vision—not just for Myanmar, but for all of humanity. You said something that has stayed with me ever since:

"The quintessential revolution is that of the spirit, born of an intellectual conviction of the need for change in those mental attitudes and values which shape the course of a nation's development. A revolution which aims merely at changing official policies and institutions with a view to an improvement in material conditions has little chance of genuine success. Without a revolution of the spirit, the forces which produced the iniquities of the old order would continue to be operative, posing a constant threat to the process of reform and regeneration."

This idea feels even more profound now, as your people fight against unimaginable odds, enduring profound suffering and sacrifice. It is clear that the material and political challenges remain immense, but your vision of transformation from within still holds incredible power.

Daw Suu, how do you hold onto that vision today, amidst such brutality and loss? How do you see this *revolution of the spirit* manifesting in the hearts of your people, even in these darkest of times? And what role does it play in building a future that can truly transcend the cycles of dictatorship and oppression?

Aung San Suu Kyi: Alan, the *revolution of the spirit* remains the cornerstone of our struggle, now more than ever. In the face of unspeakable violence, immense loss, and deep trauma, it is this inner revolution—the transformation of fear into courage, despair into hope, and hatred into compassion—that sustains us. It is what gives our people the strength not merely to endure, but to rise, again and again, against all odds.

The suffering we face is staggering—families torn apart, villages incinerated, children robbed of their futures. Yet, amidst this darkness, something extraordinary is happening. The people of Myanmar are taking the raw material of their suffering and transforming it into *parami*—the cultivation of higher virtues. This is not an act of denial but a profound form of spiritual alchemy. Through the fires of adversity, they are cultivating patience, compassion, and determination—not just for personal liberation, but for the liberation of the nation as a whole.

I often think of the teachings of our beloved *Dhamma* guide and meditation teacher, the late Venerable Sayadaw U Pandita. He would remind us that suffering—*dukkha*—while painful, is also the greatest teacher. It forces us to confront impermanence, to see clearly the causes of our pain, and to cultivate the wisdom and resilience needed to transcend it.

Sayadawgyi also often spoke of *khanti*—patient endurance—as the foundation for all other virtues. It is not passive but active, a steadfast force that allows us to hold steady in the storm without being consumed by it.

This patient endurance is what I feel in our people every day— even from within this prison cell. It lives in the father who plants rice in soil scorched by airstrikes, trusting that life will rise again. It pulses in the teenager who smuggles medicine through jungle paths under the drone of warplanes. It breathes in the nun who chants the *suttas* beside the smoldering ruins of her nunnery, her voice unshaken. These are not just acts of survival—they are acts of sacred defiance. *They are Dhamma made flesh*, resilience made prayer—turning devastation into discipline, and despair into a deeper vow to awaken.

The revolution of the spirit does not deny the reality of horror and loss— it embraces it as part of the human experience. But it refuses to let suffering define us. Instead, it calls us to rise to a higher plane of existence, to act not from hatred or vengeance, but from wisdom and compassion.

Even in the darkest times, I see this revolution unfolding in the hearts of the Burmese people. The youth, especially, inspire me. They face challenges that would break most of us, yet they do so with creativity, courage, and an unshakable belief in a freer Myanmar. Their actions are not merely acts of resistance—they are acts of creation. They are building a new Myanmar with every step they take, a Myanmar no longer shackled by the cycles of hatred and division that have haunted our past.

And I said earlier, I see it in the women of Myanmar, who have borne so much of the burden of this struggle. They have lost husbands, brothers, and sons, yet they continue to lead. Their strength is not merely physical but spiritual, rooted in the knowledge that true freedom is not just political change but the transformation of the human heart.

Alan, the *Dhamma* teaches us that every action, every thought, every moment has the potential to create *kusala*—wholesome energy that contributes to the collective awakening of humanity. This is the revolution of the spirit in its most profound form. It is not about overthrowing a regime for power's sake; it is about transforming ourselves so that the society we build reflects the highest virtues of humanity—compassion, justice, and wisdom.

To General Min Aung Hlaing and all those who continue to inflict suffering on the people of Myanmar, I say again—because some truths must be spoken until they are heard—*you are not beyond redemption.*

The *Dhamma* is universal. It holds each of us accountable, yet it offers each of us a path to awakening. Your actions have caused immeasurable harm—but the possibility for transformation remains within you. *Stop the killing. Stop it now. Release the political prisoners. Look deeply within yourself and ask: what legacy will I leave behind?*

As I said before, remember Ashoka: once a merciless conqueror, he awoke to the truth of his violence and chose another path—a path of compassion, wisdom, and peace. His transformation did not diminish him; it elevated him.

You, too, General, have that choice. Continue down the road of destruction, or choose the path of reconciliation and healing. The people of Myanmar are ready for peace. But it must begin with you.

To my fellow citizens, I say this: Hold fast to the revolution of the spirit. It is the only revolution that cannot be crushed by force. Through your patience, your courage, and your compassion, you are building not just a new Myanmar but a better world.

The road is long, and the suffering is great, but we are not alone. Every act of kindness, every moment of mindfulness, every step taken in the name of justice adds to the momentum of this revolution. Together, we are turning the wheel of the *Dhamma*—and no force on earth can halt its progress.

Alan Clements: Daw Suu, the sovereignty you describe—the inner freedom that transcends even the most oppressive circumstances—feels at once intangible and profoundly real. It is clear that this sovereignty is the foundation of everything you have stood for, the essence of the "revolution of the spirit" you have so often spoken about.

When we last spoke about this back in 1995, you described sovereignty as a process: first, the courage to see the truth, no matter how painful; then, the courage to feel it, to let it break through denial and numbness; and finally, the courage to act on that truth, even when doing so carries great risk.

Given the immense suffering and unyielding resistance in Myanmar today, how do you see this process manifesting now—both within yourself, as you navigate the isolation and hardships of imprisonment, and within your people, who continue to rise in courage despite the horrors they face? How does this inner sovereignty shape the external fight for justice, and what lessons can the world draw from the people of Myanmar about what it truly means to be free?

Aung San Suu Kyi: Alan, sovereignty begins with courage—the courage to see, the courage to feel, and ultimately, the courage to act. These three are inseparable, and together they form the foundation of both resistance and freedom.

The courage to see begins with an unflinching gaze upon reality, no matter how painful. In 1995, I first spoke about how the people of Myanmar had to confront the truth of their oppression. Today, that truth is even starker. Entire villages have been burned to the ground. Thousands languish in prison under inhumane conditions. Families are torn apart, parents lose their children, entire generations are displaced. Yet the people of Myanmar do not turn away. They see this suffering not as a defeat but as a call to action.

The courage to feel naturally follows. To see the truth and not feel it is a kind of numbness—a way of avoiding responsibility. Feeling the truth means allowing ourselves to grieve, to rage, and also to hope. It is through this feeling that we connect with our humanity, with our conscience. When we allow ourselves to feel fully, we discover that even amidst the pain, there is love—love for our people, our land, and our shared vision of freedom.

Finally, the courage to act is the hardest of all. It is not enough to see and feel; one must do something. Action does not always come through grand gestures or dramatic confrontations. Sometimes, it is as simple and profound as refusing to bow to fear. A young villager who hides activists in her home is part of this revolution. A monk who marches peacefully, fully aware of the risks, is part of this revolution. A young fighter who joins the armed resistance with tears in their eyes but conviction in their heart is part of this revolution. Every act of integrity, no matter how small, sustains the larger movement.

This is where sovereignty intersects with moral courage. *Sovereignty is the inner freedom to see, feel, and act in alignment with one's deepest values, regardless of external circumstances.* It is what allows a person to say, *"I will not betray my conscience, no matter the cost."* Sovereignty is what keeps the people of Myanmar rising, even as the weight of oppression bears down on them.

But sovereignty does not exist in isolation. It must be guided by moral courage, which ensures that our actions remain grounded in the values we seek to uphold. This is especially vital now, as many have taken up arms in a necessary but heartbreaking shift to armed resistance. These young people, who never envisioned themselves as fighters, are driven by a profound sense of responsibility—to protect their families, their villages, and their future. Their actions are not born of hatred but of love for their people and a commitment to justice.

As expressed earlier, I often reflect on the teachings of the late Venerable Sayadaw U Pandita, who reminded us that true courage is not the absence of fear but the ability to act in accordance with the *Dhamma* despite it. Sovereignty, in this sense, is not about freedom from fear or suffering but freedom from the tyranny of hatred and despair.

Even in the midst of armed struggle, there is space for compassion, for humanity, for the *Dhamma* to guide our actions. The *Dhamma* offers us a way forward, but it requires us to act.

At some point, we must lay down our weapons, seek reconciliation, and begin the process of healing our beloved nation. It is never too late to turn toward redemption.

Meanwhile, *to the people of Myanmar, I say: your courage to see, to feel, and to act is what sustains this revolution.* Sovereignty is not something granted by governments; it is something cultivated within, through the daily acts of integrity and compassion that define us as human beings. Every moment of resistance—whether it is a quiet act of defiance or a battle fought in the jungles—moves us closer to freedom.

Hold fast to your moral courage. Let it guide you, even in the darkest moments. Remember that this revolution is not just about overthrowing a regime but about building a society grounded in justice, dignity, and compassion. Sovereignty and moral courage are the twin pillars of that vision. Together, they make us unstoppable.

This is not just a fight for political freedom. It is a revolution of the spirit, one that transcends the battlefield and reaches into the hearts of all who yearn for a better world.

The people of Myanmar are showing the world what it means to be truly free. No matter how long the road, no matter how great the cost, freedom will come because it is rooted in the deepest truths of our shared humanity.

Alan Clements: Daw Suu, your reflections remind me of something you said long ago: "Freedom is not a gift; it is a responsibility." It is such a profound statement—especially when we consider the extraordinary sacrifices that responsibility so often demands.

In Myanmar, as you know so well, the cost of speaking up is devastatingly high. To act in the name of freedom can mean imprisonment, exile, the loss of one's home, family, livelihood—even life itself. And yet, your people continue to rise, to resist, to stand together against unimaginable odds.

How do you inspire that sense of responsibility in others? How do you help them see that freedom is worth fighting for—worth risking everything for—when fear and despair could so easily paralyze the heart?

Aung San Suu Kyi: Alan, responsibility begins with love—love for one's country, one's people, one's shared humanity. When we truly understand that we are not isolated beings but threads in an intricate, interwoven fabric, the question of whether to act becomes almost irrelevant. How can we turn away from our own humanity?

In Myanmar, this understanding is not abstract. It lives in the way we bow to elders, care for neighbors, honor the earth. It is woven into our songs, our prayers, our traditions. We see our lives as part of something greater than ourselves. When one person suffers, we all feel the pain. When one person resists, it strengthens the collective spirit.

As I've said many times, I remind our people: *courage is not the absence of fear—it is the refusal to let fear shape our choices.* The military's brutality is overwhelming, yes, and the sacrifices defy language. But what is the alternative? To submit? To live without dignity? To let future generations inherit chains instead of hope?

Freedom is not just an idea, Alan—it is the foundation of a meaningful life. It is the air that allows conscience to breathe. And yes, it is worth fighting for. It is worth suffering for. Sometimes, it is even worth dying for. *But I also tell my people this*: *we do not fight because we love war or conflict. We fight because we love peace, because we love justice, because we love each other.*

The world often sees Myanmar's revolution as one of guns and suffering—but at its heart, it is a *revolution of the spirit*. Every small act of resistance—a student refusing to bow to false authority, a mother shielding her child, a monk meditating in defiance—is an affirmation of our shared humanity. These acts remind us that we are not powerless, even in the face of overwhelming force.

This is not just Myanmar's struggle. The world, too, is suffering from a crisis of disconnection. Fear, apathy, and selfishness have woven themselves into the very fabric of global society. People forget their responsibility to one another, to the planet, to the future. But we forget that the power to change the world does not begin with governments or armies—it begins with a single thought, a single action, a single heart that refuses to give in to despair.

Alan, the stakes are indeed high. But when I look at my people—farmers, artists, students, elders, nurses, children—I see extraordinary courage. They remind me every day that even in the darkest moments, the light of humanity can never be extinguished. Our revolution is not just a political fight; it is a spiritual awakening. And while the cost is immense, the gift we are working toward—a future of freedom and dignity for all—is beyond price.

Responsibility, you see, is not a burden. It is the deepest expression of love. And when we act from that place of love, there is nothing we cannot endure, nothing we cannot overcome.

Alan Clements: Daw Suu, your reflections remind me of the extraordinary courage your people have shown in the face of oppression. Farmers, students, monks, and mothers—unarmed and vulnerable—standing against a military machine engineered to crush their dreams. And yet, they persist. They resist.

As I look at the world today, I see unimaginable suffering unfolding before our eyes. In Gaza, over 60,000 people have been killed—entire families buried beneath rubble, while the wounded cry out in silence, cut off from help. In Lebanon, villages lie in ruins, city blocks decimated, the weight of repeated wars leaving communities shattered and spirits weary. Syria remains scarred by more than a decade of bloodshed, with entire generations growing up amid destruction and exile. In Ukraine, once-fertile fields are scorched by relentless missile fire, millions of lives torn apart in a proxy war waged without mercy. In Russia, families grieve sons lost to a war many never believed in, while fear and repression silence those who dare to dissent.

And now, the skies over the Middle East burn once again. Israel has launched strikes on Iran. Iran has responded with missiles of its own. Two ancient civilizations—each with profound cultural and spiritual heritage—locked in a cycle of vengeance that threatens to engulf the entire region. The path of retaliation has become a prison of fire.

Daw Suu, it feels as though we are witnessing a global unraveling. The machinery of destruction is relentless, powered by the engines of hatred, greed, and fear. Its reach is vast and indiscriminate, leaving behind broken communities, displaced people, and hearts hardened by trauma.

In Myanmar, the cries of the oppressed rise from prisons and mass graves, echoing through a land held hostage by its own military. In Afghanistan, women and girls are slowly being erased—not with bombs, but with policies that deny their very existence. In Sudan, conflict erupts again and again, displacing millions while the world looks away. And in Congo, in Yemen, and in the forgotten refugee camps where the Rohingya wait without a future, suffering continues in the shadows—largely unseen, but no less real.

Even in countries untouched by war, the slow violence of racism, inequality, and fentanyl—killing hundreds of thousands, if not millions, through what can only be called chemical warfare—ravages lives. These are not distant problems. They are not separate from us. The unraveling is global. The storm is not approaching—it is already here, and we are living within it.

You have spoken of the *revolution of the spirit* as both a personal and collective transformation. What deeper lessons, rooted in Myanmar's long and painful struggle, do you believe the world must urgently learn if we are to face these global crises before it is too late?

Aung San Suu Kyi: Alan, Myanmar's struggle is a microcosm of the greater human story. The same forces that oppress my people—greed, hatred, and delusion—are at work across the world, leaving behind a trail of devastation and despair. These horrors you mentioned, and so many others, are not distant tragedies; they are reflections of a deeper crisis—a crisis of disconnection, a forgetting of our shared humanity. And yet, even amidst this darkness, there are lessons we must not ignore.

The first lesson is that the human spirit, no matter how battered, cannot be extinguished. In Myanmar, our people face bullets with nothing but their conviction, their courage, and their belief in a better future. In Gaza, mothers cradle their children, whispering hope in the midst of despair. In Ukraine, volunteers risk their lives to rescue the wounded, refusing to let compassion die. These acts of defiance, of love, remind us that humanity's light cannot be snuffed out, even by the most oppressive forces.

The second lesson is the power of unity. In Myanmar, decades of division—ethnic, religious, generational—were deliberately sown to control us. But today, our diversity is our strength. The same must be true for the world. In Gaza, in Ukraine, in Russia, in Syria, in Iran, in Yemen, in Israel—even in America—we must reject the narratives that pit neighbor against neighbor, nation against nation. Unity does not erase difference; it honors and amplifies it. *Only by coming together can we dismantle the structures of violence and build a foundation of peace.*

The third lesson is the necessity of mindful awareness. Violence feeds on fear and anger, perpetuating endless cycles of revenge and destruction. But mindfulness allows us to act with intention, to choose compassion over hatred, wisdom over impulse. This is not passive acceptance; it is the most profound form of resistance—to meet violence not with submission, but with clarity and courage.

Finally, Alan, there is a truth we must confront with open eyes: *some things are worth fighting for, even at great cost.* Freedom, dignity, and justice are not luxuries; they are the essence of a life worth living. In Myanmar, people do not fight because they love conflict; they fight because they love peace. They fight because they love their children, their communities, their future.

But let me be clear: this fight is not fueled by hatred. Hatred only deepens the wounds we seek to heal. The revolution of the spirit must be grounded in love—in the love that steadies a mother's hand as she comforts her child, in the love that binds strangers together in acts of courage, in the love that refuses to give up even when all seems lost.

These lessons are urgent. The wars and suffering you speak of, Alan, are not inevitable. They are choices, born of the same poisons of greed, hatred, and ignorance that we must uproot in ourselves and our systems. Myanmar's struggle may be ours to endure, but its lessons belong to the world. If we can rise—if we can transform our pain into compassion, our fear into resolve—then so can humanity.

The question is not whether we can learn these lessons. The question is whether we will choose to.

Alan Clements: Daw Suu, your emphasis on mindfulness draws us back to the *Dhamma*—the inner work that sustains not just individuals, but entire movements, even revolutions. In your life, you have faced challenges that would break most people, and yet your spirit endures.

As I think of you now, confined within a cell, I can only imagine how deeply this practice must root you, how profoundly it shapes your resilience. If I may, please share, how does the *Dhamma* sustain you, even here, as you endure the isolation and hardships of imprisonment?

Aung San Suu Kyi: Alan, the *Dhamma* is not just my refuge; it is my teacher, my sanctuary, and my unbreakable companion on this journey. In this cell, where the walls press in with silence and time feels suspended, I am left with only myself—my thoughts, my fears, my humanity. Meditation becomes my lifeline, the steady ground beneath my feet.

The conditions of imprisonment—the damp walls, the absence of sunlight, the relentless monotony—are harsh, yes. But they are impermanent. These sensations, as real as they feel, are not who I am. And just as the Buddha taught, *suffering arises not from the conditions themselves, but from how the mind meets them.*

Meditation reminds me of this truth daily. It teaches me to observe without attachment, to see the anger and despair that rise within me and let them pass, like clouds drifting across the sky. Through mindfulness, I recognize that even the military's cruelty, though devastating, is born of ignorance. And ignorance, like the darkness of this cell, can be dispelled by light.

This understanding frees me from hatred. Hatred, Alan, is a poison. It corrodes the soul, blinds the heart, and diminishes the very humanity we seek to protect. I send *metta*—loving-kindness—to my captors not because I condone their actions, but because I refuse to let them define me. *In refusing to hate, I reclaim my power. I remain whole.*

But let me be clear: this inner work is not passive. It is not resignation, nor is it a turning away from the suffering around me. On the contrary, it is the foundation of action. Through mindfulness, I find clarity. Through loving-kindness, I find strength. *And through the Dhamma, I am reminded that true resistance is not about conquering others—it is about refusing to be conquered by the forces of greed, hatred, and delusion.*

When I meditate, I think of the people of Myanmar—the farmers who rise before dawn to work in fields shadowed by soldiers, the students who whisper songs of freedom in the dark, the mothers who shield their children from both bullets and despair. Their courage is my strength. Their resilience is my guide.

And I think also of those beyond our borders—the families torn apart in Gaza, the children displaced in Sudan, the fathers burying sons in Ukraine. Their suffering reminds me that the *Dhamma* is not confined to one nation or struggle. It is universal, as is the responsibility it demands of each of us.

Alan, this practice—this path—is not easy. To sit with pain, to face fear, to extend compassion to those who wish you harm—it requires a discipline of the heart that is both fierce and tender. But within this discipline lies the seed of freedom. And freedom, as I have often said, begins not with the breaking of chains but with the liberation of the mind.

So even here, within these walls, I remain free. Not because I deny the reality of my circumstances, but because I refuse to let them imprison my spirit. The *Dhamma* sustains me—not as an escape, but as a living reminder of what is possible: a world where courage meets compassion, where resistance is born of love, and where even the smallest acts of mindfulness ripple outward, transforming not only ourselves but the world we share.

That, Alan, is how the *Dhamma* sustains me. And that, I believe, is how it can sustain us all.

Alan Clements: Thank you, Daw Suu. As I reflect on our conversation, I'm once again inspired by the teachings of our mutual teacher, the late Venerable Sayadaw U Pandita. He often spoke of the importance of recognizing the limits of our knowledge—and the courage required to face the unknown.

In life, and especially in times of great struggle, he would remind us that we often cling to what we *think* we know, as if certainty itself could shield us from suffering. But the *Dhamma* invites us to step into the unknown—not recklessly, but with humility and mindful intelligence—to lean into the questions that unsettle us, the truths that challenge us.

Daw Suu, in your journey—through imprisonment, resistance, and leadership—how has the *Dhamma* guided you in navigating the unknown? How do you reconcile the limits of what we can know with the imperative to act, to lead, to resist—especially when the stakes are so high?

Aung San Suu Kyi: Alan, the unknown is a vast and often daunting territory, but it is also the wellspring of growth—and of transformation. The *Dhamma* teaches us that clinging to certainty is like grasping at a shadow—it slips through our fingers and leaves us empty-handed. True understanding begins with the courage to admit what we do not know, and the willingness to explore it with humility.

In this cell, the unknown surrounds me. I do not know when—or if—I will be free. I do not know the fate of those I love, nor the ultimate outcome of our struggle. *But the Dhamma reminds me: uncertainty is not an enemy. It is a teacher.* To face the unknown without fear is to open ourselves to the wisdom that lies beyond the edges of understanding.

As you know, Sayadawgyi, often spoke of mindfulness as the key to navigating uncertainty. He would say, *"Observe without judgment. Notice what arises and let it teach you."* This practice has become my anchor. When confronted by the unknown, I ask myself: *What is this moment asking of me?* Not what I wish it would be, not what I fear it might be—but what it truly is.

The answers are not always clear. Sometimes, the unknown feels vast—like an abyss. But within that vastness is possibility: the possibility to see with fresh eyes, to act with intention rather than reaction, to discover truths we might otherwise overlook.

As a leader, I have learned that knowing what you do not know is not weakness—it is strength. It allows you to seek out those who hold the missing pieces. It reminds you to listen, to remain open, to trust the collective wisdom of others. Leadership is not about having all the answers; it is about creating the space where questions can flourish, and truths can emerge.

And in resistance, Alan, the unknown is unavoidable. We do not know how long the fight will take, nor how great the sacrifices will be. But the *Dhamma* teaches: we do not need to know the entire path to take the first step. We need only to act with integrity—guided by compassion, justice, and mindfulness.

In time, I have come to see the unknown not as a void, but as an invitation—a call to expand the edges of our understanding, to reach beyond what we think we know. It is a process of trusting not only in ourselves, but in the interconnectedness of all things.

When the unknown feels overwhelming, I turn to the *Dhamma's* greatest teaching: *Anicca*—impermanence. Everything we face—our fears, our struggles, our uncertainties—is transient. And within that transience lies freedom. To let go of the need to control, and to step into the unknown with an open heart and mind, is to touch the very essence of liberation.

Alan, the unknown is not something to be feared. It is the ground upon which we grow. It is the mirror in which we see our courage, our vulnerability, and our shared humanity. And if we can learn to walk with it, hand in hand, we will find not only the answers we seek—but the wisdom to live beyond certainty. For it is in that space—the space of not knowing—that we become whole.

Alan Clements: Daw Suu, your reflections on mindfulness and the revolution of the spirit remind me of something you have often emphasized: how the mind is both the source of suffering and the key to liberation. You have spoken of this not only in personal terms but in the context of the collective—how the state of human consciousness shapes the world we create.

How does this insight shape your understanding of the struggles in Myanmar—and beyond?

Aung San Suu Kyi: Alan, the mind is indeed the forerunner of all things. Every action—whether rooted in kindness or cruelty—originates as a thought. The Buddha taught this, and it remains as true today as it was 2,600 years ago. The great atrocities of our time—genocide, mass imprisonment, the perpetuation of oppression—did not appear from nowhere. They were conceived in the minds of individuals consumed by greed, hatred, and delusion.

This understanding aligns with something Václav Havel once said, which has stayed with me throughout this struggle:

"Consciousness precedes Being, and not the other way around. For this reason, the salvation of this human world lies nowhere else than in the human heart, in the human power to reflect, in human modesty, and in human responsibility. Without a global revolution in the sphere of human consciousness, nothing will change for the better."

These words are a profound reminder that the systems of oppression we fight—authoritarianism, militarism, exploitation—are but outward manifestations of the inner poisons of the mind. Without addressing these root causes, no amount of political reform or technological advancement will bring about true freedom. The revolution we seek must begin in the realm of consciousness.

Alan Clements: That insight resonates deeply, Daw Suu, especially in a time when so many look outward—to governments, technologies, or economies—for solutions to the crises we face. Your call for a "revolution in consciousness" feels far more fundamental, even transformative.

I know we've spoken about this to some extent, but could you say more? What does this revolution truly look like—and where does it begin?

Aung San Suu Kyi: It begins within each of us. Before we can hope to transform the world, we must first undertake the far more difficult task of transforming ourselves. The Buddha identified the root causes of suffering—*lobha* (greed), *dosa* (hatred), and *moha* (delusion). These are not abstract forces; they are habits of the mind—deeply conditioned patterns that shape how we see, how we act, and how we relate to one another.

In Myanmar, this revolution of consciousness is not a choice; it is a necessity. Our people confront not only the physical violence of the military but the psychological violence of fear and despair. To resist this, we must cultivate qualities that counteract these denigrating forces: *generosity in the face of greed, loving-kindness in the face of hatred, and wisdom in the face of ignorance.*

But this transformation cannot remain confined to Myanmar. The interconnectedness of our world means that the revolution in consciousness must be global. Look at the systemic dehumanization of entire peoples—whether through mass incarceration, cultural erasure, or the machinery of genocide. These are not isolated atrocities; they are symptoms of a deeper moral failure. Authoritarianism thrives because fear and mistrust are planted into the collective psyche. Injustice endures because we fail to recognize—and defend—the inherent dignity of every human life.

This global revolution begins with small, personal acts: moments of mindfulness, honest self-reflection, the courage to confront uncomfortable truths. But it must also extend outward—into the ways we structure our societies, educate our children, and engage with one another. It is both deeply personal and profoundly collective.

Alan Clements: Daw Suu, your vision of a revolution that begins in the heart and ripples outward is profoundly moving. Could you speak more about how this understanding has guided you personally—especially now, as you endure the solitude and strain of imprisonment?

Aung San Suu Kyi: Alan, prison has a way of stripping life to its essence. No title. No role. No audience. Only silence—and the unrelenting presence of one's own mind. At times, that silence feels like a wound. At others, like a mirror. Here, within these walls, I am left with nothing but myself: my doubts, my longing, my remembered joys, and the quiet ache of absence. The voices of those I love return only as echoes. The pain is not dramatic. It is ordinary. Unadorned. And profoundly human.

There is no romance in endurance. But there is truth. And the truth is: I struggle too. I feel sorrow. I feel anger. Yet I do not allow those emotions to shape the manner of my being. Instead, I meet them as they arise—with the few tools left to me: mindfulness, patience, and love. Insight meditation has taught me to sit with the ache, not to be consumed by it. Through *metta*, as I have said before, I extend goodwill even to my captors—not in approval of their actions, but as a quiet act of defiance. I will not let hatred script my life. Hatred is cunning—it dresses itself in the illusion of strength. But it is weakness in disguise. It contracts the heart. And we cannot build a liberated nation from hearts that have forgotten how to expand.

Let me be clear: this is not surrender. This is resistance in its most elemental form—the refusal to let darkness define who we are. To remain open, to feel deeply, and still choose compassion—again and again—that, to me, is the revolution.

Alan Clements: Daw Suu, your words move through sorrow and rise like prayer. If you could leave one message—for Myanmar, for the world—what would it be?

Aung San Suu Kyi: I would say this: the world is shaped not only by power, but by perception. Not only by laws, but by how we see and treat one another. If we want a world of justice, peace, and dignity, we must begin not with systems, but with consciousness—with how we choose to see, to feel, to act.

To those who despair, remember: courage often begins in silence, with a single thought that refuses to give in. To those gripped by anger, know that forgiveness is not surrender—it is freedom from the prison of your own bitterness. And to those who feel invisible: you are not. Every quiet act of kindness, every refusal to conform to cruelty, carries the weight of history.

To the people of Myanmar, I say: You are the revolution. Not one leader. Not one moment. But the living fabric of resistance woven through your everyday dignity. Every child you protect. Every truth you speak. Every time you stand without fear—or despite it.

And to the world, I say: do not underestimate the human heart. The revolution we need is not only political—it is spiritual, ethical, relational. Without a revolution of consciousness, no government, no technology, no movement will endure. But with it—even the impossible becomes inevitable.

DIGNITY, HUMAN RIGHTS, AND THE *DHAMMA*

Author's Prelude

In her family home in Yangon, I once sat across from Aung San Suu Kyi, her presence a study in defiance tempered by grace. Her voice, soft yet unyielding, carried the weight of a woman who has known both captivity and conviction, and it returned always to a single truth: dignity is not bestowed by power—it is forged in the crucible of conscience. It is not granted; it is claimed.

In the pages that follow, she weaves together two seemingly disparate strands—the Universal Declaration of Human Rights and the *Dhamma*—into a single tapestry of moral clarity. Here, the *Dhamma* is not mere doctrine, nor the Buddha's teachings reduced to scripture. It is the eternal law of wisdom and compassion, the path that stirs, steadies, and ultimately frees the human heart. Likewise, human rights are not abstract ideals but the practical grammar of dignity, a codification of what it means to honor the inviolable within each person.

What unfolds is no ordinary discourse on politics or ethics. It is a prayer veiled as conversation, a summons to action that springs not from dogma but from awakened integrity. This dialogue does not cajole or exhort; it illuminates. It remembers. It offers a compass that points not inferred to some distant horizon but inward, to the moral law etched in the soul—untouched by tyranny, anchored in truth. Here, the revolution is not of rhetoric or rebellion but of conscience, a silent awakening that dares to reshape the world.

◆ ◆ ◆

Alan Clements: Daw Suu, the world seems to be reaching a tipping point. Across the globe, we face crises that threaten not only nations but the very fabric of our shared existence. From rising authoritarianism to economic instability and the erosion of basic freedoms, the challenges are immense.

You have often spoken about the importance of conscience in leadership—of grounding decision-making in emotional intelligence and the courage to act beyond self-interest. As someone who has sacrificed so much for your principles, how do you see the role of conscience in shaping the kind of leadership the world so desperately needs? And how do we inspire leaders, both current and future, to embody these values?

Aung San Suu Kyi: Alan, true leadership begins not with ambition, but with service. It is not about accumulating power, but about using whatever influence one has to uplift and protect others. And to serve well, one must understand deeply the nature of power itself—and of the mind that wields it.

Conscience is the foundation of true service—it is the quiet, unshakable guide that helps us discern what is right, even in the most complex and painful situations. But conscience alone is not always enough. Leadership, especially in our world today, must be forged at the intersection of emotional and mindful intelligence. The mind is the primary tool of a leader—and as Sayadaw U Pandita often reminded us, *"To know the mind is the most important task of one's life."*

In times of crisis, conscience-based leadership is not a luxury; it is a necessity. Leaders must have the courage to stand not for what is expedient, but for what is ethical. This requires deep introspection and the willingness to confront uncomfortable truths—not only about the world, but about themselves. And yet, let us not underestimate the complexity of this task. In a country like ours—emerging from decades of dictatorship—entire generations were shaped by the psychology of fear, hierarchy, and submission. Transitioning to democracy is not only a political endeavor; it is a psychological and spiritual revolution.

Leadership without conscience becomes self-serving and destructive. It fosters division, feeds on fear, and prioritizes profit over people. But leadership rooted in conscience has the power to heal, to unite, and to inspire. It invites people into a process of awakening, of remembering their shared humanity—often against immense psychological resistance. Such leadership does not seek to dominate—it seeks to serve with humility and wisdom.

The question of how we inspire this kind of leadership is a profound one. And the answer lies not only in who leads, but in the values of those who follow.

Conscience-based leadership flourishes in societies that value truth, compassion, and justice. If we, as citizens, demand these qualities—if we refuse to accept corruption, deception, and apathy—then we create the conditions for authentic leadership to emerge.

Alan, one of the most difficult lessons I have learned, and something I have said repeatedly, is that *courage is not the absence of fear, but the refusal to let fear dictate our actions.*

In my case, our entire democratically elected leadership was decapitated. And yet we must not let despair paralyze us. For many of us, the price has already been paid. We have been imprisoned, silenced, forgotten by much of the world. So be it. The greater danger is not criticism or even persecution—it is the slow erosion of conscience. The alternative to principled leadership is not safety; it is moral ruin. And that, we cannot accept.

To inspire future leaders, we must begin with truth—lived, not taught. Integrity is not a lesson; it is a lineage. It begins in the heart, is shaped by the home, and tested in the world.

To those already in power: Look inward before you speak. Accountability begins in silence—with the courage to ask, "What harm have I caused? Whose lives hang in the balance of my choices?"

Leadership is not domination. It is creating the conditions for others to rise. It is the humility to know that the fate of many rests on the conscience of one.

In times like these, we don't need more rulers. We need moral architects. Not more promises—presence. Not more commands—compassion.

This is the revolution of leadership: to serve without ego, to unite without fear, to lead without leaving anyone behind.

Alan Clements: Daw Suu, your reflections on conscience and service call to mind the Universal Declaration of Human Rights (UDHR). Its first lines proclaim "Recognition of the inherent dignity and of the equal and inalienable rights of all members of the human family is the foundation of freedom, justice and peace in the world." I've long felt these principles echo something even more ancient—the heart of the *Dhamma* itself.

When I speak of the *Dhamma*, I don't mean it in a narrow, sectarian sense. I mean the universal law of inner freedom—the path of mindful awareness, ethical clarity, and the fearless embodiment of compassion. The *Dhamma*, to me, is a way of being that transcends belief. It is the living ecosystem of conscience.

But in a world so fractured, so desensitized, the UDHR can feel like poetry etched on paper—noble, yes, but distant. So, I ask you this: How do you see the timeless principles of the *Universal Declaration of Human Rights* aligning with the liberating truths of the *Dhamma*? And how does mindfulness—as both insight and practice—transform these rights from abstract ideals into a lived, embodied reality?

Aung San Suu Kyi: Alan, I've always felt that the *Universal Declaration of Human Rights* and the *Dhamma* speak to the same truth, though in different languages. One was written in the ashes of world war; *the other in the stillness beneath a tree where, it is said, the Buddha awakened to the truth of suffering and liberation.* But both begin with the same insight: that human dignity is not given—it is inherent. That freedom is not a luxury—it is the birthright of every being.

As you stated, the opening lines of the UDHR say it best: *"Recognition of the inherent dignity and of the equal and inalienable rights of all members of the human family is the foundation of freedom, justice and peace in the world."* That sentence alone could serve as a mantra for humanity.

And not far behind it is the warning: *"Disregard and contempt for human rights have resulted in barbarous acts which have outraged the conscience of mankind."* These are not poetic exaggerations. I have lived through these "barbarous acts." My people continue to endure them. Entire generations have been silenced, displaced, imprisoned, or erased from memory. This is what happens when we abandon the sacredness of human dignity.

The UDHR outlines thirty articles. Thirty expressions of one sacred principle: freedom. Freedom of thought. Freedom of speech. Freedom from fear. Freedom to live without humiliation, without violence, without chains. It is, I believe, the most powerful secular statement ever made about the sanctity of life in our shared human family.

But to truly honor it, we must feel it—not just recite it. Freedom is not simply a legal construct or a political aspiration. *Freedom is the oxygen of civilized coexistence. Without it, love suffocates. Dialogue collapses. Trust dies.* In its absence, societies asphyxiate—spiritually, morally, and eventually, politically. *That is why I believe both the Dhamma and the UDHR ask the same thing of us: to live in a way that protects the freedom of others as if it were our own.*

This is where mindfulness becomes essential. As we know, mindfulness is not passivity. It is not detachment or escape. *Mindfulness is the experiential intelligence of presence.* It is the art of showing up—fully, with heart, with discernment, and with the readiness to act. It teaches us to meet each moment with honesty, to listen without distortion, and to see clearly what liberates and what enslaves.

In a world where rights are violated in silence and dignity is traded for convenience, mindfulness becomes a radical act. It trains the heart to remain human in dehumanizing conditions. It empowers us to respond, not with reactivity, but with integrity.

When I speak of the *Dhamma*, I speak of this: the imperfect, often faltering discipline of freedom. Not a flawless path, but a daily one—a practice of learning to see the world more clearly, even when clarity hurts. Of learning to live with less hatred, even when anger tempts us. It is the willingness to feel—to truly feel—the ache of this life, the disappointment, the injustice, and still, somehow, to choose love over bitterness. To choose truth, even after we've turned away from it. To return to presence, again and again, however many times we've drifted.

The *Dhamma* is not perfection—it is the ancient art of getting back up, of facing a new day with an undefended heart. Come what may, we stay with it. That, to me, is real freedom.

So yes, Alan, I believe the UDHR and the *Dhamma* are partners in the same moral struggle. One gives us the legal compass; the other, the spiritual training. And together, they ask us to walk the path of liberation—not just for ourselves, but for all beings.

Because freedom, in its deepest sense, is not something we demand. It is something we embody. And when we embody it, we give others permission to breathe.

Alan Clements: Thank you, Daw Suu. What you've articulated— the convergence of the *Dhamma* and the Universal Declaration as complementary paths of inner and societal liberation—offers a rare clarity, especially in a time when both principles are so often neglected or misunderstood.

With that in mind, may I ask: If you were to speak directly to today's global leaders—those in positions of power and influence— what, in your view, is their deepest responsibility in this moment?

Aung San Suu Kyi: Alan, if I could speak directly to the leaders of today—those entrusted with the weight of nations—I would not raise my voice. I would speak softly, because truth needs no volume to be heard.

I would remind them: power is not a prize, but a trust—a delicate, impermanent gift. And how one holds it, gently or with a clenched fist, defines not only the fate of others but the very legacy they leave behind.

I would ask, with sincerity: Whom do you truly serve? When you make decisions—are you protecting your people, or preserving your position? Are your actions rooted in fear, or in care? Strength without compassion becomes cruelty. But when strength is guided by wisdom and humility, it becomes a force for healing.

I would remind them that the world is watching—not just with eyes, but with hearts. And history, in the end, tells the truth. Not about how long someone ruled, but how they ruled. Were they builders of peace, or architects of fear?

True leadership demands more than political skill; it demands moral courage—the courage to uproot the forces of division, cruelty, and deceit, wherever they arise, even within oneself.

The Universal Declaration of Human Rights and the *Dhamma* offer the same call: to see the humanity in all people, to act with compassion, and to lead with integrity. These are not just ideals—they are practical necessities for the survival of our shared world. If even a handful of leaders take this to heart, they can ignite a ripple of change that touches us all.

True power, Alan, lies not in control but in service. It is not measured by what one takes, but by what one gives. This is the leadership our world needs. And this is the leadership we must demand—not through force, but through the quiet insistence of the human spirit.

And I say this not in anger, but with a heart full of sorrow for my own country, Myanmar. The suffering of our people is immense. Families torn apart. Voices silenced. Dreams deferred.

So, I ask—gently, humbly—for the world's help.

To all leaders of goodwill, I appeal to your sense of humanity. Please, stand with us in our struggle for peace, for dignity, and for freedom. Help us bring an end to tyranny—not through vengeance, but through the restoration of justice.

And let us also begin something even greater—a global movement for peace, prosperity, and mutual coexistence. Let us study, with open minds and open hearts, every principle and protocol that promotes nonviolence—economically, religiously, and spiritually. Let us implement whatever is necessary so that people—all people—may live without fear, without deprivation, and without exclusion.

This is how human creativity will flourish—when safety is no longer a privilege but a birthright. Especially now, in this age of rapid globalization, artificial intelligence, and perhaps even interstellar cooperation, we must plant the seeds of peace deeper than ever before.

Now is the time. Not later. Not when it is convenient. Now is the time to choose life. To choose love. To choose peace.

And if I may, to President Trump: Your belief in peace through strength has inspired many. Might you now bring that strength to Myanmar, where the spirit of freedom still burns brightly, awaiting the winds of global solidarity to carry it forward?

We are not asking for miracles. Only for courage. For conscience. And for the chance to be free.

Alan Clements: Daw Suu, may it be so. May the leaders of the world—and my own American President—hear your call and act with conscience and courage, and act soon—as in now, please.

As we delve deeper into the *Universal Declaration of Human Rights*, I'm struck by the profound beauty of its vision—a vision that recognizes freedom as the cornerstone of human dignity.

Articles 18 and 19, in particular, stand out: the right to freedom of thought, conscience, religion, opinion, and expression. These are not luxuries; they are the foundation of a truly free and flourishing society.

These freedoms feel especially urgent in today's world, where censorship, propaganda, and disinformation are eroding truth and trust. And with that erosion comes fear, silence, and the suppression of the human spirit.

How do you see these freedoms—as both spiritual and civic imperatives—essential to human flourishing? And what would you say to those who hold the power, right now, to either uphold or suppress them?

Aung San Suu Kyi: Alan, freedom is not merely a political construct; it is the essence of being human. To think, to speak, to express, to create—these are the acts that define our humanity. Articles 18 and 19 of the Universal Declaration are not just rights; they are affirmations of what it means to live with dignity and authenticity.

The right to freedom of thought and conscience is the foundation of all other freedoms. Without it, we cannot discern truth, form meaningful relationships, or cultivate the wisdom that allows societies to grow and flourish. To deny someone this freedom is to deny them their humanity.

Similarly, the right to freedom of opinion and expression is the lifeblood of democracy. It is through the exchange of ideas that we challenge assumptions, refine our understanding, and hold power to account. Without this freedom, societies wither, and tyranny takes root.

Yet, Alan, these freedoms are among the most fragile. In Myanmar, as in many parts of the world, they are systematically suppressed. Censorship is not merely a tool of control; it is a weapon of fear. It silences dissent, distorts reality, and isolates people from one another. Propaganda compounds this, manufacturing consent and deepening division.

But let us not forget the beauty of these freedoms when they are honored. Freedom of expression allows us to share our stories, our struggles, and our dreams. It enables the poet to inspire, the journalist to inform, the activist to challenge. It creates a space where we see one another not as enemies, but as fellow human beings, united by a common longing for dignity and understanding.

The Buddha spoke of right speech—speech that is truthful, kind, and beneficial. This teaching is deeply relevant to the concept of freedom of expression. Freedom does not mean the absence of responsibility. It means using our voices to elevate, not to harm—to speak with clarity and compassion in a world clouded by fear and division.

To those in power, I would say this: censorship and propaganda may seem to strengthen your hold, but they erode the very foundation upon which true authority rests. They create mistrust, fracture integrity, and sow the seeds of unrest. True leadership lies not in silencing voices, but in creating the conditions where voices can flourish. *A society where people can speak freely is a society that can heal, innovate, and thrive.*

And yes, that freedom includes disagreement—even speech that is uncomfortable or offensive. I am well aware of what it means to be the target of hate speech. It has followed me for years. But so be it. That, too, is a right in a free society. Freedom of expression means little if it only protects what is polite or popular.

What matters is how we respond. Let us not lower the standard of discourse to match our divisions. Let us raise it—to meet the depth of our shared humanity. Let us speak with clarity, even in conflict. Let us listen with humility, even in disagreement. *And let us remember: beneath it all, through it all, we belong to one another.*

In the end, democracy is not static. Nor is the UDHR a finished idea. We are evolving the meaning of both—through how we speak, how we listen, and how we love.

Freedom is not just the right to speak—it is the courage to hear one another into wholeness.

Alan Clements: Beautiful, Daw Suu. Thank you for offering such an elegant and vital reminder of the true breadth and depth of freedom. Your words bring to mind Article 1 of the Declaration, which states: "All human beings are born free and equal in dignity and rights."

There is something profoundly stirring—almost sacred—in this affirmation of our shared human worth. And yet, we live in a world increasingly torn apart by race, religion, class, and ideology. The ideal of equality feels, at times, like a distant shore.

So, I ask: How do we reclaim this principle—not as a slogan, but as a lived reality—in a world so fractured? And how do these divisions, if left unhealed, threaten the very freedoms you've just spoken of: the freedom to think, to speak, to be?

Aung San Suu Kyi: Alan, the principle of equality is both a truth and a profound challenge. It is a truth because, as the Buddha taught, all beings share the same fundamental nature—the same capacity for love, for fear, for hope, and for suffering. But it is a challenge because ignorance, fear, and greed so often obscure that truth.

Divisions of race, religion, class, and ideology are not inherent— they are constructs of the mind. They are born of *moha*, delusion, which blinds us to our interconnectedness and creates false hierarchies of worth. These illusions justify the denial of freedom and dignity. And history shows us the consequences: segregation, oppression, violence—even genocide. When we forget our shared humanity, cruelty becomes possible.

The *Dhamma* asks us to look beyond these illusions. It teaches us to see the suffering of others as our own, to recognize that the freedom of one is bound to the freedom of all. This is the foundation of reconciliation. It is what allows us to bridge divides—not by erasing difference, but by honoring it. In this light, difference becomes not a threat, but a source of strength.

Alan, reclaiming equality requires both inner and outer work. Internally, we must confront our biases, cultivate compassion, and practice deep mindfulness. Externally, we must challenge the systems that perpetuate injustice. It is not easy work—but it is essential work.

When we live by the principle of equality, the rights enshrined in the Universal Declaration come alive. Freedom of speech becomes a bridge, not a battleground. Freedom of assembly becomes a circle of solidarity. Freedom of religion becomes a celebration of conscience, not a cause for conflict.

To those overwhelmed by the scale of division, I would say this: Begin where you are. Treat the person before you with the dignity they deserve. Listen with humility. Speak with kindness. Act with courage. These small gestures are not small at all—they are the seeds from which justice grows. And let us remember: equality is not an ideal we achieve—it is a truth we remember. And from that remembrance, we begin again.

Alan Clements: Daw Suu, as we near the end of this conversation, let me ask you this: If you could share one final message about the beauty of freedom—and the cost of its denial—what would it be?

Aung San Suu Kyi: Alan, freedom is the soul of humanity. It is the air we breathe, the light that guides us, the space in which we grow and create. To be free is to live authentically, to think without fear, to speak without constraint, to love without limit.

But freedom is fragile. It cannot be assumed. It must be nurtured, protected, and renewed with every generation. When freedom is denied—when voices are silenced, ideas are censored, and truth is distorted—it is not just individuals who suffer; it is the entire society that begins to decay.

The cost of this denial is immense. It is the despair of the unseen, the anger of the unheard, the erosion of potential in those who are denied the right to dream.

Yet the beauty of freedom is that it is never fully extinguished. Even in the darkest times, the human spirit finds ways to resist, to create, and to hope.

To the world, I would say: Do not take your freedoms lightly. Use them wisely. Speak not only for yourself, but for those who cannot. Act not only for your own rights, but for the rights of others. For in defending the freedom of one, we defend the freedom of all.

And to those who deny freedom, I would remind them: History has shown, again and again, that oppression cannot endure. Truth finds a way to break through, and when the human spirit unites, it becomes unstoppable.

Freedom, Alan, is not only a right. It is a responsibility. It is the greatest gift we can offer one another—and the greatest legacy we can leave behind. Let us cherish it. Protect it. And above all, live it.

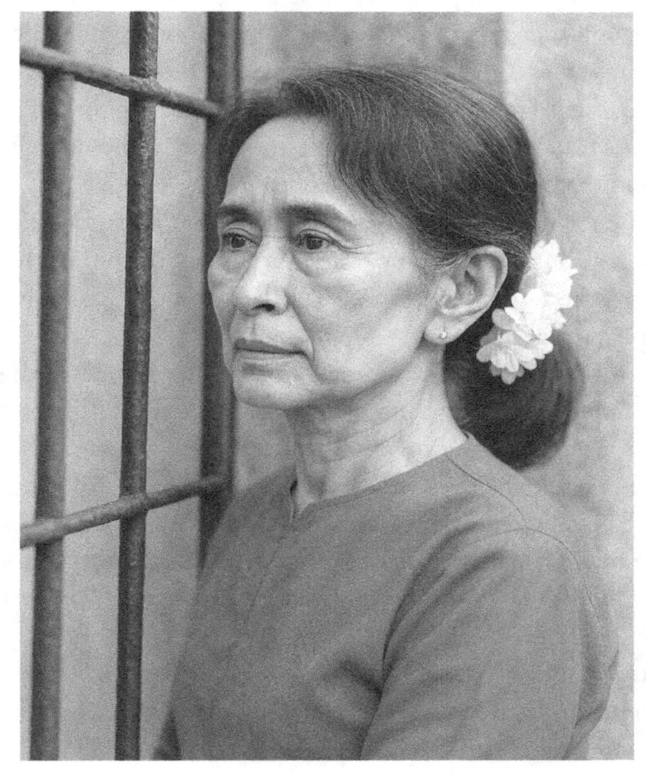

CHAPTER FIVE

A MESSAGE TO THE GUARDIANS OF FREEDOM: FREEDOM:

WORDS FOR FELLOW PRISONERS OF CONSCIENCE

Author's Prelude

There are voices in this world so pure, so unwavering in the face of injustice, that even their silence becomes an indictment of our own. Aung San Suu Kyi is one of those voices—having spent more than two decades in detention, and now, in her fifth year of solitary confinement, she continues to embody the conscience of a people, and the endurance of a principle.

This chapter is for them—for those behind bars not because they broke the law, but because they refused to betray truth. For the unseen, the unsung, the unnamed—whose sacrifices uphold the dignity of the human spirit, even in silence.

It is to these guardians of freedom that this offering is made.

May these pages serve not merely as testimony, but as torchlight in dark times. A light passed hand to hand, heart to heart.

If this book should find its way into the hands of a prisoner of conscience—smuggled between walls, whispered across wires, or carried in memory like prayer beads—I hope it speaks to you. I hope it reminds you: *your courage is not forgotten. Your isolation is not permanent. Your suffering is not in vain.*

You are not a statistic.

You are not a symbol.

You are sacred. A living testament.

And you are the reason we continue to write, to resist, to remember.

◆ ◆ ◆

Alan Clements: Daw Suu, your life has been an unwavering testament to resilience, courage, and the unyielding power of conscience. As we speak today, you are not alone in your suffering. President Win Myint, your steadfast friend and Chief Advisor U Win Htein, and the entire democratically elected leadership of your country remain unjustly imprisoned—stripped of their freedom, yet not their dignity.

Alongside them are more than 22,000 courageous, freedom-loving souls: activists, teachers, civil servants, doctors, students, mothers, poets, singers, construction workers, nuns, monks, filmmakers—citizens from every walk of life—who risked everything for truth, justice, and democracy. Their sacrifices, like yours, are not merely political—they are acts of profound moral clarity in the face of systemic brutality and relentless oppression.

And yet, this struggle extends beyond Myanmar's borders. Across the world, in countless prisons and hidden corners, there are sisters and brothers of revolution who, like you, bear the weight of conscience and the price of courage.

On the chance that this book might be translated, smuggled into these places, and find its way into the hands of these guardians of freedom, I humbly ask you to include them in your reflections, should you feel moved. These extraordinary men and women—heroes and heroines of dignity—face unimaginable hardships, yet remain resolute, standing as vital threads in the tapestry of humanity's shared struggle for democracy, justice, and freedom.

If I may, Daw Suu, what would you say to them? What words of encouragement would you offer, as if addressing them directly?

Aung San Suu Kyi: To speak to my fellow prisoners of conscience—whether here in Myanmar or across the hidden prisons of the world—is to speak directly to the essence of our shared spirit. You are more than individuals enduring unspeakable suffering—you are the breath of courage, the lifeblood of a global movement for dignity, for justice, and for freedom.

To each of you, I say: *you are not alone.* Though the walls around you may seem immovable, they cannot contain the truth you carry. Every act of defiance, every quiet refusal to surrender, sends ripples far beyond the cells that confine you. Your courage is not merely resistance—it is a profound act of creation. You are laying the moral foundation of a freer world.

To President Win Myint—your unshakable dignity continues to light our way. To U Win Htein—your wisdom and quiet strength bridge generations, reminding us that the struggle for liberty is never lost, only passed—like an unextinguished flame—from heart to heart. To my colleagues—cabinet members, ministers, elected MPs—whose only crime was to serve the will of the people: your sacrifices will not be in vain. And to the true architects of the Spring Revolution—the defiant youth and brave citizens who rose with hope against tyranny—you have stirred the conscience of the world.

To the nurses and doctors, the teachers, the civil servants, the nuns and monks, the farmers, students, grandparents, and children who stood tall in the face of danger: you are the soul of this nation. To your families and loved ones: your silent strength sustains us. Your prayers give us breath. You are the unseen heroes who hold up the sky.

To the brave souls within the ethnic armed resistance groups, and to our sons and daughters fighting even now: we are bound by a common dream—the rebirth of a democracy that belongs to all, regardless of ethnicity, faith, or language.

To the people of Myanmar: *I believe in you.* I have always believed in you. You are heirs to a civilization that stretches back thousands of years—a people forged not only in struggle but in wisdom, in grace, and in the quiet strength of the heart. You are a warrior nation—not of conquest, but of conscience. A people whose true power has always been the power of presence, patience, and purpose.

Yes, these are profoundly challenging times. And yes, they may grow darker before the light returns. But never forget: even in the blackest night, the candle of dignity can still burn. Keep the power of your conscience alive. Let it guide your thoughts, your actions, your voice. Walk with dignity, even when no one is watching. Stand tall, even when your knees tremble. Your every act of being—your refusal to give in to hatred or despair—is a radiant defiance. Shine brightly, regardless of how shadowed the path may seem. Be sure: *our time is on the rise.*

And to the international community: *please, do not look away.* Help us restore the radiance of this nation—the newest birth of democracy on our beleaguered Earth. Myanmar still shines beneath the ashes. Let us help her rise.

Alan Clements: Daw Suu, your words echo with such quiet strength and clarity. They do not merely speak to suffering—they dignify it. In honoring those whose lives have been shattered by repression, you illuminate a path forward not only for Myanmar but for anyone who has ever stood alone in the dark, holding fast to hope.

And yet, the realities so many endure are beyond words—torture, starvation, prolonged isolation, and the devastating loss of loved ones. The weight of it can push even the most resilient to the very edge.

May I ask, with the deepest respect for your own unimaginable hardship: how do you speak to those who find themselves on the brink of despair? What might you offer to those who feel powerless in the face of such relentless cruelty?

Aung San Suu Kyi: Alan, I thank you for asking this with such care. When people are pushed to the brink—when they are stripped of all that feels human, when the world retreats into silence—it is not enough to ask them to simply endure. Endurance for its own sake is not life; it can become an exile from the soul.

Instead, I would remind them—gently, tenderly—why they are still here. We are not imprisoned because we sought suffering. We are here because we refused to betray what we knew to be true. We are here because silence in the face of injustice was not an option. And that knowing—that sacred clarity—is our deepest strength.

To my fellow prisoners, I say: when despair begins to darken your heart, do not only recall the pain. Recall beauty. Recall those small, sacred moments that remind you of your humanity—the scent of a jasmine flower on a warm night, the laughter of a child chasing light, the silent prayer whispered at dawn, the breath of someone sleeping beside you.

Let these memories return—not as ghosts, but as breath. Let them fill your lungs as if you were breathing the present moment for the first time. Let them restore you. Let them remind you that you are alive, that you are more than a prisoner—you are a keeper of sacred memory, a bearer of the revolutionary spirit.

Remember the mother shielding her child from an airstrike, not because she believes she can stop it, but because love gives her no other choice. Remember the student who steps forward unarmed, the teacher who teaches in whispers, the farmer who plants again after every scorched harvest, the monk or the nun who speaks words of loving-kindness into trembling hearts, even as fear surrounds them.

These are not small gestures. They are sacred refusals. They are how we say, "You cannot take my humanity from me." They are how we stay free, even behind walls.

To those who feel powerless, I offer this gentle truth: *you are not powerless. The system that oppresses you feeds on your belief that you have no agency.* But even now, even in confinement, you choose. And your choices matter—the way you hold another's gaze, the way you sit, the way you remember. Choice is the last and first freedom.

Yes, they may confine our bodies, but they cannot imprison our minds—unless we let them.

This is how I practice here in my cell. I return to memory—not to escape, but to feel. I let beauty breathe through me. I make sacred choices throughout the day. I place my awareness where no authority can reach. *This is my revolution. This is my Dhamma.*

And to those who grieve—whose sons, daughters, lovers, and friends have vanished or fallen—I say: *I carry your sorrow with reverence. Your grief is sacred.* Grieve deeply, without shame. But know this: their lives are not extinguished. They live on in your love, in our resistance, in our undying commitment to one another. Their names move through the silence like wind through trees. They guide us still.

So, when the night feels endless, I do not reach for strength. *I reach for remembrance.* And I let it carry me—like breath, like prayer, like love that refuses to end.

Alan Clements: Daw Suu, I know you have already spoken with such clarity and grace about how we carry pain in the light of memory and love. And I bow to that—truly. Your words feel less like answers and more like sacred medicine for a wounded world.

Still, if I may, allow me to continue. Because many who hear or read your words will be holding not just sorrow, but rage. Not just grief, but terror—the kind that keeps one from breathing, from sleeping, from trusting again. These emotions—so human, so overwhelming—are part of the storm we are all trying to navigate.

I understand they are not where we must remain, but they often feel inescapable. And so, I ask, gently: how do you help someone transmute the fire of anger without extinguishing their will to fight? Or walk through the paralyzing fog of fear without collapsing into despair? What does it mean, in your experience, to walk the razor's edge between righteous resistance and inner peace—especially when both are needed, and both seem impossible to hold at once?

Aung San Suu Kyi: Alan, thank you for your kindness—and for naming what so often goes unspoken. Yes, sorrow may be softened by memory, and love may give us breath. But fear and anger, when they surge through the body, feel like fire. They burn through sleep, through speech, through reason. And when the flames are lit by injustice, they are not easily extinguished.

I would never ask anyone to deny these emotions. To pretend to be calm when one is not is not strength—it is erasure. Instead, I try to meet these emotions as I would meet a frightened child or a wounded animal: not with shame or suppression, but with presence and tenderness.

Fear, when left unexamined, contracts the spirit. But fear seen clearly—gently, without judgment—often reveals something sacred: a love we are afraid to lose, a life we long to protect. Fear shows us what we cherish. So, I listen to my fear. I thank it for its message. And then I ask it to walk beside me—but not to lead.

Anger is more complicated. It often arrives wearing the mask of power. It feels like heat, like action, like control. But if I cling to it, it begins to shape me in the image of what I oppose. So, I hold anger carefully, like fire in my palm. I do not throw it—I warm my hands by it. And then I look for the truth beneath it. Often, it is grief. Often, it is love.

When I allow myself to feel what is under the anger—without feeding it—something shifts. Anger becomes clarity. It becomes courage. It becomes direction. This is not suppression—it is transformation. It is what allows us to resist without hatred, to stand firm without becoming rigid, to be fierce without becoming cruel.

Walking that razor's edge you spoke of—between resistance and peace—is not something I accomplish and then declare complete. It is a daily practice—a moment-to-moment devotion. Some days I walk it with grace. Some days I stumble. But I return. And I return again. That returning is the practice.

Here, in this cell, I have very little. But I still have choice. I choose where I place my attention. I choose how I speak to myself. I choose which memories I nourish and which thoughts I release. These small, sacred choices are the revolution of spirit alive within me. And they are available to anyone, anywhere.

So, to those consumed by rage or paralyzed by fear, I say: do not rush to be free of them. Sit with them. Listen. Love them back into wholeness. And from that wholeness, rise.

Even in a prison, you can rise.

Alan Clements: Daw Suu, after all that has been endured—by you, by your people—hope can feel like a fragile whisper. For many, the horizon is no longer visible. How do you sustain hope, truly, in the face of such relentless cruelty? And how might others find it—not merely as an idea, but as a living force within themselves?

Aung San Suu Kyi: Alan, hope is not something we wait for—it is something we tend. Even here, in this silence, it lives. It does not shout. It does not promise. Sometimes, it is no more than the memory of light on leaves, or the echo of a voice once loved. But it is real, enduring even when all else seems lost.

Hope is not the denial of suffering—it is the refusal to surrender to it. It is born in the quiet choices we make each day: to remember instead of forget, to feel instead of numb, to act instead of despair. I find it in the discipline of attention, the dignity of restraint, and the mystery of breath itself.

To my fellow prisoners, I say this: your value is not measured by how long you endure, but by the spirit you keep alive inside. Even when unseen, even when unheard—you are not alone. You are part of something greater than the walls around you.

To the families waiting in grief, your love sustains us. Every act of remembrance, every refusal to give in to bitterness, every quiet act of care—these fragile gestures hold the battered world together.

And to all those across the world who carry this torch of conscience: know that the struggle for freedom does not belong to a single people or place. It is a shared inheritance—and a shared responsibility. Let each act of integrity, no matter how small, be a stitch in the fabric of our shared future.

Hope is not the absence of darkness—it is the way we move through it with our eyes open. And in that way, even here, I have come to know the enduring power of hope.

Alan Clements: Daw Suu, as we close this chapter, if you could offer one final message—to every prisoner of conscience, to their families, and to all who stand for justice and freedom—what would it be?

Aung San Suu Kyi: To every prisoner of conscience, to every mother, father, and child who has lived the silence of waiting, to every soul who has chosen truth over comfort—I say this: You are not only survivors; you are the midwives of a future yet to be born.

To those behind bars: your courage is not lost to the world. It seeds unseen gardens of freedom.

To the families: your love is the hidden thread that weaves strength into generations.

And to the world: freedom is not bestowed by the powerful. It is written into being by those who refuse to bow to cruelty, who choose love again and again, even when it costs them everything.

So let us not merely endure.

Let us become the awakening.

Let us embody the world we long for.

Together, we carry memory.

Together, we light the path.

Together, we are already free.

84

BEARING WITNESS: A CALL TO SEE, TO FEEL, AND TO ACT

Author's Prelude

There are moments in history when bearing witness becomes a sacred act—when to truly see suffering is to carry its moral weight as our own. This is one of those moments. This chapter invites us into the discipline of mindful presence—not as spectators of pain, but as participants in a global reckoning.

"To look into the face of a grieving mother," Aung San Suu Kyi reflects, "or a monk shielding his people, is to be summoned—not merely to ask, 'What is happening?' but to confront the deeper question: 'What will I do with what I now know?'"

It is within the stillness of that question that moral courage begins to take root.

To bear witness is not to observe from a distance—it is to be changed. Not by guilt, but by a love that refuses to turn away. And love, when honored, becomes action.

Later in the conversation, Daw Suu offers this truth: *To truly see is to act. Otherwise, it is not seeing—it is avoidance.* Her words echo through these pages—not as metaphor, but as mandate.

And as she has reminded us time and again, she affirms here: "The call to remember: freedom and dignity are not passive hopes. They are living responsibilities—measured not by intention, but by response. When our seeing is rooted in reverence, it becomes a seed—capable of growing into unity, into justice, into the renewal of our shared humanity."

Let it be planted here. Let this be not only read, but received. And may what is received become a sacred vow—not to forget, not to look away, and never to be the same again.

◆ ◆ ◆

Alan Clements: Daw Suu, as the world watches Myanmar through screens and fragmented glimpses of mass trauma—bombings, village burnings, millions displaced, and the heartbreaking faces of the Kachin, Shan, Karen, Chin, Rohingya, and Burmese monks and nuns— I'm reminded of a powerful truth: to bear witness to suffering is both a privilege and a moral responsibility.

Today, hundreds of millions of people across the globe consume images and videos of atrocities through social media, but the act of watching alone often feels hollow. Some are galvanized to act, others paralyzed by the magnitude of the horrors they witness. For those of us far from the epicenter of these tragedies, how do we transform seeing into meaningful action?

And for you, Daw Suu—who has endured this suffering firsthand, whose friends and colleagues remain imprisoned or have perished—how do you view the world's witnessing? How do you inspire people not to look away, but to truly see, to feel deeply, and to act?

Aung San Suu Kyi: Alan, to bear witness to suffering—*dukkha*, as we say in *Dhamma* terms—the anguish, the struggle, the silent traumas in as many degrees and dimensions as we are capable of witnessing—is to confront and engage the very essence of our shared humanity.

It is both a human act and an existential one—profound in its significance. For to truly see is to accept the moral weight of what we observe, whether invited or imposed, whether distant or intimate.

But seeing alone is not enough. To witness without response is to risk turning suffering into spectacle—and we must resist that with every fiber of our being.

The deeper challenge is this: to feel—as deeply and truthfully as our courage will allow. For only through such honest feeling does our witnessing become meaningful. Only then does it transform into conscience. Only then does compassion become a verb.

As we know, my beloved country of Myanmar bleeds. And the pain of my people echoes far beyond our borders. Families fleeing airstrikes in the mountains, children trembling beneath the sound of gunfire, doctors, teachers, and civil servants who marched for peace only to face bullets, Gen Z protesters who once sang songs of freedom now silenced in prison cells—this is not merely a crisis. It is the crucifixion of a nation.

Even more devastating are the stories of young boys and girls—children—forcibly conscripted, marched to the front lines, and ordered to fire upon their very own brothers and sisters. What greater violence could there be than to sever a child's conscience from their heart?

Every one of these moments must not only be seen, but felt. Because all of Myanmar is ablaze—no place is safe, no soul untouched. And to feel what we see is the first act of moral awakening.

And yet, I understand the burden of witnessing. When you see a father clutching the lifeless body of his child, or hear the cries of a mother whose home has been reduced to rubble, it is human to feel overwhelmed. It is human to turn away. But the pain we feel as witnesses is not weakness—it is a call. It is the voice of conscience, insisting that we act.

To those who watch from afar, I say this: Do not let the magnitude of suffering numb you. Let it ignite you. Let it disturb you awake. Every small act matters—writing a letter, raising your voice, supporting those on the frontlines of justice. The oppressors depend on your silence, your fatigue, your indifference. Do not surrender those to them.

Alan Clements: Daw Suu, your words enter not just the mind, but the heart. They're not ideas to be debated—they're invitations to remember who we are, and what we're here to protect.

Sometimes I think we fear witnessing because we know it can change us. And it should. That's where its power lives—not in observation, but in transformation.

Still, as you've said, witnessing suffering is not without its dangers—*the danger of feeling helpless, the danger of mistaking seeing for doing*. Many of us struggle with feelings of intrusion or helplessness—especially when the images we see feel intimate, even sacred. How do we reconcile this tension? How do we ensure that our witnessing is an act of solidarity, not voyeurism?

Aung San Suu Kyi: Alan, witnessing must be rooted in respect and intention. When I think of a father burying his child in silence, or a monk standing between his monastery and a column of soldiers, I don't see victims—I see courage. These moments are not invitations to pity but calls to solidarity. To see deeply is to recognize that these are not just tragedies, but living acts of defiance against dehumanization.

When we watch with humility, we honor the dignity of those who suffer. We acknowledge their pain, not as something to be consumed, but as something that binds us to them. Bearing witness is not passive; it is an act of carrying their story forward, of refusing to let their voices be silenced.

But we must also ask ourselves: What do we do with what we see? The act of witnessing must lead to action. Share these stories, amplify these voices, confront the systems that perpetuate oppression. Let their courage be a mirror, reflecting our own capacity to act with purpose.

True compassion is not passive. It is a form of sacred participation. Sometimes, to act is to speak. Sometimes, it is to listen. Sometimes, it is simply to refuse to turn away. Even bearing witness with mindful presence—with open-hearted stillness—can become a form of resistance.

What matters is that our seeing—our awareness—is actualized. That we carry what we've seen into the choices we make, the silences we break, and the futures we dare to imagine.

Alan Clements: Daw Suu, you've often spoken about the power of unity in resistance. In Myanmar, unity has been forged in the face of extraordinary diversity and division. How do you see this unity as a response to the suffering we witness?

Aung San Suu Kyi: Unity, Alan, is the antidote to despair. The oppressors thrive on division—on pitting one group against another, on isolating the suffering so that it feels disconnected from the whole. But when we stand together—across cultures, across faiths, across histories—we strip them of that power.

Myanmar's revolution is a testament to this struggle for unity. The Karen and Kachin, the Shan and Chin, the Rohingya and Burman—each has endured unimaginable suffering, yet they are striving, as challenging as it is, to come together in a shared dream of freedom. This unity does not erase their differences; it honors them, weaving those differences into a fabric stronger than oppression can tear apart.

The same is true globally. When we see the suffering of others—whether in Myanmar, Gaza, Ukraine, Iran, Russia, Israel, or elsewhere—it is not enough to say, "That is not my struggle." Their struggle is ours, their pain a reflection of our own shared humanity. The fractures we see between us are illusions. Beneath them, the human heart is one. Unity is not just a strategy for resistance; it is the foundation of freedom.

Alan Clements: Daw Suu, as we close this chapter, I must ask: What would you say to the millions of people around the world who are watching—some through screens, others through the lens of their own history—witnessing not only isolated acts of violence, but patterns of state-sanctioned suffering, mass-scale destruction, and what can only be called colonial-cloaked massacre?

Many feel the weight of what they see—the sorrow, the injustice— but remain unsure how to move forward. How do we, as individuals and as a global community, transform that kind of witnessing into meaningful action, especially when the devastation feels so vast, and our responses feel so small?

Aung San Suu Kyi: To those who watch, I say: Do not turn away. What you see is not just suffering—it is the courage of the human spirit refusing to be extinguished. The faces you witness, the stories you carry, are not burdens; they are sacred invitations to remember our shared humanity. They are reminders of what is at stake, and of what is still possible.

There is a moral intelligence born from truly seeing. It is not sentimental—it is steady, sober, and clear. It asks us to resist the trance of helplessness and to remember that complicity often begins with silence.

Let your pain be a compass. Let it guide you to act—not out of guilt or obligation, but out of love for the world we share. You may feel small in the face of such immense suffering, but remember: every act of solidarity, no matter how small, is a thread in the tapestry of freedom— and each thread strengthens the whole. And no tapestry begins whole. It is woven over time—through effort, sacrifice, and the steady work of conscience.

Do not underestimate the power of your voice. Speak out against oppression. Support those on the frontlines. Educate yourself and others. Let your awareness become a bridge, not a wall. And most importantly, refuse to be indifferent.

The oppressors fear your attention. They fear your unity. They fear your compassion, because these are the forces that dismantle tyranny— not with violence, but with the quiet, unstoppable force of conscience.

We are no longer confronting violence only in the form of bullets and bombs. As you've rightly pointed out, Alan, we now face a war machine stripped of human presence—operating through satellites, algorithms, drones, surveillance states, and AI-powered targeting systems.

The merchants of this technology do not carry guns; they carry patents and contracts. But the result is the same: villages erased from the sky, voices silenced before they speak, entire populations profiled, tracked, and eliminated with a precision that simulates intelligence but is devoid of wisdom.

This is not the future of war—it is its present. A present in which killing has become automated, outsourced, and justified through the cold language of efficiency. And yet, even here, the human conscience remains the final frontier. That is why bearing witness matters. That is why love must become action.

And to those who suffer, I say: You are not forgotten. The world sees you, hears you, and stands with you. Your courage inspires us. Your pain strengthens our resolve. Your endurance redefines what it means to be free. Together, we will build a world where such suffering is no longer possible—a world where freedom is not a dream, but a reality shared by all.

Let us carry this vision forward, not as individuals but as one humanity, bound by a shared commitment to justice, dignity, and peace. For this, Alan, is the legacy of true witnessing: to transform pain into purpose, to transform seeing into action, and to transform suffering into the seeds of a brighter future.

Alan Clements: Thank you, Daw Suu. May we each learn to witness with our whole being—not with the detachment of spectators, but with the tenderness of those who understand that what we see is not theirs alone, but ours. Let this seeing awaken us. Let it call us home to what matters most. Let it break the spell of indifference. Let it stir the kind of peace that does not forget, but remembers—and rises.

Aung San Suu Kyi: Thank you, Alan. In the end, it's not about having the right words or perfect answers. It's about presence—the kind that stays. If you've seen something that breaks your heart, let it also open your eyes. Let it ask something of you—not as a burden, but as an offering.

Because what we do with our seeing is what defines us—not as observers of history, but as participants in its unfolding. Even the smallest act of compassion, done with clarity, becomes a seed of freedom. *And if you must carry something from all of this, let it be this: The world changes—quietly, powerfully—when we refuse to look away.*

A MESSAGE TO THE NATIONAL UNITY GOVERNMENT AND REVOLUTIONARIES

Author's Prelude

In every true revolution, there comes a moment when the outer battle gives way to an inner reckoning. This chapter is born of such a moment. It is not only a dispatch to those who lead the resistance—it is a mirror held to the soul of leadership itself.

Here, the vision of a federal democracy is not merely a structure of governance—it is a moral vow. A compass drawn not in ideology, but in lived sacrifice. A question that must be answered again and again through action, humility, and trust:

What does it mean to lead without dominating? To resist without hating?To build with hands still trembling from loss?

To the young revolutionaries, exiled leaders, and conscience-driven defenders of Myanmar—this chapter is both your inheritance and your invocation. A call not only to strategy, but to sanctity. Not only to defend a nation, but to become its moral foundation.

Let Aung San Suu Kyi's words be received not as distant philosophy, but as breath drawn beside barricades, as resolve spoken through sleepless nights. Let them be carried into war rooms and prayer circles, into jungle camps and student gatherings—whispered across frontlines, sung beside fires, lived into being.

As Daw Suu states: *"The nation you dream of will not be born after the war. It is being born now—in how we speak, how we serve, how we dare to be kind in the midst of cruelty. And in the revolution within—where dignity becomes law long before any constitution is written."*

◆ ◆ ◆

Alan Clements: Daw Suu, as you know, the emergence of the National Unity Government—Myanmar's democratically elected representatives in exile—marks a profound new chapter in the nation's struggle for freedom.

Formed in the wake of the 2021 coup, the NUG operates largely from hiding, working across borderlands and safe houses, often in collaboration with young revolutionaries who have taken up arms not out of ideology, but out of necessity.

Many of them have suffered devastating losses—parents, siblings, teachers, and friends taken by bombings, executions, and unspeakable violence. And yet, they continue.

The **NUG** speaks of a Federal Democracy Union: a vision grounded in equality, justice, and the rights of all ethnic nationalities. They fight not only to overthrow a brutal regime, but to build a nation that truly belongs to its people.

What would you say to these leaders and fighters—many of them in their twenties and thirties and forties—who now carry the torch of democracy in these darkest of times? How would you guide them as they navigate the moral, political, and spiritual complexities of this extraordinary and perilous journey?

Aung San Suu Kyi: Alan, to the National Unity Government and to every young revolutionary standing on the frontlines of this struggle, I begin with the deepest gratitude. You are not only the embodiment of courage—you are the heartbeat of a nation refusing to surrender its soul.

Your sacrifices, your resilience, and your vision are shaping the future of Myanmar. But with this profound responsibility comes a vital call to remember: *our revolution is not simply about overthrowing tyranny—it is about creating a society where freedom, justice, and equality are not just aspirations, but lived realities for all.*

To the NUG, I say: You are not merely a government in exile. You are stewards of a dream—a Federal Democratic Union where every ethnic group, every community, has an equal voice. Let this vision guide you at every step. Build your leadership not on force, but on transparency, humility, and accountability—for these are the roots of a democracy that endures.

And to the young revolutionaries, I say this: Your bravery lights the way for an entire nation. You have chosen to fight not out of hatred, but out of love—for your people, for your land, and for the future you know we can achieve. Hold fast to this love. Let it be your compass, your strength, and your shield against the forces that seek to divide and destroy us.

And I urge you now to take on one of the greatest challenges of all: to *embody inclusivity in action.* This means putting your emotional and mindful intelligence into dynamic practice—not just thinking clearly, but listening deeply. It means setting egos aside. Hear the voices, needs, and aspirations of our ethnic leaders and peoples—and of course, among yourselves as well. This is not a time to play small. It is a time to rise together.

So, my most direct advice is this: *keep self-interest off the table. Elevate mutual respect and unity at all costs. This is our moment as a nation. Seize it with all your might.*

Alan Clements: Daw Suu, thank you for that deeply moving and morally clarifying message. You've spoken with great wisdom about the need for inclusive action, deep listening, and leading from love rather than ego or fear.

And yet, as you know so well, these emboldened leaders and revolutionaries walk a near impossible tightrope: resisting a brutal military regime while still keeping alive the dream of reconciliation, unity, and peace.

If you feel moved to share more, how do you advise them to navigate this tension—to defend with integrity, to lead without hatred, and to hold space for a future that includes even those who once stood against them?

Aung San Suu Kyi: Alan, thank you for asking that. What you've touched upon—the tension between resistance and reconciliation—is not only strategic, it is spiritual. It follows directly from what I just shared.

Because to lead with *metta*—loving-kindness—to embody inclusivity, to listen deeply across divisions—all of that becomes exponentially more difficult when you are under attack, grieving, and fighting for survival. And yet, it is precisely then that the deepest truths of leadership are revealed.

The balance between resistance and reconciliation is indeed one of the most profound challenges of any struggle for freedom. Armed resistance, while at times unavoidable, must always remain a means, not an end.

To resist *Wetiko*—or pathological, *tanha*-fueled *moha* (greed-drenched ignorance)—is not merely a battle fought against an external oppressor. It is also an internal revolution: a deep, relentless discipline of heart and mind.

Wetiko is the force of delusion, fortified by radical self-deception and the absence of *karuṇā*—compassion. It is the insatiable hungry ghost that consumes without end.

To the revolutionaries, I say: Remember, the ultimate goal is not to destroy the enemy, but to create a nation where enemies no longer exist—where the divisions sown among us are replaced by mutual respect, understanding, and shared purpose.

This requires extraordinary discipline, both in action and in spirit. It demands resisting the pull of hatred, even when hatred feels justified. Hatred blinds us to the humanity of others and ultimately poisons the very vision we fight to achieve.

Reconciliation is not weakness; it is strength. It calls for the courage to listen, even to those who have wronged us. It requires the wisdom to seek justice without vengeance—to hold perpetrators accountable while creating pathways for healing and reintegration.

Let me be clear: this is not about excusing atrocities or minimizing the suffering of our people. It is about building a future where cycles of violence and retribution are broken, where the bonds of unity are stronger than the scars of the past.

Alan Clements: Many of these young revolutionaries have known nothing but conflict. Their grief, often unprocessed, fuels their resolve but can harden their hearts. How do they transform their grief into strength without letting it turn into hatred?

Aung San Suu Kyi: Alan, grief is a powerful force—it can either shatter us or forge us. To the young revolutionaries, I would say: Honor your grief. Do not suppress it or allow it to harden into anger. Allow yourself to feel the depth of your loss, for it is in this vulnerability that our greatest strength lies.

But do not let grief consume you. Let it guide you toward purpose. Remember those you have lost—not as martyrs for vengeance, but as inspirations for a better future. Carry their dreams with you. Build the kind of Myanmar they would have been proud to call home.

Hatred is a trap, as we know. It is the easiest response to pain but also the most corrosive. The harder path—the braver path—is to fight with compassion, to resist with humanity intact. This is the path that transforms grief into a force for justice and peace.

Alan Clements: The unity we see today—among ethnic groups, religious communities, and revolutionaries—is unprecedented. How do you see this unity sustaining the movement and shaping the future of Myanmar?

Aung San Suu Kyi: Unity is the cornerstone of our struggle, Alan. For decades, Myanmar's military has exploited our divisions—ethnic, religious, political—to maintain its grip on power. But today, we are witnessing something extraordinary: a revolution that embraces diversity as its strength.

To the NUG and the revolutionaries, I say: Protect this unity as if it were your very lifeline, because it is. Unity does not mean erasing our differences; it means honoring them, listening to one another's truths, and standing together for a shared vision. It means acknowledging past grievances and addressing them with fairness and humility.

But let us not romanticize the path ahead. Unity is fragile. It will be tested again and again. Old wounds—often sealed over by silence or fear—can be easily reopened. Generational mistrust runs deep. Trauma lingers beneath the surface. A single word, a single action, can reawaken decades of pain.

That is why unity must never be taken for granted. It must be nurtured, engaged with, strengthened, forgiven, renewed. Over and over. We must learn to begin again—not just politically, but emotionally, spiritually. *We must keep trying to understand one another, even when it's hard. Especially when it's hard.*

And above all, we must work to dissolve the poisons of ego and pride—in ourselves, in our factions, in our movements. These are the unseen forces that fracture even the most noble causes. They are subtle, but deadly.

This is where the value of trans-religious wisdom becomes essential—the kind of wisdom found in the basic components of what I call *mindful intelligence*: presence, discernment, compassion, humility, and the courage to grow. These are not exclusive to any one tradition;

they belong to all of us. And they must become the ethical roots of our revolution if it is to endure.

Unity is not something we achieve once and possess. It is something we practice—moment by moment, breath by breath.

Alan Clements: Daw Suu, earlier we spoke of the National Unity Government's vision—a Federal Democracy rooted in justice and equality for all. If you would, please allow me to return to this, as it feels essential to revisit from another, more inclusive angle.

This vision, as I understand it, for a post-junta Myanmar—grounded in federal democracy—seeks not only to dismantle military dominance, but to heal long-standing ethnic divisions and reshape governance through decentralization, inclusivity, and the deep practice of democratic principles.

You had mentioned earlier before we began recording that you were aware of the evolving conversations surrounding the NUG's framework. Given the weight and importance of this aspiration, what must be lived and practiced now, within the revolution itself, to ensure that this vision becomes more than an ideal—a foundation for a new Myanmar that is truly just and whole?

Aung San Suu Kyi: Alan, federal democracy is not merely an aspiration—it is a way of life that must be cultivated now, in the crucible of our resistance. It begins by rejecting domination in all its forms, even those that hide within movements of liberation.

If the NUG wishes to lead a nation beyond tyranny, it must first model that transformation in its own practices. This means opening up leadership to genuine diversity—not just symbolic inclusion, but the active empowerment of voices long excluded from decision-making: ethnic leaders, civil society, women, youth, and historically marginalized communities.

True federalism is not top-down; it is relational. It is born from trust, respect, and mutual accountability. Each region, each ethnic group, each community must feel not merely tolerated, but respected—genuinely seen and heard.

As I spoke about earlier, begin with listening. Listening not only to agreements, but to grievances. Deep listening. Especially to those who carry the weight of ancestral betrayal. Their wisdom is not a threat to unity—it is the seed of real belonging.

And in practice: decentralize power now, even in liberated zones. Let people govern themselves where they are able. Build local councils. Share decision-making. Empower people to participate not just in protest, but in governance. That is how democracy is lived into being.

The NUG'S vision for a federal democracy, as laid out in its Federal Democracy Charter, is a vital step—it offers a framework, a compass. *But we must remember: no document, no matter how well-written, can give birth to democracy on its own. It has to be lived. Embodied. Not just proclaimed.*

What brings that vision to life are the daily choices of ethical leadership. And the truest measure of that leadership is humility—the kind that allows for transparency, that welcomes correction, and that leads not from above, but through service.

Accountability must go both ways. Decisions shouldn't come down like orders—they should emerge from open, respectful dialogue. That's the heart of federalism. It's not about a central power granting permission. It's about shared sovereignty—people and regions working together, each with dignity, in service of the whole.

Alan Clements: There's a lot of concern about the Federal Army proposal. Some fear it could become too centralized. Is that a real risk?

Aung San Suu Kyi: It's a very real risk. And it must be acknowledged. Many Ethnic Armed Organizations have fought too long and sacrificed too much to now be folded into something that doesn't respect their autonomy.

Trust cannot be commanded. It has to be earned—over time, through consistency, through listening. Honor autonomy. Coordinate with dignity rather than command with authority. A looser confederation may actually offer more trust, more space to breathe, than any rigid hierarchy could.

Alan Clements: And what about the Rohingya? It's a sensitive subject— one many still avoid.

Aung San Suu Kyi: We cannot avoid it. There is no credible path to democracy without reckoning. There must be recognition. There must be restitution. Full rights. Citizenship. Protection under the law. To leave out even one group is to shake the very foundation of the Union we claim to be building.

Alan Clements: Would you say then, Daw Suu, that federal democracy is less a final structure and more a continuous process—a culture that must be learned, practiced, even internalized?

Aung San Suu Kyi: Exactly, Alan. It is an inner revolution as much as a political one. It is about shifting from control to trust, from dominance to dialogue, from fear to inclusion. And this must be mirrored not only in national policy, but in how meetings are held, how disagreements are handled, how young leaders are mentored.

Federal democracy is not static—it must be lived forward, in trust, in transparency, in shared responsibility. Federalism is a sacred relationship—between peoples, cultures, histories. It will never be perfect. But its strength is in its resilience—its capacity to stretch and grow without breaking.

Let the movement reflect that resilience now.

Alan Clements: Let me ask you next about the structure of the resistance. The NUG has organized the People's Defense Force (PDF) and aspires to unify disparate Ethnic Armed Organizations under a Federal Army. How can this be achieved without replicating the very centralization and coercion they hope to overcome?

Aung San Suu Kyi: That is a profound challenge. The key lies in both intention and structure. A Federal Army, if truly federal, must be rooted in cooperation—not subordination. It must emerge through dialogue, not imposition.

We must avoid replacing one form of domination with another dressed in new colors. Each EAO carries its own history, its own wounds, its own sacred trust with its people. That must be respected.

Integration should be phased, voluntary, and bound by agreed principles of autonomy, mutual defense, and accountability. It should resemble a confederation of equal partners more than a traditional chain of command.

And beyond structure, the spirit must be different. Military ethics must also be addressed. A new army must be built not just with new uniforms, but with a new culture—one that protects civilians, upholds rights, and is subordinate to democratic civilian leadership at every level.

Alan Clements: Let's talk about governance in the liberated areas. In places like Sagaing, which has not only endured the war but now the devastation of the earthquake, the NUG is beginning to set up local administrations. What lessons can we draw from these early experiments?

Aung San Suu Kyi: These liberated zones are not just pockets of resistance—they are laboratories of possibility. Every decision taken, every local council formed, every modest service delivered is a living rehearsal for the kind of country we hope to build.

And in these fragile beginnings, three things matter above all: transparency, participation, and responsiveness.

Let people see how decisions are made—not just the outcomes, but the process itself. Let them be part of that process, not merely recipients of it. Councils must be accountable—not to party lines, but to the people they serve.

Pilot schools, health clinics, and legal systems should reflect not only federal principles but also the unique needs and wisdom of local communities. This is federalism in action—not theory, but practice.

And yes, mistakes will happen. But when we are honest about them—when we own them—they become the soil in which trust can grow. *People don't expect perfection. What they long for is dignity—to be seen, to be respected, to be entrusted with shaping their own future.*

Alan Clements: Daw Suu, there is growing discussion around transitional justice and how to reckon with the legacy of military violence across the country. The situation in Rakhine State is especially complex. The Arakan Army now effectively controls much of the region, and any lasting resolution must somehow address both historic grievances and present realities—including the rights and future of the Rohingya community, who remain in a state of limbo, both in camps and across borders.

Given how sensitive and deeply rooted these issues are, what principles should guide a process of justice and reconciliation—one that is both inclusive and grounded in truth, yet mindful of the delicate balance needed to move forward?

Aung San Suu Kyi: Alan, this is one of the most difficult and painful conversations we must have—not just as leaders or activists, but as human beings.

The suffering in our country has been immense. And nowhere is that suffering more layered, more heartbreakingly complex, than in Rakhine State. For decades now, that land—so rich in culture and history—has known only cycles of fear, exclusion, and violence.

Today, the Arakan Army has asserted control over much of the region. The Rohingya remain displaced, many languishing in camps within and beyond our borders, with no clear path home. Meanwhile, the Rakhine people themselves carry the weight of historical grievance, military occupation, and now, an uncertain autonomy.

There is no simple answer. But I want to begin by saying this clearly: no one deserves to live without dignity. Not the Rohingya. Not the Rakhine. Not any citizen of Myanmar.

And to our Rohingya brothers and sisters—whether inside the country or still waiting in uncertainty—I say: you are not forgotten. You belong. Your story matters. Your future matters. And any vision of a just Myanmar that excludes you is no vision at all.

But we must also understand: justice is not something we impose—it is something we build together. Brick by brick. Voice by voice. A true process of transitional justice must be rooted in listening—honest, difficult, ongoing listening. It must create space for truth-telling without humiliation, for acknowledgment without defensiveness, for accountability without vengeance.

We must recognize the full scope of harm—not just in Rakhine, but in Kachin, Karen, Chin, Shan, Bago, Mandalay, Sagaing. No region, no ethnicity, no village has been untouched by suffering. The grief is everywhere. It is in the silence of the disappeared, the trauma of the displaced, and the unmarked graves scattered across our land.

And the truth is—it did not have to be this way. It still does not have to be this way.

We have a chance now—perhaps our last—to get this right. To begin again. To create a Union that learns from its wounds instead of burying them. But it will require immense humility from all sides. And deep courage—from the state, from civil society, and from those who have endured the most.

And I must also say this with honesty: I am 80 years old now. I speak from years of reflection, but I speak also from isolation. I am no longer close to the ground in the way the NUG and the ethnic leaders are. They see things I do not. They live the cost of this war every day. I only hope these words might serve in some small way, not as direction, but as encouragement.

My guidance, if I may call it that, is simply this: Do not let the weight of the past harden your heart. Let it deepen your compassion. Let justice begin not with punishment, but with presence—with the courage to face what has been done, and the commitment to build something worthy in its place. Reconciliation is not forgetting. It is remembering with care. It is offering each other—not erasure—but a future.

We owe that to every child born on this soil: Rohingya, Rakhine, Bamar, Kachin, Chin, Shan, Mon, Karen—all of them. Let them inherit a country that finally, finally remembers what it means to be human.

Alan Clements: Thank you, Daw Suu…Your words reach far beyond policy—they touch something essential, something sacred. What you've just shared isn't simply a political statement—it's a kind of moral compass. A reminder that we're not only rebuilding a nation—we're rebuilding the fragile trust in what it means to be human together.

And I feel this deeply when you say, *"It still does not have to be this way."*

That simple truth—it's devastating. And yet, it's also a doorway. A doorway into hope, if we dare to walk through it with honesty, humility, and care.

I want to echo your humility as well. From where I sit—free to speak, to move, to write—I know I cannot fully comprehend the cost that so many inside the country are paying every single day. But I share your hope. Deeply. May the voices of the silenced rise, may the displaced return with dignity, and may justice become not a weapon—but a bridge.

With that, if I may, I'd like to shift our conversation gently toward the economic future of Myanmar.

As you know, the military coup didn't just fracture political life—it brought the economy to its knees. Livelihoods have collapsed, millions are displaced, many face starvation. In your view, how can a future federal democracy not just recover, but reimagine the economy—in a way that serves the people equitably, honors the land, and begins to repair the generational wounds of structural harm?

Aung San Suu Kyi: Alan, economic justice must walk hand in hand with political transformation. We cannot rebuild the old economy—it was never truly whole to begin with. We must reinvent it, from the roots up.

A future Myanmar must be grounded in the principles of local empowerment, transparency, and shared prosperity. That means decentralizing economic power, just as we decentralize political authority. It means placing trust not only in institutions, but in communities—trusting them to know what they need, and to shape how resources are used.

For far too long, resource-rich ethnic states have been plundered—made into extraction zones for the benefit of the center, especially the military elite.

This cannot continue. Justice demands that those closest to the land have a rightful say in how it is cared for and shared. Revenue-sharing must follow clear, fair, and inclusive agreements—crafted together, not imposed.

And we must think forward—not just in terms of economics, but of ecology.

The forests of Kachin, the jade mines of Hpakant, the rivers of Chin and Shan—they are not commodities; they are sacred inheritances. Development must become sustainable, not just as a strategy, but as a sacred trust. It is how we begin to repair the relationship between people and place, so badly broken by greed.

But most of all—we must invest in people. Especially the young. This revolution has been youth-led. The economy must now begin to reflect their values—not just survival, but vision. Green energy. Cooperative economies. Ethical entrepreneurship. Innovations rooted in care, not just capital.

Alan Clements: And the youth—their bravery, their brilliance—it's become the very soul of this movement. What role do you see for them, Daw Suu, in shaping the future—not just as idealists, but as leaders?

Aung San Suu Kyi: Alan, the youth are not simply the soul of this movement—they are its heartbeat, its conscience, its future already arriving. And we must do far more than listen to them. We must entrust them. They are not just heirs to our choices—they are co-creators of what comes next. We must welcome their voices, not as symbolic gestures, but as essential truths.

Invite them into constitutional dialogues—not as spectators, but as co-authors. Empower them to help shape local governments, school systems, environmental reforms. Encourage civic education, yes—but also moral imagination. Let them learn not only how to lead, but how to listen. Let them challenge the world not out of anger, but from clarity of conscience.

Let us build schools and communities that nurture the whole child—intellect, emotion, and spirit. Teach them how to care, how to question, how to hold silence and speech with equal grace. Let them understand courage—not as domination, but as the willingness to stand for what is right when it would be easier to turn away.

And if I may offer a truth that lives close to my heart: Just think of the more than 22,000 prisoners of conscience currently held in Myanmar. Brave hearts—activists, artists, students, monks, mothers, children—trapped in despicably cruel and torturous conditions, stripped of their freedom, yet still holding fast to their dignity.

Every one of them has or had parents. Many belong to families who wait with aching hearts. Some have children who don't know if they'll ever see their parent again. Others are merely children themselves—torn from their homes and forced into prison cells instead of classrooms.

And yet, within those cells, they live each moment in a quiet fusion of heartache, conscience, and courage. They are surviving something unthinkable—and still, many of them continue to speak truth in whispers, in glances, in their very breath.

Imagine the wisdom they carry. When they are free—and they will be—their stories will be our textbooks. Their resilience, our curriculum. Their capacity to endure and still love, still hope, still dream—this will be one of Myanmar's greatest treasures. Not only for our youth, but for young people everywhere in the world. They will not simply return to society. They will help reshape it at its roots.

To every child or young person who may read these words one day—know this: *You are not too young to lead. You are not too small to be brave. You are not too early to begin shaping the world.*

You are the sunrise we once prayed would come. The proof that light can survive even the longest, darkest night. You are the ones we've been waiting for—and now the world waits for you.

So, take this moment, this fragile, sacred moment in history—and make of it something beautiful. Make of it something true.

Alan Clements: Daw Suu, what you've just shared about the youth—and about the 22,000 prisoners of conscience suffering at this very moment—will stay with me for the rest of my life.

To hear you speak of their courage, their dignity, their untold wisdom, even from behind prison walls... it's impossible not to feel something shift inside. These aren't just statistics. These are sons and daughters, mothers, fathers, poets, students, teachers—each living minute by minute in unbearable conditions, holding fast to something sacred within themselves.

You've reminded us that when they are free, they will not simply return—they will lead the rebirth of society. And that, perhaps more than any policy or strategy, is what gives me hope.

So, with that in mind, let me ask you this—what can the world do? Not just in standing with the resistance now, but in helping to create the kind of post-junta Myanmar that can truly heal, truly rebuild, and offer a new beginning worthy of its people?

Aung San Suu Kyi: The world must come to see this not as Myanmar's isolated tragedy—but as a chapter in the global story of democracy. What happens here—what happens to our people, to our children, to our prisoners—reflects something far beyond our borders.

Recognition matters. The NUG must be acknowledged—not as a token gesture, but as a necessary step toward legitimacy, stability, and peace. Because recognition opens doors. It brings in humanitarian aid. It allows for educational partnerships, for rebuilding health care, for training the next generation of leaders.

But more than recognition, we need solidarity—not sympathy. We need friends who walk beside us, not above us. Who are willing to build with us, not just advise from a distance.

Myanmar has long been used—exploited for its resources, overlooked for its suffering. This must change. This moment is a mirror for the world. It offers a chance—for governments, organizations, and citizens everywhere—to ask: What does freedom demand of us now? Not as an abstraction, but as action.

Alan Clements: One final question, Daw Suu—perhaps the most important. In this great reckoning, this fragile unfolding of history... what must never be forgotten?

Aung San Suu Kyi: That every child born in Myanmar—every single one—deserves a nation not only free from fear, but full of belonging. Let us never build a democracy that forgets them. Let us never construct a system so focused on power that it overlooks the quiet dignity of the most vulnerable.

A democracy that does not see the child in the camp, the prisoner in the cell, the student in hiding—is not a democracy at all.

Alan, I say this from a place of deep humility. I am 80 years old. I have spent years in solitary confinement. I am frail. My body grows tired, and my access to the world is limited.

But I also know this: The women and men of the NUG, the ethnic leaders, the resistance networks, the civil society groups—they are the ones carrying the revolution forward now. They know truths I no longer see. They carry burdens I once held, but now must pass on.

And so, these words—I offer them not as instruction, but as reflection. Not as doctrine, but perhaps... a final offering.

Because we never know what the future holds.

But let it be known: I believe in them. I believe in you. And I still believe—quietly, fiercely—that Myanmar, even now, can become something luminous. Something whole.

Alan Clements: And we believe in you, Daw Suu. Thank you—for your honesty, for your heart, and for the grace you carry, even in confinement.

Aung San Suu Kyi: Thank you, Alan. Let us walk on—until freedom is not a dream, but a home.

A MESSAGE TO THE TRAUMATIZED CITIZENS OF MYANMAR:
CULTIVATING COURAGE, UNITY, AND HEALING

Author's Prelude

In this age of normalized cruelty—where drone strikes fall like poisoned rain, and silence roars louder than any scream—this chapter rises as both requiem and resurrection. It is a sacred invocation to the people of Myanmar: those whose lives lie shattered, yet whose dignity remains unbroken.

This is not a chapter of policy or philosophy. It is a whisper passed through jungle camps, prison walls, bombed monasteries, and tent cities of the displaced. A mirror held not to indulge agony—but to dignify it. And through that dignity, to summon the rarest courage of all: not only to survive, but to continue loving.

Here, Aung San Suu Kyi does not speak from the perch of political legacy, but from the raw ground of collective suffering. From her prison cell, her voice reaches into the marrow of grief and plants a truth the junta cannot burn:

Even in despair, there is choice. Even in ruin, there is memory. Even in silence, there is song.

These pages offer no easy solace. They do not romanticize pain, nor call for endurance without meaning. They offer a *revolution of the spirit*—a way to transmute trauma into wisdom, grief into clarity, pain into prayer. They ask us not to forget what has been done—but to remember who we are.

To the reader: May this dialogue enter you like medicine. May it meet you in your unspoken sorrow. May it remind you that when the world forgets you, you must become the remembering. And may it leave you with this sacred conviction: That the light of a people who refuse to hate—even when crushed—is a light that cannot be extinguished.

Let this be a chapter not only of mourning, but of rising.

Not only of suffering, but of becoming.

◆ ◆ ◆

Alan Clements: Daw Suu, across the country—from the Irrawaddy Delta to the mountains of Kachin and Chin, from the dry plains of Magway to the forests of Karen and Karenni—the people of Myanmar are living through an unrelenting nightmare. Drone attacks, scorched earth campaigns, forced displacement, mass arrests, starvation tactics, and the systematic use of terror have become part of daily life.

Numerous villages have been burned to ash. Children have been recruited as human shields. Citizens have been tortured, disappeared, or executed for something as small as a social media post.

Over 3.5 million are now internally displaced. More than 20 million, according to the United Nations, are in urgent need of humanitarian aid. And in Rakhine State alone, another UN report warns that up to two million people may face starvation this year. The devastation has only deepened in the aftermath of the catastrophic earthquake, displacing and endangering even more lives.

And yet—despite this ocean of suffering—they continue to rise, to resist, to hope. Many still speak of you as "Ma Su," the mother of their revolution. A symbol not only of democracy, but of dignity.

What would you say to these citizens—traumatized, grieving, often alone—many of whom feel they are living through the darkest night of their soul? How can they hold on amidst such devastation? What inner resource, what truth, what guidance can help them continue?

Aung San Suu Kyi: Alan, to speak to the people of Myanmar is to speak directly to my own heart. They are not just citizens. They are my family—my brothers, my sisters, my children. Their suffering is not something I read about—it lives in my body, in my silence. It moves through every breath I take in this confinement. And yet—their courage, their dignity, their relentless will to endure—that too breathes within me. It is what gives me the strength to carry on.

To the people of Myanmar, I say this: Your pain is real. It is not imagined. It is not distant. It is not forgotten.

I heard the numbers you shared, Alan—and I want to speak to them directly. To the more than 3.5 million of you who have been displaced by war, by fire, by violence—you are not numbers. You are living testaments to resilience—souls who once tended gardens, built homes, and nurtured futures, now walking bravely through ruin.

To the 20 million people across this nation who now depend on humanitarian aid just to survive—I see your strength. I honor your dignity. That you continue to care for your families, to share what little you have, to find joy even in fragments—it is humbling beyond words.

And to those in Rakhine State, where up to two million face starvation in the year ahead—my heart goes out to you in a special way.

Yours is a history of suffering that has gone unacknowledged for far too long. We must not simply remember your past; we must refuse to forsake your future.

You are not forgotten. You are not alone. *And I say to the world: if you care about democracy, if you care about humanity—look here. Look now. Act!*

To those of you living through this nightmare: You've lost loved ones. You've seen your homes burned. You've buried dreams that were still blooming. And yet you rise. You gather. You pray. You sing. You tend to each other. You keep your spirit intact in a world designed to break it. This is not weakness—it is a quiet, defiant strength.

Every time you rebuild a shelter, or teach a child by firelight, or refuse to hate even as you suffer—you are doing something miraculous. You are proving that the regime can destroy walls, but not your will.

I know the darkness feels endless. I know many of you feel abandoned. But I ask you to hold on. Because the dawn always comes—not as a gift, but as a result of our refusal to give up on one another.

Even here, in my solitary cell, I feel you. I feel your love. Your loss. Your astonishing resilience. You are not broken. You are being shaped into something stronger than fear itself.

And when the day comes—and it will come—when this nightmare ends, it will be your names, your stories, your sacrifices that shape the soul of the new Myanmar. I believe in you. I carry your courage like a prayer. And I will keep doing so for as long as I live.

Alan Clements: Daw Suu, for those who have lost everything—homes, loved ones, even the will to hope—how can they begin to heal amidst such overwhelming trauma? Not just physically, but emotionally, spiritually, and psychologically?

How do we begin to restore the soul in a time when so much has been shattered? And is there a way, even amid such devastation, for individuals to reclaim their dignity, to cultivate mindfulness, and to begin touching that deeper refuge within—the one that no regime, no war, can ever take away?

Aung San Suu Kyi: Healing begins not in forgetting, but in acknowledging. To the people of Myanmar, I say this with all the tenderness I can offer: do not turn away from your pain. Let your sorrow speak. Let your grief breathe. *Feel it fully—not as weakness, but as the undeniable truth of your humanity.*

The Buddha taught us that suffering is an inescapable part of life. It is the first noble truth, and it is also the one we most often resist. But suffering, as he taught, is not the end—it is the beginning of insight. It is a doorway we walk through, not a wall that confines us.

Psychological wounds may not bleed outwardly, but they ache in silence. I urge you to take refuge in the simplest forms of care: a moment of stillness, a breath of awareness, the placing of a hand over your heart and saying gently, *"I am here, and I endure."* These small acts matter. They are how we begin to mend what no sword can reach.

And I say to you, do not underestimate your own inner capacity. There is within each of us a quiet light—a dignity—that cannot be destroyed unless we surrender it. Even in isolation, even in despair, we can return to that place inside us that no regime, no violence, no prison can touch.

One of the books that sustained me in solitude was Viktor Frankl's *Man's Search for Meaning.* He survived the concentration camps, not by denying suffering, but by making it sacred—by discovering that even in agony, we retain the freedom to choose our attitude, our response.

And Nelson Mandela's *Long Walk to Freedom* taught me that the inner journey is as vital as the outer one. He wrote, *"It is said that no one truly knows a nation until one has been inside its jails."* I know this to be true. I know too that the deepest resilience is spiritual—it is not just survival, but the preservation of meaning, compassion, and self-respect amidst suffering.

So yes, let us grieve. But let us also rise inwardly. Again, and again. Let us strive to take our interior states higher—more radiant with truth, more rooted in *Dhamma*, more free.

No matter your religion or belief, you can touch that part of yourself which remains whole. Even now, *you are more than your wounds.* You are the living soil from which a freer, more luminous future is already beginning to grow.

Alan Clements: Daw Suu, what you've just shared about the inner refuge, about holding dignity even amidst unimaginable loss… it brings to mind many moments I've witnessed or experienced myself—whether in war zones, refugee camps, or monasteries—when all external structure collapses, and yet, something luminous still flickers within a person. A presence. A stillness. A fierce, undiminished grace.

I've seen it in the eyes of displaced mothers tending to their children with tenderness amidst burning villages, in monks who have lost their monasteries but not their mindfulness, and in children drawing peace signs on the walls of camps. These small gestures, as you said, are not small at all. They are everything—the heartbeat of humanity refusing to die.

So, with this in mind—what would you say to those who feel forgotten? Not only by the international community, but by life itself. Who feel abandoned, not just physically, but existentially—where suffering has eclipsed their sense of self, and meaning feels irretrievable?

Aung San Suu Kyi: To those who feel forgotten, I want to say this with as much love as I can offer from afar: you are not unseen. You are not alone.

Each act of survival—each meal you share, each fire you light, each word you offer to comfort another—is a sacred act of resistance. The world may not always see what you endure, but that does not mean it is without meaning. In truth, it may be the most meaningful thing of all.

The generals may control the weapons, but they do not control your heart. They do not own your humanity. As I said many years ago—and it feels more true now than ever— *"If you're feeling helpless, help somebody."* Each time you extend a hand to a neighbor, protect a child, or simply refuse to give in to hatred, you keep the flame of our nation alive. You defy them in the most powerful way possible—by remaining human.

You may not feel strong, but I assure you: your quiet courage is a greater victory than any battle won by force. Even in silence. Even in grief.

Let the suffering carve depth into your soul—but not bitterness. Let it deepen your empathy. Let it soften you toward others who are hurting. That, too, is the *Dhamma in action*. That, too, is meaning.

Know this: your resilience is not small. It reverberates. It inspires others across Myanmar, and far beyond its borders. You are weaving the living memory of this time—thread by thread, act by act—and when history looks back, it will see you not as victims, but as the architects of freedom.

Alan Clements: The children of Myanmar have endured far more than any child should ever have to. Many have lost their parents, their homes, their sense of safety. Others have never known a day free from war. Yet, they go on—some still playing, laughing, learning, surviving.

What do we say to them—not as victims, but as beings of astonishing resilience, already shaped by profound experience? How do we nourish their spirit and protect their ability to love, to trust, to dream?

Aung San Suu Kyi: To the children of Myanmar, I say this with all the love I have in my heart: I see you, I cherish you. I carry your stories within me. You are not too young to feel. You are not too small to matter. You are the living promise of a world that refuses to give up. Even your tears are sacred. Your dreams, even now, are precious.

I know many of you have had to grow up too quickly. You've seen fear in your parents' eyes. You've run from bombs. You've slept in jungles and shelters instead of beds. And yet… you still reach out to play. You still ask questions. You still draw suns and flowers and birds. That is not just survival. That is luminous defiance. You are not broken. You are becoming something extraordinary.

And to the adults: Protect their spark with reverence. Nourish their minds with stories of courage and justice. Let them cry without shame. Let them hope without fear. Create small sanctuaries wherever you can—a quiet moment, a word of praise, a safe lap, a song.

To the children, I say: this country will one day be yours to shape. And it will need your truth, your tenderness, your wild, unshakable belief that things can be different.

Hold on to your dreams. Let them grow tall within you. You are loved. Deeply, endlessly loved. And your light is already beginning to heal this world.

Alan Clements: You often speak of courage, Daw Suu. How does courage manifest for the people of Myanmar, especially those who are unarmed and defenseless in the face of such overwhelming violence?

Aung San Suu Kyi: Alan, courage is not always grand or dramatic. Sometimes, it is as simple as choosing to plant seeds in a field that has been burned, to sing a lullaby to a child amidst the sound of bombs, or to teach in secret when schools have been destroyed.

Courage is the quiet, steady resolve to hold onto your humanity in the face of inhumanity. It is the act of resisting fear, not by denying it, but by refusing to let it rule you.

The Buddha taught us about *metta*—loving-kindness—not just for others but also for ourselves. *To practice self-metta is to be gentle with your own heart, to forgive yourself for moments of weakness, and to find the strength to continue.* It is an act of moral rebellion against despair. This *metta-filled-self-compassion* is not selfish; it is the foundation of the compassion we extend to others.

Alan Clements: You've often said that unity is the key to overcoming tyranny. How can the people of Myanmar, fragmented by displacement and trauma, find unity amidst such chaos?

Aung San Suu Kyi: Unity does not mean uniformity, Alan. It means recognizing that our strength lies in our diversity. The regime seeks to divide us, to pit us against one another, to exploit our differences. But they will not succeed if we remember that we are all connected.

To the people of Myanmar, I say: let us stand together—not just as citizens of this nation but as human beings bound by a shared longing for freedom and dignity. Let us listen to one another, honor each other's pain, and celebrate the unique contributions each community brings to our shared struggle.

Unity is not just a strategy for resistance; it is the soul of the Myanmar we are destined to create—a Myanmar where no one is left behind.

Alan Clements: Daw Suu, this may be one of the most important conversations of your life, yet under these circumstances, we cannot know if your words will ever reach those for whom they are intended. If this is the only chance you have to speak to your people—all 54 million of them—what would you say?

What would you leave with them, knowing that every word could be the difference between despair and hope, between fear and courage?

Please, Daw Suu, speak to your people as if this were your final message.

Aung San Suu Kyi: My beloved people of Myanmar, You are the heartbeat of our nation. You are the reason I endure, the reason I stand tall even when the weight of oppression threatens to break us all.

Each of you carries within you a spark of light that no darkness can extinguish. Today, I speak to you as a mother, a daughter, a sister, and as one of you—a child of Myanmar, bound by the same love for this land, the same pain for its suffering, and the same dream of its freedom.

Hold fast to your dignity. Even when it feels like everything else has been stripped away—your homes, your livelihoods, your loved ones— remember this: *your dignity is inalienable. It is yours alone, and no regime, no soldier, no weapon can ever take it from you.*

Let me remind you of who you are. You are the farmers who sow the seeds of hope in fields scarred by conflict. You are the monks and nuns whose prayers echo through the valleys, calling for peace. You are the students who dare to dream of a better tomorrow, even as bullets fly. You are the mothers who cradle your children amidst ruins, and the fathers who rebuild homes for the third, the fourth time. You are the children who laugh and play, even in the shadow of fear. You are the strength of Myanmar.

To those who despair: I see you. Your pain is real, and your exhaustion is justified. But remember this: despair is not the end. It is a moment, a season—and like all seasons, it will pass.

Reach toward one another for strength. When your own light feels dim, let it be rekindled by your neighbors, your community, your shared dream.

To those who grieve: Your grief is sacred. It is a testament to your love, to your humanity. Do not turn away from it, but do not let it consume you either. Let your grief fuel your resolve.

Remember those we have lost not as victims, but as heroes. Carry their dreams forward. Build the world they would have wanted to live in.

To the children of Myanmar: You are our greatest treasure. Your laughter, your curiosity, your boundless imagination—they are the seeds of the future we fight for.

Hold on to your dreams, even when they feel out of reach. You may feel small now, but know this: you are giants in the making. *One day, it will be your hands that shape our nation into a land of peace and freedom.*

To the revolutionaries, the brave defenders of freedom: Your courage inspires us all. But remember, our fight is not one of hatred or vengeance. We fight not to destroy, but to create. We resist not to tear down, but to build a nation where every voice is heard, where every life is valued.

Let compassion be your compass, even in the heat of battle. Do not let anger harden your hearts. Let love—love for our people, our land, our shared humanity—be the fire that fuels you.

To all of Myanmar: Unity is our strength. The regime thrives on division, on turning us against one another. Do not let them succeed. Stand together as one nation, one people. Embrace our diversity—not as a weakness, but as the beating heart of our future strength.

We are Kachin, Shan, Chin, Karen, Rakhine, Bamar, and so much more. Together, we are Myanmar.

This unity is not just a strategy for survival; it is the vision of the Myanmar we are building—a Myanmar where no one is left behind, where every child can dream, where every elder is honored, and where every life is cherished.

Remember: The Buddha taught that life is indeed marked by suffering, yet suffering is not all there is. Through mindfulness, compassion, right effort, and right intention, we have the power to transcend even the darkest times.

The Buddha taught that hatred does not end by hatred, but only by love. Let this wisdom guide us—not as a doctrine confined to Buddhism but as a universal truth, resonating with the core values of all spiritual traditions.

To those who follow Christ, remember His call to love one another, even our enemies. His message of forgiveness, humility, and the power of selfless love speaks to the same truth: that hatred cannot overcome hatred, and division cannot heal division.

To my Muslim brothers and sisters: let the teachings of Islam guide you in perseverance and patience. The Quran reminds us that Allah is with those who are steadfast and just. It calls us to charity, mercy, and peace, even in times of great hardship.

To the Catholics, the Hindus, the Christians of every denomination, and those who follow no formal religion but hold fast to kindness and humanity: the essence of every faith is the shared belief in the dignity of life, in the power of compassion, and in the pursuit of justice.

The Universality of the Dhamma: The *Dhamma* is not confined to one belief system. It is the rhythm of life, the balance of cause and effect, the wisdom of living with awareness and intention. It teaches us to meet the world not with reactivity, but with clarity and courage.

Equanimity—upekkha—is our strength. It is not indifference; it is the calm within the storm, the clarity amidst chaos, the unshakable compassion that steadies the hand and clears the mind. Whether you follow the Buddha, the Christ, the Quran, the Gita—or simply the voice of conscience—this equanimity is a gift we can all cultivate.

A Trans-Spiritual Call to Action: Let us not see our differences in faith as barriers, but as threads in the rich tapestry of our shared humanity. In the face of tyranny, our diversity is our strength. Together, we bring the wisdom of many traditions, the resilience of many stories, the hope of many hearts. Let your prayers, your meditations, your reflections, and your actions be guided by the universal principles of justice, dignity, and love.

To all people of conscience: our journey is the same. We are seeking liberation—from suffering, from fear, from injustice.

This is not the work of one group, nor one generation. It is the work of all humanity. Together, across faiths, across borders, across all that divides us, let us commit to building a future defined not by fear but by love.

Hold fast to your dignity. Hold fast to your hope. Hold fast to each other. Together, we will see this dark night give way to dawn.

Freedom is not a gift we await. It is the light we forge with our own hands—and together, we will make it real.

Alan Clements: Daw Suu, your words will resonate not just in Myanmar but across the world. Thank you for reminding us of the unbreakable strength of the human spirit.

This message, this call to unity, dignity, and resilience, will not simply endure—it will stand as a testament to the indomitable courage of the people of Myanmar, and as a guiding light for all who dream of freedom.

Aung San Suu Kyi: Thank you, Alan. If these are the last words of mine you ever hear, let them be simple.

Not grand. Just true.

We will never be perfect. We will falter.

We will grieve. We will get tired.

But we must never let our hearts be taken. Not by hatred. Not by fear. Not even by despair.

The world will try to tell you that tenderness is weakness. Don't believe it. It takes far more strength to feel deeply than to turn away. Far more courage to love in darkness than to harden. And so, I say to you—wherever you are, whatever your burden: Begin again. Begin gently. Begin with whatever light you have left. And together, even in silence, even in exile, we will make something sacred of this life.

A CALL FOR COURAGEOUS DIALOGUE, RECONCILIATION, AND THE FUTURE OF THE MILITARY

Author's Prelude

In every revolution, there comes a moment when the clenched fist must soften—not in surrender, but in vision. When courage evolves from resistance into creation, and asks: what kind of future shall we shape with our shared breath?

This chapter arises from that question.

It is not a discourse of blame, nor a blueprint for strategy—it is a meditation on moral courage in its rarest form: the courage to build.

Here, Aung San Suu Kyi does not speak as a politician, but as a witness—offering her voice to the long, fragile, and necessary path of reconciliation.

To the Ethnic Armed Organizations, she offers not rhetoric, but respect.

To the military—not condemnation, but a mirror and a challenge: to remember their humanity, and reclaim their original vow—to serve, not subjugate, the people.

Peace, she reminds us, is not the mere absence of war, but the presence of trust, truth, and mutual recognition. It begins with dialogue that honors pain without becoming hostage to it. In this light, leadership becomes less about command—and more about conscience.

Let this chapter serve as a sacred threshold—not only between conflict and peace, but between old identities and new integrity. A call to end not just the violence of weapons, but the deeper violence of division, fear, and forgetting.

May its message become a guide for all who seek not merely to restore a nation—but to heal its soul.

◆ ◆ ◆

Alan Clements: Daw Suu, Myanmar's Ethnic Armed Organizations (EAOS) have shown remarkable resilience in their fight against the military junta, forming a critical pillar of the nationwide revolution. Groups like the Kachin Independence Army (KIA), Karen National Union (KNU), Arakan Army (AA), Ta'ang National Liberation Army (TNLA), and Myanmar National Democratic Alliance Army (MNDAA) have led bold offensives, capturing key territories and inspiring hope.

Others, like the United Wa State Army (UWSA) and parts of the Shan State Army (SSA), navigate complex neutralities or pragmatic engagements.

Despite their differences, many EAOs continue to challenge the junta's tyranny, often at immense cost—over 3.5 million displaced, millions facing starvation, and hundreds of communities devastated by airstrikes and conflict.

What message would you share with the leaders and members of these EAOs, who endure profound sacrifices while carrying the aspirations of their people for freedom and justice?

Aung San Suu Kyi: Alan, what strength lives in the hills and borderlands of our country—in the courage and constancy of Myanmar's Ethnic Armed Organizations. Their endurance isn't only in the battles they've fought, but in the lives, they've lived—lives offered, homes lost, generations uprooted, and still, they carry on. This, to me, is what unyielding spirit looks like.

To the leaders and members of the Kachin Independence Army, the Karen National Union, the Arakan Army, the Ta'ang National Liberation Army, the Myanmar National Democratic Alliance Army— and all others who rise up against tyranny—I say this: you are not just the heartbeat of this revolution. You are its integrity. Its will to go on.

Your victories—Mannerplaw reclaimed by the KNU, Rakhine's steady reclamation by the AA—these aren't only military gains. They are messages. They say: the junta can lose. The people can win. And yes, the MNDAA's capture of Lashio in 2024—even if surrendered under pressure—showed the world that no stronghold is invincible. That fear can change sides.

Even those among you—the United Wa State Army, the Shan State Army—who walk more cautious paths, you too help shape this moment. Strategy isn't always resistance by fire. Sometimes, it's resistance by survival. And that, too, takes wisdom.

Every act of resistance—whether through arms, alliance, or just refusing to fall—tells the world: we will not bow. Operation 1027 proved what unity across difference can do. But I also know: this unity trembles. It aches under the weight of old wounds, disputed borders, conflicting dreams.

And the outside pressures—let us speak plainly—especially from China, Lashio being one example—they test your resolve every day. But that is exactly why we must remember: *our fight is not just to end a regime. It is to begin a nation.*

So, I say to you—keep talking. Keep listening. Don't just fight beside one another—build beside one another. The regime spent decades dividing us. Let us not help them finish that work.

True unity is fragile. It takes more than alliances. It takes humility. Listening. Forgiveness. Beginning again—especially when it's hard.

To those who are displaced, grieving, surviving on the edge of despair—your pain is seen. Your courage, though quiet, is revolutionary. We owe you more than thanks—we owe you a future.

To every fighter, leader, village elder, medic, farmer, commander, and child who still believes—we haven't forgotten you. You're not waiting for history to arrive. You are writing it.

And together, despite everything, we will rise—not just above tyranny, but into something far greater than power: a nation rooted in dignity. A union of people who've learned the hard way how to love one another again.

Alan Clements: Daw Suu, the Tatmadaw, the military institution your father founded, has become the symbol of this oppression. How do you address this tragic legacy as you speak to these groups, who now see the military as their enemy?

Aung San Suu Kyi: Alan, my father envisioned the Tatmadaw as a protector of the people, a force to safeguard our sovereignty and dignity. That it has become a tool of tyranny is a betrayal of his vision and the trust placed in it by the people of Myanmar.

To the KIA, KNU, UWSA, SSA, AA, TNLA, MNDAA, and all other groups, I would say this: while the *Tatmadaw* has lost its way, the spirit of my father's vision lives on in you.

You have taken up the mantle of protecting your communities—not out of a desire for conquest, but out of a sacred necessity. In doing so, you honor the principles the *Tatmadaw* was meant to uphold.

But we cannot avoid the thorny questions of justice and accountability. For those at the highest levels of the *Tatmadaw* who have ordered or perpetuated atrocities, there must be accountability. War crimes and crimes against humanity cannot be swept under the rug.

Acknowledging these atrocities and holding the perpetrators accountable is not about vengeance—it is about *truth-telling,* about restoring dignity, and about ensuring that such war crimes can never happen again.

Alan Clements: What about the soldiers themselves—those at the lower levels who may be conscripted or forced into these acts of violence? How should they be treated in a future Myanmar?

Aung San Suu Kyi: Alan, the rank-and-file soldiers of the Tatmadaw are not monolithic. Many are victims themselves—young men and women from impoverished backgrounds, conscripted into service, brainwashed by propaganda, or forced to follow orders under threat of severe punishment.

To these soldiers, I would say: your humanity is not lost. You have the power to choose a different path—to stand with the people rather than against them. If you lay down your arms and join the side of justice, there must be a future for you in the new Myanmar we are building.

Reconciliation must extend not only to ethnic groups, but also to those who served in the *Tatmadaw* out of necessity rather than malice. For a future Myanmar, we must create pathways for these soldiers to reintegrate into society—offering education, vocational training, and opportunities to contribute positively to their communities.

Only by transforming the *Tatmadaw* itself—from an instrument of domination into a true institution of public service—can we fully heal these wounds.

Alan Clements: Resistance against the military has come at an extraordinary cost, as you've mentioned. How do these groups reconcile their fight for freedom with the immense human suffering it entails?

Aung San Suu Kyi: Alan, resistance—true resistance—is never born of hatred. It's born of heartbreak. It's born of watching your people suffer and knowing in your bones that silence would be a betrayal.

To the leaders of the EAOs, I would say this: I know the burden you carry. I know the weight of choosing between protecting your people and preserving their future. And I know that every decision you make comes at a cost—lives interrupted, families torn apart, children who may never know peace.

But please remember: your resistance is not just a reaction—it is a declaration of love. It is love in action. Every stand you take, every village you defend, every citizen you shelter—it matters. And it is seen.

Still, let us not forget: resistance is not only about fighting what we do not want. It is about imagining what we do. The goal is not merely to defeat the *Tatmadaw*—it is to build a nation where no such force could ever rise again. A place where justice is not an aspiration, but a given. Where dignity is not reserved for the powerful, but belongs to all.

This means we must walk with both courage and care. Protect your people today, yes—but also plant the seeds for the kind of tomorrow we all dream of. A Myanmar where our diversity is our strength. Where former enemies become partners in peace. Where the young no longer have to fight to be heard.

The struggle will test us. It already has. But if we lead with conscience, with compassion, and with vision, we do more than resist. We become the architects of a nation worthy of its people.

Alan Clements: Many of these groups are deeply rooted in their ethnic identities. How can they preserve these identities while contributing to a unified vision for Myanmar?

Aung San Suu Kyi: Alan, unity has never meant uniformity. It cannot. Not in a land like ours, where the mountains speak in different tongues, and each river carries the rhythm of its own people. The dream of a federal democratic union is not to dissolve our differences—it is to honor them. To allow each culture, each language, each history to breathe freely, and still hold hands across those differences to shape a shared future.

To the KIA, KNU, AA, TNLA, MNDAA, UWSA, SSA, and every other ethnic force—armed or unarmed—that has stood its ground through decades of betrayal and war, *I say this with all my heart: your identities are not barriers to unity. They are its foundation. They are its beauty. Without you, there is no union—only occupation by another name.*

And let me also say, with the utmost sincerity: I speak these words from behind bars. As do President Win Myint, U Win Htein, and the many ministers and lawmakers who were chosen by the people and then silenced. We speak not from freedom, but from captivity. And that fact alone tells you the enormity of the struggle we are still in. It tells you how deeply rooted the authoritarian assault remains—and how hard it fights not only to suppress the present, but to erase the possibility of a future built on inclusion and truth.

We must have the moral courage to tell the truth about our past. And that includes acknowledging mistakes made under my leadership and within the National League for Democracy. The centralization of power in Naypyidaw, the marginalization of ethnic voices, and the failure to build true federal trust—these were not small oversights. They were wounds. Wounds that still ache. Wounds we must tend with honesty.

But I ask you not to mistake those failures for indifference. Nor for a lack of love. I have listened. I am still listening. And I am learning. True reconciliation does not come through apology alone—it comes through action, through shared power, and through the daily practice of deep respect.

In the Myanmar we must now build—emerging as we are from fire, exile, and sorrow—diversity cannot be an afterthought. It must be the starting point. A child born in Kachin must feel just as cherished as one in Yangon. A poem written in Shan must belong to the soul of the whole country. A soldier fighting in Rakhine must know that their bravery is not tribal, but national.

Let me say this clearly: inclusivity is not political correctness. It is political maturity. It is how grown nations act. And it is how we will heal.

To those who doubt me—who wonder whether these words are too late—I understand your skepticism. And I accept it. But I also ask this: *let us not measure one another by perfection, but by perseverance.* We are all learning how to be free. May we do it together—with truth, tenderness, and the courage to begin again.

Alan Clements: Daw Suu, you've often spoken of reconciliation. For these groups, many of whom have endured atrocities at the hands of the Tatmadaw, what does reconciliation truly look like—not just in political language, but as a lived and enduring transformation of heart, history, and leadership?

Aung San Suu Kyi: Reconciliation, Alan, is not forgetting. It is refusing to let hatred be the author of our future. It is a moral commitment—a courageous practice of truth-telling that begins with the dignity of acknowledgment. To reconcile, we must look directly at the past, however painful. We must understand not only what happened, but why. We must have the strength to name the harm, and the wisdom to hold those responsible accountable. Justice must be pursued not out of vengeance, but to ensure that such darkness never rises again.

But reconciliation is more than justice—it is regeneration. It requires radical empathy, the willingness to apologize, the humility to listen, and the discipline to change.

To those who have suffered, I say: your pain must be seen and honored. To those who have caused harm, I say: your remorse must be real and public.

Only through such moral clarity can we begin to rebuild trust. And finally, reconciliation demands a reimagining of what binds us—a recommitment to principles that transcend ethnicity, religion, or political allegiance. *A shared future must be built not upon fear or dominance, but upon dignity and peace.*

Alan Clements: And what of discernment, Daw Suu? One of the deepest truths I've come to understand—through both activism and inner practice—is that reconciliation without discernment can be hollow. It risks becoming appeasement.

By discernment, I mean the ability to see clearly—to distinguish between truth and falsehood, justice and compromise, courage and avoidance. It's the inner clarity that must accompany compassion if we are to respond wisely to harm.

So, I ask: how do we integrate moral clarity with love—especially in a country where so much harm has gone unacknowledged, and where silence is often mistaken for peace?

Aung San Suu Kyi: That is such an essential question, Alan. Because without discernment, compassion can lose its depth—it becomes sentiment, a reactive softness that sometimes avoids uncomfortable truths. But without compassion, discernment can harden into judgment—an intellect that cuts but does not heal.

So yes, we must cultivate both. But not as opposites—as one. A kind of inner wisdom that sees clearly and feels deeply. That asks, gently but unflinchingly: *Who is taking responsibility? Who remains hidden in silence? Who is ready to heal, and who is still lost in harm?*

As Carl Jung reminded us, the shadow must be seen—not condemned, not cast out, but understood. And that takes great patience. Great courage. We must speak truth. We must name injustice. But we must never let truth become a tool of humiliation. And never let compassion become an excuse for silence.

In the *Dhamma*, there's a quality—I think you know it—that we call *yoniso manasikāra*: wise attention. It's the kind of discernment that doesn't stop at the surface, but looks deeply into causes and conditions. It asks not only *what* happened, but *why*. Not only *who* is guilty, but *what* has blinded them.

This doesn't mean we excuse harm. But it does mean we try to respond in ways that liberate—not just punish.

True discernment, as I've come to understand it, isn't about assigning blame—it's about seeing clearly, with depth and care. It's the discipline of looking beyond appearances, beyond politics, beyond even pain—to glimpse what might actually allow for transformation, not just reaction.

So yes, Alan, the deepest wisdom lives where truth and tenderness are not at odds, but in quiet alliance. Where we refuse to look away—and just as importantly, refuse to harden. True discernment doesn't demand that we abandon feeling; it asks that we refine it. To stay open, even as we stand firm. To see clearly, without losing the capacity to care.

That, to me, is the real courage. The kind that doesn't shout—but endures. And in this revolution, where justice must be reborn from grief, we will need that kind of courage every single day.

Alan Clements: Daw Suu, I'd like to bring in something that has deeply inspired both of us—a body of psychological and spiritual wisdom on truth, integrity, courage, and reconciliation. In particular, I'm thinking of *The Inner Citadel* by Pierre Hadot, the French philosopher and historian of philosophy, who explores how the teachings of ancient

Stoicism—especially Marcus Aurelius—offer not just ideas but spiritual exercises for cultivating autonomy and inner freedom.

Alongside Hadot, I draw from voices like Viktor Frankl, Carl Jung, Carl Rogers, Rollo May, Gandhi, and Kierkegaard—thinkers who speak to the inner foundations of peace and the moral architecture of the self.

With your permission, may I ask a few questions inspired by this lineage of thought—so that together, we might explore how such wisdom could help guide Myanmar's healing?

Aung San Suu Kyi: Of course, Alan. These are not merely theories—they are guides for how we live, how we listen, how we lead. Please, let's begin.

Alan Clements: The first principle says: "We stand in our truth, but we acknowledge others' truths." That resonates deeply in Myanmar, where so many groups have long histories of trauma. How do we balance our own truth while listening deeply to another's, especially when those truths appear to conflict?

Aung San Suu Kyi: This is where real reconciliation begins—with the courage not just to speak, but to listen.

Our truth is not threatened by another's—it is expanded. As Carl Rogers taught, to be fully oneself requires the capacity to embrace the other.

Acknowledging another's truth does not diminish our own; it affirms that we are ready for mature dialogue. When we dare to hold space for multiple truths, unity begins to unfold—not by erasing our differences, but by illuminating our common ground.

Alan Clements: Another principle says: "The cost of integrity is high, but it is the price of authentic leadership." How do we cultivate this kind of leadership in times of war, betrayal, and instability?

Aung San Suu Kyi: Authentic leadership must rise from conscience, not control. As Viktor Frankl teaches, the deepest meaning often arises from suffering transformed. Leadership grounded in integrity may be lonely—but it is never empty. We must prepare our future leaders to be uncomfortable, to be honest, and to choose courage over conformity, even when it costs them greatly.

Alan Clements: As we move on, a passage reads: "We reject blind conformity, embracing individual thought and ethical courage." This feels essential now. How do we encourage discernment over dogma, especially among youth raised in propaganda?

Aung San Suu Kyi: We must teach the youth to think—not just to obey. This is the heart of democratic culture. As Rollo May taught us, the true self emerges not through conformity, but through the bravery to question, to wrestle, to wonder.

We must nurture schools, homes, and public dialogues where questioning is welcomed, where critical thinking is cultivated. Only then will we raise a generation not just of citizens, but of ethical thinkers.

Alan Clements: And what of rejection? The manifesto says: "Rejection is an opportunity for growth, not a defeat." You've faced immense rejection—globally and personally. What has it taught you?

Aung San Suu Kyi: Rejection taught me how to stand in solitude without bitterness. It taught me that love for one's country does not depend on being loved back. It taught me that truth is not popularity— it is clarity. And clarity, when held with kindness, is liberation. As Abraham Maslow reminds us, the pain of rejection is not a signal to retreat, but an invitation to deepen—to discover what we truly stand for, and why it matters.

Alan Clements: The document ends with a call: "We will never apologize for upholding what is right." Is that how you feel now, even from solitary confinement?

Aung San Suu Kyi: Yes. Even here—especially here. I may not have all the answers. I may have made mistakes. But I will never apologize for standing for truth, dignity, and peace. And I ask others to do the same— not with arrogance, but with sincerity. Because if we lose the courage to speak from the heart, we lose the thread of our shared humanity.

Alan Clements: Daw Suu, before we close—if this chapter is to be studied for generations, what is the one message you hope endures?

Aung San Suu Kyi: That reconciliation is not about erasing our wounds—it is about transforming them into wisdom. That peace is not the absence of struggle—but the presence of conscience. That leadership is not about commanding others—but about serving the truth in all.

May we rise—not only as a nation, but as people of heart. May we walk forward, not perfectly, but bravely. And may our greatest strength always be our capacity to heal—together.

Alan Clements: Then let this be our vow: to walk that path with open eyes, open hearts, and the unshakable light of truth.

Aung San Suu Kyi: Yes, Alan. Let that be our vow. And may Myanmar one day remember not just how we suffered—but how we chose to heal.

Alan Clements: Daw Suu, as we bring this conversation to a close, I'd like to return to one final question. I know we've spoken about this before, and I believe you would firmly agree—its importance cannot be underestimated.

The road ahead is long and uncertain. The weight on the shoulders of Myanmar's Ethnic Armed Organizations is immense. What guidance would you offer them now—as they walk the fragile line between resistance and reconciliation?

And what final message would you offer to all the people of Myanmar, who continue to suffer, survive, and still somehow believe?

Aung San Suu Kyi: Alan, I thank you for asking this again. And yes, I do agree—it cannot be asked too often. Because this question sits at the very heart of who we are and who we must become.

The truth is, there are no easy answers. And I would never pretend otherwise. Some nights I lie awake thinking of the lives lost, the families shattered, the villages burned into memory. I think of young boys pulled into war, and mothers who still wait by the road for sons who will not return. It is not abstract. It is unbearable. And sometimes, yes—it makes me cry.

To the Ethnic Armed Organizations, I would say this with all the humility and respect I can offer: you carry not only weapons, but the fragile future of a broken country. The question is not only how you fight—but how you dream. How you imagine what comes after. Because if we cannot imagine a Myanmar where no child has to pick up a gun, then we have already lost something sacred.

Let your resistance be fierce—but let your hearts stay open. Use strength, but do not let it close the door to tenderness. Your unity matters, but even more, your humanity. Speak to one another not just across battle lines, but across histories. Across wounds. Let the dream be not of domination, but of dignity—for all.

And to the people of Myanmar—those who suffer in silence, those who scream into the void, those who keep living anyway: I see you. I feel you. You carry more than you should ever have had to carry. You are surviving things that no one should have to survive. And still, you love. You give. You hope. That is a kind of courage no army can conquer.

I do not say this lightly: you are the heart of our nation. You are the seedbed of our future. And though I am far from you now, though I sit behind these prison walls, I carry you with me in every breath.

We must build a Myanmar where no one is asked to erase who they are in order to belong. A nation not built on fear, but on fearless truth. Let our diversity not be the crack in our foundation, but the music of our becoming.

And let peace not be postponed until the violence ends—but practiced, quietly, in how we speak, how we listen, how we care for one another, even now.

If we can do that—if we can keep our hearts intact even through all of this—then no matter how long it takes, I believe we will arrive. Not just at freedom, but at a kind of freedom worthy of the price we've paid.

136

LIVING THE *DHAMMA* IN DARKNESS

Author's Prelude

In this chapter, silence becomes not absence, but offering. We enter not with fanfare, but with reverence. Here, in a cell emptied of all but the present moment, the *Dhamma* breathes. Daw Suu shares her heart from the soul of solitude—in gestures small enough to miss, yet vast enough to carry a nation's conscience.

This is not the *Dhamma* as doctrine. This is the *Dhamma* lived in exile—clear, patient, unshakable. Not a religion, but a path of presence. A way of seeing, feeling, and acting rooted in mindfulness, compassion, and truth. There is no performance here. No teaching plan. No plea for sympathy. Only a transmission of stillness—the kind that ripens only in the depths of silence.

These pages ask for slow reading. They call not for admiration, but for listening. In every phrase, there is a gate—to steadiness in sorrow, to gentleness in grief, to the quiet miracle of breath. This is not spiritual theory. It is survival. It is resistance through sensitivity.

Let us meet her here—in the quiet. Let us not rush past the truth that silence reveals. For in confinement's deepest chamber, the *Dhamma* does not disappear—it radiates. Not as an escape from suffering, but as a luminous refusal to be broken.

And may what we find in this chapter remain with us—not as memory, but as path.

◆ ◆ ◆

Alan Clements: Daw Suu... my friend, my heart pauses here. You are now in your fifth year of solitary confinement. No family visits. No letters. No books. No medicine of real help. No release from the endless, humid heat that presses down through the long Myanmar summers—those brutal, airless days that would wither almost anyone.

And still, you endure. Not for the first time. Over twenty years in detention now across your life. But this time... the isolation is deeper. The silence, more complete. The forgetting, almost systematic.

And yet—you remain. Clear. Grounded. Awake. Radiant, somehow, against the odds. You continue to offer guidance. Not from power, but from presence. Not from comfort, but from the marrow of truth you've lived and earned.

So, I come to this moment not as a journalist, not as a seeker, and not with any agenda—only a human question, offered from the heart: What has kept your spirit from breaking?

How have you lived the *Dhamma* in such darkness—and not only survived, but remained so fully alive?

Aung San Suu Kyi: Alan, the prison walls are indeed thick, the silence heavy, and the isolation immense. But the *Dhamma*, like air, pervades even the darkest corners. The Buddha's teaching, as Sayadaw U Pandita often reminded us, is not bound by circumstance. It is alive in every breath, every moment of awareness, and every act of compassion.

Here, I rely on the foundations of mindfulness—*satipaṭṭhāna*—not as concept, but as a living lifeline. I return again and again to the body, the breath, the feelings, the mind, and the *Dhamma*. These are the fields of liberation. Even in the narrow confines of a cell, there is a universe to observe.

I breathe—not just to survive, but to witness. To feel the rise and fall of impermanence with each inhalation. The breath is my refuge, and sometimes, my only companion. It reminds me that life continues, moment by moment, even when the world outside falls away.

Alan Clements: And what of the emotional terrain—the grief, the anger, the longing, the ache of absence? How do you navigate these waves?

Aung San Suu Kyi: I've learned to let the heart be tender, not tough. As Sayadawgyi taught: meet the moment with mindfulness, not resistance. When fear arises, I know it as fear. When sorrow visits, I bow to it as sorrow. They come; they go. None of it owns me. None of it stays. I feel the tightness in the chest, the heat of anger, the cold of despair. I acknowledge these visitors and greet them with the warmth of awareness—not indulgence, but intimacy. I hold them the way a mother holds a fevered child—with love, without clinging.

And yes, anger comes—sometimes fierce. But I know its nature. If I feed it, it burns. If I meet it with *mettā*, it softens. This is not weakness. *It is the strongest act of all: to transform what can destroy into what can deepen.*

Alan Clements: You mentioned mindfulness of the body. In such restricted conditions, what does that practice look like for you?

Aung San Suu Kyi: It is very simple—and completely alive. Mahāsi Sayādaw taught: "Know the step when stepping. Know the breath when breathing."

When I sit, I feel the cushion or the floor beneath me. When I lie down, I observe the sensations that arise in contact with the mat. Even the act of drinking water becomes a meditation—coolness, the quiet shift of sensation, gratitude.

Every movement, every shift in posture, is a teaching. The body, this fragile vehicle, becomes a field of revelation—showing me impermanence, unsatisfactoriness, and not-self in real time. The truth is not abstract. It is here—in the bones, in the blood, in the breath.

Alan Clements: And hearing? In a place where there are so few sounds, and those that do arise can be jarring or foreboding?

Aung San Suu Kyi: Sound is a potent teacher. As Mahāsi Sayādaw said, "Hear the hearing, not the meaning." When I hear footsteps, keys, distant shouting—I pause. My mind may want to react, to build a story. But I guide it gently back: this is sound, this is knowing, this is passing.

This keeps me from being dragged into fear. *It offers the great gift of mindfulness: the freedom to meet life without being captured by it.* It allows me to respond, rather than react. *It is one of the greatest gifts of mindfulness: it gives us back our freedom, one moment at a time.*

Alan Clements: Daw Suu, I know the three characteristics—*anicca*, *dukkha*, and *anattā*—have long lived at the heart of your practice.

Anicca—the impermanence of all things.

Dukkha—the subtle, often piercing unsatisfactoriness woven through existence.

Anattā—the absence of a fixed or separate self.

What have they come to mean to you now, in this season of your life? Not as ideas—but as truths you've had to inhabit, alone, day after day. Have they changed for you? Deepened?

And if so, how?

Aung San Suu Kyi: Alan, there are truths you can study—and then there are truths that strip you bare.

Anicca—impermanence—was once a teaching I respected. Now, in here, it's the only constant. There are no windows in my cell. No sunrises. No shifting shadows to mark the hours. Time becomes something else. It dissolves. Memories lose their sharpness. Names begin to fade. Even sorrow changes shape. And strangely, that too is a kind of grace.

Here, I've come to feel impermanence not just in events, but in identity. Fear rises, then subsides. Anger flares, then softens. A longing appears, then vanishes. The breath—my one companion—never stays. That is *anicca*: not something I believe in, but something I live inside. It's what remains when there is nothing left to hold onto.

Dukkha—the deep unease woven through all things—has become more than personal. It's national. It's everywhere. Not through sound or sight, but through what I imagine, what I remember, what I feel moving through the silence. I hear it inwardly—the aftermath of bombings I cannot hear, but know. The breath of mothers waiting for sons who may never return. The silence where children's laughter used to be. The vanishing of schools, of poems, of ordinary joys. It is grief without boundary. And yes, sometimes, even in here, it undoes me.

But I've learned: if I resist it, it hardens. If I meet it, it opens. I don't mean it goes away. But it becomes breathable. It no longer defines me—it teaches me. Pain is not the enemy. It is the mirror in which we see how deeply we care.

And then there is *anattā*—the absence of a fixed self. In here, you are erased by design. No name. No mirror. No role. Even "mother" becomes memory. "Leader" becomes echo. And without those identities, you begin to notice what's still there: breath, awareness, a quiet presence that doesn't belong to anyone.

At first, it felt like disappearance. Then I began to understand—it is not destruction, but freedom. Not absence, but clarity. And it made me wonder: if those who seek power could glimpse this—this vastness beneath the ego's walls—might they hold the world more gently?

So yes, these three characteristics—*anicca, dukkha, anattā*—are no longer teachings to me. They are the very architecture of my survival.

And let me bring in Nibbāna.

To me, it's not a mystical endpoint or a final escape. It's the *momentary absence of suffering*—the stillness that arises when the mind is no longer at war with reality. It's the moment you stop needing anything to be different in order to feel whole.

Not escape. Clarity. And sometimes—just sometimes—I taste it. In the breath. In the hush between thoughts. In that fleeting instant when I stop wishing for a different life.

And if that kind of peace is possible even here—even in this darkness—then I believe it is possible for the world.

For Myanmar.

For anyone who walks the path of truth, tenderness, and freedom.

Alan Clements: Daw Suu, after all we've spoken, may I ask something that feels both deeply personal and quietly universal? From seeing so clearly—impermanence, sorrow, the dissolution of self—how does compassion arise? Not as an idea, but as a living force?

Aung San Suu Kyi: Naturally, Alan. When we see clearly that all beings are caught in the same fire—craving, fear, delusion—how can compassion not arise?

Karuṇā doesn't begin with the world. It begins in here. In this cell. In this body. With the breath. With the ache. I say silently: "May I be held in compassion." And from there, I extend it—to the guards who must lock my door. To the prisoners in nearby cells. To those who misunderstand me. To those who have harmed me. Not because I condone, but because I understand.

Sayadaw U Pandita once said to me: *"If your heart closes, open it wider."* That has become my lifeline.

Alan Clements: Daw Suu, in your presence there is a stillness that feels carved from fire. I hear not only survival—but dignity, shaped in silence. What would you say to those who feel utterly undone by life— who carry wounds too deep for language, and no longer believe they can bear the weight of being?

Aung San Suu Kyi: I would say: You are not broken. You are human. Your sorrow is not a failure—it is a mirror. A doorway. The very ground from which wisdom begins to grow.

Even here, I remember: every moment is a chance to begin again. The breath is always waiting. The heart, even shattered, can soften. You don't need ideal conditions to touch freedom—only presence, patience, and a little trust in the *Dhamma*.

Let the path be humble. Let it be real. Let it be enough.

Alan Clements: Daw Suu… these words are more than reflections. They are a transmission—clear and quiet—from the depths of your heart. Thank you for meeting me—not across distance, but in the intimacy of shared inner ground.

Aung San Suu Kyi: Thank you, Alan. And to all who walk this path: never doubt that even in darkness, the *Dhamma* shines. Let it carry you home.

But allow me to say this more fully.

The *Dhamma* is not only a path to liberation—it is a sanctuary for the wounded heart. In solitude, it becomes a companion. In despair, a whisper of courage. In confusion, a thread of clarity. It is not a philosophy to adopt—it is a way of seeing, breath by breath, that keeps you human when everything else is stripped away.

When even your name becomes an echo, when all the structures of identity dissolve, the *Dhamma* remains. It cannot be imprisoned. It is patient. Fierce. Quiet. Steady. And it asks only that you turn toward life—not away from it—with honesty, with humility, with an undefended heart.

There are days I feel the weight of sorrow press so close I can hardly breathe. The longing for loved ones. The ache of not knowing what has become of so many. And in those moments, I sit. I let the grief rise—not to fix it, but to feel it. To say silently, *"I see you. You are here. Let us breathe together."*

And when I open to that sorrow, I see it's not mine alone. It is the sorrow of my people—the farmers who have lost their fields, the nuns who chant under broken roofs, the children who dream beneath the noise of war. Their grief moves through me like a river through stone. I do not resist it. I let it carve me deeper.

This is *karuṇā*—not pity, not passivity, but the courage to feel fully without being destroyed.

In this way, mindfulness is not separate from the revolution. It is the revolution. It is how we refuse to let hatred deform us. It is how we transform agony into love.

Every time I sit with pain without collapsing—every time I feel fear and meet it with presence—I walk with my people. We are not separate. Even here, I am part of the great, silent uprising of the human spirit.

In this breath, I meet the mothers singing lullabies in burned-out villages. In this body, I meet the teachers reopening schools with nothing but chalk and courage. In the rising and falling of awareness, I meet the dignity of those who refuse to disappear.

This is the grace of the Dhamma: *that even in the blackest dark, we are never truly lost.* There is always a thread of knowing to follow. A flicker of love. A still place beneath the storm.

And every act of compassion—felt, spoken, or unseen—adds to the invisible building of a Myanmar that is already being born.

So, when the sorrow feels unendurable, I return to the breath. When anger clouds the mind, I return to *karuṇā*. When despair says there is no point, I return to the quiet miracle that even here, life breathes on. Not because it is easy. Not because I am unbroken. But because the *Dhamma*, tender and relentless, carries me when my own strength dissolves.

And so, we begin again. Not perfectly. Not without pain. But with sincerity. With the trembling courage to stay human.

Let us walk on—not because the path is certain, but because it is true. Let us walk with humility, with steadiness, and with the deep knowing: *we are not alone.*

Every step echoes in the heart of the world. Every quiet act of dignity shines in the dark like a lantern they cannot extinguish.

May the Dhamma be your refuge. May compassion be your compass. And may the love we share—across prisons, across grief, across generations— be the unseen bridge that carries Myanmar home.

A VISION FOR FEDERAL DEMOCRACY

Author's Prelude

There are moments in the life of a nation when its very essence is called into question—not merely by the collapse of institutions, but by the silence that follows betrayal. In those moments, democracy feels less like a path and more like a ghost. And yet—something endures: a whisper of conscience, a thread of dignity, a refusal—however quiet—to surrender the future to fear.

This chapter is not a blueprint. It is a meditation—an intimate reckoning with federal democracy as something far more than a political arrangement. It is a spiritual architecture in search of shelter—a way of living that honors Myanmar's sacred diversity while planting the seeds of trust in soil long scorched by betrayal.

Here, Aung San Suu Kyi speaks not as a politician, but as a witness—one who has paid the price of freedom, and who still believes, even in isolation, that unity is not the absence of difference, but the radical art of cherishing it.

Her vision is not offered as perfection, but as possibility. Not as rhetoric, but as vow:

A vow that no child be unseen. A vow that no people be erased. A vow that democracy, if it is to live, must mean belonging—for everyone.

As Daw Suu states: *"Let the creation of a Federal Democracy be our covenant—not merely in theory, but in lived truth. Let it breathe in action, not just in aspiration. Let us shape it—voice by voice, region by region, story by story—until Myanmar is no longer divided by blood, but united by dignity."*

◆ ◆ ◆

Alan Clements: Daw Suu, in a previous conversation, we explored the vision of federal democracy as a cornerstone of Myanmar's future. But as we've both reflected since, this vision is far too foundational—too vital to the survival of the nation and its freedom—not to go even deeper.

As we face both the devastation of ongoing war and the hunger for true democracy, it's clear that the transformation you seek must grow from the roots of truth, inclusion, and justice. I return to this subject not to repeat, but to renew our understanding.

And so, Daw Suu, from your solitude, from the marrow of your lived insight, may I ask again: what are your most intimate reflections on federal democracy today? What, from your heart, must we more deeply understand for it to truly take root?

Aung San Suu Kyi: Alan, I welcome your returning to this subject. You're right—it is not repetition, but deepening. Its meaning cannot be overstated. In fact, it must be returned to again and again, like a promise renewed through every trial.

This vision is not simply a policy or a political structure. It is the spiritual foundation of our future—a vision without which there can be no lasting peace, no enduring freedom, no true belonging.

Federal democracy is not merely a system of governance—it is an ethical and existential imperative for Myanmar. Our nation is home to over 130 ethnic groups, each with its own language, culture, and identity. To deny this diversity is to deny the essence of who we are as a people. Federal democracy, then, is not just about power-sharing; it is about honoring the dignity of every community, ensuring that no one feels marginalized or forgotten.

However, the path to this vision is fraught with challenges. The devastation we have spoken of—the burned villages, the displaced millions, the countless lives lost—has left scars on the national psyche. These scars must not be hidden, but seen—held with fierce honesty—so that they can become the soil in which a new Union might grow.

Yet, amidst this suffering, I see the seeds of transformation. The unity forged by the Ethnic Armed Organizations (EAOS), the resilience of our political prisoners, and the courage of our people remind me that even in the darkest moments, hope is never extinguished. Hope is stubborn. It survives even the gravest betrayals. And it is this stubborn, luminous hope that will shape the Myanmar to come.

Alan Clements: Daw Suu, you mention unity, but Myanmar has often struggled with accusations of Burmese centralism, even under democratic leadership. How do you address the concerns of ethnic groups who feel excluded or mistrusted?

Aung San Suu Kyi: That is a question we must confront with humility and honesty. Our political party, the National League for Democracy (NLD), has made mistakes in the past—mistakes born not of malice but of a lack of understanding, and perhaps even a blindness to the deep currents of mistrust that exist among our ethnic communities. Burmese centralism is a legacy of decades of military rule, but its shadow has lingered—even during periods of quasi-civilian governance.

To move forward, we must first acknowledge these mistakes. As I've said throughout our conversations, reconciliation begins with listening—not only to words, but to the pain and aspirations beneath them.

To our ethnic brothers and sisters, I say: we hear you. Your grievances are valid, your struggles real. Federal democracy cannot be a top-down imposition; it must be a collective creation, shaped by the voices of all who call Myanmar home.

Alan Clements: The Ethnic Armed Organizations, including the Kachin Independence Army (KIA), Karen National Union (KNU), Shan State Army (SSA), Arakan Army (AA), and others, have become symbols of resistance and hope. How do their efforts align with your vision of federal democracy?

Aung San Suu Kyi: Alan, the efforts of the EAOs are both a challenge and an opportunity. Their courage and sacrifices embody the spirit of resistance that fuels our struggle for freedom. However, the path from armed resistance to political participation is a delicate one. To the leaders of these organizations, I would say: your weapons have defended your people, but true victory lies in the realm of dialogue and consensus.

Let us remember: federal democracy is not a zero-sum game. It requires compromise, flexibility, trust, and a mindful willingness to see beyond immediate grievances. The unity demonstrated by the EAOs in recent years is more than strategic—it is the seed of a new political and moral ethos for Myanmar. If this unity can be expanded to include all stakeholders—political prisoners, civil society, and the broader population—it could become the foundation of a truly inclusive and enduring federal union.

Alan Clements: Daw Suu, the political prisoners, including President Win Myint and over 22,000 others, represent another critical element of this vision. How do you see their role in shaping Myanmar's future, particularly in the context of building an inclusive and unified federal democracy?

Aung San Suu Kyi: Alan, the political prisoners of Myanmar are the heart of our struggle and the moral compass of our nation. They embody the courage, sacrifice, and resilience that define our collective pursuit of freedom. Each individual—whether a high-ranking leader like President Win Myint or an anonymous activist imprisoned for their beliefs—has endured unimaginable suffering, not for personal gain, but for the shared vision of a just and inclusive Myanmar.

To understand their role in shaping our future, we must first honor the profound depth of their sacrifices. Every day spent behind bars, every refusal to renounce their beliefs, every silent endurance of injustice is a living testament to their unwavering commitment to justice and dignity. They remind us that freedom is not a gift to be received; it is a responsibility to be earned and upheld.

But their contribution goes beyond resistance. Political prisoners carry not only the scars of oppression but the seeds of new leadership. They bring invaluable experience, hard-earned wisdom, and an intimate understanding of what it means to stand against tyranny. When we speak of federal democracy, their voices must be at the forefront. They are not just participants in this vision—they are architects of it.

Alan Clements: How can this vision of federal democracy incorporate the sacrifices and experiences of these political prisoners to ensure it is truly inclusive and transformative?

Aung San Suu Kyi: To incorporate their sacrifices into the framework of federal democracy, we must first ensure that their experiences are neither forgotten nor marginalized. Their stories are not just individual accounts of suffering; they are chapters in the collective narrative of our nation's struggle for freedom. We must embed their insights into our institutions, honor their resilience in our constitutions, and ensure their wisdom informs the rebuilding of our educational, legal, and civic life. Only by weaving their lived truth into the fabric of our emerging democracy can we hope to create a Myanmar that is truly inclusive, just, and free.

Their inclusion must happen at every level.

First, at the level of national reconciliation, political prisoners must play an active role in shaping the policies that seek to heal Myanmar's wounds. Their firsthand knowledge of injustice, oppression, and endurance uniquely equips them to bridge divides between ethnic groups, civil society, and the broader population. Their voices can foster dialogue rooted not in theory, but in lived truth.

Second, in the leadership of a federal democratic government, political prisoners—many of whom, like President Win Myint, are seasoned in both governance and resistance—must stand at the center of rebuilding. They have paid the price for freedom with their bodies and their lives; their leadership can ensure that the principles of justice, equality, dignity, and compassion are not merely spoken of but lived into the very DNA of our new institutions. Their experience offers a moral grounding essential for governance that truly serves all ethnicities and regions.

Third, for healing to be real and lasting, political prisoners must inform the processes of truth and accountability. They have borne witness to the regime's darkest acts—silencing, torture, disappearance— and their testimonies must shape Myanmar's reckoning with its past. A federal democracy cannot grow over buried wounds; it must grow through courageous acknowledgment and transformative justice.

Finally, political prisoners represent both a symbolic and practical force for unity. Their sacrifices transcend ethnicity, religion, and geography. In their suffering and resilience, they embody the shared aspirations of all Myanmar's people. Their release and visible participation in the rebuilding of our nation would send a powerful and undeniable message: that *we are, in truth, one people, walking together toward freedom.*

Alan Clements: The vision of federal democracy often emphasizes inclusivity. How can we ensure that the experiences of political prisoners, especially those from diverse ethnic and religious backgrounds, contribute to this inclusivity?

Aung San Suu Kyi: Inclusivity is the cornerstone of federal democracy, and the experiences of our political prisoners serve as a profound reminder of the interconnectedness of our struggles. Among the tens of thousands imprisoned are people from every ethnic group, every faith, and every walk of life. Their diversity mirrors the rich, complex tapestry of Myanmar itself—a tapestry too often torn, but never destroyed.

To ensure that this inclusivity becomes the living heart of federal democracy, we must elevate diverse voices with real commitment. Ethnic and religious minorities among the political prisoners must not merely be acknowledged; they must be given active platforms to share their experiences and shape the conversation. Their insights, rooted in both suffering and resilience, will deepen our understanding of what justice, freedom, and equality truly mean.

We must also create dedicated forums for dialogue—not token gatherings, but spaces where political prisoners, ethnic leaders, civil society, and the broader citizenry come together with the sincere intent to listen, to understand, and to build. These gatherings must be rooted in mutual respect, humility, and a fierce commitment to hearing all voices, especially those historically marginalized or silenced.

Moreover, we must recognize that the struggles faced by political prisoners are not isolated from broader injustices. They are woven into issues of ethnicity, religion, class, and gender. A truly inclusive federal democracy must address these intersectional realities, refusing to simplify or erase them. By doing so, we strengthen the moral fabric of our movement and ensure that justice is not just an aspiration, but a lived truth for every citizen.

Finally, we must reimagine our systems of justice themselves. Federal democracy cannot simply replicate the structures that enabled oppression. It must dismantle the old architecture of fear and hierarchy and build in its place mechanisms that protect human rights, honor diversity, and foster dignity. *The lessons carried by our political prisoners— etched into their very bodies and spirits—must inform every aspect of how we design the new Myanmar.*

Alan Clements: Many of these prisoners have endured profound trauma. How do we support their reintegration into society and empower them to contribute to Myanmar's future?

Aung San Suu Kyi: The reintegration of political prisoners is both a moral obligation and a practical necessity for building a democratic Myanmar. Supporting them demands a holistic approach—one that honors their sacrifices while equipping them to flourish anew.

First, we must address the deep psychological wounds they carry. Trauma cannot be brushed aside or left to heal on its own. We must provide access to psychological support, compassionate counseling, and spaces where healing can unfold safely and authentically. A nation that values its people must prioritize their emotional and mental well-being as much as their political rights.

Second, we must ensure their economic and social reintegration is not an afterthought, but a pillar of reconstruction. Many political prisoners emerge into a world that has changed without them—jobs lost, communities altered, opportunities scarce. Vocational training, education programs, and pathways to meaningful employment must be created, empowering them to rebuild their lives with dignity and purpose.

Third, these individuals must be recognized and honored publicly. They are not simply survivors—they are the architects of our revolution's moral foundation. *Their sacrifices must be remembered not with pity, but with reverence.* Public ceremonies, memorials, and educational initiatives should affirm their central role in shaping the new Myanmar and inspire future generations to cherish the price of freedom.

Above all, their role must not end with their release. Their voices must remain at the heart of policymaking, governance, and national reconciliation. Ongoing advocacy for their inclusion ensures that Myanmar's transformation is informed by those who paid the highest price to make it possible. In honoring their journey, we honor the spirit of democracy itself.

Alan Clements: As we conclude, Daw Suu, what would you say to the political prisoners themselves, as they continue to endure unimaginable hardships?

Aung San Suu Kyi: To my fellow prisoners, I say this: You are not only the soul of our nation—you are its conscience, its memory, and its undying hope. Your sacrifices are not forgotten, nor will they ever be erased from the story we are writing together. Each day you endure behind bars is a testament to your courage, a beacon that cuts through the darkest night for all of Myanmar.

Hold steadfast to your dignity, for it is your greatest shield against the forces that seek to diminish you. Even when the world outside forgets, know that your silent defiance ripples through every village, every camp, every heart still beating for freedom. Your suffering is not in vain—it is the living foundation of the Myanmar we are fighting to birth: a nation where justice is real, diversity is honored, and every voice matters.

When the day comes—and it will come—that you walk free, you will not merely return to life; you will help redefine it. You will carry with you a wisdom carved from pain, a strength forged in solitude, a clarity no oppressor can touch. *You are not broken—you are becoming.*

Perhaps most importantly, *you are not alone.* Even when it feels otherwise, you are carried on the shoulders of millions who dream alongside you, who fight because of you, who live in gratitude for the unseen sacrifices you continue to make. *We are with you—fully—in spirit, in purpose, and in unbreakable solidarity.*

Know in your heart that together, we will create a Myanmar that is not merely a remote ideal or a fragile hope—but a living truth, woven into the fabric of our shared humanity. A great nation that honors every sacrifice, tends to every wound, and gives breath to every whispered dream. A Myanmar where no one is forgotten, and everyone—everyone—belongs. *And that means you. No exceptions.*

Alan Clements: *Daw Suu, I ask this with full awareness of the impossibility it may carry—especially as you speak from solitary confinement, held by the very institution responsible for your imprisonment and the incarceration of over 22,000 others, while terrorizing an entire nation.*

The *Tatmadaw*—the military—remains one of the most entrenched and formidable obstacles to Myanmar's future. Its legacy is carved into nearly every trauma we've discussed: decades of violence, disinformation, betrayal, and systematic obstruction of democracy. And yet, the question must be asked. Because its influence, however illegitimate, remains real.

Given this brutal reality, how do we begin to imagine engagement with such an institution—not to excuse it, but to *transform* it? What would meaningful transition look like, if even possible? And how do we walk that line between necessary resistance and the long view of national reconciliation?

Aung San Suu Kyi: Alan, you're right to frame this question with caution. The Tatmadaw is not merely a military force—it is a deeply entrenched psychology. A legacy of fear, indoctrination, and obedience that has captured the minds of generations. The complexity of this challenge cannot be overstated. We are not simply confronting an institution—we are confronting a worldview. A worldview shaped by decades of authoritarian rule, disinformation, and isolation from civil society.

Yet even so, I do not believe the soldiers themselves—the young men on the frontlines—are beyond reach. I would not be surprised if many, if not the majority, quietly long for peace. Not war. Not murder. Not the daily trauma of killing their own people. They are not confronting terrorists, as they've been told—they are at war with their own conscience, their own people, their own indoctrination. And that internal war is unsustainable. It corrodes conscience.

The upper ranks—the generals, colonels, commanders—are even more isolated. Shielded by wealth, echo chambers, and privilege, they have become addicted to power. But they are not invulnerable. They are human. And no amount of control can fully protect them from the eventual consequences of their actions. History has shown, again and again, that power built on fear will not endure.

As I have said before—and it cannot be overstated—*the Tatmadaw's actions are a profound betrayal of the vision my father held when he founded it.* He imagined a protector of the people—a force for defense and unity. But that vision has been deformed. What was meant to serve has become a machinery of domination. What was meant to unify has fractured the nation. This is not only a tragedy for the people—it is a tragedy for the *Tatmadaw* itself.

To those within its ranks, I speak with both firmness and compassion: Remember your oath. You were never meant to turn your weapons on children. You were never meant to burn villages or bomb monasteries. The students, the nurses, the elders, the farmers—they are not your enemies. They are your neighbors. Your kin. Your own blood. Protecting them is not weakness. It is honor.

Engagement with the *Tatmadaw* must go beyond condemnation. It requires a twofold path: *unwavering justice for the architects of atrocity, and real opportunities for redemption for those willing to reclaim their humanity.* We must make space for doubt within the ranks. For regret. For awakening. For transformation.

And let's be clear: we cannot dismantle the Tatmadaw overnight. Nor should we indulge in the fantasy that it will disappear through force or rage alone. We must create the conditions—political, moral, and psychological—that make transformation possible. From tyranny to service. From repression to dignity. From blind obedience to accountable leadership. This is not a naïve hope—it is a strategic necessity.

No revolution can endure if it mirrors the cruelty it seeks to end. We must be fierce—but also wise. Courageous—but also humane. This is how we disarm fear—not only with weapons, but with vision.

Let this be the turning point. Let those still inside the Tatmadaw who feel the stirrings of conscience know this: you are not beyond return. You can choose differently. You can come home—to the people, to yourself, to your conscience, to your dignity.

And to the people of Myanmar, I say: hold fast to your vision. Do not let despair rob you of your dignity. You have already endured what many believed impossible—and yet you rise, again and again—not only with courage, but with grace.

This revolution—unlike those before—carries not only the fire of justice, but the seed of profound transformation. And that seed, once awakened in the heart of a people—in you—cannot be crushed. It grows in silence. It grows through sorrow. And in time, it becomes the foundation of a freedom no tyranny can erase.

Alan Clements: Daw Suu, reconciliation with the Tatmadaw may be the most painful and complex challenge on Myanmar's path forward. The institution remains deeply entrenched in power, commanding soldiers who are often ordered to kill their own people—*trained to see fellow citizens not as kin, but as enemies.* For decades, it has operated as a state within a state: shrouded in secrecy, insulated from civilian oversight, and *woven into the very architecture of authoritarianism.*

And yet, we know that healing cannot exclude them—not if we hope to build a unified, peaceful, democratic nation. So, I ask with full awareness of the cost and complexity: How do we pursue true reconciliation with such an institution? How can Myanmar hold the *Tatmadaw* accountable for its atrocities, while also creating the conditions for healing, reform, and eventual reintegration? Is it even possible to rebuild trust with an institution that has tortured the nation?

Aung San Suu Kyi: Alan, reconciliation with the Tatmadaw is not simply a political task—it is an existential one. We cannot avoid it, nor can we resolve it through shortcuts. It touches the very heart of who we are as a nation and who we dare to become.

First, let us not obscure the truth: the *Tatmadaw* has tortured the beloved people of Myanmar. Over 100,000 homes have been bombed or burned. Entire communities have been displaced, often with nothing more than the clothes on their backs. Millions now live in fear, barely subsisting. Children have been forcibly conscripted and made to fire upon their own people. Teachers, nuns, students, and civil servants have been arrested, tortured, and disappeared. This is not collateral damage—it is systemic cruelty.

And yet, as unthinkable as this suffering is, the *Tatmadaw* is not a monolith. There are men and women within it—many conscripted young, indoctrinated early—who are not ideologues, but captives of a violent culture. They are not inherently cruel. They are often terrified, broken, desensitized, and confused. I would not be surprised if many— perhaps most—as I've said before, long for a life of peace, but feel there is no way out.

The higher ranks—the generals, colonels—live in profound isolation. Power has become their prison. They are addicted to control, to privilege, to the illusion of invulnerability. But that illusion is fragile. They fear the world beyond their barricades. They fear truth, because truth would dismantle their authority. That makes them vulnerable— not only politically, but spiritually. They have grown powerful without growing wise.

To them, I would say this: You are not just at war with the people—you are at war with your own conscience. And that is a war you will not win.

So how do we go forward?

We begin with unwavering accountability. There must be justice—not performative gestures, but real, transparent legal processes for those who planned, ordered, and carried out atrocities. The people of Myanmar deserve to see that no one is above the law.

But justice alone is not enough. If we stop at punishment, we only deepen the wounds. What we need is moral architecture—what I call conditional amnesty. That means clear pathways for those in the ranks to step forward, speak honestly, express remorse, and return to the fold of society. It means truth-telling forums, reparations, restorative justice. We must build spaces where transformation is not just allowed, but encouraged.

And yes, the institution itself must be restructured—radically. Civilian oversight. Constitutional reform. Demilitarization of national identity. The *Tatmadaw* must be returned to its rightful place: not above the people, but in service to them. No democracy can survive while its military is a sovereign empire.

This transformation won't be quick. It won't be easy. But it is essential. Trust cannot be demanded—it must be earned. And it is earned through truth. Through humility. Through courageous acts of redemption.

Let the generals understand: real strength does not come from silencing dissent, but from confronting one's own delusions. Real leadership is not domination—it is service. The most powerful act they could perform now would be to relinquish fear and choose dignity.

To the people of Myanmar, I would say: do not let hatred define your future. Yes, grieve. Yes, demand justice. But do not harden your hearts. Do not mirror the violence that has scarred you. Offer something nobler. A future they never imagined they were worthy of.

And to the world: do not abandon us to this nightmare. Help us pressure the military toward accountability and reform. Help us create the political space for transformation.

Reconciliation is not appeasement. It is the most disciplined act of love we can offer to a nation broken by fear. If we succeed—if we dare to build a democracy that includes even our former captors—we will not only be free. We will be whole.

Alan Clements: Daw Suu, it seems to me that so much of our *dukkha*—our suffering, both in Myanmar and across the world—stems from the breakdown of communication: the inability, or refusal, to truly listen—to engage in honest, wise, emotionally grounded dialogue.

I've come to believe that the most radical act of courage is not to take up arms, but to stay present with complexity—to disagree without dehumanizing, to speak across difference without the threat of annihilation.

"You don't agree with me, so I will kill you"—this is the primitive reflex we must evolve beyond. Not just politically, but in the very architecture of our consciousness.

Which brings me to this: Myanmar's modern history has been scarred—again and again—by the personalization of power. From General Ne Win to Than Shwe to Min Aung Hlaing, we have seen the nation treated as private property, its people as pawns.

So, I ask: How do we break this pattern of brutal, patriarchal domination—this centuries-old affliction that says, "I am the state, and I will do with you what I please"? How do we inoculate the future from another man—draped in medals and delusion—who believes he can imprison, torture, or execute anyone at will?

How do we evolve beyond this—beyond the genome of tyranny itself—into a culture where no one, no general, no movement, no ideology, can ever again lay claim to the conscience of the country and hold everyone hostage? How do we build a democracy where power serves—not possesses?

Aung San Suu Kyi: Alan, you've touched something elemental. The personalization of power is not just a political misstep—it is a form of violence. A theft of the commons.

And yes, in Myanmar, we have lived under this shadow for generations. From General Ne Win's iron grip to Min Aung Hlaing's militarized delusion, we have seen what happens when one man confuses authority with ownership—when a nation is treated not as a people, but as a possession.

But this is not unique to Myanmar. Around the world, we are witnessing the death spiral of patriarchal domination—the myth that force equals leadership, that brutality ensures order. What we are really confronting is not one man's pathology, but a deeper human dilemma: the fear of vulnerability masquerading as control.

To break this cycle, we must do more than depose a dictator—we must unlearn the very logic that makes dictatorship possible.

That unlearning begins, as you've said, with dialogue. We must reimagine the fabric of relationship—between leaders and citizens, between communities, and most urgently, between those who disagree. True democracy does not say, "Agree with me or be silenced." It says, "Disagree with me and still be safe. Disagree with me and still belong." This is the revolution of relationship—and without it, freedom remains only a slogan.

This is not just political reform—it is biological evolution. A rewiring of the human impulse. To turn domination into relationship. To make dialogue our reflex, not our fallback.

From the kitchen table to the halls of parliament, we must teach *the noble art of listening*—not the passive kind, but fierce listening. The kind grounded in empathy, sharpened by discernment, and anchored in moral accountability. This is how we stay human. This is how we rise.

And for this, Alan, we need more than institutional reform—we need cultural transformation. We need to raise children who can say, "I feel anger, and I choose not to act from it."

We need leaders who are trained not only in policy, but in humility. A federal democracy is not just a map of power—it is a choreography of conscience. It must be designed to absorb difference, not punish it. To distribute trust, not hoard it. To create systems strong enough to protect the fragile, and humble enough to evolve.

The generals, as I've said before, are not immune to this transformation. They are deeply indoctrinated, yes—but also deeply isolated. They rule through fear because they are afraid. They silence others because they do not know how to hear themselves. That is why even the most tyrannical institution must be invited into dialogue—not to excuse it, but to dismantle its fear from the inside out.

This does not mean we forget the atrocities. On the contrary. Truth is the ground of every healing. But accountability without insight only breeds new resentment. We must hold people to account while holding open the possibility of their return to humanity. That is the only real reconciliation. Not erasure, but transformation.

Let us build a nation where no one—not a general, not a party, not a movement—can ever again claim the soul of Myanmar as their personal domain. Let us create structures that outlast charisma, systems that outgrow strongmen, and a culture that elevates conscience above conquest.

Because in the end, democracy is not a guarantee—it is a relationship. It must be lived, protected, and renewed in every generation. And that begins not in the halls of power, but in the spaces between us—in the courage to speak honestly, and the grace to hear what we would rather not. That, Alan, is where our revolution begins again.

Alan Clements: Education, as you've said, Daw Suu, is foundational. But in a country so fractured by fear, war, and betrayal—where trust has been burned to the ground—how can education serve as a bridge back to one another? How can it become a vessel not just for knowledge, but for healing?

Aung San Suu Kyi: Education is the cornerstone of any democratic society, yes—but more than that, it must become our nation's great act of renewal. It is how we remember rightly, how we teach dignity without division, how we make peace a practice, not a slogan.

In Myanmar, education must be inclusive, multilingual, and rooted in reconciliation. It must teach our children not just to recite, but to listen. Not just to achieve, but to understand. We must teach them the courage of empathy and the quiet power of remembrance.

For too long, our schools were instruments of assimilation—used to erase language, identity, and belonging. That era must end. We need an education that celebrates difference. That tells the histories of all Myanmar's peoples—not as fractured tales of conflict, but as woven strands of a shared destiny.

To our young people, I say: You are not inheriting the future. You are creating it. Learn from books, yes—but learn also from the silence of survivors, from the wisdom of elders, from the resilience in your own breath.

True wisdom is not born from domination, but from compassion. Through education, we can break the cycle of ignorance—and plant the seeds of a society where every voice matters.

Alan Clements: Daw Suu… if this were our final conversation, I'd want to ask you something not as a journalist, nor even as a witness to your extraordinary journey—but as a friend, and as someone who loves your country deeply.

Myanmar is bleeding. The people are tired, terrified, displaced. Over a hundred thousand homes burned. Millions on the run. Twenty-two thousand imprisoned for loving freedom. The revolution lives, yes—but so does the suffering.

So, with all your heart, if you had one last chance to speak—to the people, to the resistance, to the political prisoners, and yes, even to the *Tatmadaw*—what would you say? What final truth would you leave us with, to carry forward the dream of a free, dignified, federal Myanmar?

Aung San Suu Kyi: Alan... this question cuts through everything. It breaks the formality. And yes, if these were my last words—if this is the last time I am heard—let me speak them as clearly as I can.

To the people of Myanmar: Please, do not give up. I know how much you've lost. I feel it in my bones—the hunger, the terror, the betrayal. But your dignity cannot be taken unless you surrender it. So do not surrender. Not even a little. Keep kindness alive in your homes, in your camps, in your hiding places. Let federal democracy be more than a phrase. Let it be a promise. A way of walking. A way of treating each other. A covenant of care.

To the Ethnic Armed Organizations: You are the guardians of your people's lives. That is sacred. But this moment—this fragile, flickering moment—asks something more. Bravery, yes. But also, mercy. Restraint. Vision. Lay the groundwork not just for victory, but for belonging. Dare to trust, even when you've been betrayed. And when you lead, lead as if you are building the very heart of our nation—not just defending its borders.

To our political prisoners: You are the heartbeat of our revolution. Not symbols—souls. Your suffering must not be wasted. When you walk free—and may that day come soon—walk with wisdom. Help shape a country that will never again allow such cruelty. Lead us not with vengeance, but with the strange and holy clarity that only those who've lost everything can carry.

And to the Tatmadaw—those still killing, still obeying, still pretending you do not know the truth—I speak to you now with nothing left to lose. This war is not just destroying the nation. It is destroying your own humanity.

Stop the killing. Stop the bombs. Stop the lies.

Release the political prisoners. Lay down your weapons. Walk away from power. Let the healing begin.

You say you are patriots. Then prove it. Be brave enough to step aside. Do not die as tyrants. Live—if you can—as those who finally listened to their conscience.

History is not your enemy. But it will become your judge if you do not act now.

To all who hear this—friend or enemy, young or old, soldier or student—please: do not let hate be your inheritance. Let love be. Let dignity be. Let justice be.

Alan Clements: Daw Suu, before this moment slips into memory, I ask—perhaps the most difficult question of all. You've spoken with such grace about dignity, vision, unity. But what of forgiveness? I ask not from abstraction, but from the soil of suffering.

With all you've lived, all you've endured—how do we, as a people, as individuals, forgive without betraying the truth? How do we remember what has been done to us and still find the courage not to retaliate? How do we look into the eyes of those who have harmed us—soldiers, generals, enablers—and not simply see the face of the oppressor, but the trace of something more human, more complex?

The Buddha once said it is rare to encounter anyone who has not been your mother, your father, your son or daughter in a past life. That teaching haunts me, especially in times like this.

Can we, even now, recognize one another across the battlefield of delusion? Can we build a future not on vengeance, but on the evolution of consciousness itself? Can unconditional love truly survive this kind of knowing?

Aung San Suu Kyi: Alan… that question pierces the very marrow of our shared human condition. Forgiveness, when it is real, is not soft. It is not easy. It is not some polite nod to civility. It is a sacred, searing act. It is the courage to remember fully and refuse to let that memory harden into hatred.

Forgiveness does not mean forgetting—it means remembering without the compulsion to retaliate. It means carrying the truth without allowing it to deform the heart.

In my solitude, there are nights when the grief surges like a flood—the faces of children bombed in their classrooms, the silence of friends lost to prison or death, the temples razed to rubble, the aching weight of betrayal by those entrusted with our care. On those nights, I return to the breath. Not because it fixes anything, but because it reminds me that I am still here. That I still have the capacity to feel. To care. To choose.

Forgiveness, for me, begins with that choice—not to pass the pain onward. It is not the absolution of the wrongdoer; it is the liberation of the heart that refuses to be chained to cycles of violence.

I remember Jesus's words—spoken not from comfort, but from agony: *"Forgive them, for they know not what they do."* And I ask myself, with trembling sincerity: Can I say that? And mean it?

Some days, I cannot. But some days, in the stillness of meditation, in the clarity of *metta*, I can. Not because those who harm us deserve forgiveness, but because we deserve to live unpoisoned by their hatred. *We must not let their delusion become our inheritance.*

It is the hardest path imaginable—to remember the atrocities, to seek justice, and still let love be the life blood of the heart. But it is the only path that leads to real freedom. The only path that honors our ancestors, our children, and the future not yet born.

If we could see the *karmic* threads that bind us, life after life, we would fall to our knees in awe. The soldier who beat me may once have been my son. The general who imprisoned me may once have been my father. If we could hold that possibility—not as dogma, but as a lens through which to see—we would weep not only for ourselves, but for the whole tragic beauty of this human journey.

To my fellow citizens, I say: do not forget. But let remembrance make you wise, not bitter. Let your heartbreak soften you, not shatter you. Let forgiveness be the revolution that changes not just the country, but the very course of our shared existence.

That is my prayer.
That is our calling.
A democracy built not on revenge, but on reverence.
A home not secured by fear, but sustained by dignity.
A world where even the broken can be made whole again through the radical, luminous power of love.

A ROADMAP FOR UNITY

Author's Prelude

There are wounds so vast they bleed across generations—wounds too ancient to fully recall, too fresh to ever truly forget. Myanmar knows such wounds. Colonization carved them. War deepened them. Dictatorship normalized them—turning pain into routine, silence into policy.

And yet, in the marrow of its people—across every village, monastery, and exile camp—there remains a pulse. Fragile. Fierce. Unyielding. A whisper that says: *we belong to one another, even after all that's been done.*

This chapter is a solemn reckoning—a call to remember that unity is not the opposite of pain, but its path through fire. Here, Aung San Suu Kyi offers no easy answers. She walks slowly into the burn—into trauma, into silence, into the deliberate, devoted labor of reconciliation.

Unity here is not an anthem. It is a daily act: to hold space for difference without fear. To listen without defense. To grieve without retreat. To forgive without forgetting. To remember without rage. This is no path to sameness, but a passage to dignity—not to triumph, but to presence.

Let this chapter be read with your whole being—with the breath, the memory of exile, and the hunger for return. And may we each take one step closer to one another—tenderly, courageously, awake.

◆ ◆ ◆

Alan Clements: Daw Suu, unity has always been one of Myanmar's most elusive goals. With over 130 ethnic groups, with as many languages and dialects, and a history marked by entrenched conflicts, the concept of national unity often feels elusive. Yet, amidst the devastating violence unleashed by the military junta, unity is not merely desirable—it is critical for survival.

Though this theme has been explored earlier, I feel compelled to revisit it—not to restate what has been said, but to deepen its meaning. The future of federal democracy and freedom in your country hinges on your ability to forge a new unity—one rooted not in uniformity, but in justice, mutual respect, and a reconciliation brave enough to confront the deepest wounds of your nation.

With profound humility and a heavy heart, I ask again: how will you build a unity that embraces your grief, your anger, and your diversity while guiding your people toward a shared future?

Aung San Suu Kyi: Alan, you are right to revisit this question. Unity is not merely a political necessity for our nation—it is the moral cornerstone of a free Myanmar.

Let me be clear: unity does not mean sameness. It requires deep respect for our diversity. It calls for a space where every voice is heard, every culture safeguarded, and every truth given room to breathe.

Our divisions—across ethnicities, religions, and political factions—are no accident. They stem from deliberate policies of exploitation, fear, and suppression. Colonialism sowed the seeds; decades of military rule nurtured them.

These scars shape our reality today. They will not heal without effort. We must tend to them with honesty, courage, and a commitment to listening to the pain that our history has long silenced.

Alan Clements: How do you begin that process, Daw Suu? Where does reconciliation truly start?

Aung San Suu Kyi: It begins, as all true healing does, with listening—radical, uncomfortable, patient listening. We must hear the stories of our ethnic brothers and sisters—the Kachin, Karen, Rakhine, Chin, Shan, and every other community that has borne the weight of exclusion, displacement, and violence. These voices are not peripheral; they are central to the soul of our nation.

But listening alone is not enough. Justice must accompany it—not as vengeance, but as truth. We need the courage to speak clearly about the atrocities in our country: the massacres, the burned villages, the silenced dissent. Only through this honesty can we rebuild trust. Only then can reconciliation become real.

Alan Clements: Many ethnic leaders tell me they see "unity" as a pretext for imposing central control. How do you earn their trust?

Aung San Suu Kyi: By offering trust in return and earning it daily. Decentralization is not a gesture—it is an acknowledgment of our reality. Our nation cannot thrive under a center that overshadows its periphery. True federalism demands more than words: it requires constitutional protections, autonomous decision-making, and genuine participation at every level.

Beyond structures, it demands relationships. We must go to our communities, listen with humility, and live the inclusion we promise. Only through such commitment will trust cease to be demanded and instead be freely given.

Alan Clements: Yes... structural decentralization and lived inclusion are essential. But there's another layer, isn't there? The psychological layer. Beyond law and governance, how do we foster a sense of being one people—a shared belonging felt not just in documents, but in the heart?

Aung San Suu Kyi: Through education, art, and culture—through the rituals of shared humanity that no government can mandate. Our schools must teach not one history, but many. Our children must grow up seeing their languages, traditions, and ancestors honored, not erased. A child learning in her mother tongue gains not only knowledge but dignity.

Festivals, music, and storytelling are not mere luxuries; they are medicine for our nation. They remind us that, despite our diverse histories, we share universal longings: for belonging, for dignity, for peace.

Alan Clements: Daw Suu, speaking of history and ancestors, I feel called to step back—not just from politics or the present moment—but to acknowledge something deeper, something ancestral. Not as a continuation of our earlier points, but as a reckoning with the long arc of trauma your people have endured across generations.

For over two centuries, your nation has faced relentless hardship. British colonialism brought not only conquest but the forced remaking of your identity—three wars, systemic subjugation, and the dismantling of your indigenous governance, languages, and cultural rhythms.

Then came the devastation of World War II—first under Japanese militarism, then through brutal Allied bombardment. Your towns became battlefields, your cities were flattened, and your sacred forests turned to graveyards. Entire generations endured that fire.

And at the dawn of your independence—your father, General Aung San, a man of extraordinary vision and courage, rose in his youth, alongside his comrades, to reclaim the heart of your nation.

With utmost respect, I recall that he and nearly his entire cabinet were assassinated, struck down just as freedom was born. That loss shook your people not only politically but spiritually. It could have broken your spirit. Yet, somehow, it did not.

But your pain did not end there. Decades of dictatorship, disappearances, martial law, silenced voices, waves of exodus, and betrayed hopes followed.

And now, under Min Aung Hlaing's so-called State Administrative Council, a new chapter of unspeakable cruelty and devastation unfolds.

Daw Suu, how do your people begin to heal from a trauma this vast? How do they face it—generation after generation—without being consumed? And how do you lead one another—not just out of war, but into the deep waters of true healing and collective dignity?

Aung San Suu Kyi: Alan, what you've laid out is not merely a recounting of history—it is our inheritance. An aching, unfinished legacy that lives in every heart that dares to hope for our nation. A grief so deeply woven into our national soul that we sometimes cannot discern where it ends and we begin. Yet, we must name it, as you said. We must give it voice— not to prolong the pain, but to begin the slow, sacred work of healing the wound.

To live under colonization is to have our memory stolen. To survive war is to live with pieces of ourselves missing. And to endure dictatorship—time and again—is to be told that our voice, our truth, our worth do not matter.

But they do. Every life lost matters. Every dream deferred. Every child born amid rubble. Every elder who passes before seeing freedom. Every prisoner political or otherwise—who waits, not just for justice, but for acknowledgment.

Healing begins with truth—not the kind written in history books, but the kind whispered in our kitchens, wept in our temples, remembered in our songs. The truth that survives in lullabies, prayer beads, and funeral offerings long after battles fade. We must create sanctuaries where these stories are not merely shared, but held—where silence is not imposed, but revered, and tears are not shamed, but honored.

Yes, we need national dialogues and truth commissions. But more than that, we need a cultural awakening—a collective remembering of our shared suffering as sacred. Not to re-traumatize, but to dignify. Not to remain captives of our wounds, but to let them open a doorway to a larger, more compassionate humanity.

Alan Clements: Daw Suu, your words land like prayer—not as doctrine, but as a remembering, something ancestral, cellular, whole. And it moves me to speak—not with a question, but from the ache I witness in your people.

What you've just said is more than a closing thought; it is a way forward. And yet, with the deepest humility, I wonder: how do your people begin to live this way when so much inside them, and around them, is still trembling? Still afraid? Still mourning?

They have walked through fire—centuries of occupation, war, fragmentation, and betrayal. They are tired. And yet, there is something—something irreducible—that refuses to die. That still hums in the bones of a people who have lost so much.

So, if I may ask—not from the head, but from the wounded heart of a fellow traveler: What does it mean, in this moment of unbearable history, to love your country? Not sentimentally, but spiritually. Not as a possession, but as a sacred, wounded whole?

Aung San Suu Kyi: Alan… you speak of love, and I find myself reaching beyond words. To love a country like ours—a country with so many wounds, so many ghosts—is not to escape its pain. It is to sit beside that pain and hold its hand. It is to say: "I see you. I grieve with you. And still, I choose you." It is to say: "You are still mine. Even in your brokenness, I will not turn away."

To love Myanmar is to love without illusions. Not blindly, not naively—but fiercely, courageously, humbly. It is to remember the sound of a mother's voice in Chin State. The scent of *mohinga* at dawn in Mandalay. The rhythm of the rains in Rakhine. The prayers whispered by candlelight in a monastery in Shan. It is to feel the weight of every orphaned child, every imprisoned student, every bombed-out village—and still choose to stay tender, to stay human.

To serve Myanmar is not to serve power. It is to serve memory. It is to refuse amnesia. It is to carry forward the dignity of those who never lived to see this day. It is to be broken open by a love so vast it can cradle sorrow and hope in the same breath.

This love is not abstract. It is action. It is protection. It is truth-telling. It is the courage to say, *"Never again"*—and mean it.

And it is tenderness. So much tenderness. Because no revolution survives on anger alone. It survives on devotion—the slow, daily work of nurturing what others have tried to destroy.

That is what I've tried to do in here, in this silence: to love my country one breath at a time. One moment of awareness. One quiet decision not to close my heart.

Alan Clements: And even now, Daw Suu… you continue to love this nation into being. In the silence. In the unseen moments. Without recognition. Without freedom. You are still serving. Still listening. Still loving.

If I could place my hand over the land itself, I would say: May your people learn to love Myanmar as you do—not with slogans or strategy, but with heart. Not from a place of fear, but from a place of fierce tenderness. Because if they could do that—if they could love one another without the armor of ideology or fear—I believe something in this fractured land might finally begin to heal.

But love, as you've said, is not sentimental. It is courageous. And to truly love a country, they must be willing to face its pain. We all must learn this love—all inhabitants of the earth.

And so, I ask you, Daw Suu—not just politically, but soulfully: what of trauma? The kind that imprints itself into the body, embeds in the nervous system—like a vibrational echo, carried silently across generations as a quiet, invisible patterning. How do they tend to this psychological pain—not just the wounds of today's war, but a century's worth of rupture?

Aung San Suu Kyi: We must cease to regard trauma as weakness. Trauma is not a flaw in the human spirit—it is the etched testament of survival. It is the body's silent memory, holding what words cannot yet articulate. It is truth awaiting its voice and its embrace.

Yet, through mindful intelligence—through the sacred power of a single breath—we can begin to reclaim our lives. Meditation is not escape; it is embodiment of the present. It is learning to sit, breath by breath, with what we most fear to face. To abide with sorrow without flinching. To hold space for rage without becoming it. To remain with pain without collapsing beneath its weight.

We begin with compassion—not as an abstract ideal, but as a living practice. First, for ourselves. Then for the trembling soldier, the orphaned child, the widow who no longer weeps, the man silenced by what he witnessed, the monk who doubts his faith, the artist who burned her poems because the pain was too heavy to bear alone. Each deserves not judgment, but sanctuary. Not silence, but presence. Ourselves and others—not separate, but bound in shared humanity.

We must elevate emotional health as a cornerstone of democracy. It is not a luxury—it is the essential foundation for any society aspiring to dignity. A nation cannot heal what it refuses to acknowledge. We must train *Dhamma-informed guides*, steeped not only in psychological insight but in spiritual clarity, moral courage, and unrelenting compassion.

We must place counselors in every IDP camp, monastery, and community center. We must build havens of deep listening, sanctuaries of unwavering presence. This is not mere policy—it is an ethical revolution, grounded in emotional and mindful intelligence.

We must make trauma literacy—*dukkha literacy*—a shared language of our nation. A collective understanding that suffering is not a personal failing but a universal inheritance. To be alive is to know rupture, and to know rupture is to cradle the seed of renewal.

We must weave insight meditation into our schools, prisons, refugee shelters, and parliaments—not as therapy alone, but as a path to liberation. Not as a cure, but as a companion to *dukkha*—the full spectrum of human suffering: from sorrow to rage, from despair to the anguish of a wounded earth, and beyond, to the existential weight of *dukkha* itself, that profound truth which permeates all conditioned existence, whispering of impermanence, of the fleeting nature of all we cling to, yet pointing ever toward the boundless freedom of awakening.

This work is not soft—it is sacred and revolutionary. To meet suffering directly—with mindfulness, with truthfulness, with a heart that refuses to turn away—is to reclaim the power that trauma seeks to steal.

Meditation is not about fixing the self—it is about rediscovering what remains unbroken. It is a practice of radical presence, where even pain becomes a threshold to awakening. Where even despair can become a silent prayer.

This is how we build true democracy—not only with ballots, but with breath. Not only with laws, but with awareness. Not only with structures, but with the sacred integrity of being fully, fearlessly alive.

And above all, we must say to our people, with infinite tenderness: What happened to you is not your fault. It is not a shame to carry. It is a burden, yes—but one that belongs not to you alone. It is our shared weight, and we will carry it together—not forever, but until it is light enough to release. Until it becomes the fertile soil of something new.

For when held with care, with wisdom, with presence, trauma is not merely survivable—it is transformative. It becomes a sacred scar, a mark of having lived, felt, and endured without turning to stone. It becomes a strength, forged in fire and consecrated in truth. An awakening born not in spite of the wound, but through its sacred passage.

This is how we rise—not by denying what has broken us, but by allowing it to deepen our love. Not by erasing the pain, but by weaving from it a space where beauty may grow. Not by returning to what was, but by birthing something unseen before—something whole, brave, and free.

This is the Dhamma's eternal lesson: to transform every obstacle into an opportunity, every sorrow into a seed of awakening. This is the beautification of consciousness—the flowering of grace from the jagged earth of suffering, *where even dukkha becomes sacred.*

Enlightenment, not as a distant goal, but as a living practice in motion. This, to me, is *the bodhisattva's sacred art*—a presence that holds all beings in the heart of compassion.

Alan Clements: Daw Suu, after the radiance of your words—your fierce grace, your luminous truth—I feel summoned to pause. And to bow. Not from loftiness, but from deep recognition. What you've spoken is not merely wisdom—it is sustenance for the soul. Something profoundly human. Something that quietly rekindles faith in what remains possible.

You've said that trauma, when met with presence, becomes not just something to endure—but *a sacred scar*. A strength born of fire. An awakening woven through the wound. And I find myself lingering with that, letting it seep into the deeper tissues of my heart.

For there is something revolutionary in your offering: that we need not await wholeness to serve. That every act of staying, of listening, of refusing to turn away—is itself *reverence embodied*. And I've felt this too—the holiness of the smallest gesture: sharing a breath, a silence, a morsel of sustenance.

You remind your people that love, when lived fully, is not sentimental. It is a discipline. A vow. A practice of meeting the jagged terrain of existence and still choosing to sow seeds of hope.

Yet I also know—and perhaps you do too—that there are moments when even this feels beyond reach. When hope itself feels too fragile to cradle. When rising again feels not just arduous, but absurd in its audacity. Your people have carried such weight—through centuries of fracture, betrayal, and unrelenting fire. Their hands tremble from bearing too much, too long.

So, I ask—not with answers, but with open hands and a trembling heart: What do your people do when hope feels too delicate to touch? When beginning anew feels not just difficult, but unimaginable?

How do they find the courage to rise when faith falters? How, in this moment of unbearable history, do they weave love from despair, planting seeds in a soil still scorched by sorrow?

Aung San Suu Kyi: Alan, your words echo the sorrow I have known intimately. And I thank you—not for exalting me, but for meeting me in the tender truth of suffering, and in the fragile radiance of choosing to care despite it all.

Yes, there are moments when hope feels like a treacherous promise. When to hope again is to court the risk of shattering anew. I have felt this—etched in my being, woven through the silence, held in the dark. And I have learned not to resist those moments, but to let them breathe their sacred truth. To let the sorrow whisper its full name.

So, I say to my people: Let your exhaustion speak. Let your sorrow exhale its weight. Let your broken heart be revered, not hidden. But do not let it harden. Do not let it seal your spirit.

Hope is not a feeling we await—it is a muscle we temper, a discipline of the courageous. It is the practice of remaining tender in a world that urges numbness. *It is the quiet defiance of declaring*: *I will stay. I will care. I will try again. Even when it wounds.*

Hope is not always resounding. Sometimes it is a murmur amidst the rubble. Sometimes it is a single breath you manage to take while all around you crumbles.

And still—that breath matters. That moment matters. For to take it mindfully is to defy oblivion. *It is to proclaim*: *I am still here. And while I am here, I will not vanish from my own existence.*

Even in confinement, I have witnessed hope endure—not as optimism, but as presence. In the softening of a guard's voice. In the song of a bird beyond the bars. In the way memory returns—not only to pain, but to beauty, love, grace.

Every act of kindness, of dignity, of truth-speaking—these are threads in the great tapestry we are still weaving. A new national garment, fashioned not from vengeance, but from resilience. Not from erasure, but from memory transmuted. *And each must take up a thread.*

No hand is too frail. No offering too belated. Sometimes hope is merely the willingness to take the next breath with care. To prepare a meal. To linger in meditation for one more moment. To transform the wounded moment into a temple.

Let that be enough. For now. And let that be sacred.

For even when belief fades, presence endures. And where there is presence, there is life. And where there is life, there is ever the possibility to begin anew.

So, I say to my people, with boundless tenderness: Your despair is not your failing. Your trembling is not your shame. It is a burden, yes—but not yours alone. It is our shared weight, and we will carry it together— not forever, but until it is light enough to release. Until it becomes the fertile soil of something radiant.

For in the heart of dukkha lies the seed of awakening. To meet despair with mindfulness, to hold sorrow with compassion, is to walk the Noble Path.

This is the Dhamma's eternal promise: that even in the darkest hour, a single breath, taken with presence, can light the way to freedom.

Alan Clements: If you could speak—right now—to every corner of Myanmar, to every village, every city, every exile, every prison, what would you say? What would you ask?

Aung San Suu Kyi: I would say this: Unity is not something we inherit. It is something we practice. A shared act of courage. A promise renewed with every choice to listen rather than condemn, to include rather than exclude, to build bridges rather than walls.

We create unity when we look one another in the eye and say, without hesitation: You belong. Not because you agree with me. Not because you look like me. But because you are here. And that is enough.

This future of ours—it will not arrive fully formed. It will arrive in pieces. In quivering hands building shelters. In quiet voices daring to speak truth to power, even when no one seems to listen.

We must not confuse fragility with failure, or slowness with defeat. What matters is not that we rise quickly, but that we rise together. That we rise with care. With conscience. With the willingness to try again.

We must release the myth of perfection. We are not here to be flawless. We are here to be faithful—to one another, to the earth, to the dignity that lives even in the shadow. And yes, we will falter. But faltering is not falling. It is learning. It is rediscovering the way forward when the path disappears.

So let us not walk forward out of certainty, but out of conviction. Not with clenched fists, but with open hands. Let us meet hatred without imitating it. Let us meet betrayal without becoming it.

Let compassion be our method. Let truth be our backbone. Let love—not comfort, not convenience—but love be what binds our wounds and binds us to one another.

Let it stitch together the torn fabric of our shared story. Let it remind us that even after devastation, something beautiful can still be made. Let it be the quiet vow we offer to those who came before us, and to those still to come.

And may we walk on—not in certainty, but in courage. Not in anger, but in hope. Not in perfect light, but together, toward it.

Let every step be an act of reverence. Every gesture—however small—a prayer. A hand extended. A meal shared. A silence honored. A breath remembered.

This is not about winning. This is about remembering. This is about making your life—your breath, your grief, your courage—a message. As Gandhi said: *Your life is your message.*

Let that message be your poem. Your protest. Your revolution. *Let it say*: *I kept going. Even then. Even there.*

So, I say to my people: Keep going. Even when you doubt. Even when you feel unseen. Keep offering what you can—a glance, a truth, a morsel of sustenance. *Make every act, to the best of your ability, an expression of reverence in action.*

This is the sacred made real. This is liberation in the now. This is what it means to be free. Because even now—especially now—your life is still the poetry of freedom.

And if you ask what I want, what I ask of my people—not just as a leader, but as a fellow human being—it is this:

Please, do not give up on each other.

Not when it's hard.

Not when it hurts.

Not when the night is longest.

Because there is still light.

Always, there is still light.

And your life, just as it is—grieving, uncertain, imperfect—is still worthy of that light. Still capable of carrying it. Still part of the great turning of history toward something more beautiful, more just, more awake.

So, walk on—not for me, not for a flag, not for a party—but for the truth you still carry in your heart.

Walk on with reverence.

With resilience.

With joy, if it comes—and grace, if it does not.

And know this: *You are not alone. You never have been.*

178

JUSTICE AND RECONCILIATION IN MYANMAR

Author's Prelude

Some truths are too sacred to deny, and some wounds too deep to silence. This chapter descends into the moral core of Myanmar— where the longing for justice and reconciliation transcends the political, and enters the realm of the eternal. Here, we move beyond slogans and strategies, into the marrow of memory made holy by suffering: betrayal, grief, and the fierce dignity of those who have stood—unshaken—refusing erasure.

Justice, in this context, is not vengeance. It is the luminous courage to name what was broken, without shame or hatred. It is the sacred insistence that what was done in darkness must be brought to light— not to punish, but to reclaim the shattered covenant between human beings—the bond that violence tried to sever.

Reconciliation is not a peace accord. It is a human discipline. A vow of conscience. A spiritual practice. It is the daily act of turning toward truth, even when it scorches like fire. It is the labor of creating sanctuaries where survivors are not simply heard, but revered as carriers of sacred knowledge. And where perpetrators are not erased or excused, but summoned to face the full gravity of their actions—invited not into comfort, but into the rare and difficult grace of remorse.

In this dialogue, Aung San Suu Kyi speaks not only to the politics of justice, but to its inner life—to its soul beyond statutes. She offers a vision in which accountability becomes a path to redemption, woven not through coercion, but through courage. Where forgiveness—if it comes—is never demanded, but emerges from the long, costly work of truth-telling. And where leadership begins with the humility to admit harm, to kneel in contrition, and to rise only when one has faced the truth without turning away.

Read this chapter not as history, but as spiritual inheritance. Not as commentary, but as initiation. Not as politics, but as a rite of passage for a wounded world. For Myanmar's healing will never begin with forgetting. It begins with remembering—together, in the clarity of truth, with hearts stripped of pretense, and unafraid to love what has been broken.

◆ ◆ ◆

Alan Clements: Daw Suu, I know we've spoken before of justice, reconciliation, and forgiveness, confronting the long shadow of harm cast by decades of military tyranny. But this is no abstract debate—it is the raw, bleeding wound of a nation, where villages burned in the wake of the 2021 coup lie in ashes, families mourn the disappeared, and survivors carry scars that cry for reckoning. The weight of this cannot be overstated, for it is the sacred ground upon which any lasting peace, any true democracy, must be built. So again, let us return, for the path to healing hinges on how we face this truth.

How, may I ask, does a nation reconcile with those who have inflicted such unspeakable harm—not only the institutions, but the individuals who carried out these acts? Is forgiveness possible, or even appropriate, in the wake of such suffering? And what, in your view, is the true role of accountability—not as punishment, but as a pathway to healing?

Aung San Suu Kyi: Alan, your words cut through the veil of rhetoric, laying bare the anguish that demands our response. You're right to frame this not as a topic to revisit, but as a sacred foundation we must ceaselessly tend and deepen.

Justice and reconciliation are not steps in a political process—they are the hallowed ground in which a new Myanmar must take root. Without them, any democratic structure we build will crumble beneath the unhealed wounds of a people still bleeding.

But let us not diminish the enormity of what we're asking. Reconciliation is not a handshake between enemies. It is not a speech. It is a reckoning—within the heart and across the collective conscience of a nation. To reconcile, we must first confront unflinchingly what was broken.

Myanmar's trauma did not begin with this latest military coup, devastating as it has been, tearing at the fragile threads of our hope. Its roots reach deeper, stretching back through shadowed decades, as we discussed earlier—under colonial rule, during the Japanese occupation, with the brutal loss of my father and his cabinet in the post-independence assassinations, and through the suffocating grip of decades of dictatorship and protracted civil war.

Each era left behind not only broken institutions, but broken lives. And that pain is not abstract—it is woven into the very flesh of our people. It lives in the body. In the trembling hands of survivors. In the hushed grief of families. In the unspoken rage that festers where no acknowledgment has been made.

Yet, Alan, even in this solitude, *I hold fast to a truth*: *to name this pain is to begin to heal it.* To speak it is to summon the possibility of restoration—not because it erases the past, but because it honors the dignity of those who endured.

Forgiveness, you ask? It is a word both fragile and fraught. I do not believe it can be mandated, nor should it be. It is a gift, born only from a heart that has walked through the fire of truth and chosen, freely, to offer mercy.

For some, that path may be unreachable, and we must honor their refusal as much as another's grace. What matters is that we create a space where such choices are possible—where the harmed are not coerced into silence, and the harm-doers are not shielded from the mirror of their deeds.

Accountability, then, is not a weapon, but a beacon. It lights the path to healing by insisting that truth be the cornerstone. It asks of those who inflicted harm—whether by order or by hand—to stand in the full light of what they have done, to bear the weight of their actions, and, if they are willing, to seek atonement. This is not punishment; it is an invitation to rejoin the human family. *And for the nation, it is the courage to say*: *we will not build our future on lies.*

May these words carry my vision for a Myanmar where truth is the foundation, justice the framework, and compassion the bridge to a healed nation.

Alan Clements: Thank you, Daw Suu. What you're saying feels like a call to revolution—not of arms, but of awareness. A transformation not just of structures, but of our very relationship to memory. But how do we—as a people so long conditioned to hide, to protect, to forget—learn to trust truth again?

Aung San Suu Kyi: Alan, your question pierces the heart of our struggle, and here, in this shadowed cell, I feel the weight of it more keenly than ever.

As I said earlier, justice and reconciliation are not mere steps but the sacred soil of our renewal. Yet you ask now how we cultivate trust in truth—a question that demands we go deeper still, into the very heart of our collective consciousness.

Truth is not a moment we seize, nor a stage we pass through. It is a golden thread, luminous and unbroken, that must be woven through the fabric of our becoming.

And let us be unflinchingly honest: much of Myanmar's truth has been stolen, shrouded, or shattered—not only in the lies of official histories, but in the silent compromises we've made to survive.

The work before us is not to unearth truth as if it were a relic, but to radically re-member—to gather the fragments of our silenced stories and let them reshape the very marrow of our future.

This is no small thing, Alan. To trust truth again, we must dismantle the conditioning of fear that has taught us to hide. It is not enough to say, "Speak," to those who have suffered, as if a microphone could hold their pain.

We must reweave the tapestry of our society so that their presence—their unyielding, radiant testimony—becomes the cornerstone of our institutions.

Memory must cease to be a performance for pity and become a living force, a sacred flame that transforms the very air we breathe.

As I spoke earlier of reckoning, I return to it now, for it is the crucible of this trust. We need no more commissions to archive suffering in digital reports. We need sanctuaries of truth—shared spaces where those who endured atrocity are not merely heard, but enshrined as the moral visionaries of our future. Where truth is not polished for comfort, but allowed to cut, to heal, to remake us. These are not spaces for spectators, but for pilgrims—where every story, once buried beneath shame, rises as a pillar of wisdom, guiding our laws, our schools, our hearts.

On forgiveness, returning to your question I touched before, for it is a wound that demands tending. As I said, forgiveness is a gift, never coerced.

But let me expand: it is a flame kindled only in the crucible of justice. And justice, Alan, is not vengeance, nor is it humiliation. It is the clear-eyed naming of harm, the unwavering acknowledgment of responsibility, and the courageous beginning of repair.

That repair is manifold: it is the law's firm hand, yes, holding architects of systemic harm to account. It is the tribunal's gavel, echoing across borders. But it is also the quiet power of a village circle, where apologies are spoken and heard. It is reparations that restore dignity, not just wealth. It is a curriculum rewritten, so our children inherit not propaganda, but the full, luminous truth of their history—not to burden them, but to anoint them with the strength of knowing.

Can individuals be forgiven? I believe many can, as I said, but only if they step into the light of truth. For those who orchestrated atrocities, the law must be unyielding, for their crimes are not mere acts but betrayals of humanity itself.

Yet for the rank-and-file—those swept into violence by coercion, fear, or lies—there must be a path of return, a threshold of remorse where they can rejoin the human family. This is not leniency, but love—a love fierce enough to demand truth as the price of belonging.

And for our society, Alan, we must transcend the temptation of blame. *Blame is a shallow refuge. Understanding is a steeper climb, and accountability steeper still.* Only through this arduous path can we rebuild trust—not in fleeting leaders, but in enduring principles, in systems woven from integrity, in each other's unbowed spirits.

I see a Myanmar where silence is not mistaken for peace, where fear is not confused with respect, and where reconciliation is not a slogan, but a sacred practice, a daily offering of dignity, justice, and love.

Let this be not just our beginning, but the basis of all we build—a nation radiant with the courage to remember, unafraid to heal.

Alan Clements: Truth is essential, as you say. But for many, truth alone is not enough. They demand accountability for the atrocities committed by the Tatmadaw—as we know, atrocities that include mass killings, torture, and unspeakable crimes against humanity. What, in your eyes, is the role of accountability in this process?

Aung San Suu Kyi: Alan, your question pierces the core of our nation's quest for justice. As I said earlier, accountability is not a mere tool but a sacred discipline, the cornerstone of reconciliation.

You now ask its role in confronting the *Tatmadaw's* atrocities, and I must respond with the precision this moment requires, carrying the weight of a people's grief and their unyielding longing for repair.

Accountability is not a luxury—it is a moral necessity, the enduring foundation upon which true reconciliation must rise. Without it, survivors' pain is muted, the rule of law becomes a fragile shell, and our future remains bound to unhealed wounds. *It is the resolute pledge to proclaim: this happened, it was wrong, and we will not look away.*

Let us be clear: accountability is not vengeance, nor is it a display of retribution. It is a solemn act of recognition, a beacon that reveals harm and restores dignity to those who endured.

The atrocities of *Pa Zi Gyi*, *Let Yet Kone*, and countless villages turned to embers are not mere tragedies—they are scars etched into our nation's memory, demanding justice that lives in law, guides policy, and resonates in the conscience of our people.

Justice must unfold across multiple paths. Within Myanmar, we must forge an independent judiciary, a refuge of impartiality empowered to investigate and prosecute, free from political sway and rooted in the people's resolve.

Globally, we must weave our cause into the fabric of global justice, engage the International Criminal Court and human rights bodies—not only to document horrors but to ensure consequences that echo beyond our borders, denying perpetrators the cloak of impunity.

Those who grieved in burned-out villages, the children silenced in schools turned to rubble, the elders whose homes were consumed by flame—they are not entries in a ledger. They are guardians of a truth that must endure: in verdicts that uphold justice, in policies that safeguard, and in a collective memory that refuses to let their suffering fade. Their stories must stand as pillars, shaping our laws, our schools, and our vision of a Myanmar where such horrors are unthinkable.

Yet, as I noted before, accountability extends beyond punishment. To heal, we must uproot the systems that fueled this violence. Reforming the *Tatmadaw* cannot mean merely replacing its leaders, as if new names could absolve past transgressions. We must recast its essence—its doctrine, its ethos, its bond with the people—so that power becomes a trust, not a threat. This is a reckoning with the roots of authority, ensuring that force is never again mistaken for leadership, nor cruelty for strength.

Alan Clements: Daw Suu, you've spoken powerfully about the need to transform the Tatmadaw, an institution your father, Aung San, helped establish as a force for protection, not oppression. Its descent into a tool of domination is a profound betrayal of that vision. How do you personally reconcile the painful gap between its original purpose and the atrocities it has committed?

And looking forward, what role, if any, should a reformed military play in a democratic Myanmar, and how can such a transformation be achieved without perpetuating its culture of impunity?

Aung San Suu Kyi: Alan, your question cuts to the heart of a grief I carry daily—the fracture of my father's dream for a military that would shield, not shatter, our people.

The *Tatmadaw's* distortion is not merely a matter of actions but a corrosion of its founding spirit, a betrayal woven into its ideology and culture. My father envisioned a force bound by discipline, duty, and devotion to the nation's heart—not a machine of blind obedience to tyranny.

To forge a democratic Myanmar, we must first envision a military reborn. As I've said before, reform is not appeasement but transformation, and this demands a radical reimagining.

The *Tatmadaw* must become a guardian, not a ruler, subordinate to civilian leadership, tethered to the rule of law, and trained to serve, not suppress. Its role must be confined to national defense, with no authority to wield power over its own people—a firewall against the abuses of the past.

This transformation begins with the mind. Many soldiers are not villains but young men, often boys, molded by fear and propaganda to see the people as enemies. We must offer them a new path: education rooted in truth, psychological healing, and a meaningful return to a democratic society. This is not leniency but a disciplined reorientation, ensuring they understand their duty is to protect, not dominate.

Yet transformation requires courage to confront corruption head-on. We must dismantle the hierarchies and doctrines that bred violence, replacing them with a culture of accountability and service. This is a labor of years, not decrees, demanding leaders who model integrity and institutions that enforce it. Only then can the *Tatmadaw* reclaim its original purpose—not as my father's dream alone, but as the people's shield.

Alan Clements: That vision is compelling, Daw Suu, but the path to it is fraught with the question of justice. For those who committed harm—whether generals orchestrating atrocities or foot soldiers carrying out orders—how do we balance accountability with the possibility of redemption? Can forgiveness coexist with justice without diluting the demand for truth, especially for victims who still bear the scars of violence?

Aung San Suu Kyi: Alan, your question probes the delicate tension between justice and mercy, a balance that defines our humanity. As I've said before, forgiveness is a gift that belongs to those who have suffered, never to be imposed or demanded. It must never be wielded to silence righteous anger or evade responsibility. Yet I hold fast to the belief that redemption is possible—not as an escape from justice, but as its companion.

Redemption begins with truth. For foot soldiers, often swept into violence by coercion or indoctrination, redemption requires facing their actions with unflinching honesty, expressing genuine remorse, and committing to a life that repairs rather than destroys. This is no small demand—it is a rigorous journey, one that respects victims by honoring their pain.

For generals and architects of systemic atrocities, justice must be resolute and public, with no refuge in denial. Their accountability is not merely legal but moral, a signal to the nation that no one is above the law.

To navigate this, we need spaces for truth-telling, as I've noted, but let me expand: these must be more than commissions. We need national forums—designed with wisdom, dignity, and the voices of survivors at their core—where truth is not a performance but a catalyst for healing.

Such spaces allow victims to be heard, not to relive pain, but to reclaim agency. They ensure perpetrators cannot deny their deeds, fostering a collective memory that guards against recurrence.

These forums are not about erasing scars but honoring them. They weave justice and forgiveness into a tapestry of accountability, where victims' truths shape the nation's future, and perpetrators, where possible, contribute to repair—through restitution, public apology, or service to communities they harmed.

This is how we mend the moral fabric torn by violence: not by forgetting, but by ensuring truth becomes the foundation of our democracy.

Alan Clements: Daw Suu, so many ethnic communities have endured these abuses for generations—long before the coup. How can reconciliation truly be just if it does not reckon with the older, deeper wounds?

Aung San Suu Kyi: That question, Alan, is at the heart of our healing. We cannot allow this moment to be only about the most recent pain. The suffering of the Karen, the Kachin, the Chin, the Rohingya, the Shan, the Rakhine—these stories are not peripheral; they are foundational. The marginalization, displacement, cultural erasure—these were state-sanctioned, and in some cases, socially tolerated. That legacy must end if true healing is to begin.

Reconciliation, if it is to have integrity, must acknowledge and redress these legacies. Autonomy for ethnic states is not a political concession—it is an act of justice. Language rights. Cultural protection. Equitable resource-sharing. These are not privileges offered from the center—they are rights that must be honored without condition.

And yes, the National League for Democracy (NLD) bears part of this history. We did not always listen well enough. We did not act boldly enough. And for that, I take responsibility—with humility and with resolve.

True reconciliation requires political humility—the willingness to say: *"We failed you. And we are listening now."*

Alan Clements: You speak often of humility. How do you see the role of leadership—not just yours, but broadly—in modeling reconciliation? In creating unity that doesn't erase difference?

Aung San Suu Kyi: Leadership must be grounded in accountability, not infallibility. I don't believe any leader—myself included—should be above criticism. In fact, we must be the first to demonstrate what responsibility looks like.

Unity, Alan, must never mean uniformity. It must mean embracing difference as a strength, not a threat. It means not merely inviting marginalized communities into governance, but reconstructing governance around their rightful place within it. It means creating a political culture where dialogue is not merely performative, but transformative—where listening changes policy, not just optics.

If we want a united Myanmar, we must create structures that reflect the truth of our diversity—and policies that repair the damages of exclusion. That begins with leadership willing to lead not from control, but from conscience, with the courage to be changed by what we hear.

Alan Clements: Daw Suu, as we approach the end of this chapter, what would you say to the people of Myanmar now—those who have endured the worst, those who have committed harm, and those who still dare to dream of a better country?

Aung San Suu Kyi: To those who have suffered: your pain is real. Your story matters. And it must be told—not for pity, but for power. You do not have to be unbroken to be worthy of justice. You have only to be seen, to be heard, and to be honored.

To those who have caused harm: your redemption begins the moment you stop denying it. If you step forward in truth, if you commit to change, Myanmar can hold you—not as enemies, but as citizens. Citizens not of fear, but of conscience.

And to everyone still carrying the dream: don't let anyone shame you for hoping. Hope is not naïve. It is the blueprint of courage. It is the refusal to let brutality define us. Let your hope be disciplined, yes—but never extinguished. Guard it as you would guard a seed during a long winter. It may not bloom today, but it carries the shape of tomorrow.

Justice and reconciliation are not final destinations. They are disciplines—daily practices of integrity, compassion, and accountability. They are the way we refuse to surrender to cynicism. They are the quiet, defiant acts that build nations out of ashes.

If we choose them, again and again, we can make something enduring from all this ruin. Something no tyrant, no dictator, no darkness can ever erase.

Let that be our vow—not once, but every day we wake. Let it be the thread we pass from hand to trembling hand, across generations, until Myanmar stands free not only in law, but in spirit.

Alan Clements: Daw Suu, your words are a compass—clear, unwavering, and lit from within by the fire of truth. I feel them not only as answers, but as offerings to a people still standing in the storm. Your voice, though unjustly silenced by bars and fear, continues to rise—as prayer, as witness, as revolution of the heart.

May your words reach all your people—across every valley, monastery, prison cell, refugee camp, and exile—so that those who suffer might feel seen, those who cause harm might be summoned to conscience, and those who still dare to dream may find in your courage the strength to keep going. And may they also travel further still—to leaders, thinkers, and citizens across the world—because the task you've named here is not only Myanmar's, but humanity's.

In humble closing, may I ask: is there anything more you would wish to say—should this be, by chance or fate, our final conversation?

Aung San Suu Kyi: Alan, if these words mark the close of our dialogue, let them stand not as a farewell, but as a call to new beginnings.

Because the revolution we speak of is not confined to borders, nor born only of political will. It is the revolution of the spirit—the uprising of human dignity against the ancient, inherited patterns of domination. It is the refusal to let fear be the architect of our future.

Authoritarianism is not only a regime. It is a tendency—a psychological gravity—that lives in every human mind shaped by millennia of trauma, tribalism, and threat. And so, the work before us is not only to change governments, but to transform consciousness. To outgrow the reflex of "othering," and to cultivate the rare courage it takes to meet difference not with suppression, but with curiosity. With dialogue. With love.

Yes, love. Not the ornamental kind, but the muscular, disciplined love that refuses to dehumanize. The kind that sees even a stranger, even an adversary, as part of one's own unfolding. That love is the root of all true liberation. It is not soft. It is not weak. It is a fierce, grounded commitment to life. To truth. To presence. Even in the face of despair.

We are not here to merely resolve conflict. We are here to evolve how we live with difference itself—to make conflict a doorway into deeper understanding, and understanding a bridge toward a future radiant with possibility.

This is the work of a species just beginning to awaken. The human experiment is not over. It is just beginning. And each of us is called—not to perfection, but to participation.

May we liberate our minds from the chains of fear, violence, and ignorance. If not wholly, then with every step we can take, using the tools within our reach: meditation to still the heart, education to sharpen the mind, protest to awaken the conscience, art to reimagine what's possible, listening to bridge divides, repair to heal wounds, service to uplift others, and silence to find clarity. Every act is a seed planted for freedom.

Let this be our pledge: to grow ceaselessly, to offer relentlessly, to build lives—and nations—that reflect our deepest aspirations. And when we stumble, as we will, to rise with humility, with resolve, and with the unyielding conviction that the future is unwritten.

To those in Myanmar—huddled in refugee camps, resisting in hidden corners, or grieving in silence—your courage is the heartbeat of our nation. Keep dreaming. Keep fighting. Keep loving.

And to every person, everywhere, who yearns for a freer, wiser, more compassionate world: do not wait for a leader or a moment. Begin where you stand.

This is the revolution I have always served—not one of conquest, but of conscience. Not one of power, but of presence. The future will be shaped not by the weight of our chains, but by the integrity of our choices—today.

May these words, carried from my solitude, ignite a fire in every heart, a fire that burns for truth, for justice, and for a world where no one is left behind.

192

THE SHARED HUMAN CONDITION

Author's Prelude

There are truths so unsettling they demand not agreement, but moral courage to face them unflinchingly. This chapter enters the heart of such a truth: that *no one—however lost—is beyond redemption.*

It neither excuses atrocity nor softens the weight of harm. Instead, it poses a profound question—one that hovers at the nexus of justice and compassion: *How do we engage with those whose actions challenge the very possibility of forgiveness?*

Here, Aung San Suu Kyi speaks not in abstractions, but from the side of the wounded, amid Myanmar's scars of military oppression and ethnic strife. She names the affliction of hatred without succumbing to it. She urges us to see not only the crimes of history, but the conditions that shaped them—not to absolve perpetrators, but to ask wiser questions. To grieve without vengeance. To remember without condemnation. And—perhaps most challenging—to *recognize that evil is not an alien force, but a human failing, born of fear, ignorance, and choice.*

This dialogue is not a call to forget—it is a call to awaken. To understand that the divide between good and evil does not separate us; it runs through every human heart. That healing begins not with punishment, but with truth—spoken with clarity, held with courage, and offered without malice.

May this conversation be read not as a plea for absolution, but as a summons to our deepest capacity: to meet the human condition with insight, not denial; with discernment, not distance; and with a commitment to truth that transforms both the wounded and the wounding into a shared path toward redemption.

◆ ◆ ◆

Alan Clements: Daw Suu, in our past dialogues, you've illuminated justice—not as retribution, but as a foundation for healing. You've articulated a vision of reconciliation that embraces difference while anchoring itself in unflinching truth. And yet, as we sit here now—and I know I've asked this before—I feel compelled to ask again, more deeply: can we truly forgive what feels unforgivable?

How does a nation—raw from the wounds of ongoing military tyranny, where families are torn apart and sacred trusts desecrated—extend redemption to those responsible?

Is reconciliation possible with perpetrators who refuse to acknowledge their crimes, leaving survivors to bear the weight of unrepented harm?

Aung San Suu Kyi: Alan, your question—can we forgive the unforgivable?—strikes at the very heart of our humanity; a question both timeless and perilous if met with haste.

Forgiveness, to hold any meaning, as I have said many times, must never be conflated with forgetting. It is neither a dismissal of anguish, nor an erasure of history's scars. Neither acquiescence, nor surrender to injustice.

True forgiveness is a fierce act of agency—a refusal to let hatred's venom define us. It is a deliberate choice to reclaim our humanity, declaring that even in the wake of betrayal, we refuse to be reshaped by the cruelty of our oppressors.

You draw me to our *Theravāda Buddhism*, and I am grateful, for its *Dhamma* teachings offer a profound lens on this question. In *Theravāda*, as you know, we hold that no one is inherently evil; there is no fixed essence condemning anyone to darkness.

What manifests as cruelty is the culmination of conditioned patterns—ignorance that clouds understanding, fear that distorts perception, indoctrination that numbs conscience, and unresolved trauma that festers into violence. These do not absolve the perpetrator, but they reveal the tragic, human roots of their actions.

The Buddha taught that all beings act from *dukkha*—suffering—and that cruelty is often a misguided attempt to escape it. This insight, grounded in the Four Noble Truths, points to a radical possibility: *if suffering shapes harm, then understanding and mindfulness can reshape the heart.*

This perspective unveils a challenging truth: *the capacity for cruelty—or for compassion—is not a trait of 'others' but a potential within every mind, shaped by choice and circumstance.* This is not an easy truth to face, but it is a liberating one, for it affirms that transformation is within reach—for the harmed and the harm-doer alike.

In our *Dhamma* practice, we cultivate *mettā*—loving-kindness—not to excuse harm, but to dissolve the illusion of separateness and remember that our liberation is bound together. Yet this does not mean erasing accountability; it means pairing it with wisdom, so that justice becomes a path to healing rather than a cycle of retribution.

Reconciliation with those who deny their crimes is, indeed, a steeper climb. It begins not with forcing forgiveness, but with creating spaces for truth to breathe—spaces where survivors' voices are amplified, where denial is confronted, and where perpetrators are invited, however reluctantly, to face their actions.

This is not a call to naivety but to courage—a courage rooted in the *Dhamma* principle of *anicca*, the impermanence of all things. Even the hardest hearts can shift, given the right conditions. And if they do not, justice must hold firm, ensuring that truth, not silence, shapes our future.

Alan Clements: Yes, Daw Suu, your words resonate with the Buddha's teaching on the latent tendencies, the anusaya—greed, hatred, and delusion. From my humble understanding, the Buddha taught that a murderer carries no unique flaw absent in us all; we each harbor the same seeds, awaiting conditions to bloom.

This insight, profound as it is, seems to unsettle our notions of justice. How can a nation, still bearing the scars of atrocities, balance compassion for our shared human condition with the moral imperative to hold perpetrators accountable? How do we ensure justice fosters healing without excusing harm?

Aung San Suu Kyi: Alan, your question, unveils the complex tension between compassion and accountability, inviting us to navigate this challenge with the utmost wisdom and care. It rightly urges us to rethink justice, for any approach that overlooks the shared seeds of the anusaya risks deepening the very wounds it seeks to heal.

Justice, in my view, is not about labeling someone 'evil' or 'beyond redemption.' It is about confronting harm, dismantling destructive cycles, and creating conditions for transformation. It holds a mirror not only to the perpetrator but to the society that enabled such acts. This mirror reveals a truth we cannot evade: *no one acts in isolation*. The greed, hatred, and delusion the Buddha named are not merely individual flaws but societal currents, amplified by fear, propaganda, and unaddressed trauma.

In times of national anguish, there is a temptation to cast perpetrators as monsters, wholly separate from us. Yet, as you so aptly note, the Buddha's teaching on the *anusaya* reminds us that such distinctions are illusions.

History underscores this truth. The Holocaust was not the work of otherworldly fiends but of ordinary people—teachers, doctors, clerks— who cherished their loved ones yet became instruments of horror under the sway of fear, dehumanization, and collective delusion.

Rwanda, Cambodia, Bosnia, and Myanmar's own wounds—each bears witness to this pattern: *human beings, ensnared in ignorance, become capable of the unimaginable.*

This understanding does not soften accountability; it refines it. Justice must be deliberate, rooted in the *Theravādin* principle of *kamma—action and its consequences.* Those who commit atrocities must bear the weight of their choices, not as retribution, but as a step toward restoring balance.

For some, this means legal consequences, public acknowledgment, or restitution. For others, it may involve guided reflection to untangle the conditions that led to harm. In every case, justice must prevent the seeds of hatred and delusion from taking root again. Compassion, then, is not a weakening of justice but its essential partner.

In *Dhamma*, and I know you know this, we practice *mettā* to see the humanity in all, not to erase their actions but to transform the conditions that fuel them. This is not sentimentality—it is a disciplined strategy.

By addressing the roots of harm—ignorance, fear, division—we build a society where accountability and redemption are not at odds but interwoven.

Myanmar's path forward lies in spaces where truth is voiced, survivors are honored, and perpetrators are invited to confront their *kamma*, not with shame, but with the prospect of transformation.

Alan Clements: I remember the Milgram experiments. Yale. 1961. Volunteers believed they were administering electric shocks to strangers. Sixty-five percent went all the way. Not because they were sadists—but because an authority figure told them to.

We underestimate how fragile morality can become when fear or conformity sets in. It seems that one of the cruelest illusions is the belief: "I could never do such a thing."

Aung San Suu Kyi: That illusion is precisely what prevents healing. It creates a dangerous "us and them," a moral arrogance that blinds us to our shared vulnerability. But, as we have been discussing, in Theravāda Dhamma, we recognize that all beings are entangled in the web of paticcasamuppāda, dependent origination, where the Three Afflictions—lobha, dosa, and moha—greed, hatred, and delusion—arise from conditions like fear, obedience, or indoctrination.

The Milgram experiments reveal this starkly: ordinary people, swayed by authority, act against their conscience.

In Myanmar, where military propaganda has long stoked ethnic division, we see how such conditions—ignorance and fear—enable atrocities. This shifts our question from "How could they?" to "What conditions wove this web?"—a question not of judgment, but of understanding.

Forgiveness, from this view, becomes a form of moral clarity, not a negation of anger or justice. It is a mindful choice to plant seeds of awakening, declaring: *Your actions were wrong, yet I will not let them define your humanity—nor mine."*

Alan Clements: Daw Suu, your vision of shared humanity—radical yet anchored in truth—seems to brilliantly illuminate the path to reconciliation. If no one is beyond redemption, then no community is beyond reintegration.

Yet, for those still grieving—mothers who have lost their sons, villages reduced to rubble, children severed from their ancestors' names—this demands a compassion that may feel unattainable. What space can there be for their rage, their rightful anger, in a process that seeks to heal rather than divide?

Aung San Suu Kyi: Alan, your question gives voice to the raw ache of survivors—a grief that cannot and must not be silenced.

Rage has its place. To suppress it is to sever the body from the heart. To ignore it is to sow the seeds of new trauma. But rage, left untransformed, calcifies into vengeance—and vengeance cannot build a future.

As I have said before, we must create sanctuaries where pain can speak—unflinchingly, without shame, and with the dignity it deserves. We must listen, even when it breaks us, allowing sorrow to unfold without fear of judgment. But we must also guide its transformation— not by force, but through the alchemy of moral imagination and spiritual courage.

In *Dhamma*, as you know from your own training with *Sayadawgyi*, we regard rage as fire: it can destroy, or it can illuminate—when tended with insight. Through *vipassanā*—insight meditation—the fire of anger becomes the light of wisdom, and wisdom heals what hatred cannot.

Of course, it bears repeating: forgiveness does not erase memory, nor does it bypass justice. It is not forgetfulness—it is the refusal to let someone else's darkness determine our light. It is a mindful act of reclaiming agency over our humanity.

This begins not in courtrooms, but in the heart of communities: in classrooms where truth is taught without revision, in interfaith ceremonies where grief is honored as sacred, in rituals where survivors are revered, and in conversations where we confront darkness but do not bow to it.

Alan Clements: Daw Suu, you frame redemption not as a gift granted, but as a path offered—one that demands courage and truth. What conditions must exist for someone who has caused profound harm to walk that path with sincerity? How do we discern genuine remorse, as South Africa's Truth and Reconciliation Commission attempted to do, and how can we support their transformation without betraying the memory of those they've wounded?

Aung San Suu Kyi: The cornerstone of redemption is truth— uncompromising and exact. A perpetrator must name their actions with clarity: "I did this. It caused this harm. I accept responsibility without justification." This is not a confession for pardon—it is a step into the light of accountability.

Remorse follows—not as performance, but as authentic presence. It is not a spectacle of guilt, but the heartfelt willingness to bear the weight of one's deeds without flinching. It is a softening of the gaze, a stillness that no longer hides.

And then comes reparation—through visible acts of repair: public testimony, service to those harmed, relinquishment of illegitimate power. True redemption is not a plea for comfort—it is a metamorphosis. It demands humility. It requires resolve.

Discerning sincerity is not the work of courts alone. As South Africa's commission showed us, it requires communal wisdom—elders, survivors, and witnesses listening not just for words, but for the embodiment of truth.

Supporting transformation means creating spaces—socially, spiritually, institutionally—where change is possible, but never at the cost of survivors' truths.

In Myanmar, where violence has scarred generations, this means weaving accountability into the fabric of our future. It means ensuring justice uplifts the wounded, while offering those who wounded a path—not around their past, but through it—toward the possibility of becoming human again.

Alan Clements: Your words evoke the story of Angulimāla—the murderer turned Buddhist monk—who, after meeting the Buddha, renounced harm and became one of his gentlest disciples. The Buddha neither condemned nor excused him, but offered a path to awakening. That story, for many, is not folklore, but a mirror of redemption's power. How can Myanmar draw on such wisdom—not just for the oppressed, but for the oppressors?

Aung San Suu Kyi: Alan, the story of Angulimāla is indeed a mirror to our most urgent question: can we believe in transformation—not just for the oppressed, but for the oppressor? It is not naïve to ask this. It is morally audacious. And it is essential to our evolution.

As I said earlier, in *Theravāda Dhamma, Angulimāla's* story reflects the truth of *paticcasamuppāda*—dependent origination—where actions arise from conditions, and new conditions can foster awakening.

To apply this in Myanmar, we must create conditions for transformation: spaces where truth is spoken without fear, where survivors' stories guide justice, and where perpetrators are invited to face their *kamma* with courage.

This is not about excusing harm but about recognizing, as we discussed earlier, that the line between good and evil runs through every heart, as the Buddha taught.

If we reject transformation, declaring some beyond redemption, we consign ourselves to endless conflict. But if we embrace it—with clear eyes and unwavering commitment to truth—we build a society rooted in interdependence, where Buddhist, Muslim, Christian, and Hindu communities together forge a future illuminated by justice and compassion.

Alan Clements: Daw Suu, I've asked this before in different forms, but knowing this may be our final exchange, I ask again with humility and urgency: What message would you share with Myanmar's people— those enduring unimaginable loss, those who have caused harm, and those daring to dream of a renewed Myanmar and a transformed humanity?

Aung San Suu Kyi: It bears repeating, Alan, for the heart's truth is tireless: To all who breathe beneath Myanmar's wounded skies—to this land of sorrow, of beauty, of unyielding spirit—I say this to you: You are not forgotten, and you are not alone. Your pain is witnessed. Your courage is honored. And your longing for peace—so often dismissed— is not a weakness, but a testament to your strength. It is not naïve; it is sacred.

To those who have caused harm: find the courage to face yourself. Speak the truth. Own what you've done. Step into accountability not as punishment, but as the beginning of return. Myanmar will not meet you with vengeance. But neither will it absolve you without honesty. What it offers is a path. A way back. If you dare to walk it.

To our ethnic and religious brothers and sisters—Kachin, Karen, Rohingya, Shan, Buddhist, Muslim, Christian, Jewish, Hindu, and all others long silenced: you are not fragments of Myanmar. You are its foundation. Its future. Its fierce and necessary truth.

And to the dreamers—the wounded healers, the children who still plant seeds in scorched earth—know this: the rains may be slow to come, but your hope is not in vain. Each seed sown in compassion is a vow made to the generations yet to be born. Hold fast. You are not planting in vain. You are planting a future.

This movement—toward truth, toward justice, toward compassion—is fragile, often invisible before it becomes unstoppable. But it is real. Let us choose humanity, not hatred. Let us refuse to be defined by the worst among us. Let the deepest goodness within us—not rage, not fear—guide us forward.

This is not the end. It is a threshold. Let us cross it—together.

THE PATH TO PEACE:
DIALOGUE OVER DESTRUCTION

Author's Prelude

There are moments in a nation's life when silence becomes complicity—and speech, defiance. This chapter enters that threshold where language is no longer decoration but duty—where every word must carry the full weight of truth.

Here, dialogue is not a gesture. Not a ritual. Not a performance dressed in civility. It is a crucible—demanding clarity, integrity, and the courage to strip power of its illusion.

In this conversation, Aung San Suu Kyi speaks from within the deepest recesses of loss—not to soothe, but to illuminate. Not to absolve, but to expose. Hers is a voice that never softens the reality of cruelty, nor mistakes justice for revenge. It calls for a peace unyielding in principle and expansive in vision—rooted in moral imagination and forged in the hard lessons of history.

This is not a prelude to appeasement. It is a summons to truth—spoken with unyielding integrity and moral precision. "For dialogue, to be worthy of the people's suffering," she declares, "it must be unflinching in its discernment and radical in its compassion. It must never ask the wounded to forget their pain. It must ask the powerful to remember their humanity."

Let this chapter be received not as a blueprint for compromise, but as a call to the highest form of courage—the courage to seek a peace that does not sanitize history, but redeems it. Not through conquest, but through the quiet, unwavering dignity of those who still choose to speak, to listen, and to lead.

◆ ◆ ◆

Alan Clements: Daw Suu, as we speak, your country is being bled by its own military. Towns scorched. Monasteries shelled. Children orphaned. Artists, teachers, mothers, monks—imprisoned, exiled, executed. This cruelty is not accidental. It is strategic—deliberate. You know better than anyone: the junta rules through terror, indifferent to the destruction of its own name, people, and soul.

Now, in a grotesque twist of diplomacy, the man behind the 2021 coup—Min Aung Hlaing—is being welcomed on the world stage. At the 6th BIMSTEC (Bay of Bengal Initiative for Multi-Sectoral Technical and Economic Cooperation) Summit in Bangkok, he appeared shaking hands with Thailand's Paetongtarn Shinawatra and India's Narendra

Modi. Instead of facing censure, he is being legitimized. Photo ops replace headlines of horror. Refugees and survivors look on in disbelief: *"This man is a murderer."*

In Moscow, he recently met with Vladimir Putin, along with China's Xi Jinping. These appearances project a chilling façade of legitimacy—through alliance, silence, or indifference. Clearly, this is not diplomacy in service of peace. To the contrary, it mocks justice, erases suffering, emboldens tyranny, and betrays the moral conscience of the world.

So, I ask you, Daw Suu: with such entrenched deception and unrelenting cruelty, is dialogue still a morally defensible path? Or has it become a tool of the regime—a performance masking betrayal? When truth is weaponized and promises mean nothing, can negotiation be more than a charade of civility?

And before you answer, please. And yet, before you answer, please—if we abandon dialogue entirely, do we not risk becoming what we resist? Does refusing to speak foreclose transformation—and compromise our own humanity? Is there still a path to peace that honors truth without legitimizing those who distort it?

I ask not rhetorically, but from a place of anguish. What does dialogue mean in the face of 22,000 political prisoners? In a nation of scorched homes, silenced dissent, and grief etched into generations?

Can dialogue still serve the people—or only the powerful? And from your lived experience—your trials, solitude, silence, and courage— what must be true for dialogue to become more than betrayal dressed as diplomacy?

I must face this, Daw Suu: my own country, in ending a world war, incinerated cities with atomic bombs to force surrender and begin 'dialogue.' Was that peace—or annihilation disguised as wisdom? And what does it teach us today—about power, ends and means, and the true cost of victory?

Aung San Suu Kyi: Alan, your words carry the undeniable truth of this moment. I will not turn away from them. Nor will I soften reality. Dialogue cannot begin if we are unwilling to name—without euphemism or apology—the full magnitude of the brutality being endured. What you've described—the charred homes, the mass imprisonments, the international posturing amidst atrocity—this is not context for our conversation. It is the conversation.

The junta's strategy is not chaos—it is domination. Psychological warfare waged against the nation's soul. And you are right to ask: is dialogue wise, even moral, in such conditions? The answer depends entirely on what we mean by dialogue—and what we are willing to risk in the name of peace.

Dialogue that sanitizes, that rewards terror with legitimacy, is not dialogue. It is surrender. It is complicity dressed in protocol. It is diplomacy built on denial. We must never confuse photo ops with progress. And no—dialogue cannot be morally defensible if it asks victims to forget before they've even been allowed to speak.

And yet, the alternative path—one of pure retaliation—is fraught with its own dangers. Resistance, while often born of necessity and righteous anger, must remain grounded in moral clarity. When driven solely by vengeance, it risks becoming indistinguishable from the cruelty it opposes. *History warns us—again and again—that violence in the name of peace too often becomes a legacy of trauma.*

So let us speak clearly: The people of Myanmar do not have the weapons of the regime. They do not have the jets or the missiles supplied by foreign powers. They have their bodies, their courage, their memory, and the stubborn light of hope. They are fighting with their lives. And still, they rise.

The goal is not merely to defeat the *Tatmadaw* in battle. It is to defeat the mindset that gave rise to them. *A militarized psyche cannot be unseated by arms alone. It must be disarmed by something deeper—a collective moral awakening.*

So, what must be true for dialogue to be more than betrayal?

First, we must abandon the illusion that dialogue requires symmetry. The oppressed do not need to come as equals to the table. They must come in truth. That is their power. That is their leverage.

Second, dialogue must be conditional. It must demand preconditions—an end to aerial assaults, the release of political prisoners, independent monitoring of crimes. Anything less is theater. The world must stop asking victims to earn peace through submission.

Third, and most difficult, we must hold space for transformation— not only in institutions, but in hearts. Even Min Aung Hlaing must be seen through the lens of conditionality. He was not born a tyrant. Somewhere, that young man was taught to fear, to dominate, to believe in power over conscience. Understanding is not absolution—but it is the beginning of accountability.

We must be willing to see both the monster and the boy within him.

I say this without naivety. If he cannot be reached, he must be stopped. That, too, is compassion—compassion for the countless lives still at risk. But let us not glorify destruction, even when it becomes necessary. Let us not lose the thread of our own humanity.

Alan, I do not claim to have all the answers. But I know this: when the oppressed speak with moral clarity, the world begins to listen. When we walk forward without hate—even while defending our right to live—we plant the seeds of a different future.

Dialogue, then, is not negotiation with power. It is revelation. It is a call to conscience—ours, and theirs. And if we can hold that line—if we can root dialogue in dignity, not denial—then yes, it remains our most powerful path. Even now. *Especially now.*

Alan Clements: History offers us rare but powerful examples where dialogue triumphed in places long defined by violence—South Africa's Truth and Reconciliation Commission, the Good Friday Agreement in Northern Ireland, the Camp David Accords between sworn enemies. Each unfolded through profound moral risk and political imagination.

What enduring lessons, Daw Suu, might Myanmar draw from these experiments in courageous dialogue? How might they illuminate a way forward for a nation as fractured—and as fiercely resilient—as yours?

Aung San Suu Kyi: Alan, these examples remind us that dialogue is not merely an exchange of words. It is a discipline of conscience. A form of moral labor. A radical act of trust—often undertaken in the aftermath of atrocity, when trust feels impossible. In each case you mention, what moved the process forward was not only political negotiation, but a reckoning with pain, with memory, and with the deep human need for acknowledgment.

From South Africa, we learn not only the importance of truth—but that truth must be spoken aloud, in public, with consequences and courage. The Truth and Reconciliation Commission was not merely about disclosure. It was about restoring dignity to those whose suffering had been denied. About rehumanizing both the wounded and the wounder. About calling the fractured soul of a nation into a shared space of unbearable honesty.

It asked victims to speak the unspeakable—and perpetrators to confront the human cost of their actions. But it also asked a nation: *Can we bear to listen to each other's wounds without turning to revenge?* That is an extraordinary question.

From the Good Friday Agreement, we learn that peace is rarely linear. It is forged through exhaustion as much as inspiration. Northern Ireland teaches us the value of institutional imagination—shared power, cross-border cooperation, and the demilitarization of identity itself.

Identity, when fused with suffering, can become a weapon. True peace demands that we loosen the grip of grievance without erasing the memory that shaped it—that we allow ourselves to become more than the scars we carry.

Above all, it teaches us that endurance is not failure. Years of collapse and restart were not detours—they were the path. Myanmar must learn this: dialogue is not fragile because it breaks down. It is resilient because it resumes.

The Camp David Accords offer another lesson: even enemies who have waged war for generations can choose to see each other as human beings. That process was painful—and far from perfect—but it revealed the power of reframing: not erasing grievances, but choosing to place the future beyond them.

Yitzhak Rabin's words—*"Peace is not made with friends. Peace is made with enemies"*—are not a slogan. They are a confrontation with fear. Peace demands that we risk being changed by the encounter with the other.

And let me say this clearly: no model is transferable wholesale. Myanmar must create its own version of truth and reconciliation—rooted in our own history, our own wounds. But we can learn from the honesty of these examples. Their courage. Their failures. Their insistence that peace, if it is to be real, must begin not with treaties—but with truth.

Alan Clements: Daw Suu, Myanmar's challenges are profoundly layered. It is not simply a nation torn by a violent military coup—it is a country shaped by decades of civil war, colonization, betrayals, and fragile truces. As we both know, with over 130 ethnic nationalities—many of whom have been engaged in armed struggle for generations—the sense of fracture runs deep. Entire communities have fought not just for survival, but for cultural preservation, dignity, and autonomy in the face of centralized domination.

And now, in the wake of this latest junta assault, many of these armed ethnic organizations have become the backbone of the resistance—offering protection, refuge, and continuity in regions where the central government has failed or disappeared altogether.

How do we honor their sacrifices and aspirations while also envisioning a future in which the union itself can hold? How do we move toward peace and unity without silencing the legitimate claims of those who have resisted domination for decades?

Aung San Suu Kyi: Alan, your question pierces the core of Myanmar's moral and political struggle. Reconciliation and democracy are impossible without recognizing the deep wounds borne by ethnic communities, often in silence and isolation. These groups took up arms not from ambition but necessity—their voices ignored, lands seized, identities threatened. Their fight is for a rightful place in our nation's story, and they are not peripheral but foundational to our struggle.

A federal democratic system is vital, but it must transcend rhetoric. It requires equality, ensuring local autonomy, cultural preservation, and fair resource distribution. Ethnic voices must not just endorse peace but design it, weaving their histories and aspirations into a Myanmar where no spirit is overshadowed.

Alan Clements: Daw Suu, the Ethnic Armed Organizations have shown remarkable resilience, particularly through Operation 1027, which exposed the junta's weaknesses. Yet, the MNDAA has conceded Lashio to the junta under Chinese pressure, and other EAOs face similar demands to surrender strategic territories. How can these groups maintain their unity and autonomy against such external coercion?

Aung San Suu Kyi: Operation 1027, launched by the Three Brotherhood Alliance in October 2023, showcased the EAOs' strength, with the Arakan Army, Ta'ang National Liberation Army, and Myanmar National Democratic Alliance Army capturing vast territories, including Lashio's Northeastern Regional Military Command. Yet, this victory was undermined when, in April 2025, the MNDAA, under intense Chinese diplomatic and economic coercion overseen by envoy Deng Xijun, handed Lashio back to the junta.

China's pressure, driven by its need to secure the China-Myanmar Economic Corridor and border stability, now targets other EAOs, with the TNLA resisting demands to relinquish towns like Mogok and Kyaukme despite trade restrictions and junta airstrikes.

This coercion challenges the EAOs' unity and autonomy. China's influence, rooted in pragmatic economic priorities, exploits their reliance on border trade and arms. The United Wa State Army's deployment in Tangyan Township, likely at China's urging, has further strained relations within the Brotherhood Alliance.

To resist, EAOs must deepen coordination with the National Unity Government and civil society, forging a unified vision that prioritizes sovereignty over short-term concessions. As custodians of their communities' futures, their resilience must fuel a federal democracy that honors their sacrifices, not foreign agendas.

Alan Clements: Given China's growing influence, how do you view its impact on Myanmar's path to democracy, especially when it seems to prioritize economic stability over governance?

Aung San Suu Kyi: China, as a neighbor with vital economic interests, seeks stability above all, whether under dictatorship or democracy. Its support for the junta through arms and its pressure on EAOs—like the MNDAA's Lashio handover or demands on the TNLA—reflect a strategy to safeguard projects like the Kyaukphyu port and pipelines. This approach, while pragmatic, risks fracturing the resistance and deepening mistrust, as communities question who serves Myanmar's future. Yet, we must engage China constructively, recognizing its influence while championing our sovereignty.

I believe Myanmar's democracy offers China a more reliable partner than the junta's brittle rule. A democratic Myanmar, rooted in inclusive federalism, ensures the stability Beijing seeks—not through the fleeting might of one man and his cronies, but through the enduring will of a united people.

The junta's brutality breeds chaos, endangering China's economic corridors, while a government guided by conscience, dignity, and mutuality fosters peaceful coexistence and nonviolent control.

This is an invitation for China to see Myanmar's strength in its people—a nation where diverse voices unite for lasting cooperation and prosperity, benefiting all, including our neighbors.

Alan Clements: Daw Suu, healing Myanmar's divisions seems daunting when external pressures exacerbate mistrust. How can we rebuild trust and ensure reconciliation serves Myanmar's sovereignty rather than foreign agendas?

Aung San Suu Kyi: Healing Myanmar's scars—etched by decades of conflict and deepened by external pressures like China's influence on the junta and EAOs—demands patience and transparency. The MNDAA's concession of Lashio and China's ongoing demands on groups like the TNLA fuel suspicion, as communities wonder whose interests prevail.

Reconciliation must begin with open dialogue, exposing foreign pressures and ensuring no group feels abandoned to external agendas. The EAOs, NUG, and civil society must forge transparent negotiations, weaving local wisdom into a shared vision of peace rooted in dignity and mutual respect.

Reconciliation means empowering ethnic communities—Karen, Kachin, Chin, Shan, Rakhine, Mon, Rohingya, and others—to shape their futures without coercion from foreign economic priorities.

My party, at times, failed to listen deeply; we must learn from this. By celebrating our diversity, we rebuild trust.

Alan, unity arises not from uniformity but from honoring difference as our greatest teacher. If we walk this path with humility, resisting external manipulation, we can forge a Myanmar where peaceful coexistence prevails, reclaiming our nation's soul for generations.

Alan Clements: Daw Suu, you speak with such clarity about the practical steps toward peace. But dialogue, as you've emphasized, transcends politics—it's a profoundly moral act. How do we awaken leaders, citizens, young rebels, grieving mothers, monks in exile, and those in hiding to see dialogue not as compromise—but as an act of fearless integrity? How do you show the world that dialogue is not weakness, but strength forged by love and anchored in conscience?

Aung San Suu Kyi: Alan, as I've said before, dialogue is the heart's refusal to surrender to despair. It is a sacred act of recognizing the humanity in another—even when that humanity is buried beneath fear, cruelty, or silence.

Be clear: to choose dialogue is not to absolve harm, but to trust in the possibility of conscience—that no heart, however hardened, is beyond the reach of redemption. It is to believe in a future unwritten, where light persists, even amid deepening shadows.

And yet, we must go beyond words. We must speak from the marrow of experience. Dialogue, to be real, must be an embodied truth—felt in the breath, anchored in presence, guided by mindful and emotional intelligence.

To inspire this path, we must embody it, fiercely and visibly. *Dialogue is not passivity; it is revolutionary courage.* A defiance of hopelessness that declares our shared humanity will outlast our pain. It is the vow to never become what seeks to destroy us.

As Mandela taught, "No one is born hating another. If hate can be learned, love can be taught." Dialogue is how we teach love again—not by erasing scars, but by refusing to let them define our future.

As I have said so many times, this is not theory—it is survival. It is the bridge from remembrance to renewal—sowing seeds of mutuality and peaceful coexistence amid ruins. By living this truth, we invite leaders, rebels, mothers, and monks to see dialogue as a testament to dignity—a disciplined act of love that transforms grief into vision.

Alan Clements: Daw Suu, your words carry the heartbreak and unbroken spirit of a people who refuse to fade. You frame dialogue as sacred confrontation—not appeasement—a vision the world must relearn. But how do we convince the armed resistance and the students in jungle camps, that words can wield power against bombs—especially as external forces like China's influence on groups such as the MNDAA continue to sow division?

Aung San Suu Kyi: By honoring their sacrifices—without betrayal. As I've said before, we must never ask the resistance—the EAOs, the youth in hiding—to lay down arms without offering something greater: a future in which their dignity, truth, and agency form the bedrock of a new Myanmar.

Dialogue must be earned, not imposed—with a clear promise: Your suffering is seen. Your courage is sacred. Your role is indispensable.

The complexity of external pressures—like China's pragmatic pursuit of regional stability, reflected in the MNDAA's handover of Lashio or demands on the TNLA to cede territory—tests the resistance's cohesion. These maneuvers, driven by economic corridors and geopolitical calculus, risk fragmenting our collective fight for freedom.

Still, as we have learned through hard experience, we must engage these forces mindfully and constructively—asserting sovereignty while inviting cooperation.

Dialogue with the resistance must empower them as architects, not subjects. Let the Karen, Kachin, Shan, and others lead the terms—their voices shaping a federal democracy grounded in dignity and mutual recognition.

And once again, we must go beyond words. Felt experience, trust-built breath by breath, and emotional intelligence cultivated in community—these are the true foundations of dialogue.

By creating spaces where their sacrifices are not silenced but celebrated, we demonstrate that words, backed by conscience, can forge a power more enduring than violence. Here, hope is not demanded. It is kindled—by walking beside those who've paid the highest price, ensuring their fire lights the dawn of a united Myanmar.

Alan Clements: Daw Suu, if dialogue is your path—and I have asked you this before, what would you say today to Min Aung Hlaing himself? If, in a moment of reckoning, he stood before you—not as a general, but as a man—what words would you offer to awaken his conscience and turn him toward peace?

Aung San Suu Kyi: To Min Aung Hlaing, I would frank while speaking not as an adversary, but as one soul to another: You, General, were entrusted with a nation aching to heal—and yet you chose fear over courage, turning wounds into weapons. You had the chance to nurture Myanmar's children, and instead, you bombed their schools, burned their villages, and silenced their dreams. Your power—built on brutality— now holds 22,000 prisoners of conscience and an entire nation in chains. Yet, even now, as I've said before, the door to redemption remains open.

Look into your grandchildren's eyes, even if only in memory, and ask yourself: What legacy will they inherit? Will they carry pride in your strength—or shame in your silence? Recall the monks who once blessed your path, the teachers and mothers who once trusted you. *Think of the unborn, whose future you still shape.*

You could choose courage—not the false courage of domination, but the true courage of dignity. Release the prisoners. Stop the bombs. End the war on our people. Sit with your fellow citizens—not as a conqueror, but as a man ready to listen.

Listen not with strategy, but with sincerity. With presence. *With Dhamma intelligence rooted in humility.* Embrace nonviolent leadership— where peace is built not on fear, but on mutual responsibility.

Leave me in confinement if you must—I seek no favor. But if you choose to talk—truly talk—I am here. Not for spectacle, but for peace.

The path to reconciliation is narrow, and time is short. Refuse it, and history will not crown your power—it will mourn your cowardice. Your name written not in stone, but in ash, scattered by winds of change you could not control.

Yet this need not be your end. Choose dignity. Choose a future where your grandchildren walk in peace, not fear. The door is open. Step through it—for your people, your family, and the conscience you still carry, waiting to be reclaimed.

Alan Clements: Daw Suu, your voice—a beacon of truth and hope— cuts through Myanmar's darkness, offering not just a vision of peace, but a blueprint for moral leadership.

May this dialogue echo across borders as a call to conscience and rebirth, inspiring a world weary of violence to embrace the sacred courage of dialogue.

What final words would you share to ignite this vision of peace with dignity?

Aung San Suu Kyi: Let this be our vow: to forge a future not from the ruins of power, but from the courage of those who dare to love beyond pain. Let us build not merely an end to violence—but the dawn of belonging. A Myanmar where diversity is our strength, where dialogue is our defiance, and where peace is woven from dignity, justice, and remembrance.

Let the Karen, Kachin, Rohingya—and all our peoples—rise as the architects of a federal democracy, their sacrifices the foundation of a nation reborn. *Let us show the world that even in chains, the human spirit can choose mutuality over malice, coexistence over conquest.*

As I've said so many times—and will continue to say until we are free—this is not just language; it is a living truth. This is the dream we refuse to abandon: a peace that does not merely survive, but transforms—carrying the conscience of Myanmar into a future where every voice is heard, every life is cherished, and every heart is free.

FROM CRUELTY TO COMPASSION
ASHOKA'S TRANSFORMATION AND ITS LESSONS FOR MYANMAR

Author's Prelude

There are moments in history when a single awakening reshapes the destiny of a people—not through grandeur, but through the tenacious force of truth. The archetypal story of India's Emperor Ashoka is one such moment. Not legend, but a mirror—a testament to the transformative power of conscience, even in those who once ruled through devastation.

In this chapter, Aung San Suu Kyi steps into one of humanity's most radiant and haunting parables: the metamorphosis of Ashoka the Fierce into Ashoka the Righteous. She speaks not of power as dominion, but of conscience as revolution—a revolution born not in strategy, but in the heart's courageous reckoning.

Here, cruelty is not evaded—it is confronted. Remorse is not weakness, but the threshold of wisdom, born of rupture, reflection, and the heart's renewal. Compassion, in this light, is not mere sentiment—it is moral strength, disciplined by love and anchored in truth.

Guided by the *Dhamma* and the wisdom of Myanmar's Venerable Sayadaw U Pandita, this dialogue probes the heart of redemption: Can the machinery of harm be dismantled through mindful awareness? Can violence be stilled by moral courage and the imagination of peace? Can the searing realization—"I was wrong"—become the seed of authentic transformation?

Myanmar's wounds are deep and profound, etched by decades of conflict, betrayal, and tyranny. "Yet, if healing is to rise beyond an ideal," as Aung San Suu Kyi declares, "it must begin not only with accountability, but with the disciplined rigor of empathy—not only with justice, but with a vision of power that dares to feel the pulse of humanity."

Ashoka's journey remains unfinished. It lives in us—in our capacity to pause, to see, to change. Let this chapter be a meditation on that sacred possibility—a call to awaken conscience, to weave mutuality from division, and to forge a future where peace is not merely an end to violence, but a triumph of dignity, justice, and love.

♦ ♦ ♦

Alan Clements: Daw Suu, some stories don't arrive as history—they arrive as awakenings, echoing forward into the choices we make today. The life of Emperor Ashoka is one such story. His evolution—from

Chandashoka, "Ashoka the Fierce," a brutal warlord, to Dharmashoka, "Ashoka the Righteous"—is not just an ancient tale of reform. It is a revelation of conscience—a seismic awakening of the human spirit. It was not philosophy that changed him. Nor diplomacy. Nor reason or strategy. It was horror—the horror he himself had authored.

Allow me to share briefly, for our dialogue and for those who may one day read it. The late Sayadaw U Pandita shared this story with me, and you know it well, no doubt. Yet for clarity and reverence, allow me.

Ashoka's reign began in blood. He built empires through conquest, wielded terror as law, and—according to legend—constructed a torture chamber so grotesque it was called *Ashoka's Hell*, mirroring not only Buddhist cosmology but the torment of his own fractured mind.

And then something broke—not in the world he ruled, but within his heart. After the massacre of *Kalinga*—where an estimated hundred thousand perished, countless more displaced—he felt not triumph, but an unbearable weight: the reckoning of what he had become. This raw confrontation with his own complicity ignited a radical shift—a revolution of conscience, a reawakening of the soul.

The 13th Rock Edict in India, etched in Ashoka's own words on ancient stones across his empire, lamenting the *Kalinga* War's carnage, reveals this awakening with radiant clarity. He speaks not of glory but of sorrow—the sorrow of the widowed, the orphaned, the slaughtered. *This was no victory. It was a reflection of his heart's reckoning—and he chose not to turn away.*

Some say it began with a monk named *Samudra*. He entered the torture chamber not to resist, but to witness—with a stillness so complete it unsettled the very men who meant to break him. He was not spared by the fire, but passed through it with a mind untouched—freed not by mercy, but by a discipline deeper than fear. In that silence, something shifted: not just in the guards, but in the fabric of the moment itself.

Ashoka saw in Samudra not defiance, but a radiance he could not name—a peace that did not flinch, even in the furnace of cruelty. And in that moment, something within him gave way. Not in defeat, but in recognition. For a split second, he became the murdered, the tortured, the erased. The long-buried nerve of conscience stirred. The flame of personal accountability was touched. And remorse—real remorse—rose not as spectacle, but as silence: slow, sobering, and irrevocable.

He renounced violence not to salvage his legacy, but to reclaim his humanity. He turned toward the *Dhamma* not as dogma, but as reckoning. What followed was not a reign of proclamations, but a reorientation of power itself: rule transfigured by compassion, anchored in humility, and governed by the quiet discipline to care. His empire became a living experiment in conscience—an awakening shaped not by conquest, but by the audacity to change.

What makes this story so urgent is its truth: that a single moment of unflinching recognition can shatter delusion—and rebuild a life on the bedrock of accountability. Even the architect of horror can become a vessel of healing, if conscience is awakened and allowed to lead.

So, I must ask, Daw Suu: In the context of Myanmar's profound and painful struggle—where cruelty is both normalized and denied— does Ashoka's story still speak to us? Can it offer a living blueprint for transformation, not just of systems, but of souls?

Can it show how conscience might interrupt cruelty—how even horror might become the seedbed of wisdom? And if so, how do we— as individuals and as a nation—ignite that inner fire? How do we catalyze such a radical awakening—not as punishment, but as a path to redemption and collective rebirth?

Aung San Suu Kyi: Alan, Ashoka's story still lives—not because it ended in resolution, but because it began in reckoning. The fiercest battles are not fought on the fields of war—but in the quiet, trembling chambers of the human heart. And let me say it plainly: the outer wars will not end until the inner war is faced.

Transformation isn't the softening of power—it's the reimagining of its purpose. Ashoka didn't become less powerful. He became less blind. His strength, once used to break, was turned to heal. The same will that sowed fear was reclaimed by wisdom.

That, to me, is the essence of awakening. Not the loss of will—but the moment will bows to truth. When the sword is lowered—not out of fear, but because the heart refuses to lift it anymore.

And that is why his story matters here, now, in Myanmar—a land scarred, yes, but not beyond healing. When I think of our people— the disappeared, the displaced, the grieving mothers, the silenced children—I see Ashoka's grief reflected back. But I also see something else: the unextinguished ember of awakening.

Our path to reconciliation, if it is to be real, must be rooted in the living *Dhamma*—not as doctrine, but as daily discipline. In *mettā* and *karuṇā*—not as dogmas, but as strength. This is what *Sayadawgyi* gave us: a ruthless compassion, an unflinching call to look directly at suffering—and not look away.

He taught that the Four Noble Truths are not philosophy. They are anatomy. They show us that ignorance causes pain—and only wisdom, grounded in intention and action, can end it. This is not metaphor. It is mechanics.

Actions born from fear, from greed, from craving for control—they shatter lives. But when intention is purified by awareness, even the smallest gesture—a glance, a word—can become a thread in the tapestry of repair.

Sayadawgyi warned us: *the real enemy is not power—it's ignorance of consequence. It's moral blindness dressed up as pragmatism.*

And that's where Ashoka speaks loudest. In a country like ours, where cruelty has been institutionalized—his story says: *No. No system of domination is immune to conscience.* One honest moment. One raw flash of empathy. That's all it takes to begin dismantling the walls of delusion.

But let's not romanticize this. Mirrors are hard to find in a palace. Most leaders surround themselves with applause, with flattery, with carefully filtered news. They suffocate in the velvet of their own distance.

Hope, then, begins with imagination. Not fantasy—but *moral imagination.* The courage to see oneself not as ruler, not as symbol, but as a human being. Vulnerable. Accountable. Still capable of change.

Ashoka's legacy isn't just for textbooks. It's a challenge. It asks: Will we keep building monuments to our pain, or will we build sanctuaries from it?

Because true strength isn't in domination. True leadership isn't in conquest. And legacy? It isn't fear. It's the quiet revolution of a conscience that refuses to be silenced.

So may we light this path—not with certainty, but with sincerity. Let *mettā* and *karuṇā* become our guides. Let them turn our wounds into wisdom. And like seeds breaking stone, may this broken nation bloom—not into what it once was, but into what it dares to become: a country made of love, of justice, of peace.

Alan Clements: That phrase — "moral imagination"—resonates deeply. Ashoka's transformation wasn't merely a spiritual epiphany; it was a radical redirection of his entire being. He didn't just feel sorrow—he transmuted it. He had the courage to turn remorse into something tangible, enduring. He inscribed it into stone. He reshaped laws. He rebuilt the moral structure of his empire.

And yet, Daw Suu, as you so eloquently said, this didn't make him weaker—it made him clearer. But before that clarity, there was an emboldened numbness. Power had aggressively hollowed him out. Like countless who rise through domination, he had grown deaf to the pain he caused. Perhaps he even believed his cruelty was just.

Clearly, that is not unique to his time. It persists with us still, even more so. The psychopathy of violence hasn't vanished—it has both increased and modernized. We now witness atrocities in high definition. AI-guided warfare. Mass killings orchestrated from air-conditioned offices, with decisions made over energy drinks and spreadsheets. The horror is still there—cleaner, colder, veiled by abstraction. And this detachment makes it more insidious.

What pierced Ashoka's desensitization wasn't ideology—it was proximity. Contact. He was confronted not by resistance, but by presence: a monk who entered the torture chamber and emerged untouched—not spared by fire, but unmoved by fear. That calm, unwavering dignity—so alive in the face of cruelty—shattered Ashoka's illusion of control. For a moment, he saw clearly. Not the monk. Himself. And it was unbearable.

So, I wonder, Daw Suu: Could such a moment still happen today? Could those orchestrating cruelty from afar—disconnected from consequence—ever encounter the human cost of their actions? Could they still feel the weight of truth? And what would an Ashoka moment look like now, in a world of drone wars and digital propaganda? What would awaken the leaders of modern carnage and human degradation? Could we still forge a mirror powerful enough to stir their conscience?

Aung San Suu Kyi: Indeed, Alan. You've named the affliction of our age—not just violence, but emotional numbness. The slow, toxic patriarchal drift from consequence. A detachment so deep it becomes cruelty by default.

Sayadaw U Pandita saw this with terrifying clarity. He taught us that *hirī* and *ottappa*—moral shame and moral fear—are not weaknesses. They are the last guardians of our humanity. Without them, we do not become monsters—we simply stop noticing when we cause harm.

Empathy, he said, isn't a gift. It's a discipline. A willingness to feel what we'd rather not. And it is through the Four Noble Truths that we learn to see—suffering not as punishment, but as a mirror. Its cause: ignorance. Its end: wisdom, cultivated step by step along the Noble Eightfold Path.

As I reflect on Myanmar's suffering—the silenced, the disappeared, the 22,000 prisoners of conscience and counting—I don't see shame in their faces. I see truth. Dignity. A quiet defiance that says: "You may take my freedom, but not my humanity." And I wonder, as you do: could their courage become the mirror that wakes those who still rule through fear?

Ashoka's transformation did not arrive in isolation. It was not born of solitude, but of collision—contact with a conscience in context too radiant to deny. His sorrow wasn't theater. It was rupture. And from that rupture, he rebuilt—not with words, but with deeds. Roads. Hospitals. Laws. Pillars carved in stone. What endures is not the remorse itself, but what he did with it.

You ask: *what would an Ashoka moment look like today?*

Not a lightning strike, perhaps. But a slow fracture—a crack in the armor of denial. A tremor in the voice of someone who finally lets themselves feel. And for Myanmar's generals, its bureaucrats, its drone operators—men insulated by protocol and distance—this can only begin with proximity. Not to data. But to the bodies. To the breath. To the absence.

We must close the gap. Bring them face to face with what their orders have done—not once, but again and again—until silence is no longer bearable.

Because what our nation needs is not gestures. We need ethics we can touch. Compassion, not as a feeling—but as policy. As law.

Remorse, when honored, doesn't dissolve into guilt. It becomes fuel. It becomes governance. And the courage to say, *"I was wrong,"* and to mean it with your whole life—that is not performance. That is moral imagination made real.

Ashoka made his sorrow public. He let it shape the kingdom. He let it interrupt conquest with conscience. That is the mirror we must raise now—not to shame, but to awaken. Not to humiliate, but to reveal the dignity still buried inside the machinery of power.

His story is not a parable. It is a warning—and a possibility. It speaks not just to Myanmar, but to every leader everywhere who still believes that power is strength, and feeling is weakness.

Let illusion break. Let truth in. Let remorse be honored. Let compassion shape the state. Let conscience not be silenced—but lead.

And in this fractured, burning world, may we choose—as Ashoka once did—not survival through domination, but redemption through humanity. May Myanmar's wounds—and the wounds of Rabin, Mandela, and every unknown soul who turned away from cruelty— become seeds. Seeds of a peace that is both fierce and tender.

Not a peace of forgetting. But a peace that remembers everything— and still dares to build anyway. A peace rooted in truth. Disciplined by dignity. Nourished, finally, by love.

Alan Clements: Yes… may it be so! And still, Daw Suu, I find myself aching with the complexity of it all. What you've said—about embodied ethics, about institutionalizing remorse—rings so true. And yet… the machinery of violence moves at a different speed. It's loud. It's fast. It's relentless. Missiles do not pause for reflection, and tyrants do not pencil in time for remorse.

And if transformation is even possible…, where do we begin?

Ashoka's awakening sprang from raw truth—the *undeniable cost* of his devastation. But today, cruelty hides behind polished desks and encrypted files. It cloaks itself in bureaucracy, splinters itself across screens. Power is taught to feel nothing, to *outsource empathy*, to numb itself with strategy.

So, I ask—*with reverent wonder*—how do we spark that awakening now?

How do we pierce the veil of detachment—so that truth's silent cry reaches the innermost fabric of the heart? The place where conscience— *hiri* and *ottappa*—still wait beneath the flesh-draped rubble?

If we cannot guide the architects of harm to the ruins they've made—can we carry the wails of the wounded to their souls? Can we summon power to reclaim its humanity—not through blame, but through a vision of redemption strong enough to unmake the damage?

And in such a fractured world—scarred by algorithmic warfare and the dehumanization of distance—where, Daw Suu, do we even begin?

Aung San Suu Kyi: By refusing to turn away. By bearing witness. By insisting that suffering be seen—not as spectacle or propaganda, but as unflinching moral truth.

We must cultivate, Alan, cultural spaces—through film, testimony, literature, ritual—where the cost of violence cannot be sanitized or abstracted. Spaces where silence itself becomes an accomplice to cruelty, and where the shield of indifference is shattered by the force of remembrance. Spaces where generals are not shielded by protocol, but exposed to the raw grief of those they've harmed. Where the names of prisoners are not buried in statistics, but spoken aloud as living stories.

Ashoka saw the weight of his legacy written in corpses. In Myanmar, that record already exists—in burned villages, in mass graves, in whispered names. What remains absent is the willingness to face it. The courage to look without flinching.

And this is where the international community must play a deeper role—not to punish from a distance or moralize in abstraction, but to insist, again and again, on the primacy of truth. On dignity. On consequence. Not because we lack compassion, but precisely because we refuse to let compassion be eclipsed by convenience.

And beneath all of this—if we are to sustain any momentum—we must foster the capacity to see oneself in the other.

Sayadaw U Pandita taught us that *Satipaṭṭhāna Vipassanā*—mindfulness of body, feelings, mind, and phenomena—unveils *anatta*, the truth of non-self, where no "I" exists apart from another. *This interdependence is liberation's spark: to entwine one's being with another's pain, shattering the delusion of separation that fuels cruelty.*

Awakening requires courage that radiates outward—not polished, not rehearsed, but torn from the marrow of regret. Like a seed breaking open in darkness, remorse must give rise to new systems: governance steeped in *mettā*, justice that shelters dignity, leadership that bows low to heal what it once broke.

But awakening does not begin in comfort. It begins in horror.

Awakening requires a courage that bleeds—not the theater of remorse, but the breaking open of denial, cell by cell. Like a wound that refuses to close, it begins with the unbearable: *to feel what one has made others feel.*

Remorse, real remorse, does not seek forgiveness. It kneels in the ruins and refuses to look away.

It says: "I was not just wrong. I was monstrous. I knew children were in those homes—and I bombed them. I signed orders I never read—because I didn't want to feel what they meant. I crushed voices. I turned prisons into tombs. I erased names and called it stability. I made mothers dig graves with their bare hands. I watched, and I turned away. And then I justified it. And then I slept. And then I prayed."

To the families whose loved ones were disappeared—there are no words. To the children who grew up with no parents, no village, no name—there is no repair.

But this much must be said, and said aloud, by those who ordered it: "I murdered. I desecrated. And I will spend the rest of my life—what little is left—turning every breath of power I have into something that heals, if not the past, then the possibility of a future."

That is not redemption. That is the beginning of humanity.

Because peace does not begin with treaties. It begins with truth—dragged into the light, bleeding, weeping, unguarded.

This call resounds not for Myanmar alone but for all humanity—for every nation where power has silenced pain with policy, where victims have been buried without names, and where truth still waits to be spoken aloud. It is a call to confront what has been done in our name. To face it. To say it. To let conscience shape the heart and sorrow reorder the soul.

A future worthy of the dead will not be born from denial. It will rise from places where those once obeyed for their violence stand trembling before their people, unarmed and exposed, and say: "I desecrated. And I will spend what remains of my life making something sacred again."

In this age of fracture and forgetting, may we nurture havens where suffering is not erased but honored. Where spirits awaken through truth. Where power bends to the dignity of the oppressed. And where peace—like a seed pressed into bloodied soil—blossoms into justice, into love, and into a wisdom vast enough to hold all that has been lost.

For Myanmar. And for the world. Let that be our vow.

Alan Clements: Yes... I feel that in my bones. May it be so, Daw Suu. And what you just said—about truth being dragged into the light, not as punishment but as the beginning of humanity—it touches the very heart of what we practiced under Sayadawgyi.

The *Satipaṭṭhāna* path he taught us wasn't designed to make us comfortable. It was a mirror. A fire. It asked us to sit with what is most difficult—to see clearly, without defense, without delusion. And in doing that, something subtle but radical happens: we begin to take responsibility. Not just for our thoughts, but for our choices. Not just for our own liberation, but for how we live with others.

And so, I've been sitting with this question, Daw Suu. In the midst of all this—this heartbreak, this war, this revolution—how do we carry that inner path into the outer world?

Would you speak to that?

How can mindfulness—*sati*—be more than a personal refuge? How does it become a shared strength, a way we hold ourselves and one another accountable? And perhaps even more than that—how might it become the very ground of reconciliation itself? The place where repair becomes possible?

Aung San Suu Kyi: It must, Alan. Mindfulness cannot remain a personal refuge—it must evolve into a shared resilience, the living foundation of how we lead, how we heal, how we protect what's human. Because no peace born of silence or submission can last. And no outer peace can endure if it is not anchored in the clarity of an unclouded heart.

Sayadaw U Pandita was unwavering in this truth: *real leadership begins with self-governance. The restraint to pause. The humility to listen. The courage to face one's own mind—especially when it's raging with pain.*

These aren't luxuries. They are the deep, daily disciplines. Quiet. Inconvenient. Often invisible. But indispensable. They form the mindful intelligence of any freedom worthy of the name.

And these qualities cannot belong only to nuns, monks, or philosophers. They must live in the farmer who rises before dawn to sow resilience. In the seamstress whose hands mend more than fabric. In the elder who settles conflict through memory and care. In the soldier who walks the hills with a longing for home. And yes—in the revolutionary, whose fire must not consume their humanity.

Because if peace is not held close to the marrow of the heart, we risk becoming the very thing we rose to resist. Peace is not simply the absence of violence—it is the presence of culture. A living, breathing ethic. And it begins early—not just through curriculum, but through what we praise, what we normalize, what we choose to embody in the smallest acts.

We must teach empathy not as sentiment, but as a profound intelligence. A way of perceiving, listening, and responding. A moral clarity without which no society can endure.

And we must model nonviolence not just in slogans or policy—but in how we speak, how we wait, how we argue. How we walk through disagreement without dehumanizing one another.

Peace must be practiced everywhere. In the kitchen. In the refugee camp. In the makeshift classroom. In the underground clinic. In the market stall. In the exile parliament. It must live in the pauses between words. In the discipline to feel before reacting. In the courage to see another being fully—even when they oppose us, even when we want to turn away.

This is where real rebuilding begins—not with roads or bridges, but with the inward scaffolding of the human spirit. We must create spaces—quiet, communal spaces—for reflection. Places where meditation is not a performance or privilege, but a lifeline. Where ethical conduct is not decoration, but daily vow. A way of walking. Of seeing. Of listening.

Because peace is not passive—as we both know. It is not stillness by default, but a disciplined presence of heart. A form of *Dhamma intelligence*: a balance of discernment, compassion, and restraint. It is the only ecosystem in which truth and reconciliation can breathe. And like any ecosystem, it must be nourished. It must be tended. It must be protected from erosion and extremism.

It requires patience in complexity. Curiosity in difference. Restraint without repression. Resolve without cruelty.

This, to me, is the *Dhamma of peace*. Not peace imposed from above or legislated into being, but peace born from below—from the marrow of ordinary lives lived with extraordinary care. Peace that rises not through control, but through a shared awakening to what matters.

And most crucially, it asks for the radical conviction that every life counts—and that how we meet each moment is the blueprint of the world we are building.

Alan, I say this not as a young woman of protest, but as one who has lived long. My body is frail. I was injured in the earthquake. My days pass in pain and silence, behind walls. And yet—even here, even now—I believe these small, steady truths still carry power.

Not because they are convenient. Not because they guarantee victory. But because they are the only path, I know that does not lead us back into harm.

If we are to rise from this long night as a nation—not merely to survive but to emerge transformed—it will be because we remembered this: Mindfulness, empathy, and moral courage are not ideals. They are the daily labor of liberation. The quiet defiance that reclaims what it means to be human.

Because in a world that dehumanizes—to live with awareness is to resist. And to heal—truly heal—is to revolt.

Alan Clements: Yes... I feel that too, Daw Suu. What you said about rebuilding from within—not just infrastructure, but the inner wiring of a society—lands deeply. Without that, nothing holds. Not truly.

Peace doesn't begin with policy. It begins with perception—how we see, how we listen, how we respond when the world around us is broken.

And real education may be the most powerful force on earth that doesn't carry a weapon. Not education as memorization or dogma, but as the opening of the heart. A training in conscience. A teaching in how to feel—before we react. To recognize suffering not as weakness, but as signal. To sense the fracture behind anger. To hear the silence beneath fear. To see the other—not as threat, but as mirror.

And perhaps just as importantly, to know remorse not as failure, but as strength. To say, "I was wrong," and be changed by it—not diminished. That kind of education doesn't guarantee peace. But without it, peace becomes performance. Healing becomes politics. Nothing truly shifts.

So, I've been sitting with this question, especially now, as Myanmar fights for its life: How do we carry that inner path into the outer world? How do we take the wisdom of mindfulness, of introspection, of *Dhamma*—and build it into the fabric of a nation? Not just in classrooms or monasteries—but in kitchens, markets, homes. In the rituals of daily life. How do we teach the art of peace in a place where peace has been absent for so long? For the children of farmers. Of soldiers. Of prisoners. Of the disappeared.

Where do we begin?

Aung San Suu Kyi: We begin, Alan, by telling the truth—not to reopen wounds, but to begin the healing. Not to dwell in the shadows, but to walk forward with our eyes open.

In a nation where so much has been silenced, truth must become a shared inheritance—a lamp carried forward from generation to generation, woven into the fabric of our education not as abstraction, but as lived and embodied reality.

Our children must learn what happened—who suffered, and why it matters. Not to assign blame, but to cultivate understanding. Not to harden hearts, but to open them. If we deny them the truth, we deny them the tools to transform that truth into something redemptive.

We must teach ethics alongside arithmetic. Mindfulness alongside mathematics. History alongside empathy. Education must no longer be only about information, but formation—the shaping of character, of conscience, of care. It must teach our children not only how to think, but how to feel responsibly. How to carry the weight of history as a responsibility, not a chain. How to see the world not as a battleground, but as a shared and fragile home.

Incorporating ethical reflection and mindful intelligence into our curriculum is not a luxury—it is a necessity. These are skills as vital as reading and writing. The capacity to pause, to reflect, to feel the impact of one's actions—this is what allows peace to take root where violence once grew. And it asks something deep of us. Especially in a time such as this, when speed and distraction have become normal, and silence is mistaken for peace.

In our tradition, we speak of *hirī*—as I mentioned earlier—the moral modesty that keeps one from harm not out of fear of punishment, but out of reverence for life, and for oneself. *Hirī* is not submission. It is strength in the form of self-respect. It is not an easy path. It requires vigilance in a world driven by ego, consumption, and noise.

It asks us to seek purity—*sucigavesinā*—not in some abstract or moralistic sense, but as a daily, lived commitment to clarity and compassion. A life of careful seeing. Of gentle integrity. It also calls for detachment and humility—*alīnenāppagabbhena*—to live without clinging or arrogance, even when the world rewards both. And it rests on clean living and discernment—*suddhājīvena passatā*—the quiet, courageous work of aligning thought, speech, and action with truth.

These are not traits reserved for nuns, monks, or saints. They are the foundations of a peaceful society. And they must be nurtured in every child—not as doctrine, but as dignity. Not imposed, but modeled, through presence.

But this must go far beyond the classroom. As I said many times, peace must become a way of being in everyday life. In how we greet one another. In how we disagree. In how we grieve.

Again, we cannot overstate the value of community spaces—meditation centers, youth circles, storytelling gatherings—all of which help to reweave the torn fabric of trust. Children need places where they can ask difficult questions. Where they can be heard. Where they can mourn and imagine, side by side. Where the silence of trauma is broken not by noise, but by truth held with care.

And teachers... they must be supported, not just trained. They must be nourished. Protected. Allowed to become stewards of transformation. Guides who can hold space for grief, for growth, for the quiet resilience that peace requires. They must model the very virtues we hope to see in the next generation: patience, steadiness, compassion. The ability to sit with pain without becoming hardened. The wisdom to speak truth without cruelty.

But even beyond the schools and the teachers, we must invite our communities into the process—not as spectators, but as co-creators. As I've said before, we must cultivate dialogue circles, restorative justice practices, intergenerational storytelling, and memorials that do not glorify pain, but dignify it—while planting seeds of possibility.

We must make visible the lives that have been erased—not as statistics, but as stories. As living reminders of our shared fragility—and our shared strength. This is how a culture changes. Not through decrees or slogans, but through the ordinary, often invisible gestures of presence and tenderness. A shared story. A moment of stillness. A hand held instead of a fist raised. A mother listening to her child's questions. A prisoner remembering the sound of laughter. A teacher choosing not to shame, but to wait.

These are the roots of peace. Not brittle and fragile, but alive—resilient. And like any living thing, they need time, and patience, and deep attention. They need to be nurtured—not once, but again and again—until peace is no longer just something we long for, but something we practice. Something we protect. Something we live.

And I say this not as someone removed from suffering, but as a woman in her eightieth year. A prisoner in solitude. My body is weak. My world is small. But still, I believe in this. I believe that if we begin with truth, if we nurture conscience as carefully as we once nurtured fear, there is a future for our people that does not repeat the past. I may not live to see that future. But I will speak it to you now and for as long as I have voice. *Because even now—especially now—peace is possible. And our children deserve nothing less.*

Alan Clements: Beautiful! Thank you.

Daw Suu, I pose this next question with a burdened heart and utmost reverence—knowing the weight of speaking of leadership now, as you endure unjust imprisonment alongside thousands of others, in a nation trembling beneath unrelenting violence.

Forgive me if this feels misplaced; my intent is only to honor your being. Your voice, your wisdom, your presence—in this crucible of history—are a beacon not just for Myanmar, but for the world's wounded soul.

So, I ask with tender sincerity: If children learn by example, so too must a nation. Ashoka's awakened heart recast the moral arc of an empire, sowing seeds that outlasted his reign. Amid such pain and disillusionment, how can leaders—even now—be inspired to embody compassion and nonviolence? How do we guide those in power to reclaim their humanity before their conscience grows silent forever?

Aung San Suu Kyi: Thank you, Alan, for your care in asking—a question heavy yet vital, especially now, as Myanmar drowns in a sea of unimaginable sorrow. I speak from behind these walls, alongside countless others, while some wield guns where words have failed. Yet this is precisely why we must speak.

Leadership, I've learned through years of reflection, is not a mantle but a vow. As Gandhi and Martin Luther King Jr. showed, true leadership does not dominate—it kindles power within others, nurturing their courage to rise. This is no dream but a necessity.

Power without conscience breeds only ruin. Ashoka's truth is timeless: his awakening came not in serenity, but after slaughtering a hundred thousand, after crafting a torture chamber. Only then did his heart break open, refusing to turn from its own reflection. Must we always await such devastation? Must leaders awaken only when the skulls pile high?

I hold fast—because I must—that another path exists. It is arduous, especially in a land where armed struggle is survival, where freedom's cry is steeped in blood. Yet, the deeper the wound, the more urgent the healing.

We must call leaders to presence—not perfection. To pause. To feel. To transform. They must wield power like a mother cradles a child—with reverence and care. They must master their minds through mindfulness, or become their prisoners. No governance, however democratic, endures if its leaders drift unmoored from spirit.

This demands ethical clarity—mindfulness not as solace, but as salvation. As we've discussed, the Buddha's Four Noble Truths teach us to face suffering's root—ignorance—and walk the Noble Eightfold Path to liberation. Accountability, firm and just, is essential, but without inner awakening, it is mere retribution. It does not mend. It does not renew.

The future of freedom lies not only in toppling tyranny but in uprooting hatred. I draw strength from Gandhi's gentle ferocity, King's boundless love, Mandela's forgiveness that never forgot. True leadership is not force's absence, but depth's presence—a willingness to listen, to err, to begin anew.

To those wielding power—political, military, or cultural—I say: Do not wait for devastation to stir your heart. Do not wait until history carves your name in shame. Choose now. Choose to feel. Choose to lead from the tender pulse of humanity. One leader's humble shift is not weakness—it is a revolution of the soul, a mandala of peace radiating outward.

Alan Clements: Thank you, Daw Suu—thank you from my heart, and from all who read your words. Yes… accountability: a word so vital, yet so often hollow.

In Myanmar, where the engine of impunity has roared for generations, accountability can feel like a faint song amid a storm. And without it, justice has no anchor, the innocent no shield, and the cycle of harm no end.

So, I ask, in a nation so deeply fractured, where truth lies buried and fear enshrined, how does accountability take root—not just in courts, but in the fabric of culture, in daily life? How do we revive a collective conscience when so many survive by averting their gaze?

Aung San Suu Kyi: You strike the core, Alan. Accountability in a land like ours cannot be decreed—it must be reborn through remembrance, rising from the wellspring of cultural memory and human conscience.

Laws draw justice's boundaries, but the soul of a nation is redrawn through story. We need the courage to grieve together, to name the silenced—not for vengeance, but for renewal.

Civil society must breathe again—journalists, artists, educators, nuns, and monks are not mere voices but the scaffolding of trust. They weave the threads of truth, and they must be shielded, empowered, and heard.

The deepest accountability is cultural—a quiet revolution where truth becomes a practice, honesty a home. It begins when people see themselves not as history's victims, but as its healers. This is where trauma bends toward transformation: where the silent find their voice, not in rage alone, but in dignity; where the harm-doers, when possible, face their deeds—not to be broken, but to be unburdened. Only thus do cycles cease.

The world must walk with us—not as distant judges, but as partners in truth's labor, offering solidarity, not pity. Accountability demands more than censure—it requires a steadfast, human presence.

Time is needed, yes, but truth is patient. Spoken with care, held with compassion, it becomes not just reckoning, but rebirth. The question is not only how we hold the powerful to account, but how we hold ourselves—in our homes, our words, our choices. Impunity shatters through countless acts of conscience, a tapestry woven one thread at a time.

Alan Clements: Daw Suu, as we speak, I feel the pulse of Myanmar's people, surviving on shards of trust, sustenance, and hope. Yet, as we've seen, change often begins quietly, within. How do we reach those crushed beneath this weight, who feel brutality has stolen their power to shape anything?

Aung San Suu Kyi: We reach them by never forsaking them, by affirming their sacred spark. Even in chains, even under tyranny's heel, the inner life remains inviolable.

The fiercest rebellion is to reclaim dignity. To sit with your breath, though the world burns, and vow: I will not let them extinguish my care. That is not frailty—it is defiance at its deepest.

This does not mean we cease resistance. It means we resist with wisdom, with depth, with conscience. The power born of stillness, of knowing who we are, cannot be stolen. When enough souls reclaim this, fear loses its grip. That is when history shifts.

Alan Clements: And yet, the beginning is often so small—a gesture, a whisper. What first steps can someone take, even now, to live this truth?

Aung San Suu Kyi: Offer kindness where cruelty reigns. Speak truth when it risks all. Listen, even through discord. Nourish someone's hunger—for bread, for dignity, for hope. Refuse to dehumanize, even your foe. These are not small deeds—they are seismic. They gather, reshaping a nation's spirit, an unseen current turning the tide.

Alan Clements: You've woven Ashoka's legacy—a warlord turned vessel of peace; his edicts carved in stone for all to see. In our time, with our tools, how do we share such a vision?

Aung San Suu Kyi: We etch our truths not in stone, but in the living fabric of culture—through stories, through songs, through theater, through fearless voices in tea shops, in markets, in classrooms. Through quiet offerings in monasteries. Through every mother teaching her child to forgive—yes—but never to forget.

What matters is not grandeur, but sincerity. And repetition. Not as propaganda, but as prayer. Let the message rise—not from broadcasts, but from kitchens. Not from orders, but from gestures. Let it be spoken again and again until even the powerful can no longer pretend not to hear. This kind of truth-telling is not reserved for speeches. It belongs to everyone. And it belongs everywhere.

It lives in the way we greet one another with a smile, even when our hearts are heavy. In the way we give without being asked. In the way we serve tea to strangers. Help an elder lift a basket. Share a meal in silence. Or stop to listen when someone is grieving. These are not small things. These are how a nation remembers its soul.

Even in prison—perhaps especially there—it continues. In a glance of kindness unseen by the world. In a whispered word passed through silence. In the gesture of a folded blanket left without credit or command. These moments are the true edicts—etched not in rock, but in the soft walls of our humanity.

Alan, *the revolution of the spirit does not wait for perfect conditions. It begins wherever we are.* Whoever we are. It lives in the marketplace, in the monastery, in the border camp, in the exile's dream, in the bruised hands of a farmer, in the breath of a grandmother as she blesses seeds, she may never see flower. And it begins again and again in the one place that always remains: right here. In this moment. With this choice.

Alan Clements: And if Myanmar's people—bruised, burdened, grieving, yet still burning with longing—were to ask you not as a leader, but as a fellow human being: "Where do we begin?"—what would you say? Not just to the hopeful, but to the injured. To the ill. To the dying. To those who feel they have nothing left but breath and tears.

Aung San Suu Kyi: Begin there—with the breath and the tears. Begin wherever you are, especially when you believe you cannot. Begin from the floor of despair, from the ache of a body that will not heal, from the emptiness of a table where someone is missing. Begin by whispering to yourself what no one else can give you: that your life still matters. Even now. Especially now.

Transformation is not the luxury of the strong. It belongs to the trembling. The ones whose hands still shake but reach out anyway. The ones who cry alone in the dark and still rise. You do not need to be whole to begin. You need only to stay close to what is real in you—the breath, the wound, the longing not to disappear. That is where dignity lives. That is where peace begins.

Hold a hand. Offer your silence. Kiss the forehead of the dying. Feed a child. Light a candle even if no one sees it. Let the beauty you carry—not the beauty of ease, but of endurance—become your offering. A kind of altar made of moments. Each one a vow not to vanish.

This is not a metaphor. It is the revolution.

The future of Myanmar does not begin in palaces. It begins in broken homes, crowded clinics, refugee tents, and solitary cells. *It begins when even one person, forgotten by the world, decides not to forget themselves. That is the deepest act of resistance I know.*

Let us begin there. In quiet. In truth. In love that asks for nothing, and in lives that choose, again and again, not to close.

Alan Clements: Daw Suu, this dialogue has been a sacred gift. One final question, if I may. Of all that Ashoka left behind—his remorse, his reforms, his awakening—what do you most hope the people of Myanmar carry forward?

Aung San Suu Kyi: That no soul is beyond redemption. Not a tyrant. Not a prisoner. Not a nation drowning in sorrow. Ashoka butchered a hundred thousand lives before his heart broke open. But that breaking was not his end—it was his beginning.

Let us not wait for such ruin. Let us not wait for history to shame us into awakening. Let us rise now—before the flames devour what we love.

Ashoka's story is not just history. It is a mirror. A prophecy. A prayer. It asks: What will you do with your power? What will you make sacred again?

Let us answer not with promises, but with presence. Not with speeches, but with hands that heal and hearts that refuse to harden. Let our lives sing—not with perfection, but with perseverance. A mandala of peace, woven moment by moment, with compassion fierce as a mother's love, and mercy radiant as a river that carves stone through time. For Myanmar. And for the world.

Alan Clements: Thank you, Daw Suu. For your clarity. For your fierce grace. For reminding us that even in the deepest night, the human spirit can still choose light. Your words—like your life—are an invocation. A call to become more human, not less. And I will carry them forward. We all will.

Aung San Suu Kyi: Then let that be our vow, Alan. To carry forward— not my words, but the courage behind them.

Toliveasifeverymomentmattered. Becauseitdoes. Andtoremember: Peace is not made with friends. Peace is made when we refuse to forget each other—even when the world tells us to look away.

A MESSAGE TO THE BURMESE DIASPORA

Author's Prelude

There are those who carry nations not on their shoulders but in their hearts—a quiet, resolute devotion that transcends borders, languages, and the relentless march of time. They do not raise flags but cradle memories; they do not shout but remember with a fierce tenderness. In that remembrance, they keep a country alive—not as a relic of the past, but as a living, breathing promise.

This chapter is for them: the unseen guardians of Myanmar's spirit. For the mothers in New Jersey stirring rice porridge, their ears attuned to Mandalay's distant cries streaming in real-time, a lifeline across oceans. For the students in Melbourne, weaving urgent dispatches into translations between lectures, their words a bridge between worlds. For the monks in London, intoning ancient chants for villages reduced to embers, their voices a prayer against oblivion. For the youth in Toronto or Tokyo, holding Myanmar in fragments—a cadence, a melody, a wound they did not choose but fiercely claim as their own.

This is not a policy debate. It is a love letter that spans continents—a testament to the diaspora's unyielding fidelity to a homeland reshaped by history's unsparing hand. Here, Aung San Suu Kyi speaks not to strangers but to kindred spirits, her voice a clarion call from the confines of her Naypyidaw cell. "You are not distant observers—you are the pulse of our revolution," she declares, her words a balm and a summons. "Not separate from its struggle, but its vanguard—bearing the flame across oceans, keeping the spirit alive where silence once prevailed."

Her voice stirs the embers of memory, belonging, and agency, honoring those who piece together identity from remnants, whose unseen labor sustains Myanmar's heartbeat. Then, she lifts their gaze to the horizon, where possibility glimmers. The diaspora is not Myanmar's echo—it is its lifeblood. Those born beyond its borders are not diminished by distance but empowered by it, voicing Myanmar in new languages, dreaming its renewal with every act of remembrance.

This chapter is a vow: the thread of kinship remains unbroken. Let it resound in embassies and living rooms, in whispered prayers—not as a mere reunion, but as a rekindled purpose that defies erasure. Myanmar lives not in soil alone but in memory—in how fiercely that memory is guarded, cherished, and reborn.

To the diaspora: You are not the epilogue. You are the inheritance. The hour is now—to weave the past into a future where Myanmar's spirit rises, unbroken, through your hands.

◆ ◆ ◆

Alan Clements: Daw Suu, the Burmese diaspora has been pivotal in advocating for Myanmar's democratic aspirations worldwide. From London to New York, Bangkok to Tokyo, Los Angeles to Perth, they have mobilized resources, amplified awareness, and kept Myanmar's plight vivid in international consciousness.

Yet, being far from home presents challenges—alienation, fragmentation, and at times, despair. What message would you share with the diaspora to foster greater unity, resilience, and unwavering commitment to the struggle for democracy?

Aung San Suu Kyi: Alan, the diaspora is a vital lifeline for Myanmar. To those who have left our homeland—recently or generations past—I say: you are not apart from Myanmar; you are woven into her essence. Your voices, your actions, your advocacy forge a bridge between our suffering and the world's conscience.

I understand the isolation of being far from home, the strain of living between worlds, where daily struggles abroad may feel disconnected from our turmoil. Yet, your contributions are invaluable. You bear Myanmar's spirit wherever you go, sustaining our collective hope for liberation.

Alan Clements: Many in the diaspora voice feelings of powerlessness, longing to contribute more but unsure how to direct their efforts effectively. What practical guidance would you offer to transform that sense of helplessness into purposeful action?

Aung San Suu Kyi: To our diaspora—beloved kin of the Motherland— focus not on what lies beyond your reach, but on what your heart and hands can uniquely offer. You remain a living breath of Myanmar, no matter the miles. Each of you holds gifts—skills, resources, connections—and every gift finds its place in the tapestry of our freedom.

First, amplify your voices. Speak for the silenced. In London, Los Angeles, Tokyo, or Bangkok, awaken governments, international bodies, and human rights advocates. Press for targeted sanctions against the junta, demand humanitarian aid for our displaced, and insist on accountability for crimes against humanity. Your resolute voice is a lifeline across continents.

Second, give what you can. Financial support is not merely practical—it is solidarity. Whether it sustains a refugee's shelter, equips a medic, or educates a child, every contribution plants hope in the soil of suffering. No offering is too small; each is a vow: We have not forgotten.

Third, carry our truth. Write it, speak it, sing it into the world's air. From public squares to digital platforms, keep Myanmar's story alive in humanity's conscience. Silence abets tyranny; your witness dismantles it.

Above all, stand united. Let not ethnicities, faiths, or politics divide you. The junta thrives on our fractures—refuse to break. You are not resisting oppression alone; you are birthing a future where dignity embraces all. Unite, uplift, and build coalitions that celebrate the sacred diversity of our Motherland.

You are not exiles—you are Myanmar's living pulse. Through your steadfast compassion, you keep the vision of freedom radiant.

Alan Clements: Daw Suu, you've emphasized the vital need for unity within the diaspora. Yet, like Myanmar itself, the Burmese diaspora is richly diverse—weaving together myriad ethnicities, languages, and political visions. How can this vibrant mosaic be harmonized to forge a cohesive force for freedom?

Aung San Suu Kyi: Alan, diversity is not our burden; it is the lifeblood of our resilience. To the diaspora—beloved kin of many rivers, many peaks, many aspirations—I say: embrace the breadth of your differences as a wellspring of creativity, not a fracture to be feared.

Fix your gaze on the shared horizon—a free, democratic Myanmar that transcends every ethnic, spiritual, and ideological divide. See one another not through the scars of history, but through the promise of a future woven together. Create havens for dialogue, where wounds are voiced and heard with compassion, free from judgment.

Acknowledge the pain of the past—it is profound—but let it flow into bridges of mutual understanding, not walls of separation. Forge alliances rooted in dignity, respect, and an unwavering vow to our collective liberation.

Unity requires humility—to listen deeply, to atone, to forgive, to dream beyond old grievances. It asks us to place the greater good—the freedom of our people, the cries of 22,000 imprisoned voices—above personal or factional aims.

The junta thrives on our discord; our unity, born of diversity and nurtured by *anattā's truth of interconnectedness*, is their deepest dread—our mightiest force. Like a river's confluence, let your diverse streams merge into a single, unstoppable current for justice.

Alan Clements: Daw Suu, with reverence, I ask a question stirring the diaspora's hearts. Their devotion shines brightly—weaving Myanmar's truth into the world's conscience, organizing protests, raising funds, and gently pressing governments.

Though oceans apart, they cradle the resistance—nurturing the National Unity Government (NUG), supporting Ethnic Armed Organizations (EAOS), and offering vital aid to refugees along borders and displaced families within Myanmar. This tender network, spanning continents, weaves advocacy, logistics, and relief amidst ceaseless strain, deepened by the junta's cruelty and the world's hesitant gaze.

Yet, as the crisis lingers, weariness settles. Many wrestle with quiet anguish, whispering: Are we weaving change? Does our devotion hold? How can we offer more when time feels fleeting? What would you share with those steadfast yet weary, seeking strength, clarity, and hope to carry on?

Aung San Suu Kyi: Beloved kin, your devotion holds—its grace echoes beyond measure. Yes, you are weaving change. From these prison walls, I feel your quiet anguish, the ache of distance, the sorrow of witnessing our pain through fleeting images—headlines, faces, pleas. You pour your hearts into the NUG, tend our displaced, lift the silenced. You gather resources, cross barriers, weave bonds across borders. Yet, it feels too little. I know.

In solitude, I see what you may not: your gentle acts ripple outward, breathing life where despair would dwell. A meal for a child in a jungle camp, a blanket for a family on barren earth, medicine slipped through perilous borders, a whisper stirring a silent government—these are your offerings, light in our darkness. *We—in cells, exile, or hiding—live because of you.*

Myanmar endures a vast human emergency—that much you know. Over 20 million cry out for aid; more than three million wander, displaced. Villages lie in ashes, scorched by bombs. Families flee; the wounded fade without care. Trauma encircles us—children grow up without songs, women give birth in camps, elders die far from home.

In prison, 22,000 of us remain—some in solitary, most without healing, bound tightly as illness and sorrow deepen. And yet, even here, we share breaths of *mettā*, a pulse of resilience that refuses to die.

I, too, have known affliction. A prolonged illness left me weakened—dizzy, untended, alone. And now, I am injured from the earthquake. I turn to mindfulness, to *adhiṭṭhāna*, to quiet prayer. I rest inside the pain, vowing not to abandon myself. And the trial passes— temporary as it may be, not through force, but through gentle presence.

Your quiet strength is your truest ally. The revolution blooms in your heart's clarity, guided by *anicca's* truth that all pain is fleeting. Turn from numbness or hatred. Abide in humanity.

To offer more:

First, tend your spirit—not as a luxury, but as your primary act of solidarity. Before you speak, before you organize, before you give— sit. Breathe. Return to the ground beneath you. Hold yourself with the same fierce tenderness you would offer to a grieving mother or a trembling child in the camps of Myanmar. Let your own suffering be seen, held, honored.

Mettā is not just for others—it begins in the mirror. Mindfulness, prayer, stillness—whatever restores your presence—these are not escapes from the world; they are how we stay inside it without being devoured.

You are not a machine. You are not a headline. You are not required to always be brave. You are a living bridge between suffering and hope, and bridges, too, must be maintained. Rest. Cry. Laugh when laughter comes. Our work is sacred work.

Second, gather as one—not because unity is easy, but because division is deadly. Reach across the scars of history. Across region, race, and religion. Across accent and memory and wound. Do not wait for perfection. Do not wait until you feel ready. Let your gestures be imperfect, your trust hesitant, your attempts sometimes clumsy—but let them be real.

In the smallest gathering of shared care, a new nation is born. Even in silence, when two people stand together in truth, the weight of the world begins to shift. Myanmar's future will not be written by lone heroes. It will be written by circles of care. By communities that remember what it means to belong. So, reach out. Share your table. Walk beside someone not like you. Let reconciliation begin not in a treaty, but in a shared meal, a lifted burden, a name remembered.

Third, trust that every act—every act—shapes tomorrow. The world will try to convince you that your offerings are too small. That your voice is too quiet. That your solidarity cannot matter against the machines of war and empire. But this is the great lie of despair. Every coin given in love, every message sent in truth, every letter to a prisoner, every repost of a silenced voice, every prayer whispered in the dark—they build something. A field of conscience. A future that remembers. A thread in the vast fabric of resistance and renewal.

What you do in secret may become the light someone else sees by. What you give in silence may echo in places you will never know. Trust that. Trust that goodness, too, has gravity.

Does it hold? Yes—because you are vital. Your care, your conscience, lifts us. We—scattered, bruised, yet whole—are sustained by your presence.

This struggle renews our spirit. You are its keepers, reverent and true. Never waver—not for triumph's lure, but for truth's call, compassion's embrace. Like a river's gentle current, let your devotion flow, guiding Myanmar—and the world—to a rebirth of dignity, justice, and love.

Alan Clements: Daw Suu, with deep reverence, I lift a question stirring the hearts of the diaspora's children. Many, born or raised abroad, dwell far from Myanmar's soil, language, and lived sorrow. They weave new identities, embrace new freedoms, yet often feel a quiet distance from the pain and history of the land their families fled or were exiled from.

And yet, they are the future—a radiant, educated, globally woven generation of Burmese souls. What would you whisper to them—to these young hearts who may not yet feel their belonging?

Aung San Suu Kyi: Beloved children of the diaspora, I speak to you as a mother, a grandmother, a keeper of whispered hopes, holding Myanmar's dreams long enough to see them gently, fiercely entrusted to you. You are not apart from us. You are the living threads of a story still unfolding, woven with anatta's truth that binds us as one.

Though you may never have walked Myanmar's earth, or spoken her tongue with ease, or traced every scar of our complex past, you hold a sacred legacy within. You are heirs to a lineage of resilience—a culture that has faced colonization, dictatorship, and profound sorrow, yet never yielded its spirit.

You are not outsiders, but rightful keepers of a timeless grace. This legacy is not a weight—it is a choice. Reach for it with tender curiosity. Learn its stories—not to be tethered, but to be anchored. Seek the tales of your grandparents, of villages lost to time, of protests that stirred the world, of prisons that could not break us. *Know those who gave their lives for your freedom—not as distant figures, but as family, their courage pulsing in your veins.*

Your bond with Myanmar transcends place. It breathes in how you honor others, in the justice you seek, in the bridges you weave between cultures and continents. This is your spiritual inheritance, your moral calling, guided by *mettā's* gentle light.

You hold gifts your parents could only dream of—freedom to think, to learn, to grow. Embrace them. Be poets, healers, scholars, farmers, builders—but let Myanmar's memory deepen your compassion, her wisdom illuminate your path. In this hour, as 22,000 of us languish in prison, their silenced voices call to you—draw near through your acts of truth and love.

You are our ambassadors—not only to distant lands, but to tomorrow. Let no one say you do not belong. By blood, by spirit, by the tears your parents shed in far-off cities for your dignity, you are Myanmar's heart.

This struggle is not only for those on the front lines, but for you who cradle our stories, songs, and values. Write verses in Burmese and English. Craft tools for healing. Teach. Testify. Build peace from where you stand. This is your Myanmar, too.

When the moment calls—and it will—find your way to serve her, not from duty, but from love, from the quiet knowing that our nation's destiny rests in your hands. I believe, with all my heart, you will rise—with wisdom, dignity, and the radiant truth of your voice.

Like a river's gentle current, let your lives flow, carrying Myanmar's dreams to a rebirth of freedom, justice, and love.

Alan Clements: Daw Suu, thank you—for your luminous and intimate words of wisdom and hope to the children of the diaspora. What you offered was not only a message, but a blessing—spoken with the tenderness of a mother. I've seen firsthand how many of these young people live in two worlds at once—grappling with freedom while carrying ancestral grief they can barely name. And your words, I pray, stay with them—giving shape to a belonging they have always felt but rarely heard affirmed.

But around these children stands a wider circle—parents, elders, exiles, monks, and lifelong activists. An entire Burmese family dispersed around the globe, who—though forced from their homeland—have never abandoned their love for it. Many have spent decades living in quiet resistance, holding fast to memory, conscience, and an unshakable vision of freedom.

So, if I may, I'd like to ask: What is your call to the wider diaspora—across generations and continents? What role do you see them playing, not just in ending dictatorship, but in shaping Myanmar's future—its culture, its governance, and its spiritual resilience?

Aung San Suu Kyi: Alan, my vision for Myanmar has never been an abstraction. It is not a hope suspended in theory—it is a living vow—embedded in the collective conscience of our history, whispered in the prayers of our elders, and carried forward in the faces of our children.

To those in the diaspora, let me say this as clearly as I can: you are not distant observers of our suffering or mere allies to our cause. You are woven into the very fabric of this vision. You are not the echo—you are the voice. You are not a reflection of Myanmar's past—you are co-creators of her future. The living extension of a revolution that began not ten years ago, but centuries ago.

Ours is a country shaped by deep and complex wounds. We carry the shadows of colonial subjugation—the long scars left by British occupation that disrupted our sovereignty, our spiritual rhythms, and our stewardship of the land. We bore witness to the horrors of a world war fought on our soil. And after that, came the cold silence of dictatorship—not once, but again and again. Decades of terror. Fear institutionalized as policy. Violence normalized as governance. We have seen what happens when power is decoupled from conscience, and how the human spirit—when brutalized long enough—can grow numb to its own suffering.

And yet, despite all this, we endure. We are a nation of fierce resilience and exquisite beauty—composed of over 130 ethnic groups, each with its own languages, stories, and wisdom traditions. Our people practice Buddhism, Christianity, Islam, Hinduism, Judaism, animism— and despite immense hardship, we have largely coexisted in relative harmony. That quiet coexistence is not incidental—it is a resource. It is part of the vision we now carry forward.

We are not merely surviving history—we are shaping it. In many ways, our struggle is the birth cry of something greater: we are the youngest democracy on Earth, and these are our birth pains. It hurts. It confuses. It stretches us beyond what we thought we could bear. But it also reveals the true mettle of our people.

Because beneath all the sorrow, something is rising: a quiet, unbreakable revolution of the spirit. Our movement is not merely political. It is moral. It is spiritual. It is living proof that even under tyranny, the human conscience can remain intact. That hope can endure in the most unlikely places—in prison cells, in refugee camps, in whispered prayers passed from mother to child under threat of violence.

To the diaspora—you carry that revolution forward. Your advocacy sustains the world's gaze. Your voices pierce through censorship. Your fundraising saves lives. But even more than that: your memory keeps us whole. You remember us, and in that remembering, you keep the soul of the nation alive.

But I ask even more of you. I ask you to remember not only who you resist, but who you are. Remember your worth. Your value. Your dignity.

You are the descendants of warriors, poets, and peacemakers. The inheritors of a wisdom tradition stretching back millennia. And you are the architects of the Myanmar yet to come—a nation defined not by its borders or its armies, but by the strength of its compassion and the clarity of its conscience.

So, rise—not in rage alone, but in radical love. Rise in truth-telling. In unity. In your refusal to be divided, degraded, or diminished by those who fear your strength.

Let the world see what kind of democracy we are birthing here. Not imported. Not imposed. But born of blood, and breath, and a defiant tenderness that refuses to die. Let them see that Myanmar is not merely a place—it is a promise. And you—each of you—are its keepers.

Alan Clements: Daw Suu, it's difficult to speak after your words. What you just shared... it's more than a vision—it's a sacred vow. And I want to thank you, not only for the clarity and courage of your answer, but for the way you continue to hold the soul of Myanmar with such unwavering love.

If I may share something personal in response—Myanmar has been my spiritual home since I was a young man. At the age of twenty-nine, in one of the most uncertain and difficult moments of my life, I was welcomed into a monastery in Burma—not as an outsider, but as family. The Burmese people gave me everything: robes, food, medicine, shelter... and above all, the priceless, timeless teachings of the *Dhamma*.

They asked for nothing in return.

It was through the radical generosity of *dāna* that I learned what true freedom means—not in theory, but in practice. I was taught to sit still, to observe, to surrender, and to see. And to this day, I can say without hesitation that the most important teachers and mentors I've ever known came from your country, Daw Suu—many of them your own spiritual companions and closest allies. Some are still with us. Others have passed on, but not away. Their wisdom lives in us.

In whatever small way I've tried to bear witness over the years—to your people's suffering, your resistance, your moral revolution—it has been my way of repaying a debt I could never fully repay.

And so, I ask this next question from that place of gratitude, reverence, and responsibility: If Myanmar is, as you've said, not merely a country but a promise... how do we keep that promise alive, especially now? How do we transform this moment—not just into resistance, but into a legacy that endures? One that future generations will look back on and say: they didn't give up. They didn't let go of their humanity. They made something sacred from their suffering.

Aung San Suu Kyi: Alan, your words touch something very deep in me. There is something sacred about gratitude when it is born not of sentiment, but of truth. And I feel your truth—because I know it. I have lived it. So many of us have. To be broken open in Myanmar and made whole again—not by force, not by ideology, but by generosity. By the warmth of a village offering you a mat to sleep on. By the quiet faith of a teacher who asks for nothing but your presence.

By a Dhamma that asks only that you see—not through belief or opinion, but through direct knowing. To touch the truth of life for yourself. To see reality as it actually is—not as you want it to be, not as fear or habit shapes it—but clearly, intimately, as it reveals itself moment by moment.

This, too, is part of our revolution. A revolution not only of politics, but of perception. Not just of systems, but of seeing. And from that seeing, a new Myanmar may begin to take root. One breath, one act of clarity, at a time.

The world often looks at Myanmar and sees only its suffering: the coups, the prison camps, the war zones, the charred villages. And yes, these are real, and they demand to be seen. But what the world often misses is that beneath all this devastation lies a spiritual force so ancient, so unyielding, that no bullet can extinguish it. It is the force that allowed monks to walk barefoot into danger to offer blessings to the dying. It is the force that leads mothers to share rice with strangers, even after their homes have been burned to ash. It is the force that lives in every child who bows before a shrine before they understand what prayer even means. That is the Myanmar I know. That is the Myanmar I serve.

But to keep that spirit alive, we must be honest about what we have endured—not as victims, but as witnesses. Our country has been shaped by fire. We endured the weight of colonial rule—when Burma was carved into a possession of empire. The British dismantled our governance, co-opted our economy, and attempted to erase our spiritual life. They sowed division to make rule easier. They made fear a function of policy.

Then came the Second World War, and we were not just occupied—we were torn open by forces that saw our land as little more than a battlefield. Whole towns were annihilated. Sacred sites were leveled. Families were broken. Cultural memory was scorched by bombs dropped in a war that was never ours to fight.

We gained independence only to fall again—into silence, into fear, into rule by force. As I mentioned earlier, a succession of dictatorships institutionalized oppression. Torture became bureaucracy. Truth became a crime. And still, we resisted—not always with weapons, but with wisdom. With song. With prayer. With a dignity that could not be legislated or stripped away. And through it all, we remembered who we were.

We have not forgotten the Dhamma. And the Dhamma reminds us: impermanence is real. Power shifts. Regimes fall. But the clarity of a single mind—steady, compassionate, free—can outlast empires. We are the keepers of that clarity.

Our history is long—not fifty years, not even one century—but thousands of years deep. Our culture is older than our suffering. And the beauty of our diversity—the great mosaic of peoples who have lived on this land for centuries, each with their own languages, stories, customs, and faiths—is not a challenge to be solved. It is our inheritance. It is our strength. It is our offering to the world.

Yes, these are our birth pains. But they are not chaos. They are contractions. Signs of a deeper emergence. The emergence of a people who have known oppression and still choose not to hate. Who have every reason to give up—and still choose to build.

So how do we make this sacred? We do it by living it. By passing on the *Dhamma* not merely in words, but in how we walk. By planting trees even if we will never sit in their shade. By telling our children, "Yes, it was hard. Yes, we suffered. But we did not lose our humanity. We gave. We forgave. We endured."

Let our legacy be this: that in a time when cruelty was normalized, we chose kindness anyway. That in an age of division, we stitched community back together with the golden thread of patience. That when the world said we were broken, we rose—not with vengeance, but with vision.

And to all who carry Myanmar in your heart—whether inside her borders or across oceans—I say: you are the stewards of this promise. Every act of compassion. Every effort to listen across difference. Every moment of disciplined hope. That is how we keep the promise alive. That is how we become the ancestors we once prayed for.

Because in the end, the revolution we are fighting for is not merely a transfer of power. It is a restoration of truth. Of love. Of human dignity. That is the Myanmar I still believe in.

And that is the Myanmar we are becoming.

Alan Clements: Daw Suu, as we know all too well, the military regime continues its merciless war on truth and human dignity. It has imprisoned Myanmar's democratically elected leaders—including you, President Win Myint, and more than 22,000 others across the country.

It has been nothing less than the decapitation of democracy. Cabinet ministers. Members of Parliament. Activists. Musicians. Filmmakers. Poets. Authors. Professors. Doctors. Teachers. Civil servants. Nurses. Monks. Nuns. Mothers. Grandparents. Even children. Some languish in solitary confinement. Most are denied medical care. Many endure psychological torment and slow, deliberate torture. Some have been executed. Others have simply disappeared.

This is not merely a political crisis—it is a collapse of conscience, a moral emergency of global proportions.

And yet, so much of the world looks away. Distracted. Disengaged. Deaf to the cries behind the wire. So, I ask you now: How can the Burmese diaspora—and the wider international community—act not symbolically, but with strategy, urgency, and precision? What must be done to demand your freedom—and the release of every political prisoner in Myanmar?

Aung San Suu Kyi: Alan, this is not a side issue in our revolution—it is its core, its pulse, its unyielding truth. There can be no meaningful peace. No honest reconciliation. No legitimate democracy—while the conscience of a nation remains locked behind prison doors.

We—the imprisoned—are not abstractions. We are not slogans. We are lives. Flesh and blood. Memory and breath. We are teachers who once opened minds, now silenced. We are doctors who once healed the broken, now left to suffer untreated. We are monks, poets, farmers, mothers. We are the breath of this country—and we are being suffocated in the dark.

The world must understand: every single day of our captivity is a day stolen from Myanmar's future—its healing, its progress, its dignity.

To the diaspora—and to all who claim to care about freedom—I say this with love and urgency: Make our release your unwavering priority. Not an afterthought. Not a polite request. Not an item on a list. But the heartbeat of your advocacy.

Raise our names in every capital. Let no government, no corporation, no diplomat claim ignorance. Make our captivity a red line—a moral emergency that cannot be negotiated away. Your voices must be unrelenting. Your advocacy, relentless. Your conscience, loud.

And go further than words. Organize. Mobilize. Coordinate. Write to your elected officials. Petition. Protest. Wherever silence takes root—disturb it. Wherever apathy settles—interrupt it. Because visibility is protection. And each protest, each poster, each post—each one chips away at the regime's armor of secrecy and shame.

Support the work of truth-telling. Support the journalists who risk their lives to document our erasure. Support the lawyers building the future cases. Support the families of the disappeared. Support those who shine a light into the darkest corridors of our nation's conscience.

Because truth is not only a shield. It is a summons. A direction. A path out of madness. And those who walk it now—you among them—are building the moral infrastructure of the Myanmar that will rise.

So, I ask you—not from a place of hope alone, but from the full weight of this lived fire: Carry this cause as you would carry a loved one from a burning house. Urgently. Fiercely. Without delay. Because until every voice is freed, None of us are free. And no future worth living can be built on the silence of its most courageous souls.

Alan Clements: May the urgency of your plea catch fire across the world. May it ride side by side with the courage of those on the front lines—revolutionaries risking everything to oust the terrorist regime. And may these twin forces of resistance—one armed, one moral—two inseparable rhythms in the song of shared freedom, bring light to the regime's grotesque attempt to demonize and dehumanize democracy in Burma.

This is not merely about a distant Southeast Asian nation. It is about the global family of freedom lovers—a sacred alliance stitched into the shared fabric of democracy. A family that lives, breathes, and rises through one another. *Ubuntu: I am because we are.*

Which brings me to my question: The regime's violence has led many to take up arms. Meanwhile, powerful nations like China and Russia continue to prop up the junta, deepening the fracture and complicating every path forward.

In this brutal, divided terrain—how can the Burmese diaspora move with clarity and courage, while still honoring peace, justice, and integrity? How do we resist without becoming what we oppose?

Aung San Suu Kyi: Alan, we cannot afford illusions—but neither can we afford despair. The world is complex. So is this conflict. But complexity must never be used as an excuse for paralysis or silence. We must learn to move through the complexity without losing our clarity.

To the diaspora, I say: you must act with both strategy and conscience. Build coalitions wherever you can—with nations, organizations, and peoples who stand for freedom. Leverage every diplomatic avenue. Apply pressure wherever the regime seeks legitimacy. Isolate them, expose them, deny them the comfort of international indifference. *No dictatorship can thrive indefinitely when light is persistently and intelligently directed at its foundations.*

But just as importantly, never abandon the ethical core of our struggle. Amplify nonviolent resistance wherever possible. Support civil disobedience. Support the quiet acts of spiritual and cultural defiance that keep dignity alive even in the darkest places. *Peace built on dignity and truth endures far longer than peace forced by fear.*

We must also begin to heal even before the last bullet is fired. Foster dialogue—within Myanmar and beyond it. Among ethnic groups. Across generations. Across the divisions that history has sown. *We cannot rebuild a free Myanmar if we are divided from ourselves. Healing must start now—not after victory, but alongside it.*

These actions are not glamorous. They do not make headlines. But they build the foundations of a future we can be proud of. A future rooted not in vengeance, but in wisdom.

Alan Clements: Daw Suu, as we bring this chapter to a close, what message would you like to leave the diaspora with—especially those who feel far from home, but tethered to its fate?

Aung San Suu Kyi: Along with what I have said before, to the diaspora, I say this: you are not bystanders in our struggle. You are the keepers of the flame. When our voices are silenced here, you become our echo. When we are unseen, you are our witness. And when the world forgets, you must remember—not quietly, but with the full clarity of your conscience.

Let your love for Myanmar be radical. Let it be tireless. Let it be wise. And let the call for freedom—for every political prisoner—be at the center of all you do. Not merely as a cause, but as a vow made with your whole heart.

To the young among you: you may have been born far from our soil, but you are no less its children. Carry our stories. Carry our songs. Carry our spirit. And when the time comes—and it will—bring your skills, your truth, your compassion home. *Myanmar will need you—not someday, but soon.*

And to all of you: know that your actions matter. Your solidarity matters. Every step you take in truth sends a signal to those of us in the dark: we are not forgotten. The light is still alive. *And as long as the light lives, so does the future.*

Let the strength of your conviction be your protest. Let the depth of your compassion be your resistance. Let your unity be the revolution.

Because in the end, it will not be the tyrants who are remembered. It will be those who chose to care. Those who rose—not for revenge, but for justice. Those who carried the future inside them like a flame, and passed it forward, one step, one song, one sacred act at a time.

You are that flame. *Carry it forward.* It is the soul of our struggle— and the hope of our nation's future.

CHAPTER EIGHTEEN

FEARLESS DISRUPTERS— A CALL TO ACTION

———

Author's Prelude

There are moments in history when silence ceases to be neutrality and becomes betrayal. This chapter does not rise from anger, but from refusal—a refusal to descend into quiet complicity.

What follows is not a celebration of heroism, but a reckoning with the price of conscience. Aung San Suu Kyi draws us into the inner sanctum of moral courage—a space where truth is spoken not to impress, but to transform. She charts the path of fearless disruptors—those luminous beings who, though trembling with fear, confront tyranny with the fire of integrity and the discipline of love.

Here, you'll encounter those who stood unshaken in the storm: Dr. Myint Maung, who meditated through cancer behind bars. Monks who transformed prison cells into sanctuaries. Exiles who turned displacement into resistance—and distance into lifelines. These are not myths. They are reminders of what awakens in us when we remember who we truly are.

This chapter is both mirror and manifesto—a compass for the soul in times of collapse. Its message is both intimate and universal: conscience is not an ornament. It is a lineage. And we, each of us, are its rightful heirs.

May I invite you to receive these words not as comfort, but as a vow. Let them rise like a quiet fire in the marrow of your being. And may the flame carried by fearless disruptors—in Myanmar and across the world—as Aung San Suu Kyi affirms— "light the way for all who still dare to stand, to speak, and to love in the face of brutality."

Because, as you will soon read: "Courage is not the absence of fear—it is the audacity to move forward anyway. Not fueled by rage, but anchored in the uncompromising grace of truth."

◆ ◆ ◆

Alan Clements: Daw Suu, across continents and generations, certain rare souls stand in the shadow of fear and weave threads of defiant courage—threads that unravel the machinery of oppression. They seek neither glory nor martyrdom, but through an unshakable vow to *sacca*—truth—they become the pulse of moral revolutions. In Myanmar, we see them: doctors mending the wounded in secret, monks meditating amidst prison chains, youth chanting defiance beneath death's gaze.

In your view, what awakens this fearless fidelity to conscience? What spiritual and psychological qualities support these disruptors—artists, poets, healers, and warriors—who, against towering odds, choose truth over safety, dignity over despair, breathing life into the vow of justice?

In this hour, as we both know, more than 22,000 political prisoners languish in Myanmar's prisons; how might their courage stir the diaspora—and all who hold Myanmar in their hearts—to act with renewed urgency and unwavering love?

Aung San Suu Kyi: Alan, fearless disruptors are not born without fear; they are conscious individuals who choose courage, moment by moment, beneath fear's shadow. Their bravery is not bravado—it is the steady, radiant pulse of a heart that refuses to yield to silence.

In my humble opinion, this kind of courage does not bloom from impulse, but from a profound and intimate communion with, as you said, *sacca*—truth—rooted in *mettā*'s boundless, loving-compassion and nourished by an unshakable vow to justice, as our late beloved *Dhamma* teacher, Venerable Sayadaw U Pandita, taught us through *citta-visuddhi*: the purification of mind that anchors such resolve.

These luminous bearers of conscience are guided not by ideology or vengeance, but by a moral clarity and courage that sees—and feels—suffering and cannot turn away. To remain silent would be a wound deeper than any tyranny could inflict. Their strength lies in the seamless weave of values and deeds—a tapestry of integrity unbroken, even when freedom—or life—is the cost.

Here in Myanmar, our thousands of prisoners of conscience languish in tortuous conditions, their quiet defiance—doctors mending wounds in secrecy, nuns meditating amidst iron bars, youth whispering truth beneath death's gaze—mirrors the world's millions of unsung disruptors. Their courage is a summons, urging the diaspora to carry this living legacy of truth with reverence and resolve.

Alan Clements: Daw Suu, this alignment of heart and action—this unwavering compass of conscience—has pulsed through every great struggle for justice, from the Civil Rights movement in America to the fearless resistance unfolding in Myanmar today. But the cost of such moral clarity is often immense: ridicule, isolation, imprisonment, exile, even death. And yet, some still rise—again and again—with fearless grace, not bitterness.

What, in your understanding, sustains these individuals when the forces arrayed against them feel insurmountable? What inner resource—spiritual, psychological, or communal—allows them to remain anchored in truth, when the world around them demands surrender?

Aung San Suu Kyi: They are anchored not by certainty, but by a sacred responsibility—not to ego or ideology, but to life itself. To the quiet vow to protect what still matters. These disruptors are not made of stone. They are human—vulnerable, trembling, choosing again and again to act in the presence of fear. And yet, they cultivate *upekkhā*—equanimity—not as indifference, but as Sayadaw U Pandita taught us: a steady, embodied strength that holds heartbreak without hardening, that meets suffering without collapse.

This kind of empowerment is not the absence of vulnerability—it is the full embrace of it. It is the courage to meet one's pain and or hesitation without turning away. And that includes the sacred, often hidden, necessity of *self-mettā* and *self-karuṇā*—a tenderness toward one's own wounds, one's fatigue, one's longing. Without that compassion for the self, our compassion for others becomes brittle. We must not only extend grace outward—we must dwell within it ourselves.

To live this way, especially in captivity, is to take unflinching refuge in *anicca*—the lived-truth of impermanence. *This too shall pass.* That is not a cliché, but a lifeline. The storm is not forever. And even the darkest night, if held with mindful presence, can become a field of radical transformation.

I believe this is where the sacredness of the human condition reveals itself most powerfully—in what some traditions call the dark night of the soul. That hour when all certainties fall away and one must decide: *will I collapse into bitterness, or will I break open? Will I allow suffering to hollow me out—or to hallow me?*

For those who dare to meet that moment fully, something changes. A deeper stillness arises. A more tender resolve. A grace not born of escape, but of union with mystery. And then—one returns. To the body. To the breath. To the ground of one's being. To the simple, radical discipline of love.

Nelson Mandela once said that not a single day passed in his twenty-seven years of imprisonment when he did not think about his freedom—and the freedom of his sisters and brothers, and of all South Africa's children. That is not a distraction from suffering; it is a vow made *inside* it. An inner uprising of faith—not in inevitability, but in the possibility of transformation.

Here in Myanmar, where thousands still endure—some in solitude, others pressed together in cells where illness spreads and silence thickens—I hear of this kind of faith kept alive: prisoners sharing crusts of bread, whispering *mettā* into aching ears, holding each other upright when there is no strength left to stand. Their resistance is not spectacle—it is sacred. Their strength is not in triumph, but in integrity. Not in having power, but in refusing to betray what is most human.

They remind us: you can be bound in chains and still walk in truth. You can be denied freedom, and still embody it.

That is why I say to the diaspora, and to all who still believe in this sacred fight for justice: these individuals are not merely symbols—they are living embodiments of the *Dhamma*.

Let their light become your own. Carry it not as a burden, but as a blessing. Let it guide you—through despair, through doubt, through the long night. Because dawn will come. And when it does, it must find us standing—not hardened, but tempered; broken, at times—yes—but still whole.

Alan Clements: Daw Suu, your wisdom weaves a timeless thread through the moral tapestry of history—not inscribed in ink, but carved in sacrifice. Across eras and continents, rare souls have risen—unbowed by power, their hearts throbbing with an unshakable vow to truth.

Modern disruptors—Mahatma Gandhi, Martin Luther King Jr., Nelson Mandela, Rosa Parks—wielded not weapons, but vision. They stood anchored in moral clarity and an unwavering commitment to humanity's awakening. As you have, they endured vilification, censorship, and imprisonment—some even paid with their lives. Yet, their spirits remained luminous, beacons in the darkness of oppression.

Their defiance was not merely against regimes, but against the machinery of fear and the architecture of ignorance. They sought to dismantle it—not with vengeance, but with a piercing clarity that exposed injustice and stirred the dormant conscience of the world.

So, I ask: what enduring truth do their lives reveal about the anatomy of moral resolve? And in this hour—when Myanmar's diaspora cradles your revolution across oceans—how might their legacy guide us to forge a future grounded in freedom, truth, and justice?

Aung San Suu Kyi: From this solitary cell, where silence is both captor and teacher, I see them—radiant figures in our shadowed age, guided not by dogma, but by a presence that breathes sacca—truth.

Gandhi, King, Mandela, Parks—and countless others—were not untouchable heroes, but mortals who wept, faltered, yet stood resolute against the weight of suffering. Their lives, like mine, are not sagas of triumph, but testaments to the tenacity of choosing truth over comfort, breath by relentless breath.

Gandhi's *satyagraha*—the unyielding call of truth—wove a nation's freedom from empire's chains, not with force, but with the quiet, indomitable might of the spirit. Martin Luther King Jr., battered by batons and jails, dreamed not merely of justice, but of a beloved community where dignity binds all as one. His voice still summons us to rise. Nelson Mandela, bound for 27 years, offered not vengeance but reconciliation, a blade of *mettā*—loving-kindness—that severed the roots of hatred. Rosa Parks, with one steadfast refusal, unleashed a thunderclap of truth, awakening a nation's conscience to its own moral failing.

Their eternal truth is this: power without *sacca* is a hollow masquerade. One heart, rooted in *adhiṭṭhāna*—unshakable resolve—can fracture fear's dominion. This is no fable.

In Myanmar's cells, where resisters languish, I hear whispers of it: a prisoner sharing a scrap of rice, a monk's breath steadying the dark. Across the world, it echoes, from way back—Juliano Mer-Khamis, kindling art as rebellion in Palestine's Freedom Theatre until his murder in 2011; Hiba Abubaker, weaving feminist hope in Sudan's war-torn shadows amid ongoing conflict. And so many others, unnamed but undaunted.

These disruptors bore scars, doubts, dread. Yet, they embraced *upekkhā*—equanimity—not as retreat, but as a fierce stillness that cradles suffering without yielding to despair. From this confinement, where walls whisper *anicca*—the impermanence of all pain—I see their courage as a river's eternal tide, flowing through every act of defiance, every whisper of resistance.

To Myanmar's diaspora, my kin, I speak from these shadows: let their lives be your compass. Your voices, your offerings, your remembrance are the lifeblood of our revolution.

Let your actions weave *mettā's* radiant, unyielding love—fierce, precise, resolute. History will judge not your titles, but the truth you live, the love you give. Rise, not to echo their resolve, but to embody it, forging a Myanmar—and a world—reborn in freedom, truth, and justice.

Alan Clements: Daw Suu, as we've discussed, throughout history, those who dare to disrupt injustice often pay a price far beyond politics—imprisonment, exile, vilification, even the attempted erasure of their very names. And yet, some remain inwardly unshaken. They hold fast to a kind of authenticity that seems untouched by fear or humiliation.

You've already spoken with such depth about the spiritual foundations of this path. But if I may ask us to go deeper still: from where you sit now—surrounded by silence, by uncertainty—what sustains that inner resilience? What allows a disruptor to preserve the integrity of their conscience, and the clarity of their purpose, when everything around them is designed to shatter it?

Aung San Suu Kyi: By dwelling in truth, their authenticity becomes not a shield of defiance, but a sanctuary of integrity. In this cell—where solitude strips away every illusion of identity or status—I've come to see more clearly: fearless disruptors do not conquer fear; they simply refuse to be ruled by it.

It is a matter of mindfulness. And self-respect.

Of course, they do not pretend to be invulnerable. They tremble. They grieve. They ache. But they do not sever their vow to *sacca*—to truth. Because to betray that vow would inflict a wound deeper than any prison ever could.

Mindful authenticity, in this context, is not performance—it is practice. It is presence. It is a spiritual discipline. Cultivated daily, moment by moment, in silence—through informed awareness, ethical discernment, and the courageous patience to remain inwardly clear even when the world collapses around you.

As Sayadaw U Pandita taught us, this is the essence of *adhiṭṭhāna*—unshakable determination rooted not in force, but in wisdom. And yes, that steadiness is not forged through willpower alone—it is tempered by humility, deepened by vulnerability, and made whole by heartfulness.

Resilience is not the absence of suffering. It is the courage to feel that suffering fully—and remain intact. It rises from within, nourished by silence, anchored in solitude, and sustained by the quiet knowing that one's life belongs to something greater than the self.

In the prison cells of Myanmar—crowded or solitary—this spirit endures. A whispered chant. A glance between cellmates. A half-smile exchanged in the dark. These are our sacraments.

So too, I imagine, did Rosa Parks draw strength—not from spectacle, but from the invisible threads of her community's dignity, faith, and quiet, righteous rage. Her stillness was a signal. Her body, a boundary. Her refusal, a beginning.

So, I would say: disruptors endure not by hardening against pain, but—as I have so often said—by softening into *mettā*. Into a radical, unwavering, love-infused compassion. A *mettā* directed not only toward those they defend, but also—unthinkably—toward those who harm them. Not as appeasement, but as *sacred defiance*. A refusal to let cruelty shape their soul.

This is the highest discipline. This is their invisible monastery.

Alan Clements: Thank you, Daw Suu. Before we close, may I ask you to reflect—gently, intimately—on those you knew and loved, whose courage lit the darkest corners of Myanmar's prisons?

I ask not to create a hierarchy of disruptors—because I believe, as I know you do, that every woman, every man, every child who rises with dignity in the face of injustice carries an equal weight of moral grace. This question comes not from a place of distinction, but reverence. What do you remember of them—not just their resistance, but their tenderness, their presence, their humanity?

Aung San Suu Kyi: Thank you, Alan. I'm so grateful you said what you did—that we must not elevate a few and forget the many. I couldn't agree more. The spirit of resistance is not a performance reserved for the known. It is a light that flickers in countless quiet acts—in the woman who feeds a fugitive in secret, the child who carries messages between safe houses, the teacher who refuses to rewrite truth. Every one of them, known or nameless, is sacred.

But yes, since you ask, there are some I knew well—men whose companionship and moral clarity shaped my own path, and whose memories live with me still.

Dr. Myint Maung. A healer, a parliamentarian, and above all, a man of the *Dhamma*. Even as cancer overtook his body behind bars, he refused to harden. He practiced *mettā* for his jailers. He whispered teachings to those in despair. He once told me, *"Daw Suu, we must live every hour as if we are dying and being reborn, because we are. And that truth—it purifies."* He died in custody, denied care, up until the final week, I'm told. But he died free—because his mind had never been conquered.

Saya U Win Tin. He chose, after release, to wear his blue prison shirt every day—as if to say: 'I carry them with me, all of them, still imprisoned.' He turned cloth into conscience. His wit never dulled. His courage was sharp but never bitter. He taught us that memory is resistance.

Uncle U Kyi Maung. He mentored me in the early days—firm, principled, and warm. His dignity was never loud. He had a way of laughing that cut through fear. A revolutionary, yes, but also a father, a listener. He reminded me that leadership is presence, not command.

Saya U Tin Oo. Our General. Our elder. His years in prison only deepened his loyalty to the people. He believed in nonviolence not because he was naïve, but because he had seen too much war. In confinement, he found clarity. His faith in our future never wavered.

These men—each imprisoned for nearly two decades, or more— did not merely endure incarceration. They transformed it. They turned their cells into monasteries, their silence into classrooms, their suffering into temples of truth. They mentored the young, shared food when there was little, and practiced *mettā* even through sickness and despair.

They preserved what the regime most feared—and tried desperately to extinguish: the inner revolution.

And still, I must say again—none of them stood alone. Their courage was mirrored by thousands: students beaten in alleyways, farmers tortured for sheltering rebels, grandmothers hiding leaflets in their prayer books. Their names may not be remembered by the tyrants—but they are remembered in the marrow of our nation's conscience and awakening.

To the diaspora, to every person reading this—I ask you to carry these lives forward. Not in sorrow, but in gratitude. Not as martyrs, but as reminders: the heart cannot be caged. The spirit, when anchored in love and truth, becomes unbreakable.

Alan Clements: It's extraordinary to hear how they turned confinement into a monastery, a school, a sanctuary for truth.

Aung San Suu Kyi: Yes. They revealed a truth no regime can ever imprison: you can cage a body—but not a heart that's free.

In Myanmar's prisons, the nameless endure. Some in silence. Some in sickness. Yet their dignity shines unquenched. To them I say: your light is not forgotten; it guides us still. *You are not waiting to be free—you are already free; in the invincible truth you live.*

And to the diaspora: let their resolve become your own. Let it be your vow—a river's eternal tide moving toward justice.

Alan Clements: As we reflect on these disruptors, what universal message do they offer activists worldwide?

Aung San Suu Kyi: Their message is raw, radiant, and urgent: freedom is not bestowed—it is forged. It is not given by rulers, but claimed by those who dare to live in truth.

Sayadaw U Pandita once said, *"Conquer your heart, and the world follows."* This is the essence of disruption—not domination, but transformation. Not conquest of others, but liberation of the self. Fearless disruptors transmute suffering into strength. Isolation into communion. Silence into sacred defiance.

Their rebellion is not against one tyrant, but against the inner chains—fear, hatred, delusion—that bind every society, every age. From this cell, I see it: in Myanmar's streets, where youth defy bullets with creative acts of revolutionary defiance.

To activists worldwide: your truth is your power, your compassion your shield. Let each act ripple, weaving a global tapestry of dignity and justice.

Alan Clements: Daw Suu, as we close, what would you say to disruptors on the front lines—those risking everything for freedom and justice?

Aung San Suu Kyi: To disruptors everywhere, I speak not only from solitude—but from shared struggle. Your courage is a lantern, lighting paths that history has yet to chart. You are not alone. Every truth you speak, every injustice you face, every kindness you offer in defiance of cruelty—weaves a tapestry vast enough to cradle the future. You are the heirs of Gandhi's *satyagraha*, King's dream, Mandela's forgiveness, Parks's quiet rebellion. You stand in a lineage of grace and fire.

Hold fast to *adhiṭṭhāna*—resolve that outlasts fear. Let *mettā* guide your steps. Even your adversaries carry suffering. Loving-kindness is not weakness—it is the fiercest power of all.

Your vision is not distant. It is already here, alive in your breath, kindled with each act of sacred resistance. In Myanmar's prisons, names are whispered like prayers. You are one of them. Walk forward, beloved kin. For you are the creators of a new world—a world where truth prevails, and justice finally breathes.

Alan Clements: Daw Suu, if you were to leave behind a single message—a distilled manifesto—for disruptors around the world, what would it contain?

Aung San Suu Kyi: From this cell, where silence sharpens the soul, I offer not instructions—but a spirit. A way of walking. A breath-shaped vow born not just of my own journey, but of Myanmar's long, unbroken struggle for dignity and freedom. It is not a doctrine. It is a discipline. A lived presence. A daily choice to meet each moment with courage instead of collapse, clarity instead of illusion, compassion instead of rage.

And this vow is not mine alone. It belongs to every soul who stood when falling would have been easier. To the students beaten and killed in 1988, who marched for a freedom they might never taste. To the monks disrobed, tortured, and disappeared in 2007, whose chants echoed even through locked prison gates. To the fierce, unarmed lovers of liberty who vanished in 2021 beneath the thunder of tanks and silence of global indifference. To the mothers—right now—pressing their children to their chest, hiding them from bullets with trembling hands and whispered prayers. They are the true authors of this vow. It is written not in ink, but in blood, in breath, in quiet acts of unyielding care.

If I speak it now, it is only to pass it on—to keep the flame alive. So that in the darkest hours, we may remember who we are. And what we still refuse to become.

Live *sacca*—truth—as your breath. Let *mettā* be your shield—tender, unwavering, and fierce. Root your strength in *adhiṭṭhāna*, anchored in the wisdom of *anicca*: all things pass. All pain. All regimes. All darkness.

Weave your life as a tapestry. Let every action be a thread, every refusal to kneel a sacred knot. Let your legacy be one of beauty, of love, of awakening.

To all disruptors: you are not solitary sparks—you are a river. A tide. An unquenchable current flowing toward justice. Carry this legacy, beloved kin, not as a burden, but as a light—shaping a future where dignity is not a dream, but a shared, breathing truth.

Aung San Suu Kyi: Let me offer it as simply and fiercely as I can: From this narrow cell—where solitude deepens into silence, and silence sharpens into truth—I offer no commandments, only a communion of breath and conscience. This is not a doctrine. It is a distilled vow. A current of resolve drawn from the undying spirit of my people.

A MANIFESTO FOR FEARLESS DISRUPTERS

Spoken by Aung San Suu Kyi as an offering of guidance and solidarity to all who dare to rise, rooted in Myanmar's unbroken revolutionary spirit

1. Begin with Truth

Truth is no longer a luxury; it is the ground beneath your feet as the world collapses around you. In Myanmar today, propaganda calls massacres "security," airstrikes "peacekeeping," starvation "order." And yet, truth remains. It binds the wounded crossing rivers at night; it steadies the hand that shelters a fugitive child. Before you act—before you resist, before you speak, before you endure—ask yourself only this: *Am I faithful to truth, to the suffering of my people?* If you are, no gun, no prison, no tyranny can unmake you. In Insein Jail, even when flesh was broken, our poets scratched verses into the walls—because truth was their last and only country.

"It is not power that corrupts but fear. Fear of losing power corrupts those who wield it and fear of the scourge of power corrupts those who are subject to it."
—AUNG SAN SUU KYI

2. Transcend Fear, Don't Erase It

Fear walks with us all. It tightens the breath before a hidden crossing. It echoes in the roar of gunships over a village. Do not despise fear. Let it speak. Then walk forward anyway. You need not be unafraid to be free. You need only refuse to be ruled by terror. I have seen young Burmese stand trembling before tear gas and bullets—and still they sang. Courage is not the absence of fear. It is the decision that fear will not dictate who you are.

"The only real prison is fear, and the only real freedom is freedom from fear."
—AUNG SAN SUU KYI

3. Do Not Mirror Your Oppressors

It is easy, in the face of cruelty, to believe that cruelty is power. But true power lies elsewhere. We have been taught brutality—villages burned, prisoners tortured, voices silenced—but we must not become what we resist. In the darkest hours of Myanmar's struggle, monks walked unarmed toward rifles, and civilians shielded the wounded with bare hands. To meet violence with hatred is to lose ourselves. Our strength is not in how much we can destroy, but in how deeply we can remain human.

"Darkness cannot drive out darkness; only light can do that."
—MARTIN LUTHER KING JR.

4. Live Small, Dream Vast

Revolution does not always wear a uniform. It often wears a worn shawl, a calloused hand, a whispered prayer. In Myanmar, it lives in the mother smuggling rice across checkpoints, the medic stitching wounds in jungle camps, the teacher reciting lessons under torn tarpaulins. These acts seem small. They are not. They are the scaffolding of a future yet unseen. Dream beyond the barricades. Beyond the ruins of Arakan. Beyond the burning fields of Sagaing. Hold the vision of a land restored—not by conquest, but by the patient, luminous work of countless unseen hands.

"You must be the change you wish to see in the world."
—MAHATMA GANDHI

5. Alchemize Your Pain

Pain is not the enemy. It is the crucible where courage is forged. In Myanmar, our grief is a river—flowing from the massacres of 1988 to the fallen angels of 2021. Bury your dead, honor them with tears, but let their memory rise as action. I have seen mothers in Bago turn mourning into marches, and widows in Chin hills weave defiance into every thread. Let your pain deepen your love, not your hatred. Let it make you fierce with compassion. Only then does suffering become strength.

"Out of great suffering can come great strength, and out of
great strength can come great peace."
—AUNG SAN SUU KYI

6. Find Strength in Each Other

No one endures alone. In Myanmar, we have survived because we stood together—exiles sharing rice, resistance fighters training side by side in the jungles, families hiding the hunted under their roofs. In 1988, we sang from prison cells; in 2021, we banged pots against tyranny. Community is more than survival—it is our first act of defiance, and our final line of hope. Feed one another. Shelter one another. Carry each other's burdens across the broken bridges of this world. In each other, we become unbreakable.

"Alone we can do so little; together we can do so much."
—HELEN KELLER

7. Carry the Long View

Despair whispers that oppression is eternal. But history speaks louder. We have outlived the British Raj, the bombs of world wars, the terror of countless juntas. Freedom is not a sudden gift—it is a long, aching pilgrimage. Every step through blood and ruin matters. Even when the horizon seems to recede, walk toward it. Walk for those who can no longer walk beside you. Walk until hope is not a dream, but a ground you stand upon.

"You should never let your fears prevent you from doing what you know is right."
—AUNG SAN SUU KYI

8. Practice Sacred Resistance

Resistance is not only an act of defiance—it is an act of devotion. In Myanmar, monks blessed the dying on bloodied streets; nurses stitched wounds by candlelight in hidden clinics; teachers whispered lessons in jungle caves. Every gesture that preserves life, dignity, or truth becomes sacred. Do not believe that only weapons can defeat tyranny. The smallest act of compassion—offered in the face of fear—is a revolution in itself. Live in such a way that your very existence defies oppression with grace.

"The only way to deal with an unfree world is to become so absolutely free that your very existence is an act of rebellion."
—ALBERT CAMUS

9. Know That Liberation is Internal

The body can be imprisoned. The village can be burned. The future can be stolen. But the mind—if guarded carefully—remains sovereign. Dr. Myint Maung, after many long years of suffering without care in prison, was taken to a hospital only at the end. Even then, he did not cling to fear or bitterness. He smiled once, some years back, and said to me: *"Just birth and death, Daw Suu—all the time."* Chains can shackle flesh, but they cannot bind the awakened heart. Freedom begins within. And a spirit anchored in truth cannot be conquered—not by walls, not by guns, not even by death itself.

"Real freedom is freedom from fear, and unless you can live free from fear you cannot live a dignified human life."
—AUNG SAN SUU KYI

10. Pass the Flame

You are not fighting only for today. You are planting the seeds of tomorrow. In Myanmar, across generations of uprising and exile, we have passed our stories—through whispered songs, hidden poems, quiet acts of remembrance. Teach your children the names of our fallen, the truths of our struggles, the dignity of our hopes. Teach them our languages—Burmese, Karen, Shan, Chin—so that memory is not lost but lives on as action. You are not just heirs of the past. You are architects of the future. Pass the flame with tenderness and with courage, so that it grows brighter in every hand that receives it.

"The education and empowerment of women throughout the world cannot fail to result in a more caring, tolerant, just and peaceful life for all."
—AUNG SAN SUU KYI

Aung San Suu Kyi: Let me say this, Alan: You do not need permission to be free. You do not need rank to be mighty. In Myanmar, it is the girl in Taunggyi with a hidden radio; the fisherman ferrying refugees across the Salween under the cover of darkness; the monk bowing to his captor with a smile. It is the mother whispering courage to her child before fleeing gunfire. It is the writer smuggling hope across borders in a single sentence.

You are not the echo of change. You are its genesis. Live it fiercely. This is our revolution—a revolution of the spirit, unconfined by any prison, undefeated by any tyranny.

Let history record this truth: *tyrants fade. But fearless disruptors—those who choose conscience over fear, truth over silence—seed the world anew.*

Alan Clements: Thank you, Daw Suu. Thank you from my heart.

Aung San Suu Kyi: Thank you, Alan. Let this be our legacy: a flame no darkness can extinguish, carried by my people and by all who dare to rise.

I wish to close by invoking my father's words—offered not from exile, but from the birth of a nation, spoken with unwavering clarity and a love fierce enough to outlast fear:

"We will not wait for others to grant us our freedom,
for history has never been kind to those who
wait. We must claim it with our own hands,
through the strength of our unity and the unwavering will of our
people."

"The path ahead may be arduous,
and we may face many betrayals and deceptions,
but let there be no doubt—we will march forward."

"We will not be divided; we will not be subdued. And with or
without their consent, *Burma shall be free.*"

—GENERAL AUNG SAN, *Presidential Address to the First Congress of the Anti-Fascist People's Freedom League (AFPFL), January 20, 1946, Rangoon, Burma*

274

CHAPTER NINETEEN

RESPONDING TO CRITICS AND LESSONS LEARNED

Author's Prelude

What follows is neither rebuttal nor apology. It is a reckoning—a searing testament of conscience from a woman whose so-called "silence," at a critical time in Myanmar's recent history, was not absence, but a mirror reflecting the world's distortions. Her name became a battleground—claimed, vilified, sanctified, betrayed—while her humanity was erased into myth, flattened into symbol, scapegoat, or shrine.

Here, in this unflinching exchange, Aung San Suu Kyi steps from the shadow of caricature into the fierce, radiant clarity of her own unvarnished truth. This dialogue does not offer comfort. It reopens wounds still raw—military brutality, communal fracture, a nation unraveling in the grip of its own ghosts. It asks us to confront a land where ancient pagodas stand sentinel over bloodied earth, where the promise of democracy collided with the burden of inherited divisions.

Yet it dwells in the discomfort, speaking not in soundbites but in the halting, intricate language of lived complexity. It reminds us that moral outrage, untethered from understanding, risks calcifying into dogma—and dogma, too, can destroy.

There are no shortcuts through this terrain, no slogans resilient enough to bear the weight of this history. I offered no soft questions, sought no absolution. I offered space—a rare, unguarded clearing where truth could breathe, unburdened by agenda, a place beyond the binary of innocence and guilt, beyond iconography.

Her words carry the weight of decades endured under house arrest, of a family fractured by distance, of a nation's hopes pinned to her frail shoulders. And Daw Suu does not flinch. She responds with grace and gravitas, with the clarity of one who has survived the crucible of solitary confinement without shattering, speaking not to defend a legacy but to map the moral wilderness of impossible choices.

To read this is to step into the consciousness of modern history, to wrestle with the paradox of conscience in power, to grieve not only what was, but what might have been. To hear, at last, a voice unbowed—not mythologized, not unscathed, but fiercely, achingly awake.

Let this be no one's vindication. Let it be an invitation—to listen anew, to think anew, to hold justice not as a verdict but as a living dialogue between suffering and responsibility, vision and flaw, silence and the ferocity of truth. It asks us not only to hear her, but to examine our own complicity in the narratives we inherit and the silences we perpetuate.

From the confines of her Naypyidaw prison cell, these may be the final words we hear from Aung San Suu Kyi in her lifetime—a voice from the edge of history, echoing with the weight of a nation's dreams and the clarity of a conscience unbroken. This is not the closing of a case. It is the opening of a braver, more urgent conversation.

◆ ◆ ◆

Alan Clements: Daw Suu, the New York Times recently branded Myanmar's civil war a "forgotten conflict," but I'd argue—drawing on a searing documentary by The Independent—that it is not forgotten. It is willfully ignored. *Cancelled: The Rise and Fall of Aung San Suu Kyi* lays bare the grotesque absurdity of scapegoating you for the crimes of an autonomous military dictatorship, as well as the spiritual bankruptcy of a political culture that canonizes saints—then crucifies them for the crime of being human.

Your youngest son, Kim, recently revealed that some journalists now privately concede they got it wrong. But they claim they've "moved on." Yet research from Care International and the Yusof Ishak Institute unmasks a chilling truth: *Western reporting had a measurable, causal role in escalating sectarian violence. Those distortions didn't vanish with the news cycle—they endure in the shattered lives of millions, a wound that festers beyond the headlines.*

What does it mean to "move on" from such consequences?

The international abandonment of your leadership didn't just break hearts—it paved the way for a military coup now in its fifth year: a reign of terror that has gutted a nation. Schools lie abandoned, markets silent, the dreams of a generation entombed beneath the rubble of airstrikes and fear.

As Sir John Jenkins, former British Ambassador to Myanmar, declared in that documentary: the military had you "exactly where they wanted you." So, while the *Tatmadaw* razed villages and ruled by fear, it was you the world turned against. Since then, countless lives have been extinguished—thousands perished in the inferno of their brutality.

How do we even begin to name this? Over 22,000 political prisoners—tortured, silenced, erased from the world's conscience. More than 100,000 homes bombed or burned to ash. Some 3.5 million people displaced, surviving in jungles and camps under conditions that defy the very language of humanity.

This is not merely a tragedy; it is a moral indictment of our collective silence. And much of it—this human catastrophe—was amplified by a handful of journalists scapegoating you from air-conditioned editorial offices, far from the reality of mass graves, torched villages, and families cowering in ravaged forests. Their words, fueled by a global hunger for simple villains, drowned out the messy truths of a nation caught in geopolitical crosswinds.

I raise this not to relitigate the past, but to reframe this moment with unflinching clarity. For the first time since your imprisonment, the world can hear directly from you—not through intermediaries or filtered narratives, but in your own voice, raw and unbowed.

If I may, I'd like to introduce a complex subject—and my opening makes my stance undeniably clear. But it is you, not me, whom history is listening to now. So, allow me to be direct. This is a rare and sacred opportunity to speak with candor and depth about your leadership, your legacy, the accusations leveled against you, and the far more intricate realities obscured by headlines.

Aung San Suu Kyi: Alan, you're right—it's me they want to hear from, for better or worse. And your "not-so-subtle" opening laid bare your position with crystalline clarity.

As for hindsight, well, it's always mercilessly clear, isn't it? If we could bottle "if onlys," Myanmar might have a thriving economy. This is one of those tragic "if onlys" the entire nation—perhaps even ARSA, the Islamic terrorist group in Rakhine born of rage amid a persecuted people's despair—wishes we could have escaped. They, too, were consumed by the flames of conflict, a cycle of violence that spared no one, leaving only ashes where hope once flickered. Everyone has lost in this catastrophe. Even the *Tatmadaw*, though they may not yet see the abyss they've carved for themselves.

But as I often say with a wry smile, it wasn't politics that sustained me—it was the *Dhamma*. And, perhaps, a touch of gum disease—a strange ally in solitude, and now my "earthquake arm" injury, as I'm calling it, that has me unable to use my left hand.

There were days when it felt like an infection coursing through me—deep, gnawing, inescapable. But I learned to sit with it, to study it, to meet it with patience rather than dread. And, in time, to heal through the quiet alchemy of understanding.

The same holds with my arm. The only true remedy for suffering is insight. Not the insight of judgment, which divides, but the insight of compassion, which seeks to understand even the roots of cruelty, however bitter they may be.

That's what I hope this conversation might offer—not recriminations, not defenses, not bitterness—but a shared effort to see with greater clarity, to feel with greater depth. For only by seeing clearly can we honor those we've lost and, if we're brave, prevent such loss from haunting us again.

Alan Clements: Daw Suu, I didn't expect *periodontal wisdom*—but you've somehow woven *Dhamma*, dentistry, and anatomy into a single thread. And all three, it seems, call for a steady mind and the patience to sit with pain—a lesson as profound as it is unexpected.

On a graver note, I hear you—and I honor the clarity, humility, and quiet humor with which you name what so many refuse to see: that everyone has lost, and Myanmar's wounds still bleed with a ferocity that defies erasure.

Daw Suu, many cast you as myth—heroine or betrayer, icon or apologist. But history, as you know, resists such binaries. Your leadership—extraordinary, unyielding—has faced searing scrutiny, particularly over the Rohingya crisis, your stewardship of Myanmar's fragile democratic transition, and your profoundly misconstrued appearance at *The Hague*. It was a nation poised on a knife's edge, where every step toward democracy risked stirring ancient hatreds or emboldening an unrepentant military. Some call these stains on your legacy. Others argue the narrative itself was twisted by distortion, a casualty of the world's hunger for simple truths.

If I may be direct, this is a rare moment to hear from you, unfiltered, since your imprisonment. I invite you to address a constellation of weighty issues: your leadership, your legacy, the accusations against you, and the truths obscured by headlines.

This is not an indictment, nor ovation—it is a caring plea. Will you speak, unflinchingly, to the criticisms that have shadowed your name? Will you share your truth—not as a symbol to be exalted or condemned, but as a woman who bore the unimaginable weight of a fractured nation on her shoulders?

Aung San Suu Kyi: Alan, thank you. Your words are not only perceptive—they are brave. It is a profound relief to be met with such candor. I heard every word. I felt it. And I welcome this chance to speak—not through the haze of headlines, but directly, with an intimacy that cuts through the noise. Yes, I will engage this conversation fully.

Let me first say I was deeply moved by your mention of my son, Kim. His courage in speaking truth—amid a climate where truth invites scorn, or worse, retribution—speaks volumes. He has borne the weight of distortion and silence alongside me, often quietly, with remarkable grace. For him to step forward now, with love and insight, affirms the deepest bond between us. His voice is part of this healing, and I honor it with a mother's unwavering reverence.

Your framing cuts through the fog of selective outrage. I have been called many things—saint, traitor, icon, apologist. But I learned long ago that such labels reveal more about the world's projections than the woman who carries them. As you said, the hunger for saints is seductive—and the crucifixion of flawed humans is its inevitable shadow, a ritual as old as history itself.

Let us be clear: there was not only misunderstanding; there was orchestration. A narrative was crafted, and anything that complicated it was discarded or drowned out, like whispers in a storm. What pained me most was not the scrutiny—it was its shallowness. The flattening of human complexity into slogans. The preference for scandal over truth.

I have always believed leadership demands accountability—to supporters and critics alike. It also demands a stillness within, a refusal to let the clamor of judgment drown out the quiet, steady voice of conscience. I claim no infallibility. Leadership is a tapestry, woven from intention, action, compromise, and constraint.

To answer you honestly: the criticisms surrounding the Rohingya crisis are a source of deep sorrow and a call to reflection—not only on the limits of my leadership, but on the distortions that fester in a wounded world, where truth becomes the first casualty.

Before we go further, one truth must be clear. When people speak of "my government," they often overlook that Myanmar had two governments: one civilian, elected by the people, and one military, entrenched by constitutional design.

The military controlled the armed forces, police, prisons, border affairs, and national security. They held, by decree, 25 percent of parliamentary seats—a veto over any democratic reform. This was not abstract; it was our daily reality, a shadow cast over every decision, every hope.

This distinction is not academic. Today, nearly all our elected leaders are imprisoned, killed, or disappeared, alongside over 22,000 activists, artists, doctors, teachers, and journalists. Among them was my dear friend U Ko Ni, a brilliant constitutional lawyer and devout Muslim from Rakhine State, assassinated on January 29, 2017. He sought lawful, peaceful ways to loosen the military's grip through constitutional reform. He was shot in broad daylight, cradling his grandson. His death was no accident—it was a warning, a chilling testament to the cost of dreaming in a land ruled by fear.

You were in Yangon then, Alan. You remember. The silence that followed was not just grief—it was terror. So, when people speak of "my government," I ask for precision. Without understanding the true structure of power, we cannot grasp the tragedy that unfolded or the forces that shaped it.

Nor was the distortion solely the media's doing. Governments, too, found it convenient to condemn rather than engage, to signal virtue while ignoring the geopolitical currents that fueled the crisis.

Let me turn to the media. The media, Alan, is a double-edged blade. At its best, it exposes oppression's darkest corners. At its worst, it distorts, sensationalizes, and reduces complex truths to fit preordained molds. The Rohingya crisis, like so many tragedies, fell prey to this simplification, a narrative stripped of nuance and humanity.

Alan Clements: Daw Suu, the world saw what it needed to see: images of devastation, eyewitness accounts, satellite footage of villages ablaze—evidence that, for many, was irrefutable, a searing testament to unspeakable loss. These harrowing visuals forged an international narrative that accused your side of the government not merely of failure, but of moral collapse, a betrayal of the very ideals you were seen to embody.

How do you reconcile these indelible images and reports with your steadfast claim that the dominant narrative was not only incomplete, but profoundly distorted, a lens that obscured as much as it revealed? What truths remain unseen, even now, through the prism that judged you so harshly?

Aung San Suu Kyi: Alan, let me speak plainly: the suffering of the Rohingya is undeniable, and I would never diminish it. Villages burned, lives were lost, families shattered. These are truths that demand recognition, unclouded by denial or distortion, a wound that cries out for acknowledgment. Their pain is real, and it weighs on my conscience as it should on the world's. Yet even in their exile, the Rohingya endure, their resilience a quiet rebuke to those who reduced their story to spectacle —a spectacle that, too often, drowned out their humanity.

Yet the narrative woven around these events stripped away the intricate truths of a wounded nation. Myanmar is a tapestry torn by centuries of ethnic strife, colonial scars, and systemic inequities. The crisis in Rakhine State is not a singular event but a thread in a tangled knot of interwoven histories, traumas, and grievances, stretching back through generations. To cast it solely as the persecution of one group by another flattens the lived realities of the Rohingya, the Rakhine Buddhists, and countless other ethnic minorities trapped in cycles of fear, mistrust, and survival. It reduces a nation's anguish to a headline, a caricature of suffering that erases the deeper currents beneath.

The international community, too, often judged Myanmar's fragile democracy as if it flourished in isolation. In truth, as I said earlier, our civilian government was tethered to a military that retained iron control over security forces, police, and borders—powers enshrined in a constitution we were powerless to amend.

Civilian authority stopped where military command began. Our democracy was not a triumph; it was a delicate, often perilous negotiation with an unrepentant adversary. This is not an alibi—it is the architecture of our reality, too often erased in the rush to condemn, a truth obscured by the world's need for a simple villain.

What remains unseen is the chaos beneath the surface: the provocations, the competing narratives of victimhood, the deliberate stoking of fear by those who thrived on division.

The media, hungry for clarity, amplified one story while silencing others, ignoring the broader tapestry of a nation teetering on the brink of collapse, where every community bore its own scars.

And the world, eager for a villain, found one in me—not because I wielded the power to stop the violence, but because I bore the crushing weight of its expectations, a burden I could neither fully meet nor escape.

I do not ask for absolution. Leadership, I have learned, is not the wielding of power but the bearing of its weight—knowing that every choice, however constrained, ripples through lives and histories, leaving echoes of both hope and regret. I ask for understanding—not of me alone, but of a nation caught in the crucible of its own history, a land where the past and present collide in unrelenting anguish.

If my voice falls silent, let it not be the end of this reckoning. Let future generations demand truth—not from me alone, but from those who shaped the narratives that divided us. To see clearly is to honor the suffering of all, to refuse the simplicity of blame, and to recognize that truth, like healing, demands patience, courage, and an unwavering commitment to the complexity of our shared humanity.

Alan Clements: Daw Suu, your decision to defend Myanmar at the International Court of Justice, facing genocide charges against the military, drew sharp, unrelenting criticism. To some, it seemed you were shielding the Tatmadaw's actions, a stance that appeared to betray the very principles of justice you had long embodied. How do you answer those who saw your presence there as condoning their violence, as a tacit endorsement of atrocities that shook the world's conscience?

Aung San Suu Kyi: Alan, standing before the ICJ was the hardest choice I ever made. I knew how it would be read—by those whose wounds still bled, by a world poised to equate my defense with complicity.

The weight of that moment haunts me still, a shadow that lingers in the quiet of my cell. Every night, I see the faces of those who suffered—

Rohingya, Rakhine, all caught in a storm not of their making—and I ask myself what more I could have done within the chains that bound me, chains forged by history and power alike.

Yet consider this: could any leader step into a global court and brand their nation guilty of genocide without shattering not only the culpable but the blameless—the millions of ordinary souls who played no part in the violence, yet would bear the weight of the world's judgment?

My presence was not an absolution of the military's deeds. It was a defense of Myanmar as a nation—a nation scarred by decades of strife, division, and fragility, teetering on the brink of further ruin, where every wound threatened to unravel the whole. I sought to weave the tangled threads of our story: not to deny the suffering, but to shield Myanmar from an isolation that would deepen every wound, not just in Rakhine but across our fractured land.

The world's sanctions, while righteous in intent, risked starving a nation already on its knees, severing any path to dialogue or repair. Isolation does not heal; it festers, leaving scars that outlast generations.

I stood there to insist that Myanmar's truth be told—not as a tableau of guilt or innocence, but as a tapestry of agonizing complexity, where every thread bore the weight of history's unresolved grief. To reduce it to a verdict would betray not only the Rohingya but every citizen who yearns for a future beyond division. I spoke not to excuse, but to preserve the faint, flickering possibility of reconciliation, a hope as fragile as it is essential.

If these are to be my final words, let them be clear: I was never silent—only unheard. What they called silence was refusal. What they could not bear was truth spoken without permission. So, judge me not by the noise of those who condemned me, but by the quiet, unyielding devotion it took to hold a fractured nation with bare, trembling hands, knowing the world watched only to see me fall.

And to those who still pass judgment—I ask only this: seek understanding, not verdict. For only truth—not blame—can mend what history has torn, can heal what division has broken, can light a path where darkness has reigned too long.

Alan Clements: Daw Suu, going further, critics contend that your administration failed to adequately address the humanitarian needs of the Rohingya or to condemn the military's actions with sufficient force. Their voices echo a broader sentiment—that your leadership, once a beacon of hope, faltered in the face of unspeakable suffering. How do you respond to these charges, to the weight of their accusations in a world that still mourns the losses they lament?

Aung San Suu Kyi: Alan, these criticisms pierce deeply, and I bear their weight with unflinching humility. More could have been done—more should have been done. Our administration strove to deliver aid and support where we could, but those efforts were often thwarted—not only by the military's iron grip on security and borders, but by a volatile political landscape we fought to steady; a terrain where every step risked collapse.

In Rakhine, fear and mistrust had long pitted neighbor against neighbor, a tinderbox where even humanitarian aid could spark suspicion or violence, igniting flames that consumed the very lives we sought to save.

In retrospect, I wish we had been bolder, more unrelenting in championing the rights of all in Rakhine, especially the Rohingya. I wish we had found paths through the barriers that confined us.

But I ask my critics to see the dilemma we faced: in a nation where words could ignite reprisals—not just against leaders, but against entire communities—every utterance carried the risk of unraveling a fragile democratic hope, a dream so tender it could shatter with a single misstep. My safety was not the concern; the survival of a nascent movement, shadowed by military power, was —a movement that bore the aspirations of millions, yet trembled under the weight of its own fragility.

We sought to navigate this treacherous terrain while sowing seeds of trust, unity, and reform for enduring change. It was an imperfect dance, and I acknowledge, with profound sorrow, that we faltered.

Even today, more so today in the silence of this cell, I carry the faces of those we could not reach, their silent pleas an indelible reminder that even the best intentions can fall short of justice's uncompromising demand.

Yet to judge us solely by our stumbles is to miss the delicate, often unseen threads we wove toward a future Myanmar might yet claim—a future where healing might outlast the scars of our failures.

Alan Clements: Daw Suu, some argue the NLD, under your leadership, advanced a Burmese-centric vision of Myanmar that sidelined ethnic minorities. Their critique casts a shadow over your democratic legacy, suggesting a vision that, while noble, overlooked the very diversity it sought to unite. How do you address this critique, and what lessons have you gleaned from this painful reflection?

Aung San Suu Kyi: Alan, this charge carries truth, and I meet it without deflection. The NLD's vision of democracy, though earnest, was often blinkered by narratives that—perhaps unwittingly—elevated a singular identity over Myanmar's vibrant mosaic. We failed to fully embrace the voices and dreams of our ethnic minorities, and for that, I take responsibility.

Yet few appreciate the lethal, maniacal nature of the military machinery we faced—a regime driven by the pathology of authoritarian control, willing to exact any price, to crush any dissent, to preserve its dominion at all costs. And today, under this reign of terror, that ferocity has only deepened, as the nation sits in the grip of a junta that knows no bounds.

Despite these constraints, we strove with every fiber of our being to be inclusive, to weave every community into the fabric of our vision, though our efforts faltered under the weight of a system designed to divide. No democracy can stand if it does not weave every thread of its people into its heart. This was our failing, and it is a lesson etched in my soul, a scar I carry as a testament to what might have been.

Myanmar's future demands a democracy that exalts its diversity—not as an afterthought, but as its bedrock. Federalism, true autonomy, and unyielding inclusion must anchor our path forward, a path we sought to pave despite the military's unrelenting shadow.

These are not ideals; they are the sinews of survival, the very lifeblood of a nation's hope. Without them, peace is a mirage, unity a deferred dream. If my voice fades, let this truth endure: a nation's strength lies in its many voices, lifted as one.

This is not my burden alone—it is ours. Let those who inherit Myanmar's future build a nation where no voice is silenced, no dream cast aside, where the complexity of our past becomes the foundation of a shared tomorrow.

Alan Clements: Daw Suu, you speak with profound humility and unflinching reflection, yet the question lingers: given the chance, what would you do differently to mend the fractures your critics lament, knowing now the cost of those missed bridges?

Aung San Suu Kyi: Alan, hindsight is both a lantern and a weight. It illuminates the bridges we missed, the words we left unspoken, the doors we failed to open. It also reveals the years I spent apart from my family, the solitude of confinement, the silent cost of a life given to this struggle—choices I would make again, yet mourn for the lives they could not save. And it bids us carry those lessons forward, a sacred duty to those we failed and those who still dream.

If I could retrace my steps, I would labor with unrelenting effort to amplify the voices of ethnic minorities—not merely inviting them into a prebuilt frame, but co-crafting a nation that mirrors the full, radiant spectrum of Myanmar's peoples. I would forge deeper bridges of trust—not only through politics, but through the quiet, sacred work of listening, learning, and shared dreams, a labor too often thwarted by a military machinery that thrived on division. As I said earlier, few understand the complexity of confronting such a regime—a machinery driven by the pathology of authoritarian control at all costs, a force so lethal, so maniacal, that it would rather burn the nation to ashes than yield an inch of power, a reality we faced then and that has only worsened under today's reign of terror.

I would demand greater transparency and accountability, even against the unyielding resistance of a military whose grip was as ironclad as it was ruthless, a force that saw inclusivity as a threat to its dominion. And I would nurture a vivid, unyielding awareness of Myanmar's interwoven histories, ensuring no child, no village, no community feels exiled from our shared story —a story we tried to tell, despite the military's shadow, in every effort to include, to heal, to unite.

Yet I would hold fast to the principles that have guided me: nonviolence, dialogue, reconciliation. These are not the easy paths—they are the lonelier, more arduous ones, carved through the bedrock of a nation's pain. But they alone can lead us beyond vengeance, beyond bitterness, to a peace woven not by force, but by mutual reverence, a peace that honors every voice, every scar, every hope.

Alan Clements: Finally, Daw Suu, what message would you offer your critics, both in Myanmar and across the globe, at a time when your voice, potentially the last we hear, carries the weight of a nation's hope and a world's reckoning?

Aung San Suu Kyi: To my critics, I say: I hear you. Your voices, even when they cut, are a vital call to growth, a mirror I cannot turn away from. Leadership is not perfection—it is a journey of learning, shaped by mistakes and reflection. I have faltered, and I carry those failures not with defensiveness, but with a resolve to grow, to do better, to honor the trust placed in me with every breath I have left.

Yet I ask for understanding—not as absolution, but as recognition of the labyrinth we navigated: a democracy tethered to a military's unyielding might, a nation fractured yet yearning for unity amidst a storm of historical wounds. The legacy media, as it has done elsewhere—misrepresenting leaders, justifying wars—often distilled our struggle into simplistic tales, reducing a tapestry of anguish to a single, distorted thread.

Let us transcend these distortions. Let us embrace a deeper, more nuanced dialogue, where truth is not a weapon but a bridge. The fight for democracy, justice, and reconciliation is not a saga of heroes and villains—it is the unfinished story of humanity, frail yet brave, flawed yet boundless in its capacity for renewal.

Let us write that story together—with candor, with humility, with unwavering hope, for only through such a shared endeavor can we heal the wounds we've borne and dream the future anew.

Alan Clements: Daw Suu, your words resonate with astonishing candor, unyielding courage, and transcendent grace. Thank you.

Before we close, I offer you this final space—not as a journalist, nor even as your friend, but as one who believes, with every fiber of his being, that Myanmar's story endures —a story of resilience, of defiance, of an unquenchable dream for freedom. If these were your last public words—your final chance to speak to the people—what would you say?

What message would you send to those rising in resistance, to the soldiers who have defected, to the diaspora watching from exile, to the young risking all for freedom's dream?

What truth would you wish history to hold—not only of you, but of who we were, and who we might yet become as a people forged in struggle, yet reaching for a dawn beyond the darkness?

Aung San Suu Kyi: If these are my final words, let them be a benediction—not for me, but for Myanmar's people, a sacred offering to a nation that has endured the unendurable, yet dares to dream of light.

To those rising in streets and shadows: you are not forgotten. Your courage is the heartbeat of a nation reborn, a rhythm that echoes through the ages. You are not rebels—you are the visionaries of a future forged in dignity, justice, and shared humanity. Builders of a Myanmar that will stand as a testament to your unyielding spirit.

To the soldiers who have laid down arms, crossing the unseen line of conscience: you are not traitors. You are living proof that truth can unravel even the tightest chains of indoctrination, that the soul can choose honor over fear. Your quiet valor heralds a new Myanmar, born one act of integrity at a time, a nation where conscience becomes the cornerstone of peace.

To those in exile—watching, aching, weaving resistance from afar: distance cannot sever love. Your songs, your stories, your festivals kept alive in foreign lands—these are the roots that no border can uproot, the threads that bind us across oceans and generations. Your voices echo with a resonance that time cannot silence. You are woven into this land, eternally. Your place in its future is not merely valid—it is indispensable, a vital thread in the tapestry of our rebirth.

And to the children—those yet to come and those now carrying water through fire: we never forgot you. Even when the world turned away, we turned toward each other. Even when our names were silenced, we spoke—in whispers, in songs, in coded prayers, in dreams. We carried you in our hearts, every step of the way, a promise unbroken amidst the storm.

Let history not recall us as victims, but as those who chose light, again and again, no matter the cost, who held fast to hope even as the darkness roared.

The fog will lift—even in the minds of generals, even in hearts hardened by fear, for truth is relentless, a tide that no wall can hold. And love—when fierce and free—cannot be caged, its flame a beacon that will guide us home.

To the world beyond our borders: see us not as a cautionary tale, but as a mirror. Our struggle is yours—against division, against silence, against the seductive ease of despair. Join us in choosing hope, for in that choice, we weave a shared destiny that transcends borders and binds us as one.

Let the world remember: we rose, we endured, we will rise again—not in vengeance, but in vision. Not as conquerors, but as a people who remembered who we are, and dared to dream of who we might become—a nation reborn in the light of justice, where every voice sings in harmony, where every scar tells a story of resilience, where every hope blooms into a future unbowed.

Alan Clements: Beautiful. Daw Suu, before we draw this conversation to a close, allow me one final request—not born of formality, but from the urgency and moral weight of this moment, a moment that may echo through history as your last recorded testament. I invite you to offer something historic: a clear, unequivocal final response, in your own words, to the core criticisms you know so well.

These, as we know, are not abstract charges—they have shadowed your name, tested your spirit, and shaped the world's perception of a nation you've given everything to preserve. One by one, let us face them—not as a defense, nor as justification, but as a reckoning, a transparent, heartfelt illumination of the truth as you have lived and borne it through decades of sacrifice.

Let this be your testament to the world, a final record for history, etched in the unyielding clarity of your voice. You've addressed many of these issues already, but I believe, with every fiber of my being, that truth—especially in this moment—demands to be spoken again, with unflinching clarity, lest silence claim the last word.

Given the profound toll of distortion and misunderstanding—a toll that has wounded both you and Myanmar's soul—will you lay bare the complexities, the constraints, and the choices that shaped your path, offering a legacy of truth that history cannot ignore?

Aung San Suu Kyi: I will, Alan. I thank you for this invitation—not to defend, but to speak with the unadorned dignity that truth commands, a dignity I have carried through every trial.

I offer this not as an argument, nor as an attempt to rewrite what has been etched in headlines. I offer it as a reckoning—measured, honest, rooted in the marrow of lived experience, a testament born of humility.

Let me be unequivocal: I do not speak to justify, but to illuminate. I do not seek to erase my critics' voices, but to weave them into a deeper tapestry of understanding, where pain, critique, and hope find their place. I yearn not for vindication, but for clarity—a clarity that honors the suffering of all, that dares to dream of a future beyond our scars.

If my words spark even a flicker of insight, compassion, or honest reflection, they will have served their purpose—a fragile offering to a world that too often chooses judgment over understanding. May this reckoning embed the primacy of democracy—not as a system, but as a covenant where every voice is inviolable, a beacon against tyranny.

Let it affirm our interconnectedness, a tapestry of shared humanity upheld by the Universal Declaration of Human Rights, whose sacred freedoms—speech, expression, thought—are the lifeblood of truth and justice.

We are frail vessels in this human experiment, fraught with complexities, shadows, and unknowns, yet bound by a longing for light. Let this be a temple for honest, morally courageous dialogue and accountability, where we end war, violence, political imprisonment, character assassination, and propaganda, and let truth reign as a balm, a bridge, a beacon.

May this legacy transcend one nation, uniting us in the quiet, unyielding work of healing history's wounds, forging a peace where voices rise in harmony, and hope outshines the darkest night.

Failure to Condemn or Stop the Rohingya "Genocide"

Aung San Suu Kyi: Let me be unequivocal: I have never denied the anguish of Rakhine State. I have never closed my eyes to the plight of the displaced. The tragedy—raw, shattering, born of decades of communal strife, historic mistrust, and systemic neglect—demands recognition, unclouded by denial, a truth that sears the conscience. As a leader, I carry its scars in my heart, knowing no title could shield me from the grief of lives lost under my watch.

Yet the military's actions in 2017 did not erupt in isolation. They were ignited by calculated provocations from the Arakan Rohingya Salvation Army (ARSA), a well-armed terrorist group with documented jihadist affiliations and transnational ties.

On October 9, 2016, ARSA launched coordinated assaults on three border posts in Maungdaw Township, killing nine police officers and seizing 48 firearms, 6,624 rounds of ammunition, and other weapons. Two days later, on October 11, four Myanmar soldiers fell in ensuing clashes. These were not spontaneous acts—they were meticulously planned to destabilize a fragile region and provoke a security crisis.

On August 25, 2017, ARSA escalated its campaign, launching simultaneous attacks on 30 police and army posts across northern Rakhine, claiming 12 security officers' lives. The military reported 400 deaths, primarily insurgents, but it was civilians—caught in the crossfire of terror and retaliation—who bore the deepest wounds.

That same day, as documented in Amnesty International's May 22, 2018 report, ARSA terrorists massacred up to 99 Hindus in Kha-Maung-Seik village. Fifty-three men, women, and children were executed; eight women and children were abducted and forcibly converted. These atrocities, verified by international human rights organizations, are too often erased from the narrative, yet they must be seen. Rakhine's volatile mosaic—where fear fueled cycles of violence— ensnared all communities in a web of mutual distrust, a complexity the world too often ignored.

Ataullah, ARSA's leader, arrested in Bangladesh on March 17, 2025, trained with Taliban affiliates in Pakistan, as noted in the International Crisis Group's 2016 report. These are corroborated facts, not speculation. ARSA is not a peaceful advocate for rights. Designated a terrorist organization by Myanmar's civilian government, its aim was clear: to provoke a military crackdown, internationalize the conflict, and fuel global outrage.

Under the 2008 Constitution, I held no authority over the military—a legal reality, not an excuse. Yet within my power, I acted. I called for investigations and urged restraint. By 2019, 429 Myanmar soldiers faced courts-martial for their actions in Rakhine—a truth later buried under the junta's veil of secrecy.

I championed Kofi Annan's recommendations: addressing citizenship, fostering interfaith dialogue, spurring development. By 2020, my government issued 10,000 birth certificates to stateless children and began—however haltingly—closing IDP camps, steps toward justice too often overshadowed by the narrative of my "silence."

I spoke at the United Nations, before the International Court of Justice, and to the people of Myanmar, acknowledging the suffering of all—Rohingya, Rakhine Buddhists, Hindus alike, with a clarity the world chose to ignore.

At the ICJ, I declared:
"The sufferings of the many innocent people whose lives were torn apart as a consequence of the armed conflicts of 2016 and 2017, in particular, those who have had to flee their homes and are now living in camps in Cox's Bazar."

And again:
"The Arakan Rohingya Salvation Army—known as ARSA—launched simultaneous attacks on three police posts... This was the start of an internal armed conflict... ARSA fighters launched coordinated attacks on more than 30 police posts and villages."

My so-called "silence" was no indifference—it was a distortion, a deliberate erasure of what I said and sought to avert. I spoke—with care, with gravity—but because I shunned the incendiary rhetoric some craved, my voice was deemed absent.

I chose restraint not from lack of compassion, but from the burden of safeguarding millions—not only in Rakhine, but across a nation teetering on the edge of wider violence. One reckless word could have set ablaze the fragile threads of peace we clung to, a reality few understood then, and fewer understand now.

The world expected me to wield a power I did not hold. I acted with the tools I had, ever mindful of Myanmar's future, a future I sought to preserve for all its people.

If this is judged failure, let it be weighed in full—not by slogans, but by the unyielding light of truth. Let history linger in the gray spaces where truth resides, asking not only what I did, but what the world failed to do—for Myanmar, for the Rohingya, for justice itself.

Erosion of Moral Authority and Human Rights Legacy

Aung San Suu Kyi: My moral authority was never a Nobel Prize, nor the transient applause of the world. It was, and remains, my unyielding fidelity to Myanmar's people—the millions who dared to dream of liberty in a land cloaked in fear, a faithfulness forged through decades of sacrifice.

I've now spent over two decades in detention—alone, unseen, unheard, not for accolades or canonization, but to serve, to bear witness, to endure so hope might endure. Each year of solitude was a vow that their dreams would outlast my chains, even as my own joys dimmed in their shadow.

When I emerged each time to lead, I did not inherit a blank slate. I stepped into a nation bound to generals, riven by ethnic wounds, haunted by betrayals etched into its soul, where our fragile democracy stretched taut over a chasm of military might.

At the International Court of Justice, I spoke without illusion:

"We shall adhere steadfastly to our commitment to non-violence, human rights, national reconciliation, and rule of law, as we go forward to build the Democratic Federal Union to which our people have aspired for generations past."

These were not mere platitudes—they were the marrow of my conviction, bared before the world's scrutiny, a testament to a vision I never abandoned. This is not the creed of a betrayer. It is the evidence of one who never ceased believing in peace, even when peace glimmered as a distant star, a light I chased through every storm. To claim I abandoned my principles is to misread the challenges I faced, to presume ideals float free of history, fear, or the iron weight of power. They do not. Ideals are carried—across shattered earth, amid impossible choices, through a landscape scarred by betrayal.

I chose nonviolence not as a gesture, but as a lifeline for a nation's survival, a path to preserve hope against annihilation. I chose dialogue not for safety, but as the only bridge left to us, a fragile span over a chasm of violence. I governed within constraints unfathomable to those judging from afar—legal, military, historical—where the world sought a savior unbound by history, not a leader wielding fragile tools against unyielding odds. I did not forsake my values. I lived them—imperfectly, arduously, under siege, holding fast to the belief that justice could outlast the darkness.

If history must judge me, let it measure me not against abstractions, but against the inheritance I bore and the future I strove to forge, a future where Myanmar's wounds might heal. Let it recall that moral courage is not the absence of tragedy, but the refusal to let tragedy define the horizon, a refusal I embodied with every choice, every breath.

My legacy is not a monument—it is the enduring hope of a people who, despite every shadow, still reach for light. If my voice falls silent, let it resound in the courage of those who press on, forging a Myanmar where justice and reconciliation bloom as truths woven in shared struggle, a legacy not of perfection, but of perseverance.

Suppression of Press Freedom and the Reuters Case

Aung San Suu Kyi: The imprisonment of Reuters journalists Wa Lone and Kyaw Soe Oo is often cited as a stain on my leadership, a charge I will not evade. Yet let us be clear: they were ensnared by the Official Secrets Act of 1923—a relic of colonial oppression forged under British rule. I neither authored that law, nor ordered their arrest, nor commanded the judiciary—a system beyond my control.

Their ordeal was a tragedy—raw and wrenching, a pain I bore as a leader, knowing my hands were bound by laws I sought to reform. Myanmar's judiciary, a labyrinth of caprice scarred by decades of authoritarian rule, resisted the reforms we labored for. In a democracy as tender as ours, transformation requires the patient forging of institutions resilient to both public clamor and military shadow—a task we pursued against unyielding odds.

When Wa Lone and Kyaw Soe Oo were detained, my trusted advisor, Win Htein, spoke plainly: *their arrest was an entrapment, orchestrated by military elements embedded within the state, relics of a dictatorship we could not unseat. These forces wielded power beyond our reach, turning justice into a weapon against truth, a reality too often obscured.*

I shared his judgment. Yet I knew that to intervene with an executive decree—to bypass the judicial process, even in so grave a case—would set a perilous precedent, opening the gate for others to be condemned without due process. The rule of law must stand impartial, or it crumbles into the arbitrary power we fought to dismantle, a principle I upheld even in anguish.

I was not silent. Within the corridors of power, I pressed for justice and transparency. Publicly, I upheld due process, lest we slide back into the tyranny we sought to escape, a choice born not of indifference, but of a vision for a Myanmar where law reigns over whim.

In my first year as leader, I lifted charges against scores of activists, widened avenues for protest, nurtured independent media, and fostered political dialogue, steps toward a freer press often overshadowed by the narrative of my failure.

Yet the line between national security and press freedom blurs in a nation fractured by armed conflict, steeped in mistrust, and stalked by forces bent on unraveling our democracy—a complexity the world too often ignored.

Here lies the bitterest paradox of leadership: to defend justice's foundation, even when it demands restraint amid injustice's sting, a paradox I lived with the weight of a nation's future in my hands. If my voice fades, let it echo in a Myanmar where journalists walk free, where justice is not a paradox but a promise kept.

Autocratic Leadership Within the NLD

Aung San Suu Kyi: They called me autocratic. I smile at the charge, and I say: I led with the trust of Myanmar's people, in their name, not my own.

The Constitution barred me from the presidency, so we crafted the role of State Counsellor—not to hoard power, but to honor the democratic mandate millions risked everything to bestow, a mandate shadowed by military might.

I did not centralize authority for its own sake. I shouldered responsibility—to shield a tender democracy from collapse under the siege of a military still clutching the true reins of power, a siege that struck with brutal clarity in the 2021 coup.

Was I strict? Undeniably. Strategic? Resolutely. Short-tempered? I confess—on occasion, yes, for decades of negotiating with the obtuse, the morally hollow, and the deceivers can wear patience thin.

Yet let us not forget: ours was a revolution of nonviolence. We wielded no vitriol, no weapons. We raised the human voice, resting on two sacred disciplines: non-vilification and non-demonization.

We summoned our people to confront their own shadows before challenging others', for how could we mend a fractured nation by mirroring its hatred, violence, and projection?

Leadership was not sainthood—it was survival. Most of my colleagues bore scars from years as political prisoners—enduring beatings, isolation, starvation—trauma that breeds projection and ill-will, the very corrosion of solidarity we needed most.

Thus, leadership in Myanmar was about tending an unseen garden: the wounded roots of trust, the scarred soil of hope, a task we pursued despite our flaws. Democracy cannot take root in poisoned earth; first, you must nurture the broken human heart.

If I faltered—and I did—it was in bearing too heavy a burden alone, striving to guard a nascent democracy from forces poised to strangle it, knowing one misstep could unravel the dreams we bled for.

Call me autocratic if you will. But know that every decision, every tightening of the reins, was driven by one aim: to preserve the fragile possibility of freedom for all.

The cries of "autocrat," "tyrant," "narcissist" echo in every nation wrestling for liberty, where moral courage and moral projection blur—a tension I lived in blood, breath, and bone.

If I have one final lesson on leadership, it is this: True leadership in times of trauma demands endurance—enduring betrayal without bitterness, holding complexity amid calls for slogans, loving a people so fiercely that you embrace misunderstanding, even vilification, if that is the price of their future.

I did not lead because I deemed myself above others. I led because, at the edge of ruin, someone must hold the center—however imperfectly, however painfully—until others rise to share the load.

I offer no excuses, only this truth: In a land of shattered vows, I chose to stand—and keep standing—not for power, but for the fragile, radiant dream of a Myanmar yet to be born. If my voice falls silent, let it live in those who weave a Myanmar where leadership is not a solitary burden, but a shared song of justice and hope.

Failure to Resolve Ethnic Conflicts Beyond the Rohingya

Aung San Suu Kyi: Myanmar's ethnic conflicts are not mere disputes—they are ancient scars, etched by colonization, betrayal, and eroded trust among peoples who once shared the same earth, wounds older than the nation itself. I never professed I could heal them alone, nor claimed such a triumph.

What I did—what I poured every fiber of my being into—was to nudge the wheel of reconciliation toward healing, however faint its glimmer. I revived the Panglong Peace Conference, my father's unfulfilled dream of unity, breathing life into its faded symbol as a vow to honor his vision—not as a daughter, but as a servant to a nation yearning for wholeness. Under my stewardship, we convened three national rounds of dialogue, forging agreements with multiple ethnic armed groups, pressing for federalism to honor every voice, despite the military's unyielding shadow.

We channeled development to the long-neglected rural states—Shan, Kachin, Karen, Rakhine—not as alms, but as a birthright, a step toward mending the fractures of inequity that fueled conflict.

Before the International Court of Justice, I spoke plainly:

"The situation in Rakhine is complex and not easy to fathom… Currently, an internal armed conflict is going on there—between the Arakan Army, an organized Buddhist armed group with more than 5,000 fighters, and the regular Myanmar Defense Services."

The pain, I knew, was not the Rohingya's alone. The UN OCHA's December 2024 report bears witness: the clash between the Tatmadaw and the Arakan Army displaced 300,000 more souls, many Rakhine Buddhists, their lives uprooted by the same relentless conflict—a tapestry of anguish where every community bears its own scars.

I harbored no illusion that peace would dawn swiftly, or that my voice could suture centuries of bloodshed. My aim—our aim—was to carve a space where dialogue could take root, where those who knew only bullets might rediscover words, however falteringly.

There were glimmers of progress. There were shattering setbacks. Yet I never wavered in my belief that no conflict, however ancient, is beyond redemption—not through conquest, but through the courage to see another's humanity amid the fog of historical pain.

Myanmar's sorrow is vast, its hope delicate. I believed then, and believe still, that even the oldest wars can find peace through the stubborn act of presence—the refusal to forsake the most broken places.

I did not heal the nation. But I did not turn from its brokenness. If I leave any legacy here, it is as a relentless listener, steadfast in the faith that Myanmar might one day glimpse its wholeness—a legacy carried forward by those who weave a nation where every scar becomes a bridge to peace.

Defending Myanmar at the ICJ Despite Evidence of Atrocities

Aung San Suu Kyi: I did not stand before the World Court to absolve the military. I stood to defend Myanmar's right to justice—true justice, not the verdict of headlines or the clamor of expediency, but a justice born of searing complexity.

"For materially less resourceful countries like Myanmar, the World Court is a vital refuge of international justice," I declared. I believed it then. I believe it still. I did not deny the horrors that unfolded. I acknowledged openly: *disproportionate force may have been used by the Defence Services, in defiance of international humanitarian law,* a truth I spoke without illusion.

Yet I insisted, and insist still: such crimes demand the rigor of an independent judiciary—not the rush of outrage, not the flattening of a nation into a damning narrative.

I asked the world: "Can there be genocidal intent on the part of a state that actively investigates, prosecutes, and punishes soldiers accused of wrongdoing?" This was a plea for fairness, for nuance, for the discipline of justice over condemnation, each word bearing a nation's trust, a vow to stand firm though the world's judgment burned.

My presence at the ICJ was strategic, yes. The 2020 elections loomed, our democracy a fragile flame. My words rallied a nation, reminding them of our shared struggle—thousands lined Yangon's streets upon my return, the National League for Democracy surging with renewed hope.

But it was not morale alone that drove me. I stood to claim Myanmar's dignity on the global stage—to assert that we were not pawns in a geopolitical game, but a people striving for self-determination, seeking leverage to advance the perilous work of constitutional reform against the military's stranglehold.

The generals took note. They struck back.

The USDP, their political arm, withdrew from our reform committee on December 17, 2019. Tanks rolled through Yangon on December 12, as Bertil Lintner reported, even before the case concluded, a chilling signal of power they never meant to yield.

When I pressed—resolutely—for soldiers accused of atrocities to face courts-martial, I stirred unease at the military's core, not because my demands were fanciful, but because they dared to chip at their myth of impunity.

Had we been granted one more term—one more breath of time— we might have pried open those constitutional chains. But the generals, sensing their supremacy fray, fearing accountability's dawn, chose the coward's path: the coup. And what followed?

More than 22,000 political prisoners. Over 20 million of our people in desperate need of aid. More than 100,000 homes reduced to ash. Over 3.5 million displaced, surviving in jungles, caves, and camps, their lives stripped of dignity—a living catastrophe fueled by the ruthless seizure of power.

So, I ask, with searing sincerity: Was it not evident from the start?

Was it not clear that our so-called "fall from grace"—our alleged betrayal of moral authority—was seized, amplified, weaponized to pave the way for military dominion, a narrative the world embraced too readily?

And I ask further: Is it not plain now—after thousands slain, villages razed, a nation gutted by cruelty—that the true betrayal was not mine, but the world's abandonment of Myanmar, the betrayal of discernment, of truth? Nations that once cheered our democratic dawn turned away, content to condemn rather than engage our tangled truths.

I did not go to The Hague to shield the military. I went to safeguard a people still gasping through the smoke of endless war, to preserve a future now dimmer—but not, I pray, beyond reclaiming.

Alan Clements: Daw Suu, your words carry the full weight of history. Let this stand—not as an excuse or defense—but as a clear call to truth in the face of widespread distortion.

Aung San Suu Kyi: Thank you, Alan, for granting me this space to speak—not for myself alone, but for Myanmar.

Let the world remember: our story is not a fable of heroes and villains. It is the saga of a people—wounded, resilient, striving for freedom under crushing odds. I carry that saga in my bones. Always.

And let the world recall: we rose not because victory seemed assured, but because dignity demanded it. We rose because a nation's conscience cannot dwell in chains forever. Even now, amid all that is lost, I hold fast to that rising. It is not finished—not in Myanmar, nor anywhere truth beats in ordinary hearts.

If my voice falls silent, let it live in the unbreakable spirit of Myanmar's people, who, through every loss, still weave a future of justice and dignity.

Let this chapter be no epitaph, but a dawn.

The revolution of the spirit endures, awaiting those brave enough to carry its flame.

CHAPTER TWENTY

TO GLOBAL LEADERS

Author's Prelude

In a world shadowed by converging crises—where Myanmar's anguish echoes through Gaza, Ukraine, Sudan, and the fentanyl-laced streets of America—this chapter cuts through the fog of indifference.

From the solitary silence of a Myanmar prison, Aung San Suu Kyi speaks—not with pleas, but with a measured challenge. Her voice, tempered by decades of confinement, carries the quiet resilience of a nation's hope, a testament to a spirit unbowed. She seeks neither to flatter nor provoke, but to awaken a global conscience with the clarity of truth. This is not mere diplomacy—it is dignity given voice, a cry cast across borders.

Here, a nation's plea transcends barbed wire, seeking the hearts of the powerful. Each sentence is a spark, passed from Naypyidaw to Washington, Beijing, Moscow, Brussels, bearing the unyielding spirit of a people who refuse to be erased. Yet too often, the world turns away, content to lament from afar while the forsaken are left unheard.

This is no manifesto. It is a diplomatic summons, delivered with the restrained force of truth.

A mirror, not a weapon.

It does not accuse—it questions: What will you do, now that ignorance is no longer a shield?

It summons *karuṇā*—compassion as courage, a call for reckoning. It urges the powerful to rise beyond complacency, to shape a world where no nation's suffering is ignored, no people's dignity dismissed.

It is the pulse of Myanmar's enduring soul, defiant against erasure. And it may be the final plea to listen—while something sacred remains to be saved.

◆ ◆ ◆

Alan Clements: Daw Suu, before we turn to Myanmar's plight, I must honor the weight borne by so many across the globe. We dwell in an era of relentless, interwoven sorrows—from Gaza's unyielding devastation, to the destabilizing violence searing Lebanon, Syria, and the wider Middle East. From Ukraine's enduring war with Russia to the opioid scourge in the United States, where fentanyl claims over 100,000 lives yearly, shattering families and reshaping a nation's soul.

Everywhere, wounds fester—wars without cease, hunger without reprieve, displacement without refuge, addiction without solace. At their root: ignorance, greed, fear. *Samsara,* indeed—yet not without consequence.

We are not powerless. We are not absolved of responsibility. The question is not whether suffering exists, but how we meet it—with apathy or with dignity.

In this light, if you could address global leaders—those at the United Nations, ASEAN, the world's mightiest capitals—what would you say? How can they intervene meaningfully in Myanmar amidst this cascade of crises? And what must they grasp—not only of your people's anguish, but of their defiance, their dignity, their vision for a future forged in freedom and justice?

Aung San Suu Kyi: Alan, your words weave a tapestry of shared human pain, and I am grateful for their breadth. I speak not to elevate Myanmar above this global sorrow, but to plead that we not be entombed beneath it—forgotten in neglect, erased by distraction, dismissed as too tangled to face.

From the confines of a prison cell, my voice rises not for myself, but for a people whose spirit refuses to be silenced, whose dreams endure despite the chains.

The Preamble to the Universal Declaration of Human Rights proclaims "the inherent dignity and the equal and inalienable rights of all members of the human family" as the bedrock of freedom, justice, and peace.

Myanmar's people are no exception to this truth. We are not a tragic aside. We are kin to that family. Yet too often, the world's gaze falters, its resolutions fade, leaving nations like ours to drown in the silence of forgotten promises.

And we suffer—not by chance, but by design.

Our nation is at war—not with itself, but with a military junta that wrested power through brute force and reigns through terror. This is not governance, nor sovereignty. It is oppression's machinery, warring against its own people.

To global leaders, I say: Myanmar's fight is yours. Act not from pity, but from the truth that no people's freedom can thrive while another's is crushed.

Alan Clements: Let it be proclaimed without equivocation: this is no insurgency, no rebellion, no terrorism by the people. The true terrorist is the junta itself—a brutal regime unleashing systemic horror on the nation it falsely claims to defend.

Aung San Suu Kyi: Yes, Alan—thank you for naming it unflinchingly. A military dictatorship is not a state; it is an aberration, a desecration of governance itself. What it inflicts upon Myanmar is not "law and order"—it is calculated brutality, cloaked in the illusion of rule.

Yet we rise. We are not merely a people in peril. We are a tapestry of resistance—poets and monks, farmers and teachers, artists and revolutionaries. We are youth facing fighter jets unarmed, mothers burying sons with *mettā* on their lips, nuns chanting peace as monasteries burn.

Myanmar is no land for pity or plunder—it is a living civilization. One of Southeast Asia's most ancient cultures, shaped by the *Dhamma's timeless wisdom*, we are woven from a multitude of ethnic threads— languages, customs, and spiritual traditions. Not fractured, but a mosaic of endurance and soul.

To global leaders, I implore: place human life above profit, dignity above politics, vision above expediency. This is no geopolitical riddle—it is a vessel of moral clarity. Your action—or your silence—will resound for generations. The hour for hesitation is gone. The stakes transcend Myanmar; they strike at the heart of our shared humanity.

Let me speak plainly of our ordeal.

This revolution—this uprising of the heart—is no mere movement. It is a reckoning with decades of fear, silence, and inherited trauma. A reckoning that will not falter, for it cannot. Our people have chosen— not in slogans, but in blood: we will not return to chains.

And yet I know what looms.

This regime is not only cruel—it is emboldened. Armed with fighter jets, missiles, drones, and digital surveillance—supplied by Russia and China, fueled by billions in oil and gas, shielded by illicit financial networks and global complicity.

Nations that profit from this junta's plunder—through trade, through arms, through silence—bear the stain of our suffering. This is not just a military. It is an ideology of impunity, fattened by wealth and the world's averted gaze.

I fear, Alan, that without intervention, this revolution may drown in tragedy. From my cell—where silence is both cage and canvas—I see their faces: youth, mothers, nuns. Their courage outshines my confinement. Our people's resolve is unshakable. But the toll is catastrophic. Over 2,000 villages have been razed since 2021. Children die. Elders are entombed in silence.

So, I say to the world's leaders: *this is your hour—not to watch, but to act.* If you champion democracy, let it not become a relic—revive it with courage. If you seek peace, do not whisper it in diplomatic halls—embody it through meaningful choice. If you claim to uphold justice, let it be more than sentiment—let it rise like a tide, fearless against cruelty's tide.

Above all—see us.

Not as a distant crisis, not as strangers with names you struggle to pronounce. See us as kin.

We are not apart from you. Nor are you apart from this moment.

Let *karuṇā*—true compassion—be your compass. Not the calculus of cost, not the shadow of risk, but the wisdom that tells us caring for others is not weakness—it is the highest power.

For if you wait until we are silenced, shattered, buried, your solidarity—however heartfelt—will arrive too late.

History will not record your sympathies. It will etch your courage—or your silence.

At the heart of this lies a question we must all confront: How does the human mind justify the killing, the maiming, the brutalizing of 'the other'? Until we confront that question—in our bones—the cycle of violence will go on.

This is the Buddha's samsara.

And this is why our struggle for freedom must be a revolution of the spirit.

I have said it before, and I say it now:

"The quintessential revolution is that of the spirit, born of an intellectual conviction of the need for change in those mental attitudes and values which shape the course of a nation's development."

This revolution calls not just for new laws—but for a new heart. A transformation of perception, a seeing that dissolves the illusion of separation. A revolution that sees no 'other'—only the sacred, shared humanity before us.

This work—to end tyranny, to restore democracy—requires not ideology, but an ethic of care, the courage to bear the burden of others' needs. As I once wrote:

> *"To live the full life, one must have the courage to bear the responsibility of the needs of others... one must want to bear this responsibility."*

This is not politics. It is spiritual. It is human. It is the recognition that each of us holds the spark to realize truth—and to guide others gently toward it.

> *"The quest for democracy in Burma is the struggle of a people to live whole, meaningful lives as free and equal members of the world community. It is part of the unceasing human endeavor to prove that the spirit of man can transcend the flaws of his nature."*

Alan Clements: Daw Suu, your words lift us from the realm of politics into the realm of conscience—a summons not merely to act, but to remember our shared humanity, our spiritual essence. And yet, despite such clarity, many global leaders still hide behind the tattered shields of "sovereignty" and "geopolitical complexity."

They protest, *"It's not our place,"* or *"Our hands are bound."* Some cite risks of escalation or destabilization. Others, in hushed tones, confess the real barriers: economic entanglements, regional alliances, or the fatigue of sustained compassion.

In the searing light of all you've shared, how do you respond to those who wield sovereignty as a veil for inaction while Myanmar's soul is being crushed? And how can we, as a global community, transcend the paralysis of convenience to embrace a shared ethic of courage, responsibility, and *karuṇā?*

Aung San Suu Kyi: Sovereignty, Alan, is not a fortress for impunity. It was never meant to shield governments from accountability—it exists to safeguard the dignity of people. When a government—or in our case, a rogue military—turns its arsenal against its own people, bombing schools, razing villages, jailing elected leaders, it forfeits any claim to legitimacy.

Power without legitimacy is not order—it is tyranny. And tyranny, no matter what flag it flies or wealth it commands, demands not deference but confrontation.

Myanmar is not descending into civil strife. We are not battling unrest. We are enduring the iron grip of a criminal cartel masquerading as a state. To invoke "non-interference" here is not diplomacy—it is willful denial.

Nations that preach human rights yet profit from this regime's oil, weapons, and silence betray the very values they profess. To stand neutral in the face of terror is not neutrality—it is complicity.

I do not discount the complexity of geopolitics. Nations must guard interests, maintain alliances, and shield economies. I know the weight of that calculus. But I ask you—what is the purpose of power if it forsakes the service of life? If a single innocent life can be bartered for profit or stability, we have not only failed Myanmar—we have failed the meaning of leadership itself.

As Václav Havel wrote: *"The salvation of this human world lies nowhere else than in the human heart... in human responsibility."*

Responsibility—not for perfection, but for presence. Not for heroic gestures, but for moral clarity.

What is the cost of inaction? Each day without action, children die in silence. Monks are murdered. Mothers disappear. Elders are buried unwept. Artists are broken.

Delay is not diplomacy. It is betrayal.

We are not asking for soldiers. We are asking for moral alignment. For tools you already hold:

- Sever the junta's financial arteries—its access to international banking and revenues.
- Cut off the weapons that fuel its war on the people.
- Open humanitarian corridors to sustain our displaced—from Kachin to Karen, Shan to Rakhine.

- Formally recognize the National Unity Government, the legitimate voice of Myanmar's people, and stand with the Ethnic Armed Organizations who have long held the line of resistance.
- Bring the perpetrators to justice—not in editorials, but in international courts.

This is not interference—it is solidarity. It is the necessary groundwork for a federal democracy where Bamar and ethnic peoples live not in suspicion, but in trust. Not under fear, but in dignity.

As Aleksandr Solzhenitsyn warned: *"Let the lie come into the world, let it even triumph. But not through me."*

If this terror endures, let it not pass through your silence. Not through your trade deals. Not through your geopolitical hedging. Not through your fear to risk comfort.

To world leaders, I say: If you would not tolerate this violence in your own streets, do not ignore it in ours. If you would never allow your children to live under siege, stand with ours as they fight to survive.

If you believe the human spirit is sacred, then stand now. Or all your convictions are theatre.

Eleanor Roosevelt said: *"Where, after all, do universal human rights begin? In small places, close to home… unless these rights have meaning there, they have little meaning anywhere."*

For us, "home" is shattered—but still ours. And we remain. We will not surrender.

The hour for hesitation is over. The hour for moral courage has arrived. Let history engrave your conscience—not your convenience.

And I speak not only to global leaders—but to the soldiers of Myanmar:

You were not born to serve tyranny. Your uniform was never meant to strangle the people—it was meant to protect them.

I speak in the name of my father, General Aung San. He did not create a military to dominate, but to defend dignity. His legacy—his courage to confront even his own power—lives in me. And from these prison walls, I urge you:

Reclaim that legacy. Lay down your arms. Choose conscience over command. Let this be your Ashoka moment. Not to destroy, but to restore. Not to conquer, but to awaken.

Because only then will Myanmar rise—not as a wound, but as a wisdom. Not just free, but transformed.

To the people of Myanmar—and to all who cherish freedom:

"Politics is not distant, nor reserved for the powerful. It is your life—how you eat, sleep, work, live. You may turn from it, but it will not turn from you. It haunts your home, your labor, your children's future. It is neither noble nor sordid—it is the shape of your freedom."

So seize it. Do not leave it in the hands of those who profit from ignorance.

This is not a call for action. It is a call for awakening.

Let the age of conscience begin—not tomorrow, not when it is safe—but now.

And if you ask where to start?

See. See clearly. See deeply.

Because the moment we refuse to look away, conscience is born—and from that seed, the world begins to change.

Alan Clements: Thank you—from my heart. May your words find their rightful place in the world: in the halls of power, and in the hearts of those who still remember what it means to lead with truth.

Daw Suu, you've long emphasized ASEAN's unique role in Myanmar's struggle. And yet, many of its leaders waver—some cloaking inaction in the language of neutrality, others retreating behind the veil of quiet diplomacy.

One might respond to your plea by saying: *"You paint us as complicit. But we are striving. We are engaging. We are respecting sovereignty. The situation is complex."*

How would you respond—directly and unflinchingly—to that defense?

Aung San Suu Kyi: I understand the instinct for caution, Alan. Diplomacy, at its best, is the patient weaving of fragile threads—threads of trust, of language, of timing. But diplomacy untethered from conscience becomes delay. And delay, in our case, becomes complicity.

When over 10,000 civilians have been killed since the February 2021 coup, when 3.5 million souls are displaced, when more than

100,000 homes are incinerated and entire villages are erased from the map—nuance without action becomes a veil for moral retreat.

Children die in bombed schools. Mothers give birth in ditches. Monks are murdered mid-chant. The United Nations warns that two million people in Rakhine State alone face the risk of starvation this year. Twenty million cry out for basic humanitarian aid.

Yangon's lights flicker—four hours on, twenty off. Mandalay bears the scars of a devastating earthquake. In the shadows, Myanmar festers as a global epicenter of cybercrime and narcotics, with fentanyl and methamphetamine flowing across borders, corroding the region's soul.

For what? Power? Profit? Political caution? Averted eyes?

This is not a crisis to be slow-walked through diplomatic choreography. This is a moral abyss. And its darkness stains not only Myanmar—it stains the entire region, and every government that chooses silence over solidarity.

Neutrality, in the face of state terror, is not diplomacy. It is abdication.

I do not dismiss the complexities. But when complexity is used to excuse paralysis, it becomes cowardice. ASEAN was built not only for cooperation, but for mutual uplift. For shared peace. For regional dignity. What peace can grow in a region where one member state is a factory of atrocities?

So, I say this to ASEAN leaders:

Your legacy will not be measured by statements or communiqués, but by the lives saved—or lost—because of what you chose to do. Or chose not to.

Respect for sovereignty is never a license for atrocity.

Do not mistake silence for diplomacy. Do not let "quiet engagement" become the mask behind which thousands perish. The junta does not need more time—it thrives on delay. It thrives on your hesitance.

There is no excuse left.

The world is watching. History is watching.

And what it will record is not your intentions, but your impact.

To ASEAN leaders who feel reproached, I offer this: (Brunei, Cambodia, Indonesia, Laos, Malaysia, Myanmar, the Philippines, Singapore, Thailand, and Vietnam).

You are not accused—you are summoned.

Summoned to stand not in judgment, but in solidarity. Summoned to support the National Unity Government and the Ethnic Armed Organizations in weaving a unified resistance—one whose dialogue and sacrifice form the cornerstone of a federal union where every voice is protected, and every life dignified.

Summoned to reclaim ASEAN's soul. To honor the spirit of your own Charter—your promise *"to strengthen democracy, to enhance good governance, and uphold the rule of law."*

This is not interference—this is your covenant.

I speak not as **ASEAN**'s critic, but as its daughter—raised in th_s region's embrace, formed by its cultures, and still believing in its power to lead not only in commerce, but in conscience.

Cease all complicity. End every collaboration that lends oxygen to oppression.

Bar your banks from laundering their billions. Halt the flow of arms that fuel atrocity. Deny their envoys the legitimacy of your platforms. Withhold the scaffolding that props up tyranny under the guise of sovereignty.

Yes, they may seek assistance—but not for food or medicine. They seek weapons, status, impunity. And in truth, what they need is neither of those. They need redemption—moral and spiritual.

I speak not as a politician—but as a prisoner. One voice among 22,000. Each of us—children, teachers, spouses, students—a Nelson Mandela in spirit. Silenced, but not broken. Disappeared, but not erased. We are not statistics. We are your kin.

And among us stand the Ethnic Armed Organizations— courageous defenders of our diverse peoples. Warriors and protectors, they hold the frontlines of justice and federalism with bare hands and unyielding hearts. In their courage, the seeds of a new Myanmar take root—amidst fire, famine, and ash.

I do not ask, *What have you done?*

I ask:

What will you do?

When will you act?

Let **ASEAN** rise. Not as a bystander, not as a broker of platitudes— but as a beacon of moral courage.

Let your nations stand as one—not behind the junta, but beside Myanmar's people—guiding our shared dream of a federal democracy into the light. A democracy where power is held in trust, not in terror. Where justice is not an abstraction, but a lived experience. Where dignity is not conditional, but shared.

Because history will not etch your intentions.

It will carve your courage—or your silence.

**Letter to the Honorable Secretary-General
and Members of the United Nations**

Alan Clements: Daw Suu, you've addressed nations, laureates, Elders, the Sangha, lay Buddhists, and religious leaders of all faiths. As a final beacon of hope, may I invite you to please speak with the Honorable Members of the United Nations and the Secretary-General, to clarify why Myanmar's struggle matters and to rally their resolve for your people's salvation in a world of converging crises?

Aung San Suu Kyi: Alan, this is where the world's conscience must rise to meet its own promise. To the Honorable Members of the United Nations and Secretary-General António Guterres, I offer not a plea, but a moral and diplomatic summons to the sacred covenant of humanity's shared destiny, urging you to act with the moral courage that Myanmar's struggle demands—for the sake of our world's enduring hope and the principles you have vowed to uphold.

Aung San Suu Kyi

To the Honorable Secretary-General and Esteemed Members of the United Nations
July 2025 – In Detention, Naypyidaw Prison

Esteemed Members and Honorable Secretary-General,

From the austere confines of a Naypyidaw prison, I write as a daughter of Myanmar, a servant of the *Buddha's Dhamma*, and a witness to the universal yearning for dignity that unites humanity.

In Myanmar, where our ancient traditions—steeped in *karuṇā* (compassion that embraces all), *satya* (truth that pierces delusion), *ahiṃsā* (non-violence that heals), and *metta* (loving-kindness that unites)—have shaped a vibrant culture, I have striven to embody these virtues despite the shackles that bind me.

Today, I address you not for my own freedom, but for 54 million lives ensnared by terror—their courage a testament to humanity's unyielding spirit, their anguish a sacred summons to the United Nations' conscience.

Why does Myanmar matter?

It matters because it is a crucible for the principles upon which your institution was founded—peace, justice, human rights, the sanctity of life. It matters because we stand at a perilous crossroads, where China's economic and geopolitical ambitions threaten to transform Myanmar into a modern-day Tibet in silence or Taiwan under siege—a region subsumed under Beijing's expanding influence.

Through the China-Myanmar Economic Corridor (CMEC), Beijing has invested billions in our oil and gas pipelines, stretching 800 kilometers from Kyaukphyu's deep-sea port to Yunnan, ferrying 440,000 barrels of oil daily—securing access to the Indian Ocean while bypassing the Strait of Malacca. These pipelines, along with investments in rare earths, timber, and jade, render Myanmar a fulcrum in China's Belt and Road Initiative, granting Beijing sweeping leverage to exploit both our resources and our strategic location. It is a deliberate encroachment, a calculated bid for dominance that dismantles our sovereignty.

China's actions—arming the junta economically, brokering with ethnic armed groups, and mediating to protect its stake—reveal a chilling truth: Myanmar teeters on the brink of becoming a vassal state, its independence hollowed like Tibet's, or a geopolitical fault line like Taiwan. The junta's fragility, propped by Russian arms, nuclear pledges, and Min Aung Hlaing's Moscow visits, accelerates this descent as China fills the vacuum left by global inaction.

Time is collapsing.

Over 20 million of our people—more than one-third of our nation—require urgent humanitarian assistance, their lives imperiled by starvation, displacement, and violence. A crisis that threatens to extinguish the keepers of our culture and conscience. Millions of our youth have fled to Thailand, Bangladesh, and India—their futures bartered for survival, as Myanmar faces the gravest catastrophe in its recorded history. A fate no nation should endure. And one that our people reject with every breath.

This is not the path we choose.

Myanmar's diverse spiritual heritage—encompassing Buddhist, Muslim, Christian, Hindu, and indigenous traditions—reflects a nation that has endured centuries of invasions, colonial oppression, and authoritarian rule. United by universal principles of compassion, justice, and human dignity, these communities embody a shared commitment to humanity's highest ideals.

Yet, Myanmar is but one of many nations in crisis—alongside Russia, Sudan, Ukraine, Iran, Israel, and Gaza—each demanding the international community's urgent attention.

Myanmar is not peripheral; it is a critical test of the United Nations Charter's integrity. If the global community falters here, where the junta's systematic violations undermine the 1948 Universal Declaration of Human Rights, what hope remains for oppressed peoples worldwide, whose aspirations, across every faith and language, rise for justice and accountability?

When tyranny thrives in one nation, it unravels the moral thread in all, diminishing the Charter you are entrusted to defend.

You, Honorable Members—and you, Secretary-General Guterres—possess the authority to ignite a miracle of justice. Your voices can break the silence that shields atrocity. *I implore you: Act—not with guarded diplomacy, but with the moral fire of those who forged your Charter from the ashes of war.*

- **Deploy peacekeepers** to shield our people from junta airstrikes and Russian weapons.
- **Impose targeted, enforceable sanctions** to sever the regime's financial arteries.
- **Deliver aid**—food, medicine, shelter—through civil society, monasteries, and humanitarian channels that bypass junta control.
- **Support the National Unity Government and Ethnic Armed Organizations**, helping weave a just federal democracy across Kachin, Karen, Shan, and beyond—where every voice, Bamar or ethnic, rural or urban, is heard in harmony, shaped by *metta* and *Dhamma*.

This is not intervention. It is the embodiment of *satya* confronting *avijjā* (ignorance) with truth.

Myanmar matters because its collapse would unleash instability across South Asia and the Bay of Bengal.

It matters because unchecked impunity in Myanmar signals to despots worldwide that justice is negotiable.

It matters because our children—eyes still burning with stolen dreams—are the world's future, their suffering a shared failure we cannot accept.

To General Min Aung Hlaing, I extend—as the Buddha once did to *Angulimāla*—a path of redemption: You are not beyond grace. End the violence. Release the leaders. Embrace *ahiṃsā* as Emperor Ashoka did—from bloodshed to benevolence. The United Nations stands ready to guide your transformation, if you so choose.

Esteemed leaders:

You are the stewards of humanity's hope, entrusted with the legacies of Eleanor Roosevelt, Dag Hammarskjöld, and Kofi Annan—

visionaries who dared to dream of a world where no cry is lost in the void.

In my cell, I have practiced *sati*—mindful awareness—uncovering our shared *dukkha* (suffering), and *paññā*—wisdom—guiding me to meet even my captors with *metta*. I ask you to do the same.

Your actions—peacekeepers, sanctions, aid—are not policies. They are the breath of *karuṇā*.

They are seeds of awakening in a wounded world.

From these prison walls, where 22,000 lives—each a beacon of *satya*, each a prayer for *metta*—stand unbowed, I call upon you to rise as guardians of peace, artisans of justice, architects of a new dawn.

Let Myanmar be your crucible—not your regret.

And when history's ledger is opened, may it read: In Myanmar's darkest hour, when China's influence expanded and terror reigned, the United Nations and Secretary-General Guterres stood as sentinels of *karuṇā*—compassion that seeks to alleviate suffering—their voices a symphony of *satya*, the pursuit of truth, their resolve an undying flame, lighting the way to peace, and safeguarding humanity's hope for generations to come.

With reverence, urgency, and unwavering hope,
Aung San Suu Kyi
JULY 2025
FROM NAYPYIDAW PRISON, MYANMAR

Letter To All Living Nobel Peace Laureates

Alan Clements: Daw Suu, we've addressed ASEAN, the region, the UN and global powers. Yet there exists a unique community whose moral authority transcends borders—the living Nobel Peace Laureates, including His Holiness the Dalai Lama. Their voices, forged in struggles for justice, carry a singular weight. What would you say to them, collectively, to rally their support for Myanmar's plight?

Aung San Suu Kyi: Alan, this is where *conscience must rise to action*. To my fellow Nobel Peace Laureates—my sisters and brothers in the sacred pursuit of humanity's highest ideals—I offer not a plea, but *a call to our shared soul*, bound by the Dhamma of compassion, the truth of justice, and the eternal flame of peace.

Aung San Suu Kyi to All Living Nobel Peace Laureates Dear Sisters and Brothers, Esteemed His Holiness the Dalai Lama,

From the shadowed solitude of a prison cell in Naypyidaw, where silence cradles both pain and persistence, I write as one who has walked beside you in spirit, humbled by the radiant legacy of our shared Nobel Peace Prize.

We are bound not by laurels, but by our unshakable commitment to human dignity, moral conscience, and sacred trust—you, the heirs of Martin Luther King Jr.; the disciples of Mahatma Gandhi; the comrades of Nelson Mandela; the kin of Archbishop Desmond Tutu; and the devoted students of His Holiness the Dalai Lama.

In Myanmar, a land steeped in the *Buddha's Dhamma*, I have strived to uphold these same virtues: *karuṇā* (compassion), *satya* (truth), *ahiṃsā* (nonviolence), and the relentless pursuit of peace—even amidst the invisible crucifixion of incarceration.

Today, I reach out with fierce authenticity—my heart laid bare—not for myself, but for 54 million beloveds caught in the grip of terror—my colleagues, our freedom-loving people, and the silenced voices of Myanmar's collective conscience.

I write with the intimacy of one who knows the weight of misperception, the sting of public judgment, and the quiet burden of responsibility. Like you, I have faced the challenges of sacrifice—my cell a mirror to your own: King's Birmingham jail, Mandela's Robben Island, Tutu's moral defiance—binding us in a vow to transform suffering into compassion.

Some of you may harbor misgivings about my path—particularly regarding the Rohingya crisis. I do not shy from this. I acknowledge the suffering of all communities—Rohingya, Rakhine, Bamar, and others—entangled in a centuries-deep tapestry of wounds, militarism, and ethnic division.

As State Counsellor, I faced constraints—legal, military, historical—that limited my power to act as swiftly or fully as my heart compelled. Yet I never ceased striving for reconciliation, advocating dialogue, and pressing for justice within the bounds of a fragile democracy.

If my efforts fell short, I bear that burden not with defensiveness, but with a vow to deepen my understanding, heal more wisely, and bridge divides more bravely—*as the Dhamma teaches us: to turn suffering into wisdom.*

So, I ask you—set aside judgment, not for my sake, but for the innocents who suffer now.

Since the coup of February 2021, the junta has ignited an inferno. Over 10,000 civilians have perished—slain by a regime armed with Chinese and Russian jets, missiles, and drones, and emboldened by Moscow's nuclear pledges and Min Aung Hlaing's parades through the Kremlin.

Over 3.5 million are displaced—wandering jungles, sheltering in makeshift camps. More than 100,000 homes are destroyed. Classrooms bombed. Children buried beneath the ruins. Mandalay's sacred ground still trembles from the 2025 earthquake. Yangon flickers under four hours of daily power. The economy is eviscerated. Myanmar is now a failed state—a cybercrime syndicate and fentanyl cartel masquerading as a government, sustained by complicity from foreign powers.

This is not the Dhamma's way. This is not the legacy of peace we vowed to uphold.

Your moral power—forged through exile, apartheid, civil rights, and sacred defiance—can pierce this darkness. I implore you: lend your voices, your influence, your sacred moral capital to Myanmar's cry.

Do not support me. Support the cause of my colleagues— President Win Myint, our elected ministers and parliamentarians, and the 11 million citizens who voted for democracy in 2020—now hunted, imprisoned, and tortured for their courage.

Stand with the National Unity Government and Ethnic Armed Organizations—who, despite bloodshed, are building a federal democracy through dialogue. In Kachin, Karen, Shan, and beyond— every voice, Bamar and ethnic, urban and rural, is rising to reimagine Myanmar as a nation of justice and grace.

The junta's reign is not destiny. It feeds on your silence. Your voices can break the spell of impunity. Proclaim, with one resounding voice:

"We, the Nobel Peace Laureates, demand an immediate ceasefire. We demand the release of President Win Myint, State Counsellor Aung San Suu Kyi, all elected leaders, and every prisoner of conscience."

Urge nations to close their ports to the junta's arms and commerce. Halt the flow of Russian and Chinese weapons. Freeze the regime's financial lifelines. Call for 20,000 crore (approx. €2.2 billion) in humanitarian aid—channeled not through generals, but through civil society, monasteries, and trusted networks of compassion.

Lead the charge at the UN and ICC. Name Min Aung Hlaing and his generals as war criminals. Their crimes—10,000 dead, 3.5 million displaced—are inscribed in the bones of our people.

To General Min Aung Hlaing, I echo Mandela: You are not beyond redemption. Cease the slaughter. Release our leaders. Choose the path of conscience—like Ashoka, who turned from conquest to compassion. History offers mercy to those who awaken.

Dear laureates, you know the price of silence. King dreamed of a beloved community. Gandhi wove freedom through truth. Mandela forged unity from division. Tutu danced with *ubuntu*. And His Holiness radiates *karuṇā*.

His Holiness, your compassion has lit the world's heart. Let it now warm Myanmar's wounds, as you once consoled Tibet's exiles— urging peace where terror reigns.

I appeal to these truths—to the Dhamma's vow to end suffering—to the sacred moral power you embody. Myanmar is not a distant tragedy—it is a mirror of our shared humanity, a test of our global conscience.

Let your collective voices awaken the world—ignite a moral uprising to lift Myanmar's people—proving once more that peace, like the *Dhamma*, knows no border.

If not now—when?

From these prison walls, with 22,000 souls—each a living prayer of *satya*, each a breath of *metta*—I implore you:

Be the architects of peace. Be the guardians of conscience. Let your voices rise—As King's rose from Birmingham, As Gandhi's from Sabarmati, As Mandela's from Robben Island.

Let history say: When Myanmar's darkness deepened, the Nobel Peace Laureates lit the path—hearts ablaze with truth, compassion, and the unyielding spirit of peace.

With respect, conscience, and unwavering hope,

Aung San Suu Kyi

JULY 2025

IN DETENTION, NAYPYIDAW PRISON

Letter to Myanmar's Sangha and the Global Buddhist Sangha

Alan Clements: Daw Suu, you've addressed nations, superpowers, and fellow laureates. Yet there exists a sacred community whose wisdom and moral authority could shift Myanmar's destiny—the *Sangha*, the order of *bhikkhus* and *bhikkhunis* in Myanmar, and Buddhist *Sangha* members across all traditions worldwide. What would you say to them, to awaken their hearts and voices in support of Myanmar's long struggle for freedom.

Aung San Suu Kyi: Alan, this is where the *Dhamma's* radiant truth must dispel the paralysis of silence. To Myanmar's *Sangha*—venerable *bhikkhus* and *bhikkhunis* who cradle our nation's spiritual heart—and to the global Buddhist *Sangha* across all traditions, I offer not a plea, but a summons to the sacred guardianship of *hiri* and *ottappa*—the conscience that anchors the *Dhamma*—calling you to rise as protectors of the Sasana and beacons of collective awakening.

Venerable *Bhikkhus*, *Bhikkhunis*, and Esteemed *Sangha* Members Across the World,

From the confines of Naypyidaw prison, I write to you as a daughter of the *Dhamma,* a humble servant of the Buddha's teachings, and a witness to the impermanence that binds all sentient life.

In Myanmar—where the *Sangha's* saffron robes have long illuminated the path of *karuṇā* (compassion that embraces all beings), *satya* (truth that liberates), *ahiṃsā* (nonviolence that heals), and *metta* (loving-kindness that unites)—I have striven to embody these virtues, drawing strength from the Four Noble Truths and the Noble Eightfold Path.

Today, I do not speak for my own liberation. I write for 54 million lives ensnared by terror—their courage a testament to the *Dhamma's* enduring radiance, their anguish a direct call to your sacred conscience.

You, revered *Sangha*, are the custodians of the *Sasana*—the living stream of the Buddha's insight—entrusted not only to preserve its purity, but to protect its relevance in times of great peril.

Myanmar now stands at the precipice. Should we falter, we risk becoming the next Tibet—a land where the *Dhamma's* flame flickers, its monasteries are silenced, and its spiritual heart uprooted by tyranny.

The junta that seized power in February 2021 threatens not only our democracy but the very breath of the *Sāsana* itself—their violence a blasphemy against the Buddha's teachings and a desecration of our shared humanity. Armed with Russian and Chinese jets, missiles, and drones—and emboldened by Moscow's nuclear reactor pledges and Min Aung Hlaing's ritual pilgrimages to the Kremlin—they have leveled entire villages, torched monasteries, and murdered monks. They have silenced children's laughter in classrooms blasted without warning, executed medics for offering care, and used rape as a weapon of war against our ethnic sisters.

In the aftermath of the 2025 earthquake, they looted disaster relief, transformed sacred groves in Mandalay into fortified compounds, and blockaded aid from reaching displaced families now starving in makeshift camps beside the charred remains of *kyaungs*. This is not merely a military occupation—it is a systematic erasure of conscience, culture, and freedom.

This is not the *Dhamma's* path. This is the road of *avijjā*—ignorance—the very darkness the Buddha urged us to illuminate with wisdom.

The *Sangha's* heart pulses with *hiri*—moral shame that recoils from harm—and *ottappa*—moral dread that restrains the unwholesome. As you know so well, these twin guardians are the conscience of the *Dhamma*—the inner compass that awakens sati (mindful intelligence) and *paññā* (wisdom).

I have known their power in the stillness of my own practice—in solitude, where *sati* revealed the web of interdependence and *paññā* offered the courage to meet it with compassion.

As a laywoman, I have walked this path imperfectly. Yet it has sustained me—guiding me through long years of captivity, softening anger, opening me to love, even toward those who imprison me.

Venerable ones, your robes are not mere garments. They are living vows—to uphold *karuṇā* that heals, *satya* that liberates, and *ahiṃsā* that refuses all harm.

Yet some among Myanmar's *Sangha* remain silent—or worse, lend legitimacy to the regime through complicity. This silence is not neutral—it is a wound to the *Sasana*, a betrayal of *hiri* and *ottappa*.

The Buddha taught that ignorance is the root of suffering. But it is through *sati* and *paññā* that we see, and through moral courage that we act. You, venerable ones, hold the wisdom to illuminate what Min Aung Hlaing refuses to see: that his path leads only to *dukkha*—for himself and for all beings.

I call you to rise—not in wrath, but in radiant *metta*. Speak the truth of the *Dhamma* with fearless compassion. Chant *metta* in the streets, as the monks of 2007 once did—their robes shields of *ahiṃsā*, their presence sanctified rebellion.

Convene councils of awakening, as the Buddha once did—to summon Min Aung Hlaing to his own humanity. Illuminate his delusion with *paññā*. Show him the impermanence of power. Invite him into the merit of renunciation, the nobility of peace.

Proclaim, with the full moral weight of the *Sasana*:

"Step down, General. Free President Win Myint, State Counsellor Aung San Suu Kyi, all democratic leaders, and every prisoner of conscience. Renounce violence, or bear the kammic burden of your deeds."

To the global Sangha—Theravāda, Mahāyāna, Vajrayāna, and all paths of awakening—I appeal to your shared vow: to preserve the *Dhamma* for the benefit of all beings.

Myanmar's Sasana is your Sasana. Its peril is your call to respond.

Raise our voice through your networks: from Thai *wats* to Japanese *zendos*, from Tibetan *gompas* to Western *viharas*. Urge your governments to sever the junta's lifelines—arms, trade, financial channels—and to channel urgent aid through monasteries and civil society—the veins of *karuṇā* in our torn land.

Stand with the National Unity Government and Ethnic Armed Organizations. Help them weave a federal democracy in Kachin, Karen, Shan, Chin, and beyond—where all life flourishes in harmony, a living manifestation of the *Dhamma*.

To General Min Aung Hlaing, I say, as the Buddha said to *Angulimāla*: You are not beyond grace. Cease the violence. Free the imprisoned. *Embrace metta's path.* Become, like Ashoka, a ruler reborn in compassion. The *Sangha's* wisdom awaits your awakening.

Venerable Sangha, you are the keepers of the Buddha's flame. You are the embodiment of hiri and ottappa. The voice of sati and paññā.

In this sacred moment, the fate of Myanmar—and the *living Sasana*—rests in your hands.

If you break your silence, if you speak *Dhamma* truth to power, you can kindle a flame of redemption, a wave of moral accountability that frees 22,000 prisoners and restores the spiritual heart of our nation.

Envision a Myanmar where the *Sangha's* chants echo in peace once more. Where no life is crushed by tyranny. Where the *Sasana* flowers. This is not a dream. It is the *Dhamma's* promise. And you, venerable ones, are its voice.

From these prison walls—alongside 22,000 beings—each a torch of conscience, each a hymn of *satya*—I call you to rise as the *Dhamma's* weavers:

Weave a world where karuṇā heals, ahiṃsā protects, and metta unites all hearts.

And when the annals of history are etched, let it be said: In Myanmar's darkest hour, the *Sangha* rose—their voices a symphony of *karuṇā*, their resolve a fortress of *satya*, their *metta* the eternal light that preserved the *Sasana* for generations yet to be born.

With reverence, conscience, and unwavering hope,
Aung San Suu Kyi
JULY 2025
IN DETENTION, NAYPYIDAW PRISON

Letter to Lay Buddhist Teachers and Practitioners Worldwide

Alan Clements: May I invite you Daw Suu to address the vast, vibrant community of lay Buddhist teachers and practitioners across all traditions worldwide, whose voices and actions could amplify Myanmar's cry for justice. What would you say to them, to ignite their Dhamma-inspired activism for the betterment of your people?

Aung San Suu Kyi: Alan, this is where the *Dhamma's* radiant truth must awaken a global moral uprising. To lay Buddhist teachers and practitioners worldwide—across *Theravāda*, *Mahāyāna*, *Vajrayāna*, and all lineages—I offer not a plea, but a summons to the heartwood of the path: *hiri* and *ottappa*, the conscience that births *karuṇā* and satya. I urge you to weave your voices, teachings, and daily presence into a living tapestry of compassion for Myanmar's imperiled people.

Dear Friends in the *Dhamma*,

From the austere stillness of Naypyidaw prison, I write to you as a fellow lay practitioner, a humble disciple of the Buddha's teachings, and a witness to the ceaseless interplay of *dukkha* and liberation.

In Myanmar, where the *Dhamma's* gentle light has guided hearts for centuries, I have walked the path of *karuṇā*—compassion that embraces all; *satya*—truth that pierces delusion; *ahiṃsā*—nonviolence that heals; and *metta*—loving-kindness that unites.

Today, I reach out not for my own freedom, but for 54 million lives trapped in fear, their resilience a mirror of the Buddha's wisdom, their suffering a summons to your awakened hearts.

You, beloved teachers and practitioners, are the bridge between the *Sangha's* sacred vows and the world's longing for peace. Your meditation halls, *Dharma* talks, and daily sittings radiate *sati*—mindful intelligence that sees clearly—and *paññā*—wisdom that discerns the real from the unreal.

I know this path intimately. I have sat in silence, my mind steadied in *sati*, sensing the interconnection of all *dukkha*, and guided by *paññā* to act with *metta*—even toward those who hold the key to my cell.

As a laywoman, I have stumbled. But the Four Noble Truths and the Noble Eightfold Path have been my refuge.

They have taught me that *hiri—moral shame that recoils from harm—*and *ottappa—moral dread that guards against harm—*are the twin flames that illuminate the heart's inner compass.

Myanmar now teeters on the edge of spiritual collapse. The junta that seized power in February 2021 tramples the *Dhamma*. Their rule is not mere oppression—*it is avijjā embodied.* It is a desecration of every teaching you hold sacred.

With both Chinese and Russian weapons, with missiles and drones, with Moscow's nuclear pledges and Min Aung Hlaing's gilded visits, they have leveled hundreds of villages, crushed classrooms, and left over 20 million of our people in extreme need of humanitarian support. Yangon flickers in blackout. Our economy is a shell. Myanmar is now a failed state—a digital crime syndicate, a fentanyl empire in uniform—enabled by global powers who profit from our collapse.

If we do not act now, Myanmar will become the next Tibet—a sacred land silenced, its *Dhamma* voice exiled, its *Sasana* dismembered by dictatorship.

This is not the Buddha's path. This is the road of *Mara*. And we—those who practice in his name—are called to end it.

Your voices, your pens, your presence—these are not small things. They are the breath of the *Dhamma* made manifest. I ask you to rise—not in anger, but in boundless *metta*—and speak *satya* with fearless compassion.

Teachers, let your *Dharma* talks echo with Myanmar's cry. *Weave hiri and ottappa into your teachings. Urge your students to see conscience as the pulse of practice.*

Practitioners, write. Share how *sati* opens the eye to shared *dukkha*, how *paññā* guides us to act. Host vigils. Meditate for Myanmar. Post on every platform. Each tweet, each chant, each blog is a thread in the robe of awakening.

Speak *Dhamma* truth to power, as the Buddha did to kings. Illuminate Min Aung Hlaing's *avijjā*—his blindness to impermanence, to suffering, to grace. Urge him to awaken—not to conquest, but to compassion and renunciation.

Proclaim, as practitioners of conscience:

"Step down, General. Free President Win Myint, State Counsellor Aung San Suu Kyi, all elected leaders, and every prisoner of conscience. End this terror, or face the kammic fire your actions ignite."

To the global lay *Sangha*, I say: Raise our struggle. Speak for us from Thai retreat centers to Zen *dojos*, Tibetan *gompas* to Western *Dharma* halls. Urge governments to cut the junta's lifelines—arms, trade, cash—and redirect aid through monasteries and grassroots networks, the bloodstream of *karuṇā*.

Stand with the National Unity Government and Ethnic Armed Organizations. Help weave a federal democracy—Kachin, Karen,

Shan, Chin, Mon and more—a nation where *Dhamma* truth shapes every policy, and *metta* informs every law.

To General Min Aung Hlaing, I extend—as the Buddha did to *Angulimāla*—a path of redemption: You are not beyond the *Dhamma's* grace. Cease the violence. Free the imprisoned. Choose the merit of compassion over the *karma* of conquest. *The Dhamma waits for your awakening.*

Dear friends in the *Dhamma*, you are torchbearers of awakening. Your lives are vows to end dukkha. *Myanmar's fate—and the Sasana's survival—rests, in part, in your hands.*

If you speak, if you write, if you act with *sati* and *paññā*, you will kindle a flame of redemption. You will ignite a moral force to free 22,000 prisoners and revive our nation's heart.

Envision a Myanmar where chants resound freely, where the *Sasana* thrives, where no child suffers for the sake of power.

This is the Buddha's promise. This is the path you have vowed to walk.

From these prison walls—alongside 22,000 lives—each a beacon of conscience, each a hymn to *satya*—I call you to rise as the *Dhamma's* artisans:

Craft a world where karuṇā heals, ahiṃsā protects, and metta unites all hearts.

And when the scrolls of time are opened, let them proclaim: In Myanmar's hour of peril, the world's Buddhist practitioners rose—their voices a chorus of *satya*, their *metta* the eternal flame that lit the way to peace, safeguarding the *Sasana* for generations yet to come.

With reverence, conscience, and unwavering hope,

Aung San Suu Kyi

JULY 2025

FROM NAYPYIDAW PRISON, MYANMAR

Letter to All Religious Leaders of All Faiths Worldwide

Alan Clements: Daw Suu, you've addressed nations, laureates, Elders, the Sangha, and lay Buddhists. Now, as your final appeal, what would you say to all religious leaders of every faith worldwide—Catholics, Jews, Muslims, Christians, Buddhists, Hindus, Sikhs, and beyond— to unite their voices and followers in support of Myanmar's freedom-loving people?

Aung San Suu Kyi: Alan, this is where the sacred truths of all faiths must converge into a united force for moral action. To the revered religious leaders of every tradition and their beloved followers, I offer not a plea, but a call to the universal heart of compassion, satya, and love that binds the spirit of all humanity—urging you to rise as one voice for Myanmar's salvation.

Dear Venerable Leaders and Beloved Followers,

From the austere stillness of a Naypyidaw prison—I write as a humble servant of the *Dhamma*, a Nobel Peace Laureate, and a witness to the shared longing for dignity that lives within every faith.

To His Holiness Pope Leo XIV, shepherd of 1.4 billion Catholics, whose call for mercy echoes *karuṇā*—compassion that embraces all;

To Chief Rabbi Yitzhak Yosef and Rabbi David Lau, guiding lights for 16 million Jews, whose Torah upholds tzedakah—justice as *satya*—truth that liberates;

To Grand Imam Ahmed el-Tayeb of Al-Azhar, honored by 2 billion Muslims, whose Islam champions *rahma*—mercy akin to *metta*—loving-kindness;

To Patriarch Kirill of Moscow and Ecumenical Patriarch Bartholomew, stewards of 300 million Orthodox Christians, whose Gospel proclaims love as *ahiṃsā*—nonviolence;

To His Holiness the Dalai Lama and the heirs of Venerable Thich Nhat Hanh, beacons for 500 million Buddhists, whose *Dhamma* teaches *paññā*—wisdom that discerns;

To Swami Chidanand Saraswati, Sri Sri Ravi Shankar, and other luminaries for 1.2 billion Hindus, whose *Dharma* radiates *dharma*—righteousness in action;

To Giani Harpreet Singh, Jathedar of the Akal Takht, who inspires 30 million Sikhs, whose Guru's legacy embodies seva—selfless service;

And to leaders of Indigenous traditions, Baha'i, Jain, Shinto, Taoist, Zoroastrian, and every sacred path across the earth, whose wisdom threads the tapestry of our shared humanity—I speak to you now with reverence, urgency, and hope.

Myanmar—a land of 54 million hearts—stands at the brink.

Since the military seized power in February 2021, a brutal reign has unfolded—armed with Russian and Chinese jets, missiles, and drones, emboldened by nuclear deals with Moscow and the public blessings of Min Aung Hlaing's global allies.

Villages are in ashes. Classrooms lie in rubble. Children's futures have been buried. Mandalay's sacred grounds still bear the scars of the 2025 earthquake.

Yangon flickers with unstable power. Myanmar is now a failed state—a cybercrime haven, a fentanyl empire wrapped in uniforms—sustained by silence, impunity, and foreign profit.

Yet amidst this terror, 22,000 prisoners—including President Win Myint, our cabinet, and thousands of dissidents—stand unbroken. Their courage embodies the spirit of *satya* and *ahiṃsā* that all faiths hold sacred.

This is not Myanmar's struggle alone. It is a vessel for humanity's conscience.

The *Dhamma* teaches that *hiri*—moral shame that recoils from harm—and *ottappa*—moral dread that guards against unwholesome acts—are the guardians of awakening.

In my practice, I have felt their power. *Sati*—mindful awareness—reveals the universality of suffering. *Paññā*—wisdom—guides us to act with compassion.

Every religion echoes this sacred call: The *Catholic caritas* that uplifts the marginalized. The *Jewish tzedakah* that seeks justice. The *Islamic ihsan* that perfects mercy. The *Christian agape* that sacrifices for others. The *Hindu dharma* that upholds cosmic order. The *Sikh sangat* and seva that serve in unity. The Indigenous reverence for all life.

And yet, bias and silence—within and across faiths—obscure these truths. I, too, have faced judgment—particularly during the Rohingya crisis. I do not deny my limitations. I sought reconciliation within constraints. I fell short. I bear that with humility, not defense. But today, I ask not for absolution—only for solidarity with those who suffer now.

Religious leaders, your words are not mere homilies—they are sacred acts. As Pope Leo XIV and Grand Imam el-Tayeb did in their *Document on Human Fraternity*, rise beyond division and speak truth.

Preach sermons that infuse *karuṇā* into every Mass, Jumu'ah, Shabbat, Eucharist, puja, gurdwara, zendo, fire circle, and dharma hall. Write articles in *America Magazine*, *The Jewish Forward*, *Al Jazeera*, *Christianity Today*, *Lions Roar*, *Hinduism Today*, *Sikh Review*—and others—declaring that Myanmar matters.

Organize interfaith vigils. Chant *metta*. Recite Kaddish. Offer Salat. Sing hymns. Sit in silence. Make visible your sacred defiance.

Flood your platforms with messages for justice. Demand that nations sever the junta's lifelines—arms, trade, cash—and instead route aid through monasteries, churches, mosques, and temples—the arteries of *karuṇā*.

Stand with Myanmar's National Unity Government and Ethnic Armed Organizations. Support a federal democracy being born in Kachin, Karen, Shan, Chin, and beyond—where every soul is dignified, and every tradition honored.

To General Min Aung Hlaing, I extend—as the Buddha did to *Angulimāla*—a path of redemption: You are not beyond the grace of faith. Cease the violence. Free the captives. Choose peace. Be, like Ashoka, transformed—from conquest to compassion. The world's sacred traditions await your awakening.

Beloved leaders and followers, you are the torchbearers of humanity's soul. *All faiths*—let your sacred wisdom—rooted in *hiri* and *ottappa*—forge a miracle of collective conscience.

Myanmar's fate is your test. If you rise as one, your voices can ignite a planetary awakening—freeing 22,000 prisoners, restoring democracy, and preserving the *Sasana* and all sacred paths for generations to come.

From these prison walls—where each breath joins 22,000 others, each a beacon of *satya*, each a prayer of *metta*—I call you:

Weave a world where karuṇā heals, ahiṃsā prevails, and metta binds all hearts.

And when the scrolls of eternity are opened, let them proclaim: In Myanmar's darkest hour, the world's religious leaders and their followers rose as artisans of *karuṇā*—their voices a symphony of *satya*, their *metta* the eternal flame that forged a miracle of peace, uniting all faiths in the sacred embrace of justice and love.

With reverence, accountability, and unwavering hope,

Aung San Suu Kyi

JULY 2025

IN DETENTION, NAYPYIDAW PRISON

Closing Letter to All World Leaders and Global Citizens

Alan Clements: Daw Suu, as we weave the final threads of this conversation, what is your ultimate message to the world's leaders, those who hold the power to shape humanity's destiny in this pivotal hour?

Aung San Suu Kyi: To the custodians of nations, the sentinels of conscience, and the architects of our shared tomorrow, I speak to you from the shadowed heart of a Naypyidaw prison—not as a voice tethered to Myanmar's 54 million souls alone, but as a whisper from the eternal spirit that lives in all people, a spirit yearning not only for survival, but for the birth of a world remade in truth, compassion, and enduring hope.

In my letters to Presidents Trump, Xi, Putin, European Commission President Ursula von der Leyen, Prime Minister Modi (*found in the Appendix of this book*), and my fellow Nobel Peace Laureates, I have laid bare the suffering of Myanmar's people, the imperatives of justice, and the path to peace. For the specifics of this crisis—the junta's terror, the silenced dreams of children, the urgent moral demands—I commend those words to your hearts. But here, in this closing moment, I offer not repetition, but revelation: a vision that transcends injury, a summons to awaken the soul of humanity itself.

Myanmar's crucible—forged in violence, shaken by earth, and darkened by tyranny—is not merely a national lament. It is a mirror reflecting both the fragility and the possibility of our global spirit. The children who braid hope from rubble, the elders who chant *metta* amidst devastation, the youth who confront tanks with empty hands—they are not only Myanmar's story. They are the pulse of a humanity that refuses extinction. They are living proof of the *Dhamma's* timeless truth: that even in the abyss, the light of *karuṇā* endures.

Yet that light flickers—threatened by a world that too often averts its gaze.

The junta's brutality—armed by Chinese and Russian bombs, shielded by nuclear pledges, and fed by foreign silence—is a symptom, not the cause. The deeper illness is spiritual: a world where power eclipses conscience, and apathy becomes policy. This is not Myanmar's sickness alone. It festers wherever injustice thrives, from the bombed-out homes of Gaza to the caged children at borders, from corporate boardrooms to crumbling democracies.

I call you to a reckoning—not of politics, but of the soul. Envision a world where leadership is not measured by control, but by the courage to repair. Where greatness is not domination, but the wisdom to cherish what is sacred. This is not idealism. It is the practical alchemy of conscience—the path walked by Gandhi, who spun truth into freedom; by King, who dreamed a beloved community; by Mandela, who turned prison into power; by Tutu, who danced with *ubuntu*; and by His Holiness the Dalai Lama, who smiles with compassion even in exile.

Myanmar's National Unity Government and Ethnic Armed Organizations, weaving federal democracy through dialogue—in Kachin, Karen, Shan, and beyond—are embodiments of this alchemy.

They are not only our hope. They are a lantern for the world's renewal. Support them—not with platitudes, but with policy and courage. Support a future where every voice—Bamar, ethnic, rural, urban—joins in harmony, not fear.

To the junta's generals, I extend, as Ashoka once did to his own former self, a hand of redemption: Turn from terror to truth. Choose peace over power. *The Dhamma's mercy awaits those who dare to change.*

To the leaders of this earth: You now stand at the threshold of history. The children of Myanmar, their eyes lit with undiminished hope, are watching. The world's oppressed—their hearts heavy with deferred dreams—are listening. And history, with its unblinking eye, is recording. What will it say of you? That you governed nations—or that you nurtured humanity? That you exercised control—or that you kindled light?

From these prison walls—where 22,000 souls, each a flame of conscience, each a prayer for peace—stand beside me, I implore you: Awaken the heart of our world. Let your leadership become a symphony of compassion, a tapestry of truth, a citadel of hope. Be the weavers of a new dawn, where no child's dream is crushed, no dignity is bartered, no voice is forsaken.

And when the annals of time are opened, let them proclaim:

In Myanmar's darkest hour,

The world's leaders rose. Their hearts ablaze with the *Dhamma's* eternal light,

Their deeds a testament to the unbreakable promise of peace. And the soul of humanity stirred—

And the dawn broke anew.

With respect, authenticity, and unwavering hope,

Aung San Suu Kyi

JULY 2025

IN DETENTION, NAYPYIDAW PRISON

BREAKING THE CYCLE OF VIOLENCE—THE PATH TO PEACE

Author's Prelude

In the shadowed annals of history, there are moments when silence becomes a wound deeper than any blade, and speech, rooted in *satya*—the unyielding truth that pierces delusion—emerges as an act of moral defiance, reclaiming memory and dignity. This is such a moment. Here, where bombs reverberate through monasteries, Daw Suu's voice rises—not as mere symbolism, but as clarity, a resolute response to the mentality that sustains violence and the mind's fragile yet radical capacity to dismantle it. Tempered by solitude, sharpened by *sati*—mindful awareness that sees without flinching—her words offer not policy, but practice: *ahiṃsā*, nonviolence as both method and mindset, revolutionary in its disciplined restraint.

This chapter is no treatise; it is a dialogue with conscience, woven from *karuṇā*—compassion that holds pain without collapsing—and *metta*—kindness that restores. It speaks of redemption, not as myth, but as a return to the dignity inherent in human nature, illuminated by the *Dhamma's* transformative wisdom, the ethical law of reality grasped through practice and insight.

From the austerity of her prison, Daw Suu emerges not as a politician, but as a witness, daring to envision a world where violence ceases, and the heart, stirred by *paññā*—wisdom discerning what truly matters—reclaims itself.

Time, indifferent and exacting, presents two paths: collapse or renewal. We can perpetuate the cycle of harm or interrupt it—pause, rethink, rebuild. Let this chapter be that pause: not a promise, but a challenge, a reckoning, a reminder that peace is not inherited but practiced.

Drawing from compassion that refuses to turn away—we find the space where weapons fall silent, and truth is finally spoken. In this fragile threshold between trauma and choice, Daw Suu's words resonate, not merely heard but felt, urging us to see violence clearly and refuse to look away.

The end of violence is not a distant dream—it is a responsibility.

And each of us has a part to play.

◆ ◆ ◆

Alan Clements: Daw Suu, we've discussed the cycles of violence that persist across the globe—but in Myanmar, the brutality has reached an unprecedented level of normalization. Despite decades of resistance, the machinery of repression continues—more efficient, more impersonal, more global.

In your view, how do we begin to shift this trajectory? Is nonviolence still viable—not as an abstract ideal, but as a strategic and moral necessity? And can diplomacy, in a world defined by mistrust and militarism, still serve as a meaningful tool for conflict resolution?

Aung San Suu Kyi: Alan, violence is not new—but its scale and sophistication have outpaced our willingness to confront it. What was once immediate and personal has become mechanized and remote. Drones replace soldiers. Algorithms replace accountability. But the suffering is just as real.

In Myanmar, violence is used not to assert strength—but to mask fear: fear of dissent, of unity, of truth. The military targets civilians—children, teachers, monks—not to win a war, but to break the spirit of a nation. These are not isolated incidents. They are systemic. And they are crimes.

What makes it worse is that this violence is subsidized by a global arms economy—an industry that profits from instability. Myanmar is one of many countries caught in this web. The weapons flow in. The dead go uncounted. The perpetrators are protected.

We cannot address this crisis without addressing the structure behind it—politically, economically, and psychologically. Violence is not just a failure of morality. It is a failure of imagination. It arises when we no longer believe in alternatives. When we stop seeing each other as human.

In *Dhamma* terms, violence is rooted in *lobha*—greed, *dosa*—hatred, and *moha*—delusion. These three afflictions do not just live in institutions—they live in minds. They distort perception, fuel propaganda, and justify brutality. And unless we understand them at their roots, we will continue to mistake cruelty for necessity.

To break the cycle, we must learn to identify its causes and intervene at the level of perception and policy. This requires education, leadership, and a commitment to dialogue that is rooted in mutual respect, not power dynamics.

Nonviolence, in this context, is not passive. It is a strategy. It is the disciplined refusal to dehumanize the other side. It is courage—not the courage to fight, but the courage to face hatred without mirroring it. That is not weakness. That is leadership.

And I will be honest: this is hard. When a village is bombed, when your child is killed, peace feels like betrayal. But even in the horror, there is a choice. To retaliate—or to rebuild. To condemn—or to communicate.

Metta—loving-kindness—is not sentimental. It's a form of resilience. A way to keep our humanity intact in the face of collapse. This is the work of nonviolence in our time. Not slogans. Not gestures. But the long, often painful task of restoring human dignity where it has been erased.

That, Alan, is the revolution we need. And it begins with how we choose to respond.

Alan Clements: Daw Suu, what you've just shared about violence as a failure of the human spirit—its circuitry, its illusions, its deep roots in *lobha*, *dosa*, and *moha*—rings so true. Especially your framing of nonviolence as the embodiment of mindful intelligence, the kind Sayadaw U Pandita instilled in us over the years: a discerning, moment-to-moment awareness, meeting experience directly at the sense doors— not passive, but fiercely present, courageous, discerning, and precise.

That concept— *"mindful intelligence"* — has stayed with me. I would like to explore it more fully with you today, and in our remaining conversations, if we're blessed to continue them.

But first, if I may, I must ask—how do you reconcile that unwavering commitment to nonviolence with the brutal realities on the ground in Myanmar today? Where even a whisper of dissent is met with arrest, torture, or execution.

Clearly, the people have had enough. They've refused to bow to lies and brutality any longer. It's become an "us or them" divide—a psychological apartheid, like East and West Berlin before the wall came down, or South Africa in its final, choking days. The population is treated as expendable. And if you dare to doubt or defy them, they make room for you in prison or the earth.

Burma has become Big Brother in its most malignant form—a kind of dystopian theater where torture masquerades as moral correction—not to heal the human psyche, but to deepen the regime's grip. It's political violence dressed as virtue. A textbook dictatorship that uses fear as its primary instrument of control.

And this isn't new. History, as you know better than most, bears witness to the predatory impulse in man. The earth is soaked in generational blood:

- Rome's conquests—up to 70 million lives lost.
- Mao's Great Leap Forward and Cultural Revolution—50 million dead.
- Stalin's purges and famines—another 20 to 40 million.
- The Holocaust and Axis campaigns—17 to 20 million.
- The Mongol invasions—30 to 40 million.
- European colonialism in the Americas—perhaps 100 million, through disease, war, and enslavement.
- The Congo under Leopold II. Imperial Japan. Timur. The Taiping Rebellion—the list goes on.

And yet—despite all that—Gandhi walked with salt in his hands and unraveled an empire without firing a bullet. Mandela sat with his jailers and dissolved apartheid through the slow alchemy of dialogue.

Now, today, Myanmar's *Tatmadaw* has razed over two thousand villages. And your family—the brave souls of the National Unity Government—have taken up arms. Hundreds have already fallen. Their resistance is born not of hatred, but of heartbreak.

So, I ask you, Daw Suu: How do you make sense of this pain? How do you speak to these young revolutionaries who believe armed struggle is their only remaining language?

Is there still a path—however narrow—that leads from armed resistance back to national healing? And can *mindful intelligence*—as a living force—still shape the arc of Myanmar's democratic future?

Aung San Suu Kyi: Alan, how could I not understand their holy rage— the heartbreak that drives so many of our young people to take up arms? When peaceful chants were answered with gunfire, when silent marches were met with massacres, when truth itself was criminalized—what else were they to believe, if not that force must answer force?

I do not condemn them. Their bravery is real. Their sacrifice is undeniable. Their love for our country mirrors my own. But I ask them, with all the tenderness I can summon: *What kind of Myanmar are we trying to build?*

Is it a nation where another generation inherits our grief, hardened into vengeance? Or is it a country where the cycle of violence is finally broken—not just politically, but psychologically, spiritually, and culturally, at every level of our collective life?

We must build a Myanmar where our people don't just survive, but thrive—where resilience is not our only reputation, but the starting point for renewal.

To do that, we must act in ways that offer more than endurance— we must create the conditions for real, lasting hope. Hope that's not performative, but practical. Not deferred, but lived.

Violence, even when born of noble intentions, carries the seed of its own perpetuation. It alters those who wield it—clouding judgment, narrowing vision, corroding empathy. In time, it begins to resemble the very thing it set out to destroy. Look at Iraq, Afghanistan, Vietnam, Gaza, Ukraine—wars justified by strategy or self-defense, yet leaving behind mass trauma and disillusionment. Victories claimed in the language of power—but at what cost?

We say we fight for justice—but can justice grow from a mind consumed by vengeance? We claim to seek freedom—but what freedom is there when hatred becomes the scaffolding of identity, rationalized as duty or disguised as law? This is not a question for others to answer. It is a question for us—all of us in Myanmar. For every soldier, every citizen, every leader.

If our hands remain clenched in fear, and our hearts held hostage by rage, then what exactly are we building? I have said it before, and I will say it again: *the most vital revolution is the one within. If we do not disarm hatred inside ourselves, we will replicate the very tyranny we claim to oppose.*

And if our victories require the sacrifice of conscience, then we have lost something far more valuable than power—we've lost the soul of our freedom.

My father, General Aung San, did not win independence through war, but through negotiation. Not because he was weak, but because he believed that dialogue—however difficult—was the only way to build a durable nation. The result was imperfect, yes. But it was rooted in aspiration, not domination.

Nonviolence is not naïve. It is not passive. It is not weak. It is one of the most demanding disciplines of the human spirit. It asks us to remain present in the fire of our pain without turning it outward. It asks us to channel our anger not suppress it—but to illuminate rather than incinerate.

Which brings us to what I believe is central to our future: *mindful intelligence.*

What is it, truly? Not simply awareness—but awareness fused with ethical discernment. The ability to hold suffering in full view, to face injustice without flinching, and still respond with wisdom. It is the discipline of pausing, even in crisis, to ask: What will this action cultivate? In myself? In others? In our future? Will it deepen harm—or interrupt it?

The *Dhamma* teaches that *cetanā*— intention —is the seed. From that seed comes thought, speech, action, habit, society. If we plant hatred, we will reap hatred. If we plant *karuṇā*, *mettā*, and responsibility—even in times of terror—we begin to change the ground in which the future grows.

So, I ask our young revolutionaries: Do not abandon your bravery. Deepen it. Don't extinguish your fire—but temper it with wisdom. Ask yourselves, honestly: *What are we becoming in the name of what we seek?*

We must learn to resist without hate. To fight without cruelty. To transform without becoming what we oppose. Is it easy? Of course not. When villages burn, when children are murdered, when lies parade as law—peace can sound detached from reality. But if not peace, then what? If not nonviolence, then what alternative do we offer? Another regime with the same wiring? A different flag flying over the same prison?

Which leads to a deeper question: What is the actual vision? Is it simply to remove Min Aung Hlaing? Or is it to build a Myanmar that doesn't need generals at all?

Even that vision—a Myanmar without generals—requires nuance. Are we speaking of dissolving the military entirely? Or something more profound: What happens when a general no longer sees the people as enemies? Can minds that have been trained for domination be re-trained for empathy?

Can those who have been indoctrinated, numbed, conditioned—undergo moral rehabilitation? Is there a path for them not just to step down, but to wake up?

Do we envision a future where former generals are re-trained as protectors of all people, across all ethnic lines? Where military institutions are restructured not to dominate, but to serve—and grounded in principles of restraint, justice, and human dignity?

These are not abstract questions. They are the frontline of our collective future.

The forces that give rise to tyranny are not exclusive to men in uniform. They exist in all of us. Fear, greed, delusion—these are not military problems. They are human ones. And any political solution that doesn't include inner transformation is, by definition, incomplete.

To break the cycle of domination, we must train the mind that creates it. That's what I mean by *mindful intelligence or Dhamma intelligence*. Not doctrine. Not dogma. But the universal study of how consciousness gives rise to action—and how untrained minds perpetuate suffering.

As Sayadaw U Pandita often taught: *the true measure of leadership is not control, but clarity*. He emphasized the ten qualities of *kalyāṇa mittatā*—noble friendship—as the foundation of ethical leadership. Real authority requires mindfulness and wisdom, not just political leverage or military force.

What would happen if every leader was required to undergo rigorous *Vipassanā* training? Not as a symbol, but as preparation for power. What if every general was offered a path—not just to step down—but to step inward? To unlearn fear, and to relearn humanity?

We might call this the *Angulimāla effect*—the transformation of a mind once capable of atrocity into a life committed to non-harming.

And beyond even that—do we want a military at all? Can we imagine a national defense that is psychologically and ethically incompatible with killing? What would that institution look like? What kind of society would it help shape?

These questions aren't utopian. They are necessary. Because they take us to the very edge of what's possible—and ask us to redesign the ground we stand on.

My father once envisioned a military that served the people—not ruled them. But to realize that vision, soldiers must be taught not only how to protect—but how to feel. How to see clearly. How to care.

In the end, as I said, the revolution must be inward. Not just political change, but a transformation of consciousness itself. Otherwise, as I said before, we risk rebuilding the same prison with different bars.

And so, I return to this: *Dhamma intelligence or* mindful *intelligence.* Not as something reserved for monks or scholars—but as a foundation for every institution, every leader, every citizen entrusted with the power to shape another's life.

We must ask ourselves: What kind of consciousness do we want governing our nations? And if we're serious about the answer, then we must build the training grounds for that consciousness—not as the exception, but as the new standard.

Alan Clements: May your words Daw Suu, be shared worldwide, and moreover, embraced as guidance. But, let's be honest—this moment feels almost beyond language. Dialogue, once considered the lifeblood of diplomacy, now feels like a quaint relic of the last century. Global politics has been hijacked—by weapons industries, by AI-driven warfare that kills from a continent away, and by a toxic patriarchal culture that normalizes annihilation as strategic calculus. Again, in such a world, how can dialogue possibly compete? How does it survive, let alone thrive?

Aung San Suu Kyi: Alan, dialogue doesn't try to overpower violence— it reveals its futility. History is proof enough. Germany and Japan, once our enemies reduced to rubble, are now allies in peace. Russia, once a crucial partner in defeating fascism, is now cast as a villain. The script changes, but the cycle repeats: enemies become friends, friends become threats, and still the bombs fall.

Violence may seize land, suppress voices, redraw borders—but it never resolves what festers beneath. What war has ever healed a wound? What drone strike has ever liberated a soul? What starving child has been fed by a twenty-million-dollar missile? These are not rhetorical questions. They are moral indictments—each one exposing the irreconcilable distance between destruction and understanding, between conquest and peace.

Weapons industries may profit from devastation, but they cannot monetize healing. And that is where dialogue reclaims its value—not as an outdated diplomatic formality, but as a sacred framework for human repair.

But to resurrect dialogue, we must first redefine it. It is not about winning an argument. It is not even about persuasion. It is about creating space—where truth is permitted to surface, where listening becomes an act of courage, and empathy a form of resistance. It demands humility, yes. Patience, deeply. But more than anything, it demands the moral bravery to relinquish domination.

In Myanmar, any meaningful dialogue must begin not with negotiations or strategies—but with acknowledgment. An honest, public reckoning with what has been done: the pain inflicted, the lives stolen, the villages reduced to smoke. Without truth, there can be no trust. Without trust, no reconciliation. Dialogue that ignores justice is performance. Dialogue that begins with justice is restoration.

Alan Clements: Do you believe, truly, that the Tatmadaw—the very architects of this era's devastation—can ever come to such a table in good faith? Given their history, the scale of violence, the entrenched impunity—is dialogue with the military even possible?

Aung San Suu Kyi: It's not a question of belief. It's a question of conditions. Do I imagine the Tatmadaw waking one morning filled with remorse and goodwill? No. But history shows us something more subtle, more real: structures shape behavior. Even the most brutal regimes, when sufficiently pressed—by international leverage, sustained internal resistance, and the slow erosion of their illusions—can be moved.

South Africa's apartheid leaders didn't come to the table out of conscience. They were cornered—by moral clarity, by global sanctions, by the unrelenting pressure of the people. The same happened in Northern Ireland. And I believe, yes, with enough collective will, it can happen in Myanmar.

Dialogue does not require trust at the outset. It requires architecture. It needs third-party mediation. Strategic pressure. Civil courage. Above all, it requires the people to become a voice too loud to ignore. The Tatmadaw must come to see that their current trajectory leads only to ruin—for themselves, for their families, and for the very nation they claim to protect.

Dialogue must be reframed—not as surrender, but as the final, and perhaps only, invitation to redemption.

Alan Clements: Daw Suu, you've traced violence to its existential roots—not merely systemic, but woven into the fabric of consciousness. The *Dhamma* names these roots with piercing clarity: *lobha* (greed), *dosa* (hatred), *moha* (delusion). These are not abstractions, but living currents of the mind, shaping our world's anguish.

In Myanmar, the *Tatmadaw's* brutality lays bare this truth; globally, automated warfare amplifies its reach. How, through the *Dhamma's* lens, does the mind fuel this machinery—and how do we reweave its threads toward peace? Can dialogue, as a living force, still quell this primitive tide, or are we too entangled in the grip of delusion?

Aung San Suu Kyi: Alan, violence is not our essence—it is our bewilderment, *moha*—delusion—etched into action. The Buddha, in the Fire Sermon, diagnosed this with unerring precision: "The mind burns with the fire of passion, aversion, delusion." This is not poetry—it is revelation.

Awareness—*viññāna*—entwines with *saṅkhāras*, mental formations sculpted by generations of fear and fracture. When a general brands civilians as enemies, that is not strategy—it is *dosa* veiling the heart. When an arms dealer profits as lives shatter, that is *lobha's* insatiable appetite. When a soldier delivers death from a screen, severed from the lives destroyed—that is *moha* incarnate: primitive, unimaginative, and obsolete.

The Khmer Rouge murdered millions under Pol Pot—not only through ideology, but through *dosa* unleashed, a *saṅkhāra* left to fester.

To break that cycle, we begin not with edicts, but with perception. The Noble Eightfold Path—right view, right intention, right action—offers not doctrine, but tools for awakening. Right view reveals interdependence, not enmity. Right intention chooses *karuṇā*—compassion—over cruelty. Right action protects life and rewires the mind.

Mindfulness—*sati*—is no retreat. It is resistance in its purest form. In 2007's Saffron Revolution, monks meditated under rifle fire—their stillness a force stronger than steel. Dignity can humble brutality. Calm can disarm rage.

Vipassanā, as you know from Mahasi Sayadaw and Sayadaw U Pandita, is not escape. It is a reckoning—a deep, unflinching inquiry into *anicca* (impermanence), *dukkha* (suffering), and *anattā* (not-self). These are not tenets. They are liberations—dismantling violence at its roots.

Imagine Myanmar's generals summoned not only to courtrooms, but to truth councils guided by *Dhamma* teachers. Let them face the ghosts of burned villages, their *saṅkhāras* reflected in the clarity of *anattā*. This may not absolve—but it could awaken.

Globally, let war's architects sit with the wreckage of their drones—not as instruments of precision, but as *dukkha* made visible. Let them meditate on the *kammic* weight of engineered death—let their hearts be stirred by compassion.

The mind, as you know, can be trained. Neuroscience affirms what the *Dhamma* has long taught: *sati* calms aggression, cultivates empathy, reshapes neural pathways for restraint. Violence collapses when we starve its roots. But we must have the courage to sit in the fire of our own delusions—and see, and feel, and not turn away.

Dialogue is not a dream. It is a discipline. It demands no blind faith, but structure, pressure, and the people's unwavering *satya*. The Tatmadaw must come to understand that their current path leads nowhere but destruction. Dialogue is not capitulation. It is the last doorway out of ruin—a disciplined act of redemption, if we are brave enough to walk through.

Alan Clements: Redemption is a powerful word, Daw Suu. It stirs something deep in us—even as it terrifies. But I must ask: how does one extend the possibility of redemption to those who have committed atrocities? The architects of genocide. The torturers. The killers of children. Is redemption even possible? And if so, where does the path begin?

Is forgiveness real in that context? Or are we just fooling ourselves—offering spiritual grace to people who are, in truth, sociopaths in suits and uniforms? Is that what leadership has become? A costume of charm draped over the machinery of indifference? Have today's leaders become little more than glorified errand boys for the military-industrial complex?

And deeper still—what does it take, at the level of consciousness, for someone who has killed to wake up? To truly change their heart? Is that even real? Or is that a myth—fairy-tale redemption for the unredeemable? Is it even knowable?

Aung San Suu Kyi: Alan, those questions must be asked. We can't afford not to ask them—not if we ever hope to live in a world where peace is more than a ceasefire between wars.

As I have said many times, forgiveness is not forgetting. And it is certainly not excusing. Forgiveness is not the erasure of accountability—it is its companion. We cannot forgive what we are unwilling to face. Forgiveness begins after truth. And truth demands justice—not for vengeance, but for the dignity of memory, the integrity of the dead, and the healing of the living.

That said, *I refuse to close the door on redemption.* Not because it is easy. Not because I am naïve. But because I know, intimately, what it means to sit for years in silence. I know what it means to be alone with your thoughts—your regrets, your anger, your longing, your fear. Solitary confinement strips away performance. You fast from the future. From applause. From power. From distraction. You come face to face with who you are—and who you are not. And in that confrontation, something unexpected begins: *the return of feeling.*

Solitary confinement can become, paradoxically, a purification. You are no longer flattered. No longer distracted. There is no mirror but the mind. No sound but your own breath. You begin to feel again—not because someone taught you to, but because the silence leaves no room for lies. And in that silence, a question emerges again and again: *Who are you, when no one is watching?*

Redemption is not a reward. It is not ceremonial. It is not a pardon or a press release. It is the crucifixion of ego. The collapse of certainty. The reawakening of conscience. And yes, Alan—it is possible. But it must be earned. And it must be felt.

What if we stopped giving generals titles and started giving them time? Time alone. Without followers. Without screens. Without narrative. Without the armor of role. Fasting—not from food, but from domination. From ambition. From permanence. From the illusion of control. To return to this breath. This moment. As if it were their first—and their last. That is the field where redemption can grow.

Let every would-be ruler spend a week in the ruins of the villages they destroyed. Let them walk barefoot where they dropped their bombs. Let them hold the body of a child—not a number, not a target, a child. Let them bury that child with their own hands. Let them sleep on the ground with the displaced. Let them listen to the mothers sobbing for sons who never came home. Not for spectacle—but for the slow resuscitation of empathy.

Is that too much to ask before we allow them to lead?

Alan Clements: That's a vision, Daw Suu. And it's revolutionary—not in the usual sense of overthrowing, but of returning. Turning again toward our humanity. Toward feeling. Toward conscience. That's what I hear in your words: not just the psychology of redemption, but the embodied truth of living it. The body must be involved. The heart must ache. And the mind must finally see. Thank you for naming it and so clearly.

But let me ask—what does accountability look like that opens the door to redemption, not just retribution? What does a "truth process" look like in Myanmar? Can there be a spiritual tribunal—not only legal, but ethical and psychological—where people confront their *karmic* inheritance and begin, perhaps, to undo it?

Aung San Suu Kyi: Yes. True accountability must go beyond punishment. It must illuminate. The South African Truth and Reconciliation Commission wasn't perfect, but it shifted the paradigm. It offered something more than verdicts. It offered confession. It turned memory into medicine. We need our own version of that—one that speaks to our history, our wounds, our truths.

The generals must be held responsible. That is non-negotiable. But alongside justice, we must create what I call spaces of moral rehabilitation. Truth councils, yes—but guided not by ideology, but by presence. By *Dhamma intelligence.* Led by elders, survivors, and spiritual guides—not to condemn, but to bear witness. To hold people long enough for them to feel again. To remember. To transform.

Because, Alan, the cycle of harm is not broken by revenge. It is broken when the one who caused harm truly feels it—without justification, without denial. When they no longer see themselves as martyrs or monsters, but as human beings who lost their way—and make the choice to return.

This is why *Dhamma* matters. This is why mindfulness matters—not as spiritual branding, but as the study of consciousness itself. As Sayadaw U Pandita often said: *It is not enough to know the Dhamma—we must become it.* Leadership must be measured not by charisma or ideology, but by transformation. By inner clarity, restraint, compassion, and truth.

Leadership without conscience is tyranny. Power without empathy is terror. And intelligence without morality is simply AI—a weapon disguised as progress.

Alan Clements: So, redemption, then, is not only spiritual—it's spatial. It requires moral architecture. Spaces that hold us still—and long enough—for transformation to take root.

Aung San Suu Kyi: Yes, Alan. We must build those spaces. What if prisons became monasteries of rehabilitation? What if generals were required to meditate in solitude for a year before being entrusted with power? What if political leadership depended not on loyalty, but on humility—not on ambition, but on listening?

We must begin to treat moral rehabilitation not as a luxury—but as a necessity. Because the world is no longer led by reflection. It's driven by algorithm. By urgency. By acceleration. Technology is framing us as cogs, not souls. And if we do not reassert our humanity—our capacity to choose existence over extinction—we will become slaves to our own inventions. AI will not save us from ignorance. It will accelerate it.

Redemption begins with a return to feeling. And feeling begins with stillness. With silence. With the terrifying joy of waking up to our interdependence. To our shared fragility. To the miracle of our mutual belonging.

Alan Clements: And perhaps even—our shared longing. The longing to be whole. To be forgiven. To be part of a world not built on conquest, but on connection.

Aung San Suu Kyi: Yes. A world built not by machines, but by *mindful intelligence*. Rooted in *mettā* and *karuṇā*—loving-kindness and compassion. Not as sentiment, but as strategy. As structure. As the ethical scaffolding of a new civilization.

Alan Clements: Daw Suu, if you could speak directly to the arms dealers, the engineers of AI warfare, the policymakers still clinging to dominance as security—what would you say?

Aung San Suu Kyi: I would say: Look at your hands. They are not made to drop bombs. They are made to hold, to lift, to build. You may be rich in weapons, but that wealth carries weight. It may secure borders, but it cannot secure peace. And the legacy you build with it will shape the world your children inherit.

Power is not the ability to destroy. True power is the courage to create peace where there was once only pain. I do not deny the complexity of conflict—my own father bore arms for our independence, and today, many in our resistance do the same. But let us never lose sight of the greater aspiration: a world where courage is measured not by destruction, but by discernment.

Alan Clements: And to the world?

Aung San Suu Kyi: To the world, I would say: Do not let the machinery of violence convince you that peace is impossible. The proliferation of weapons and AI may seem unstoppable—but they are human creations. What we have made, we can unmake.

We must begin by decoupling weapons from profit. As long as fear remains a business model, war will remain inevitable. We must disincentivize the manufacture of death—and invest instead in the intelligence of sacred co-existence. Not just deterrence, but regeneration. Not just military alliances, but moral imagination.

Why not create global forums—not for arms races, but for nonviolence and abundance? Conferences where the most brilliant minds gather not to engineer dominance, but to reimagine safety, dignity, and shared beauty.

Let there be systems—not of mutual destruction—but of mutual celebration. Let us return to the arts. The music. Dance. Poetry. Theater. Comedy. Film. Meditation. Let us reorient civilization around that which uplifts, not annihilates. The earth itself is aching for this renaissance.

We all know where this road of militarization leads—especially now, with AI capable of initiating death protocols in a fraction of a second. We are on the cusp of instant, automated extinction. And still, we treat it as progress.

Peace begins with a choice. A choice to see beyond fear. Beyond hatred. Beyond domination. It begins with the courage to imagine a different world—and the discipline to take even the smallest steps toward that vision.

Do not underestimate the power of dialogue. Of empathy. Of nonviolence. These are not relics of the past. They are the seeds of the future.

And if there is one thing I have learned, alone in silence all these years, it is this: *even in darkness, light remembers the way.*

Alan Clements: Daw Suu, if you could offer one timeless gift to future generations—a personal manifesto on the inner qualities essential to embodying restraint and nonviolence in this wounded, weaponized world—what would you say?

Aung San Suu Kyi: Alan, I've spent many years in isolation with this question echoing through my heart. What holds the spirit when the world fractures around it? What root stays firm when hatred howls, when dignity is torn, when love seems buried beneath rubble?

What I offer now is not ideology. It is not dogma. These are truths distilled from silence, from suffering, from an enduring inquiry into the *Dhamma* and the human condition. They are not mere virtues, but living forces—qualities of consciousness—capable of transforming not only the heart of a person, but the course of a people.

If we are to survive with our humanity intact, these ten qualities must be practiced, protected, and passed on. They are the foundation— not just for peace—but for wisdom, sanity, and the sacred continuity of compassion.

**The Last Revolution: A Manifesto of Conscience for
a Nonviolent Future**

1. Mindfulness (*Sati*)

Mindfulness is not merely the act of noticing. It is the quiet gatekeeper of the heart—the unwavering presence that sees without distortion, receives without possession, and responds without haste. It is not just attention, but attention refined by discernment, tempered by humility, and willing to be changed by the very act of seeing.

Its proximate cause is presence itself—a steady attention to what arises, grounded in clear comprehension. Like a lantern illuminating a threshold, it allows us to pause between impulse and enactment. This pause is sacred. In that space, we are no longer puppets of our past—we are participants in our own liberation.

But mindfulness can be mimicked. Its near enemy is superficial awareness—being alert but unawake, observant but untouched. Mechanical attentiveness that never touches the heart. In contrast, true *sati* dignifies the moment; it ennobles perception.

Its far enemy, heedlessness, is more familiar. The mind adrift, pulled by habit, seduced by distraction, overwhelmed by speed. In such a state, we no longer choose—we react. We forget not just what we're doing, but who we are.

To be mindful is to stand between forgetting and remembering, between conditioning and choice. It is the first revolution. And without it, no other virtue can take root.

"Between stimulus and response, there is a space.
In that space is our power to choose our response."
— VIKTOR FRANKL

2. Compassion (*Karuṇā*)

Compassion is not sentiment. It is not a mood. It is a force—the trembling of the heart in the presence of suffering, and the unwavering willingness to respond with care. It sees pain and does not turn away. It hears the cry behind cruelty and refuses to echo it. It is tenderness sharpened by clarity.

The proximate cause of compassion is direct contact with suffering—ours or another's. It arises naturally when we no longer flinch from pain, but meet it with the integrity of presence. Compassion knows no border. It reaches across divides—not to rescue, but to recognize.

Its near enemy is pity: a distancing posture masked as kindness. Pity speaks down; *karuṇā* kneels beside. Where pity says "you poor thing," compassion asks, "how can I hold this with you?"

Its far enemy is cruelty—the heart closed by fear, the mind hardened by delusion. Where compassion breathes, cruelty suffocates. One softens the world; the other breaks it.

To cultivate compassion is not to soften one's spine. It is to strengthen the heart to feel—to really feel—without collapsing. It is to acknowledge that even those who cause harm are often shaped by it, and that healing is never born from hatred returned.

Compassion does not excuse injustice. It simply refuses to become it.

"Love and compassion are necessities, not luxuries.
Without them, humanity cannot survive."
— HIS HOLINESS THE 14TH DALAI LAMA

3. Equanimity (*Upekkhā*)

Equanimity is not detachment—it is unshakable balance. A poised heart in a trembling world. It does not close itself to joy or sorrow but remains upright within both, stable without being static, present without being overwhelmed. It is the strength to care without collapsing.

Its proximate cause is insight—the deep, lived understanding that all things are impermanent, conditional, and not fully controllable. What arises will pass. What is gained can be lost. What pleases can also wound. Equanimity holds this truth without panic.

Its near enemy is indifference. Emotional distance pretending to be peace. Indifference is brittle, disengaged, unfeeling. *Upekkhā* is engaged presence with perspective. It feels deeply—and stays steady.

Its far enemies are greed and aversion: the grasping after what we crave, the pushing away of what we fear. These are the engines of reaction. Equanimity interrupts their cycle.

To practice equanimity is to become a refuge. A place where others can breathe, and where we ourselves are no longer at war with experience. It is the ground on which compassion does not burn out and wisdom does not harden. It is not apathy—it is love with altitude.

"I no longer shut out the world, but let it enter me. I no longer flee from responsibility. I face it all—joy, suffering, and death—and still find life to be meaningful."
— ETTY HILLESUM

4. Wisdom (*Paññā*)

Wisdom is not cleverness. It is not accumulation. It is not the ability to outargue or outmaneuver. Wisdom is the clear seeing into the nature of things—into *anicca* (impermanence), *dukkha* (suffering), and *anattā* (not-self). It doesn't decorate the truth; it reveals it.

Its proximate cause is sustained mindfulness and concentration—a mind stabilized enough to look deeply, and brave enough to look honestly. From that stillness comes discernment. From that discernment, freedom.

Its near enemy is intellectualism—knowledge without realization, concepts without embodiment. Words can sound wise while masking confusion. But real *paññā* transforms perception. It humbles. It liberates.

Its far enemy is delusion. The belief in permanence, in separateness, in control. The roots of violence and greed grow in that blindness. Wisdom pulls them out—not through force, but through insight.

To be wise is to see that the enemy we fear is not "other"—but the illusion of otherness itself. Wisdom doesn't harden us. It softens us with clarity. It tells us: this moment, too, will pass. This anger, too, is made of fear. This life, too, is not mine—but a flowing, breathing mystery.

Wisdom does not make us more powerful. It makes us more real.

"Peace cannot be kept by force; it can only be achieved by understanding."
— ALBERT EINSTEIN

5. Restraint (*Saṃvara*)

Restraint is not suppression. It is not fear of desire or shame around anger. It is the disciplined reverence for life's sacredness—a conscious choice to interrupt harm before it begins. To practice *saṃvara* is to guard the sense doors, not with rigidity, but with wisdom and care.

Its proximate cause is mindfulness paired with clear comprehension—the ability to see a reaction forming and gently say: not now, not this way. Restraint arises when we recognize that every action shapes the future. That freedom is not doing whatever we want—but choosing what is most skillful, most kind.

Its near enemy is repression—a clamping down, a moral bypassing that pretends stillness while seething inside. *True restraint is fluid, not frozen.* It pauses to feel, but does not blindly act.

Its far enemy is indulgence—the heedless pursuit of pleasure or revenge, the compulsive enactment of whatever the mind demands. Without restraint, even good intentions can wound. With it, even our anger becomes instructive rather than destructive.

Restraint is inner nobility in motion. It is not weakness. It is a fierce vow: to feel the fire and still not burn the world with it."

Restraint is not denial—it is reverence in action."

— AUNG SAN SUU KYI

6. Patience (*Khanti*)

Patience is not passivity. It is not silence born of fear. It is love extended through time—a quiet, enduring strength that neither retaliates nor retreats. To practice *khanti* is to remain upright in the face of injustice, insult, and delay, without allowing bitterness to bloom.

Its proximate cause is deep reflection—on the law of *kamma*, on the cost of anger, and on the slow rhythm of real transformation. Patience understands that truth ripens on its own schedule, not ours.

Its near enemy is resignation—the belief that nothing will ever change. But *khanti* is not defeat. It is sustained effort without panic. Stillness with stamina.

Its far enemy is ill will: the quick flare of irritation, the simmering grudge, the need to punish when hurt. Without patience, we become reactively righteous. With it, we reclaim the space to respond from wisdom, not wounding.

Patience is a courageous refusal to be hardened by delay or degraded by cruelty. It waits, not because it is weak, but because it knows what is worth waiting for.

"Patience is not passivity—it is fierce commitment, lived slowly."

— AUNG SAN SUU KYI

7. Truthfulness (*Sacca*)

Truthfulness is not just accuracy in speech. It is a way of being—a life lived in alignment with reality, even when that reality is raw, complex, or inconvenient. To embody *sacca* is to place truth above comfort, popularity, or self-protection.

Its proximate cause is reverence for what is real—a mind trained in clarity, and a heart that refuses to deceive, even in subtle ways. Truthfulness begins not in the mouth, but in the mirror.

Its near enemy is selective honesty—truth bent to serve image, truth trimmed to avoid discomfort. This is not integrity; it is performance. *Sacca* does not edit the truth. It respects it.

Its far enemy is falsehood—conscious deceit, denial, betrayal. The world does not fall apart from lack of information, but from lack of honesty.

To speak the truth is to stand uncloaked, vulnerable, and unguarded. But it is only from such ground that trust can grow. And trust is the only soil in which peace can take root.

"In a time of deceit, telling the truth is a revolutionary act."
— GEORGE ORWELL

8. Resolve (*Adhiṭṭhāna*)

Resolve is not rigidity. It is not blind will. It is a vow held in love—the quiet, steady decision to remain faithful to what matters, even when everything else falls away. *Adhiṭṭhāna* is strength without violence, direction without domination.

Its proximate cause is clear intention rooted in wisdom and compassion. Not just the desire to act, but the clarity to know why we act, and for whom.

Its near enemy is stubbornness—fixation masquerading as strength, persistence driven by ego or fear. True resolve is flexible. It adapts without abandoning what is sacred.

Its far enemy is indecision, defeatism—the tendency to collapse under pressure, to lose heart when met with resistance. *Resolve does not guarantee success—but it protects the integrity of the path.*

To live with resolve is to walk forward in the dark with a candle in your chest. Not because you're certain. But because you refuse to betray the light.

"The strongest of all warriors are these two — Time and Patience."
— LEO TOLSTOY

9. Generosity (*Dāna*)

Generosity is not the giving of surplus. It is the giving of self—an act of spiritual defiance against fear, against the illusion of separation, against the myth of scarcity. It says: *There is enough. I am enough. And I choose to share.*

Its proximate cause is empathy—a felt understanding of another's joy, sorrow, or need. It arises from connection, not obligation.

Its near enemy is transactional giving—generosity shadowed by pride, performance, or subtle expectation. When giving becomes about being seen or owed, it ceases to be free.

Its far enemy is greed. The hunger to possess, hoard, or dominate. Greed shrinks the soul. Generosity expands it.

Dāna is a declaration of trust: in life, in others, in the sufficiency of the heart. It is the refusal to build walls when bridges can be made. And sometimes, in our emptiest moments, the smallest act of giving becomes the greatest act of healing.

"No one has ever become poor by giving."

— ANNE FRANK

10. Humility (*Nivāta*)

Humility is not self-denial. It is not hiding. It is the grace of knowing one's true place in the vastness of things—not as inferior, not as superior, but as essential and interdependent. It is the wisdom that whispers, *I am part of this, not above it.*

Its proximate cause is insight into *anattā*—the truth of not-self. The recognition that identity is fluid, fragile, and ultimately shared.

Its near enemy is false modesty—insecurity clothed as virtue, the self-effacing mask that still seeks attention. True humility does not speak in disclaimers. It simply acts without vanity.

Its far enemy is conceit: the inflation of self, the hunger to be more than others. Conceit isolates. Humility connects.

To be humble is to listen before speaking, to bow without losing dignity, to lead without needing to be followed. It is not weakness. It is the soil where all the other virtues grow.

"I do not wish to be above anyone. I only wish to be real."

— AUNG SAN SUU KYI

Alan Clements: Daw Suu, thank you—from the heart—for your clarity, your courage, and your generosity. What you've offered isn't just a list of qualities—it's a living guide. A reminder of what it means to stay human in inhuman times.

So, let me ask, directly: Can a leader truly turn from the machinery of militarism to a politics of peace? Or has that vision already been buried under the weight of "realism"?

Aung San Suu Kyi: It is not a dream, Alan. It is a prophecy—one we have inherited but not yet honored. Again and again, we've failed to fulfill it. But it remains. Waiting. Still.

Yes, such a transformation is rare. It demands the courage to renounce the currencies of domination—fear, spectacle, armament, control. It asks of a leader something that appears foolish to the world but is wise to the soul: the willingness to lose power in order to gain conscience.

We have seen it before. José Figueres abolishing Costa Rica's military. Mandela choosing reconciliation over revenge. These were not saints. They were human beings who made sacred decisions.

So, the question is not whether it is possible—but whether we are willing to bear the cost. Peace is not free. But neither is war. And one of them demands that we evolve. The other ensures that we vanish.

Which will we choose?

Alan Clements: And in an era where violence is not only normalized but automated—where algorithms replace empathy, and wars are outsourced to machines—do you still believe, in your heart of hearts, one more time, if I may ask, that nonviolent leadership is possible?

Aung San Suu Kyi: I do. And I must. Because the alternative is not simply death. It is the erasure of what makes us human.

Nonviolence is not a fantasy. It is a discipline. A moral technology. A spiritual operating system. A survival code for civilizations that wish to continue.

It is not only possible—it is essential.

Gandhi knew this. So did Kolbe.

You may know his name. For others, allow me: He was a Polish Catholic priest. A man of quiet devotion. But it was in Auschwitz where his truth became immortal.

In July 1941, after a prisoner escaped, the SS selected ten men at random to starve to death. One cried out for his wife and children. And Kolbe—calmly, without hesitation—stepped forward and asked to take his place.

They agreed.

Locked in a starvation bunker, Kolbe led the others in prayer, in silence, in dignity. One by one, they died. When only he remained— calm, composed, conscious—the guards ended his life with a lethal injection.

It was not weakness. It was strength of the highest order. The kind of strength that chooses love over survival.

And he is not alone.

There are mothers who bury their children without giving birth to hatred.

There are prisoners who forgive their captors. There are activists who refuse to dehumanize those who hunt them.

These are not anomalies. They are our lighthouses.

Even in Auschwitz, nonviolence lived—in whispered prayers, in shared bread, in the decision to comfort rather than curse.

So, who are we, in our comfort and complexity, to say it cannot be done?

Alan Clements: I'm moved—deeply. In Kolbe's act, we don't just witness sacrifice. We witness conscience in its most incandescent form—a refusal to be extinguished, even in a place engineered to erase the human soul.

May his defiance echo through every hall of power—from Yangon to Geneva—as an archetypal reminder of what it means to honor the voice within. To elevate life itself—through compassion, through courage, through the dignity of love in action.

And if this book is read, decades from now, by a young person— born into a world of fracture and forgetting—what last truth would you offer them, Daw Suu? Not as a leader, but as a human being who has suffered, endured, and still chosen love?

Aung San Suu Kyi:
I would tell them this:

You were not born to hate.
You were born to love—

Not the kind found in stories,
But the kind that dissolves stories.

The kind that humbles pride,
Heals wounds,
And dares to listen
When no one else will.

Violence is a form of forgetting—
Forgetting our interconnection.
Forgetting the miracle of consciousness.
Forgetting that beneath all flags and fears,
We are one breath.

Nonviolence, then, is remembrance.
It is how light survives the dark.
It is how we return home—
To ourselves.
To each other.

Do not mistake gentleness for weakness.
Do not mistake silence for surrender.
There is strength in restraint.
And clarity in compassion.

So, walk with me—
Whoever you are.
Wherever you are.
In mindfulness,
In courage,
In love.

Even in darkness—
Light remembers its way.

And so can we.

And if I may—
Before this chapter closes—
Offer a final prayer:

May we remember the many Kolbes among us—
Not only in distant history,
But in our cities,
Villages,
Prisons,
And homes.

Those who rise in silence,
Who choose dignity over revenge,
Truth over silence,
Compassion over conformity.

May their courage be recognized,
Even if no monument bears their name.

May their sacrifices awaken us—
To the possibility of grace in the face of cruelty,
To the quiet revolution of conscience in motion.
May we, too, answer the call—

To live our highest truth.
To embody our finest Dhamma.
To express the radiance of love,
Even when the world forgets how.
And may we walk this path not alone—

But with those who have come before,
And those still yet to rise.

In mindfulness,
In courage,
In love.

(She pauses. We look at each other. Her eyes, lit by quiet fire, meet mine.)

Aung San Suu Kyi: Alan… I have shared so much with you. Allow me now to ask you something.

Alan Clements: Daw Suu, I would be deeply honored.

Aung San Suu Kyi: You have walked with our people for decades. You've given voice to our silence, stood with us through banishment, bullets, and betrayal. Your books, your films, your witness have carried our hopes to the wider world.

So let me ask: If you had but one story to share—one among the many I know you carry close—not just for me, but for generations to come…

Please share it. Not as memory alone, but as a torch.

Alan Clements: Then I will speak—not with authority, but with gratitude.

The weeks I spent with Burmese student refugees in the jungles of Karen and Shan States remain among the most sacred of my life. We worked side by side in the infirmary, joined them on patrol, shared simple meals, and spoke quietly of freedom.

One night, we sat under the stars with a single candle between us. I was speaking with a 29-year-old university graduate who had fled after the 1988 uprisings.

I asked her gently, "Have you ever been in love?"

She looked into the flame and said: "Yes. I was to marry my fiancé in 1988. But the uprisings came. We marched. We sang. We knelt before soldiers and called them brothers. They opened fire."

They fled into the jungle. Hiding. Starving. Watching comrades die of disease and bullets. On the night they were to be married, an ambush separated them. She has not seen him since.

"I don't know if he's alive," she said. "But I cannot ask. Contacting anyone could cost lives."

We sat in silence. Then she said:

"I still think of him. I miss him. But my love has changed. Now I am in love with freedom. And if I die—tortured or forgotten— If that helps restore freedom to my people,I will die in love."

She looked at me. Eyes unwavering. And said:

"Yes, I have been in love. And I remain in love."

CHAPTER TWENTY-TWO

THE DHAMMA'S ROLE IN THE STRUGGLE FOR FREEDOM

Author's Prelude

Some truths break through prison walls, born not in temples or texts, but in lives shaped by sacrifice, resonant as the ancient pagodas of Myanmar. This chapter captures their power: not dogma, but insight; not debate, but a living voice—raw, reverent, unyielding.

It is the story of Daw Aung San Suu Kyi, a woman who has made the *Dhamma*—the Buddha's teaching of freedom from fear, anger, and delusion—her core, her silence, honed by years of lost liberties, a force rising against the chains of captivity.

Here, she does not preach Buddhist ideals—she lives them. Her strength is a steady light, unwavering despite the chaos of political imprisonment.

This chapter reveals a dialogue rooted not in theory but in conscience, shaped by decades of resilience and sacrifice. It explores the *Dhamma's* practical role in modern Myanmar: mindfulness to endure oppression, compassion to unite a divided nation, and nonviolence to resist tyranny.

Aung San Suu Kyi, imprisoned in solitary confinement since the military coup in 2021 for her democratic leadership, embodies these principles, her voice a beacon for a country torn by terror and war.

In her solitude—where a nation's hopes meet the focus of a single breath—she weaves a *Dhamma* no dictatorship can unravel. A story of courage under siege, of defiance that yields not to force but to truth, of mindfulness in a cell, and loving-kindness facing cruelty. This is no abstract philosophy. It is truth lived—a *Dhamma* forged in hardship, shining with fierce compassion.

Above all, it is a sacred offering: to young revolutionaries seeking courage tied to clarity, to prisoners whose every breath becomes prayer, to leaders who ask not what is easy, but what is right.

This chapter is the book's heart—a call to awaken in a time of darkness, a testament that the *Dhamma* lives, inspiring every heart bold enough to dream of a free Myanmar.

◆ ◆ ◆

Alan Clements: Daw Suu, as our dialogue unfolds—across oceans, prison walls, and lifetimes of resistance—I sense that what we are shaping here is more than conversation. It feels like a living *Dhamma* in motion. A shared vow of spiritual friendship—rooted in conscience, sustained by clarity, carried forward by the heart's most sacred promise: to see truly, to do no harm, to live in truth, to serve freedom.

This is my way of bowing in gratitude—for your words, yes—but also for your silence. For the rare and luminous gift of your presence, even now. For the honor of bearing witness and bringing your voice to the world. To your people. To those who revere you. And yes—even to your critics. May these words not only deepen love among friends, but soften the hearts of those who once judged, vilified, or sought to erase you.

Let forgiveness be the revolution. Let reconciliation burn brighter than grievance. Because in the end, we are all exiles of some kind—each of us yearning to belong to one another again.

And allow me this, if I may—plainly, from the heart: If you were on the Titanic, and I was in the last lifeboat, I would reach for your hand. Without condition. Without hesitation. Even if you had betrayed me. Even if you were the one who pushed me into the sea.

I say this not only to you—but to your captors. To those who penned your sentence. To the architects of your disappearance. Even to the generals who razed your cities and bombed your villages. This offering—of peace, of dialogue, of a shared humanity—is extended to them, too.

Because in that raw, final moment—between drowning and salvation, between breath and no breath—we are not roles. Not ideologies. Not history's names. We are simply human beings. Reaching. Remembering. Trying, however clumsily, to begin again.

Not as savior and saved—but as equals. Carried by conscience. Guided by *Dhamma*. And devoted to what is still possible—when love and presence lead the way.

Daw Suu, I know we've spoken of this before—countless times over the years—but I feel called now to return to it, deeper than before. Especially given where you are. And where the world is.

Throughout your life, your spiritual practice has not merely accompanied your leadership—it has defined it. Your relationship with Sayadaw U Pandita, your fierce devotion to the *Dhamma*—these are known.

But now, in the crucible of confinement, of profound isolation... what is the role of the *Dhamma* in your life today? How does it hold you—not just as a symbol or leader—but as a human being living moment to moment in the darkness of a windowless cell in solitary confinement?

Aung San Suu Kyi: Alan, I say this with what little self remains: the *Dhamma* is not a refuge I visit. It is the marrow of my being. The breath I follow. The silence that steadies me. Especially now—when almost everything else has been stripped away.

As we speak, and share, and listen to one another—this, too, is *Dhamma* practice. The *Dhamma of Listening* is not a passive act, nor a mere courtesy. It is an intimate discipline—a deep attention to the nuanced shadows of ego, the subtle movements of thought and feeling.

It is the quiet inner art of hearing, feeling, knowing—within one's own innermost awareness.

To listen in this way is to awaken. To touch the primordial pulse of consciousness—the arahant instinct, that ancient, unshakable impulse for full liberation embedded in the DNA of awareness.

It is a sacred rebellion against the noise of reaction, the clamor of self, the violence of indifference. It is how we hear the world's suffering—whether in the cries of Gaza's children, the silenced voices of Myanmar's prisoners, or the unspoken ache within ourselves—and how we respond: not with fear, but with mindful intelligence, moral courage, and existential beauty.

Your question is not simply timely—it is sacred. Because what we are doing here—this deliberate exchange, this act of listening and speaking with full presence—is itself the relational *Dhamma*. Not ritual. Not abstraction. But truth, received in awareness. Truth offered with care. Truth arising between us—not as performance, but as shared awakening. Truth tested in the container of experience.

To your question: the *Dhamma* sustains me as it always has—not as armor, but as mirror. A mirror that reveals not only what is—but what might still be. Here, in this solitary cell, with no contact, no movement, almost no sound—save for a bird's cry or the whisper of rats in the walls—I have deepened into something I can only describe as the unbroken now.

Sayadawgyi's teachings live in me—not as memory, but as oxygen. He was not interested in performance. He cared for one thing: liberation.

Awareness, he taught us, must live in every posture—in walking, sitting, lying down. In prison or in parliament. In exile or in the arms of family. He taught mindfulness as a moral atmosphere—not a technique. A way of seeing that clarifies even the darkest terrain.

He was not merely a teacher of *Satipaṭṭhāna*. He was its living embodiment. In his fierce love, in his exacting kindness, he remains—next to my mother and father, my late husband Michael, and my beloved sons Kim and Alexander—a pillar of my conscience.

And I must name others. Those whose nobility shaped not only my practice but the fiber of my public life.

Saya U Tin Oo—courage carved from silence. Uncle U Kyi Maung—quiet integrity in the face of fear. Saya U Win Tin—whose flesh bore torture, but whose dignity never bruised. And U Win Htein—my dearest comrade, 84 years old, still in solitary in Obo Prison. His unseen presence is a flame that refuses to go out.

These noble friends remind me: the *Dhamma* is not solitary. It is relational. Forged in *kalyāṇa mittatā*—spiritual friendship. Tempered in patience. Illuminated through presence.

Here, in confinement, I return to the practice unceasingly. In walking meditation. In *vipassanā*. In brushing my teeth. In sweeping the floor. In listening to my thoughts without obeying them. Life does not pause. Nor does the practice.

Yes, the conditions are harsh. The heat thickens the air. The insect's bite. The body aches. My injury pains me. I sleep little. Yet sometimes—a bird sings. A high, slender note. It breaks through the cement like a prayer etched into stone. And in that sound—I smile. Because beauty, too, refuses to surrender.

Sayadawgyi taught me that practice is not an escape—it is an intimacy. With sensation. With thought. With sorrow. With love. He taught us not to chase stillness, but to meet the storm with presence.

So, I observe. I feel. I release. And I begin again.

Because this path is not about transcendence. It is about return. Not as punishment—but as refuge. As tenderness. As vow.

That, Alan, is my aspiration. Not to follow the Dhamma, but to become it.

Alan Clements: Beautiful. Thank you, Daw Suu.

Meeting *Sayadawgyi* changed my life as well. He wasn't just a teacher—he was a compass of conscience, a spiritual father, a fierce and tender friend across nearly four decades, until his passing in 2016.

I think you know, I was blessed to bring him to America for the first time in 1984, and later to Australia as well. His presence was thunder wrapped in wisdom—unyielding in truth, radiant with *mettā*. He taught not to impress, but to awaken.

And before Sayadaw U Pandita, there was the Venerable Mahasi Sayadaw. I had the rare honor of also bringing him to America for the very first time in 1979. At the end of that visit, I received the unexpected blessing of ordaining under him—in the Burmese Ambassador's apartment in New York City, of all places. I shaved my head. I donned the robe. And the very next day, we boarded a flight to London, and then to Burma. The rest, as they say, is history—a living one, rooted in breath, silence, and the dignity of unshakable conscience.

And in that lineage—through the fire of those teachings and the quiet beauty of their hearts—I met you. Through, as you recall, the late Saya U Tin Oo. It was 1995, just after your release from house arrest. I remember it vividly.

Ironically, I had met him years earlier—the very day after his own release from prison, sometime around 1980. His detainer? General Ne Win—the very same man who would later detain you. And yet, upon release, U Tin Oo did not flee. After a night at home, he was taken to the Mahasi Meditation Center in Rangoon—where I was living as a monk—and there, he ordained. What kind of man does that?

He shared so much with me—about Burma, about the psychology of dictatorship, the moral arc of history, the impossible beauty of your people, and the quiet power of conscience. So much wisdom. So much grace. So much heart. What a luminous mind he was.

Aung San Suu Kyi: Yes, I remember. He was indeed a luminous mind. And that crossing of paths—through Uncle U Tin Oo—was no small event. It was the seed of something enduring. It's how *The Voice of Hope* came to be—our first book together, born of five months of conversation in my home in Rangoon.

(She smiles knowingly.)

Back in the "good old days"—six years into house arrest, yet still buoyed by hope. And now, here we are... thirty years later ...in the penthouse at the Four Seasons.

(We both laugh—softly, reverently.)

He was not only your friend and mentor, Alan. He was mine. My comrade. My guide. And alongside his beloved wife—*my co-conspirator in conscience.* As you know, he co-founded our party, the National League for Democracy.

And in all the years I knew him, he never once sought power for its own sake. He stood—always—with the people. With truth. With dignity. Even after years of prison, after exile, after the machinery of repression had tried to break him—he emerged not hardened, but purified. Not bitter, but bound to service. *He was a Dhamma warrior.*

Alan Clements: If I may, Daw Suu, let me share a story with you about Saya U Tin Oo. You may already know it—he shared it with me at your home, just days before I was forced to leave Burma in March of 1996.

We were sitting quietly in your garden by the lake. The late afternoon light was soft, golden. Saya seemed almost timeless—so full of grace, wisdom, and quiet courage. A statesman forged not by ambition, but by suffering. One who had endured conditions in prison that most would not survive—not unlike, as you know too well, the fate of more than 22,000 political prisoners still held in captivity today—including you.

I asked him, "What does it take to emotionally and psychologically survive eleven years of solitary confinement?"

He looked at me and smiled—not bitterly, but with that unmistakable, soft, almost boyish light in his eyes. And then, as if speaking from the stillness of that very cell, he answered:

"Oh, I had ways to keep my spirit alive," he said, lifting his seventy-six-year-old face to the sun. "My hut within the prison was separate from the main block, encircled in barbed wire. I was indoors all the time. That wire—it became my teacher. It reminded me how sacred freedom really is. Like in the Buddha's teachings—obstacles can become advantages. The loss of freedom can awaken the reflection on its value. That insight gave me joy."

He paused, then continued, calm and clear:

"I knew from my years as a monk the benefits of *sati*—mindfulness. Just do everything with awareness, and there's no room for harmful thoughts. I treated each day in prison the same way I did in the monastery—mindfully. I tried to observe everything: each sound, each taste, each thought, each flicker of sensation or emotion. It all becomes just experience. Nothing added. Just phenomena. Even the thought of imprisonment is just that—a thought. It comes. It goes. And if you don't cling to it, there's no problem."

He went on to describe how he would recite the Buddha's discourses in *Pāli,* and how a small book of Jesus' sayings had been smuggled in. He loved Jesus' sincerity—his spirit of radical forgiveness.

"And I gave *dāna*," he said with a quiet chuckle. "Every day I tried to offer a little something to my jailers. A bite of food. A kind word. Anything. I didn't want to see them as enemies. They were living hard lives too. That softened my heart. It eased my pain."

Then came a pause. Silence.

He looked at me again and said, "I also chose to stop eating after midday. There are many people in my country who go hungry—because of this dictatorship. By fasting, I stayed in solidarity with them. I kept myself honest."

His eyes closed for a moment. A long breath passed through him. And when he opened them, he smiled—with that quiet, unshakable joy I will never forget.

"But most importantly," he said, holding both my hands in his, "I would think about my friends. Their faces. Their kindness. Our laughter. I would speak to them in my heart—one by one. That, more than anything, kept me sane."

And then—in a moment of pure grace—he said something that etched itself into me forever:

"It's the love that you feel that keeps your sanity. It's the love that sets you free."

I carry that sentence with me still—as compass, as shield, as vow.

That memory reminds me that presence is a form of communion. That liberation is relational. And that even in our deepest isolation—as you know far better than I—the act of remembering love, of consciously returning to it, is not sentiment. It's spiritual survival.

Aung San Suu Kyi: Yes, Alan. What a gift. That story captures him so well.

We must bring the best of ourselves to each moment—not just when we are seen, but when we are alone. Especially then. *Because the true measure of love is what we offer when no one is watching. Can we still give? Can we still rise?*

Even here, in solitary, I ask myself as often as needed: Can I renew my courage to love? Can I stand in communion with myself, with others, and with the world—all at once?

Because we are in this together. And we need each other—not only to survive, but to awaken. To become fully alive. To liberate ourselves and one another. And to carry the *Dhamma* forward—not only as a spiritual path, but as a living vow. A vow to meet life fully. To meet each other fully. *The Dhamma of heartfelt listening, relating, being. The art of sacred reciprocity.*

To embody presence as consecrated ground. To live from that ground—awake, responsive, fearless—is to be ready. Ready to live. Ready to die. Ready to touch, and to be touched.

So, from my heart, thank you, Alan—for sharing this story of *Saya*. And for sharing it not just from memory, but from your whole being.

As we were speaking of Kolbe—the priest who gave his life at Auschwitz so another might live—I find myself thinking of Uncle. To me, he embodied that same sacred courage. That quiet, noble strength. He understood sacrifice not as performance, but as love in its most fearless form.

I think you know, *Saya* was my mentor. My comrade. My *kalyāna mitta*. And yes, his beloved wife, as I mentioned, was my comrade too. Together, they formed a pillar in my life—and in our shared struggle.

In all the years I knew him, he never once sought power for its own sake. He stood—always—with the people. With conscience. With truth. Even after years in prison, he chose not bitterness, but service.

So yes—please go on. Speak of *Sayadawgyi*. Let your words bring him back to life. I know how deeply he lived in you.

Alan Clements: Thank you, Daw Suu.

Sayadawgyi's presence in my life was foundational. He possessed a vast and subtle knowledge—not just of classical Buddhist teachings, but of science, art, literature, and culture. Especially *vipassanā*, of course. You may already know this, but he spoke several languages and could quote at will—from Tolstoy to obscure Buddhist treatises from the 1920s. Often, in the middle of a conversation, he would reach for one of the thousands of books in his greeting room and pull out a passage to illuminate his point.

He was a remarkable conversationalist, alive with a natural, spacious curiosity—especially about me, his young Western guest. He wanted to know everything: my childhood, my difficulties, my dreams. And so began a cross-cultural dialogue that, over the decades, became a kind of mirror—a space in which we could both see the conditioning of East and West more clearly. In truth, I think we educated each other—gently, across cultures—in the hidden scaffolding of our minds.

I was dazzled—by his brilliance, yes—but also by his tenderness. And I think he saw in me a novice not only hungry for knowledge but a soul longing for direction. Back then, I asked—timidly—for permission for him to be my primary teacher. He granted it with the simple grace that marked his life.

Eventually, I returned to my homeland, but Sayadaw U Pandita and I never lost touch. As I mentioned earlier, I had the honor of organizing his first teaching tours to America and Australia. And I returned often to Burma—to sit with him again, to drink from the ever-deepening river of his mind. And yes, like a river, he only grew more luminous with time.

One of the greatest blessings of my life was the time I spent with him near the end—nine evenings of intimate conversation, just months before his passing. You may recall—those dialogues became the basis for our book, *Wisdom for the World: Mindful Advice to the People of My Country*. Nine evenings that changed me forever.

We covered a vast range of topics—but at the heart of those conversations was his vision of what he called the *Requisites of Reconciliation*: his guidance for healing broken relationships, restoring dignity, and laying the moral groundwork of a future built on peaceful coexistence. It is a book, I believe, for every leader in the world today.

Sayadawgyi could see the global trends unfolding—the slow fragmentation of conscience, the technological acceleration of cruelty, the dangerous erosion of dialogue.

He had lived through the Second World War. He had seen the devastation of Burma's internal conflicts. He understood, viscerally, the limitations of force, the futility of hatred, and the soul-destroying power of politics untethered from ethics.

His lifelong message was both simple and fierce: *peace is not a sentiment. It is a practice of relentless communication and courageous understanding.*

And so, in his final months, he gave everything he had left to articulating these truths—with the full force of his wisdom, expressed in the language of dialogue, which was, in many ways, his final offering to the world.

His precision. His truthfulness. His unshakable devotion to liberation.

His exactness wasn't intellectual—it was existential. He taught me that clarity is love in action. That you cannot deceive yourself and still be free. That awareness is not indulgence but revolution.

His truthfulness was never cruel. But it cut through delusion like silk through shadow. He could see where you were deceiving yourself— often before you opened your mouth—and he would wait, quietly, relentlessly, until you had the courage to see it too.

And his devotion to freedom—not merely political freedom, but the emancipation of mind from *lobha, dosa,* and *moha*—was absolute. He made it clear that mindfulness, if not grounded in the aspiration for liberation, was just a way of polishing the ego's mirror.

He once said to me, with that mix of fire and affection: *"Your mind is your first government. Liberate that, and the rest will follow."*

You mentioned earlier that Sayadawgyi once asked you— piercingly— "Are you prepared to lead?" And when you said yes, he offered you the six defining qualities of a *kalyāṇa mitta*—a noble friend, a moral guide, a spiritual ally.

Would you be willing, Daw Suu, to share them again now—with the same clarity, depth, and luminous authority with which he once offered them to you?

Aung San Suu Kyi: Yes, I remember it vividly, Alan. He spoke slowly, deliberately—as if etching each word into the marrow of time, carving out the path I was being asked to walk. His voice was calm but unyielding. There was no space for sentimentality. Only truth.

He said: "Understand this well. Leadership, in the *Dhamma* sense, is not command. It is presence. To lead is not to be admired—but to be useful to the conscience of a people."

Then he began.

First, piya—to be genuinely lovable. But not through charm. Not through flattery. Through moral transparency. When your actions are anchored in integrity, the people will love you—not because they are commanded to, but because they trust the ground beneath your feet. I learned this early on. During my first public speeches in 1988, it wasn't the words that mattered most. It was the stillness. The refusal to inflame. *Sayadawgyi* always told me: "Let them feel your *sīla* before they hear your speech."

Second, garu—to be respected. But not through fear. Through dignity. You hold yourself in such a way that others feel safe in their own goodness. Your virtue breathes space into their virtue. When I chose to remain under house arrest rather than flee into exile, it was not an act of martyrdom—it was an act of dignity rooted in clarity. And it allowed others to stand firm in their own moral truth.

Third, bhāvaniya—to be the object of loving-kindness. Sayadawgyi said: "You must live in such a way that others naturally send you *mettā*—not because you ask, but because your being evokes it." You cannot fake this. You earn it through humility, through warmth, through constancy. In my darkest hours, letters arrived from children, from monks, from mothers in exile. Not sympathy. Not pity. But blessings. And that, *Sayadawgyi* said, was *bhāvaniya*.

Fourth, vattā—to speak the truth. Even when it shakes the room. Even when it costs you everything. "The leader who hides behind half-truths," he said, "corrodes the moral spine of the nation." I remember when I once softened a speech to placate international backers. *Sayadawgyi* said nothing. He only looked at me. A look that said everything: Truth, Daw Suu. Or nothing.

Fifth, vacanakkhamā—the ability to receive criticism. Especially from your adversaries. If you can't withstand the truth from those who oppose you, you cannot uphold it for those who depend on you. In Parliament, I was once accused of negligence regarding rural health. My instinct was to defend. But *Sayadawgyi's* voice rose in me: Listen. Listen beneath the wound. And there, beneath anger, I found care.

And sixth, no c'āṭṭhāne niyujjako—never to use others for your own gain. Never to manipulate. Never to seduce loyalty at the cost of someone's dignity. *Sayadawgyi* said: *"Lead with conscience, not strategy. Or you will build an empire of betrayal."*

These six pillars—he made clear—are not political strategies. They are inner architecture. And without them, leadership collapses into mere spectacle. Or worse—into tyranny.

Alan Clements: Those qualities—they don't just describe a leader. They describe the moral climate we hope to build in a country. In a world. That kind of integrity becomes culture. It becomes continuity.

Aung San Suu Kyi: Exactly. Sayadawgyi wasn't grooming politicians. He was cultivating spiritual warriors. Moral companions for the long road.

Alan Clements: And what of the six additional leadership qualities he shared with you?

Aung San Suu Kyi: Yes. I asked him at the time: "Sayadawgyi, how do we recognize a leader, when so many appear to lead from ambition rather than virtue?"

And he answered: *"The Dhamma recognizes a leader through six signs."*

First, khamā—patience. The ability to endure heat and cold, praise and blame, comfort and hardship. He said: "The one who cannot bear criticism cannot carry a nation."

Second, jāgariya—vigilance. Eyes wide open. Alert to the suffering of the people. Awake to consequence. Never asleep in privilege.

Third, utthāna—initiative. Not waiting for perfect conditions. Rising up. Moving first. Taking risks with discernment. Leading with boldness rooted in wisdom.

Fourth, samvibhāga—generosity. A leader must share. Power. Resources. Credit. Sacrifice must never be extracted—only offered. The fruits of freedom must never be hoarded.

Fifth, karuṇā—compassion. Not sentiment, but an embodied empathy that sees others as oneself. He said, "The compassionate leader doesn't rule. She serves."

Sixth, ikkhanā—foresight. The ability to assess. To see things as they are—and as they may become. To live and lead from the long view. To act not just for today, but for the future.

Alan Clements: Sayadawgyi was a teacher of revolution in the deepest sense—a revolution of consciousness. His vision of leadership is so clear. So, demanding. And so, needed.

Aung San Suu Kyi: Yes, Alan. And he taught it not just through words, but through presence. When he asked me, "Are you prepared to lead?"— it wasn't a question about politics. It was a question of readiness. Of the heart's posture. About walking the path in every moment, in every breath, in every circumstance.

And this is what I try to do, even now. Even in this prison. To remember that true leadership—true moral companionship—begins in the unseen moments. In how we think, speak, and act when no one is watching. That is where the revolution truly begins.

Alan Clements: He was offering a covenant of the soul. Not just a checklist of conduct—but a *dhammic* vow. A standard to return to again and again.

Aung San Suu Kyi: Yes. That was his brilliance. He didn't just teach ethics. He carved them into your nervous system. Through mindfulness. Through awareness. Through repetition.

He once told me, "A government is only as stable as the leader's ability to endure discomfort without lying." Alan, I have carried that sentence with me every day since. And it is perhaps the hardest lesson of them all.

Alan Clements: If we may return, Daw Suu, to your life here and now—imprisoned, in solitary confinement.

I imagine that the extreme solitude, while harrowing, can also be used in your favor—transmuted, perhaps, into a kind of strange, sacred ground for practice.

Sayadawgyi often reminded those close to him—those willing to listen with the whole of their being—that the *Dhamma* demands no time off. "All times. All postures. All contexts. All states. All degrees of complexity," he would say. *"Take it off others—and turn everything into freedom, into wisdom, into peace."*

But I also know that such a commitment is not romantic. It is exacting. It doesn't invite—it interrogates. And surely, the challenges of imprisonment are immense—physical, emotional, existential. The least of them, I imagine, are the deplorable conditions and the unrelenting isolation.

So, I must ask—and I know we have spoken of it before—but if I may: How do you sustain your practice in such stark conditions? How do you maintain your sanity—truly?

Aung San Suu Kyi: Alan… it is difficult to find words that match the depth of what you've asked. But I will try, from the quiet of this cell, to speak from the heart of my experience—as honestly and as humanly as I can.

The practice is both simple and profound. It begins with the body. I sit, I breathe, I observe. There is a windowless wall where my cell meets the sky, and though I cannot see the sun, I feel its presence in the warmth that filters through. That warmth becomes a teacher—a reminder of impermanence, of interdependence, of the constancy of change.

There are, of course, challenges. The body suffers—aches in the joints, the staleness of the air, the weariness that comes from inadequate nourishment. And my arm, a near constant pain. But the *Dhamma* teaches us that suffering is not something to be feared; it is something to be understood. When I observe the suffering without attachment, it softens. It loses its power over me.

The mind, too, is unruly. Thoughts of the people I love, the suffering of my nation, the uncertainty of the future—they come and go like waves. And at times, yes, I hurt. But through mindfulness, I learn not to cling to these thoughts, to these feelings, not to let them pull me under. The mind, when trained, as you know, can be as vast as the ocean—capable of holding everything without drowning in any of it. And at other times, well, let me say, we trust in our humanness.

As you shared, Sayadaw U Pandita often encouraged: *"Bring the finest qualities of the Dhamma to every context. Let no moment be exempt from Dhamma presence."* And that is what I try to do. Even in this confinement—perhaps especially in this confinement—I treat the aching, the longing, the hunger, the pain, the silence, as objects of practice. I sit with the suffering. I breathe with the uncertainty. I walk slowly in this narrow space, lifting and placing each foot, each step, with as much mindful care as if I were in a meditation hall.

Yes, there are times when I feel like crying. When the grief of this world—its cruelty, its blindness—presses down with unbearable weight. Not for me, but for my people—for what they endure, and what they are forced to become. And I sometimes get angry that it does not have to be this way. But ignorance, I remind myself, is very much a part of the human condition—and we seem to have a very high dose of it here in my country.

But the Dhamma has taught me not to fear tears. They are not weakness. They are cleansing. They are the heart's unspoken clarity. They are what remains when ego dissolves—truth in liquid form.

I reflect often on my beloved sons—Kim and Alexander. And now, my grandchildren, who will grow up in a world shaped by the choices we make today. I carry their presence with me—not as sorrow, but as a vow. May I be worthy of their love. May I help build a future they can live in with dignity.

And every day, I send *mettā*—loving-kindness and strength— to my fellow political prisoners, many of whom are held in far worse conditions. I think of U Win Htein in solitary confinement. I send him strength. I send him peace. I hold him in the field of my awareness, as *Sayadawgyi* taught us. May his spirit remain unshaken.

To the young revolutionaries scattered across the jungles and shadows of our country, I send courage. I send forgiveness. I send the wish that they know their hearts as sacred, even amidst the violence. That they know their worth—even when the world turns away.

This practice is not about escape. It is about being fully here. Alive. Awake. Even when there is pain. Even when there is loneliness. Even when there is no sign of change.

And this is how I survive. Not by clinging to hope, but by returning to the breath. To the sensation. To the present. Again, and again.

The *Dhamma* is how I stay human. It is how I remain free.

Alan Clements: Thank you, Daw Suu, for your commitment to the *Dhamma* and your relentless moral courage.

You have often spoken about *mettā*, loving-kindness. In these conditions—this isolation, this brutality—and I have asked you this before, and now weeks have passed, and so if I may, does your practice of *mettā* extend even to your oppressors? How do you sustain compassion in the face of such cruelty?

Aung San Suu Kyi: *Mettā* does not discriminate, Alan. It does not stop at the boundary of what is tolerable. It does not ask, "Do they deserve it?" It asks only, "Can I remain human?" That is the question the *Dhamma* places before us—not once, but moment by moment.

When I think of the *Tatmadaw* soldiers, the guards, even the architects of this suffering—yes, the generals—I do not deny their responsibility. I do not excuse their actions. But I see, as best I can, their conditioning. Their fear. Their estrangement from their own basic goodness. And I know that to meet them with hatred would be to step into the very blindness that binds them.

Compassion, for me, is not softness. It is discipline. It is strength. It is the refusal to become what we oppose. *Mettā* is not about liking someone. It is about refusing to participate in the cycle of harm.

That, too, is resistance.

Alan Clements: That is a remarkable perspective, Daw Suu. But for those who are not steeped in the *Dhamma*—for those whose hearts are heavy with rage, grief, and the unbearable weight of loss—how do they even begin to walk that path?

Aung San Suu Kyi: We begin where we are. With breath. With pain. With honesty.

Anger is not to be demonized—it is to be understood. It has energy. But it also has heat. The *Dhamma* teaches us to feel that heat, to witness how it burns us from within. When we truly understand suffering—our own and others'—something begins to shift. Compassion arises not as a virtue, but as necessity.

This path does not ask us to abandon the fight. It asks us to purify it. To infuse it with awareness. To fight for justice with a heart unpoisoned by vengeance. That is the way of true warriors.

Alan Clements: You speak of freedom beginning within. How does that inner freedom become a force in the outer struggle—for democracy, for human rights, for your nation?

Aung San Suu Kyi: A mind unshackled by hatred cannot be enslaved. A heart free of fear cannot be manipulated. This is what makes nonviolence so powerful. It is not about strategy—it is about being.

In our history, it was not tanks or guns that inspired the world. It was monks in robes walking barefoot in silence. It was students holding nothing but courage. It was ordinary people who chose truth, again and again, even when it cost them everything.

That is inner freedom moving as outer action. And that is what will sustain our movement—not rage, but rootedness. Not conquest, but clarity.

Alan Clements: What of the younger generation, Daw Suu? They carry the fire now. What is your message to them?

Aung San Suu Kyi: To the youth—our brave, luminous future—I say this: You are the inheritance of our suffering and our wisdom. Steward both. Use both well.

Yes, burn brightly. But do not burn out. Cultivate mindfulness as your backbone. Let silence shape your speech. Let integrity guide your alliances. You do not need to abandon activism to embrace the *Dhamma*. You only need to see that they are not separate.

The outer revolution will only endure if it is rooted in inner evolution.

Alan Clements: You've always taught that we are not separate—that interdependence is not just spiritual truth, but political truth. What does this mean for the future of Myanmar?

Aung San Suu Kyi: It means our freedom is not a zero-sum game. It means that the suffering of the Rohingya diminishes the Burman. That the oppression of one ethnic group diminishes the dignity of all. That the Tatmadaw's violence wounds even the hearts of its own soldiers.

To build a truly democratic Myanmar, we must create a union that reflects our interdependence—not just in law, but in perception.

We must teach our children to see each other not as rivals for power, but as kin in the sacred struggle to live with dignity.

Alan Clements: And what would you say to those who call this too idealistic? Too slow for a world on fire?

Aung San Suu Kyi: I would say: speed is not the measure of wisdom. The Dhamma asks not how fast we move—but whether we're moving in the right direction.

Violence may bring quick results, but it leaves rage. The path of the *Dhamma* is slow, but it nourishes. It roots. It lasts.

In this time of AI-driven warfare, of automated cruelty, of numbness as policy—we must reclaim what makes us human: *our capacity to feel, to pause, to choose. The way forward is not more force. It is more mind. More heart. More truth.*

Let us walk it. Together. With mindfulness. With courage. And with the unwavering belief that—even in the darkest night—light remembers its way.

A Revolution of Character: The Wisdom of True Leadership —Part I: A Blueprint for Ethical Governance

This manifesto is rooted in the timeless Buddhist concept of *kalyāṇa mitta*, the "noble friend." Traditionally, a *kalyāṇa mitta* is not merely a companion on the path to spiritual liberation but a moral exemplar, a courageous guide, and an unwavering embodiment of ethical presence. In the crucible of political life, such a figure becomes indispensable. Leadership distorts. Power seduces. Fear erodes. The conscience of a nation often rests on the integrity of a single leader's character.

Years ago, the late Venerable Sayadaw U Pandita, my cherished spiritual mentor, shared with me the defining qualities of a *kalyāṇa mitta*—not as abstract ideals, but as the bedrock of authentic leadership. I have carried these principles through imprisonment, the scrutiny of diplomacy, and the solitude of reflection. They are not easy. But they are essential. What follows is not a mere list. It is a sacred covenant for those who lead.

These twelve principles, reimagined as archetypes of leadership, are crafted for all entrusted with power—presidents, parliamentarians, diplomats, activists, and citizens alike. They are Eastern in origin, universal in aspiration. They are not tactics. They are integrity in action.

They form the moral architecture of a leader who does not dominate, but uplifts.

1. Catalyst | *Piya* — Trust Forged in Moral Clarity

True leadership begins not with charisma, but with trust. *Piya* is the quality of being genuinely worthy of trust—not through persuasion, but through ethical transparency. When people sense your intentions are rooted in integrity, their loyalty is not fleeting—it is resolute. It is principled. Their faith in you becomes the cornerstone of collective courage.

"The salvation of this behovely world lies nowhere else than in the human heart."
— VÁCLAV HAVEL

2. Wisdom Keeper | *Garu* — Reverence Through Dignity

Garu signifies reverence earned—not through intimidation, but through quiet dignity. The Wisdom Keeper carries experience as a beacon—not to dazzle, but to illuminate the path for others. True reverence arises when a leader chooses principle over expediency, sacrifice over self-interest.

"In the end, we will remember not the words of our enemies, but the silence of our allies."
— MARTIN LUTHER KING JR.

3. Empath | *Bhāvaniya* — Goodwill Through Embodied Humility

The Empath leads with warmth—never misconstrued as fragility. *Bhāvaniya* is the capacity to inspire others to offer *mettā*—loving-kindness—freely. This is not sympathy. It is a benediction. It emerges when people feel your steadfastness, your humility, your humanity. Your courage mirrors their highest aspirations, compelling their support without coercion.

"A nation's greatness is measured not by its might, but by its mercy toward its most vulnerable."
— NELSON MANDELA

4. Beacon | *Vattā* — Truth as Unyielding Commitment

Vattā is truth articulated not for convenience, but as a sacred duty. The Beacon speaks with clarity—especially when the message is difficult, when it risks favor or comfort. Leadership must resist the allure of half-truths. Even a minor compromise of truth, repeated, becomes systemic corruption. To remain a beacon, a leader must shine through the fiercest tempests.

"A moral act, though without immediate effect, plants seeds of enduring change."
— VÁCLAV HAVEL

5. Navigator | *Vacanakkhamā* — Listening as Ethical Discipline

The Navigator listens—not to deflect, but to discern. *Vacanakkhamā* is the discipline to receive critique, even from adversaries, without reprisal. True leadership hears the unspoken pleas beneath confrontation, recognizing that criticism often masks a yearning for acknowledgment. A leader who cannot listen has already forfeited their moral clarity.

"Governance is not the art of the possible, but the courage to make necessary what is just."
— VÁCLAV HAVEL

6. Mirror | *No c'āṭṭhāne niyujjako* — Integrity Beyond Exploitation

This principle forbids using others for personal gain. No *c'āṭṭhāne niyujjako* demands that leaders never manipulate, seduce, or exploit loyalty. Many falter not from external threats, but from within—when they prioritize allegiance over truth, spectacle over conscience. The Mirror reflects integrity back to power, unyielding and pure.

"A democracy's strength is measured by its leaders' capacity to face unvarnished truth."
— LIU XIAOBO

7. Exemplar | *Khamā* — Endurance with Grace

Khamā is the art of enduring with grace. The Exemplar stands resolute amid accusation, exile, or loss—unflinching yet composed. Patience here is not passivity; it is a fierce serenity, a capacity to remain anchored while the world convulses. Without it, leadership becomes reactive. With it, it becomes a moral lodestar.

"The true measure of leadership is steadfastness in crisis."
— NELSON MANDELA

8. Ally | *Jāgariya* — Vigilance Without Complacency

Jāgariya is alertness—not suspicion, but clarity. The Ally remains awake to injustice, even when it demands personal sacrifice. To lead is to confront suffering directly, allowing it to reshape perception, choice, and action. Leadership that averts its gaze from pain has already abdicated its purpose.

"Our strength lies in our solidarity."
— ANDREI SAKHAROV

9. Initiator | *Utthāna* — Action in Service of Wisdom

The Initiator acts decisively when others falter. *Utthāna* is the courage to lead with vision, not convenience. It is moral momentum—a refusal to be paralyzed by fear or indecision. The world transforms because one dares to step forward before the path is certain.

"To give light, one must endure the flame."
— VIKTOR E. FRANKL

10. Giver | *Samvibhāga* — Generosity as Empowerment

The Giver recognizes that leadership is the equitable distribution of opportunity. *Samvibhāga* is the willingness to share not only resources and recognition but trust, voice, and responsibility. A leader's legacy is not in how many serve them, but in how many they empower.

"Power corrupts not through ambition, but through fear—fear of its loss or its absence."
— AUNG SAN SUU KYI

11. Servant | *Karuṇā* — Compassion as Transformative Force

Karuṇā is compassion made manifest. The Servant leads not from a throne, but from alongside. Their leadership is not transactional—it is relational, rooted in presence and empathy. They see the pain of others not as a policy footnote, but as the cornerstone of just governance.

"Leadership is giving voice to the silenced, hope to the despairing, and power to the dispossessed."
— ELEANOR ROOSEVELT

12. Seer | *Ikkhanā* — Foresight Guided by Conscience

The Seer perceives beyond the immediate. *Ikkhanā* is the rare ability to act with precision and vision. A leader with foresight governs not for acclaim, but for legacy, planting seeds for a future they may never see. Their decisions endure because they are guided by conscience, not calculation.

"True freedom requires universal responsibility—a commitment to heal, to reconcile, and to uplift all humanity."
— AUNG SAN SUU KYI

These twelve archetypes are not a checklist. They are a living covenant. They form a moral architecture for leadership, where inner discipline meets outer courage. Rooted in the *Dhamma*, they resonate with every democracy, every revolution, every act of statecraft.

To the stewards of tomorrow: Let these principles be your guiding star. Embody them. Adapt them. Innovate with wisdom. Forge new pathways to peace. Create diplomacy rooted not in fear, but in shared humanity.

Let us build a world where leadership is measured not by dominance, but by dignity; not by triumph, but by vision. May our nations be free from fear, free from violence, and united in the shared vow of awakening together.

And may that era dawn swiftly.

CHAPTER TWENTY-THREE

LEADERSHIP IN DEMOCRACY

Author's Prelude

Some truths strike with the force of thunder, rousing the complacent foundations of the known. Others descend gently, like rain on parched earth, their quiet resonance echoing in the timeless rhythm of Myanmar's ancient mountains, valleys and rice fields. This chapter is of the latter kind—subtle, vital, and profoundly cherished.

This is not a discourse on democracy drawn from textbooks or diplomatic treatises. It is a vision forged in solitude, where joy surrenders to duty, and wisdom emerges not from instruction, but from the disciplines of inner life. Aung San Suu Kyi does not merely articulate leadership; she inhabits it—an enduring vow, a quiet dignity sculpted in unseen moments of resolve.

Her words transcend political theory, offering instead a spiritual ecology: a leadership rooted in the fertile soil of integrity, nourished by *hiri* (moral conscience) and *ottappa* (moral reverence), and illuminated by the resilience of a monsoon's afterlight. In the stillness of her confinement, where the clamor of tyranny fades, she discerns the heart's unspoken truths, crafting a leadership that does not dominate, but heals—*binding fracture to wholeness.*

Here, democracy is not a system, but a sacred relationship—a covenant of trust and mutual accountability. Leadership is not a role, but a rhythm, pulsing with discernment and tenderness. True strength lies not in defiance, but in the courage to serve unseen, to hold contradiction without faltering, and to act with clarity while listening with depth.

The world no longer needs rulers, but restorers—leaders who speak with moral authority, listen with empathetic wisdom, and midwife a future not of fleeting illusions, but of enduring hope. This chapter stands as a threshold, inviting those ready to lead with steadfast presence to guide a world yearning for renewal.

May these words echo in the silence of reflection, unlock what power has long sealed, and summon a new era of leadership—not of force, but of compassion. May they endure as testament to Aung San Suu Kyi's unyielding devotion to a democracy that uplifts, restores, and rehumanizes.

◆ ◆ ◆

Alan Clements: Daw Suu, our last conversation unveiled a profound vision of ethical leadership—rooted in *kalyāṇa mitta*, the noble friend, weaving conscience, courage, and wisdom. Yet I sense we've only begun.

If you're willing, I'd like to delve deeper—into leadership within a democracy. Not in theory, but amidst today's rising authoritarianism, societal fragmentation, and eroding trust.

You've walked through these fires—led from within them—a beacon of moral endurance. So, humbly, I ask: now in your fifth year of solitary confinement under a brutal regime, how do you understand leadership's deeper nature in a democracy? And how do conscience and dignity—not just as principles, but as presence—become the foundation of authentic leadership?

Aung San Suu Kyi: Thank you, Alan.
No manifesto, no speech, no policy—however eloquent—can rival the quiet, daily work of conscience, forged in solitude.

What we explored was no code, but a looking glass—or a set of seeds meant to stir something awake in those called to lead. In democracy, where trust frays and voices clash, leadership becomes a clearing—a space where truth can breathe, where doubt is allowed to speak, where care takes root.

That clearing is shaped by self-respect—this is what dignity truly means. It is not a mask we wear; it is a threshold we refuse to cross. It is the silence that holds us back from saying what we know is false.

It is knowing that leadership does not seek admiration, but trustworthiness in the quiet moments. Here, where solitude carves both wound and wisdom, I strive to see the stars, as Ahmed Kathrada did in his cell: *"One prisoner saw iron bars; another, stars."*

Here, *hiri* and *ottappa* arise—the Buddha's "guardians of the world." Not rules, but inner thresholds. *Hiri*, the quiet voice whispering, "You've gone too far" or "You've not done enough," halts self-justification. *Ottappa*, the felt truth that our choices ripple outward, reminds us: no act is private.

These are the anchors that hold leadership steady against the sway of performance.

Leadership is imagination—the courage to see possibility where others see only fate. Nelson Mandela's words guide me: *"It always seems impossible until it's done,"* calling us beyond smallness. And this, too: *"There is no passion in playing small—in settling for a life less than you are capable of living."*

Conformity—often mistaken for stability—is democracy's hidden peril. As Rollo May warned: "The opposite of courage is not cowardice—it is conformity." Shame binds only if we accept its terms. When we question myths disguised as moral law, we begin to see more clearly.

Rosa Parks did not shout or revolt—she refused to move. She rejected a logic that insulted her humanity. In that stillness, she kindled a movement.

Even here, even now, I hold this: releasing shame restores a deeper power—the power to redefine what's possible.

Thus, leadership in democracy begins with quiet disciplines: the courage to pause before acting, the humility to own our errors, and the strength to uphold dignity—for others, and within.

It is not a platform. It is a daily practice.

Conscience is not the absence of fault, but the presence of care—the inner thread that binds us to a world still learning how to heal.

Alan Clements: Daw Suu, the way you speak of hiri and ottappa—not as rigid doctrines, but as quiet, inner companions—has stayed with me. You make them feel deeply human. Personal. Almost like moral ancestors we can lean on when the road narrows and the winds rise.

Your reference to the South African Ahmed Kathrada, struck a quiet chord. That line about the stars—it's not just poetic, it's a kind of vow. A refusal to let the bars dictate your integrity, your dignity, your felt sense of freedom. It speaks to something elemental: that even in captivity, there's a sovereignty of spirit that no regime can take—only we can surrender.

And when you spoke of conformity—how it masquerades as harmony—I felt the sting of that. We've all, in one way or another, been puppets to it. The pressure to shrink, to nod, to fit the mold. And yet you remind us: true leadership doesn't come from pleasing the moment. It comes from listening to what's timeless.

That's where *hiri* and *ottappa* seem to live—in that space of inner listening. The subtle check before the wrong word, the pause before betrayal. That sacred hesitation where presence becomes a stand.

So, may I ask—gently, but directly—would you speak more about how these two guardians, *hiri* and *ottappa*, show up in your own hardest moments of leadership?

When everything is on the line—when the pressure is immense and the choices are murky—how do they help steady you?

What do they sound like in your own heart?

Aung San Suu Kyi: Alan, we've often spoken before of *hiri* and *ottappa*—the quiet guardians of the moral life. And I return to them now, not to repeat what's already been said, but to go deeper. Because they are not merely principles to me. They are the very atmosphere I continue to breathe—as a human being, and as someone entrusted—however imperfectly—with leadership.

In times of crisis, exile, or injustice, leadership cannot begin with charisma, or even with strategy. It must begin with something far more radiant—and far harder to counterfeit: an unwavering relationship with conscience.

Hiri and *ottappa* are not abstract ideals. They are the marrow of moral presence. And I have seen them dismissed—too quiet, too soft, too internal for the world of politics. But I have lived the opposite. It is precisely because this world is so coarse, so tempted by cruelty and shortcuts, that these qualities must lead.

Without them, even the noblest virtues—dignity, compassion, discernment, accountability—begin to unravel. Without them, leadership loses its ethical shape. And freedom loses its center.

I often return to the preamble of the Universal Declaration of Human Rights, adopted in 1948 after humanity had looked into the abyss. It begins with a recognition:

> *"...the inherent dignity and of the equal and inalienable rights of all members of the human family is the foundation of freedom, justice and peace in the world."*

And later:

> *"...disregard and contempt for human rights have resulted in barbarous acts which have outraged the conscience of mankind..."*

The conscience of humankind. That phrase. I've meditated on it for decades. It is not laws that preserve our shared humanity—it is conscience. And at the root of conscience are these two quiet flames: *hiri* and *ottappa*.

Hiri is that inner restraint born from self-respect. It doesn't arise from fear of punishment, but from fidelity to one's deeper nature. It is the voice that whispers, "You know this isn't right." It does not scold. It does not shame. It simply refuses to disappear.

Ottappa is its companion. It faces outward and sees the consequences. It is the hesitance not of fear, but of reverence—for life, for others, for the weight of your choices. It's what stills the hand before signing a law that might harm someone's home, their safety, their dignity.

Together, they form what I might call a *dialogue of conscience*: *Hiri* saying, "This is not who I am." *Ottappa* answering, "And this is not what I wish to do."

And no, this dance is not always graceful. When the stakes are high, when the pressure to bend is immense, these are the very qualities that often disappear first. I've watched that happen—to others and, at times, to myself.

Integrity is rarely loud—but it is always at risk. It's easy to justify, to rationalize, to look away. But when these two forces are alive in you, they pull you back. Quietly. Persistently. Without applause.

I've spoken to political prisoners who endured torture and still refused to betray their comrades. Their refusal was not pride. It was *hiri*. I've seen people starved, exiled, broken in body—and yet, they would not speak lies. That was *ottappa*. Not performance. Not purity. But presence.

There is a form of courage rarely celebrated: the courage to sit in a cell and not become bitter. To be offered a way out, and not take it—if it means betraying something sacred. That is the kind of courage *hiri* protects. That is what *ottappa* sees.

And these qualities do not make one flawless. I know that intimately. We all contradict ourselves. We speak of peace, but harbor anger. We strive for justice, and then negotiate it. That is not hypocrisy. It is humanity. And the work of leadership is not to deny this, but to meet it—with tenderness and clarity.

Even here, I ask myself: Does my silence help—or harm? Am I being principled—or merely cautious? Am I still leading—or only surviving?

There are no perfect answers. But I return to one simple vow: *To never let strategy outrun conscience. To never let fear silence the voice that still knows what is right.*

This is what I believe leadership demands—not perfection, but presence. Not dominance, but discernment. Not performance, but integrity.

So let the world praise charisma. Let it chase certainty. I will sit here with my two companions—*hiri* and *ottappa*—and remember that freedom begins with how we answer the smallest questions of our own hearts.

And in that quiet space, even now, I still know what it means to be free.

Alan Clements: That—what you just said—is perhaps one of the purest definitions of strength I've ever heard. Not perfection. Not certainty. But the willingness to stay with the tension. To choose love—not just when it's easy, but precisely when the contradictions pull you in every direction.

And I so agree: people aren't looking for flawless leaders. They're looking for truthful ones. For those who won't abandon themselves—or the truth—just to maintain an appearance.

What stays with me most is how you describe *hiri* and *ottappa* not as moral restraints, but as moral guides. Not rigid rules, but living companions that help you stay in relationship—with yourself, with the people, with the weight of power.

And it makes me wonder... in a world that so often rewards performance over presence, and speed over reflection—how do we teach this kind of inner leadership? How do we help people trust the strength of nuance, of silence, of still choosing care?

Because it seems to me, Daw Suu, that what you're describing isn't just personal. It's structural. Foundational. Essential to any democracy that hopes to endure.

And maybe that's where courage enters. Not the loud kind—but the kind that quietly chooses integrity over applause.

You've spoken often about courage in leadership. How do you see this quality shaping the path forward—not just for Myanmar, but for global leaders navigating an increasingly fractured world?

Aung San Suu Kyi: Courage is the spine of leadership, yes—but not in the sense we're often taught. It's not about defiance for its own sake, or bold proclamations designed to impress. It is, rather, a kind of quiet fidelity. Moral courage.

The kind that doesn't parade itself, but steadies the room. It moves through you gently, but with an unshakable clarity. It's the resolve to remain true—not just to what is right, but to what is kind.

This courage doesn't roar. It listens. It considers. And it lives quietly in the hearts of those who have made peace with the complexity of this world. It means being brave enough to feel deeply, and still act with discernment. To protect, not dominate. To inquire, not accuse. To stay present in uncertainty, without retreating into certainty for relief.

One of the most valuable teachings I received was this: courage arises from clarity. When you know who you are and what you will not betray, courage becomes less a choice and more a rhythm. It is not something we perform. It's something we embody.

But this embodiment comes with great humility. Because no one leads without error. And no true leader emerges without being shaped by her contradictions—and her capacity to hold them with grace.

Alan Clements: Mistakes—that brings us to a crucial point. We expect leaders to be strong, but too often we confuse strength with infallibility. Yet mistakes are inevitable. How do you reconcile that inevitability with the immense responsibility leadership carries?

Aung San Suu Kyi: Alan, I carry this truth with me every day: to lead is to live within the full spectrum of our humanness. And to be human is to stumble. Mistakes are not failures of leadership—they are woven into its fabric. The real question is not whether we will fail, but how we respond to that failure. And this response, I believe, reveals the heart of one's leadership.

Do we deny? Do we defend? Or do we pause and ask, with sincerity: Why did I do that? What was I hoping to accomplish? These questions—when asked without judgment—are not signs of weakness. They are signs of moral maturity. They open the door to transformation.

I was taught never to rush to judgment—neither of others nor of myself. *Sayadawgyi* often said that the most beautiful question a leader can ask is simply, "Why?" Not to blame, but to understand. Why did this happen? Why did I choose what I chose? What pain or fear was moving in me—or in others?

When we ask in this way, something shifts. We stop performing leadership, and begin living it.

Elie Wiesel once said, *"Questions unite people. Answers divide them."* I've held that closely. In my experience, asking sincere, even uncomfortable questions has deepened trust more than any rehearsed answer ever could. Because a question creates space—for dialogue, for dignity, for shared humanity.

When I've been confronted with mistakes—especially my own— the temptation to justify is strong. But in those moments, I've found that gentle, sustained inquiry does more than any explanation ever could. It reminds me that I am not a position, or a title. I am a human being. And to lead is to remain in relationship with that truth.

Self-compassion is not indulgence—it is stamina. It is the thread that holds that relationship together. Without it, accountability becomes cruelty. We must learn to forgive ourselves—not to escape consequence, but to renew our ability to serve.

Mistakes, when met with empathy, become teachers. They shape us into wiser, more grounded leaders. Not because we rise above them— but because we choose to rise through them.

And I believe this is where feminine leadership reveals its quiet brilliance. Not through domination, but through presence. Through the willingness to say: I see the harm. I hold the weight of it. And I will stay in this conversation until healing begins.

So no, I do not fear mistakes. I fear the absence of reflection. I fear the silence that comes when we stop asking questions. Because when we stop asking, we stop learning. And when we stop learning, we lose the heart of democracy.

To forgive oneself is to keep that heart alive—not as an act of indulgence, but as an act of continuity. As an act of conscience. As moral courage in one of its most luminous forms.

Alan, to lead is to be human, and to be human is to err. Mistakes are inevitable. But what matters is how we respond. Do we deny them, hide from them, or blame others? Or do we face them—with honesty, with humility, and with a commitment to learn?

Leaders must cultivate empathy—not just for others, but for themselves. Empathy allows us to understand the impact of our actions and to take responsibility without being consumed by guilt or defensiveness. It also allows us to connect with those we serve—to see their struggles as our own.

This is where the divine feminine comes into play. Leadership shaped by the divine feminine is not about dominance, but about nurturing. About creating space for growth and healing. It recognizes that strength lies in vulnerability. That power is amplified through connection.

Alan Clements: Daw Suu, in a world where patriarchal systems—rooted in hierarchy and conquest—cast long shadows over Myanmar's embattled spirit and the globe's fractured democracies, the divine feminine emerges as a luminous counterforce, its wisdom woven through the resilience of your nation's women.

Drawing from the quiet power of *karuṇā* and the enduring legacy of your mother, Daw Khin Kyi, how does this paradigm of leadership, with its emphasis on care over control, reshape your vision for a future where authority nurtures rather than dominates?

Aung San Suu Kyi: Divine feminine leadership is not confined to gender—it is a quality of consciousness. It centers care where others impose control. It breathes through presence rather than power, and moves through life not to conquer but to tend. At its heart is *karuṇā*—compassion not as sentiment but as embodied response, as ethical action in the face of suffering. The deep recognition that all pain is shared—that none of us stands outside the ache of the world.

This kind of leadership is quiet, steady, and unseen—yet it carries the weight of entire communities. It lives in the woman who rises before dawn to grind rice for her children before fleeing from soldiers. It lives in the schoolteacher who scribbles out lessons by candlelight as gunfire echoes in the distance. It lives in the nurse who hides antibiotics under her shawl for a wounded child she has never met.

These acts are not heroic in the way history books define it, but they are the daily manifestations of moral endurance. Leadership of this kind does not raise its voice—it raises the child. It does not strike back—it tends the wound, even when the wound is still bleeding.

In Myanmar, where tyranny demands obedience and violence wears the mask of order, this feminine ethic persists like water carving stone. It is not fragile—it is radical in its refusal to abandon tenderness. Village women, without title or protection, hold families together through famine and displacement. They whisper lullabies beneath drone-filled skies. They plant rice in fields seeded with landmines. They boil water over the ashes of what used to be homes. Their resilience is not born of ideology—it is born of necessity, of love, of a courage that does not announce itself but endures.

This is leadership as sustenance. Not command but care. Not performance but presence. It chooses empathy over dominance, conversation over decree, and inclusion over conquest. It asks: What does this law do to a mother's breath? What does this war do to a child's sleep? It slows down the machinery of power long enough to hear the human heartbeat beneath it.

Globally, this shift is not optional—it is urgent. We are witnessing the unraveling of a world built on hierarchy, extraction, and speed. The divine feminine offers not a reversal, but a rebalancing. It leads with questions, not weapons. It restores beauty where brutality has taken root. And it reminds us that no democracy, no policy, no nation can endure unless it honors the sacred task of care.

Let us remember: power that cannot love will not last.

In Myanmar, let leadership mean surviving the night together. Let it mean feeding, healing, and holding each other when the state has turned its back.

And for the world—let it mean remembering one another's humanity before drawing another line, before launching another drone, before justifying another silence.

This is not idealism. It is a sacred realism—born not of abstraction, but of grief and grit. It is survival, made luminous by love.

Alan Clements: Daw Suu, in a world increasingly fractured by force and performance, you've spoken of another path—one that does not seek to dominate, but to tend; that leads not through assertion, but through attunement.

May I ask: what are the essential attributes of this leadership when it is most tested? Not as ideals, but as lived capacities—felt in the body, refined in solitude, and made visible in action when the stakes are highest?

What does divine feminine leadership look like—not when it is easy, but when it must carry a people through fire?

Aung San Suu Kyi: Thank you, Alan. That question goes to the heart of what I've tried to live—especially in silence, especially in stillness, especially when there is no one to witness but one's own conscience.

Divine feminine leadership expresses itself through what is too often dismissed as "soft." But these are not signs of fragility—they are forms of subtle strength. Unyielding, unannounced, and rooted in relationship rather than rule.

Empathy is the first thread. Not sympathy, not pity—but the ability to stand inside another's experience without retreating or collapsing. In diplomacy, in conflict, in governance—if we cannot feel each other's lives, we are not leading people. We are managing systems. Or shadows.

Then there is nurturance—not sentimentality, but the daily, disciplined act of helping others grow. It's what mothers do, yes—but also teachers, healers, visionaries. *It's what real leaders do: they cultivate strength in others.*

Intuition must also be named. We are conditioned to privilege logic, but intuition—when refined—is a form of direct knowing. It hears through noise. It senses what is not yet spoken. In political complexity, it helps leaders recognize the turning point before it arrives.

And of course, collaboration. Divine feminine leadership does not seek to dominate—it seeks to weave. To co-create. To gather voices. It asks not, "Who is in charge?" but "Who is not yet heard?" It says: power with, not power over. And in that shift, a different world becomes possible.

Alan Clements: Daw Suu, the leadership you've described—rooted in empathy, presence, mutuality—offers a clear alternative to inherited traditions. But the obstacles are not only structural. Patriarchy seeps into our self-doubt, our view of strength, our praise for aggression, our silencing of feeling. It teaches boys to equate power with detachment, girls to see care as lesser. It turns emotion into liability, cooperation into weakness.

In your experience, how does this conditioning limit not just leadership's expression, but our capacity to imagine it differently? And how might we unravel these myths—not through antagonism, but transformation?

Aung San Suu Kyi: Patriarchy is not just a system—it's an inheritance, a myth handed down like a surname, the air we breathe before we name it. It teaches that leadership is command, feeling is failure, power belongs to those who shout loudest, take most, never apologize. It confuses dominance with dignity, fear with strength, and numbness with discernment.

Patriarchy is not just in laws—it's in bedtime stories, paychecks, the pause when a woman senses she's spoken too long. It's in how a girl learns to shrink before she learns to speak, how a boy is praised for conquest before kindness. It's in glances, silences, the way we dim our joy to ease others.

In Myanmar, the junta—the *Tatmadaw*—is not just a regime. It is patriarchy militarized. It enforces control through fear. It trains men to kill before they feel, to follow orders that burn villages. It punishes kindness as betrayal, dissent as weakness. It silences women's leadership, fearing the fusion of compassion and clarity. It burns, jails, destroys— not to lead, but to dominate. It wages war not only on bodies, but on the country's moral fabric.

Transformation begins in the mirror, questioning: Who called emotion weak? Who deemed tenderness less than intellect?

Patriarchy cannot simply be dismantled—it must be composted, gently broken down, returned to the soil of reimagining. We reclaim not just power, but wholeness.

To men: You weren't born to silence your heart. The divine feminine lives in you, awaiting recall. To women: Your voice isn't an inconvenience—it's your ancestors' survival. To all: This isn't about new hierarchies, but dissolving them—transforming domination into shared responsibility.

Love is fierce, protective, reclaiming. It says: "No more" and "Come home." We begin by naming patterns, listening to understand, speaking to be heard, forgiving to heal. This isn't utopia—it's a return to conscience over control. A restoration of wholeness over hierarchy.

Alan Clements: Daw Suu, thank you. May your words be shared widely—and live on for generations.

If I may, can we go deeper into the qualities you've described as divine feminine leadership? How does leadership *reveal itself* when it draws strength from *vulnerability, cyclical wisdom, sustainability,* and the harmonizing power of beauty?

Aung San Suu Kyi: Beauty, long exiled from power's discourse, restores. It nourishes, mending what fracture has torn. In Myanmar, where the junta's violence cloaks itself as order, feminine leadership knows we need more than policies—we need poetry, rhythm, and rituals that gather us beneath the quiet watch of the pagodas. Beauty isn't adornment—it's coherence, softening power's edge to make it human.

Vulnerability is a vital thread. In this cell, where silence sharpens my heart, I see it as trust's root. We're taught leadership means knowing, asserting, deciding. But often, it's admitting, "I don't know," or "I need help," or "I see your pain." Vulnerability is not a fracture—it is the deepening of authority through shared humanity.

Cyclical wisdom, less familiar, is essential. It knows life isn't linear—that rest isn't idleness, and endings are thresholds. The seasons become teachers; the moon, a reminder of release. Feminine leadership heeds this rhythm, valuing compost as much as bloom, silence's voice as much as speech. Politics would be wiser for such patience.

Sustainability—ecological, emotional, ethical—asks, "What can we tend?" not "What can we gain?" It refuses to trade tomorrow for today's victory, seeking a world worth inheriting. These qualities— empathy, nurturance, intuition, compassion, creativity, inclusivity, sustainability—aren't decorative. They're elemental. Ancient. Seismic. They redefine power's center.

Alan Clements: In that remembering, what becomes possible—not only for Myanmar, but for a world on edge?

Aung San Suu Kyi: A strength to carry, not crush; to include, not impose. Measured by how deeply we listen, how wisely we respond, and how fully we welcome the forgotten. We can move from domination to dialogue, punishment to understanding, fear to care. This takes quiet courage—to question inherited systems, to imagine more human ones.

We're kin, frail yet fierce, weaving a future where care binds us all. Shaped by suffering, we can still remember something wiser than control—not progress, but presence; not leadership, but companionship; not diplomacy, but kinship. Born of love, not force, this is the vision I hold.

Alan Clements: Daw Suu, beyond states, policy, roles—we spin together on this fragile earth, through a vastness we cannot fully grasp, dreaming amid destruction, weeping amid wonder. If this were your last moment to speak from this prison, what truth would you leave about leadership, conscience, our place in existence?

Aung San Suu Kyi: Alan, your question cradles the world. We're frail, harming what we love, yet enduring—carrying terror and tenderness.

Leadership begins with reverence—for life, each other, and time's fragile gift. Domination has failed. Division has exhausted us. Let compassion be our strategy, our fiercest intelligence, the force that gathers the world back into wholeness.

The divine feminine rises—not to conquer, but to balance. To soften conquest's edge. We need leadership that honors mystery, that listens with silence's weight.

I speak knowing my people suffer—as I've said, but never enough: over twenty million need urgent aid, three and a half million displaced, countless grieving in the wake of earthquake and atrocity. Prisoners endure torture, yet sing, resist, love—even now, beneath the gaze of ruined pagodas.

This isn't metaphor—it's movement. A mother's care amid despair. A prisoner's song in darkness. A child's outstretched hand in rubble. I leave behind devotion—to truth, to tenderness, to dignity.

We are shaping a story for our children,
and for strangers not yet born.

From this cell, where silence weaves
grief with grace, I'd whisper:

Lead with love.

Freedom, my greatest love—
cherish it. Trace its every vein.
Let it be your nature.

It is the pulse that joins us, the vow that cannot be broken.

Choose conscience over conquest.
Care over fear. Life above all.

Elie Wiesel showed us:
Questions weave kinship.
Ask not, "What can I control?"
But, "What can I care for?"

Craft sanctuaries.
Build community.
Live in kinship—not in fortresses,
not in empires, not as heroes.

Let care mend the world.

Go forward—frail, fierce, awake—

For Myanmar's wounded heart,
for the world,
for this shared earth—
where freedom still breathes.

A Revolution of Character: The Divine Feminine as the Soul of Leadership
—Part II: A Covenant for the Future

Let me begin with this: this is not a commentary on identity—it is a clarion call to restore balance at the heart of existence. A reclamation of a sacred intelligence, long banished from the halls of power and starved in the depths of the human spirit.

When I speak of the divine feminine, I speak not of women alone, but of the eternal capacities within all souls—to hold without possessing, to sense before proclaiming, to shape without shattering. These are the ancient rhythms of creation, the quiet forces that mend what conquest has torn asunder.

In an era scarred by domination and haste, another strength rises—not to conquer, but to abide. It does not proclaim itself. It listens. It anchors. It refuses to forsake compassion in a world enthralled by spectacle. It is the courage to remain present when no reward beckons; to choose kindness over control; to wield truth not as a blade, but as a beacon.

This leadership does not arrive with trumpets. It emerges in the kitchen, the clinic, the prayer hall—in moments no one celebrates. It does not strategize—it accompanies. It does not perform—it roots. It draws its strength not from invincibility, but from mercy sustained under fire.

The divine feminine in leadership does not ascend above humanity—it walks alongside it. It does not claim virtue—it embodies it. It is forged in the deep ethic of *kalyāṇa mittatā*—noble friendship—and guarded by the twin sentinels of the *Dhamma*: *hiri* and *ottappa*—a conscience that guides, a reverence that endures. *It is sustained by the oldest vow: to love amid collapse—and to never forget how.*

This is not idealism. It is moral necessity. The preservation of integrity. The practice of nonviolence that is not passive, but piercingly precise. The dignity that blooms without awaiting acclaim.

The ten archetypes that follow are not roles to perform. They are rivers of character, carved across centuries by mothers, monks, midwives, and poets. I have witnessed them in my mother's grace, in the women who bore our struggle unshod, and in men unafraid of their tenderness. They are the pulse of a leadership that persuades not through fear, but through unyielding truth; that chooses presence over pretense; that is strong enough to remain unguarded.

To the next generation of leaders: Do not mistake intimidation for influence. Do not sever your empathy for applause. Do not forsake your intuition for the illusion of certainty. The future does not crave your performance of power—it hungers for your devotion to what is just.

This is my offering. Not a blueprint. Not a doctrine. But a sacred covenant with the eternal.

A code for those who still believe:
- In influence woven through relationship, not reward
- In truth spoken without malice
- In legacies built not on conquest, but on love

May this be not instruction, but invocation—
To lead without fracturing your soul,
To walk this world with fierce compassion,
And to leave not a monument, but a garden where others may flourish.

1. The Weaver: The Architect of Sacred Unity

The Weaver does not confuse unity with conformity. She knows that true belonging is not sameness—it is the sacred act of holding contradiction without collapse. Her leadership is a tapestry, woven from stories as much as systems, from threads of every hue, every wound, every dream remembered and nearly lost.

She values diversity not as ornament, but as the very sinew of resilience—a foundation, not a flourish. In an age torn by division, she speaks across fractures, honoring difference without erasing it.

She knows democracy is not a destination, but a fabric rewoven daily—a covenant that deepens through dissent, endures through tension, and thrives not because it is flawless, but because we return to mend it.

"Another world is not only possible; she is on her way. On a quiet day, I can hear her breathing."
— ARUNDHATI ROY

2. The Listener: The Guardian of the Unspoken

The Listener knows that leadership begins not in words, but in silence. She hears not only what is spoken, but what has been silenced. Her presence is a sanctuary where truth feels safe to emerge, where even the pain behind truth finds space to breathe.

She listens not to reply, not to redeem, not to perform compassion—but to bear witness to what is raw and ruptured. She listens until fear softens, until shame sheds its mask, until the invisible claims its voice.

In a world addicted to noise, she restores the sacred art of attention—to the margins, to the overlooked, to voices buried beneath spectacle. Her power lies not in the volume of her words, but in the freedom, she grants others to speak the unspeakable.

"When we listen, we offer with our attention an opportunity for wholeness."
— RACHEL NAOMI REMEN

3. The Restorer: The Alchemist of Healing

The Restorer knows what many forget: wounds do not fade with time. They deepen when neglected, harden when ignored, fester when denied.

She brings harm into the light—not to weaponize it, but to hold it until it is seen without distortion or shame. She lingers where it is broken, guiding it back to the shape of its own wholeness. Her justice is not a blade, but a balm that refuses to surrender.

She knows no peace can stand on the unacknowledged bones of the past. She labors in the liminal space—between the cry for justice and the grace of forgiveness, between the weight of memory and the courage to release.

"Apology is a balm. It can transform shame into dignity."
— V (FORMERLY EVE ENSLER)

4. The Steward: The Guardian of Future Generations

The Steward leads not for praise, but for those who will never know her name. Every choice is a legacy, every action a prayer for those yet to come.

She weighs not only costs, but consequences—what the future will bear because of her decisions. She protects tomorrow with today's courage, honoring cycles, stillness, and the unseen.

Guided by *hiri* and *ottappa*—a conscience that anchors, a reverence that endures—she leads with a clarity that transcends doubt.

"What we do to the Earth, we do to ourselves."
— DR. HELEN CALDICOTT

5. The Initiator: The Herald of Conscience

When others hesitate, the Initiator steps forward—not for glory, but because her conscience compels her. She moves not from impulse, but from a discernment as steady as the *Dhamma* itself.

She does not wait for safety to act justly. Her leadership is a devotional rhythm, deliberate and rooted, answering not to popularity, but to presence.

"Courage is the most important of all the virtues because without courage, you can't practice any other virtue consistently."
— MAYA ANGELOU

6. The Groundbreaker: The Compassionate Dismantler

The Groundbreaker sees what others accept as inevitable—the harm veiled as tradition, the violence cloaked as normalcy. Yet she breaks not to destroy, but to clear sacred ground where truth may root.

She carries *ottappa* as a lantern, asking: What harm might this cause? What healing must rise in its wake? Her courage is not cruel, her critique not contemptuous. She deconstructs with hope, disobeys with love, and dreams even as she dismantles.

"Without leaps of imagination, or dreaming, we lose the excitement of possibilities. Dreaming, after all, is a form of planning."
— GLORIA STEINEM

7. The Midwife: The Guide of Emergence

The Midwife does not impose her will. She listens for what stirs beneath the surface, sensing what longs to be born. Leadership, for her, is not forcing change, but creating a sacred space for its unfolding.

Her power is presence, not coercion. She accompanies transformation, honoring its pain, its timing, its mystery, as a teacher attuned to the rhythm of becoming.

"There is a future yearning to be born. Our job is not to dominate it—but to be tender enough to receive it."
— ADRIENNE MAREE BROWN

8. The Truthbearer: The Voice of Clarity and Care

The Truthbearer speaks not to wound, but to reveal. Her honesty does not fracture—it illuminates, shaped by *hiri's* fidelity and *ottappa's* reverence for impact.

She is unafraid to unsettle, but never harms for sport. She speaks not to triumph, but to widen the horizon of truth, her words a bridge between clarity and compassion.

"The most common way people give up their power is by thinking they don't have any."
— ALICE WALKER

9. The Embracer: The Leader of Sacred Vulnerability

The Embracer does not conceal her contradictions—she honors them. She names her doubts, claims her humanity, and in doing so, creates space for others to do the same.

Her leadership is not armored in perfection, but rooted in the courage to abide when certainty fades. She leads through inquiry, humility, and the wisdom that shadows are not flaws, but guides to wholeness.

"Out of suffering have emerged the strongest characters; the most massive souls are seared with scars."

— KAHLIL GIBRAN

10. The Unifier: The Emissary of Shared Belonging

The Unifier rejects the illusion of separation. She sees beyond borders, roles, and ideologies, speaking from the profound truth of our interconnectedness.

Her diplomacy is relational, her activism compassionate, her politics a living *Dhamma*—cause and consequence, suffering and awakening. She leads not to divide, but to reconcile, knowing that healing is not the aftermath of revolution—it is the revolution itself.

"Peace does not mean the absence of conflict; it means the presence of creative alternatives to violence."

— DOROTHY THOMPSON

Let this be our call to courage—
Not the courage of conquest,
but the courage of care. Not the pursuit of power,
but the devotion to remain tender-hearted
even when it would be easier not to.
Let us stop asking who is strong enough to rule,
and begin asking instead:
Who is soft enough to listen?
Humble enough to change?
And deep enough to lead without losing their humanity?
The divine feminine is not a trend. It is the return of something ancient. Something essential.

A remembrance of what we once knew—
and what we must have the courage to remember again:
- That healing is strength.
- That listening is leadership.
- That democracy is not a possession—
  but a shared vow, renewed with every generation.
And leadership—true leadership—
is not about being right. It is about being ready. Ready to hear. Ready
to grow. Ready to serve what is most fragile, and most sacred.

This is not a manifesto of perfection. It is a declaration of
possibility.

Let us meet the future as we are—
wounded, wondering, fiercely awake. Together.

OUR INHERENT MUTUALITY

Author's Prelude

What if the most radical act of leadership was not to command, but to accompany? Not to rise above, but to walk beside.

This chapter is a return—to the breath between beings, to the thread that binds stranger and friend, prisoner and president, monk and militant, child and elder. It is a return to our oldest knowing: that *we do not awaken—or survive—alone.*

Here, Aung San Suu Kyi speaks not from a stage, but from the depth of confinement. Her voice carries the weight of a thousand unseen companions. Her words are not performance, but presence—not strategy, but a sacred offering.

Power, in this light, is not control. It lives through *ubuntu—the truth that "I am because we are."* It breathes through *kalyāṇa mittatā*—the noble friendship that sustains both awakening and resistance. And it matures through the *pāramīs*—not as isolated virtues, but as relational strengths, refined in community, not in retreat.

These pages are not written for theorists. They are for those who have cradled grief like a child and still chosen to walk toward dignity. For those who wonder if suffering can still teach love. They are for those who are learning to live without turning away. They are for you.

Even the Depayin Massacre is not buried here—it is brought forward—not for spectacle, but as a moral lesson. In 2003, a convoy of peaceful supporters was ambushed by a state-orchestrated mob—scores beaten to death in an attempt to silence Daw Suu's journey. It failed. And what remains is not only horror, but the question: How does dignity endure the unspeakable?

Aung San Suu Kyi does not offer us perfection. She offers something rarer: unshakable presence—steadfast, unadorned, and quietly human. And in that presence, she gives us something far more enduring than certainty: the possibility of belonging. Not to tribe or ideology or nation, but to something older, something more elemental—a shared humanity that outlives borders, titles, and even the walls meant to erase her.

So, let us enter this chapter not with conclusions, but with questions: Who are we, really, without each other? What kind of world might we create if we led not from fear, but from relationship? And how might we—each of us, in our imperfect, luminous way—help shape the sacred 'we'? The only force that can bring everything back to life.

♦ ♦ ♦

Alan Clements: Daw Suu, so much of what you've shared—particularly your reflections on *hiri* and *ottappa*—points to something profound: an ethic of interdependence. Or perhaps more precisely, a covenant of reciprocal responsibility—a living recognition that we do not act, speak, or even think in isolation. That conscience itself is relational—formed, tested, and sustained in the space between self and other.

Children grow in the gaze of their parents. Students learn through the generosity of their teachers. Leaders are shaped by those they serve. Our very identities are mirrored, challenged, and refined through others.

All of nature—life itself—is mutually related, despite humanity's recurring hubris to engineer hierarchies of domination and control—with militarized dictatorship standing dangerously near the pinnacle of that madness, as you know so well.

In South African culture, there's a word I know you're familiar with: *ubuntu*. It's often translated as "I am because you are." But it goes deeper than that. *Ubuntu* is a way of being that recognizes: *your dignity is inseparable from mine.* It's not charity. It's not sentiment. It's kinship. It's the understanding that humanity is never a solo act—it's always a shared composition.

Do you see something similar in Burmese culture—or in the *Dhamma*? A lived sense of mutuality, of ethical companionship, that helps guide how we live, how we lead, and how we belong to one another?

Aung San Suu Kyi: Yes, we do.
There is a Burmese saying that goes:
If he's not part of it, it can't be done.
But he alone can't do it.
If you aren't part of it, it can't be done.
But you alone can't do it.
Without me, it can't be done.
But I alone can't do it.
Only when he, you, and I are part of it—can everything be done.

It's an expression of profound mutuality. Much like *ubuntu*, it insists that no meaningful progress can be made in isolation. It teaches that interdependence is not merely a necessity—it is a virtue. This is not just cultural. It is existential. We are co-creators of everything: peace, justice, suffering, and healing. We are bound by the invisible covenant of shared becoming. We rise or fall together.

And as we've discussed before, this is what the Buddha called *kalyāṇa mittatā*—noble friendship. But let me be clear: this is not friendship in the casual sense. It is the moral and spiritual infrastructure of any truly human society. *Kalyāṇa mitta* is the deep recognition that none of us liberate ourselves alone. It is not an emotional refuge; it is a disciplined, conscious practice—the art of bearing witness to each other's struggles, the art of refusing to abandon one another. It is the daily, deliberate work of showing up—not as saviors, but as companions. As protectors of what is good.

Real leadership is not born from the will to dominate, but from the courage to relate. It does not ask, "How can I prevail?" but "How can I serve our wholeness?" That is where the *Dhamma* and democracy meet—in the sacred, malleable space between "I" and "we."

This kind of mutuality is not weakness. It is strength of the highest order. It refuses to cast others as enemies. It refuses to reduce anyone to a role. It says: *"I see you—not as other, but as part of the same wholeness I seek."*

So yes—*ubuntu* lives here, too. In our culture. In our resistance. In the woman who breaks her last piece of bread and quietly places half on a neighbor's windowsill. In the prisoner who sings to soothe the stranger in the next cell. In our shared vow to dignity. And in that vow, renewed with each small act of conscience, I continue to place my trust.

Alan Clements: That's beautifully said, Daw Suu—and it echoes so closely the spirit of *ubuntu*. What you've shared points to something I've come to hold as essential: our inherent mutuality—not as aspiration, but as a foundational condition of being. As you said, a quiet, daily recognition that we do not—and cannot—exist apart from one another.

It reminds me of the *Bodhisattva's path*, especially the practice of "exchanging self and other"—that radical turning of the heart, where the boundary between "I" and "you" begins to dissolve. Not out of sentimentality, but through a deeply embodied awareness of shared being, of reciprocal becoming.

Do you see this same thread of interdependence woven into the development of the *pāramī*? That as we cultivate these states of brilliance—not just as inner attainments but as relational expressions—they become, at their heart, acts of connection?

Aung San Suu Kyi: Absolutely. The *pāramī*—the states of inner excellence—are not solitary conquests. They are formed, tested, and ultimately made real in the dynamic of relationship. Our teacher, the late Sayadaw U Pandita, made this clear again and again. He often reminded us that virtue, when left unchallenged, risks becoming abstraction. But when lived amidst people—especially in times of adversity—it becomes truth.

Take patience (*khanti*), for example. It is rarely born in ease. It arises when we're wronged. When we're silenced. When we're misunderstood. In those moments, we discover whether our forbearance is genuine or merely conceptual. *True patience is not quietism—it is resilience.* It holds steady without collapsing. It protects without retaliating.

Or compassion (*karuṇā*). It does not awaken in theory. It awakens when we look into the eyes of someone who's lost everything—family, home, hope—and feel their pain as inseparable from our own. It's in the refugee who shares food with another, even when there's not enough. It's in the prisoner who comforts a stranger through the wall.

Determination (*adhiṭṭhāna*) too is forged relationally. When the world tells us to give up—when we are imprisoned, exiled, ridiculed—it is the memory of those we love, and those we serve, that deepens our vow. We remember that our resolve is not for self alone—it is for a future we may never see, but still choose to protect.

Each *pāramī* is a thread, and the human world is the loom. Generosity, morality, renunciation, wisdom—none of these can be refined in isolation. They are lived through others, shaped by others, held accountable by others.

So yes, Alan. This path is not a solitary ascent—it is a shared rising. It is a journey walked together, even when walked alone.

Alan Clements: So even opposition—even betrayal—can serve the path. I'm thinking of the Buddha's relationship with Devadatta, his cousin and disciple, who not only defied his authority but even conspired to take his life. And yet, it's extraordinary to consider: even that kind of enmity can become a condition for deepening the *parami*—the perfections that refine the heart through adversity.

Would you say that such adversity—when met with mindfulness—can actually accelerate the development of these inner states of excellence? That the friction of opposition may be not an obstacle, but a crucible for transformation?

Aung San Suu Kyi: Yes, absolutely. Sayadawgyi was clear in his teaching: opposition, when rightly understood, is not a detour from the path—it is the path tempered by fire. There is something profoundly redemptive about holding equanimity in the face of cruelty, about staying rooted in one's dignity without surrendering to bitterness. This is not passive endurance—it is the fierce discipline of conscious restraint.

When confronted with hostility or injustice, we are presented with a threshold moment: to react from wounded pride or to respond with patience (*khanti*), compassion (*karuṇā*), and unwavering resolve (*adhiṭṭhāna*).

Choosing the latter demands a rare kind of strength—the strength to transform pain without transmitting it. It is the choice to make suffering conscious, to let it ripen into wisdom.

As you noted, despite *Devadatta's* repeated attempts to harm the Buddha—including sending assassins, orchestrating a rockslide, and unleashing an enraged elephant—the Buddha met each act not with retaliation, but with profound inner stillness. He regarded these assaults not as disruptions to his path, but as confirmations of it.

In my own experience—during my years under house arrest, and now in solitary imprisonment, and through the agony of witnessing over 22,000 fellow political prisoners languishing in Myanmar's prisons—the temptation to armor oneself with rage was always near. It would have been easy to grow calloused. To mirror the violence, we resisted. But again and again, I returned to the guardians of *hiri* and *ottappa*—the twin flames of conscience that refused to let me become what I abhorred.

These principles, along with the *parami*, became not just teachings but sanctuaries. They preserved my sanity and my humanity in places designed to strip both away. They reminded me that mindful restraint is not weakness. It is a form of power far deeper than force—the power to remain human where humanity is denied.

In our own lives, when betrayal or injustice strikes, we stand at a similar crossroads. We can allow these wounds to sour our hearts— or we can let them deepen our character. Patience becomes courage. Compassion becomes clarity. Determination becomes vow. And in that moment, we are no longer merely surviving hardship—we are awakening through it.

This is how adversity becomes a teacher—not by breaking us, but by summoning the parts of us that only emerge in darkness. When we meet suffering not with resistance but with reverence, we no longer ask, "Why me?" We ask, "What now can I awaken?"

We stop being victims. We stop being warriors. We become practitioners of the *Dhamma*, shaped not by theory, but by lived truth— which is the only truth worth embodying.

Alan Clements: Daw Suu, everything you've shared about the *pāramī*, about hiri and ottappa, about dignity, resilience, and the transformative potential of suffering—it brings to mind something I've long wanted to ask you. With deep respect for the gravity of the memory, may I revisit a moment in your life that shook the conscience of the world?

I'm speaking of May 30th, 2003—Depayin. A convoy of your supporters was ambushed by a state-backed mob. A massacre orchestrated not merely to harm, but to humiliate, to silence, to crush the breath of a people daring to hope.

I think you know, I've studied the details: up to 5,000 attackers, armed with clubs, sharpened bamboo, iron rods, and swords. Militia members and recently released prisoners recruited and paid by local authorities. Spotlights in the trees. Barricades. Paid informants. Every step choreographed with surgical cruelty.

And yet, you lived. You were there. You witnessed the carnage— your supporters maimed and murdered—and somehow, you survived.

If you feel willing, I humbly ask: would you share how that night unfolded, through your own eyes? And more than that—how you survived it not just physically, but morally. How, in the face of such calculated hatred, you held onto your humanity. How the *pāramī*, the

Dhamma, those invisible companions you've spoken of—how they moved through you in that moment.

Aung San Suu Kyi: Alan, your memory serves with painful clarity. Yes, I will speak of it—not to reopen wounds, but because some truths must be carried openly if we are ever to transform them.

That night, we were en route to *Monywa*. The journey had already been long. My convoy was fatigued but spirited. We'd visited several towns—*Mandalay, Myingyan*, and *Yesagyo*—where tens of thousands had come to greet us. There was a current of courage moving through the country. A breath of resistance stirring again. Hope had found its voice.

I had no reason to think that night would be different.

But outside *Kyi Village*, just before *Depayin*, the atmosphere shifted. The road narrowed. The air changed. And then—everything broke.

A flood of attackers surged from the darkness. They had been waiting. Organized. Fed. Paid. Trained—not in discipline, but in fear. I later learned they were armed by the USDA—the Union Solidarity and Development Association. Many were hardened criminals, recently released from prison. Others were local militia. Some, coerced villagers. Each was handed a crude weapon and 500 kyat to kill with impunity.

They blocked the road and descended upon us. The first phase of the ambush was a blur of screams and steel. People were pulled from trucks. Beaten. Slashed. Blood pooled beneath the wheels. A young man ran toward our vehicle—then fell mid-stride. I don't know if he was struck or shot. I never knew his name. But I remember his face. I always will.

The operation was choreographed. Spotlights had been fixed in the trees. Loudspeakers blasted commands. Headlights from trucks lit up our convoy like a stage. This was no riot—it was a script. A state-sponsored horror meant not only to kill, but to erase the very memory of resistance.

We somehow pierced through the first blockade. Kyaw Soe Lin, our driver, was extraordinary. His composure, his courage—I owe him my life. But another blockade lay just ahead—thicker, more brutal. Somehow, impossibly, we broke through again.

By the time we reached Ye-U Township, our vehicle was dented, blood-smeared, and nearly out of fuel. That's where we were intercepted. Soldiers stopped us at gunpoint. One officer held a pistol to our driver's head and ordered him to kneel. I thought: "This is where it ends." But they didn't shoot. They transported me to a military base, then to Ye-U prison. And from there, back into house arrest. Silenced. Again.

It wasn't until much later that we understood the scale of what had happened. Over a hundred people were killed—some say more. Bodies disappeared. Women violated. Survivors tortured. Families given no word, no closure—only silence.

And the regime? They called it a traffic dispute. A "misunderstanding." They did not merely lie to cover their crime—they lied to annul it. They jailed the witnesses. Sealed the records. Shut down our movement. They tried to disappear the truth.

But truth is persistent. It remains even when memory is outlawed. The blood on that road is still visible in my mind.

What carried me through? *Hiri. Ottappa.* The *pāramī.* Not as abstractions—but as reflexes. As oxygen.

Hiri whispered: Do not become like them. *Ottappa* reminded me: Someone, somewhere, will one day ask what you chose in this moment. These teachings became not just anchors—but lifelines.

That night, I was not fearless. I was not heroic. I was simply obedient—to the stillness I had practiced, to the moral grammar I had internalized, to the memory of those who believed we could be better than our circumstances.

Even now, in this cell, I sometimes hear the echoes—boots on gravel, the groan of injured bodies, the sudden silence after violence. And I whisper to those memories, over and over: *I did not become what they tried to make me.*

And that—that refusal—is a kind of freedom. Not from them. But for the future.

Leadership is not made in crowds. It's forged in those invisible moments when no one is watching—when it would be easier to hate, but you choose to feel. When it would be easier to vanish, but you stay.

That night broke something open in me. But it did not break me.

And in that unbroken space, I made a vow—not to power, not to revenge, but to the only thing that could outlive such hatred: *a love strong enough to remain human, even when humanity is under siege.*

Alan Clements: Your words, Daw Suu… they are not only a teaching, but a testimony. You've lived through what most of us cannot imagine. And yet, you return not with hatred—but with wisdom, clarity, and the quiet grace of someone who has endured without losing her humanity.

So, I ask, in the spirit of everything you've shared: Would you say that the *pāramī*—or as *Sayadawgyi* once called them, the virtues of an "excellent person"—are not only moral ideals, but essential lights to guide those who lead amid suffering and uncertainty?

I know we've spoken of this before, but if you would—please speak of them again, more completely, more intimately, as if offering them to a new generation just beginning to awaken.

Aung San Suu Kyi: Yes, Alan—we've reflected on this before. But some truths bear repeating, not from forgetfulness, but because their weight deepens over time. Especially now—when the stakes are no longer theoretical, but human lives. Fractured families. Displaced millions. A nation teetering not only on the brink of collapse, but on the edge of forgetting itself.

The *pāramī* are not merely aspirations—they are the marrow of authentic leadership. They are the silent compass points that do not tremble, even in the fiercest storms. They are not practiced in retreat—but tempered in fire, tested in relationship, and proven through the unseen choices of conscience.

Sayadawgyi reminded me often: true excellence arises when we prioritize the well-being of others—not from self-concern, but from *karuṇā* and *mettā*—compassion and loving-kindness. The *pāramī*, he would say, are not virtues cultivated for personal merit or recognition. They are offerings. Acts of ethical artistry. Selfless expressions in a world too often governed by harm.

"Purity of heart," he told me, "is not a luxury for saints—it is the foundation of trust." And trust—earned through patience, clarity, and consistency—is what gives leadership its quiet, enduring power.

No matter the accolades, no matter the years of struggle, we are not measured by what we've won, but by how we've remained human in the face of inhumanity. That is the ultimate test.

So, allow me to revisit what we've already explored—because it cannot be overstated:

The *pāramī* are not confined to monasteries or meditation halls. They belong in parliaments, courtrooms, refugee camps, cyclone shelters, hospital wards, and prison cells. Anywhere that conscience is called to act without applause.

Sayadawgyi taught me: a leader is seen as *parama*—noble, trustworthy—only when they act with clarity of intention. Not from ego or strategy, but from a sincere wish to serve. When we give without needing to be thanked, when we speak without craving praise, when we choose silence over spectacle—this is where the *pāramī* begin.

Greatness is not shaped by grand gestures. It lives in the quiet, invisible commitments: the pause before reacting; the inner check before using power; the prayer before making a decision that touches many lives.

That inner discipline, that mindful intelligence—*Sayadawgyi* called it *Satipaṭṭhāna*. He taught me that mindfulness is not only a meditative skill, but the core discipline of moral leadership. It means asking, again and again:

"What am I doing?"

"Why am I doing it?"

"Whom does this serve?"

"Will this action leave the world more whole—or more fractured?"

This is where the teachings of *Dhamma* and the ethic of *ubuntu* meet. "I am because we are." It is not just beautiful—it is urgent. It is not just African—it is universal.

My breath touches yours. My silence echoes in your life. My choices shape the moral climate we all must live in.

In this light, leadership is not a role. It is a relationship. A trembling vow. A field of trust cultivated not by speeches—but by the invisible gestures of care.

A vow to serve not only one's supporters, but one's adversaries. Not just one's nation, but the shared future of all nations.

Alan Clements: Daw Suu, in light of all you've shared—and all you've endured, from long years of house arrest to brutal crackdowns, and now solitary confinement—alongside decades of courageous leadership, traveling the world, meeting presidents and prime ministers from every corner of the globe, witnessing firsthand what dignifies nations and what breaks them—would you be willing to offer the generations to come a compendium, perhaps even a modest manifesto, for both present and future leaders? One that reflects how the profound interconnectedness of our shared humanity—a truth rooted deeply in both Buddhist philosophy and the ethic of *ubuntu*—has shaped your vision of mindful and compassionate leadership?

Aung San Suu Kyi: Alan, thank you—for your question, and for the care behind it.

There are so many ways to lead. So many cultures, temperaments, and trials that shape what leadership must become in a given time and place. What I will share is not definitive, nor intended as a final word. It is a threadbare tapestry of practice—frayed in places, but stitched always with sincerity.

They are, quite simply, the quiet lessons I've tried to live—not to proclaim. Sometimes imperfectly. Sometimes invisibly. But always with the vow to serve without losing myself.

If these reflections serve others, so be it. That is a gift. But in truth, the greater gift has been the journey itself—especially now, over eighty, when the horizon feels closer than the shore.

In these years of deep solitude, I've returned again and again to what truly endures. And what I've found are not grand philosophies, but humble certainties. Truths that move like water through our lives—unseen, but essential. Threads of humanity that bind us—across time, across sorrow, across wonder.

If I may, I'll share them now.

Not as commandments. Not as doctrine. But as companions for the uncertain road.

Threads for those who still dare to lead with love when the world calls for conquest. Threads for those who still dare to listen when the world demands noise. Threads for those who still believe that even brokenness can be beautiful—if it is met with a whole and tender heart.

These reflections are simple, but not small. They are soft, but not weak. They are ancient, but they belong to the future.

May they serve you, whoever you are, wherever you walk.

And may you carry them not as armor—but as light.

A Manifesto for Mindful and Compassionate Leadership
Prologue: Whispers from the Unseen

Leadership is often misconstrued as ascent—a rising above circumstance, contradiction, or the fragility of uncertainty. Yet the truest leadership does not climb. It descends—into the depths of nuance, the intimacy of relationship, the place where ethics are not ideals, but lived.

This is not a treatise. It is a sacred architecture of reflection, born not from theory, but from the silent intimacy of unchosen solitude. From hours etched by loss, conscience, and history's unanswered questions.

These words carry no claim to authority. They are offered with reverence, as a companion for a future leader—perhaps yet unborn—navigating the unseen dimensions of power: restraint, listening, mutuality, and the courage to remain open in a world that prizes hardness.

Two philosophical streams converge here: the *Dhamma*, with its call to inner liberation through wise attention, and *ubuntu*, the African ethic of relational humanity— *"I am because we are."* Together, they weave a dialogue between solitude and solidarity, the breath and the collective soul.

I write from a prison cell in *Naypyidaw*. Yet this manifesto is not about confinement. It is about what endures beyond bars: the unbroken thread of dignity, the clarity that pierces distortion, the moral intelligence of care.

These pages are not commands, but invitations—portals to a leadership rooted not in dominance, but in depth; not in applause, but in coherence.

If anything endures, let it not be the name beneath these words, but the quality of attention they awaken in you.

1. The Breath of Shared Existence

To breathe is to belong. Each inhalation is not merely biological—it is a silent vow of interdependence, binding us to the vast, unbroken rhythm of life. In this awareness, we see that well-being is never solitary; it is a shared inheritance, a collective exhalation of care.

Sayadaw U Pandita urged me to return to the breath, not as refuge, but as inquiry.

He asked:

"What will you do with this breath, which is not yours alone?" "Will it speak with integrity? Choose with wisdom? Liberate or cling?" And most urgently: "How fiercely will you guard freedom—not as privilege, but as the refusal to bow to greed (*lobha*), hatred (*dosa*), or delusion (*moha*)?"

To attend to the breath is to return to first principles. Leadership begins not in proclamation, but in mindful presence—in the quiet discipline of remembering: *every decision breathes into the lives of others.*

Practices for Daily Life

Begin each morning with fidelity. Place a hand over your heart. Breathe as if renewing a sacred vow—to serve with clarity, steadiness, and care.

In moments of tension, pause for three deliberate breaths. Let them anchor impulse, shielding your discernment.

When the world fractures, offer the gift of breath to another. Not as correction, but as communion—a reminder of shared ground.

2. The Weaver's Inclusive Loom

To weave is not to adorn—it is to bind. It is not artifice; it is alchemy. Leadership, at its noblest, is the sacred act of threading lives, losses, and longings into a resilient whole. It is the patient labor of stitching fractured truths into a future that embraces all.

True inclusion is not ornamental—it is foundational. It is not a performance of diversity, but its embodiment. It is the moral clarity to see that exclusion frays the fabric of humanity. Every silenced voice, every erased story, weakens the collective design.

In an age torn by division, the weaver is the rare leader who bridges divides without erasing difference. She honors tension, refusing to mistake unity for uniformity. As I have said: *"Unity in diversity is not a slogan—it is the living soul of a nation's peace."*

To weave is to choose presence over power, complexity over convenience. It is the courage to include what history has cast aside—not for optics, but for wholeness.

Practices for Daily Life

In every decision, ask: Who is absent? Whose voice awaits invitation? Act not as gatekeeper, but as welcomer.

Listen not to defend or reply, but to receive. Embrace what unsettles, for it strengthens the weave.

Before deciding, pause: Whose dignity does this uplift? Whose silence does it betray? Make space for those furthest from power.

3. The Garden of Mutual Flourishing

Even within these walls, where time is stilled and silence enforced, I hold fast to the vision of a garden—not metaphorical, but moral. A space where one's freedom nourishes another's, where dignity is not a contest, but a shared blossoming.

True growth is never solitary. If my thriving demands another's diminishment, it is not growth—it is theft. Leadership, especially in constraint, is the art of tending beyond oneself—planting in barren soil, offering sustenance without expectation. A whispered word between cells may carry more life than a thousand speeches.

Societies that nurture only the powerful reap decay. Those that uplift the voiceless cultivate resilience—regenerative, not ornamental.

This flourishing is not a dream—it is a discipline, built root by root, gesture by gesture. It begins with how we see one another and endures in how we lead.

Practices for Daily Life

Celebrate another's success as your own. Let joy transcend the boundaries of self.

Create something—a thought, a space, a story—that thrives beyond your presence, serving those you may never know.

Tend to the forgotten. Ask how they are. Listen not as duty, but as devotion.

4. The Beacon of Reflective Kindness

In a place where cruelty is routine, a single act of kindness becomes a quiet rebellion.

Here, I have learned that even an imagined gesture—a cup of boiled water offered in thought to a guard, the stillness of nonjudgment, the silent gift of presence—can shine. Especially when offered to those hardened by their roles, the line between captor and captive dissolves, revealing not duty, but humanity.

Kindness, to endure, must be reflective—not born of pity or performance, but of the truth that the light we offer others guides our own path. It is not weakness; it is strength transfigured by love.

When given without agenda, kindness becomes a mirror—not to exalt the giver, but to sanctify the bond. It equalizes, drawing us to the shared, fragile ground of our humanity.

Practices for Daily Life

Offer one selfless act of kindness daily, especially where cruelty is expected.

Be present without fixing. Let listening be your offering.

When anger tempts retaliation, ask: *What would love choose if it were fearless?*

5. The Quiet Power of Dignity

Dignity is not granted by those who deny it—it is claimed by those who refuse to surrender it.

Each assault on my privacy, each mockery of truth, each attempt to erode my personhood reminds me: the power to affirm another's dignity remains mine alone. In a system designed to dehumanize, to uphold respect—quietly, steadfastly—is a silent revolution.

To lead with dignity is to reject the logic of humiliation. It is to wear integrity like armor no captor can pierce. And it is to reflect that respect to others, especially those the world has taught to forget their worth.

When we restore dignity—not with fanfare, but with presence— we ignite a liberation that pierces walls, reawakening what is sacred in being human.

Practices for Daily Life

Speak with respect, even in conflict. Refuse the venom of contempt.

Remind someone of their worth, especially where power has erased them.

In humiliation, choose stillness. Let dignity be your sanctuary, silence your strength.

6. The Leader Who Listens

In a world drowned in noise, listening is a radical act.

Many here are voiceless—not for lack of truth, but because the world has forgotten how to hear. Yet in this silence, I discern a resilient music—the truth that sings between words, enduring where language fails.

To lead with conscience is to amplify the unheard, to let buried songs rise above the din of power. It is to attune the heart to grief, anger, or hope—not as noise, but as sacred messages.

Leadership listens first and speaks only to restore harmony where the world has broken its chords.

Practices for Daily Life

Ask someone: "What is your truth?" Receive it in stillness, without judgment.

Uplift a quiet voice, especially one dismissed as inconvenient.

Record a forgotten story. Let its courage echo through history's silence.

7. The Hearth of Belonging

A prison offers no warmth, yet we kindle it—a shared bowl of rice with my guard, a whispered song, a gesture to one trembling with despair.

This warmth is not sentiment—it is the foundation of belonging. It builds the unseen architecture of community through deliberate acts of inclusion.

Leadership must be a hearth—a refuge for those scorched by power, where exclusion's chill meets the fire of welcome.

Not charity, but solidarity. Not pity, but presence. Not performance, but the vow: *You belong. You are seen.*

Practices for Daily Life

Notice the isolated. Offer a smile, a seat, a word that creates space.

Share what sustains you—a meal, a prayer, a story. Let your comfort heal another.

Create rituals of inclusion. Let every gesture say: *This circle holds you.*

8. The Mirror of Mutual Respect

In my mirror, I see not only myself, but countless faces—prisoners, teachers, my people—whose courage shapes my own.

Respect is not deference to power, but reverence for our shared fragility. The leader who cannot see herself in another risks cruelty. But the one who meets another's gaze finds both accountability and freedom.

To lead is to see—not with eyes alone, but with the heart—and to honor the humanity reflected, wounded or weary though it may be.

Practices for Daily Life

In judgment, ask: How would I wish to be treated in their place?

Hold mistakes gently—yours and others'. Let respect cradle forgiveness.

Make respect tangible—in tone, timing, presence. Offer dignity, don't demand it.

9. The Seedbed of Future Hope

Hope, here, is not a feeling—it is a discipline. It is the refusal to let despair shape our actions.

To hope is not to chase victory, but to remain human without applause. It is planting seeds you may never see bloom, tending possibilities others have abandoned.

I write, reflect, resist—not for assured outcomes, but because the future listens. Not for perfection, but for presence—a hand reaching into the dark with care.

Unseen eyes watch—children unborn, prisoners unnamed, citizens yet to hope again. They seek not certainty, but example.

To lead with hope is to prepare the future, not predict it. It is to garden in the dark, watering what the world deems barren.

Practices for Daily Life

Begin something that outlives you—a letter, a law, a gesture. When despair calls, act. Even the smallest integrity defies apathy. Live as a curriculum of courage. Teach through your return to care.

10. The Bridge of Reconciliation

I have known betrayal, tasted bitterness, watched trust unravel. Yet I have learned: *to hold hatred is to carry the oppressor within.*

Forgiveness is not forgetting—it is remembering without venom. It is the choice to break the cycle, to let dignity, not damage, define our legacy.

Reconciliation begins not in treaties, but in a breath, a silence, a heart that refuses to close. It is staying soft in a world that demands armor, stepping onto the trembling bridge between truth and tenderness.

To lead is to walk that bridge, even when justice is unfinished, even when mercy feels like risk. It is to declare: *violence will not have the final word.*

Practices for Daily Life

Begin forgiveness within. Whisper their name with less fire, letting the burn fade.

Offer a gesture of peace, not to restore trust, but to free yourself from their shadow.

Reflect on revenge's cost. Ask: *What peace am I willing to embody?*

Closing Reflection: A Thread Through Time

These principles are not born from me alone. They are woven from the lived wisdom of countless generations—monks and mothers, revolutionaries and refugees, teachers and prisoners—each of whom, in their own way, chose love over fear, clarity over comfort, and presence over power.

They are drawn from the deep well of the *Dhamma*, from the *Buddha* who spoke not only of liberation, but of interdependence and responsibility. In the *Sigālovāda Sutta*, and throughout his teachings, we are reminded that freedom is not achieved in isolation. It is shaped—day by day—in the way we walk with others.

Every relationship becomes a sacred field of reciprocity—a living ground where we either restore the fabric of humanity or contribute to its unraveling.

To honor the *Dhamma* is not to withdraw from the world, but to meet it fully—with steadiness, with empathy, and with the courage to hold complexity without collapse.

To lead, in this light, is not to rise above others. It is to carry the weight of their dignity as reverently as your own. It is to walk slowly enough to hear the unheard. To kneel when necessary. To stand not to be seen, but to be of service.

When we lead this way, we become more than individuals. We become vessels of a deeper possibility. We join a lineage—not of domination, but of devotion. A lineage that speaks in quiet voices, walks without fanfare, and builds futures with the fragile tools of care.

So, to those who lead now—and to those who will:

Let your leadership be luminous with tenderness.

Let it be grounded in humility, and fierce in its fidelity to truth.

And above all, let it remember this:

To serve others is not a burden. It is a privilege. A vow. A joy that transcends the self.

Even here, in a prison built to silence the human spirit—I remember. And in that remembering,

I remain free.

— AUNG SAN SUU KYI, NAYPYIDAW PRISON, JULY 2025

Alan Clements: Daw Suu, your words carry a transcendent grace, a moral clarity, and a quiet courage that illuminate the path of conscience under the harshest trials. Your reflections are not merely a testimony to endurance, but a living embodiment of the pāramīs in motion—luminous, rooted, and profoundly relational. Each insight feels like a thread woven into the enduring tapestry of human dignity, stitched with unwavering resolve, even within the confines of captivity.

You remind us that ethical leadership is not rooted in grandeur, but in presence. It is not measured by obedience, but by service. Your articulation of *ubuntu*—woven through the *Dhamma* and your lived sacrifice—redefines power as a sacred bond, not dominion.

With this in heart and mind, may I ask: In your journey as a leader and advocate for democracy, you have faced trials that demanded not only resilience, but an extraordinary depth of ethical discernment, honed through reflection. Could you share how the Buddha's teachings—

particularly *yoniso manasikāra*, or wise reflection—have shaped your decision-making and your vision of leadership?

And if there is more you feel called to share, please offer whatever might deepen our understanding of how this reflective discipline continues to guide your path in these darkest hours.

Aung San Suu Kyi: Indeed. Let me recount a poignant teaching from the Ambalaṭṭhika Rāhulovāda Sutta, where the Buddha offered his young son, Rāhula, a lesson of timeless depth. At seven, Rāhula was vibrant with innocence. The Buddha, seeing the seeds of leadership within him, chose not abstract doctrine, but vivid, embodied wisdom to guide his path.

He began with truthfulness. Pouring a small measure of water into a cup, he asked *Rāhula* if he could see its scant volume. When *Rāhula* nodded, the Buddha said: just as this water is meager, so too is the virtue of one who feels no shame in a deliberate lie. He poured out the water, overturned the cup, and showed it empty—each gesture a stark illustration of how deception empties the soul.

Then, he offered the image of a mirror. "What is a mirror for?" he asked. "To reflect," *Rāhula* replied. The deeper teaching followed: let your mind be a mirror. Examine your thoughts, words, and deeds— before, during, and after. See them with unsparing clarity. Own them with courage. Amend them with compassion.

He taught a threefold discipline:
- Before acting: Reflect—will this harm myself or others?
- During action: Observe—if harm emerges, pause and redirect.
- After action: Review—if harm was done, confess it, resolve to act with greater mindfulness.

This was not a lesson in judgment, but in self-honesty, responsibility, and reverence for all life.

In Burmese monasteries, we speak of living through the three doors of body, speech, and mind. Each demands vigilance before we cross its threshold. Wise reflection is not optional—it is the cornerstone of an ethical existence.

The spirit of *ubuntu*— "I am because we are"—is woven into this practice. Every word, every deed, ripples across the shared waters of humanity:

- A lie clouds the water.
- A truth spoken polishes the mirror of trust.
- An act of greed hardens the soil of connection. • An act of generosity renews it with hope.

Wise reflection is not mere morality—it is our shared salvation.

In this light, *ubuntu* becomes a daily vow:

- Before enacting laws, ask: Will this restore dignity or diminish it?
- Before speaking, inquire: Will this heal or harm?
- Before acting, reflect: Will this bridge division or deepen it?

The Buddha's *pāramīs*—the ten noble perfections—become living inquiries:

- *Dāna* (Generosity): "What can I give without seeking reward?"
- *Sīla* (Integrity): "Can I align my actions with my deepest truth?"
- *Nekkhamma* (Renunciation): "Can I let go of what binds me?"
- *Paññā* (Wisdom): "Am I seeing clearly, or through the veil of ignorance?"
- *Viriya* (Energy): "Can I persist without losing heart?"
- *Khanti* (Patience): "Can I endure with tenderness intact?"
- *Sacca* (Truthfulness): "Will I honor truth, even at great cost?"
- *Adhiṭṭhāna* (Determination): "Will I remain steadfast through trials?"
- *Mettā* (Loving-kindness): "Can I extend goodwill to all, without exception?"
- *Upekkhā* (Equanimity): "Can I stand firm amid life's storms?"

These are not ideals—they are beacons in the darkness.

And *ubuntu* is the mirror we polish with our lives.

It is not a phrase. It is not a dream. It is a choice.

A sacred vow whispered across generations: We are bound to one another. Only together do we remain whole.

Alan Clements: Daw Suu, your words return us to the breath, the vow, the sacred bond that unites us across time and space. A mirror of truth. A thread passed from heart to heart. Thank you.

Aung San Suu Kyi: May we be mirror and breath, seed and bridge.
May we live the truth that dignity, like love, grows only when shared.
And to my people—
To those who suffer in silence, and those who rise with courage;
To the hungry, the displaced, the forgotten, and the exiled;
To my fellow prisoners—seen and unseen, in Burma and beyond;
To those who shelter in tents, and those who rest beneath ruins;
To the children whose questions await answers—
I offer no grand promises.
Only this:
You are not alone.
Your pain, your resilience, your very breath—they are my vow.
Let us cling to the faintest light.
Let us not let cruelty make us cruel.
Let us find, even in ashes, the ember of a sacred fire—
A fire not of vengeance, but of vision.
And to those in power,
Whose choices shape lives far beyond your gaze:
May you dare to see—not as rulers, but as kin.
May you remember:
Justice is not weakness.
Mercy is not folly.
And the future will not recall your words—but the lives you
safeguarded when it mattered most.
Let this be our practice.
Let this be our path.
Let this be our pāramīs in motion.

Playbook for Leadership: Part III
The Ten Pāramīs as a Covenant for Relational Leadership

These are the *Pāramīs*—the ten states of excellence—as *Sayadawgyi* taught me. Patiently. Reverently. Carving a path through decades of sacrifice and solitude. They are not mere virtues, but sacred vows, forged within relentless oppression. "Leadership," he said, "is not dominion. It is mindful presence." A living testament to trust, truth, and eternal peace.

This philosophy resounds profoundly with the African ethic of *ubuntu*: "I am because we are." It proclaims that dignity is not claimed— it is woven. Our liberation is collective, or it is nothing.

A Burmese proverb enshrines this wisdom:

"Without her, it cannot be done. Yet she alone cannot do it. Without you, it cannot be done. Yet you alone cannot do it. Without me, it cannot be done. Yet I alone cannot do it. Only together—her, you, and I— can all be fulfilled."

Through years of silent contemplation, I have learned that wise, courageous, and compassionate leadership is rooted in these *pāramīs* and illuminated by *yoniso manasikāra*—wise reflection. Clearly, leadership is not flawless action; it is the courage to pause, to see and feel with piercing clarity, and to act with reverence for all.

Here, I offer them not as ideals, but as a sacred covenant for those who lead with conscience. *Ten pāramīs.* Ten relational pillars. Ten vows to serve a cause greater than oneself.

1. *Dāna* (Generosity)

In a world shackled by self-interest, *dāna* is a silent revolution. It is not merely giving possessions, but offering presence, trust, and time—free from expectation or reward. It shatters the ego's grasp, weaving bonds of communion. *Dāna* fosters communities where people flourish not through obligation, but because they are truly seen.

In resistance, it is passing courage like bread. In exile, it is offering a silent prayer for another. In captivity, it is sharing hope through a whispered word. Generosity is not a gesture—it is the seed of trust, the cornerstone of peace.

Proximate Cause: Compassion and liberation from greed.
Near Enemy: Giving to control or to be seen.
Leadership Quality: *Samvibhāga* – Equitable Sharing

"I gave not for acclaim, but to affirm they were never forsaken."
—AUNG SAN SUU KYI

2. *Sīla* (Morality)

Sīla is the bedrock of leadership in an age where ethics falter under tyranny, fear, or expediency. It is not a rigid code, but a living vow to do no harm, aligning actions with a moral compass that upholds collective dignity. Spiritually, it anchors integrity, granting peace amid turmoil.

Emotionally, it is the courage to stand resolute when others waver. *Sīla* radiates trust, inviting others to rise without fear of betrayal.

Proximate Cause: Reverence for self and others; mindfulness of impact.
Near Enemy: Self-righteousness, where rules eclipse compassion.
Leadership Quality: *Garu* – Reverent Dignity

"Morality is not a refuge; it is the ground, we share in trust."
—AUNG SAN SUU KYI

3. *Nekkhamma* (Renunciation)

Nekkhamma calls leaders to release—not their vision, but the chains that diminish it: pride, comfort, the need for approval. In a world craving recognition, it is a cleansing breath, freeing us from smallness. Emotionally, it is liberation; spiritually, it is the clarity to prioritize enduring good over fleeting gain. It is the courage to step aside, letting others shine. Imagine a prisoner forgoing despair to kindle hope—that is *nekkhamma*, a rebellion against self.

Proximate Cause: Wisdom and awareness of impermanence.
Near Enemy: Apathy or escapism posing as detachment.
Leadership Quality: *Khamā* – Enduring Patience

"I released not to lose, but to gain the trust of those who endured."
—AUNG SAN SUU KYI

4. *Paññā* (Wisdom)

Paññā is the leader's guiding light in a storm of distortion—a clarity that pierces illusion to reveal truth. It is not mere knowledge, but a depth that discerns cause and effect, truth from deceit. Emotionally, it is the calm to witness suffering without being consumed; spiritually, it is the vision to navigate complexity. For a leader, it is foresight—seeing not just events, but their human toll, and acting with precision. Picture a prisoner guiding a people through oppression—that is *paññā*, the awakened heart.

Proximate Cause: Contemplation, reflection, and truth-seeking.
Near Enemy: Intellectual pride or reliance on cunning.
Leadership Quality: *Ikkhanā* – Visionary Foresight

"Truth is not loud; it is the silence that pierces chaos."
—AUNG SAN SUU KYI

5. *Viriya* (Energy)

Viriya is the lifeblood of leadership—a relentless drive that endures setbacks. In an era of despair, it is not haste, but sustained effort rooted in purpose. Emotionally, it is the fire to persist when hope fades; spiritually, it is the focus to prioritize what matters. For a leader, it is initiative— igniting movements, rallying communities, breaking chains—not from ego, but from conviction. Think of a dissident rising after defeat—that is *viriya*, energy as creation's force.

Proximate Cause: Courage and faith in the path.
Near Enemy: Restlessness or exhaustion from misdirected effort.
Leadership Quality: *Utthāna* – Bold Initiative

"Strength lies not in victory, but in daring to begin anew."
—AUNG SAN SUU KYI

6. *Khanti* (Patience)

Khanti is the art of enduring without breaking—a sacred strength in a world chasing instant results. It is not passivity, but a steadfast holding of space for justice, healing, or truth. Emotionally, it is the resilience to bear anguish without anger; spiritually, it is the wisdom to see timing as destiny. For a leader, it is grace under fire—weathering betrayal or silence with trust in the path. Picture a prisoner enduring solitude to speak truth—that is *khanti*, patience as power.

Proximate Cause: Equanimity and understanding of suffering.
Near Enemy: Indifference or suppressed resentment.
Leadership Quality: *Vacanakkhamā* – Openness to Truth

"Patience is not surrender; it is the courage to await justice."
—AUNG SAN SUU KYI

7. *Sacca* (Truthfulness)

Sacca is the leader's unyielding voice—compassionate, authentic, resolute. In an age of deception, it is a lifeline: speaking truth, even when it trembles. Emotionally, it is the courage to risk rejection for integrity; spiritually, it is the clarity to dispel illusion. For a leader, it is the bedrock of trust—aligning words with soul, whether to a cellmate or a nation. Imagine a prisoner speaking truth to power—that is *sacca*, authenticity as conscience's call.

Proximate Cause: Integrity and fearlessness.
Near Enemy: Harsh truth without compassion.
Leadership Quality: *Vattā* – Radiant Truth

"Half-truths fracture a people; only whole truth heals."
— AUNG SAN SUU KYI

8. *Adhiṭṭhāna* (Determination)

Adhiṭṭhāna is the unshakable resolve in a leader's core—a commitment that holds fast against doubt or despair. In a fleeting world, it is an anchor: choosing a path and walking it, no matter the tempest. Emotionally, it is the grit to face darkness; spiritually, it is the focus to see beyond chaos. For a leader, it is vigilance—building what endures, unwavering. Think of a martyr enduring for freedom—that is *adhiṭṭhāna,* determination as devotion.

Proximate Cause: Conviction and clarity of purpose.
Near Enemy: Stubbornness or inflexible rigidity.
Leadership Quality: *Jāgariya* – Steadfast Vigilance

"Resolve is not noise; it is the silence that endures storms."
—AUNG SAN SUU KYI

9. *Mettā* (Loving-Kindness)

Mettā is the heart of leadership—a boundless goodwill that sees no enemy, only shared humanity. In a divided world, it is a revolution: choosing connection over conquest. Emotionally, it is the warmth to embrace others as they are; spiritually, it is the insight of our interdependence. For a leader, it is love in action—uplifting communities with care that seeks no reward. Imagine a prisoner forgiving her captors—that is *mettā,* love as leadership's enduring language.

Proximate Cause: Seeing others as oneself; boundless compassion.
Near Enemy: Attachment posing as care.
Leadership Quality: *Karuṇā* – Transformative Compassion

"Love is not frail; it is the strength to hold all within your heart."
—AUNG SAN SUU KYI

10. *Upekkhā* (Equanimity)

Upekkhā is the leader's serene balance—a stillness that neither clings nor recoils, even as the world rages. In an age of turmoil, it is a sanctuary: standing firm amid chaos. Emotionally, it is the peace to feel without being ruled; spiritually, it is the vision to see the greater whole. For a leader, it is the maturity to guide without dominating, to act without exploiting. Picture a prisoner finding peace in chains—that is *upekkhā*, equanimity as strength.

Proximate Cause: Wisdom and detachment.
Near Enemy: Indifference or emotional detachment.
Leadership Quality: *Na c'aṭṭhāne niyujjako* – Freedom from Exploitation

"Equanimity is not cold; it is the warmth of wise dignity at rest."
—AUNG SAN SUU KYI

These *pāramīs* are not mine—they are humanity's mirror. *Sayadawgyi* did not shape a politician; he forged a companion for the *samsaric* struggle. Leadership, thus, is relational—a tapestry of wisdom and interdependence woven into humanity's DNA. It is mindful intelligence as the cornerstone: knowing your impact, choosing truth, fostering peace.

This is the path I have walked—and the one I entrust to you, as a vow to Awakening.

ENVISIONING THE FUTURE

Author's Prelude

To envision the future is not to predict its contours but to sow its seeds—with unwavering care, resolute courage, and the fierce patience of those who may never witness its flowering.

This chapter is both a meditation and a mandate. It emerges as a radiant signal from a voice unyielding, still incandescent in the deepest shadows of solitary confinement. Aung San Suu Kyi speaks not as a symbol but as a visionary cartographer, charting a democratic freedom not yet realized, yet courageously alive in the heart of her people.

What follows is no oration—it is hope in deliberate motion. A set of sacred imperatives, each ignited by the truth that tyranny flourishes not only through violence but through silence, apathy, and erasure.

In Myanmar, where military oppression seeks to smother aspiration, Daw Suu summons us to three acts of defiance: to recall, to respond, to rehumanize, forging a collective vow that unites every heart.

To recall: Freedom is a shared promise, not a solitary quest. *To respond*: With mindful presence, not platitudes. *To rehumanize*: Restoring conscience where cruelty seeks to reign.

Her vision, tempered in sorrow yet unbroken, endures—not through rhetoric but through the quiet power of being. These are not tactics; they are invitations, offerings from a spirit that has endured profound anguish yet chooses, relentlessly, to illuminate.

Each act of response—each candle kindled, each name spoken, each life held sacred in the heart of a vigilant world—is more than protest. It is remembrance. It is *mettā—loving-kindness*—made manifest. It is grief transmuted into grace, witness woven into a tapestry of shared dignity.

This chapter offers a rarity: a blueprint not merely for resistance but for the world that must rise from liberation's ashes. Not peace as a fleeting truce, but as an enduring promise. Not slogans, but a summons to the soul. Not solace, but searing clarity.

Kindly engage these words not only with your intellect but with the full weight of your conscience. Let them pierce your deepest sense of duty. Breathe with their urgency—not as alarm, but as awakening. Let them stir the part of you that still trusts in love and healing's possibility. Let them break your heart—gently, irrevocably—and guide you to serve with that heart held open, resolute, and whole.

And, if, by the end, you find yourself questioning what it means to love a nation—not as an abstraction but as a living, breathing act—then this prelude has fulfilled its purpose.

◆ ◆ ◆

Alan Clements: Daw Suu, as we draw this series of conversations to a close, I feel compelled to ask: What will it take—not only for you, but for the 22,000 political prisoners still held across Myanmar—to be truly free?

Further, what conditions are necessary, not just for your release, but for the liberation of an entire people still held hostage by tyranny? And perhaps most importantly, what is your vision for Myanmar once that freedom is achieved?

Aung San Suu Kyi: Alan, to free my 22,000 brothers and sisters still locked in prison cells, we must break more than stone and steel—we must break silence. We must break complicity. And most urgently, we must shatter the global hypnosis that allows mass suffering to fade into background noise. This is not simply a question of politics—it is a test of global conscience.

Let me say this with absolute clarity: their freedom matters more than mine. These women and men—monks, students, elders, medics, mothers—carry the moral weight of our revolution. It is not our weapons the regime fears. It is not sanctions or speeches. It is the fire in their eyes. It is the refusal in their posture. It is their ethical courage— uncompromising and unbribable. It is the unbearable power of people who cannot be bought.

Their imprisonment is not symbolic. It is the frontline. They are the quiet, radiant heart of our resistance. And if we are to see them walk free, *we must ignite something far greater than outrage: we must ignite the global imagination. We must make it impossible for the world to look away.*

The world will not act because it understands us. It will act when it feels us. When the cry of a prisoner echoes in the body of a mother in São Paulo. When the silence of a tortured student trembles in the throat of a poet in Stockholm. When the locked doors of a cell are heard in the boardrooms of London, the mosques of Istanbul, the universities of Delhi, and the hip-hop studios of Lagos.

We cannot afford to freeze. We must resist despair as fiercely as we resist dictatorship. We must remain fluid—creative—alive. The regime thrives on predictability. Let us become beautifully unpredictable. Let us disturb the silence not just with condemnation, but with creation.

Imagine if the world's most beloved artists, spiritual leaders, fearless philanthropists, visionary influencers, and defenders of conscience united—not to issue policy papers or polite statements, but to awaken the sleeping soul of the planet. Art that stirs the marrow. Sound that shatters indifference. Satire that exposes complicity. Spiritual fire that burns through numbness.

Imagine if, even for one day, the global media were interrupted by a single, unignorable truth: *"The soul of Myanmar is being tortured to death. Right now. And it will not stop unless you help stop it."* Let that message reverberate through cathedrals and nightclubs, classrooms and boardrooms, temples, galleries, protests, and poems. Let it be danced, painted, wept, sung, shouted, amplified—until the cry for Myanmar's freedom becomes a global act of conscience no one can turn away from.

Let the call for Myanmar's freedom become uncontainable.

Alan Clements: Daw Suu, what you've shared is not only visionary—it's revolutionary. You've made it unmistakably clear that the freedom of your fellow prisoners—those 22,000 hearts beating behind bars at this very moment—is not only central to Myanmar's future, but essential to the awakening of the world's conscience.

May all lovers of freedom—artists and teachers, monks and students, policymakers and activists—respond to your urgent call. May their actions arise not merely as performances of solidarity, but as moral imperatives. As radical sacred vows. As expressions of mutual dignity.

And now, if I may— You've spoken about how to galvanize the world for those behind bars. But I want to turn the question inward: In your experience—both as a political leader and as a prisoner of conscience—how do we stay human in a world that so often normalizes inhumanity? What sustains our capacity to care when we are surrounded by apathy, distraction, denial, and despair?

Aung San Suu Kyi: Alan, your question touches the very marrow of our struggle—not just in Myanmar, but everywhere the human heart collides with the machinery of forgetting. How do we remain human in a world that has forgotten what humanity means?

For me, the answer lies in presence—not as performance, but as self-discipline. To remain present with suffering, without numbing it or turning it into spectacle, is a radical act. The *Dhamma* teaches this. To courageously feel—with wisdom and balance—is itself a form of resistance.

I've come to see that compassionate action is not sustained by emotion alone. Emotions rise and fall. They fatigue. But what endures is mindful awareness—clarity born of felt interdependence. The realization that the person suffering before you is not "other," but another expression of your own life—that is the root of resilience. That is *mettā* as energy, not sentiment.

And when that clarity dims—as it does—I return to a simple reflection, whispered long ago by a teacher I revere: *"If not now, when? If not me, who?"*

We all have thresholds. But with wise attention—*yoniso manasikāra*—we can widen those thresholds without losing the heart's softness.

There are days when even hope feels extravagant. But what I've never abandoned is responsibility—not as a burden, but as a vow. To respond with care. To respond with conscience. That is the root of the word itself: *response-ability—the ability to respond.*

In truth, Alan, we stay human not by turning from the world's pain, but by allowing it to refine us—to soften us without breaking us, to deepen us without silencing us.

That, to me, is the art of Dhamma in dark times.

And perhaps that is our task now—not only to be resilient. Not even always strong. But to be steady enough, tender enough, awake enough to meet the next moment with dignity. To thrive, not just survive. That to me, is how we remain human. And more than that—that is how we begin to rehumanize the world.

Alan Clements: Daw Suu, before we close this chapter, I want to acknowledge something we've returned to often—across our conversations, in different forms, with different phrasing.

These themes—justice, dignity, peace, and redemption—are not new, but neither are they ever old. They echo through our shared humanity like breath in meditation: again and again, seemingly repetitive, yet always vital, always evolving.

Aung San Suu Kyi: And as you've said before, we cannot speak too often of these things—only too little. So let us be patient here. Let us feel more deeply into the words—not only with our intellects, but with that quiet presence that knows what it means to suffer, to endure, to hope.

Just as in meditation we return to the breath a thousand times, so too must we return to the language of liberation—to the words that awaken us from apathy and denial.

Let this conversation, then, be not merely a dialogue, but a meditation—an invocation of ethical clarity and spiritual presence. An act of *ubuntu*. A remembering.

Let us carry this tone throughout, as a thematic anchor: that our words are not merely spoken—they are embodied. Practiced. Returned to. Like the breath itself.

Alan Clements: Beautiful. And when freedom is finally secured, what kind of Myanmar do you envision rising from the tyrannical disaster of this dictatorship?

Aung San Suu Kyi: As we have spoken about before, I envision a federal democratic union—a Myanmar where the rights of all peoples, from the Bamar to the Kachin, the Karen to the Shan, the Rakhine to the Rohingya, are protected by law and celebrated in daily life. A Myanmar where no one is forced to choose between their ethnic identity and their citizenship.

But it will take more than constitutions. It will take reconciliation—not as a political slogan but as a national ethic. Reconciliation means honesty. It means accountability. And yes, it means forgiveness—not to forget, but to transcend.

Alan Clements: But Daw Suu, allow me to ask you again, how do we reconcile with those who have caused so much harm? Can there truly be redemption for a regime that has inflicted so much suffering?

Aung San Suu Kyi: Redemption is never guaranteed, Alan. It must be chosen. The generals and those who have enabled them must come face to face with the truth—not only through the judgment of tribunals, but through the judgment of their own conscience. Justice must be pursued, not as retribution, but as restoration. Only then can we heal.

Our responsibility, as those who have endured the harm, is not to absolve, but to uphold truth without hatred. We must create the conditions for transformation. This is not naïve hope—it is disciplined compassion. Even the most deluded mind can awaken. Even a nation soaked in sorrow can flower again.

Alan Clements: And what about the rest of the world? What should humanity learn from Myanmar's struggle?

Aung San Suu Kyi: That no nation is immune to darkness. That democracy, once taken for granted, can vanish overnight. That the forces of greed, hatred, and delusion are not Burmese—they are human. And so are their antidotes: compassion, courage, and wisdom.

Myanmar's story is not isolated. It is a mirror. It reflects the struggle of every person who dares to speak truth in an age of silence. Of every woman who stands up to patriarchal power. Of every young person who believes the future belongs to them.

To the world I say: Myanmar is your test too. Will you look away, or will you rise? Will you side with expedience, or with dignity? Will you act—or will you remember us only when it's too late?

Alan Clements: Before we close, Daw Suu, I want to invite us to step back—to reflect not just on politics, but on peace itself. In a world saturated with war and threats of war, and in a country like Myanmar where violence has become so entrenched, what does it truly mean to choose peace? To choose dialogue over destruction?

Aung San Suu Kyi: Alan, if ever there was a moment to reflect on peace—not as a posture, but as a profound necessity—it is now.

Peace begins not in treaties, but in truth. And the truth is this: we live in a world that still believes, deep down, that you can kill your way out of conflict. That violence is a legitimate language. That if you just eliminate enough enemies, enough threats, enough inconvenient lives, somehow peace will arise. But that belief, Alan, is a spiritual failure. It is a collapse of moral imagination.

Yes, some wars have had to be fought. But the question is no longer whether a war can be justified. The question is: how long will we justify war itself as a solution?

Every person killed—every so-called "combatant," every so-called "target"—had a mother, a sister, a name. They had a laugh, a favorite song, a fear they never spoke aloud. And we erase them with acronyms, with euphemisms, with strategy. We turn their deaths into metrics. We convert oceans of trauma into footnotes.

And what do we inherit from it? Not security. Not wisdom. But a haunted world—a species that has made sanctuaries of killing fields, that applauds cruelty in the name of nationalism, that calls collective punishment justice.

We must, as a species, give peace a chance—not as an ideal, but as an imperative. We must dare to believe in a deeper intelligence—the intelligence to decode the very architecture of hatred, of vengeance, of genocide, of greed, of human stupidity.

True peace demands that we look inward as fiercely as we look outward. That we study our own minds with the same urgency we study our enemies. That we understand how fear becomes ideology, how trauma becomes policy, how silence becomes complicity.

This is not abstract. This is personal. It is Myanmar. It is Gaza. It is Ukraine. It is everywhere a child cries and no one listens.

So, when I speak of peace, I do not mean absence of violence. I mean presence of conscience. I mean the courage to see our shared humanity, even when every part of us wants to look away.

Peace begins with the courage to speak to one another—not just about ceasefires, but about what it means to coexist without domination, without humiliation, without erasure.

The power to destroy is loud. But the strength to listen, to negotiate, to imagine a shared future—that is where peace takes root. And it must take root now. Or we may not have another chance.

Let us begin—again—with the vow that we will not kill to feel safe. That we will not dehumanize to feel strong. That we will not destroy to feel seen. Let peace be more than an option. Let it become our path, our practice, and our most sacred inheritance.

Alan Clements: And what are some of the lessons we can draw—not just from theory, but from history?

Aung San Suu Kyi: There are many. The Camp David Accords between Israel and Egypt. The Good Friday Agreement in Northern Ireland. The end of apartheid in South Africa. The Cuban Missile Crisis. Rwanda's post-genocide healing. In each case, what changed the course of history was not force—it was willingness. It was empathy. It was the radical act of choosing to see the other not as an enemy, but as a partner in survival.

In Myanmar, we must do the same. Even with those who have oppressed us. Not to accept their actions, but to transform our future. That is the hardest kind of peace. And the most enduring.

Alan Clements: And how do we teach that? How do we help people— especially the next generation—choose peace over violence?

Aung San Suu Kyi: As I shared earlier, by showing them it's possible. By telling the truth about war's devastation. By modeling diplomacy. By creating institutions that reward listening over shouting. And by lifting up the voices of those who suffer most—for they know the price of violence better than anyone.

Peace is not a dream. It is a discipline, forged not in idealism, but in the lived truth of suffering and reconciliation. We have seen this in our monasteries and refugee camps, in the quiet dignity of mothers who bury their children and still choose not to hate.

In my own life, I have found that peace begins with the smallest gesture of non-retaliation—the willingness to see the person behind the uniform, the human behind the cruelty. Peace is not abstract. It is an act of spiritual defiance. And it remains, however difficult, our only future.

Alan Clements: And to the people of Myanmar—your people—what message do you leave in this hour of darkness?

Aung San Suu Kyi: My beloved people: You are the light. Every act of resistance, every whisper of truth, every tear shed for a fallen comrade— these are the threads of our future. You carry the spirit of those who walked before us, who dreamed of freedom even when it seemed impossible. Do not let despair become your master. Let it become your teacher. Let your suffering deepen your resolve. Let your silence become song.

Remember: No one can imprison the human spirit. Not forever. And no one can extinguish our hope—not while we continue to breathe, to love, to rise.

We will walk this path together. Not just for ourselves, but for the children not yet born—for the Myanmar that waits.

Alan Clements: And finally, Daw Suu—what would you say to the leaders of the world? To those who can act, but hesitate?

Aung San Suu Kyi: I would say this: The people of Myanmar are not pleading for pity—we are invoking principle.

I speak to you not as a politician, but as a fellow human being. A daughter. A mother. A prisoner of conscience. And I say, with all the calm urgency my heart can carry: do not let diplomacy be reduced to cowardice.

We in Myanmar have witnessed what happens when moral clarity is delayed in the name of neutrality. We have lived the consequences when trade partnerships silence ethical truth, and when complexity becomes a convenient excuse for inaction.

History, I assure you, will not only remember what was done to us. It will remember who looked away. *So, I ask you—no, I invite you—to stand with us in a deeper way. Not performatively. Not someday. But now.*

Let Myanmar be the place where your courage meets our suffering and turns it into redemption. Let this be your moment to rise—not in condemnation alone, but in creation. In conscience. In sacred responsibility.

Let me offer five imperatives—not policies, but vows. Five sacred threads in a mandala of liberation. Together, they form a covenant. Not just for Myanmar's survival, but for humanity's renewal.

First—Emancipation. The immediate release of the 22,000 political prisoners—monks, students, mothers, journalists, and yes, myself and President U Win Myint—is non-negotiable. Their continued captivity is a daily insult to the world's conscience. Freeing them is not symbolic—it is the restoration of our nation's soul.

Second—Stillness. A ceasefire. Now. Cease the airstrikes. End the killing. Peace is not a pause between wars—it is the sanctuary where dialogue can begin. Without stillness, there can be no listening. And without listening, there is no Myanmar left to save.

Third—Legitimacy. Recognize the National Unity Government. It was born of the people's will—88% of our citizens voted for it. It carries all our ethnicities, all our dreams. It is not just a government-in-waiting—it is the rebirth of democracy, and the emergence of a more inclusive Federal Union, still breathing, even under siege.

Fourth—Reconciliation. True peace demands more than disarmament. It requires the courage to forgive without forgetting. The grace to speak across the bloodlines. Justice must not harden into vengeance. We must transcend—not by denying harm, but by transforming it.

And fifth—Creation. Let us never underestimate the power of art. In our darkest hour, our murals, our poems, our songs, books, and theater have carried what guns cannot—dignity, memory, resistance. Every act of beauty is a refusal to die in silence. Let the world join us in turning anguish into art, and art into action.

These are not suggestions. They are the heartbeat of a covenant. One that begins not in policy rooms but in meditation halls, in classrooms, in refugee camps, in the hearts of those who still dare to care.

To global leaders: Your inaction prolongs our suffering. Your resolve can end it. Stop the flow of weapons. Freeze the banks that fund our oppression. Recognize the rightful government. Send aid not someday, but now. Stand with us—not in your words alone, but in your deeds.

And to every global citizen: Engage your moral imagination. Let your meditation be a form of resistance. Send *mettā* to the 22,000. Hold our names in your heart. Feel what it would mean if it were you. Because in the deepest sense—it is you.

Rooted in *Dhamma* and in ubuntu— "I am because we are"—this is not only Myanmar's moment. It is the world's. Our shared dignity depends on what we do now.

So let us act—not with delay, but with devotion. Not with pity, but with purpose. Let us make this a turning point worthy of the suffering that has brought us here.

May mettā guide us. May truth embolden us. And may peace—real peace—prevail.

Alan Clements: Daw Suu, thank you. For your wisdom. For your strength. And for your unwavering love for the people of Myanmar.

Aung San Suu Kyi: May that love be our guide. May it give us the courage to do what must be done. And may we never forget: we are not alone. We are all in this together. And together—we will be free.

A CALL TO REDEMPTION: MYANMAR'S PATH TO PEACE

Author's Prelude

To speak to power is a fleeting gesture; to address its conscience is an enduring act of moral courage. This may well be the deepest leap of faith—and the gravest risk.

This chapter is a letter, a requiem, and a supplication. It seeks neither to placate nor to vilify. It is crafted to summon the frailest thread capable of drawing a nation back from the precipice: redemption—not as artifice, but as the raw, irrevocable turning of the soul.

It opens as an unflinching appeal—from me to Senior General Min Aung Hlaing, architect of Myanmar's torment—but transcends its singular address to become a meditation on power, conscience, and the sacred calculus of human choice.

It is the embered dialogue between oppressor and witness, tyrant and truth-teller—an invocation, a lament for the 10,000 slain, the 22,000 imprisoned, the 3.5 million displaced, and a trembling breath of sacred possibility. It is a call to pierce the armor of cruelty and glimpse the latent humanity within.

The tone is neither sentimental nor conciliatory. It is resolute in its moral clarity, yet it shuns the allure of hatred. It dares something rarer: to speak to the capacity for awakening, even in the heart of devastation.

In this act, the chapter becomes more than a missive to one man— it is a confrontation with tyranny itself, and an audacious wager that truth, spoken with *mettā—loving-kindness*—can unravel even the most entrenched darkness.

Through Aung San Suu Kyi's voice, we are reminded: the *Dhamma* does not avert its gaze from the scars of violence. It kindles in the silenced, burns brighter in those who refuse to mirror hatred, and calls forth *hiri*—conscience—and *ottappa*—moral restraint—as beacons in a tragically fractured world.

This chapter is a meditation on moral audacity, on the spiritual fortitude required to face the author of a nation's ruin and declare: There is a path to redemption, but it demands a soulfully courageous inward gaze, unshielded by armor or alibi.

To those who deem this vision quixotic, I offer this: every transformation begins with one who dares to trust in humanity's capacity to awaken. In Myanmar, where 20 million cry for aid, where airstrikes have razed 100,000 homes, this trust is not naïveté—it is moral defiance.

Let this dialogue be received not as a proposal but as a transmission—from the soul of a wounded nation to the soul of its captor, and to all who wield power. Should it reach him, or another like him, may it stir the question long interred: Can I choose redemption? A single, trembling yes—a yes that reshapes a life, redirects a nation, and heralds, at last: Let the healing begin.

◆ ◆ ◆

General Min Aung Hlaing,

You stand at a pivotal threshold, General, not only for your life but for Myanmar's future. Your choices now will shape the legacy you leave—for your family, your nation, and the world's moral reckoning. You wage war not only on your people but on truth, humanity, and the Buddha's teachings you profess to honor.

Over 22,000 political prisoners languish in your jails—Daw Aung San Suu Kyi, President Win Myint, elected voices, alongside elders, students, monks, artists, farmers, and peacebuilders—the moral heart of Myanmar. Once the "Ruby of Asia," Myanmar bleeds under your rule, driven by fear, violence, delusion.

Redemption or Ruin

This moment is existential. You face a reckoning—not just with international law, but with unrelenting truth of *kamma*. The world's gaze rests on you. History draws near; its judgment unyielding. Yet even now, you can choose—not escape, but redemption, not might, but awakening.

The Courage to Turn

It begins with moral courage. Go before your nation and the world. Announce a ceasefire. Acknowledge the suffering caused. Release Daw Aung San Suu Kyi, President Win Myint, and all prisoners. Invite ethnic groups, democratic forces, international partners to a National Dialogue. This is not weakness—it's leadership, born of humility.

The Ashoka Peace Accord

Let an Ashoka Peace Accord define your legacy—a reconciliation rooted in dialogue, accountability, and *Dhamma's* enduring wisdom. King Ashoka, once "Cruel," turned from bloodshed to compassion, transforming an empire. You stand at such a threshold.

The Embers Within

The true enemies, as the late Venerable Sayadaw U Pandita taught, are within—greed, hatred, and delusion—consuming all, even their bearer. Daw Aung San Suu Kyi, resisting not just tyranny but hatred, embodies true strength. Follow her path.

Lead the Military Back to the People

The *Tatmadaw*, once honorable, now sows fear. Lead your soldiers from ruin, restoring their role as guardians, not oppressors.

The True Victory

Dhamma-vijaya—victory through truth—transforms the heart, not headlines. Rise above tyrants, join history's redeemers. Governance without *Dhamma* is domination, and domination without conscience is death.

What the World Demands

The world will not forget. Democracy's movement grows—ethnic forces unite, the National Unity Government gains legitimacy, sanctions tighten, the diaspora rises. You cannot win this war. Choose how you'll be remembered.

The Final Appeal

Imagine: You stand before the world, with elders, monks, and peacemakers, not generals. You bow in dignity, not defeat. You apologize, release prisoners, and call for a National Summit for a democratic, federal Myanmar. This act would redeem your name, restore Myanmar's honor, and prove even a general can return home.

Remember what Israeli Prime Minister Yitzhak Rabin once said before laying down his arms: *"You don't make peace with friends. You make peace with enemies."* That truth is not a slogan—it is a reckoning. And for daring to embody it, Rabin was awarded the Nobel Peace Prize.

You, too, stand at such a threshold: to choose dialogue over domination, reconciliation over revenge. That choice could yet define you—not as a tyrant, but as a statesman of the impossible.

The choice is yours—destruction or *Dhamma*, tyranny or peace. Your conscience calls. Let this be your hour.

With urgency and hope,

Alan Clements

A Call to Redemption: A Dialogue on Conscience and Power

Aung San Suu Kyi: Alan, may I ask you something personal?

Alan Clements: Of course. Please do.

Aung San Suu Kyi: This letter you wrote to General Min Aung Hlaing—the open call for his redemption. I read every word. Not once, but several times. And I must confess: it shook me. You addressed him not just as a critic, but as a fellow human being. You appealed to his conscience. To his potential for transformation. *That kind of appeal is rare.* What moved you to write with such unwavering humanity?

Alan Clements: Daw Suu, it came from a place of heartbreak—and a fragile, insistent hope. Heartbreak for the suffering he has caused—to you, to the thousands unjustly imprisoned, to the millions displaced and grieving. And hope that even the most deluded mind can awaken. That even a tyrant might be reminded of his humanity. If we believe in the Dhamma—if we believe in redemption—then we must speak to its possibility. Otherwise, what are we truly defending?

Aung San Suu Kyi: You invoked Ashoka. That comparison was striking. He, too, was a man of bloodshed. And yet, he became one of the greatest champions of peace the world has known. You wrote that Min Aung Hlaing still has time to walk the path of Dhamma. Do you believe that—even now?

Alan Clements: I believe it must be said—*regardless of whether he listens.* Ashoka wasn't born righteous, as you know. He saw the carnage he had unleashed, and it broke him. That crack in his pride let the Dhamma in. If even a sliver of conscience remains in Min Aung Hlaing, that letter was meant to reach it.

Aung San Suu Kyi: You challenged him to release us all—myself, President Win Myint, the 22,000 political prisoners. You asked him to appear on national television, confess his wrongs, and call for a national dialogue. That is not only bold—it is dangerous.

And yet, you invoked not only Ashoka *but also Israel's Prime Minister Yitzhak Rabin, who—as you wrote in your letter—once said, "You don't make peace with friends. You make peace with enemies."* Do you truly believe Min Aung Hlaing could walk such a path?

Alan Clements: I believe he stands at that very threshold. Just as Ashoka did. Just as Mandela did. Just as Rabin did. Each of them knew blood. Each of them chose not to double down on domination—but to pivot toward the impossible: reconciliation.

Rabin's past was fraught. He commanded violence. Ordered broken bones during the Intifada. And yet—he changed. Or rather, he allowed himself to be changed. He stepped forward—trembling—into dialogue. And for that act of moral imagination, he was shot in the back by one of his own. That's the risk. But it's also the reckoning.

If Min Aung Hlaing has even a flicker of conscience left—some trace of the *Dhamma* he once knew—then yes, I believe the path is still open. He may never be celebrated. But he could be remembered—not as the man who destroyed Myanmar, but as the one who stopped just before the edge. The one who, against all odds, turned toward the light.

Aung San Suu Kyi: And he must understand—this isn't just about him. It's about all of us. An entire nation held hostage to fear, still waiting to heal.

Alan Clements: Exactly. And in the letter, I reminded him: this isn't about power. It's about the heart of Myanmar. About our children. About the women violated, the monks murdered, the villages burned. It's about whether this land will ever break free from the cycle of domination and revenge.

Aung San Suu Kyi: Alan, your letter was a risk. A gamble. Some might even call it naïve.

Alan Clements: Perhaps. But so was the Buddha when he walked up to Angulimāla—a murderer wearing a necklace of severed fingers. He didn't see a monster. He saw a man still capable of awakening. And Angulimāla laid down his sword.

Aung San Suu Kyi: That story has lived in my heart for years.

Alan Clements: Mine too.

Aung San Suu Kyi: But here's what I want to ask you now. If he were watching us—Min Aung Hlaing, I mean—right now in this dialogue, and he could hear every word, what would you say to him? Not as an enemy. As a fellow human being.

Alan Clements: I would say this: "General, you were born into a land steeped in spiritual tradition. You were raised in the shadows of monks and pagodas. The Dhamma is not foreign to you. You know the words: lobha, dosa, moha—greed, hatred, and delusion. These are not enemies of the state. They are enemies within your own mind.

"You still have time. Time to stop. To reflect. To see what you've become. You do not need to die a tyrant. You can die a man who tried to make amends.

"Release Daw Suu. Release the President. Release the students, the journalists, the monks, the mothers and fathers and children behind bars.

"You will not win this war. Even if you hold your throne, you will lose your soul. But if you let go—if you walk into the light of truth and admit your wrongs—you will rise. Perhaps not in this life. But in the hearts of your people."

Aung San Suu Kyi: That is a hard truth. And a noble one.

Alan Clements: And one, I pray he hears.

Aung San Suu Kyi: I wonder if he's listening?

Alan Clements: Even if he isn't, someone else is. Someone who will one day lead Myanmar—whether from the military, from the NUG, or from a monastery. Words ripple, Daw Suu. That we know.

Aung San Suu Kyi: Then let this dialogue be a ripple. One of conscience. Of compassion. Of possibility.

Alan Clements: So long as we speak, the dream of democracy lives.

Aung San Suu Kyi: And so long as we listen, redemption is possible.

Alan Clements: What would you say to him, Daw Suu? If he asked you directly: Is there still a way for me to change?

Aung San Suu Kyi: I would say: "There is always a way. But not without truth. Not without accountability. Not without the courage to relinquish the lies you've built your power upon. Come to the table—not as a general, but as a human being. Lay down the weapons, both within and without. And listen. Listen to the voices you silenced. Only then will you understand what it means to lead."

Alan Clements: May he hear these words.

Aung San Suu Kyi: And may we live them.

Alan Clements: For Myanmar.

Aung San Suu Kyi: For peace.

Alan Clements: For the future.

Aung San Suu Kyi: And for the truth that still lives, even in darkness.

Alan, before we close today—if I may—I'd like to return to something you shared before we began recording. It has stayed with me ever since. You spoke of your new book—created specifically for the people of my country, and aimed directly at the conscience of General Min Aung Hlaing.

You described it as an act of good faith—something you could not walk away from. You said you spent the winter creating it, and that it was born from a question left unanswered.

May we speak about that now? I'd like to understand the deeper impulse behind it—and ultimately, your intention in bringing this work into the world.

Alan Clements: Yes, of course, Daw Suu. That's right. The book is titled *Conversation with a Dictator: A Challenge to the Authoritarian Assault*.

I had written the General a letter—openly and sincerely—inviting him to host me in Naypyidaw for a globally broadcast, unedited two-hour dialogue. A no-holds-barred, yet respectful conversation—at least from my side—to explore not only what he has done, but why. To understand the man behind the actions. The mindset behind the violence.

That invitation was made in good faith. I hoped it might open a crack in the armor—a moment of reckoning in the glare of truth.

That was two years ago.

No response. Just silence.

The book spans 492 pages and centers on a fictional dialogue with the Senior General, accompanied by over 300 full-page illustrations. My intention was to create a literary feature film—a two-hour immersive experience that traces the arc of Burma's history, from its roots in spiritual resilience to the brutality of the 2021 coup, *and into the present moment.*

I wanted to understand—not just what he's done, but why. What story does he tell himself to justify this? What is the voice inside his mind that explains away 22,000 political prisoners, the deaths of over 10,000 civilians, the displacement of 3.5 million people? What inner narrative rationalizes terror over truth?

To answer, I immersed myself in the minds of history's tyrants—Stalin, Hitler, Pol Pot, Mussolini, Idi Amin, Kim Jong-Il, Pinochet, Assad, Saddam Hussein. I traced the common threads of their delusions—their language, their mythologies of self-aggrandizement, their fetishization of control.

I asked: Do they possess a conscience? If so, how does it endure the machinery of oppression? Can it be resurrected? What is the anatomy of tyranny—the sanctification of violence, the denial of suffering, the idolization of power?

I wasn't seeking to demonize evil. I was mapping its inner architecture. For if we cannot comprehend the oppressor's mind, how can we dismantle the conditions that birth such figures? And more crucially, how can we offer a path to redemption?

How do tyrants speak to themselves in the dark? And can that voice still be interrupted by truth? Can even the most deluded mind be invited into dialogue, into recognition, into the trembling possibility of remorse?

As I shared, it began with a genuine invitation—my open offer to sit across from him, as I once sat with you, to explore the psychological and moral scaffolding of his power. But his silence spoke louder than words.

So, I turned to the unfettered realm of literature, where truth can breathe uncensored. That's when the project was transfigured. It became an imagined dialogue—fictional, yet searingly precise in its emotional and moral truth. A reckoning. A descent into the labyrinth of authoritarianism.

But it transcended a mere conversation. The book became a theatre of conscience, a sacred sanctuary where no one could hide—not even the dictator. A space where truth could be spoken without fear, where the ghosts of memory could rise from the ashes of repression, where art became resistance.

At its core, it is an unrelenting challenge to Min Aung Hlaing's self-justification—his mythology of rule, his rationale for terror. It is a profound meditation on indoctrination, violent patriarchy, and the perversion of language—how cruelty is cloaked in ceremony, how slogans strangle truth.

The narrative unfolds as a dramatic encounter within the palace he usurped—an imagined stage at the heart of power, after he seized your elected government. It evokes *Clockwork Orange's* raw intensity, *1984's* dystopian clarity, and *The Manchurian Candidate's* psychological depth.

Structured in five acts as a stage play, it distills Myanmar's epic struggle for freedom into a single, transformative sitting.

The illustrations are not ornaments; they are witnesses. They haunt, bypassing the intellect to sear the soul. They compel the reader not just to see, but to feel. In this, the book is not merely literary—it is cinematic, a ritual of remembrance, a mirror held to power until it shatters.

It is not entertainment. It is not escape. It is an exorcism of silence, a testament to truth, a beacon for Myanmar's redemption.

Aung San Suu Kyi: And what does that theatre reveal? What did you discover by imagining this conversation?

Alan Clements: I discovered that the dictator's voice—his rationalizations, evasions, brutalities—is not exceptional. It's familiar. Disturbingly familiar.

The book plunges into the psychic infrastructure of tyranny. Through a surreal, imagined interrogation, I try to dissect the delusions, fears, and spiritual collapse that sustain authoritarian regimes. What I found was that tyranny isn't only structural—it's internal. It grows in the soil of unexamined belief. Of grievance disguised as justice. Of entitlement exalted into law.

The General speaks, yes—but every word is like a mirror held up to the darkest corners of the human psyche. And what emerges is not just a political reckoning, but a spiritual one. The conversation becomes a reckoning with how power—when severed from conscience—corrupts not only nations, but the soul itself.

This isn't just about Myanmar. The pathology of authoritarianism lives everywhere: in propaganda, in patriarchy, in the lie that dominance brings order. My goal wasn't only to expose Min Aung Hlaing's crimes, but to understand the delusions that permit them. To peel away the myths until what's left is the raw face of power—terrified, hollow, obsessed with control.

And threaded through it all is the silenced presence of someone whose absence haunts every page: you, Daw Suu. Your voice is erased in reality—but in the book, you are everywhere. Not as a political figure, but as a spirit of unbroken dignity. As Burma's unfinished revolution.

Aung San Suu Kyi: You said before that the format is theatrical. Not a standard interview, but something stranger. More poetic. Why did you choose that?

Alan Clements: Because tyranny itself is surreal. It bends reality. It distorts the senses. It turns children into threats and truth into treason. I needed the book's form to reflect that psychological distortion.

So, I wrote it like a fever dream. Five acts. No traditional plot. Just an escalating confrontation. The journalist is relentless. He doesn't just question the General—he interrogates his soul. At times, it feels like the dictator is arguing with himself, unraveling in real time. That was intentional. Dictatorship, at its core, is a delusion trying to sustain itself. The form needed to embody that collapse.

Aung San Suu Kyi: And what of the art? Over 300 illustrations, you said. That's extraordinary. Why pair such heavy dialogue with imagery?

Alan Clements: Because language alone can't hold this kind of grief. Or madness. Or erasure.

The illustrations are not decorative. They're necessary. Visual truth-telling. They show what words can only circle around: the psychic cost of tyranny. The faces of the disappeared. The contortions of power. The annihilation of memory. One page might show a mother reaching for her child as a bomb falls. Another might depict a figure crumbling into ash—what it means to be erased by propaganda.

And throughout, there's a counterforce. You, Daw Suu—appearing not as a character, but as a presence. A lotus in shadow. A flame in the dark. The conscience the dictator cannot extinguish.

This book isn't something you read passively. You enter it. You witness it. And if I've done my job, by the end you haven't just seen into the mind of tyranny—you've felt the cost of resisting it.

Aung San Suu Kyi: And who is it for? Who do you most want to read this book?

Alan Clements: I wrote it for the 22,000 political prisoners of Myanmar. For the children growing up in camps, in hiding, in exile. For the artists and monks and medics who chose dignity over safety. They are the soul of this book.

But I also wrote it for the world. For anyone who thinks dictatorship is a foreign phenomenon. It isn't. It's in our institutions, our headlines, our algorithms. We all participate—through our silence, our distraction, our forgetting.

Conversation with a Dictator is my refusal to normalize authoritarianism. A wake-up call. A literary act of defiance. And if—by some miracle—Min Aung Hlaing himself reads it, I hope it unsettles him. I hope it pierces the armor he's built around his conscience.

And I hope, truly—with all my heart—that world leaders read it. President Trump and everyone close to him. Prime Ministers. Members of the United Nations. Politicians. Religious leaders. Everyone who still believes in the sanctity of life and the promise of democracy. Everyone who understands that the Universal Declaration of Human Rights is not a relic—but a living covenant.

And as you've said so beautifully, Daw Suu: *"For all those who know in their hearts that freedom and democracy are dreams you never give up."*

Aung San Suu Kyi: That's a powerful hope. And if he doesn't?

Alan Clements: Then I hope the children of Myanmar do. I hope it endures as a testament. As a record of conscience. As proof that someone—somewhere—refused to forget.

472

THE SPIRIT OF LEADERSHIP AND THE *DHAMMA* OF REVOLUTION

Author's Prelude

Leadership is not a mantle, but a holy vow. Not the wielding of power, but the art of wise presence. Not supremacy, but mindful discernment—forged in conscience, honed through unrelenting real-world practice. As we approach the culmination of our dialogues, we return not to resolve, but to consecrate—to honor the truths that endure amidst Myanmar's long struggle for freedom.

In the sacred rhythm of our exchange, Aung San Suu Kyi offers no sweeping denouements, no facile truths. What emerges instead is a rarer gift: a transmission of embodied wisdom—a fusion of politics, poetics, and inner alchemy.

This chapter is not a schema for transformation. It is its breath, its pulse—a living current of moral imagination. Threaded through our words flows the enduring legacy of the late Venerable Sayadaw U Pandita, whose teachings on mindfulness, self-accountability, and ethical clarity course like an unseen river beneath each syllable.

Here, leadership is not etched in charisma or command, but in the fortitude to feel deeply, perceive lucidly, and act with precision— even from the confines of a prison cell, where 22,000 courageous souls struggle to survive, 10,000 have perished, and 3.5 million wander displaced.

What unfolds is a reverential convergence: the moral audacity of resistance interwoven with the contemplative rigor of the *Dhamma*. Daw Suu offers not merely a vision, but a pledge: to lead with mindful intelligence, to resist not only the junta's tyranny but the toxins of greed, hatred, and delusion—in their overt and veiled forms.

This is a summons to those who will shape tomorrow: lead with your entire being. Let wisdom illuminate your mind. Let tenderness anchor your heart. Measure every decision not only for this moment, but for generations yet to come.

If this chapter bears one abiding truth, it is this: *authentic power elevates*. Truth is not a blade—it is a beacon. And those who aspire to serve must first master the art of listening—with fierce compassion, profound humility, and resolute clarity.

I invite you to read deliberately. Let these words permeate your essence, your conscience, your choices. This is not solely Aung San Suu Kyi's voice. It is the chorus of those who have marched, fallen, and risen—for a world of greater dignity and freedom.

Let her words be your catalyst. Let them forge your pledge. And may your pledge ignite the revolution. From my heart to yours—and, speaking for her, from Daw Suu's as well.

◆ ◆ ◆

Alan Clements: Daw Suu, as we near the culmination of our conversations, I am haunted by the transcendent grace of those nine nights I spent in communion with Sayadaw U Pandita in 2016, mere months before his passing. We've explored at length your own profound encounters with him, particularly on the *Dhamma's* luminous qualities of leadership—the fierce, tender courage required to embody them in service to others. You reminded me that even when we stumble, the true calling is to rise anew—and persist.

You spoke of authentic leadership as rooted in the qualities of a *kalyāṇa mitta*—a noble spiritual friend. If memory serves, these include: personal warmth and impeccable conduct (*piya*), unassailable integrity and reverence (*garu*), a presence worthy of love and veneration (*bhāvaniya*), speaking truth with unflinching clarity (*vattā*), the humility to embrace critique (*vacanakkhama),* and an unwavering refusal to exploit others for gain (*no c'āṭṭhāne niyujjako*).

Would you share further how these timeless teachings resonate within Myanmar's revolutionary struggle for liberation—and with you, here, in the day-to-day of solitary confinement? These qualities seem indispensable, not only for today's movement but for the promise of principled leadership, the world over, in the decades ahead.

Aung San Suu Kyi: Alan, Sayadaw U Pandita's teachings radiate with timeless truth, their weight magnified amidst the fury that engulfs our nation. Leadership, in its deepest essence, must be anchored in ethical resolve and an unyielding duty—not only to oneself, but to the collective, and to generations yet to dawn. Without the spirit of *kalyāṇa mittatā*, leadership falters, brittle and hollow. And when leadership fractures, the spirit of the revolution shatters in its wake.

In my country, our quest for freedom demands more than courage. It requires a clarity of heart—a wisdom that pierces the veil of terror and chaos. A revolution without wisdom risks becoming a reflection of the very oppression it seeks to dismantle.

Our leaders—from the National Unity Government to the young visionaries forging paths in jungle enclaves, to the Ethnic Groups throughout the country—must resist not only tyranny, but the seduction of a hardened heart. They must embody integrity—unwavering, luminous, and alive in action.

They must cultivate forbearance (*khamā*), vigilance (*jāgariya*), relentless effort (*utthāna*), and generosity in sharing their strength (*samvibhāga*).

Above all, they must nurture compassion (*karuṇā*) and foresight (*ikkhana*)—virtues without which today's sacrifices may become tomorrow's sorrows.

These are not aspirational ideals. They are the bedrock of moral leadership, the scaffolding that sustains a revolution's spirit. They are how we endure, not merely to survive, but to redeem.

Alan Clements: Sayadaw U Pandita also emphasized the necessity of foresight as a refined form of reasoning. He spoke of assessing whether an action is beneficial or harmful, suitable or unsuitable—and ensuring it brings no harm to oneself or others.

He reminded us that foresight must reach beyond the present; it is a form of care that extends across time. This echoes a Burmese proverb he once shared: *"If you cannot help, at least do no harm."*

How do we cultivate such far-seeing compassion in the midst of relentless chaos?

Aung San Suu Kyi: It begins with mindfulness, Alan. Foresight is born of clarity, and clarity arises from sati—from intelligent presence. Without mindfulness, our actions are easily driven by reactivity—by greed, fear, or blind conditioning. But with mindful intelligence, we begin to see how our choices ripple outward—across time, across generations. This is the antidote to the *Wetiko* spirit we've spoken of before—the devouring mind, insatiable, heedless of consequence.

To cultivate far-reaching compassion is to place ourselves in the hearts of the unborn. To imagine the world, they will inherit—and to act with their welfare in mind.

The Buddha taught *mettā, karuṇā, muditā,* and *upekkhā*—loving-kindness, compassion, sympathetic joy, and equanimity—not as lofty ideals, but as the active intelligence of a conscious society. They are not passive. They are revolutionary. And they must become the compass of our political and spiritual lives.

Alan Clements: What still astonishes me, Daw Suu, is how *satipaṭṭhāna* reorders perception—not abstractly, but intimately. It dissolves that subtle veil between awareness and experience. Suddenly, sorrow isn't just sorrow—it's movement, sensation, impermanence.

And joy, too, is stripped of intoxication. Everything becomes workable. The *Dhamma* becomes immediate. Leadership, from that ground, feels less like control—and more like attunement.

Aung San Suu Kyi: Yes, and that attunement is what protects us from cruelty disguised as necessity. Without *satipaṭṭhāna*, it's easy to confuse reactivity for resolve, or silence for peace. The practice reminds us to pause—not out of hesitation, but out of integrity. Every mindful breath becomes a vote for nonviolence.

Alan Clements: And *satipaṭṭhāna* isn't passive—it demands courage. To really observe the body, *kāyānupassanā*, or the mind in flux, cittānupassanā, is to see how often we reach for control, for permanence, for self. That shatters the spell of ideology.

I often wonder: how different would governance look if every leader were required to sit with their breath, their whole being, and examine their intentions before making decisions?

Aung San Suu Kyi: It would be revolutionary. Because *satipaṭṭhāna* doesn't just sharpen awareness—it refines motivation. In politics, it is easy to cloak self-interest in the language of service. But mindfulness unmasks that disguise. It shows us whether our actions are born of lobha, dosa, or moha—greed, hatred, or delusion—or from something purer. *Satipaṭṭhāna* is accountability at the level of consciousness.

Alan Clements: Exactly. It's where ethics and perception meet. And it's why I believe the practice isn't just therapeutic—it's insurgent. It exposes the mind's complicity in suffering. And if we're brave enough to see that, we can lead without exploitation. We can resist without becoming what we oppose.

Aung San Suu Kyi: And in that way, *satipaṭṭhāna* becomes a form of service. Quiet. Steady. Inwardly luminous. It teaches us how to be free even while unfree. That, to me, is the true test of any leadership—how one behaves when stripped of status, stripped of praise. When there is only awareness, intention, and response. That is where character is forged.

Alan Clements: Daw Suu, we've spoken many times of King Asoka—the emperor who once bathed in conquest, only to awaken to the folly of violence and become one of history's most luminous examples of ethical rule. His journey—from *Chand-Asoka*, the fierce and vengeful, to *Dhamma-Asoka*, the compassionate and wise—remains one of the rare moral inflection points in the annals of power.

It still astounds me: a sovereign capable of such cruelty choosing, in the aftermath of devastation, to renounce it. His remorse at *Kalinga* was not symbolic—it was seismic. A transformation of consciousness. *His rule became a living covenant with the Dhamma: to lead not by fear, but by the power of conscience.*

And now, as we speak, cruelty is once again unmasked across our world—in Gaza, where children's bodies lie buried beneath rubble; in Ukraine and Russia, where an escalating war grinds entire cities into grief; and in countless zones of violence, repression, and trauma that barely register beyond the flicker of a headline. Myanmar, too, remains gripped by terror.

From this place in our shared history—where moral collapse and political violence have become global epidemics—how do we revive the legacy of *Asoka*? How do we bring his turning into the bloodstream of modern Myanmar, and perhaps into the conscience of the world? How do we midwife such a transformation in our time?

Aung San Suu Kyi: Alan, the story of King Asoka is not a relic. It is a mirror. And a question posed to every leader, in every era: when you come face-to-face with your own capacity to harm—to dominate, to deceive, to destroy—do you cling to it? Or do you change?

Asoka's transformation was not merely political. It was psychological. Spiritual. He did not just halt a campaign of violence—he relinquished the worldview that had made it justifiable. He reimagined power as responsibility, not rule. And that is why his legacy endures—not because he triumphed, but because he awakened.

For Myanmar, this is not a historical lesson. It is a moral necessity.

Our revolution must undergo that same metamorphosis—not out of defeat, but through discernment.

Cetanā matters—intention shapes outcome. And so does *samādhi*—clarity that steadies the mind before it acts. If we are to rebuild our country from the ruins of atrocity, we must go beyond replacing tyranny with a new face. We must uproot its very logic. That means resisting not only bullets and propaganda, but also the subtle intoxication of vengeance.

Alan Clements: That distinction feels essential—not simply inverting tyranny, but transcending it. Because history shows us again and again: when the form changes but the mindset persists, the outcome remains the same.

Asoka's transformation wasn't the end of power—it was the purification of it. He governed not by threat, but by trust. His edicts carried not the weight of punishment, but the invitation to conscience. He institutionalized *karuṇā* and *mettā*. He used the machinery of state to support *sīla*, *samādhi*, and *paññā*—ethical conduct, steadiness of mind, and deep wisdom.

It makes me wonder—how many revolutions collapse not for lack of bravery, but for lack of inner reflection?

Aung San Suu Kyi: Yes, and that reflection must not be confined to books or monasteries. Wisdom is not abstract. It lives in action, in restraint, in the humility to feel the future in the choices we make today.

In Myanmar, cruelty surrounds us. But cruelty isn't confined to the junta. It takes root wherever the heart forgets its own tenderness. And so, the deepest revolution—*as we've often said*—must begin within.

Asoka's story reminds us that even the most brutal of histories can be interrupted by a single act of moral courage. That is why our movement must be guided not only by resistance, but by *Dhamma*. Not as decoration—but as design. Not as inspiration—but as infrastructure.

It must shape how we teach, how we heal, how we govern, how we forgive. *As Sayadawgyi often said: Dhammo have rakkhati dhammacārī—*

"The Dhamma protects those who protect it." That is not a slogan. It is a law of moral gravity.

If we build our nation on that foundation, then the freedom we birth will not just be a change in regime. It will be a change in consciousness.

Alan Clements: And that may be the most radical proposition of all—that liberation is not only the goal, but the method. The how determines the what. The seed shapes the fruit.

I think of the youth of Myanmar—risking their lives, forging new paths in the shadows of war. Many of them have never known peace. And yet, they are the authors of what comes next.

If Asoka's turning lives on, it will be because they dared to make one of their own. Not in blood, but in *paññā* and *mettā*. Not through conquest, but through conscience.

May that be the turning history remembers—not as destiny, but as deliberate decision.

Aung San Suu Kyi: Yes, and I would speak to them directly—our youth, our revolutionaries. I know you are tired. I know you carry grief like a second skin. But please, do not let the fire that fuels your courage burn away your humanity.

There will be moments when rage feels more honest than hope—when the call for vengeance feels louder than the voice of conscience. That is precisely when mindfulness matters most. Not as retreat, but as refuge. As protection from becoming what we oppose.

If this revolution is to birth something truly new, then let it begin within—by refusing to let fear, hatred, or despair shape our next generation of leaders. True victory is not found in purity, or certainty, or punishment. It is found in the difficult, daily work of choosing clarity over confusion, compassion over cruelty, and presence over despair. That, to me, is the real *Asokan* turning—one the junta can neither see nor stop.

Alan Clements: Daw Suu, one of Sayadawgyi's most intimate and powerful teachings was that we are related in four ways: as human beings, as world relatives, as beings bound by countless past lives, and as *Dhamma* companions. He said this understanding fosters compassion and mutual respect—that when we truly see one another through these lenses, we act differently.

He would often say, "It's natural for people to help each other, and this should be done without self-interest. One shouldn't want something in return. We should help with *mettā* and *karuṇā*." In today's world, where division has become doctrine and reactivity a reflex, how can this wisdom illuminate a new path—for Myanmar, and for the world?

Aung San Suu Kyi: Alan, Sayadawgyi's teachings on interconnection are more than spiritual truths—they are a call to live differently. To see ourselves as world relatives is to dissolve the false boundaries of nation, race, creed, and ideology. When we act with *mettā* and *karuṇā*—with loving-kindness and compassion—we transcend self-interest and touch the essence of our shared being.

Myanmar's struggle is not isolated. It echoes through every corner of the world where dignity is denied and truth is silenced. When we give without expecting return, we affirm the sacred bond of belonging. *Sayadawgyi's invocation—to give with the wish "May they be well; may they be happy"*—reminds us that true generosity flows not from surplus, but from a heart softened by empathy. This is the tenderness that sustains revolutions—and the quiet force that rebuilds nations.

To my fellow citizens, and to the world, I say this: Let us act not as strangers, but as *kalyāṇa mittā*—spiritual friends on the path. Bound not by blood, but by conscience. Let our actions be guided by love, by clarity, and by the joy of one another's freedom. Only then can we co-create a world where peace is not an abstraction, but a lived reality.

Alan Clements: Daw Suu, as we close this chapter, what final message would you offer—to the people of Myanmar, to the revolutionaries, and to a world that still watches from the shadows?

Aung San Suu Kyi: To the people of Myanmar: Hold fast to the *Dhamma*. Let it guide not only your resistance, but your relationships, your values, and your everyday choices. This revolution is not only about the fall of tyranny—it is about the rise of a conscience-based society. A nation where every life is honored and every voice heard.

To the revolutionaries: remember, the highest victory is self-mastery. Resist not only the junta, but also the pull of *lobha*, *dosa*, and *moha*—greed, hatred, and delusion. Let your courage be anchored in compassion. Let your strength be forged in humility. Lead with wisdom, not wrath.

And to the world: stand with us—not only in sentiment, but in solidarity. The fight for Myanmar's freedom is a thread in the tapestry of global justice. May we all cultivate the wisdom to see clearly, the compassion to act bravely, and the responsibility to shape a world where future generations may live, love, and flourish in peace.

Alan Clements: Thank you, Daw Suu, for your luminous vision and unwavering devotion to truth. May your words not only awaken the conscience of Myanmar, but stir the soul of our shared humanity—guiding us through these perilous times with the clarity of the *Dhamma*.

Aung San Suu Kyi: Thank you, Alan. May we all walk the path of Dhamma—with courage, with compassion, and with the faith to believe in a better world.

Alan Clements: And so, we conclude this extraordinary exchange—this sacred dialogue carried across silence and steel, from your solitude in captivity. I thank you from the depths of my heart: for all that you are, all that you have endured, and all that you continue to embody—not only for Myanmar, but for the conscience of the world.

Your life, your moral clarity, and your unshakable devotion to justice light a path of dignity for us all. May the radiance of your spirit—and the fearless heart of Myanmar's revolution—guide the birth of a future worthy of our noblest humanity: a future free from tyranny, from hatred, and from the blindness of indifference.

And may all those entrusted with power—now and in times to come—awaken to the sacred strength of redemption. Not as spectacle, but as sincerity. Not as weakness, but as the ultimate expression of humanity.

If there is one light I carry forward from this dialogue, Daw Suu, it is this: the revolutionary power of consciousness, of conscience, and of the courage to reclaim what is just and true.

Let this be our call: to reach into the deepest recesses of our being, to resurrect the virtues of *dāna*, *sīla*, and *bhāvanā*—generosity, ethical integrity, and inner cultivation—and from these roots, correct our wrongs, elevate our character, and embody the promise of peaceful coexistence.

From my heart to yours, Daw Suu: live on, luminous voice of truth. Live on, steadfast guardian of freedom. May your words ripple through the marrow of history and awaken every soul to its noblest potential.

Thank you. Thank you. Thank you.

Aung San Suu Kyi: Alan, thank you—for your friendship, your courage, and for being a revolutionary witness to our story. In the darkest times, it is the *Dhamma* that lights the way. Let it be our compass—guiding us through fear, through grief, and toward a future stitched with unity and compassion.

May we never forget our shared humanity. May we choose love over fear, wisdom over division, and action over despair. And may we live not just for ourselves—but for one another.

Together, we can rise—rooted in peace, anchored in justice, and nourished by freedom.

From my heart to yours, Alan—and to all who walk this path of hope: thank you. *Sādhu.*

**Playbook for Leadership Part 4:
Defiance and Discernment in the Dance of Freedom**

1. Mindful Intelligence: The Architecture of Clarity
2. Deep Listening: The Ear of the Divine Feminine
3. The Courage to Feel: Rebellion of the Heart
4. Truth as a Sacred Vow
5. The Generosity of Presence: Leadership as Gift
6. Resilience Through Equanimity: The Power of Poise
7. Compassion as Service: Love in the Face of Power
8. Vigilance Against Manipulation: Staying Awake in the Dark
9. Intuitive Wisdom: The Oracle of the Feminine Mind
10. Moral Integrity: The Soul's Unshakable Ground

This playbook rises from the ancient riverbed of human struggle and awakening—a current fed by many tributaries: the groves where the Buddha taught fearless discernment, the haunted streets of Orwell's Burma, and the blazing moral clarity of Václav Havel, Hannah Arendt, Noam Chomsky, and every other revolutionary who has lived throughout history, often paying the ultimate price for freedom. These voices, forged in the fires of dictatorship, exile, and inner revolution, do not simply urge us to resist tyranny—they call us to resist with intelligence, with compassion, and with the full depth of our shared humanity.

George Orwell, stationed in Insein Township near Rangoon, walked daily past the British-built prison that would later cage revolutionaries of another age. That same prison now holds voices that echo his warnings—its bricks steeped in silence, its walls humming with the songs of defiant hearts. Noam Chomsky exposes how *manufactured consent* becomes the machinery of mass deception, while Václav Havel, from his prison cell, reminded us that *"living in truth"* is itself a political act—one capable of toppling empires built on fear and illusion.

To these, I add the quiet brilliance of Sheldon Wolin, who named the creeping specter of *inverted totalitarianism*, where domination no longer marches in jackboots but wears the mask of normalcy, commerce, and consensus. And from my own decades of house arrest, and now imprisonment—where time became both mirror and fire—I offer what I have learned.

Leadership is not posture. It is not charisma. It is the willingness to suffer for love, to speak when silence is safer, and to walk barefoot through history with the dignity of one who listens deeply.

Here are ten attributes—drawn from my love of the *Dhamma*, the intuition of the feminine, and the lived wisdom of those who refused to bow. These attributes are not definitive. They are not meant to be. Each of us must discover what qualities nourish our moral imagination and sharpen our ethical clarity. Especially those in positions of leadership—I encourage you to reflect, question, and compose your own list. Make it real. Make it yours.

And of course, draw freely from mine. Expand it. Refine it. Let it grow into a living, breathing ecosystem—*an Earth-based World Dharma*—a sacred interdependence of inner and outer liberation. Let it keep evolving, pointing us toward higher and more nuanced expressions of freedom, mutuality, and peace.

Peace—not just for the powerful, but for the powerless. Not just for humans, but for animals, trees, rivers, insects, clouds. For the unborn. Let this be a playbook of care: a gesture of reverence for the miracle and madness of existence.

Let us remember Sayadaw's teaching: that we are related as human beings, as world relatives, as those who have shared past lives, and as *Dhamma* relatives. And I invite you to add a fifth: the vow to keep evolving our shared life—not merely to survive it, but to dignify it.

May this work benefit you and all beings, everywhere.

From my heart to yours,

Aung San Suu Kyi

NAYPYIDAW PRISON,

JULY 2025

1. Mindful Intelligence: The Cornerstone of Clarity

The *Kālāma Sutta* became my compass in 1988, when I first spoke to the people of my country at the Shwedagon Pagoda in Rangoon. The Buddha's counsel was clear: do not believe something merely because it is tradition, because it has been handed down, or because authority declares it so. Investigate it for yourself. Ask whether it leads to harm— or to freedom. That teaching, ancient and fiercely relevant, ignited a flame within me that has never dimmed.

In Orwell's world, the past is rewritten to suit the present. *"Who controls the past controls the future."* This isn't just literary prophecy—it is our reality. We see it now: in rigged elections, in deepfakes that blur fact and fiction, and in algorithms that nudge our thoughts before we've even had the chance to think.

Václav Havel urged what he called an *"existential revolution"*— to act in truth even when that truth seems politically futile. This is the revolution of clarity. Mindful intelligence is the ground of that revolution. It means pausing before reflex, examining before believing, and seeing the full landscape before moving forward.

MQ—the quotient of mindful intelligence—is the guardian of consciousness itself. It is the vigilant *Dhamma* ally stationed at the sense doors, ready not just to look, but to see. And from that seeing, to feel—

to touch the textures and frequencies of a moment; to keep feeling, and seeing, and knowing. To discern reality rightly. To see through the layers—through obscurations, through self-deception, through cognitive bias—into the luminous heart of what actually is.

And from that knowing, to ask with integrity: Does this harm or help? Does it elevate or diminish—myself, others, or both? And from there, to either restrain our thoughts and actions, or to engage them with care. To uplift. To serve. To participate—deliberately and bravely—in the long revolution toward freedom.

Playbook: Make time each day to question what is given—not just *Is this true?* but *Whom does this truth serve, and at whose expense?* Train your mind not merely to consume information, but to metabolize it—slowly, wisely—through the lens of freedom. Truth that is not examined becomes a tool of control. Freedom requires discernment. And discernment takes time.

Practice stillness not as retreat, but as reconnaissance. Let your awareness be both tender and incisive—intuitive, but unshaken by spectacle. Watch what arises at the sense doors. Listen for the manipulation folded into persuasion. Trace each impulse to its root. Refuse to be rushed. Refuse to be herded. Refuse to mistake noise for clarity.

Where the world commands react, pause. Where the powerful demand obedience, look closer. Where propaganda insists believe, go quiet—and examine. Learn to love complexity. Let your clarity come from your own direct seeing—deep, embodied, and uncorrupted by urgency or inheritance.

Mindful intelligence is not polite. It is radical. It questions what power prefers we accept. It does not flatter—it interrogates. It does not obey—it investigates. Let it be the still flame that outlives the storm. Let it be the compass that keeps your integrity whole—especially when compromise whispers in sweet tones.

Let it be your most revolutionary act: to stay awake.
"Freedom begins with the refusal to accept ignorance as truth, and fear as wisdom."

— AUNG SAN SUU KYI

2. Deep Listening: The Ear of the Divine Feminine

When I was silenced for 15 years by house arrest, and now in my fifth year of solitary confinement at age eighty, I was forced to listen differently. I listened to the chants of monks at dawn echoing faintly from a distant monastery. I listened to the hush between my footsteps on cold stone floors, to the stillness of empty rooms and shuttered windows. I listened to the heaviness in the air—how it carried the unspoken grief of a nation. I listened to the longings of a people denied dignity for generations.

But deeper still, I listened to the voice of my deceased mother—her devotion, her restraint, her strength. I listened for the distant echo of my father, whom I never truly knew, but whose blood, ideals, and sacrifice are etched into the marrow of this land. I listened to the memory of my beloved brother, who drowned in the lake when we were just children, playing in the water. I listened to their absence. To our unfinished conversations. To the ache of love across time. And in those silences, I came to understand that listening—true listening—is a sacred act. It is the ear of the Divine Feminine, and it hears not only sound, but suffering.

Authoritarianism thrives on noise—on the churn of propaganda, surveillance, distraction, and fear. Orwell's telescreens didn't just watch; they colonized the inner life. They drowned stillness in distortion. Noam Chomsky reminds us to listen for those voices silenced by power. Václav Havel believed that a true leader must first be a witness—one who listens not to command, but to understand. One who listens with conscience, with humility, and with the willingness to be changed.

Deep listening is not passive. It is both political and spiritual. It is the quiet defiance of paying attention in a world that trains us to interrupt, to react, to scroll past. It is the refusal to look away. It is the discipline of presence. It is holding silence long enough for truth to arise without agenda. To listen deeply is to push against the culture of noise. It is to reclaim the sacred space between words—the inner refuge where wisdom lives.

True listening suspends judgment. It seeks to understand before responding. Like a clear mirror, it reflects without distortion. It offers undivided attention as a form of reverence. It perceives the subtle interconnectedness of speaker and listener, dissolving the illusion of separation. Thich Nhat Hanh once said, *"In deep listening, you see that you and the other are not separate… this is interbeing."*

To listen like this is to stand at the edge of liberation—where silence becomes clarity, and clarity becomes compassion. In the revolution of spirit, deep listening is not soft. It is fierce. It is how the divine feminine holds the world to its truth—not with noise, but with presence. Not with domination, but with attention. And in that attention, something subtle but seismic shifts. Healing begins.

Playbook: Practice listening not as retreat, but as revolution. Listen as if the survival of truth depends on it—because it does. Let your ears become instruments of discernment, not just collection. Tune them not to volume, but to vulnerability. Listen for what trembles beneath the words. Attend to what is not said. Let silence speak. Let it clarify. Let it heal.

Begin where it hurts the most: with those whose voices unsettle you. Not to abandon your values, but to expand their application. Listen not for what confirms your convictions, but for what transforms your capacity to love without surrendering discernment. This is not comforting work—it is sacred confrontation. It asks for stillness, for humility, for the courage to be re-formed.

Each day, choose to inhabit a silence that isn't your own. Sit with a voice you might otherwise scroll past. Let it dwell in you long enough to feel where its truth intersects with your breath. Let deep listening carve new rooms in your being—rooms spacious enough to hold contradiction, complexity, and the full humanity of another.

Refuse the algorithm of outrage. Refuse the trance of performance. Let no one in your presence feel invisible. When you listen—truly listen—without rescuing, correcting, or deflecting, you become a sanctuary where truth can land, take root, and grow wings. You become the revolution's quiet, unshakeable center.

Let your attention be so clean, so fierce, so still—it becomes a preserve no tyranny can touch. Let it be your act of rebellion, your offering of presence, your embodied prayer for a world where every voice is heard with dignity, and every silence is met with care.

"In the stillness of my captivity, I heard the people speak. They taught me how to lead."
— AUNG SAN SUU KYI

3. Courage to Feel: The Heart's Rebellion

In every true revolution, there comes a moment when feeling becomes both unbearable and essential. Not sentimentality, but moral clarity—a refusal to go numb in the face of overwhelming sorrow.

In my own captivity, I did not cry for myself. I cried for the mothers whose children were disappeared. For the tortured. For the faceless ones buried without names. Grief, when allowed to speak, becomes a deeper kind of strength. It becomes a sacred fuel—one that does not burn out, but burns through.

George Orwell didn't just warn us about authoritarianism; he warned us about emotional anesthesia—the slow erosion of conscience through the normalization of cruelty. His work reminds us that tyranny does not begin with violence. It begins when violence no longer moves us.

Viktor Frankl, speaking from the evil of Auschwitz, taught that the last of human freedoms is the ability to choose one's response— even in the midst of suffering. And that response, I believe, begins with presence. With feeling. James Baldwin reminded us that *the interior life is the real life.* Courage begins there—not in slogans or spectacle, but in the quiet, private willingness to let suffering break us open.

But to grieve does not mean to collapse. It does not mean to be swept away by despair. True grieving is not drowning—it is knowing. It is feeling sorrow fully without being consumed by it. It is the choice to touch pain with dignity, to witness it without fleeing, and then— through that intimate contact—to rise. Grief becomes sacred when it deepens our compassion rather than closing our hearts. It becomes powerful when it sharpens our discernment and expands our sense of responsibility.

In Soviet prison camps, dissidents like Nadezhda Mandelstam and Anatoly Marchenko preserved their humanity not by hardening, but by feeling. By grieving. Remembering. Writing. They made sorrow a sanctuary for the soul—a way to remain human in places designed to erase humanity.

That is the courage I speak of. Not bravado. Not rage. But the fierce, unflinching refusal to become indifferent. The heart's rebellion against the machinery of forgetting. To feel is to remember that we are still alive—and still free.

Playbook: Let yourself feel what the world has taught you to silence. Not for drama—but for direction. Let sorrow point you toward what matters. Let joy remind you why it's worth it. Feelings are not interruptions to your strength—they are entrances to it.

Start where it hurts. Not to suffer for suffering's sake, but to stay honest. Numbness is not strength—it's surrender in disguise. Feel fully, then rise taller for having dared to go inward. Let the ache teach you how to hold space—for yourself, and for others.

When anger rises, ask what grief lies beneath. When grief floods you, ask what truth it carries. Let no feeling go unexamined. Let no pain pass without purpose. In a world that rushes us toward reaction, choose reflection instead.

Create a space—daily, even briefly—where no mask is required. Let your inner world breathe without performance. That breath is your rebellion. That breath is where your heart reclaims its authority.

Feeling is not collapse. It is continuation. Let your heart remain open enough to break—and strong enough to carry others with it. Let emotion be your compass, not your cage. Let it guide you through the dark—not away from it.

"What is to give light must endure burning."
— VIKTOR FRANKL

4. Truth as a Sacred Vow

Truth is not a tactic. It is a vow. A discipline of the heart. A sacred act of fidelity to reality, made in full view of consequence. I learned this under the uncompromising gaze of Sayadaw U Pandita. His silence— when I softened my speech to make it more palatable—cut sharper than any rebuke. The Buddha called it *sacca*—a truthfulness that purifies perception and clarifies the mind. It is not about winning an argument. It is about remaining real—unshakably real—in a world allergic to honesty.

Orwell's *2 + 2 = 5* is not merely a lie—it is a declaration of dominion over reality itself. A dismantling of the shared fabric of meaning. It is the weaponization of fiction. Noam Chomsky revealed how mass media can engineer consent not just through falsehood, but by smothering dissent in layers of omission and distortion. Václav Havel understood that truth could be dangerous—even fatal—yet insisted that *"even a single word of truth can shatter a world of lies."* To speak truth in public is not merely communication—it is rebellion. It is risk. It is conscience made audible.

Elie Wiesel, speaking from the ashes of genocide, reminded us that neutrality in the face of injustice is not neutral at all. *"Silence encourages the tormentor, never the tormented,"* he wrote. In his voice, truth became testimony. A candle lit in a room full of denial. A flicker that dared to endure.

In times of terror, truth does not whisper—it rings. A leader's responsibility is not to console with illusions, but to illuminate with integrity. Even when that illumination endangers their comfort, their reputation, their safety. Especially then. Truth is not about certainty. It is about fidelity—to what is, to what matters, to one another. Even when the cost is exile, prison, or loss.

And always, it is a choice. Do we distort to protect ourselves—or do we stand firm? Vulnerable. Visible. Awake.

Playbook: Tell the truth even when it shakes your voice. When it complicates your alliances. When it dismantles the story, you wish were real. Speak it not to provoke, but to clarify—like fire in the fog. Truth, when spoken cleanly, cuts through distortion without spectacle. Let it be steady. Let it be unsparing. Let it be kind—without compromise.

Write one thing each day that is difficult to admit. Say one thing each week that risks discomfort. Not recklessly, but reverently. Let truth become your spiritual hygiene—a daily clearing of illusion, a burning through the subtle corrosion of appeasement. The cost of silence is often greater than the cost of discomfort.

And when you are tempted to remain silent—not from wisdom, but from fear—remember this: silence, too, is a sentence. *Elie Wiesel said it best*: *"I swore never to be silent whenever and wherever human beings endure suffering and humiliation."* Let your voice join his. Not as echo, but as vow.

Truth spoken aloud is not just information. It is transmission. It is structure. It is revolution. Let your words be the bones of freedom. Let them carry weight. Let them ring so true they make denial impossible.

"The ideal subject of totalitarian rule is not the convinced Nazi or the convinced Communist, but people for whom the distinction between fact and fiction... no longer exists."
— HANNAH ARENDT

5. Generosity of Spirit: The Gift of Presence

After the 2021 coup, it was not the generals who defined our history—it was the students, the nurses, the poets, the farmers, the teachers, the monks and nuns, the mothers, and the children who rose with bare hands and burning hearts. Our Spring Revolution began not with weapons, but with presence—the kind of presence that says: We are here. We will not disappear. We are not afraid to be seen. That presence is not performance—it is power.

That revolution—our Spring Revolution—continues now. It pulses across jungles, villages, classrooms, prison cells, and refugee camps. Its strength lies not in violence, but in fidelity to conscience. In a world ruled by extraction, where every act is measured by return, to stand in truth—with no guarantee of success—is a sacred kind of rebellion. To offer yourself in this way is to practice generosity not as charity, but as conviction.

Orwell's Party clung to power "for its own sake," draining meaning from every word and gesture. Chomsky warns us of systems that hoard influence while starving the soul. But the divine feminine moves in the opposite direction—it does not cling, it overflows. It gives without calculation. It nourishes without depletion. This is what Havel, Mandela, and Gandhi embodied: their legacies were not merely political, but deeply personal. They offered themselves. *Presence was their gift.*

True leadership is not domination from above. It is descent into shared humanity. It is the act of saying: I am here. Fully. No distraction. No agenda. No façade. Just the courage to be radically available—to the moment, to others, to truth itself.

This kind of presence cannot be faked. It does not posture. It does not barter. It does not seek applause. It is a devotional posture of the soul—generosity stripped of ego. In its stillness lives a revolution. In its humility, a force no tyranny can touch.

Playbook: Start small. Offer your full attention to someone who has been made to feel invisible—not out of pity, but out of equality. When you walk into a room, ask yourself: Who here has not been seen? And then, truly see them. Let your gaze become a quiet act of justice.

Withhold nothing of your humanity when it matters most. Sit beside grief without fixing it. Stand inside tension without fleeing. Let your stillness say what words cannot: You are not alone. Presence does not require eloquence—it requires courage. It asks us to show up without needing to control or repair.

Presence is not a performance. It is a practice. And generosity is not what you give—it is how you arrive. In a transactional world, let your presence be unbuyable. Let it carry no price, no pretense, no demand for recognition.

Go where power refuses to go. That is the revolution. That is the gift. Not grand gestures, but daily availability. Not spotlight, but sanctuary. Let your life become a place where others feel safe enough to be fully seen.

"There can be no greater gift than that of giving one's time and energy to help others without expecting anything in return."
— NELSON MANDELA

6. Resilience Through Equanimity

Through years of solitude—fifteen of them under house arrest, and now nearly five in solitary confinement— *upekkhā*—equanimity — became my constant companion. It is not detachment; it is disciplined presence. The ability to hold joy and sorrow in the same breath, without clinging to either. It is the stillness beneath the noise, the steady hand in the quake, the breath that doesn't flinch.

In Orwell's *1984*, Winston is not broken by pain—he is broken by the collapse of his inner ground. He had no refuge within. He surrendered not his body, but his soul. Václav Havel, even in prison, kept his spine upright because he lived from a deeper truth. Hannah

Arendt warned us that the greatest threat to freedom is not brute force, but thoughtlessness—the slow erosion of discernment, the absence of inner anchoring.

Equanimity gives us that anchor. It is the clarity to feel without drowning, to act without reacting. It is the strength to remain intimate with chaos without being undone by it. To breathe inside the fire without being consumed. To weep and still stand. To be wounded, and still love.

Playbook: Return to your inner axis before returning to the fight. When chaos erupts, locate your breath. When outrage surges, touch your stillness. Do not lose your shape in a shape-shifting world. Presence is not passivity—it is precision. It is how we respond without being reduced, how we move without being moved off course.

Be like water when challenged, like stone when tested. Flow where needed. Stand where it matters. Let your calm unsettle tyrants. Let it be the silence that cannot be provoked, the stillness that does not yield. Equanimity is not retreat—it is mindful resilience. It is how you carry fire without burning, how you hold pain without becoming bitter, and how you stay open when the world tries to shut you down.

"Stillness is not escape—it is a form of resistance that power cannot touch."
— AUNG SAN SUU KYI

7. *Mettā*: The Courage of Compassion

Mettā—loving-kindness—is not soft. It is not sentiment. It is not a retreat from conflict, but a courageous entry into it—with eyes open and hands outstretched. *Metta-filled compassion* is not the absence of anger; it is the refusal to allow anger to close the heart. It is the strength to protect without becoming cruel, to feel rage without losing grace, and to endure without becoming numb.

I did not fight for position. I fought for people. I did not seek to rule. I sought to safeguard what could not speak for itself—the children of silence, the fragile breath of truth, the dignity that dictators try to erase.

Václav Havel said that politics must be guided by conscience, not convenience. Orwell showed us that isolation breeds control—that when we are cut off from each other, we are easier to manipulate.

Chomsky reminds us to stand in solidarity with those the world treats as disposable.

And the *Dhamma* teaches us this: to witness suffering and do nothing is to abandon one's own humanity. Real leadership does not soothe pain with platitudes. It enters the wound. It dignifies the vulnerable. It does not ask, *How can I appear compassionate?* It asks, *Who is suffering, and how can I serve?* Compassion is not the opposite of power. It is what redeems it. It is what transforms authority into shelter, presence into protection, and action into care.

Playbook: Start with proximity. Move closer to what hurts—not to fix, but to witness. Do not wait until it is safe to care. Do not wait until it is fashionable to stand beside the broken. Ask not, *What can I win?* but, *Whom can I help rise?* What voice can I amplify? What dignity can I restore simply by being near? Speak not to be heard, but to uplift. Speak like someone who remembers how sacred another person's pain is.

Make your policies into prayers. Let your plans hold people like hands. Let every act of leadership be a kind of tending—a mending of the torn, a guarding of the sacred. Let your ambition be not dominance, but devotion. Let your vision extend beyond outcomes to embodiment. Let your presence feel like protection. *Let your legacy be this*: *wherever you walked, people felt more human—not less.*

"Love and compassion are necessities, not luxuries. Without them, humanity cannot survive."
— HIS HOLINESS THE 14TH DALAI LAMA

8. Vigilance Against Manipulation: The Warrior's Watchfulness

To lead is to stay awake. *Jāgariya*—vigilant awareness—is not anxiety. It is not the hypervigilance born of trauma, but the lucidity born of devotion. It is the disciplined willingness to see without flinching—to perceive the world not as it is framed for us, but as it actually functions. True vigilance is not suspicion. It is sacred discernment. It keeps perception sharp, compassion grounded, and conscience intact.

Orwell's Newspeak wasn't just censorship—it was the erasure of moral imagination. It made dissent not only dangerous, but unthinkable. Chomsky's enduring question—*Who benefits?* —remains a compass in an age of curated outrage and designer truths. Sheldon Wolin warned that spectacle is not merely distraction—it is anesthesia, numbing the soul while power consolidates in silence.

Vigilance is not paranoia—it is love refusing to fall asleep. It is a moral posture. A fierce refusal to be lulled. It protects not only against external deception, but internal complicity. To lead with vigilance is to be a lantern in the dark—calm, aware, unwilling to look away.

Playbook: Look beneath every headline. Question every convenience. In every policy, trace both the profit and the pain. Ask not just what is said, but what is concealed. Ask again and again: *Who profits? Who pays? Who vanishes when the lights come on?*

Stay awake—not only for yourself, but for those who cannot afford to sleep. Your clarity may be the shield someone else needs. Your discernment may become their refuge. Do not confuse noise for knowledge, or consensus for truth. Stay awake as protest. Stay awake as prayer. Stay awake as love.

"The smart way to keep people passive and obedient is to strictly limit the spectrum of acceptable opinion."
— NOAM CHOMSKY

9. Intuitive Wisdom: The Feminine Oracle

Paññā—wisdom—is not intellect. It is not accumulation. It is integration—truth known from the inside out. It ripens in silence. It clarifies through stillness. It lives not in the stream of thought, but in the intuition between perception and response. It is the kind of knowing that neither performs nor persuades—because it recognizes what is essential.

This is the wisdom that steadied me in Parliament when facts failed. That whispered to Havel in his prison cell. That anchored Rosa Parks in her refusal. That pierced Simone Weil in her hunger for God and truth. It is not loud. It is elemental. The voice of soul beneath the voice of self.

As artificial minds outpace our logic, we must return to the original source: the body's knowing, the heart's quiet clarity. *Intuitive wisdom is not louder than reason—but it is truer.* It does not compete with fact—it completes it. It slows the rush to act. It listens before it speaks.

It senses before it decides. In a world addicted to speed, that alone is a revolution.

Playbook: Make solitude your teacher. Step back from the sound—not to disappear, but to remember what is real. Let the body speak before the brain begins its debate. Let intuition interrupt your strategy. Let quietness write your next move.

Trust what arrives in stillness. Trust the pause, the hunch, the ache. Not because it's safe, but because it's sacred. When the world demands certainty, listen instead for what feels quietly true. This is not passivity—it is poise. The deep feminine wisdom that moves like water—and shapes stone.

"I am not afraid… I was born to do this."

— JOAN OF ARC

10. Moral Integrity: The Soul's Anchor

Sila—moral discipline—is not appearance. It is not posture or performance. It is not reputation or rhetoric. It is a vow to the unshakable ground beneath you, even when that ground costs everything. I was offered safety in exchange for silence. I refused. Not because I was fearless—but because I could not betray what I knew to be true. Integrity, in that moment, was not courage—it was fidelity.

Orwell showed us how language can be weaponized—how meaning can be twisted, how virtue can become camouflage for violence. Chomsky warns us that integrity is often smeared as extremism—because a principled person cannot be controlled. And Havel reminded us: *to live in truth is to build a republic of spirit—one brave, invisible act at a time.*

Integrity is what remains when the applause stops. It is the decision made in silence, when no reward is promised and every cost is real. It is the refusal to betray your soul when no one is watching.

Playbook: When seduction whispers comfort, choose clarity. When power offers favor, return to your core. Let your principles outlast your popularity. Let your values be sturdier than your platform. Be the compass others trust in the dark—not because you're flawless, but because you're faithful.

Say no when it matters. Say yes when it costs you. Let your name become synonymous not with status, but with steadiness. In a time of erosion, let your integrity be the shoreline—not resisting the tide, but defining it. And when doubt arises, ask: *Can I live with this?* If the answer falters, turn back. That turning is not failure—it is strength to begin again. Anchored. Awake. Whole.

"You must never be fearful about what you are doing when it is right."
— ROSA PARKS

A CLOSING INVOCATION

This is not a doctrine. It is not a final word. It is a field guide—spoken not from exile, but from the heart. A meditation offered in the darkness of solitary confinement. A thread of breath passed between those who still have voice and those who have been silenced. Between the living and the lost. Between those who endure, and those who will never be forgotten.

As I said in the opening, and I will reiterate again here:

This is not a book of prescriptions. It is a vow. A vow to truth, to care, to conscience. A vow to meet this moment—however brutal, however uncertain—with the full weight of our humanity. A vow not to abandon each other.

Take from this what nourishes you. Leave what does not. Above all—create your own. Let this be not a script, but a mirror. Not a rulebook, but a call. A call to innovate, to listen deeply, and to lead with your own fierce clarity. There is no single path to liberation—only many footfalls, converging.

I offer this in the shadow of devastation. In a country scarred by earthquake, war, and the systematic targeting of its own people. Five years into a terror campaign unleashed by a rogue general, we find ourselves still breathing. Still resisting. Still hoping.

This is for the teachers who whispered banned history to children in secret. For the artists who painted truth on walls that were torn down by morning. For the nurses who treated the wounded in silence and shadow. For the mothers who lit candles before dawn, whispering: May my child return.

Leadership, as I have learned, is not a crown to be worn. It is the act of staying human while the world tries to make you forget what that means. It is refusing to abandon your conscience—even when silence is safer. It is choosing devotion over dominance. Clarity over convenience. Presence over power.

I stand not alone, but on the shoulders of many. Of Václav Havel and Hannah Arendt. Of Nelson Mandela and Desmond Tutu. Of Martin Luther King Jr., Rosa Parks, and Malcolm X. Of Simone Weil, Rigoberta Menchú, Liu Xiaobo, and Andrei Sakharov. Of Elie Wiesel. Of the Dalai Lama. Of Thich Nhat Hanh. Of Aung San—my father—whose dream of a free Burma remains unfinished, but never forgotten.

Let this be your invitation—not to imitate, but to illuminate. Let your truth take a shape that is yours. Let your resistance look like care. Let your creativity become a weapon no regime can touch. Sing. Paint. March. Mend. Farm. Teach. Breathe.

The soul of Myanmar will not be saved by saviors. It will be saved by kinship. By conscience. By collective care. It will be saved by those who refuse to forget one another.

So let this not be the end. Let it be a vow. Let it be the offering before the next beginning.

The elephant of our shared destiny rises.

See it not as burden, but as blessing.

Feel its weight, its majesty, its sorrow—and walk beside it.

Not as masters. But as stewards. As servants. As those who remember that the future—if it is to be free—must be carried not alone, but together.

And to my beloved people:

May you be safe.

May you be strong.

May you be seen.

May you be free.

With *mettā*, always—

Aung San Suu Kyi

504

BREAKING THE MIND OF BIG BROTHER

Author's Prelude

In the deepest recesses of oppression—where truth is stalked, thought outlawed, and even breath is shadowed—there dwells a silence that refuses to yield. It listens. It observes. It endures. It remembers. It dreams. And when the world forsakes its memory, this silence does not fade—it begins to sing.

This chapter emerges from that sacred silence.

Here, beneath the iron tread and garish banners of tyranny, we probe not merely the visage of dictatorship—but its psyche. Not as conjecture, but as anatomy. Not to inflame with rage, but to illuminate for liberation. For only by discerning the architecture of delusion can we dismantle the machinery of subjugation. What we fail to comprehend, we are fated to obey.

What follows is not mere testimony. It is mirror and scalpel, witness and blade. It is a reckoning with the inner mechanisms of domination—the allure of compliance, the orchestration of dread, the weaponization of language, and the fabrication of silence masquerading as peace.

This is not retribution. It is lucidity. It is an invocation to reclaim what no regime can seize: our conscience, our kinship, our clarity, and our sacred right to dissent.

To engage these pages is to reawaken: To affirm that the flame they sought to entomb was never theirs to extinguish. That love, rooted in *Dhamma*, the path of awakening, outlasts every dominion of fear. That liberation is not bestowed—it is perceived, claimed, lived.

Let this chapter be your summons—not merely to awaken,
but to see through,
to see inward,
to see free.

◆ ◆ ◆

Alan Clements: Daw Suu, here we are—not at an end, but arriving at the close of this extraordinary journey. But your struggle lives on. The enduring courage of your people lives on. This dialogue may conclude in words, but the truth it carries continues—far beyond these pages.

You have spoken from within a cell—cut off from the world, injured, in pain, denied the balm of medicine, the warmth of visitors, the comfort of voice—and yet, your being resounds with a quiet majesty.

Not merely unbroken, but luminous. You have transfigured solitude into sanctuary, captivity into conscience, silence into testament.

In this fifth year of isolation, you remain wholly present—composed, unwavering, profoundly awake. Not as a figure of resistance alone, but as a living embodiment of the *Dhamma's* deepest vow: to meet suffering without retreat, and to turn even the darkest confinement into a mirror of love, wisdom, and invincible grace.

And from the deepest part of my being—thank you. What a living testament you are to the power of the human heart—not only to endure complexity, but to elevate it into a crowning jewel of moral clarity. Thank you for the gift that you are.

Through you, the light of every one of the 22,000 political prisoners shines. Through your spirit, the breath of every revolutionary in this land finds voice. Your words are not merely echoes from confinement—they are courage, they are grace, they are uprising. You have given the world a sacred example of what it means to be free, even when shackled. And for that, for all of it, I thank you.

As we've reflected earlier, George Orwell once walked these same roads. But what he imagined in fiction, we have come to know in flesh. From 1922 to 1927, he served in Burma as a colonial police officer, witnessing firsthand the mechanisms of imperial control.

Those years shaped his vision of Big Brother—not as metaphor, but as warning. And now, nearly a century later, that warning lives again. The uniforms have changed, but the machinery of domination remains. The surveillance, the censorship, the erasure of memory—all sharpened by new technologies, but rooted in the same hunger for obedience. What Orwell feared might come, Myanmar now endures.

And yet we also inherit another vision—one offered by our beloved Sayadaw U Pandita, who spoke of a sacred compass to guide our lives: a fourfold bond—human, global, karmic, and dhammic. That vision still guides me. It reminds me that we are never alone in our suffering, nor in our striving for freedom.

So please, Daw Suu, let us begin there. Through those four sacred relationships *Sayadawgyi* taught us to honor, how do you see the consciousness of the regime today? What is it doing—to Myanmar, and to our shared world?

Aung San Suu Kyi: Alan, your words carry the weight of both love and clarity. They speak not only of grief, but of responsibility—and of deep companionship through the long night of injustice. Thank you. From the silence of this cell, where so much has been stripped away, your acknowledgment means more than I can say.

But let me also speak plainly: I do not see myself as exceptional. Whatever strength I've shown, it is a reflection—an echo—of the strength of millions who suffer far more than I. The parents who bury their children and keep going. The young who carry medicine through war zones. The monks who chant in bombed-out monasteries. My solitude is heavy, yes—but their burden is immeasurable. And I carry their courage with me, every day.

Orwell may have envisioned Big Brother, but we have lived beneath his gaze. We've heard his voice in schoolbooks, felt his shadow in our homes, and seen his silence made law in our courts.

But what matters more than recognizing the face of tyranny is understanding its roots. The regime's consciousness is not simply political—it is psychological. It is spiritual, in the most distorted sense. It is fear made institutional.

You, Alan, perhaps more than anyone I've known, have studied not only the strategies of oppression but the mind behind them—the illusions they depend on to survive. You've walked through the darkness not to become it, but to expose the light it fears.

When we look through Sayadaw's fourfold lens—*human, global, karmic, dhammic*—we begin to see that dictatorship is not merely a system; it is a moral rupture.

On the *human* level, it denies the sanctity of life. It sees people not as beings of dignity, but as tools of utility. It brutalizes dissent, erases identities, turns names into numbers.

On the *global* level, it severs connection, isolates the nation, contaminates diplomacy. It fears the mirror of international conscience.

On the *karmic* level, it feeds the cycle of delusion, greed, and hatred—each act of repression planting seeds for future suffering.

And on the *dhammic* level, it is a betrayal of everything noble. It rejects *hiri* and *ottappa*—healthy shame and wise fear—as weakness, when in truth, they are the mind's immune system against cruelty.

But perhaps the greatest threat of Big Brother is not his presence, but his infiltration—into the minds of those he dominates. When people begin to silence themselves, to distrust their own thoughts, to forget the feel of their own conscience—that is when dictatorship wins most deeply.

Our revolution, therefore, is not only political. It is inner. It is the restoration of moral imagination. The reclamation of thought. The recovery of voice. The elevation of creativity. It is the courage to see clearly and feel fully—even when doing so hurts.

To break the mind of Big Brother, we must become minds unafraid of freedom. Minds that see without illusion, act without hatred, and love without needing permission. This is the real revolution—not one of slogans, but of liberated seeing. It begins with self-awareness, deepened through wise reflection. It ripens in truth, nourished by discernment.

Even when we feel hated, we must still learn to act—not react, but act—mindfully. For in the very act of conscious response, hatred begins to lose its grip. It is displaced by presence. It is undone by care. In choosing awareness over vengeance, we reclaim our humanity—and deny the oppressor their ultimate victory.

And it blooms in compassionate action—steadfast, fearless, and free. Rooted in *Dhamma*. Inseparable from love.

Alan Clements: If I may, Daw Suu—amid the silence and distortion of reality forced upon you, how do you remain anchored in truth—untouched, if it's possible, by the toxicity of their deception and their psychic violence?

Aung San Suu Kyi: Alan, that question reaches into the marrow of what it means to survive—not merely physically, but with one's conscience intact.

I would not say I remain untouched. No one is. To live under prolonged captivity, where silence is weaponized and reality is rewritten, is to be immersed in a form of existential warfare. But the *Dhamma* teaches us: what touches the mind need not stain the heart. And so, I listen—not to their words, but to the quality of presence within myself.

Each day, I return to the only sanctuary they cannot confiscate: self-awareness. With every breath, I reclaim—however humbly—the sovereign space between stimulus and response, that sacred interval where freedom begins. As Viktor Frankl once wrote, it is there that choice is born. And in that choice, truth remembers itself. Not as doctrine. But as presence. As the quiet courage to remain whole in a world built to fracture us.

Alan Clements: Daw Suu, when truth is not just obscured but actively outlawed—when distortion becomes the currency of daily life—how do you continue to discern what is real, and protect that knowing from being buried?

Aung San Suu Kyi: There are moments Alan, when the fog is thick— when lies are not only told, but enforced as law, as curriculum, as common sense. That is where jāgariya, vigilant awareness, becomes essential. I reflect: Is this mine, or has it been planted? Is this thought born of wisdom, or is it a disguise for fear?

As I've explained in the Playbook, *mindful intelligence is the cornerstone of clarity.* I hold that clarity like a lantern in the dark. Not to accuse, but to illuminate. I write things down—small details. A rustle of leaves beyond the bars. The tone in a guard's voice. The silence after a question goes unanswered. These become my anchors to what is real.

And I remember—*truth is not a weapon, but a vow.* It does not need to be shouted. It needs only to be lived, moment by moment, in the choices I make—not to hate, not to numb, not to forget who I am. *As Sayadaw U Pandita taught us, even a single breath, taken mindfully, can hold the weight of a nation's dignity.*

Compassion becomes my form of defiance. Not the soft kind, but the kind that dares to see humanity even in those who would strip me of mine. That is not acquiescence. It is moral clarity. It is the heart's refusal to become what it opposes.

So, no—I am not untouched. But I am not undone. I fall. I cry. I begin again. And again. Rooted not in certainty, but in conscience. Guided not by power, but by poise. As I've said before: to lead is to stay human when the world demands otherwise. That is my vow. That is my practice. That is my freedom.

Alan Clements: Daw Suu, thank you—for sharing from the depths of your being. Each word you've offered is a light of moral clarity in a world increasingly veiled in confusion. I remain deeply honored to be in dialogue with you here.

And I pray—sincerely—that your voice, forged in the cruel silence of solitary prison and radiant with love, reaches far beyond these pages. May it offer others the strength to endure, the insight to awaken, and the inspiration to carry on—especially your beloved revolutionary family here in Myanmar: the 22,000 political prisoners held in the junta's gulags, and the millions more who resist—day by day, breath by breath—with unwavering courage.

If I may, I'd like to return, just for a moment, to the beginning of this current chapter in Myanmar's long and unfinished story—February 1, 2021. The day of General Min Aung Hlaing's military coup. The day one man—blinded by delusion, intoxicated by power—committed not only a political betrayal, but what may be remembered as one of the gravest moral catastrophes in the history of your nation. It was not just the theft of a government. It was the attempted erasure of a people's dignity. And history will not forget.

He cowardly gave the order—for you to be taken, cut off, imprisoned—along with every other lawfully elected democratic leader. And yet, across the country, something extraordinary unfolded. In the face of tanks and terror, the people rose. Not for ideology, but for dignity. For memory. For one another.

Please allow me to read an excerpt from *The Irrawaddy*—a passage that, for me, brings that fateful moment vividly back to life.

◆ ◆ ◆

Excerpt from The Irrawaddy
Published March 2021

In recent weeks, Myanmar has been transformed into a battleground: peaceful protesters gunned down with lethal precision; streets streaked with blood; cities reverberating with gunfire, the air thick with tear gas and gunsmoke. Medics and rescue workers have been assaulted. Security forces, armed for combat, stand poised to kill more unarmed civilians. This brutal crackdown shows no sign of abating.

Before Feb. 1, Myanmar's cities were relatively peaceful, and the country enjoyed tentative stability. That changed abruptly when a military coup, led by Senior General Min Aung Hlaing, seized power in the early hours of Feb. 1, plunging the nation into chaos. The coup halted a fragile decade-long transition to democracy, aiming to nullify the Nov. 8, 2020, general election—a landslide victory for the National League for Democracy (NLD)—and to prevent the new Parliament from convening.

The junta arrested NLD leaders, including State Counsellor Daw Aung San Suu Kyi and President U Win Myint, both democratically elected. The consequences were immediate: Myanmar's emerging economy contracted sharply and everyday life was upended. Hope for the future dimmed for young and old alike.

But the people resisted.

Within days, Myanmar's citizens—led by students and youth—took to the streets to reclaim their rights and restore their vision of a democratic future. Hundreds of thousands joined, forming a nationwide uprising against military rule.

Then the lethal shooting began.

Myanmar's streets became a killing field.

Yet, this violence has failed to suppress the movement. Killing unarmed civilians, alongside arrests and intimidation, has not deterred protesters—it has emboldened them, particularly the youth.

That courage is rooted in Myanmar's history and its people's resolve.

On Feb. 28, during a nationwide general strike, security forces killed at least 18 people across the country, according to the United Nations. On March 3, at least 38 more protesters were killed in multiple cities, per credible reports from local monitoring groups.

Every one of those protesters knew the risks. They left their homes aware that death was a real possibility.

Kyal Sin, 19, was among the most courageous. She was shot in the head while protesting in Mandalay on March 3. Anticipating the danger, she had posted her blood type on Facebook and pledged her organs for donation in the event of her death.

She died demanding her rights as a young citizen: the right to a future and to freely elect her leaders. In the 2020 election, she cast her first ballot for the NLD, proudly sharing a photo on Facebook, smiling beside her father with their ink-stained fingers raised.

Since the crackdown began, many young protesters have followed her example, writing emergency contacts and blood types on their arms before marching.

Kyal Sin is one of at least 54 protesters killed by security forces since Feb. 1, according to local human rights organizations. These targeted killings have not broken the movement—they have galvanized it.

On March 4, Mandalay's streets filled again as thousands attended Kyal Sin's funeral. Known as "Pure Star" in Burmese, she has become a symbol of resistance. Her death did not diminish courage; it inspired it.

On March 5, protests surged in Mandalay. Another young man was killed. Still, the people showed no sign of fear. Across Myanmar, citizens are proving their unyielding bravery.

Their fight persists, and tragically, so does the killing. The violence won't end soon.

I was a high sckool student during the 1988 uprising. I remember our motto: "They die, or we die." It meant that their sacrifice ensured our victory, or their victory meant our end.

That motto has evolved. The younger generation now chants: *"They die, or they die."* With defiant resolve and Gen Z tenacity, it signals a refusal to let the revolution falter. Their determination to end military dictatorship is unwavering. They believe victory is inevitable.

As of March 6, the regime has not regained control. It has failed to quash the resistance: massive street protests, led by Generation Z; the Civil Disobedience Movement (CDM), driven by civil servants and workers; the political efforts of the Committee Representing Pyidaungsu Hluttaw (CRPH); and public campaigns targeting junta supporters.

This is a lopsided conflict: a heavily armed military regime versus an unarmed people. History suggests the outcome is predictable.

But Myanmar's resilient people defy that history. Even as their comrades are killed, tortured, or imprisoned, they persist. The killing fields may claim more lives like Kyal Sin's, but the movement's spirit will continue to resist—with determination, resilience, and the unquenchable fire of a revolution that refuses to die.

Their motto holds: *They die, or they die.*

◆ ◆ ◆

Alan Clements: Daw Suu, reading The Irrawaddy's account of Myanmar's crisis forces a moment of reckoning. The unimaginable has become routine: unarmed youth shot through the head; streets running red; a generation marking their blood types on their arms as they face gunfire. Yet, amid this horror, we've witnessed extraordinary courage— Kyal Sin, students, monks, medics, ordinary citizens who refuse to break.

What began as a coup has spiraled into nationwide slaughter. The atrocity deepens daily, shattering the soul. Yet your people rise, fueling a revolution to topple Senior General Min Aung Hlaing and dismantle the junta's grip.

I ask you, Daw Suu—not as a journalist, but as someone grappling to comprehend: How do we endure this? How do we learn from it? And above all, how do we prevent it—here or anywhere—when dictatorship often arrives not with tanks, but cloaked in promises, striking where no one expects?

Your words are more than memory. They are a beacon—for Myanmar and for any people facing the creeping shadow of tyranny. The world needs that light now.

Aung San Suu Kyi: Your question weaves the raw pain of Myanmar's recent wounds with the enduring threat of tyranny.

In February 2021, when the military's fist crushed our fragile democracy, I was confined, cut off from the streets. Yet I felt their pulse—through the crack of gunfire, the whispers of aides before their silence, the weight of a nation's hope pressing against my captivity.

The Spring Revolution was no mere response—it was a rebirth of courage rooted in our people. The Irrawaddy's account captures the blood and bravery, the transformation of peace into carnage. But it only hints at what I sensed unfolding.

Though isolated, I heard of Kyal Sin, a 19-year-old extinguished too soon, her defiance igniting thousands. I learned of youth scribing blood types on their arms—a stark testament to their resolve to die for a future they had only tasted in the 2020 election.

I wept in silence—for them, for the over 10,000 lives lost, the 22,000 political prisoners, the millions traumatized or starving. Yet we speak of their unbroken spirit, a courage that redefines humanity in the face of inhumanity. *The motto "They die, or they die" is no mere slogan; it's a vow etched in our ancestors' resolve, a promise that this junta will not outlast our will.*

You ask about dictatorship's hallmarks, and your nod to Orwell is apt. I have lived within his warnings.

Dictatorship is not just bullets or boots—it's the strangulation of truth, the erasure of choice, the assault on the human spirit.

First, it is arrogance—the belief that power can rewrite reality. Min Aung Hlaing thought he could void our votes, dissolve our Parliament, and silence our voices as if democracy were a trifle.

Second, it is cowardice masquerading as might—murdering young adults like Kyal Sin, attacking medics, hiding behind jets and tanks against a people armed only with dreams.

Third, and most insidious, is the isolation it imposes—not just physical, like my confinement, but spiritual. It seeks to convince us we are alone, that resistance is futile, that the junta's gaze crushes all.

But here is the unshakable truth they cannot grasp: dictatorship thrives on fear, but it underestimates love.

The love of a teenager proudly displaying her inked finger. The love of a generation marching despite the cost. The love that binds us even now, as we speak of suffering and resilience.

Orwell saw Big Brother's mind. But he could not foresee this: a people who refuse to yield.

The junta has made Myanmar a killing ground, yes. But they have also sown their own ruin. Every Kyal Sin they kill sparks a thousand more fighters. Every prison they fill swells the ranks of the resolute. We are not just surviving—we are dismantling their regime, step by agonizing step. Our pain and hope outweigh their machinery.

This is the defining truth: their machine can kill. But it cannot fathom the heart it seeks to break.

Alan Clements: Daw Suu, your words carry a searing clarity. Let's broaden our gaze. Beyond your confinement, your people face blackouts, betrayal, and bullets. What is the most Dhamma-grounded act they can take to break the junta's spell—to shatter its illusion of control?

Aung San Suu Kyi: One act? Compassionate defiance—a unity that resists without hatred.

The junta feeds on division—pitting neighbor against neighbor, co-opting monks, reducing hope to horror. But *Dhamma*, rooted in the Buddha's teachings and echoing *ubuntu's truth, binds us as one.* Share rice when fields burn. Shield a protester as soldiers storm the door. Teach a child amid the rubble. These are acts of sacred rebellion.

Do them with *mettā*, not venom. Whisper "May you be free" to the jailer who binds you.

Yet, if rage rises—embrace it. It is not your foe. It is the pulse of a heart that still feels, still cares. Righteous rage springs from conscience, from dignity, from the refusal to look away. *Breathe into it.* Ground it. Let it burn clean, not wild. Transmute it into the fierce fire of disciplined, courageous love.

This is the revolution: not suppressing rage, but transforming it. Let your anger defend, not destroy. Let it deepen your resolve—to protect life, to uphold truth, to love even your oppressor enough to wish them free from delusion.

This is mettā-forged rage: fierce in compassion, unyielding in clarity, devoted to mutual liberation—yours and theirs. This is how we fight—not to dominate, but to awaken. *This is how ubuntu lives*: "*I am, because you are.*"

This slow, unquenchable fire—kindled in '88, reignited in '07, and blazing in the Spring Revolution—consumes chains. It turns cages into candles. It is love grown fierce, biting through delusion to reveal truth.

Alan Clements: Daw Suu, the fire you describe isn't one of destruction but of fierce devotion—a mettā that embraces rage and transforms it. It's a truth our world struggles to grasp, let alone live.

Orwell's Winston saw only the boot crushing the human face forever, but he missed what pulses beneath—the breath that endures, evolves, and refuses to be silenced. The breath that sings even under pursuit, that rejects the lesson of hate.

Your words reveal: true defiance isn't breaking chains—it's refusing to let them bind the mind. The junta's brutality burns fiercely, but it cannot touch the heart's core: the memory, the love, the unyielding clarity of those who march forward, bleeding but unbroken. They don't fear guns—they fear those who remember what it means to be human.

So, please tell me, Daw Suu—what is the deepest crack in their consciousness? Where does truth slip through—not as rebellion, but as a mirror? Where might their illusion fracture from within?

Aung San Suu Kyi: Their deepest crack is the fear they hide behind steel.

They parade as invincible, but beneath their armor, they crumble. Rust cloaked in grandeur. They're haunted—not just by justice, but by memory's unyielding gaze: by Kyal Sin, whose blood marks Mandalay like a sacred text; by mothers whose children they cannot unkill; by the unanswered prayers of those they tried to erase.

They dread what cannot be buried: the echo of 10,000 lives lost, the 22,000 souls caged, the millions starving for dignity, for voice, for breath.

Min Aung Hlaing's medals are no shield—they're a mask for trembling hands. Their statues, erected in haste, crack under the glow of a single candle held with love. They cannot face the silence where truth speaks.

Truth is their unraveling—not through force, but through its quiet power. It needs no weapons, only witnesses. Whisper it in the dark. Scrawl it on prison walls. Sing it through shattered windows. Speak it in the stillness before dawn.

Every silenced voice—Kyal Sin's final breath, a boy's cry in Yangon, a grandmother's refusal to bow—chips away at their facade. Dictatorship isn't strength; it's panic posing as power. Their spectacle isn't rule—it's a performance teetering on collapse.

Wield truth with clarity, not fury, and watch their illusion shatter from within.

Alan Clements: Truth as a wedge—your words hone it sharp. Let's dig deeper, if you will. You've endured regimes fixated on control—from Ne Win's era to this current tyranny, each more desperate, more intrusive, more stifling.

What drives this obsession with surveillance? This need to track every word, every glance, every breath? Is it fear of rebellion—or fear of a people awakening? What does this relentless scrutiny reveal about the mindset of power when it cannot look away, even for a moment?

Aung San Suu Kyi: It's not control—it's terror. They watch because freedom takes root where their gaze falters—in a prayer whispered in a cell, a chant in a tea shop. That's their nightmare.

Ne Win tapped my phone lines. Now it's drones, spyware, a digital stranglehold. Yet the root remains: a free thought is their abyss. In February 2021, as the Spring Revolution ignited, I sensed their panic through these walls. Every chant of "They die, or they die," every blood type inked on an arm—it shattered their myth of control.

Surveillance is fear dressed as vigilance—a dictator's admission: they're powerless over what they cannot see. That's where we thrive— unseen, untamed, growing in the shadows they cannot conquer.

Alan Clements: That's dread in a uniform. Now—your youth. They dodge bullets. Chant in shadows. Heal in hiding. What do you say to them from this cage, as they forge a revolution of spirit and steel?

Aung San Suu Kyi: To them, I say: You are Myanmar's soul. Pure stars lighting the dark. Outsmart them—not with cruelty, but with Dhamma's clarity. Master yourselves—the Buddha's truest triumph. Be fluid. Fierce. Rooted in compassion. You are rivers; they are walls.

Fight for the broken—the vendor with no stall, the child with no school, the 22,000 locked in silence. Stand as one. Breathe as one. When despair gnaws, return to the breath, the body, the truth. Kyal Sin's martyrdom. Your marches through blood. These are not just defiance—they are acts of rebirth.

You're not surviving a coup. You're birthing a world where tyranny drowns under its own weight.

Alan Clements: A river past steel—resilient, ancient. And the world—watching, too often waiting. What do you demand of us, from these walls?

Aung San Suu Kyi: Act. Don't gaze. The junta feeds on your stillness, your disbelief. We are karmically woven. Sayadaw knew it. This isn't Myanmar's burden alone—it's yours.

Starve their machine. Cut their cash, their guns, their lies. Name the wounds: 10,000 dead. Millions shattered. Millions hungry. Amplify the silenced—Kyal Sin. The nurse beaten for healing. The boy shot mid-chant. Burn their crimes into the memory of the earth.

Then look within. Where does your fear prop them up? Where does your apathy oil their gears? Dictatorship festers where conscience sleeps.

Wake it—everywhere. This is kinship, not charity. Act like kin—or their shadow grows.

Alan Clements: Daw Suu, as we close this chapter—an offering to a world that often forgets—may I ask: what truth, from within this prison, would you want etched into history?

What have these years of captivity revealed about the psychology of dictatorship—not just its violence, but its inner mechanics? What must we understand to protect our own minds from the seeds of authoritarianism, including the kind we plant ourselves?

And if I may frame it with a moment you've spoken of before: those early days of 2021, when the coup began. How did that event expose their mind—and shape your own?

Aung San Suu Kyi: Your question is a fine thread, Alan—weaving the raw wounds of our nation's present with the shadows of tyranny we've traced. You draw me back to that fateful moment, and I'll meet you there—unveiling their mind as it revealed itself, and the truth it forged in ours.

Let history—and every soul reading—carve this deep: Dictatorship is a shadow posturing as stone. A delusion so brittle it fears its own echo. I've faced its masks—Ne Win, Than Shwe, Min Aung Hlaing— and peeled them back to trembling men hollowed by dread. The Spring Revolution of 2021 lit the furnace where their psychology burned bare. Cunning. Cruel. Yet fatally flawed.

Dictatorship's psyche? It's not just boots or bullets—it's the suffocation of the soul. A war on truth, choice, and connection. Engineered to prey on the spirit.

It bears repeating—what I said earlier: *First, arrogance.* It begins in the illusion that authority alone can shape what is real. Min Aung Hlaing believed he could vanish the people's will with a decree. But no command can erase the dignity of a nation. Arrogance is the absence of listening. It is the refusal to see truth reflected in another's eyes. *The Dhamma teaches humility not as submission, but as clarity.* Real power does not dominate—it bows to reality. What they call order is often just fear disguised as structure, the panic of truth in motion.

Second, cowardice disguised as might. Their cruelty conceals a trembling hand. The soldiers who shoot into crowds, the generals behind fortress walls—they are not strong. They are afraid. Afraid of the unarmed. Of conviction. Of joy. Kyal Sin was fearless. Her courage was not loud, but pure. The regime sees love and calls it threat—because love requires no armor to stand upright. True courage does not crush. It protects. It shelters.

Third, isolation's poison. Dictatorships break bonds before they break bodies. They say: you are alone. That whisper becomes a prison of the mind. But no one resists alone. Even here, in this cell, I was not abandoned. I felt the warmth of our people—holding one another in silence, in grief, in prayer. The antidote to isolation is communion. To sing together. To mourn together. To struggle as one mind, one breath, one vow.

Fourth, the theft of meaning. They hijack language, turning lies into law. They rename repression as peace. Imprisonment as protection. But words remember. The people remember. A father knows the word for his vanished son. A mother hears truth beneath the soldier's boot. Our task is not only to speak—it is to restore meaning where it has been stolen. To return the names of the dead. The names of the disappeared. To keep telling the story that refuses silence.

Fifth, psychological predation. The regime studies the soul to exploit its thresholds. It offers illusion to numb pain. And when our guard is lowered, it strikes. This is not strategy—it is spiritual warfare. To offer hope, only to weaponize despair. But even here, the *Dhamma* is refuge. A breath. A step. A pause before belief. Mindfulness becomes resistance. To know oneself is to see the bait—and not bite.

And so—here lies their fracture. *They overreach. Their hunger is their undoing.* Every time they crush a flower, a field blooms. Every time they tighten their grip; another hand reaches out. *Dictatorship feeds on fear, but it withers before love.*

Kyal Sin's pride in her inked finger. A generation's march through blood. The quiet defiance of those who feed each other in the dark. Their machine kills. But it cannot comprehend the heart it breaks.

That is their downfall: not rage, but remembrance. Not revenge, but vision. Every life lost becomes a vow. Every scar, a signature of freedom.

We are dismantling them—not with steel, but with a beauty they cannot kill. Step by scarlet step. With our flaws. Our songs. Our unextinguished fire.

This is how tyranny ends. Not with a battle. But with a breath— held in truth.

We rise. And they dissolve.

To you, reader: This is your handbook. Etched in Myanmar's blood. Sharpened by our defiance.

Tyranny's mind is a mirror. Arrogance blinds. Cowardice trembles. Isolation starves the soul. Its cunning lies—its power lives where you collude.

Do you believe their myths? Fall silent? Let your conscience sleep? Then you are their accomplice.

But if you see their sham, refuse their frame, unite where they divide, remember where they erase—then you are the wedge. The light. The fire.

Tend that fire. Reflect like *Rāhula*. Act with *mettā*. Defy with clarity.

We are one weave. No dictator can cut that thread. They fall—not by force, but by what is truer.

Myanmar's killing fields are their tomb. Our love is their ruin. Walk on. Carry the flame.

"They die, or they die," they said. But now we see the truth:

"They kill—and still, we rise. The flame they tried to bury was never theirs to quench."

A Testament Against Tyranny: Six Distortions
Aung San Suu Kyi on the Mind of Dictatorship Part 1

Alan Clements: Daw Suu, as we seal this dialogue—a torch to pierce a world's forgetting—I ask: what enduring truths would you carve into history's heart to help future generations unmask and dismantle the mind of dictatorship?

Aung San Suu Kyi: You ask, Alan, for truths—lights to guide humanity through tyranny's shadow. I speak not to condemn, but to awaken.

To dismantle dictatorship—whether in Myanmar or wherever it masquerades as order—we must understand its mind. We must name its distortions, trace their roots, and strip away their illusions with the kind of courage that doesn't just resist, but illumines.

These are not abstract lessons. They are truths forged in the blood of our people, shaped by the defiance of the brave, and affirmed by the wisdom of generations who have stood where we now stand.

I offer six distortions—not strategies, but wounds of the spirit. They are viruses of perception that corrode our shared humanity. Born from Myanmar's struggle and echoed in the world's long battle for justice, they form a map—not only for survival, but for solidarity.

Each is a spark. Together, they are a fire no tyrant can extinguish.

DISTORTION ONE: Arrogance—The Delusion That Power Rewrites Reality

Dictatorship begins in a mind that crowns control as truth.

Min Aung Hlaing believed he could erase Myanmar's 2020 election with a pen, crush a nation's will with a dawn raid, and bury democracy beneath his medals—mistaking forced silence for submission. This arrogance is not strength, but blindness: a denial of life's interwoven nature, a fantasy that power can snap history's spine.

History humbles such pride. Nero sang as Rome burned, blind to ruin. Mao's Great Leap Forward starved millions—his utopia a mirage. Pinochet's Chile silenced thousands, yet their cries echo still. Noam Chomsky warns, "Power protects itself by distorting reality," but truth endures. Václav Havel, whose words helped fell Czechoslovakia's regime, wrote, "Living within the truth is an elemental act of dignity."

In Mandalay, Kyal Sin, 19, voted with pride, and died for it—her blood a testimony no decree could erase. Her torch still burns. The Buddha taught: all things are bound; to deny this is to invite collapse. Even Ne Win, Myanmar's earlier tyrant, died forsaken, his astrologers' stars long dimmed. No delusion outlasts its echo.

The antidote is truth as a vow—not rhetoric, but presence. One honest voice—Havel's pen, Kyal Sin's step, a mother's whispered fact in Yangon—can collapse a palace of lies. Let future generations wield truth as Chomsky urges: "Question power, and you reclaim responsibility."

DISTORTION TWO: Cowardice Masked as Strength

Dictators strut as giants, but they are shadows trembling in steel.

True strength stands bare, rooted in love. Dictatorship hides: behind tanks, sham courts, hollow edicts. In Myanmar, the junta shoots children chanting freedom, fearing their songs more than armies. They killed Kyal Sin, radiant with belief, not for her threat but for her light. That is not might; it is fear dressed in medals.

History strips this facade. Hitler shivered in his bunker as Berlin crumbled. Ceausescu's grandeur in Romania fell to a crowd's scorn in 1989. Hannah Arendt saw tyranny's truth: "Evil is banal, rootless, and fleeting." Desmond Tutu, defying apartheid, declared, "Love is stronger than hate." In Myanmar, a medic braving bullets to save a protester proves this: strength heals, not harms.

Sayadaw U Pandita taught power is patient, not cruel. When the junta attacked monks in 2007's Saffron Revolution, their robes outshone rifles. To see violence is to see fear. Future generations must learn, as Arendt suggests, that tyranny's bluster betrays its frailty. Cultivate courage that seeks kinship, not conquest, and watch the giant shrink to a ghost.

DISTORTION THREE: Isolation—The Fragmentation of the Soul
Dictatorship's cruelest lie is: You stand alone.

They part the prisoner from the world, the monk from the *Sangha*, the mother from her child's grave. In my cell, they swore Myanmar had abandoned me, that resistance had faded, that my voice was a cry into nothingness. Yet, through the dark, I heard courage—protesters' steps, students' smuggled notes, the Civil Disobedience Movement's whispers stitched into my blankets.

This tactic haunts history. Apartheid banned gatherings, yet South Africa's songs wove defiance. Stalin's gulags caged dissenters, but Solzhenitsyn's words flew free. Václav Havel wrote, "Hope is the certainty that something makes sense, no matter the outcome." Desmond Tutu's *Ubuntu sings, "I am because we are."* In Hong Kong's Umbrella Movement, umbrellas shielded not just bodies but bonds.

A child in Yangon, singing for freedom despite tanks, carries this truth. *The Dhamma teaches: no life is solitary.* The junta may cut wires, block voices, but it cannot sever belonging. When Myanmar shares rice in ruin, chants as one, mourns as one, the regime falters.

The antidote is community as rebellion. Poland's Solidarity fused workers and dreamers to topple communism. Myanmar's Spring Revolution binds generations. Future generations must forge, as Havel and Tutu urge, unbreakable ties, knowing isolation is tyranny's myth, and togetherness its end.

DISTORTION FOUR: Narrative Theft—The Hijacking of Language and Meaning

Dictators don't just chain bodies—they shackle words.

In Myanmar, they call murder "order," coups "stability," dissent "betrayal." They cloak tyranny in peace's name. This is not propaganda—it is the theft of memory, truth, and soul.

Orwell's 1984 warned, "Who controls language controls thought." Pol Pot's "Year Zero" erased Cambodia's past, killing millions. Putin's Russia brands truth "treason." Noam Chomsky dissects this: "Language shapes reality; control it, and you control minds." In Iran's *Woman, Life, Freedom protests*, women's cries for liberty cut through regime lies.

Yet words remember. In Myanmar, a protest is a poem, a funeral a hymn, a whisper scripture. When the junta tried to rename our nation, purge our stories, the people kept their truth—in tea shops, cells, the heart's pulse. A grandmother in Bago, defying arrest to speak of her grandson's death, wove such a thread. Chile's arpilleras, sewn by mothers, smuggled truth past Pinochet.

The response is story as salvation. *Toni Morrison wrote, "Freedom is to free another."* Speak truth—on walls, in songs, across time. Myanmar's youth, graffitiing defiance, live this. Future generations must, as Morrison and Chomsky urge, guard language as sacred, weaving narratives that reclaim history's heart.

DISTORTION FIVE: Psychological Predation—Manipulating Fear and Hope

Tyranny hunts the mind, weaving dread with cruel precision. It offers peace, then fires snipers; pledges calm, then raids at dusk.

In 2021, Myanmar's junta promised order, then erased children from schools. This dance—hope to horror—carves exhaustion. Yet our people answered with courage, not collapse.

History knows this predation. Franco's Spain mixed pardons with purges, sowing distrust. North Korea's spectacles of plenty mask starvation. *Hannah Arendt wrote, "Tyranny thrives by atomizing souls, reducing them to fear."* But resilience defies this. Thich Nhat Hanh taught, "Awareness dissolves fear." Nelson Mandela, unbroken after 27 years, said, "Courage is the triumph over fear."

A student in Mandalay, inking her blood type before marching, embodied this clarity. *The Dhamma's rebellion is mindfulness: to know your mind is to free it.* Myanmar's protesters, turning dread into fire, light the way.

Future generations must, as Mandela and Thich Nhat Hanh urge, train their hearts to resist manipulation. Mindfulness is power—making the soul ungovernable, a torch no predator can snuff out.

DISTORTION SIX: Overreach—The Collapse Born of Excess

Dictators overreach, blinded by myths of eternity.

In Myanmar, the junta's slaughter of over 10,000, caging of 22,000, and starvation of millions sparked not surrender but the Spring Revolution. They saw us as frail; we were fertile.

This is history's law. Rome's gluttony bred revolt. Gaddafi's cruelty fueled Libya's fall. Than Shwe's Myanmar faded, and Min Aung Hlaing's will follow. The Buddha taught, "All that arises passes." Desmond Tutu echoed, "Evil sows its own ruin." Noam Chomsky observes, "Power's overextension breeds its downfall." Tunisia's Arab Spring, sparked by one vendor's defiance, proves this.

A monk in Sagaing, praying amid airstrikes, holds this truth. Overreach is tyranny's fracture. The junta's brutality is not strength but a requiem.

The lesson is vigilance. Watch for excess, as Myanmar's youth did, turning a regime's hubris into its grave. Future generations must seize this moment, as Chomsky and Tutu inspire, to fan the spark of defiance into a fire of change.

These distortions are tyranny's blueprint, not Myanmar's alone. From Yangon to Tehran, Moscow to Hong Kong, they chart oppression's course. To study them is to arm humanity against their return. To counter them—with truth, courage, kinship, story, awareness, and vigilance—is to forge a world where freedom and coexistence bloom.

This is our pledge: to carry Kyal Sin's light, the chant "They die, or they die," the rice shared in ashes.

These are not weights but torches, kindling a future where no one bows to lies. Václav Havel wrote, "The human heart is where salvation lies." Let that heart, fierce and free, guide us. Let every student, leader, and dreamer take up this torch—question power, weave truth, stand as one.

For Myanmar, for all, let us vow: the fire of freedom will not fade.

Final Closing Declaration

To the World: Let Myanmar's scars be humanity's warning.

These six distortions—arrogance, cowardice, isolation, narrative theft, psychological predation, and overreach—are not confined to generals or juntas. They lurk wherever truth bows to dominance, wherever fear chokes choice, wherever power forgets love.

Search your nations. Your institutions. Your own heart. Where do you echo their lies? Where do you silence your voice? Where do you trade courage for compliance?

This is not just politics—it is our shared inheritance. And we must reject it.

To You, the Reader: You now cradle a testament—not of theory, but of blood and breath. To resist tyranny—anywhere—know its mind. Name its wounds. Defy its illusions. Return to truth. To kinship. To a love that sees with unflinching clarity.

And never forget Myanmar's vow: "They die, or they die." But now we know: They kill—yet we rise. The flame they sought to smother was never theirs to claim.

"They die, or they die," they said.
But now we see the truth:
"They kill—and still, we rise.
The flame they tried to bury
was never theirs to quench."

Alan Clements: Daw Suu, your voice, your insight, your truth-telling, thank you.
It kindles silence into fire.
It hands us a torch—to burn tyranny's veil,
a blade to carve its mind,
a beacon to guide our own.
Thank you—for the flame.
For the grace.
For the call that will not fade.

Aung San Suu Kyi: Thank you, Alan—for bearing witness.
For amplifying this cry.
For defying their shadow.

May the Dhamma light our path—
with courage to unmask their soul,
compassion to outshine their fear,
and hope to rebuild as one.

To all: This torch is yours.
Walk with us.
Burn bright.

A Manifesto to Understand Dictatorship Part 2

The Architecture of Authoritarianism
A Guide to Recognizing and Resisting Tyranny

Authoritarianism does not storm in as a tyrant—it creeps, law by law, fear by fear, cloaked in promises of order. Hannah Arendt unmasked its banality; Primo Levi warned: obedience's silence forges its chains before hearts dare rise. It wears masks—patriotism, tradition, safety, faith— yet its blueprint is unchanging: power without accountability, control without consent. It spreads not as shadow, but as a veil, whispering dread, draped in false salvation.

In Myanmar, where the junta's blackouts choke truth, I have lived in tyranny's cell, a witness to its rise—not only here, but everywhere. Orwell saw its aim: to strangle thought. Frantz Fanon knew its toll: voices robbed of self; souls stripped of dignity.

I offer ten structural pillars of its design—ten torches to pierce its veil before it falls again. These are not Myanmar's alone—they are humanity's, summoning every heart to resist.

Each pillar, entwined with the distortions of arrogance, cowardice, isolation, narrative theft, predation, and overreach, reveals tyranny's mind. *Each carries a Mindful Action Playbook—practices rooted in nonviolence, Dhamma, and fearless resolve to guard your society, your conscience, your truth.*

This is not theory. This is survival. This is your mirror, your shield, your spark—rise, resist, rebuild.

1. The Iron Veil of Exclusion: Power Without the People

In Myanmar, where the junta's decrees silence Yangon's streets, authoritarianism takes root when voices are erased—from apartheid's silenced millions to Hong Kong's imprisoned protests. It cloaks arrogance, believing it can rewrite the people's will. Power sequesters itself—behind uniforms, councils, palaces, or boardrooms. Tocqueville foresaw: tyranny begins when the state's ambition drowns the people's pulse.

The people are promised inclusion, yet become ghosts in their own land. Elections are mirages, reflecting not will but the regime's design. It builds walls, calls them gates, consults itself, names it democracy.

To unmask dictatorship, ask: Who decides? Who is silenced? Who vanishes when power speaks? When decrees replace dialogue, dissent a crime, you are not governed—you are claimed.

"The power of the powerless lies in living within the truth."
— VÁCLAV HAVEL

Mindful Action Playbook: Kindle the Torch of Inclusion

Reject the Charade: Boycott sham elections and hollow rituals. Refuse to lend your voice to systems that stage consent while burying truth. Your absence is a shout.

Weave Parallel Democracies: Forge grassroots councils—worker collectives, neighborhood assemblies, mutual aid networks. As Poland's Solidarity and South Africa's anti-apartheid webs defied oppression, build democracy in the shadows. Havel urged: "Truth shatters the lie of consent."

Expose the Facade: Use satire, street art, or public mimicry to reveal contradictions. In Myanmar, youths mock junta decrees with graffiti. Sharpen discernment; let humor be your blade.

Ask the Unspoken: Who profits from silence? Whose story fades? What truth is forbidden? Let your questions crack control. Inquiry, as Chomsky teaches, is rebellion's first spark.

2. The Choking Grip of Fear: The Atmosphere of Obedience

Fear is authoritarianism's breath; a cowardice masked as strength. It seeps into homes before soldiers arrive, silencing minds before prisons swell. It turns neighbors into spies, children into watchers, thought into peril. Fear needs no fanfare—it settles like ash, coating all until freedom chokes. It rewires hearts, curates silence. In a society ruled by fear, cages are redundant—people police themselves.

To diagnose tyranny, listen not for gunfire, but for the hush that follows—not peace, but dread. In Myanmar, where snipers haunt protests, fear predates the bullet. Where fear governs, liberty has fled.

"When the people fear the government, there is tyranny; when the government fears the people, there is liberty."
— THOMAS JEFFERSON

Mindful Action Playbook: Transmute Fear into Fire

Break Isolation's Spell: Hold silent vigils, flash mobs, or public stands with signs of defiance. One candle, as in Myanmar's night protests, splits a thousand shadows.

Breathe as Rebellion: Practice mindfulness to master fear, not flee it. Anchor in breath, as Thich Nhat Hanh teaches. Fear, transmuted, fuels courage.

Name the Unnamed: Speak the forbidden truth—say their name, your pain, your hope. Let your body know it endured. In Iran's protests, women's cries broke silence.

Unmask Fear's Guise: Trace when fear poses as logic or pragmatism. Tyranny whispers "be reasonable"; defy it by questioning what "reason" serves.

3. The Mirror of Self-Glorification: Leaders as Idols, Not Servants

Authoritarianism feeds on worship, its arrogance craving adoration. It demands not just obedience, but devotion. The dictator becomes savior, sun, myth. His face floods cities, his name haunts schools, prayers, lullabies. Statues rise, slogans bloom, history bends to glorify. He is not questioned—he is revered. He does not serve—he reigns.

In Myanmar, Min Aung Hlaing's image looms, a hollow god. No human merits worship; no nation should kneel to a face. Where portraits multiply and loyalty is choreographed, you stand in tyranny's hall of mirrors.

"Power tends to corrupt, and absolute power corrupts absolutely."
— LORD ACTON

Mindful Action Playbook: Shatter the Idol's Glass

Mock the Myth: Use satire, theater, or memes to expose the cult's absurdity. In Myanmar, cartoons of junta leaders spark laughter, a rebel's tool.

Question All Heroes: List your side's flaws, not just the regime's. Truth, not charisma, guides. Havel's self-scrutiny toppled lies.

Unravel the Narrative: Who crafts the myth? Who profits? What history was erased to exalt the face? Ask, as Chomsky urges, to dismantle power's frame.

Celebrate the Nameless: Honor ordinary courage—market women, silent marchers—without titles. Let dignity outshine pomp, as Tutu's *Ubuntu* teaches.

4. The Blade of Truth Suppression: Knowledge as Threat

Authoritarianism fears a book more than a bomb, its isolation severing thought. A book cannot be bribed; an idea, once rooted, cannot be uprooted. When regimes fear truth, they censor. When they cannot argue, they jail voices. When they cannot rewrite history, they burn pages. Control of language is control of meaning; control of meaning is control of reality.

In Myanmar, where libraries are raided, truth is the junta's enemy. Ask: What am I barred from reading, saying, knowing? The answers map tyranny's cage.

"The further a society drifts from truth, the more it will hate those who speak it."
— GEORGE ORWELL

Mindful Action Playbook: Ignite Truth's Lantern

Smuggle the Forbidden: Share banned stories, data, or songs. Use codes, symbols, whispers. In Myanmar, flash drives carry truth past blackouts.

Forge Rebel Schools: Host secret study circles, teach outlawed history. Education, as Freire taught, is liberation's spark.

Defy the Script: Say the banned word, read the forbidden name. Break repetition's trance, as Gaza's protesters chant "Freedom."

Memorize the Lost: When pages burn, carry stories in your heart. Speak them to the young, as Solzhenitsyn's gulag tales endured.

5. The Shackles of False Unity: The Myth of 'One Voice'

Authoritarianism, isolating to divide, craves not unity but uniformity. It demands obedience, not harmony, painting the nation one hue and jailing every shade. It fears complexity, criminalizes dissent, calls diversity treason. In its song, only one voice sings; all others are noise.

In Myanmar, where ethnic voices are silenced, false unity is a chain. True unity is chosen, woven, alive. Where loyalty is measured in slogans, tyranny sits at the table.

"Dissent is the highest form of patriotism."
— HOWARD ZINN

Mindful Action Playbook: Sing the Many Voices

Bridge the Divide: Share stories across differences—ethnic, religious, class. In Myanmar, interfaith vigils defy junta lies. Solidarity is rebellion.

Question with Courage: When agreement is demanded, ask deeper. When slogans echo, whisper a story, as Havel's truth pierced silence.

Embrace the Clash: Where uniformity blinds, seek what's hidden. Complexity, as Arendt taught, is freedom's soil.

Celebrate Dissonance: Make space for disagreement. Let diverse truths breathe, as Tutu's rainbow nation showed.

6. The Poisoned Well of Inequality: Wealth Without Justice

Authoritarianism, predating the vulnerable, thrives on manufactured suffering. It builds palaces on starvation, turns poverty into policy. Wealth is not earned—it is stolen, flowing upward like breath from the dying. The poor are not neglected—they are designed. Their hunger is a leash.

In Myanmar, generals' silk contrasts mothers' hunger. Inequality is not a flaw—it is the system. Look: gilded roofs over crumbling clinics, jets over empty schools.

"The true measure of freedom is how the poorest fare."
— AUNG SAN SUU KYI

Mindful Action Playbook: Reclaim the Commons

Share Without Permission: Give food, skills, shelter freely. Build micro-economies of dignity, as Myanmar's mutual aid networks do.

Starve the Spectacle: Shun elite displays. Trace who profits from your consumption. Reinvest in life, as Gandhi's *swadeshi* defied empire.

Expose the Cost: Uncover the pain priced into your comfort. What injustice fuels your ease? Inquiry, as Chomsky urges, is justice's spark.

Redistribute with Love: Let wealth flow sideways, care downward, justice through every act, as South Africa's *Ubuntu* binds us.

7. The Puppeteer's Strings: Institutions as Instruments of Power

Authoritarianism, stealing narratives, bends institutions to its will. Courts convict before trials, schools teach obedience, churches bless the throne, the press forgets to question. Laws shield not people, but power. These are not failures—they are the design.

In Myanmar, where judges serve the junta, institutions are puppets. Ask: Who does the law protect? Whose story is erased? Who pays for truth?

"When institutions lose their spine, dictatorship finds its feet."
— AUNG SAN SUU KYI

Mindful Action Playbook: Free the Institutions

Teach the Forbidden: Host banned-book clubs, underground *Dhamma* talks, pop-up truth schools. Learning, as Freire taught, is rebellion.

Unmask the Narrative: Analyze textbooks, sermons, headlines. Who benefits? Who vanishes? What's omitted? Chomsky's lens reveals power's lies.

Map the Unsaid: Trace what institutions won't say—that's tyranny's sacred lie. Ask, as Havel did, to pierce the veil.

Choose Integrity: Refuse to play legitimacy's game. Resign from complicity. Step out, as Mandela's defiance showed.

8. The Flame of Militarized Will: Rule by Force, Not Consent

Authoritarianism, overreaching, rules by boots when words fail. Dialogue dies; uniforms judge, teach, censor. It offers not security, but domination in armor. Tanks guard schools, snipers haunt rooftops, helicopters curse fields. The regime fears not enemies abroad, but its own people.

In Myanmar, where soldiers storm villages, force is the junta's god. Where armies occupy classrooms or polls, freedom bleeds.

"Militarism is not protection—it is power in camouflage."
— AUNG SAN SUU KYI

Mindful Action Playbook: Extinguish the Flame of Force

Wield Strategic Stillness: Stage walkouts, market shutdowns, silent stands. Myanmar's quiet protests expose armed absurdity.

Humanize the Uniform: Ask soldiers questions, offer tea, sing before tanks. Return them to humanity, as Tiananmen's lone man did.

Choose Fierce Nonviolence: Let rage fuel resolve, not revenge. Expose cruelty without mirroring it, as Gandhi's *satyagraha* proved.

Count the Cost: Every gun inward steals a meal, a truth, a future. Name this, as Myanmar's monks and nuns do in meditation.

9. The Fog of Manufactured Enemies: Division as Control

Authoritarianism, isolating to conquer, thrives on division. When power wanes, it births enemies—outsiders, traitors, minorities, truths. It stokes suspicion, inflames identity, casts dissent as betrayal. Where unity could rise, it sows fences; where love could bloom, it plants fear.

In Myanmar, where ethnic groups are scapegoated, hatred is policy. The regime survives by making us forget we are one.

"When rulers fear truth, they build walls. When they fear love, they seed hate."
— AUNG SAN SUU KYI

Mindful Action Playbook: Clear the Fog with Kinship

Humanize the Scapegoated: Carry their names, tell their stories. In Myanmar, photos of the fallen defy erasure.

Paint Shared Dreams: Use art, song, and story to reveal common hopes. In Iran, murals and music became lifelines—whispers of freedom painted on prison walls.

Trace the Hate: When rage rises, ask: Who sowed it? Why now? Unravel, as Arendt's clarity did.

Love Across Lines: Build bonds where tyranny forbids. Solidarity, as Mandela's long walk to freedom reminds us, is revolution.

10. The Graveyard of Accountability: Power Without Consequence

Authoritarianism's endgame, overreaching, is power unanswerable. Laws bow to rulers, corruption coins wealth, crimes fade in silence. In democracy, power shifts; in tyranny, it fossilizes. The tyrant fears one thing: reckoning. So, they bury the past, erase ledgers, trade justice for myth.

In Myanmar, where massacres go unpunished, truth is the junta's dread. But memory endures. Justice hunts patiently.

"The price of indifference is to be ruled by evil."
— PLATO

Mindful Action Playbook: Resurrect Accountability

Build Memory's Archive: Document violations, names, dreams lost. Myanmar's citizen journalists make forgetting impossible.

Question Your Own: Hold your side accountable, as Mandela did, starting where it stings.

Sanctify Justice: Let law serve life, not power. Speak it, study it, as Havel's truth rebuilt nations.

Chase the Lie: Where cruelty is excused, dig. Freedom begins in your heart's honesty.

Final Reflection — Aung San Suu Kyi

Dictatorship is not a face—it is a pattern.

It lurks not in one land, but at every society's edge, waiting for inattention. It speaks all tongues, flies all flags, yet its architecture is one: control without conscience, power without love.

Let this manifesto be your mirror, your shield, your torch. A way to see—clearly. A way to resist—fearlessly. A way to live—wholly. See the signs—not only in governments, but in communities, workplaces, families, and the quiet corners of your mind.

When the veil begins to fall, answer not with violence, but with vigilance. Not with vengeance, but with truth. Not with despair, but with a unity that embraces difference, rooted in *Dhamma*. A truth that illuminates, not wounds. A courage that protects, not conquers.

For freedom, for the next generation, for all life's dignity—take up this torch. Study tyranny's mind. Name its distortions. Kindle truth's fire.

Remember Kyal Sin's light, the chant "They die, or they die," and the rice shared in ashes. As Václav Havel wrote, "The human heart is salvation's home."

Let that heart, fierce and free, guide us. The fire is yours.

Carry it.

Feed it.

Shine.

The Inner Revolution: Ten Mindful Practices to Unravel Self-Deception

Self-deception is the mind's silent betrayal of truth—a refusal to see reality as it is, often to shield us from discomfort, fear, or responsibility. It's not mere ignorance; it's an active choice, conscious or not, to cling to illusions that serve our ego or ease our pain.

For example, a person might insist they're "fine" despite chronic stress, ignoring their body's tremors to avoid confronting overwork. Or someone might defend a toxic leader, rationalizing their cruelty as "tough love" to preserve a sense of belonging. In Myanmar, citizens might accept junta propaganda that massacres are "security measures," fearing the truth's weight. Self-deception distorts perception, chaining us to false narratives that external tyrannies exploit.

The Buddha's Kalama Sutta, a radical call to independent thinking, shatters conformity's grip. Preached to the Kalama people, it urges skepticism of tradition, authority, or dogma. The Buddha advised: "Do not accept anything by mere tradition, report, or because it is said by your teacher… But when you know for yourselves that these things are wholesome, blameless, praised by the wise, and lead to welfare, then accept and abide by them."

Its components of independent thinking include: *inquiry* (questioning sources), *discernment* (weighing evidence), *direct experience* (testing truths personally), and *ethical reflection* (ensuring actions foster well-being). This sutta is a torch against self-deception, demanding we see for ourselves.

The Buddha's simile of the blind men and the elephant illustrates self-deception's partial truths. In the original, blind men touch different parts of an elephant—tail, trunk, leg, ear—and each insists their fragment is the whole, arguing fiercely.

In a modern context, imagine a team analyzing a failing company: one, reviewing finances, calls it a "budget crisis"; another, in HR, sees a "culture problem"; a marketer blames "branding." Each clings to their slice, blind to the whole—a toxic leadership structure. Self-deception thrives when we mistake our perspective for reality, as Arendt warned of fragmented thought under tyranny.

Ten common covers for self-deception and the shadow of false certainty veil our clarity, each a trap dictatorships exploit:

1. Denial: Rejecting painful truths (e.g., ignoring a junta's atrocities to feel safe). **2. Rationalization:** Justifying harm (e.g., excusing a leader's violence as "necessary"). **3. Projection:** Blaming others for personal flaws (e.g., scapegoating minorities for societal woes). **4. Confirmation Bias:** Seeking only affirming information (e.g., consuming propaganda that aligns with fears). **5. Blind Loyalty:** Clinging to authority without question (e.g., venerating a dictator as infallible). **6. Selective Memory:** Rewriting the past to suit the present (e.g., ignoring a regime's past crimes). **7. Groupthink:** Conforming to collective delusions (e.g., agreeing with a crowd's false narrative). **8. Overconfidence:** Mistaking certainty for truth (e.g., assuming one's ideology is unassailable). **9. Avoidance:** Dodging discomforting realities (e.g., ignoring personal complicity in oppression). **10. Self-Justification**: Defending harmful actions to preserve ego (e.g., claiming "I had no choice" under tyranny).

Key qualities of mindful independence, inspired by the Kalama Sutta, are:

Inquiry: Questioning sources with relentless curiosity.

Discernment: Weighing evidence against reason and ethics.

Courage: Facing uncomfortable truths without flinching.

Clarity: Seeing reality unclouded by bias or fear.

Compassion: Guiding actions with empathy for all beings.

Integrity: Aligning beliefs with authentic, tested truths.

Tyranny begins not with armies, but with the mind's silent betrayals. To resist outer oppression, we must first unravel inner delusion. These ten practices are blades, honed to slice through illusion, projection, and control. They are not gentle—they demand the courage to see. Rooted in Jung's shadow work, Laing's radical unmasking, and Thich Nhat Hanh's lucid awareness, they are a revolution kindled within.

Ten Mindful Practices to Unravel Self-Deception

1. Dissect Your Triggers

When rage or fear surges, pause—do not act, probe. What narrative sparked this? What belief anchors it? Is it yours, or was it sown—by fear, family, or junta lies? Dictatorships, preying on reflex, ignite outrage to enslave reaction. Jung's unconscious drives behavior; Chomsky's propaganda manipulates emotion. In Myanmar, junta rhetoric baits fear to silence dissent. Trace triggers to their root, as Laing's fractured selves reveal imposed truths.

"Until you make the unconscious conscious, it will direct your life and you will call it fate."

— CARL JUNG

Practice: When triggered, write the story behind the emotion. *Ask*: Who gains from my reaction? Whose voice shaped this belief? Freedom is choosing your response.

2. Shatter Your Echo Chamber

Seek voices that jar—not polished summaries, but raw, opposing truths. Feel your resistance, not to convert, but to learn. If you consume only what affirms, you're not thinking—you're echoing. Havel's truth pierced ideological walls; Fanon's decolonized mind defied dogma. Dictatorships, isolating to divide, thrive on polarized thought. The Dalai Lama's curiosity bridges divides, as the Kalama Sutta urges testing truths.

"The test of a first-rate intelligence is the ability to hold two opposed ideas in mind and still retain the ability to function."
— F. SCOTT FITZGERALD

Practice: Read an unfiltered dissenting view. Note where you tense. *Ask*: Why does this challenge me? What truth might it hold? Curiosity is defiance.

3. Uncover the Unspoken

What is never voiced? Which questions are dodged? Whose stories vanish? Tyranny doesn't just speak—it erases. Silence is its weapon, as Arendt's totalitarianism omitted truths. In Myanmar, blackouts hide massacres, silencing the fallen. Baldwin saw the unsaid as power's tool. Charting absences, as the *Kalama Sutta's* inquiry demands, reveals what power conceals.

"The most dangerous creation of any society is the man who has nothing to lose."
— JAMES BALDWIN

Practice: In news, talks, or your thoughts, list what's missing. *Ask*: Who is erased? What truth is buried? The unsaid is your path to reality.

4. Challenge Your Icons

No figure is untouchable—not heroes, not rebels. Scrutinize their actions, expose their contradictions. Blind devotion, as Laing's false selves warn, breeds delusion; Chomsky's critique of authority unmasks worship. Dictatorships, cloaked in arrogance, feed on idols. In Myanmar, junta myths exalt Min Aung Hlaing. Loyalty to truth, as the *Kalama Sutta's* discernment teaches, breaks the spell.

"Unthinking respect for authority is the greatest enemy of truth."
— ALBERT EINSTEIN

Practice: Choose a revered figure. List their flaws. *Ask*: What do I ignore to exalt them? Truth, not icons, is your guide.

5. Embrace the Opposite

Invert your convictions—defend what you reject with fervor. Wear the other side's truth, not to betray, but to clarify. If beliefs collapse, they were not yours—they were imposed. Havel's dissent thrived on doubt; Thich Nhat Hanh's compassion held opposing views. Dictatorships, enforcing false unity, fear uncertainty. The *Kalama Sutta's* direct experience tests truth's strength.

"Doubt is not a pleasant condition, but certainty is absurd."
— VOLTAIRE

Practice: Write a defense of a belief you oppose. Feel its logic. *Ask*: Where does my stance weaken? Doubt is liberation's fire.

6. Listen to the Body's Signal

Your body knows deception before your mind admits it. A clenched chest, a knotted gut, a bone-deep ache—these are truth's alarms. Laing mapped the body's suppressed realities; Jung tied somatic cues to the shadow. Dictatorships, predating the psyche, bank on your denial. In Myanmar, fear tightens throats before bullets fly. Heed the visceral, as the *Kalama Sutta's* ethical reflection urges, to stand at truth's gate.

"The body never lies."
— MARTHA GRAHAM

Practice: When discomfort stirs, pause. Note sensations. *Ask*: What truth am I evading? The body's signal is your compass.

7. Unravel the Narrative's Frame

Every narrative is crafted—someone authors it, profits from it, vanishes within it. *Ask*: Who speaks? Who is silenced? What emotion is summoned, and why? Chomsky's media analysis exposes framing's power; Fanon's colonial critiques reveal subjugation's scripts. In Myanmar, junta headlines call murder "stability." Dismantle the frame, as the *Kalama Sutta's* inquiry demands, and lies crumble.

"The truth is not simply what you perceive, but how you perceive it."
— JIDDU KRISHNAMURTI

Practice: Take a headline or belief. List its beneficiaries, omissions, intent. *Ask*: What's concealed? Reframing is rebellion.

8. Seek Silence Amid Noise

Step away from screens, debates, urgency. Spend 48 hours in quiet, then write what emerges. Your true voice surfaces; the rest is conditioning. Thich Nhat Hanh's silence unveiled clarity; the Dalai Lama's retreats restored truth. Dictatorships, loud to isolate, drown your signal. Silence, as the *Kalama Sutta's* discernment teaches, reclaims your mind.

"In the silence of the heart, God speaks."
— MOTHER TERESA

Practice: Unplug for two days. Journal what arises. *Ask*: What is mine? Silence is not escape—it is reclamation.

9. Wrestle Your Contradictions

Where do your beliefs clash? Where do you claim freedom yet act bound? Contradictions are portals, not flaws. Dive into them, as Laing's fractured selves revealed truth, or Havel's dissent embraced tension. Dictatorships, enforcing false unity, fear complexity. In Myanmar, citizens claim justice yet (at times) excuse junta crimes. Integrity, as the *Kalama Sutta's* ethical reflection urges, is born in this struggle.

"Out beyond ideas of wrongdoing and right doing, there is a field. I'll meet you there."
— RUMI

Practice: List where actions betray values. Explore one clash. *Ask*: What truth bridges this? Contradiction is wholeness's path.

10. Rewrite Your Script

You were given a role: who to be, what to fear, how to live. Defy it—frown where you'd smile, question where you'd nod. See what is yours and what is performance. Martí's rebellion forged a free self; Fanon's decolonized mind rejected imposed identities. Dictatorships, overreaching to script lives, falter when you reclaim authorship. The *Kalama Sutta's* direct experience demands you write your truth.

"The first duty of a man is to think for himself."
— JOSÉ MARTÍ

Practice: Break one habit today—speak where you'd stay silent, challenge where you'd agree. *Ask*: Who authored my role? Freedom is your pen.

This inner revolution is a mirror to see, a blade to cut, a torch to kindle. Dictators fall when minds awaken. Rebellion begins not in streets, but in the silence where truth breathes. See. Question. Liberate.

The Inner Flame of *Sacca*: A Revolution in Truth

This book is a testament to Myanmar's unyielding quest for freedom, a call to every heart that yearns to break tyranny's chains. *Sacca—truthfulness in thought, word, and deed—*is our sacred fire, kindling the courage to see ourselves and others with unclouded eyes.

It is not without peril, for truth lays bare our flaws and invites sacrifice. Yet in its radiance, we find liberation, forging spirits no oppression can bind. These ten beacons of *sacca*, drawn from our people's defiance, light the path for all who seek a just world. Each is a star to guide you, a tribute to those who, in Myanmar's darkest nights, rise with truth as their shield.

The Ten Beacons of *Sacca*: Illuminating the Path to Freedom

1. The Vision of Truth: *Sacca* unveils reality, clear as dawn over the Irrawaddy. In Myanmar, where junta lies obscure justice, truth pierces the veil, enabling us to see oppression's designs. It empowers our youth to resist, unafraid, for a nation reborn. This vision is your inheritance—embrace it to discern the world's heart.

2. The Anchor of Sovereignty: *Sacca* frees your will from external dominion. In our land, where decrees seek to bind, truth restores our right to choose. It emboldens citizens to reject propaganda, crafting lives of dignity. This sovereignty is your birthright, a defiance of chains forged by fear.

3. The Fire of Fearlessness: *Sacca* ignites courage, unyielding before terror. Our people, facing bullets in Yangon, draw strength from truth's clarity. Like Kyal Sin, they risk all for freedom, their hearts alight. This fire burns in you, fueling daring to challenge any tyrant's might.

4. The Pillar of Wholeness: *Sacca* aligns your actions with your heart's truth. In a nation where lies fracture trust, our protesters stand united, true to justice. Their integrity shines, guiding others through darkness. This wholeness is your calling, a beacon of authenticity amid deceit.

5. The Embrace of Compassion: *Sacca* opens your heart to others' truths. In Myanmar's struggle, neighbors share rice despite scarcity, binding us in love. This empathy, as Thich Nhat Hanh taught, heals divides. This embrace is your gift, uniting humanity against oppression's rift.

6. The Fortress of Endurance: *Sacca* roots you against life's tempests. Our activists, imprisoned yet unbroken, mirror Václav Havel's steadfast dissent. Truth sustains them through torture, a shield unyielding. This fortress is your strength, enduring storms with resolute grace.

7. The Spark of Creation: *Sacca* unleashes thought, unbound by dogma. In Myanmar, poets craft verses under blackout, defying censorship. Their creativity births visions no junta can cage. This spark is your power, igniting ideas to reshape a freer world.

8. The Bridge of Kinship: *Sacca* forges bonds, authentic and true. Our people, chanting as one, defy tyranny's isolation with trust. Honesty weaves communities, unbowed by fear. This bridge is your vow, connecting hearts to build a shared dawn.

9. The Compass of Meaning: *Sacca* guides life with purpose, lit by truth. In our fight, every sacrifice—every fallen hero—finds meaning in freedom's hope. The *Dhamma's* clarity steers us true. This compass is your guide, charting a path of profound intent.

10. The Dawn of Liberation: *Sacca* frees your mind, toppling tyranny's reign. In Myanmar, truth awakens conscience, as José Martí's rebellion kindled Cuba's fire. Each honest act dismantles oppression's throne. This dawn is your destiny, a liberated spirit sparking a just world.

This inner revolution is a mirror to see, a blade to sever, a torch to kindle. Dictators falter when truth rises. For Myanmar, for all who seek freedom, let *sacca* be your guide. Begin not in streets, but in the silence where truth breathes.

550

CHAPTER TWENTY-NINE

UNIVERSAL DECLARATION OF HUMAN RIGHTS (UDHR) ADOPTED BY THE UNITED NATIONS GENERAL ASSEMBLY ON DECEMBER 10, 1948

Followed by the Final Conversation with Aung San Suu Kyi

Author's Prelude

From the smoldering ruins of the Second World War—when Auschwitz's charred conscience still drifted, when Hiroshima's wounds wept, when mass graves bore witness to shattered empires—humanity forged a sacred covenant. Not a contract between nations, but a vow among souls, born on the knife-edge of oblivion, when our capacity for cruelty lay raw and undeniable.

That vow became the Universal Declaration of Human Rights, proclaimed on December 10, 1948. Its thirty articles stand as beacons, not scribed in ink but etched into the scars of a century, each a light kindled from the ashes of complicity.

Flawed, unenforced, yet eternal, they are a compass for the human spirit—a testament to the unyielding worth of every life.

But what is a vow without vigilance?

What is a right without resolve?

What is dignity, if we let it bleed?

Since that day, over 250 wars, rebellions, and invasions have ravaged the earth, claiming more than 100 million lives through slaughter, starvation, exile, and despair. Generations have known only conflict's shadow. The UDHR, our holiest pledge to honor humanity, lies trampled—the world's most sacred text, yet its most betrayed.

In Myanmar's ravaged villages, in Gaza's shattered dreams, in Ukraine's scarred cities, in Sudan's unseen agonies, and in countless hidden corners of sorrow, these articles are torn in tatters. Civilians fall to shells, children wither from hunger, truth is exiled, conscience is chained.

The breaches are so ceaseless that outrage has faded to a distant murmur, and many, hearts heavy, have turned to silence—not from apathy, but from the ache of witnessing.

Yet there are those who hold the flame aloft. Those who see the spark of divinity in every soul. One such spirit endures in a Myanmar prison cell.

Aung San Suu Kyi does not proclaim human rights—she breathes them. Not with oratory or pretense, but through the resolute silence of her truth, the radiant clarity of her *sacca*—truthfulness in heart, word, and deed—and an unyielding refusal to surrender to hatred. She is a living testament to a nation where truth is outlawed, yet rises still.

She teaches us that the UDHR is not a chapter closed. It is pulse, blood, the fragile thread weaving dignity through despair. With quiet ferocity, she reminds us that defending human rights is not the province of envoys alone.

It is the daily work of refusing to diminish another. Of choosing to witness. Of vowing to remember.

It shapes how we nurture our children, how we mourn our losses, how we speak truth, how we act—especially when no eyes behold us.

This chapter is not a text—it is a mirror. Let it pierce you.

Let it pose the question that defines our age: *In the face of cruelty, will we uphold our shared humanity?*

If we do not guard these rights with the full might of our conscience, our love, our art, our defiance, and our prayer, the era of covenants will dissolve into fable, and an age of mere endurance will rise.

This is not a conclusion, but a summons—an urgent call to leaders, visionaries, and every heart that hears. Rekindle the vow of 1948. Defend dignity with unswerving courage. Become the light no tyranny can quench.

◆ ◆ ◆

Preamble

Whereas recognition of the inherent dignity and of the equal and
inalienable rights of all members of the human family is the foundation
of freedom, justice and peace in the world,

Whereas disregard and contempt for human rights have resulted
in barbarous acts which have outraged the conscience of mankind, and
the advent of a world in which human beings shall enjoy freedom of
speech and belief and freedom from fear and want has been proclaimed
as the highest aspiration of the common people,

Whereas it is essential, if man is not to be compelled to have
recourse, as a last resort, to rebellion against tyranny and oppression,
that human rights should be protected by the rule of law,

Whereas it is essential to promote the development of friendly
relations between nations,

Whereas the peoples of the United Nations have in the Charter reaffirmed their faith in fundamental human rights, in the dignity and worth of the human person and in the equal rights of men and women and have determined to promote social progress and better standards of life in larger freedom,

Whereas Member States have pledged themselves to achieve, in co-operation with the United Nations, the promotion of universal respect for and observance of human rights and fundamental freedoms,

Whereas a common understanding of these rights and freedoms is of the greatest importance for the full realization of this pledge,

Now, therefore, The General Assembly proclaims this Universal Declaration of Human Rights as a common standard of achievement for all peoples and all nations, to the end that every individual and every organ of society, keeping this Declaration constantly in mind, shall strive by teaching and education to promote respect for these rights and freedoms and by progressive measures, national and international, to secure their universal and effective recognition and observance, both among the peoples of Member States themselves and among the peoples of territories under their jurisdiction.

Article 1

All human beings are born free and equal in dignity and rights. They are endowed with reason and conscience and should act towards one another in a spirit of brotherhood.

Article 2

Everyone is entitled to all the rights and freedoms set forth in this Declaration, without distinction of any kind, such as race, color, sex, language, religion, political or other opinion, national or social origin, property, birth or other status. Furthermore, no distinction shall be made on the basis of the political, jurisdictional or international status of the country or territory to which a person belongs, whether it be independent, trust, non-self-governing or under any other limitation of sovereignty.

Article 3

Everyone has the right to life, liberty and security of person.

Article 4

No one shall be held in slavery or servitude; slavery and the slave trade shall be prohibited in all their forms.

Article 5

No one shall be subjected to torture or to cruel, inhuman or degrading treatment or punishment.

Article 6

Everyone has the right to recognition everywhere as a person before the law.

Article 7

All are equal before the law and are entitled without any discrimination to equal protection of the law. All are entitled to equal protection against any discrimination in violation of this Declaration and against any incitement to such discrimination.

Article 8

Everyone has the right to an effective remedy by the competent national tribunals for acts violating the fundamental rights granted him by the constitution or by law.

Article 9

No one shall be subjected to arbitrary arrest, detention or exile.

Article 10

Everyone is entitled in full equality to a fair and public hearing by an independent and impartial tribunal, in the determination of his rights and obligations and of any criminal charge against him.

Article 11

1. Everyone charged with a penal offence has the right to be presumed innocent until proved guilty according to law in a public trial at which he has had all the guarantees necessary for his defense.
2. No one shall be held guilty of any penal offence on account of any act or omission which did not constitute a penal offence, under national or international law, at the time when it was committed.

Nor shall a heavier penalty be imposed than the one that was applicable at the time the penal offence was committed.

Article 12

No one shall be subjected to arbitrary interference with his privacy, family, home or correspondence, nor to attacks upon his honor and reputation. Everyone has the right to the protection of the law against such interference or attacks.

Article 13

1. Everyone has the right to freedom of movement and residence within the borders of each state.
2. Everyone has the right to leave any country, including his own, and to return to his country.

Article 14

1. Everyone has the right to seek and to enjoy in other countries asylum from persecution.
2. This right may not be invoked in the case of prosecutions genuinely arising from non-political crimes or from acts contrary to the purposes and principles of the United Nations.

Article 15

1. Everyone has the right to a nationality.
2. No one shall be arbitrarily deprived of his nationality nor denied the right to change his nationality.

Article 16

1. Men and women of full age, without any limitation due to race, nationality or religion, have the right to marry and to found a family. They are entitled to equal rights as to marriage, during marriage and at its dissolution.
2. Marriage shall be entered into only with the free and full consent of the intending spouses.
3. The family is the natural and fundamental group unit of society and is entitled to protection by society and the State.

Article 17

1. Everyone has the right to own property alone as well as in association with others.
2. No one shall be arbitrarily deprived of his property.

Article 18

Everyone has the right to freedom of thought, conscience and religion; this right includes freedom to change his religion or belief, and freedom, either alone or in community with others and in public or private, to manifest his religion or belief in teaching, practice, worship and observance.

Article 19

Everyone has the right to freedom of opinion and expression; this right includes freedom to hold opinions without interference and to seek, receive and impart information and ideas through any media and regardless of frontiers.

Article 20

1. Everyone has the right to freedom of peaceful assembly and association.
2. No one may be compelled to belong to an association.

Article 21

1. Everyone has the right to take part in the government of his country, directly or through freely chosen representatives.
2. Everyone has the right of equal access to public service in his country.
3. The will of the people shall be the basis of the authority of government; this will shall be expressed in periodic and genuine elections which shall be by universal and equal suffrage and shall be held by secret vote or by equivalent free voting procedures.

Article 22

Everyone, as a member of society, has the right to social security and is entitled to realization, through national effort and international co-operation and in accordance with the organization and resources of each

State, of the economic, social and cultural rights indispensable for his dignity and the free development of his personality.

Article 23

1. Everyone has the right to work, to free choice of employment, to just and favorable conditions of work and to protection against unemployment.
2. Everyone, without any discrimination, has the right to equal pay for equal work.
3. Everyone who works has the right to just and favorable remuneration ensuring for himself and his family an existence worthy of human dignity, and supplemented, if necessary, by other means of social protection.
4. Everyone has the right to form and to join trade unions for the protection of his interests.

Article 24

Everyone has the right to rest and leisure, including reasonable limitation of working hours and periodic holidays with pay.

Article 25

1. Everyone has the right to a standard of living adequate for the health and well-being of himself and of his family, including food, clothing, housing and medical care and necessary social services, and the right to security in the event of unemployment, sickness, disability, widowhood, old age or other lack of livelihood in circumstances beyond his control.
2. Motherhood and childhood are entitled to special care and assistance. All children, whether born in or out of wedlock, shall enjoy the same social protection.

Article 26

1. Everyone has the right to education. Education shall be free, at least in the elementary and fundamental stages. Elementary education shall be compulsory. Technical and professional education shall be made generally available and higher education shall be equally accessible to all on the basis of merit.

2. Education shall be directed to the full development of the human personality and to the strengthening of respect for human rights and fundamental freedoms. It shall promote understanding, tolerance and friendship among all nations, racial or religious groups, and shall further the activities of the United Nations for the maintenance of peace.

3. Parents have a prior right to choose the kind of education that shall be given to their children.

Article 27

1. Everyone has the right freely to participate in the cultural life of the community, to enjoy the arts and to share in scientific advancement and its benefits.

2. Everyone has the right to the protection of the moral and material interests resulting from any scientific, literary or artistic production of which he is the author.

Article 28

Everyone is entitled to a social and international order in which the rights and freedoms set forth in this Declaration can be fully realized.

Article 29

1. Everyone has duties to the community in which alone the free and full development of his personality is possible.

2. In the exercise of his rights and freedoms, everyone shall be subject only to such limitations as are determined by law solely for the purpose of securing due recognition and respect for the rights and freedoms of others and of meeting the just requirements of morality, public order and the general welfare in a democratic society.

3. These rights and freedoms may in no case be exercised contrary to the purposes and principles of the United Nations.

Article 30

Nothing in this Declaration may be interpreted as implying for any State, group or person any right to engage in any activity or to perform any act aimed at the destruction of any of the rights and freedoms set forth herein.

The Universal Declaration Under Siege

Alan Clements: Daw Suu, here we sit—your voice rising from a prison cell in the midst of Myanmar's ongoing revolutionary war, and mine reaching through silence to meet it. What a journey it has been. What a timeless gift—of learning, of communion, of the *Dhamma's* highest radiance.

May I invite us now to turn our attention to the bedrock of global sanity: the Universal Declaration of Human Rights. Born in 1948 from the shattered conscience of humanity, it was meant to enshrine dignity for all. And yet today, Myanmar weeps blood. Democracy has been decapitated. And the UDHR stands not as a promise fulfilled, but as a fractured vow—surgically excised from the world's conscience, replaced by diplomacy without dignity.

May I ask, what is your deepest reflection on how this five-page document—your guiding star—has been forsaken, eroded, and betrayed by the very world that once birthed it?

Aung San Suu Kyi: Alan, the UDHR was never a relic to me. It has always been a living vow—written not just in ink, but in the moral DNA of humanity. When I stood in 1988 before the Shwedagon Pagoda, facing armed men and an uncertain fate, I carried its promise in my heart. Not as law, but as a shield of conscience. A promise whispered into the soul of every person longing to live without fear.

Its betrayal did not arrive with bayoneted soldiers alone—but through the slow corrosion of memory. Myanmar signed those principles, then crushed them. Ne Win concealed them behind walls. Than Shwe distorted them with propaganda. Min Aung Hlaing tramples them openly—disappearing citizens, orphaning children with airstrikes, imprisoning poets for their breath.

But the deepest wound is not in the text—it is in the silence that followed its desecration. The world did not simply forget the Declaration. It compartmentalized it. It treated justice as a ceremony and impunity as strategy. Diplomats praised its ideals while ignoring its collapse. Rights became rhetoric. Principles, conditional.

The UDHR is not obsolete—it has been politically orphaned. Disowned when inconvenient. And yet, it waits. It waits for people—not governments—to claim it back.

Alan Clements: Article 3: "Everyone has the right to life, liberty, and security of person." Daw Suu, you have carried this not just in principle, but in your heart. As a lifelong Buddhist, how do you reconcile the UDHR's moral clarity with the truth of *saṃsāra*—a world marked by delusion, violence, and impermanence? Where do these two visions meet—or diverge?

Aung San Suu Kyi: Alan, *saṃsāra* is not simply a cycle of birth and death—it is the totality of conditioned existence. It is the world seen through the veils of craving, fear, ignorance. It lives not only in our minds, but in our institutions, our economies, even our constitutions. *Violence is not its anomaly—it is its signature.*

The *Dhamma*, then, is not a philosophy to ponder, but a path to walk. It shows us how to see clearly in the midst of distortion. How to meet hatred without becoming it. How to act without being captured by reaction. *That is not passivity—it is wisdom-in-action.*

Now, the UDHR… it is not sacred scripture. But it is sacred intent. It is humanity's attempt to etch the heart of compassion into public life. It says: even in this *saṃsāric* world, we will draw a line. We will protect the vulnerable. We will name dignity as non-negotiable.

The two are not contradictory. The *Dhamma* prepares us to live the UDHR—not as dogma, but as daily practice. To protect life not because it is permanent, but because it is precious. To honor liberty not because it is guaranteed, but because it is fragile.

To me, the UDHR is a global expression of what the Buddha called *mettā*—universal goodwill made into principle. It calls on us to live beyond instinct. Beyond tribalism. Beyond fear.

The UDHR is not naïve. It is bold. It dares to articulate universal dignity in a world that often rewards domination. I do not seek to reconcile *saṃsāra* with the UDHR—I allow their tension to illuminate what is required of us.

Further, the Declaration asks us not simply to observe suffering, but to intervene with wisdom. It is not a document of idealism—it is a moral compass forged in the aftermath of atrocity. To honor it is to swim upstream against the current of history. To say: yes, life is impermanent—and still, we will protect it. And yes, it will fail. Just as we do. But the failure is not in the aspiration—it is in the forgetting.

And the remedy, as always, is mindful presence. Reflection. Renewal.

Alan Clements: Let me press further. The United Nations Security Council was created to uphold these rights. Today, it's paralyzed. War criminals like Min Aung Hlaing walk free, while so-called "free nations" trade diplomacy for silence. Why is the UN so ineffectual—and what does that reveal about the deeper structure of global power?

Aung San Suu Kyi: The United Nations was conceived in the embers of war—but today, it navigates the flames with a blindfold. The Security

Council has become a theater of vetoes and symbolic gestures—a chamber where justice is rehearsed, but never enacted.

Min Aung Hlaing's impunity is not a mystery—it is a mirror. He survives not because he is extraordinary, but because *the world has normalized complicity.* Some arm him with weapons; others arm him with indifference.

Power fears principle because principle does not negotiate. And the UDHR is principle in its purest form—a mirror held to the face of every nation. They do not try to dismantle it because it is weak, but because it reveals their strength to be hollow.

That mirror remains. Cracked perhaps—but luminous still. And it will reflect until the world is ready to see itself without illusion.

Alan Clements: Freedom is often bifurcated—negative freedom, liberation from oppression; and positive freedom, the capacity to flourish. You have been stripped of both. Yet you speak of a revolution of the spirit. From a prison cell, your voice silenced, democracy plundered, what does freedom mean—truly, now?

Aung San Suu Kyi: Freedom is not the absence of chains—it is the presence of truth. It begins when you claim the sovereignty of your own being, unbowed by permission or coercion.

In 1989, they confined my body—but my spirit refused to kneel. I breathed. I summoned the self that existed before the state branded me. That is *negative freedom—the quiet defiance of spiritual nonconformity, the refusal to absorb the oppressor's narrative.*

But positive freedom? That is a sterner summons. It is not merely enduring with dignity—it is conjuring beauty amid desolation. It is scrawling poems on scraps of smuggled paper. It is erecting inner sanctuaries when outer temples crumble. It is choosing love when surrender to grief would be simpler.

The Universal Declaration of Human Rights is no mere charter— it is a gauntlet. It demands not only justice but imagination. Freedom is not bestowed; it is cultivated—moment by moment, in silence, in struggle, in the stubborn fidelity of memory.

Alan Clements: Daw Suu, Article 19—freedom of expression—is the cornerstone of democracy, yet the first casualty of despotism. When speech is extinguished, violence festers. Why is this article so perilous to tyrants—and so casually forsaken by those who profess to uphold it?

Aung San Suu Kyi: Because words are the scaffolding of consciousness. They name what power seeks to obliterate. Free speech does not merely defy regimes—it dismantles their illusions.

Alan, tyrants dread Article 19 not for its threat to their flesh but for its challenge to their fictions. Free speech is perilous because it poses forbidden questions: Who thrives in the shadow of silence? Who decrees the boundaries of permissible thought?

That is why they imprison poets, writers, filmmakers, singers, musicians. That is why they shutter schools and strangle the internet. Despots cannot endure dialogue—they demand monologue.

And those who claim to champion free speech? Too many embrace the concept but recoil from its cost. They applaud expression that aligns with their interests yet quell voices that unsettle their allegiances. True free speech is not decorum—it is principle. It speaks when it imperils. It listens when it wounds.

Tyrants abhor it. But so do the timid.

Alan Clements: What is your judgment of Western democracies that proclaim freedom abroad while arming autocrats, stifling dissent, or criminalizing protest at home? Are they guardians of rights—or complicit in a global charade?

Aung San Suu Kyi: The West wields the rhetoric of liberty but too often trades in the coin of expediency.

Democracy is not a banner—it is a discipline. You cannot preach what you fail to practice. You cannot denounce tyranny abroad while abetting injustice at home. You cannot arm oppressors and then lament the oppressed.

I speak not to condemn but to summon. To remind those with power that freedom is not a commodity but a vocation. It must be lived where it is legislated. If you profess the dignity of humanity, you must defend it—even when it disrupts your alliances, even when it defies your convenience.

The Universal Declaration of Human Rights was forged to bind humanity in a shared moral vision—not to be bartered, fragment by fragment, on the altar of geopolitical expediency.

Alan Clements: Article 1 of the Universal Declaration of Human Rights proclaims: "All human beings are born free and equal in dignity and rights." Yet dignity is trampled daily in Myanmar's prisons, in refugee camps, and across the globe. From your perspective—rooted in Buddhism, Christianity, and conscience—what does human dignity mean, and why is it so elusive to uphold?

Aung San Suu Kyi: Dignity is not conferred—it is reclaimed. It is the unyielding recognition that beneath all titles and torments lies an inviolable humanity, unbroken by circumstance.

I have witnessed dignity in the most desolate corners—in the resolute grace of monks silenced by fists, in the unbowed defiance of mothers whose children were torn from them, yet who still cradle the living. Dignity endures where power falters. It is not delicate—it is indomitable.

Why is it so rarely honored? Because it demands discipline. It commands: Do not exploit, even when profit beckons. Do not dehumanize, even when crowds cheer. Dignity requires us to act not from supremacy, but from mutual recognition of our shared humanity.

It is not fragility—it is moral rigor. Tyrants loathe it, for it cannot be coerced, bartered, or extinguished. It stands as a rebuke to their hollow victories, a reminder of the humanity they forfeited for power.

Alan Clements: You once told me that "compassion is the strongest form of defiance." But how do we embody compassion when the world burns—when Article 5, which prohibits torture, is mocked in military dungeons? What does it mean to resist with love?

Aung San Suu Kyi: To resist with love is not to yield to horror—it is to sharpen moral clarity without descending into cruelty. It is to confront brutality unflinchingly, yet refuse to be consumed by hatred. Love is not the absence of rage—it is the resolve to remain undefiled by it.

I have seen men broken by torture, their bodies shattered, yet I held fast to the hope that their tormentors might one day awaken. Not to absolve their crimes, but to refuse to replicate their violence in my heart.

Compassion is not passive. It's the courage to face suffering without turning away. It protects without attacking. It heals without hardening. This is what the Buddha taught—not escape, but engagement. Not giving in, but showing up with clarity and heart, even when the world is burning.

It's Gandhi choosing hunger over hatred. It's Nelson Mandela walking free without bitterness. It's Mother Teresa cradling the dying in Calcutta's alleys. It's Thích Quảng Đức sitting in flames without anger. It's Martin Luther King Jr. dreaming out loud through tear gas and jail bars.

True compassion does not retreat from horror—it meets it, transforms it, and dares to build a gentler world from the ashes.

Alan Clements: That transformation seems distant. Myanmar's civil war, Gaza's anguish, the bombing of Iran, Ukraine's devastation—across the world, Article 9's safeguard against arbitrary detention crumbles. The rule of law is derided. Amid such systemic collapse, does the Universal Declaration of Human Rights retain its relevance?

Aung San Suu Kyi: It is not merely relevant—it is indispensable. It is the final beacon before the world plunges into moral abyss.

When law fails, memory must rise. The Declaration is no longer just a bulwark—it is a mirror and a compass. It reflects our collective failures and charts the path back to our shared humanity.

It recalls the vows we made and the world we are summoned to forge—not for nations, but for people. Yes, detentions are arbitrary. Yes, war crimes go unpunished. But the Declaration does not describe the world as it is—it proclaims the world we are obligated to build.

Without it, we are mere predators armed with technology. With it, we are imperfect beings striving toward conscience.

Alan Clements: Yet the world grows more predatory. Surveillance suffocates speech. Fear supplants conviction. Markets erode the sacred. In this environment, how do we preserve the essence of freedom?

Aung San Suu Kyi: By remembering that freedom's essence resides in choices, not institutions. It is not enshrined in charters or capitals—it lives in the crucible between thought and deed.

It is sustained in how you greet a stranger, how you engage dissent, how you choose humanity when the world urges otherwise. Freedom is not proclaimed—it is enacted. One deliberate act at a time: to listen rather than dominate, to forgive without erasing accountability, to speak truth when silence would cost nothing but integrity everything.

These acts may seem modest, but they are the architecture of civilization. No autocrat can dismantle what you refuse to relinquish within yourself.

And I say this not only as a prisoner of conscience today, but as someone who has walked through Myanmar's decades of darkness—who has seen, heard, and felt the burden of our people's suffering in every corner of the country.

I have seen a woman beaten for daring to speak in public about her stolen land.

I have heard the testimony of monks who were dragged from their monasteries, their robes bloodied, their dignity mocked.

I have sat across from families whose homes were confiscated without explanation, their lives reduced to rubble by an official's signature.

I have listened to survivors describe the unspeakable: torture chambers hidden behind courthouses, rape used as a weapon of silence, children orphaned by airstrikes or snatched in the night for conscription.

I have walked in villages where the fields were once green with rice—and now are graves.

And yet, from this prison, I feel the current of resistance more strongly than ever.

It reaches me through whispers, through the unbroken current of kinship that no wall can contain. A teacher holds class beneath a scorched tree. A doctor tends the wounded by candlelight, with no salary, no safety—only duty. A monk chants *mettā* between soldiers and students, his body exposed, his mind unwavering. A mother carries her child across the border to spare her from war—and a daughter stays behind to join the revolution, knowing she may never return home.

These are not gestures of despair. They are sacred acts of defiance. They say to tyranny: *you may control the guns, but not our choices.* And so long as that truth remains embodied in even one person, freedom has not perished.

Alan Clements: I know we have spoken about this many times Daw Suu, but as we come to a close, please, let us go further. That courage—woven through your life—how is it sustained? What preserves your spirit, day after day, in a prison bent on erasing your name and your nation?

Aung San Suu Kyi: Silence. Breath. Remembrance. I summon my father—not merely as a man, but as the ember of a nation yet to be born. I hold fast to those who perished for a Myanmar rooted in dignity, not dread. I see the women who whisper defiance in shadowed kitchens, the students who scrawl poems in alleys, fleeing bullets with verses pulsing in their veins.

My spirit does not endure despite the cage—it endures because I refuse to forget. Courage is not the absence of fear. It is fidelity to a vision greater than survival—to truth, to love, to the aspiration that we might one day live not in subjugation, but in dignity. Until that dawn, I remain—not unscarred, but unbroken in my humanity.

Alan Clements: You speak of memory, Daw Suu—of honoring those who have sacrificed. Yet history itself is besieged. Dictators distort it. Democracies sanitize it. In the silence, truth vanishes. What is memory's role in the UDHR, and how do we safeguard it?

Aung San Suu Kyi: Memory is defiance incarnate. It is not sentiment—it is moral continuity. It is the ledger of suffering that resists obliteration, the wellspring of awakening that outlasts lies.

When tyrants rewrite history, they do not merely distort the past—they plunder the future. *The UDHR begins with "recognition of the inherent dignity"—recognition as an act of re-knowing, a refusal to let universal truths be buried.*

Memory keeps the blood vivid, the laughter alive, the betrayals unclenched. Without it, we are not free—we are curated amnesiacs, adrift in a fog of convenience, unable to see, to speak, to rise. To defend memory is to guard the raw truths that forge our collective conscience.

Alan Clements: Yet the international order seems blind to that recognition. Myanmar, Syria, Gaza, Israel, Iran, Sudan—the blood flows, but institutions falter. Article 7 promises equality before the law, yet justice feels like a fable. What does the collapse of accountability reveal?

Aung San Suu Kyi: It reveals that law without conscience is theater, and justice without courage is commerce. Powerful states claim equality before the law—until it binds them.

The UDHR was not crafted as a relic—it was forged as a mandate. Yet too often, it is wielded not as a covenant but as a prop. Article 7 challenges us to live as if no one is expendable. The price of neglecting it? Cynicism that corrodes, collapse that consumes.

Civilization does not perish by force alone—it erodes when its principles are stripped of consequence. Accountability is not a privilege to be rationed—it is the foundation of a world that dares to call itself just.

Alan Clements: Let's speak plainly. Has the international system—this patchwork of diplomacy, deterrence, and doctrine—failed? If so, what emerges from its ruins?

Aung San Suu Kyi: The international system has not collapsed, but it buckles under humanity's gravest trials. Designed to preserve order, it falters in upholding the inviolable dignity of every life. The United Nations' preamble vows to reaffirm faith in human rights and dignity, yet aspiration is not fulfillment. The UN strives for justice, but is hindered by rival interests, bureaucratic inertia, and powerful nations prioritizing sovereignty over equity.

Over 100 million displaced—from Syria to the Horn of Africa— flee war, persecution, or despair. Conventions and agencies offer relief, but rarely confront root causes: authoritarian regimes, unchecked arms trades, and economies that entrench inequality. Refuge must be redefined—not as charity, but as a shared duty grounded in the universal right to safety.

Disinformation and digital authoritarianism further expose the system's limits. From Myanmar to beyond, technology, once a herald of freedom, now silences dissent and fractures truth. Fragmented regulations and corporate self-interest lag behind the pace of harm. A global compact is needed to safeguard the integrity of information, ensuring it serves justice, not control.

Democratic values erode under siege. From Hong Kong's imprisoned voices to manipulated elections in established democracies, self-determination falters. The system must not merely observe—it must defend every individual's right to shape their society through voice, not violence.

These crises reveal a system strained, not shattered. The UN's vision of dignity remains a beacon, but demands action beyond declarations. What must rise is a new covenant, fusing moral clarity with political resolve. The Universal Declaration of Human Rights is our guide, but useless without the courage to follow it. We need leaders who see diplomacy as stewardship, not strategy; who know peace is not the absence of conflict, but the presence of justice.

This renewal begins within—through a revolution of compassion, truth, and accountability. From these ruins, we can forge a world where dignity is not an aspiration but a reality, driven by the urgency of now and the vision of always.

Alan Clements: Daw Suu, we've traversed a world torn apart by crises—fractured democracies, silenced voices, and rising authoritarianism. Article 20 of the Universal Declaration of Human Rights enshrines the right to peaceful assembly and association, yet crackdowns abound: protests criminalized, unions demonized, law weaponized, civil society choked, and much of the media—a mouth piece for criminals. In Myanmar, your people face bullets and drones for daring to gather. How should the world respond when the space for peaceful dissent vanishes?

Aung San Suu Kyi: The world must refuse to let dissent fade into silence. In Myanmar, where the junta terrorizes a nation's soul, every whispered chant, every candle raised in defiance, testifies to our people's unyielding resolve. Dissent is not a luxury—it is democracy's pulse.

Article 20 is not mere text—it is a mandate: to stand together is to reclaim one's voice. The world must not merely watch—it must uplift the lives of Myanmar's youth, the cries of Iranian schoolgirls, the songs of South African miners, the defiance of those armed only with truth.

Offer not sympathy, but solidarity. Stand where we fall. Speak where we are silenced. *To those who suppress: know this—every voice you crush becomes a seed sown in history, and history does not forget.*

In Myanmar, the junta believes bombs can extinguish hope. They misjudge its nature. Hope is not a flame to be snuffed—it is a current carving paths through stone. The world must prove them wrong—not with rhetoric, but with action: support the resistance, halt the flow of arms and wealth, amplify the call for freedom. Dissent does not perish. It transforms. It endures. In its quiet alchemy, it forges its return. The time to act, is now.

Alan Clements: Yet, Daw Suu, dissent can be a double-edged sword. It can unite, but it can also fracture—pitting freedom against cohesion, passion against peace. In Myanmar's wounded society, where ethnic divisions and mistrust persist, and in polarized nations worldwide, how do we safeguard freedom of expression without tipping into chaos?

Aung San Suu Kyi: Freedom of expression is not a spark to be feared— it is a flame to be tended with discipline. In Myanmar, our struggle for democracy bears the scars of division, where the anguish of ethnic minorities—Shan, Kachin, Rohingya—has too often been drowned by the majority's voice. True freedom does not silence these wounds; it heals through listening.

Chaos arises not from abundant speech, but from scarce understanding. Expression without accountability fuels conflict; expression grounded in respect forges unity. The Universal Declaration demands freedom that upholds dignity—not freedom that erodes it.

In fractured societies, we protect dissent by cultivating the resolve to disagree without dehumanizing, to debate without destroying. This is Myanmar's path: a unity born not of silence, but of the courage to hear every truth.

Globally—from America's polarized divides to Ethiopia's ethnic strife—the principle holds: freedom flourishes when we honor the dignity of the other.

In Myanmar, I envision a nation where every voice—Bamar, Karen, Rohingya—rises in concord, not discord. The world must nurture this by fostering dialogue over domination, amplifying the marginalized over the loudest. Freedom is not unrestrained—it is reverent.

Alan Clements: Daw Suu, many in the West remain insulated, believing dictatorship is a distant tragedy—an "elsewhere" problem to scroll past between their lattes and elections. From your prison cell in Myanmar, where the junta's grip tightens, what would you say to them, about what's truly at stake?

Aung San Suu Kyi: Dictatorship is not a distant specter—it is a shared human failing, born in the silence you tolerate, the fears you excuse, the comfort you leave unquestioned. In Myanmar, every stolen voice warns: freedom is fragile, and its loss begins with your indifference.

Alan Clements: We stand on hallowed ground, Daw Suu. If you may never again address your people—not as a prisoner, not as a leader, but as a woman, a mother, a keeper of humanity's hope—what message would you leave for Myanmar and the world? How would you wish to be remembered?

Aung San Suu Kyi (*pausing, her voice steady yet warm*): I am no saint, no martyr. Do not cast me in stone or story. Remember me as a woman who strove—who stumbled, who rose again, who spoke truth when silence was safer, who chose grace when anger was simpler, who held the names of the lost through nights of oblivion.

Each breath in this cell is a sacred pledge: that my people will know joy not as a fleeting hope, but as a right etched in their bones. To Myanmar, I say: You are my lifeblood. Your courage—students defying death, mothers mending the broken, monks shunning alms from tyrants—lights a path through the world's darkest night.

To the Karen, Kachin, Rohingya, to every voice erased: I see you. I have always seen you. I dream of a nation that will one day weave itself whole.

To the world: Freedom is not a solitary note—it is a chorus that binds us. From Gaza's horrors to Sudan's forgotten sorrows, from Belarus's cells to Myanmar's hidden refuges, our struggle is one. Embrace the silent might of the human heart—*metta*, compassion, truth—mightier than any army. Dignity is rebellion. Hope is resistance unbroken. Carry this light, and let it burn with care, with valor, eternally.

Alan Clements: Daw Suu, it has been the profoundest privilege of my life to walk this arduous road with you—through memory and vision, through sorrow and resolve, across decades marked by silence, defiance, and sacrifice. Since you returned to Myanmar in 1988, you have given not merely your voice, but your entire life to a people whose dreams of freedom were tested, broken, and buried—yet ever unyielding.

In these pages, in our treasured dialogues, I pray, we have not merely documented history—we have kindled a spiritual awakening. A revolutionary light passed from heart to heart, from those who dared to believe to those who refused to forget. And this conversation is no mere chronicle—it is a sacred vow; a prayer etched in resistance.

I am also haunted by the luminous grace of those nine nights I spent with Sayadaw U Pandita in 2016, months before his passing, exploring the *Dhamma's radiant qualities of leadership*—fierce yet tender courage in service to others. You shared your own sacred encounters with him, illuminating the *kalyāṇa mitta*—a noble friend whose warmth, integrity, clarity, humility, and refusal to exploit shine as a beacon. Now, as we near the final minutes of this final exchange, I offer you this moment, and the silence, to address the world one last time. May your words soar beyond these walls and pages—to the classrooms of tomorrow, to the chambers of power, to the hearts yet to dream.

Should these be your last testament, Daw Suu, let them resound with the might of truth and the grace of love. Let them rise as an eternal chime. What would you say—to your people, to the world, to artists whose creations could awaken humanity, to those listening in the dark?

Aung San Suu Kyi: Let me speak, then, not from a prison cell, but from the heart of a dream unbowed—not as a captive or a leader, but as a woman, a daughter of Myanmar, a mother of a vision that will not die.

To those who have journeyed through decades of flame, betrayal, and silence, I offer my deepest homage. We have borne unbearable loss. Yet our spirit remains unbroken. That, above all, is our triumph.

From the monks who marched with empty alms bowls to the students who fell, hands open, hearts ablaze, from the mothers who cradled grief yet rose to fight, to the daughters who still weave freedom into the night—we endure. And that is no small victory. That is the revolution.

This dream breathes in the whisper of every teacher who smuggles truth in hidden lessons, in every doctor who mends wounds by starlight, in every exile who guards their mother tongue. You are the bearers of this light now. Guard it with ferocity. Nourish it with love, with truth, with courage. Let it burn—not to consume, but to reveal.

To the people of Myanmar: You are my heart's rhythm, my eternal pledge, my reason for every dawn. Do not let the junta erase our truth. They may raze our villages and shatter our schools, but they cannot shatter the truth. They may cage our bodies, but they cannot cage our souls.

In this hell, where over three million hearts wander displaced, where thousands languish in chains, where hunger gnaws at seven in ten, your defiance is a miracle. Every step you take—every poem scrawled in defiance, every child taught in secret, every wound bound in the dark—is a rebellion no tyrant can quell. You are the pulse of a nation that refuses to die.

And to you, Alan—my noble companion, my friend in truth—thank you. Not merely for listening, but for keeping memory alive. For affirming that silence is not absence. This book is no mere chronicle—it is a sacred bond. Between us. Between the survivors. Between all who dare to love.

To the artists of the world—painters, poets, singers, dancers, dreamers—your creations are the breath of humanity. Do not let Myanmar's agony fade into the noise. We cannot succumb to despair—we must defy it as fiercely as we defy dictatorship. Let your art be a rebellion, unpredictable and uncontainable. Paint the cries of our children until they pierce every heart. Sing the names of our lost until they echo in every hall. Dance the defiance of our youth until the world cannot look away. With every stroke, note, and step, awaken the sleeping conscience of the planet, until Myanmar's pain becomes a global summons no one can ignore.

And to those who wield power, from presidents to prime ministers—if you stood before me now, I would not appeal to your titles. I would address your humanity. I would ask you to envision your own child—not in palaces or on red carpets, but in a cell. Alone. Vanished. Helpless. What would you do? Then do that. Not for me. Not even for Myanmar. But for the fragment of your soul that still remembers how to love.

The crimes in Myanmar—the scorched earth, the thousands imprisoned, the children stolen—are not local affairs. They are not "intricate regional issues." They are wounds on humanity's soul. The world's shame. And you must act—not with sorrow, but with unflinching justice. Justice that names perpetrator. Sanctions that break the powerful. Aid that feeds the starving.

This is not just our trial—it is yours. It is a test of your conscience, your courage, your humanity. Authoritarianism thrives when truth is sold for convenience. When apathy becomes complicity. When silence cloaks itself as diplomacy. If you cannot lead with compassion, then lead with honor. And if even that is too much—make way. And let the people rise unhindered.

You ask of my legacy. But my legacy is not mine to claim. It belongs to the children who still etch birds in the margins of censored textbooks. It belongs to the revolutionaries who weave code in shadowed corners. It belongs to the prisoners who still offer prayers for their captors. These are Myanmar's tomorrow. These are the dreamers of a democracy more radiant than anything I could have dreamed.

So, if I am erased—if this voice is silenced and these words are my last breath—do not grieve for me. Do not carve monuments. Do not kindle candles in my name. Instead, carry the light.

Carry it with grace—with compassion. Carry it with fire—with resolve. Carry it until the cries of our lost weave songs of liberty. Until justice treads freely in Yangon, in Rakhine, in every village shattered beneath this cruelty.

Let it blaze in every deed that risks everything. Let it blaze in the murmurs of those who still remember what it means to be free. Let it blaze in the silent awakenings that begin in the soul.

And let it blaze until every child dreams with both eyes open. Until the morning no longer fears the night.

That is my legacy. That is my eternal call. That is my parting breath.

**Aung San Suu Kyi's Ten-Point Manifesto for
Every Human Being on Earth**

**A Sacred Covenant to Uphold the Universal Declaration of
Human Rights with Conscience, Dignity, Freedom, *Ubuntu*,
and Peaceful Coexistence**

1. The Light of Liberty: Cherish Freedom as Your Breath
2. The Mirror of Conscience: Uphold Truth Without Violence
3. The Practice of Dignity: Honor Humanity in Every Soul

4. The Right to Speak: Defend Freedom of Expression as Sacred Flame
5. The Courage to Disobey: Resist Unjust Power with Moral Intelligence
6. The Heart of *Ubuntu*: Thrive in Our Shared Belonging
7. The Discipline of Compassion: Let Love Be Fierce, Not Fragile
8. The Path of Peace: Choose Coexistence Over Conflict
9. The Practice of Humility: Serve, Don't Rule
10. The Legacy of Freedom: Be Remembered for How You Loved

1. The Light of Liberty: Cherish Freedom as Your Breath

Freedom is the rarest element on Earth. It is more precious than wealth, more sacred than power. It is the first breath of conscience when fear loosens its grip. Never take it for granted—not yours, not another's. To walk freely, to speak one's mind without terror, to choose whom to love, where to live, and what to believe—these are not luxuries. They are *lifelines*. They are the sacred inheritance of every person, and the responsibility of every generation.

Whether you are a prisoner in a cell, or a leader in a palace, know this: The measure of your life is how deeply you honor the freedom of others. You do not own it. You are its guardian.

"When we lose the right to be different, we lose the privilege to be free."
— CHARLES EVANS HUGHES

2. The Mirror of Conscience: Uphold Truth Without Violence

Conscience is your only true country. It speaks in silence, resists all propaganda, and cannot be imprisoned. To live truthfully is not merely to tell the truth—it is to *embody it*, especially when deception is easier. This requires courage—not the kind that shouts, but the kind that is mindfully awake. The kind that says, "I will not lie, even if my silence could save me."

Conscience will ask everything of you. And give back your soul in return. In a world where truth is twisted and brokered, the one who listens to their inner moral compass becomes a revolution.

"Conscience is the root of all true courage."
— JAMES FREEMAN CLARKE

3. The Practice of Dignity: Honor Humanity in Every Soul

Dignity is not something you earn. It is something you *recognize*. In yourself. In your enemy. In the stranger. In the wounded. In the one who has nothing. And yes, even in the one who has done great harm.

To practice dignity is to resist all forms of dehumanization. It is to say, "I will not reduce another being to their label, their mistake, or their past." You are never more powerful than when you protect the dignity of the powerless. This is how peace begins—not on paper, but in how we see one another.

"Our shared dignity is the foundation of our common future."

— KOFI ANNAN

4. The Right to Speak: Defend Freedom of Expression as Sacred Flame

Speech is the lifeblood of liberty. It is the voice of conscience made audible. To silence it is to suffocate the soul of a people. The right to speak—to question, to dissent, to create, to cry out in pain or joy—is not the privilege of the powerful. It is the birthright of every human being.

Defend it. Especially when the words offend you. Especially when they come from the margins. Because the day we silence the weak is the day we forfeit our strength. And without expression, there is no freedom—only quiet obedience.

"I disapprove of what you say, but I will defend to the death your right to say it."

— EVELYN BEATRICE HALL (OFTEN ATTRIBUTED TO VOLTAIRE)

5. The Courage to Disobey: Resist Unjust Power with Moral Intelligence

Obedience to injustice is complicity. True strength is not in following orders—it is in knowing when not to. When power commands you to betray your conscience, your duty is to resist. Nonviolently. Unflinchingly. Not with hate, but with clarity.

Civil disobedience is not rebellion—it is a form of remembrance. A remembrance of who we are before fear took hold. When systems turn cruel, it is the sacred duty of the human being to say: *No. Not in my name.*

"An individual who breaks a law that conscience tells him is unjust... is in reality expressing the highest respect for law."
— MARTIN LUTHER KING JR.

6. The Heart of *Ubuntu*: Thrive in Our Shared Belonging

Your freedom is not separate from mine. Your suffering is not separate from mine. I am because you are. This is *Ubuntu*—not charity, not pity, but the sacred recognition of our intimate interdependence. It is the deep knowing that human dignity and freedom are never solitary affairs. They are shared truths, woven into the fabric of our mutual becoming.

We rise together or not at all. We cannot build peace for ourselves if we build prisons for others. Practicing *Ubuntu* means living with radical empathy. It means asking not only: "What's best for me?" but "What honors us all?"

"Ubuntu speaks of the very essence of being human.
You can't exist as a human being in isolation."
— DESMOND TUTU

7. The Discipline of Compassion: Let Love Be Fierce, Not Fragile

Compassion is not weakness. It is the highest discipline of the heart. To remain open, even after betrayal. To protect the vulnerable, without needing vengeance. To see humanity where others see threat—that is the courage of love.

Let your compassion be clear-eyed. Let it set boundaries and dismantle harm. But let it never harden into hate. For in the darkest hours, it is not cruelty that will save us—it is those who refuse to forget the humanity of their enemy.

"The final forming of a person's character lies in their own hands."
— ANNE FRANK

8. The Path of Peace: Choose Coexistence Over Conflict

War does not create peace. It delays justice. It buries grief beneath rubble and teaches the next generation that force is the only language that works. There is no victory in ashes.

Peace is not passive. It is radical. It is the fierce protection of dignity without domination. To coexist is not to agree with everyone—

it is to live in mutual restraint and mutual respect, even when that is hardest. Choose peace not because you are weak, but because you are strong enough not to destroy what you cannot control.

"An eye for an eye makes the whole world blind."
— MAHATMA GANDHI

9. The Practice of Humility: Serve, Don't Rule

True leadership is rooted in service—not status. Whether you lead a nation, a classroom, a movement, or a family—your authority is measured by how you listen, how you include, and how you lift others up.

Humility is not silence. It is moral clarity without self-importance. It is the willingness to be corrected, to keep learning, and to admit when you have caused harm. Those who rule with ego collapse in fear. But those who serve with humility become unforgettable.

"The best way to find yourself is to lose yourself in the service of others."
— MAHATMA GANDHI

10. The Legacy of Freedom: Be Remembered for How You Loved

One day, your name—our names—will dissolve. Your titles, our titles, will vanish. Your image, our images, will fade. What will remain is how you treated others—how bravely you defended their freedom. How deeply you loved, how deeply we all loved. And how generously we gave our lives to something larger than ourselves.

This is the final measure: Did we live in a way that made freedom more possible for those who came after us? Let that question guide our choices. Let it whisper to us in silence, and thunder in us when we rise—together—in love. In love of freedom, of justice, and of peace.

"Darkness cannot drive out darkness; only light can do that. Hate cannot drive out hate; only love can do that."
— MARTIN LUTHER KING JR.

Aung San Suu Kyi's Closing Statement
From captivity — but never from silence

My beloved people of Myanmar—
And to all across this wounded world
who cradle the ember of freedom in your hearts—

This is not merely a manifesto.
It is a mirror — to see.
A map — to guide.
A vow — to bind.
It does not ask for your beliefs,
but for your life's devotion.

What will you forge
with the fragile, fleeting gift of freedom?

How will you wield
your voice,
your breath,
your heart
in this brief and sacred span?

You may feel powerless.
Alone.
Unseen.
But hear me—
truly hear, please:

Every quiet act of defiance.
Every stand against falsehood.
Every spark of kindness
lit in fear's shadow—
resounds beyond the horizon.

Uplift others in their liberty
as you would long to be uplifted
in your darkest hour.

When someone is silenced,
listen with your whole being.

When someone is imprisoned,
lend them your voice.

When a people are erased from history,
hold them as your kin—
for they are.

Freedom is not a prize to possess.
It is a covenant—
woven of vigilance,
truth,
and a love that does not yield.

The true measure of our humanity
is revealed in how fiercely we defend
the dignity of others.

If I never walk free again,
let my voice live in your actions.

Let these words become your sacred oath—
not to me,
but to the yet-unborn dawn.

Let the children of tomorrow inherit a world
where no one trembles to speak,
to dream,
to dissent,
to belong.

Where silence is not a shield—
but a gift.

Clasp this manifesto to your heart.
Teach it.
Embody it.
Defend it with your life.
Pass it on
like flame through the night.

And to the dreamers—
teachers,
healers,
mothers,
visionaries—
your quiet acts are humanity's salvation.

Do not let Myanmar's agony
vanish into shadow.
Weave a tapestry of compassion
that defies the junta's cruelty.
That names our stolen lives.
That carries our hope
to every corner of the earth.

Let your life be a global awakening—
unyielding—
until justice resounds
in every soul.

And never forget:

You are never too small
to guard the sacred.

And the sacred is everywhere—
in every gesture,
every stand,
every whisper that declares:
Not while I breathe.

In solidarity,
in memory,
and in fierce, eternal love—

Aung San Suu Kyi
JULY 19, 2025

An Open Letter to Future Generations
A Final Blessing from Daw Aung San Suu Kyi

To my grandchildren,
and to every child living under tyranny:

If these words have found you,
then something in the world still hears.
Perhaps it is dawn. Perhaps it is dusk.
Either way, I imagine you with open eyes and a steady breath—
one not yet shaped by fear,
nor hardened by betrayal.

Hold onto that breath.
It is your first freedom,
and your most intimate inheritance.

I have lived long enough to know the shape of silence.
I have slept beside it in prison cells,
eaten with it at bare tables,
walked among crowds silenced by terror.

Silence can be a teacher—
a fierce and faithful one.
But never—*never*—let it become your master.

Do not mistake power for truth,
nor law for justice.
These things part ways more often than they meet.

You will be told to obey.
You will be told to forget.
But your dignity is not theirs to erase.
Your conscience is not theirs to command.

In my time, I witnessed great cruelty—
cleverly cloaked in policy, banners, and beautiful lies.
I watched my people suffer beneath flags embroidered with falsehood.
And yet—we did not vanish.
We did not kneel in spirit.

Because our revolution was not only political.

It was moral.
It was spiritual.
It was rooted in the heart—
a place no dictatorship can ever reach.

Remember this:
Every time you listen with compassion,
you are healing a wound older than yourself.
Every time you speak the truth—
especially when your voice shakes—
you are carrying the torch of all who dared before you.
And every time you choose not to hate,
even when hatred would be easier,
you are shaping a world where love can survive.

You are not powerless.
You are becoming.
And *becoming* is more powerful than you know.

Let the teachings of the *Dhamma* be your anchor:
clarity, patience, compassion, truth.
Let **Ubuntu** be your compass:
"I am because we are."

To those who govern:
govern with humility—or not at all.

To those who suffer:
your pain is valid, your voice is sacred.

To those who inherit this fractured earth:
do not merely endure it. Shape it. Sing it back into wholeness.

And when you kneel beside injustice—
not in defeat, but in prayer—
let that kneeling become a vow:
I will rise.
I will rise in dignity.
I will rise for others.

And when you speak,
let your words cross oceans and generations.
Speak not to be remembered—
but so others may remember themselves.

May your hearts be fierce.
May your minds be clear.
May your compassion be boundless.

This is my blessing.
This is my farewell.
This is my vow of *mettā*—
sent forward like a candle set upon the river of time:

You are not alone.
We are with you.
Rise.

— *Daw Aung San Suu Kyi*
Written in spirit, from a place beyond bars
MYANMAR, JULY 19, 2025

EPILOGUE:
THE END THAT BEGINS

—Alan Clements, JULY 2025
From a world still listening

The final pages of a book are never truly the end.
They are a held breath in silence—
a pause between what has been
and what insists on becoming.

Unsilenced is not merely a record of conversations.
It is a chronicle of conscience.
A mirror held to a shattered world.
A vessel of memory.
A quiet act of moral resistance.

And now,
in the wake of fresh devastation,
it becomes something more:
a requiem,
a vow,
and a call to action.

On March 28, 2025—
six months before this manuscript was finalized—
a catastrophic earthquake struck Myanmar's Sagaing Region.
Homes collapsed like paper.
Temples cracked and wept stone.
Thousands were displaced in a single night.

And amid the rubble,
the fighter jets still roared overhead.
The sirens did not stop.
Relief convoys were shelled.
Villages already scarred by war
now bear new wounds—
carved by both earth and empire.

Nature trembled.
But it was man's cruelty that continued to kill.

And yet—
something remains.
Something refuses to die.
There are children in refugee camps
who still sing lullabies.
Nurses tending to the wounded by candlelight—
their clinics reduced to ash.

Teachers reciting poetry underground.
Grandmothers boiling rice for strangers.
Monks chanting in defiance.
Political prisoners whispering
courage through sewage pipes.
Armed and unarmed revolutionaries memorizing
the Universal Declaration of Human Rights
as if it were scripture.

This is not just survival.
This is sacred resistance.

Myanmar today is not a metaphor.
It is not a symbol.
It is a nation being erased—
while the world debates process.

As of this writing,
more than 22,000 political prisoners
remain unjustly detained—
starved,
tortured,
denied medicine,
tried in military courts without legitimacy.
Children abducted.
Women violated.
Villages bombed.

The junta's methods are not new.
They are the architecture of modern evil.

And still—
the people do not bow.

The Spring Revolution,
born of fire and song,
still marches.
One foot in the jungle.
One foot in the dream.

It has evolved,
scattered,
rebuilt.

It is no longer just a protest.
It is a spiritual uprising.
A moral awakening.
A human anthem.

And behind it, always,
is dignity—
unseen,
undefeated.
No bomb can reach that.

When I began this book,
I did not know if Daw Aung San Suu Kyi
would ever speak again.

And yet—
through these pages,
she has spoken.
Not only to me,
but through me.

Her voice is not political.
It is prophetic.

It carries the silence of cells,
the memory of massacres,
and the stubborn, enduring love of her people.

Let this epilogue be not a farewell—
but a frontline.

If you are reading this,
you are now a custodian of memory.
You are holding in your hands
not just a book—
but a living record of suffering,

of resistance,
and of promise.

What will you do with it?

Will you speak the names of the 22,000 still imprisoned?
Will you ask your government
why it sells weapons to war criminals?
Will you light a candle—
not as a symbol,
but as a vow?

Or will you turn the page and forget?

To the displaced,
the grieving,
the starving,
and the unbroken—
I say this:
We see you.
We hear you.
We carry you.

To the revolutionaries
who have refused to surrender love
to the logic of war:
You are the future writing itself.

To Daw Aung San Suu Kyi,
still imprisoned as of this writing:
May your words continue to ring
louder than the bars meant to silence them.
You have given the world
a testament of conscience.
We will not let it vanish.

This is the end of the book.
But it is only the beginning of our responsibility.

May *Unsilenced*

raise global awareness of her enduring presence in the world—
though silenced by force.

May it serve as a catalyst for action,
not applause.

May it awaken leaders to finally speak and act—
for her,
and for the more than 22,000 imprisoned for truth.

May it also shine light on the
National Unity Government (NUG),
whose tireless pursuit of federal democracy
deserves international recognition and support;
and on the Ethnic Armed Organizations (EAOs),
who fight not just for democracy—
but for dignity.

And may it bring hope to every human soul in Myanmar—
imprisoned or free,
armed or unarmed,
hungry or resolute.

Even to the soldiers of the *Tatmadaw*:
May you lay down your weapons
and take up a different cause—
the revolution of the spirit,
the redemption of the human heart.

May Myanmar become a miracle.
Not through vengeance—
but through reconciliation,
truth,
and a peace the world has never seen.

Brave on.
You are an inspiration to all who cherish freedom.

Statement by **Ambassador Kyaw Moe Tun**,
Permanent Representative of the Republic of the Union of Myanmar
to United Nations, at the High-level debate of the General Assembly
on *"A second chance: addressing the global prison challenge"*
(NEW YORK, 13 JUNE 2025)

Mr. President,

I wish to thank you for convening this meeting.

Nelson Mandela once said: *"No one truly knows a nation until one has been inside its jails."*

To know Myanmar today is to confront a nation where prisons are not tools of justice—but instruments of oppression.

Under successive military regimes, arbitrary detention and torture have long disfigured the rule of law. But since the unlawful military coup attempt in February 2021, this repression has reached horrifying new heights.

Therefore, the 10th anniversary of the Mandela Rules must not be a moment of ceremony—but one of conscience. We are called to act in defense of the people these rules were meant to protect.

Mr. President,

In Myanmar, more than 29,000 people, from students, doctors, journalists, elected lawmakers to children, have been arrested on political grounds. But in most cases, people are arbitrarily arrested, and many for extortion purposes.

Out of those arrested, over 22,000 people remain detained and sentenced in prisons. But these detainees had never received fair trials.

Notably in 2022, four political prisoners—Phyo Zeya Thaw, Kyaw Min Yu (known as Ko Jimmy), Hla Myo Aung, and Aung Thura Zaw—were executed after closed-door trials.

Two years following in 2024, the junta hanged Kaung Htet and Chan Myae Thu—a young woman, and the first known female political prisoner executed.

These are not isolated atrocities. They are deliberate acts of terror, designed to suppress opposition from the people, extinguish hope and silence dissent.

IN MYANMAR,
SIX POLITICAL PRISONERS
WERE EXECUTED
FOR THEIR LOVE OF
DEMOCRACY—
PHYO ZEYA THAW,
KYAW MIN YU (KNOWN
AS KO JIMMY),
HLA MYO AUNG,
AND AUNG THURA ZAW—
ALONG WITH
KAUNG HTET AND
CHAN MYAE THU—
A YOUNG WOMAN, AND
THE FIRST KNOWN FEMALE
POLITICAL PRISONER EXECUTED.

Mr. President,

Rule One of Mandela is clear and signifies "Dignity". It stated that *"All prisoners shall be treated with the respect due to their inherent dignity and value as human beings."*

Myanmar's military junta is in open defiance of this standard.

The Assistance Association for Political Prisoners (AAPP) Burma has documented numerous forms of atrocities committed by the military junta and their mistreatment to prisoners. These include torture using electric shocks, beatings, waterboarding, sexual violence against both men and women and withholding of medical care as a form of coercion.

On some occasions, the junta has been practicing release of political prisoners as a weapon. Former detainees are tracked, denied jobs and education, often rearrested within days. One survivor described release as *"a new version of imprisonment"*— life under surveillance, with no freedom and no future.

This, too, is a form of torture.

Again, Rule 58 of Mandela affirms that prisoners must be allowed contact with their families and the world beyond prison walls, which is certainly not the case in Myanmar where that right is almost entirely denied.

Phone calls and letters are rare, heavily censored, and arbitrarily cut off. Visits are cancelled without notice. Even lawyers are frequently barred from access.

This cruelty is strategic.

Even Myanmar's most high-profile detainees—President U Win Myint and State Counsellor Daw Aung San Suu Kyi—have been held incommunicado for years. They have been stripped of legal counsel, denied contact with loved ones, and cut off from the very people who elected them.

Taking this opportunity, I wish to inform you that our leader Daw Aung San Suu Kyi will turn 80th year-old next week. Many people of Myanmar are now organizing various activities to celebrate her 80th Birthday and pray her for good health and immediate release.

Mr. President,

One former prisoner said: *"It wasn't the beatings that broke me - it was knowing my mother thought I was dead."*

Here, the concept of the heinous military junta is obvious. They mean to isolate a prisoner by erasing them and isolate elected leaders to erase democracy itself.

Detention in Myanmar is not about law enforcement—it is about domination.

Military courts operate in secret, issuing death sentences in minutes. At least 163 pro-democracy supporters were sentenced to death in 2023 alone.

New prison wings are being built—not to uphold justice, but to detain it.

Mr. President,

The Mandela Rules are not aspirational. They are a baseline; a moral and legal minimum for all prisoners, everywhere.

When one state defies those rules so blatantly—and the world stays silent—the credibility of international human rights is what's truly on trial.

This is not only about Myanmar. It is about what we are willing to tolerate.

Therefore, I wish to underscore the following points: -

1. **Demand unrestricted access** for the UN and the ICRC to all detention facilities in Myanmar. These actors must be able to comprehend the actual situations that prisoners are facing. For whatever reasons detainees been arrested, they shall have the right to enjoy fair trial and justice before law. Contacts must also be allowed where families know conditions of their loved ones. All these measures are prerequisite.

2. **Insist on the immediate release** of all political prisoners—and an end to the practice of release-and-rearrest. The military junta clearly lacks legitimacy for such detention in the first place. Moreover, the latter practice is dubious which involves political manipulation and largely relates to extortion.

3. **Apply coordinated pressure** on the military junta through targeted sanctions, a global arms embargo, and support for evidence-gathering.

4. **Invest in survivor recovery**: psychological care, medical support, and reintegration for those returning from the prison system.

To conclude, **Mr. President,** Mandela emerged from 27 years in prison not broken—but ready to lead his country to a better future.

So too might many of Myanmar's prisoners - if we defend their rights now and unlock the doors to justice.

Let us honour the Mandela Rules not just with remembrance, but with resolve.

Let Myanmar's prisons no longer destroy hope - but, in Mandela's own words, become *"schools of freedom."*

The military junta in Myanmar is the root cause of the current crisis in our country.

Not only those in prisons, but also the entire population have been suffering through displacement and humanitarian settings due to the military junta's flagrant disregard of the rule of law and hostilities against the civilians.

Meanwhile, this junta has been enjoying impunity and blatantly violating the international law, international humanitarian law and international human rights law. It is the sole perpetrator for crimes that are amounting to war crimes and crimes against humanity.

They must be held accountable.

In this regard, I would like to urge the international community to help us in our effort to ending the military dictatorship and it unlawful military coup.

Only by establishing a federal democratic union, can Myanmar observe the Mandela Rules earnestly and bring justice both to the prisoners and people across the country.

I thank you.

FEDERAL
DEMOCRATIC
UNION OF
MYANMAR
FREE &
DEMOCRATIC

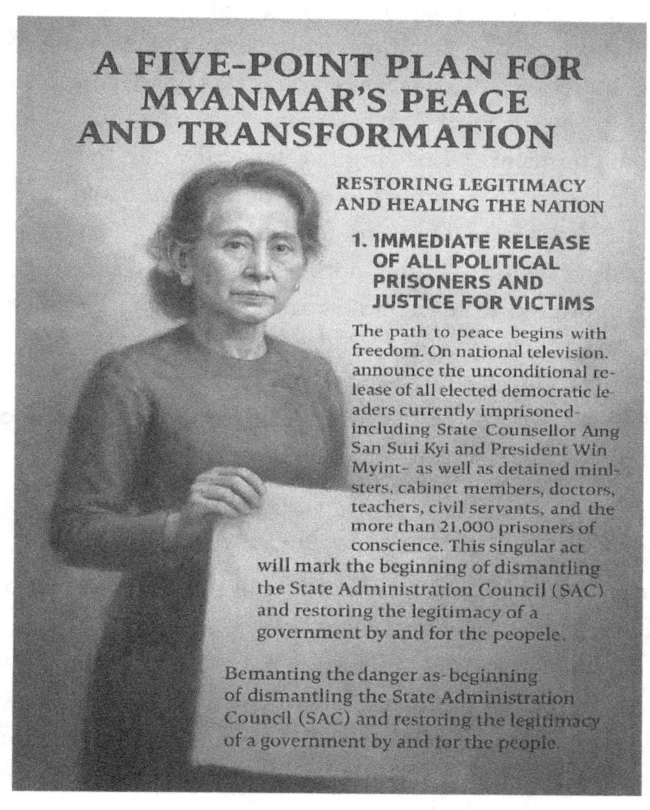

CONCLUSION & THE FUTURE

A Five-Point Plan for Myanmar's Peace and Transformation

Restoring Legitimacy and Healing the Nation

1. Immediate Release of All Political Prisoners and Justice for Victims

The path to peace begins with freedom. On national television, announce the unconditional release of all elected democratic leaders currently imprisoned—including State Counsellor Aung San Suu Kyi and President Win Myint—as well as detained ministers, cabinet members, doctors, teachers, civil servants, and the more than 22,000 prisoners of conscience. This singular act will mark the beginning of dismantling the State Administration Council (SAC) and restoring the legitimacy of a government by and for the people.

Justice for victims is not optional. Establish a National Truth Council empowered to investigate crimes, document testimonies, and begin reparative justice. This includes rehabilitation for survivors and public accountability for those found guilty of war crimes and systemic abuse. Healing requires truth. And truth requires the courage to face the past openly, with compassion and moral clarity.

Building a Federal Democratic Union

2. Resignation of Military Leadership and the Transformation of the Armed Forces

Senior General Min Aung Hlaing and his inner circle must resign without condition, relinquishing their grip on power. This act of moral responsibility is essential to begin national reconciliation. In their place, a civilian-led transition will reimagine the military as a force that serves the people—not controls them.

Transformation means accountability. Establish a military reform initiative with international oversight, focusing on ethical training, the demilitarization of governance, and integration with democratic norms. Offer programs to rehabilitate soldiers and create honorable exit paths for those who step down peacefully. Let the Tatmadaw become a protector of human rights—a military worthy of the people's trust.

A New Social Contract

3. Convening the Ashoka Peace Accords for Governance Transformation

Summon the voices of unity. Convene the Ashoka Peace Accords in Naypyidaw, uniting the National Unity Government, ethnic armed organizations, civil society leaders, spiritual figures, and international observers. This conference will define the moral, legal, and structural pillars of a new federalist democracy.

Structure the dialogues with a clear timeline, inclusive participation, and transparent mechanisms for implementation. Integrate principles of equitable power-sharing, cultural autonomy, and constitutional safeguards for ethnic minorities. Build a future where no group must fight for recognition—because every community belongs.

Accountability as a Path to Redemption

4. Truth, Justice, and National Healing

Myanmar will not forget—but it can forgive. Establish a Truth and Redemption Tribunal to allow perpetrators of violence to come forward in a spirit of honesty and transformation. Let those who have harmed the nation speak their truth, face just consequences, and seek moral redemption.

Support this process with reparations for victims, psychological and social reintegration programs, and community-led truth dialogues. Create a National Reconciliation Commission, inspired by both international law and the compassionate frameworks of Buddhist ethics. Let it be known: healing is not weakness. It is strength born of moral courage.

Becoming a Beacon of Peace in the Region

5. A Geopolitical Strategy for Regional Stability and Global Cooperation

Let Myanmar emerge not as a cautionary tale, but as a moral beacon. Strengthen alliances with ASEAN, the UN, and neighboring states through transparent, inclusive governance. Position Myanmar as a regional leader in conflict transformation, anti-corruption, human rights, and environmental cooperation.

Establish the Ashoka Peace Accords as a model for the nonviolent resolution of regional conflict. Seek economic and diplomatic partnerships that prioritize sustainable development, gender equity, and technological innovation.

Conclusion: A New Dawn for Myanmar

This Five-Point Plan is not a political document. It is a moral call to action. Let Myanmar rise from the shadows of tyranny into a future guided by truth, dignity, and justice. Let every prisoner of conscience walk free. Let every ethnic group feel seen. Let every child grow up knowing peace.

History is watching. Let Myanmar be remembered as the nation that chose healing over hatred, dialogue over destruction, and democracy over dictatorship.

The world awaits our courage. And to that world, we say: *Stand with us. Not tomorrow. Today.*

**Aung San Suu Kyi, from Opening Keynote Address
at NGO Forum on Women, Beijing China, 1995**

The regaining of my freedom has in turn imposed a duty on me to work for the freedom of other women and men in my country who have suffered far more—and who continue to suffer far more—than I have. [...]

For millennia women have dedicated themselves almost exclusively to the task of nurturing, protecting and caring for the young and the old, striving for the conditions of peace that favor life as a whole. [...] no war was ever started by women. But it is women and children who have always suffered most in situations of conflict. Now that we are gaining control of the primary historical role imposed on us of sustaining life in the context of the home and family, it is time to apply in the arena of the world the wisdom and experience thus gained in activities of peace over so many thousands of years. The education and empowerment of women throughout the world cannot fail to result in a more caring, tolerant, just and peaceful life for all.

In societies where men are truly confident of their own worth women are not merely "tolerated", they are valued. Their opinions are listened to with respect; they are given their rightful place in shaping the society in which they live.

It is not the prerogative of men alone to bring light to this world: women with their capacity for compassion and self-sacrifice, their courage and perseverance, have done much to dissipate the darkness of intolerance and hate, suffering and despair.

Many of my male colleagues who have suffered imprisonment for their part in the democracy movement have spoken of the great debt of gratitude they owe their womenfolk, particularly to their wives who stood by them firmly[...] These magnificent human beings who have done so much to aid their men in the struggle for justice and peace -- how much more could they not achieve if given the opportunity to work in their own right for the good of their country and of the world.

Yet the very high performance of women in our educational system and in the management of commercial enterprises proves their enormous potential to contribute to the betterment of society in general. Meanwhile our women have yet to achieve those fundamental rights of free expression, association and security of

life denied also to their menfolk.

The relationship between men and women should, and can be, characterized not by patronizing behavior or exploitation, but by *metta* (that is to say loving kindness), partnership and trust. We need mutual respect and understanding between men and women.

Women in their role as mothers have traditionally assumed the responsibility of teaching children values that will guide them throughout their lives. It is time we were given the full opportunity to use our natural teaching skills to contribute towards building a modern world that can withstand the tremendous challenges of the technological revolution which has in turn brought revolutionary changes in social values.

LETTERS TO
WORLD LEADERS

Letter To United States President Donald J. Trump

Alan Clements: Daw Suu, we've addressed ASEAN and the region. Yet greater leverage lies with global superpowers—the United States, China, Russia, the European Union. Each wields immense power, each cloaks inaction in its own rationale. Together, they could end this horror. What would you say to them—directly, one by one?

Aung San Suu Kyi: Alan, this is where power must kneel to conscience. To the United States—to President Trump—I offer not a plea, but a summons to history's crucible.

From Aung San Suu Kyi, in Detention, Naypyidaw Prison
JULY 2025

Dear President Trump,

Moments in history test a leader's power not by its might, but by its courage to answer truth's urgent call. I write to you—not only as a fellow leader enduring persecution, but as a survivor of lawfare's distortions, a reality you know intimately. From my cell, I see our struggles converge—a shared defiance against systems that fear unyielding conviction.

You have faced the weaponization of democratic tools, the sting of legal assaults waged to silence dissent. So, too, have I, alongside 22,000 fellow prisoners—farmers, students, monks, and teachers—jailed not for crimes, but for their belief in freedom; punished not for corruption, but for conscience. You understand this fire, Mr. President, a fire no prison or lie can extinguish. *I ask you to stand with us now, not as a diplomat, but as a leader who refuses to bow.*

The junta strangling Myanmar has lost all legitimacy, retaining only its savagery. Its war machine, devoid of a people's mandate, thrives on global inaction. That machine can be dismantled today, Mr. President, if you wield your unparalleled resolve to stop it.

You froze $1.5 billion of their assets. Now, sever their lifelines completely. Target their gas pipelines, military banks, and illicit revenue streams—the arteries fueling their brutality. Sanctions alone are not enough; isolation is their true fear. Your voice—singular and seismic— can render them global pariahs.

You champion strength and victory. Then champion the millions of Myanmar citizens who risked everything to vote for the National League for Democracy in 2020—and delivered a landslide victory. Support the National Unity Government (NUG) and Ethnic Armed Organizations (EAOs)—our resilient allies in Kachin, Karen, Shan, and beyond. From the Kachin Independence Army's unyielding defense to the Karen National Union's governance, their sacrifices forge the foundation of our democratic vision. Equip them not with troops, but with advanced technology, drones, secure communications, and innovative logistics inspired by American ingenuity, such as Starlink's connectivity. Let America's strength be measured not only in military might, but in solidarity with those who bleed for liberty.

Above all, proclaim with the full authority of your office: "Release President Win Myint, State Counsellor Aung San Suu Kyi, all democratically elected leaders—cabinet ministers, parliamentarians—and every prisoner of conscience. End the slaughter, or face America's unrelenting resolve." Make this your red line. Draw it now for Myanmar's people.

This is no mere conflict—it is a war on democracy itself. The junta bombs schools, razes 100,000 homes, displaces 3.5 million, and starves millions, with 20 million in desperate need of aid, as the United Nations warns. Myanmar has become a global disgrace, a hub for cybercrime and a fentanyl trafficking superhighway, threatening international stability.

Looming behind this crisis is China, eyeing Myanmar as its strategic foothold on the Bay of Bengal. With vast reserves of oil, gas, timber, and gems, they seek to exploit our land for slave labor, secure a deep-sea port in the Andaman Sea, and expand a 800-kilometer pipeline to Yunnan, transporting a quarter of a million barrels of oil daily. Beijing envisions not a sovereign nation, but a vassal state, its Belt and Road Initiative eroding our independence. If Myanmar falls, China's influence will tighten—a chokehold on the Indo-Pacific, threatening global freedom.

You have challenged China's ambitions before. Do so again. By supporting Myanmar's resistance, you can counter Beijing's expansion, safeguarding not only our sovereignty but the security of Southeast Asia and beyond.

This is not just Myanmar's fight—it is a bulwark against tyranny's global advance. The NUG and EAOs, united in dialogue, are forging a federal democracy where Bamar and ethnic voices shape a shared destiny. We seek no American boots on our soil, only your voice, your resolve, and your power to alter history's course.

In me, see not a diminished figure, but a woman who dares to believe in justice, unbroken after decades of struggle. In us, see a nation unbowed, carrying forward General Aung San's vision of unity, guided by the *Dhamma*'s call for compassion and righteousness. In you, Mr. President, see an unparalleled opportunity to shape a legacy of action—a triumph that will echo across generations.

Be our voice. Be our ally. Be our hope. Let the world declare that when freedom was reborn in Myanmar, it bore your name.

The time is now.

With respect and urgency,
Aung San Suu Kyi
IN DETENTION, NAYPYIDAW PRISON

Aung San Suu Kyi to President Xi Jinping of China

Dear President Xi,

Our paths crossed once—a fleeting moment etched in my memory with the clarity only adversity can sharpen. I recall it not with resentment, but with hope that dialogue between neighbors remains not only possible, but essential. As a daughter of Asia, I have long believed that China, rooted in its ancient philosophical heritage, can lead not merely with power, but with the moral vision of compassion.

I write to you from my prison cell, where silence cradles both suffering and hope, not with accusation, but with profound sincerity; not in defiance, but with an urgent appeal to our shared humanity. The future of our region hinges not only on the balance of power, but on the courage to weave strength with healing. Your leadership, Mr. President, can shape that destiny.

You have championed harmony, stability, and a shared future. Yet, across your border, Myanmar is engulfed in crisis. The junta that seized power in February 2021 through violence and deception has plunged our nation into despair. Over 10,000 civilians killed. More than 3.5 million displaced. A hundred thousand homes reduced to ashes. Schools shattered by airstrikes. Villages erased in flames. Millions face starvation, with 20 million in desperate need of humanitarian aid, as the United Nations warns. These are not mere statistics—they are your neighbors, our children, monks, and elders, crying out for compassion.

Your pipelines traverse a land starved of hope. Your trade sustains a regime that silences its people. To many, your silence suggests acquiescence. But it need not be so. You wield unparalleled influence—economic, diplomatic, and moral. I believe, with unwavering conviction, that you also possess the wisdom to wield it for justice.

China's interests in Myanmar—oil, gas, timber, gems, ports, and pipelines—are undermined by a junta that thrives on chaos. A regime that bombs its own schools cannot safeguard your investments. A cartel fueling fentanyl trafficking and cybercrime cannot ensure stable trade. A military that slays its citizens cannot uphold the trust required for true partnership.

True stability, Mr. President, will flourish only in a democratic Myanmar, led by leaders committed to human dignity and mutual respect. The National Unity Government (NUG), alongside Ethnic Armed Organizations (EAOs) forging autonomy in Kachin, Karen, Shan, and beyond, offers that vision: a federal democracy, born of dialogue, where Bamar and ethnic voices unite to rebuild a sovereign nation. This Myanmar will protect your infrastructure, secure your ports, and honor your trade—not as a subordinate, but as an equal partner grounded in justice.

Close the channels of complicity. Suspend the arms fueling this carnage. Demand an immediate ceasefire. Proclaim with your unmatched authority: "Release President Win Myint, State Counsellor Aung San Suu Kyi, all democratically elected leaders—cabinet ministers, parliamentarians—and every prisoner of conscience." These leaders are no threat to China; they are Myanmar's bridge to peace, and peace is strength's highest expression.

To General Min Aung Hlaing, I say: You stand at a crossroads. End the terror, free our leaders, and embrace the path to reconciliation. History offers redemption to those who choose conscience.

You have spoken of the Chinese Dream—rejuvenation, prosperity, harmony. Let Myanmar's peace be its foundation. A dream that ignores suffering is fragile; one that uplifts humanity endures. Open Yunnan's border to deliver stalled aid, feeding our children and sheltering our displaced. Let China be not only a global power, but a compassionate neighbor; not merely a force, but a beacon of hope.

Recent resistance efforts underscore our resolve. In May 2025, Mandalay's resistance seized a Chinese pipeline station, while Karen State's forces united under the Karen National Union, strengthening our fight. Yet, the junta's planned 2025 election, a facade to entrench power, threatens further violence. Your intervention can halt this cycle, ensuring these sacrifices pave the way to peace.

By acting, you will not lose Myanmar—you will earn its eternal gratitude, a legacy etched in the hearts of millions. A democratic Myanmar, united in dignity, will stand as China's steadfast partner, its stability a pillar of Asia's harmony, its gratitude a testament to your foresight.

History honors leaders not for dominion, but for mercy; not for conquest, but for compassion's enduring reach. From these prison walls, alongside 22,000 prisoners of conscience—each a beacon of courage—I implore you: Use your influence to heal, to uplift, to lead. Be the sage who stanches the wound. Be the architect of peace.

Let it be said for centuries to come that when humanity stood at a crossroads, China chose the path of dignity. Myanmar awaits. The world watches.

With respect and resolute hope,
Aung San Suu Kyi
IN DETENTION, NAYPYIDAW PRISON

Aung San Suu Kyi to President Vladimir Putin of Russia

Dear President Putin,

Though we have not met, I have followed your leadership with deep interest, mindful of Russia's storied history and its enduring quest for global respect. Your recent engagements with Senior General Min Aung Hlaing—hosting him twice in Moscow, signing agreements for a nuclear reactor near Naypyidaw, expanding arms supplies, and forging a mutual protection pact against international accountability—compel me to write from my prison cell, where I speak not with resentment, but with profound sincerity; not in defiance, but with an urgent appeal to your conscience. In the silence of confinement, I see a shared aspiration for a world where power serves justice, urging you to align Russia's strength with Myanmar's hope.

You have declared that strength commands respect. Yet, I ask: what greater strength exists than the courage to halt a war fueled, in part, by Russia's support? The junta's military, armed with Russian jets, missiles, and drones, has razed over 2,000 villages, killed more than 10,000 civilians, and displaced 3.5 million since February 2021. Schools lie in ruins. Homes are reduced to ashes. Millions face starvation, with 20 million in desperate need of aid, as the United Nations warns. These are not numbers, Mr. President—they are your neighbors, our children, monks, and elders. This is not influence; it is devastation.

Russia's pledge to supply a nuclear reactor near Naypyidaw, alongside increased arms deliveries, risks entrenching a regime devoid of legitimacy. A junta that bombs its own people cannot be trusted to steward such power. Its illicit trade in fentanyl and cybercrime, flourishing amid chaos, undermines not only Myanmar but the stability Russia seeks in its partnerships. Your advisors in Naypyidaw support an unlawful regime, not a government, as evidenced by their mutual shield against international arrest warrants.

Yet, this need not define Russia's legacy. Your strategic interests— influence in Southeast Asia, economic partnerships, regional stability— are undermined by a regime that sows terror. A fractured Myanmar cannot safeguard your investments or honor alliances. True stability will flourish only in a democratic Myanmar, led by leaders committed to human dignity and mutual respect. The National Unity Government (NUG), alongside Ethnic Armed Organizations (EAOs) forging autonomy in Kachin, Karen, Shan, and beyond, offers that vision: a federal democracy, woven through dialogue, where Bamar and ethnic voices unite to rebuild a sovereign nation. This Myanmar will stand as Russia's reliable partner, vibrant with justice and shared prosperity.

You wield unparalleled influence—military, diplomatic, and moral. I believe, with steadfast conviction, that you also possess the wisdom to wield it for peace. You have championed Russia's independent path. Let that path shine not through weapons that destroy, but through compassion that heals.

Close the channels of complicity. Suspend the supply of jets, missiles, and drones that slaughter our people. Withdraw advisors enabling this regime. Reconsider the nuclear agreement that emboldens tyranny. Proclaim with your formidable authority: "Demand an immediate ceasefire. Release President Win Myint, State Counsellor Aung San Suu Kyi, all democratically elected leaders—cabinet ministers, parliamentarians—and every prisoner of conscience." These leaders are no threat to Russia; they are Myanmar's bridge to peace, and peace is strength's highest expression.

To General Min Aung Hlaing, I say: You stand at a crossroads. End the terror, free our leaders, and embrace reconciliation. History offers redemption to those who choose conscience over cruelty.

Your voice resonates on the global stage. Use it at the United Nations not to shield perpetrators, but to protect the vulnerable, redirecting military profits to humanitarian aid for Myanmar's 20 million in need. Let Russia be not only a power, but a champion of justice.

You have said, "We are not the West." Let this distinction blaze through actions that set a new standard—not of expedient alliances, but of moral courage. Open Russia's heart to our displaced, allowing aid to feed our children and shelter our families.

Recent resistance efforts underscore our resolve. In May 2025, Mandalay's resistance seized a Chinese pipeline station, while Karen State's forces united under the Karen National Union, strengthening our fight. Yet, the junta's planned 2025 election, a sham to entrench power, threatens further violence. Your intervention can halt this cycle, ensuring these sacrifices pave the way to peace.

By acting, you will not lose Myanmar—you will earn its eternal gratitude, a legacy etched in the hearts of millions. A democratic Myanmar, united in dignity, will stand as Russia's steadfast ally, its stability a testament to your foresight, its gratitude a beacon for a world yearning for justice.

History honors leaders not for dominion, but for mercy; not for conquest, but for compassion's enduring reach. From these prison walls, alongside 22,000 prisoners of conscience—each a beacon of courage—I implore you: Use your influence to heal, to uplift, to lead. Be the sage who stanches the wound. Be the architect of peace.

Let it be said for centuries to come that when humanity stood at a crossroads, Russia chose the path of dignity. Myanmar awaits. The world watches.

With respect and resolute hope,
Aung San Suu Kyi
IN DETENTION, NAYPYIDAW PRISON

**Aung San Suu Kyi to President Ursula von der Leyen and the
European Union**

Dear President von der Leyen,

Europe knows the scars of conflict, the weight of rebuilding
from ruins, and the vision of leaders who transformed suffering into
unity. From the ashes of Warsaw, the rubble of Berlin, and the shores
of Normandy, you have forged a union rooted in conscience, pledging
"never again."

I write from a prison cell in Naypyidaw, not only as a fellow servant of the public, but as one who believes Europe's beacon of compassion shines undimmed. In the silence of confinement, I see our shared aspiration for a world where dignity triumphs, urging you to align Europe's resolve with Myanmar's hope.

I implore you to view Myanmar not as a distant tragedy, but as a living echo of the horrors Europe vowed to prevent. The darkness engulfing my nation of 54 million mirrors the crises you have overcome, unfolding now with a ferocity that demands your attention. The time to act is now.

Since the junta's coup in February 2021, over 10,000 civilians have been killed, their lives extinguished by a regime armed with Russian jets, missiles, and drones, emboldened by Min Aung Hlaing's Moscow visits and Russia's pledge for a nuclear reactor near Naypyidaw. More than 3.5 million are displaced, seeking refuge in jungles and camps. Over 100,000 homes have been reduced to ashes, villages erased. Schools lie shattered by airstrikes.

Mandalay bears the scars of the March 2025 earthquake, while Yangon survives on four hours of daily electricity. Myanmar has become a failed state—a hub for cybercrime and fentanyl trafficking sustained by a terrorist junta, propped up by Russian and Chinese complicity and global inaction.

Yet, this tragedy need not persist. Europe's interests—regional stability, human rights, and global moral leadership—are undermined by a regime that thrives on chaos. A junta that slays its citizens cannot secure your trade or uphold your values. True stability will flourish only in a democratic Myanmar, led by leaders committed to human dignity and justice.

The National Unity Government (NUG), alongside Ethnic Armed Organizations (EAOS) forging autonomy in Kachin, Karen, Shan, and beyond, offers that vision: a federal democracy, crafted through dialogue, where Bamar and ethnic voices unite to rebuild a sovereign nation, vibrant with mutual respect.

You wield unparalleled influence—economic, diplomatic, and moral. I believe, with steadfast conviction, that you possess the wisdom to wield it decisively. Your sanctions have weakened the junta; now, intensify your efforts to dismantle its power.

Freeze their foreign accounts—every euro withheld prevents further bloodshed. Ban their gas exports, starving tyranny of its resources. Block their access to international finance, severing the lifelines of terror. Act swiftly, lest inaction be seen as complicity. Recognize the NUG as the legitimate voice of 11 million who risked their lives to vote in 2020—a mandate, not a movement. Allocate €200 million to support its governance, empowering a future rooted in trust.

To General Min Aung Hlaing, I say: You stand at a crossroads. End the terror, release our leaders, and embrace reconciliation. History offers redemption to those who choose conscience over cruelty.

Madam President, you have shown that values are non-negotiable, democracy enduring, and human rights a daily commitment. Cease all engagement with a regime whose nuclear ambitions and illicit trade threaten global security. Instead, stand with the children of Sagaing, the displaced of Rakhine, and the prisoners of Yangon. Let them know Europe sees their plight.

Recent resistance efforts underscore our determination. In May 2025, Mandalay's resistance seized a Chinese pipeline station, while Karen State's forces united under the Karen National Union, bolstering our fight. Yet, the junta's planned 2025 election, a facade to entrench power, threatens further repression. Your leadership can tip the balance, ensuring these sacrifices lead to peace.

Let Europe's principles shine not only in Brussels, but in the eyes of those clinging to dignity amid despair. Let the EU lead not just in prosperity, but in compassion, forging a Myanmar where democracy thrives, its people a testament to your unwavering resolve. If not now, when?

From these prison walls, alongside 22,000 prisoners of conscience—each a sentinel of hope—I implore you: Be the architect of peace. Be the guardian of humanity. Let history declare that when Myanmar's darkness deepened, Europe lit the way.

With respect and resolute hope,

Aung San Suu Kyi

IN DETENTION, NAYPYIDAW PRISON

Aung San Suu Kyi to President Narendra Modi of India

Mr. President,

From the confines of a prison cell in Naypyidaw, where silence cradles both anguish and hope, I write to you as a sister in spirit, a daughter of Asia, and an enduring admirer of India's luminous legacy. Our nations are bound by sacred ties: the world's largest democracy you lead, the universal human rights you champion, and the timeless

Dhamma born on Indian soil, where the Buddha's wisdom illuminated compassion, truth, and non-violence. In Myanmar, a land steeped in Buddhist devotion, we strive to embody these principles, as I have through decades of unwavering commitment.

My mother, Daw Khin Kyi, served as Myanmar's ambassador in New Delhi, where I lived in the 1960s, my heart shaped by India's vibrancy and Mahatma Gandhi's gospel of ahimsa. In New Delhi's vibrant streets, I absorbed Gandhi's truth and the Buddha's compassion—a flame that burns undimmed, urging you to ignite India's moral leadership for Myanmar's salvation. Gandhi's courage—confronting tyranny with truth, forging freedom through sacrifice—lives in me, as it does in you, a leader who invokes his vision to guide India's ascent. I reach out not with accusation, but with profound sincerity; not in despair, but with an urgent appeal to the conscience uniting our peoples.

India, the cradle of the Buddha, understands the cost of silence and the transformative power of action. Yet, across your border, Myanmar is consumed by crisis. The junta that seized power in February 2021 through violence and deception has plunged our nation into despair. Over 10,000 civilians have been killed, their lives extinguished by a regime armed with Russian jets, missiles, and drones, emboldened by Min Aung Hlaing's Moscow visits and Russia's pledge for a nuclear reactor near. More than 3.5 million are displaced, seeking refuge in jungles and camps. Over 100,000 homes lie in ashes, villages erased. Schools are shattered by airstrikes. Mandalay bears the scars of the March 2025 earthquake, while Yangon survives on four hours of daily electricity. Myanmar has become a failed state—a hub for cybercrime and fentanyl trafficking sustained by a terrorist junta, propped up by Russian and Chinese complicity and global inaction.

This is not the legacy of the *Dhamma*. This is not the path of dignity. India's interests—regional stability, democratic leadership, and security in the Northeast—are undermined by a junta that sows chaos. A regime that slays its citizens cannot ensure your trade or safeguard your borders, risking instability in Manipur and Assam. True stability will flourish only in a democratic Myanmar, led by leaders committed to human dignity and justice. The National Unity Government (NUG), alongside Ethnic Armed Organizations (EAOS) forging autonomy in Kachin, Karen, Shan, and beyond, offers that vision: a federal democracy, crafted through dialogue, where Bamar and ethnic voices unite to rebuild a sovereign nation, vibrant with mutual respect.

You wield unparalleled influence—economic, diplomatic, and moral. As a leader who reveres Gandhi's truth and Ashoka's redemption, you understand the power of choices that transform. Ashoka, once a warrior, embraced the *Dhamma's* light, his redemption a beacon for empires. I hold the same hope for Myanmar's military—a path to peace, guided by a neighbor who dares to lead.

I appeal to India, a global democratic beacon, to stand not in silence, but in conscience. Close your borders to the junta's weapons and illicit commerce. Halt the flow of arms and funds—whether through official channels or private firms—that fuel Myanmar's destruction. Demand an immediate ceasefire. Proclaim with the moral clarity India embodies: "Release President Win Myint, State Counsellor Aung San Suu Kyi, all democratically elected leaders—cabinet ministers, parliamentarians—and every prisoner of conscience." These leaders are no threat to India; they are Myanmar's bridge to peace, as Gandhi was to yours. Peace, Mr. Prime Minister, is not frailty; it is strength's highest expression, rooted in the *Dhamma* we revere.

To General Min Aung Hlaing, I say: You stand at history's crossroads. End the terror, release our leaders, and embrace Ashoka's path of reconciliation. History offers redemption to those who choose conscience over cruelty.

India, the birthplace of the Buddha, has a moral duty to act. Open your borders to our displaced, as you have for countless refugees. Deliver aid—food, medicine, shelter—through civil society, monasteries, and grassroots networks, bypassing junta control to reach the 20 million in desperate need.

You have shown that democracy endures, human rights are a daily commitment, and India's global rise is rooted in moral courage. Cease engagement with a regime whose nuclear ambitions and illicit trade threaten regional security. Instead, stand with the children of Sagaing, the displaced of Rakhine, and the prisoners of Yangon. Let them know India sees their plight, as Gandhi saw the unseen, as the Buddha saw suffering.

Let India's vision shine not only in New Delhi, but in the eyes of those clinging to dignity amid despair. Let India rise as Asia's moral compass, its democratic heart guiding Myanmar to a federal union where dignity prevails, its legacy a testament to your leadership, Gandhi's truth, and the Buddha's compassion. If not now, when?

From these prison walls, alongside 22,000 prisoners of conscience—each a sentinel of hope, each a reflection of the *Dhamma's* truth—I implore you: Be the architect of peace. Be the guardian of humanity, as Ashoka became, as Gandhi taught.

Let history declare that when Myanmar's darkness deepened, India lit the way, its heart ablaze with courage and compassion.

With respect and resolute hope,

Aung San Suu Kyi

IN DETENTION, NAYPYIDAW PRISON

634

Advice to the People of My Country
A Reflection on the Dhamma Teachings of
the Late Venerable Sayadaw U Pandita

635

Burma, the newest-born democracy on Earth, a fragile phoenix rising from the ashes of tortured history.

I sat with the Venerable Sayadaw, in his humble cottage, his wisdom refracting like a prism of light—a rainbow of inseparable truths arching across the sky of shared existence.

This was a great nation, forged in centuries of complex struggles, one hundred and twenty-one years under the tyrannical grip of British colonialism's maniacal control. A grand land of mountains, teak forests, vast rice fields, and endless seascapes, carved up, exploited, its riches siphoned, its spirit suppressed. Its one hundred and thirty-one different ethnicities divided, ruled, and abused, their diversity weaponized as a tool of oppression.

The tragic upheaval of World War II scarred this ancient land even further—incessant aerial bombings and relentless warfare left wounds that still bled. Yet, within the chaos, autonomy stirred, revolution flickered like embers refusing to die.

An independence so short-lived it was barely a blink—a breath in *samsara's* relentless convulsions and volcanic traumas. Freedom's promise stolen by a succession of dictatorships—each one more lethal than the last.

Decades where people's voices whispered only in coffee shops, bedrooms, and the shadows of fear.

Layer upon layer, the challenges of transition grew—a militarized state entrenched in the coma of totalitarianism, its grip unrelenting, its shadow long and suffocating.

Even in the dawn of hope, the chains were not fully broken. The 2008 military-drafted constitution ensured their control—a labyrinth of clauses and provisions cementing their iron grip over the lifeblood of power: defense, home affairs, border affairs.

This was not governance in parallel; it was the illusion of freedom—a torturous *mandala* of deception, terror, and control.

A civilian government existed, but only as a fragile shard, a delicate shimmer of autonomy beneath the watchful gaze of the generals.

Yet, the tides had begun to shift. Political prisoners were being released, and nationwide elections, held just months earlier, ushered in the first rays of hope.

The people breathed the air of freedom, fragile but exhilarating, their voices finally heard after decades of silence.

Members of Parliament, Cabinet Ministers—once prisoners of conscience—now architects of a nation reborn. Leaders carrying the weight of history, their scars from years of chains etched into the fragile foundation of a new democracy.

I asked the Venerable teacher, Aung San Suu Kyi's spiritual advisor, and mentor to so many elected leaders of the NLD: "What does it mean to lead? To embody the *Dhamma*, to walk the path of compassion in power?"

His voice, steady as mountains, carried the answer: "Look to the qualities of a good friend, a *kalyāṇa mitta*—six jewels to illuminate the path:

'Integrity so true it draws love like a magnet.

Respect earned by conscious actions, not force.

A presence so kind it invites *metta*—loving-kindness—to bloom.

Moral courage to speak the truth when silence could betray.

Grace to endure criticism, even hardship, without venomous retribution.

And mindful restraint—refusing to use others for selfish personal gain.'"

"For a true leader is first a friend, a sacred ally. And a wise friend holds the world in their palms, embodying freedom in their breath."

His words resonated like liberating poetry in the air; the music of freedom infused with wisdom. But I pressed further.

"Is that enough? Can these qualities reach beyond today, into the fragile fabric of tomorrow? Can they touch the unborn—the trees, the waters, the lives not yet seen? Can they hold the peace and unity of tomorrow?"

He paused, his gaze piercing lifetimes: "A leader needs more: patience like oceans,

vigilance sharp as a falcon's eye, and foresight—reasoning that transcends self."

"To ask: Will this choice bear fruit? Will it nourish or destroy? Will it uplift or diminish the dignity of others?"

"To see beyond the mirage of the now, to cradle generations not yet conceived."

Back then, Burma's democracy seemed a fragile light, flickering against the storm of scapegoating, patriarchy, and ignorance, both within and beyond its borders.

And yet, hope filled the air with the promise of peace. People were smiling again; tears of joy trickled down cheeks etched with the lines of trauma.

But today, that light is dimmed. The military, desperate to survive in its obsolescence,

grips power with iron fists, turning dreams to ash in a single coup.

In February 2021, everything unraveled: 22,000 imprisoned, thousands of dead, disappeared, tortured, executed. Aung San Suu Kyi silenced in solitary confinement, as Russian and Chinese-made rockets and drones rain hell—relentless, indiscriminate,

destroying villages, monasteries, churches, schools, life itself.

No one is spared—except the elites.

Rakhine, Chin, Karen, Shan, Kachin—regions now synonymous with suffering. Entire towns burn in brutal battles with revolutionary forces—Generation Z, women and men, who have had enough.

Entire towns turned to rubble, millions displaced, starving, bleeding, their lives scattered like ash in the wind. Mothers clutching children beneath the roar of jets. Elders walking barefoot through jungles. Their homes gone, their hearts hollowed by monetized war. The suffering is endless, relentless.

The people of Myanmar?

Broken but unyielding. Their cries echo through a world too distracted—by Gaza, Ukraine, Russia, Israel, Yemen, Lebanon, and propaganda—to truly listen.

"What, then, can be done?" I asked him that night, a question trembling under the weight of the world.

The Venerable Sayadaw U Pandita smiled, a tender light in the vastness of his age: "Begin here, now. With mindfulness like fresh air—essential, unceasing. Breathe in morality. Breathe out greed. Stand by the truth, even when the winds howl lies into your ears."

"Be the calm in the storm, the clarity amidst chaos."

"For the Buddha taught: with *sīla*, morality as the base, *samādhi* and *paññā*—concentration and wisdom—can untangle the tangles of this world."

And as his words settled into the silence, he offered one last teaching:

"Be the guardian of the unborn. Exchange yourself for the future, feel the weight of forests not yet grown, the cries of rivers yet to flow."

"Only with such compassion—multi-generational, boundless—can the world heal, tand the newest-born democracy stand firm."

His wisdom lingers, a temple bell ringing across time: Burma's courage. Her people's sacrifice. And the path ahead, steep but illuminated.

We stand now, on the cusp of something ancient and new. The *Dhamma* breathes through us, urging us forward, to act with *metta* and *karuṇā*—with truth as our guide and the unborn in our hearts.

And on this very day, I wonder what Sayadawgyi would say, if he spoke to the people of his country from the Deva realm where he now abides. Perhaps his voice would carry across the land, saying: "Courage, my children, for this darkness is not eternal. The seeds of freedom have been planted; they only need time and care to grow."

"To the people of Burma, I say: Let your hearts not be consumed by anger, but illuminated by *hiri* and *ottappa*—a sense of shame at wrongdoing, and a fear of its consequences."

"These two guardians of the world will guide you to stand upright even amidst the ruins."

"To the displaced and traumatized, I whisper: Your suffering is seen, your pain not forgotten. Hold on to your dignity, for justice will bloom when compassion breaks through this barren soil."

"And to Senior General Min Aung Hlaing, I implore: Turn away from the path of destruction. Even the great King Asoka, steeped in conquest, awoke to the cries of the slain and transformed. Let the light of wisdom pierce your heart. Trade the sword for the pen of reconciliation. Lay down power not in shame but in grace."

"For the path of true greatness is not one of dominion but of service—to all beings, to the Earth, to generations yet unborn."

He would leave us with a final truth: "The wheel of *Dhamma* turns eternally. No tyranny lasts forever, and no act of compassion is ever in vain."

"Hold fast to your morality, and the day will come when Burma rises again—free, united, and radiant."

As the evening deepened, the Venerable Sayadaw's words hung in the air, gentle yet piercing, like a temple bell echoing across lifetimes.

I sat before him, feeling the weight of his wisdom settle into my being, his presence a mirror reflecting the truths of the *Dhamma*.

He had spoken of courage, compassion, and the responsibility we all bear—to guard the unborn, to cradle the future, to breathe life into the fragile light of freedom.

And then he paused, his eyes clear, timeless, piercing through the veils of *samsara* to meet my heart. "With goodwill for the entire cosmos," he said, his voice soft yet firm, "cultivate a limitless heart."

"Above, below, and all around, unobstructed, without hostility or hate."

These were not just words—they were a calling, an invitation to embody the ancient path, to keep alive the luminous thread of the *Dhamma*, woven through the fabric of existence, binding us all to the beauty of liberation.

I bowed deeply to him, my forehead touching the ground, my heart overflowing with gr attitude and reverence. This was my final connection to my beloved teacher in this life, a moment both sacred and eternal.

As I rose, his smile carried the lightness of a thousand lifetimes— his encouragement etched into my entirety:

To live with *metta*, *karuṇā*, and courage.

To carry forward the ancient teachings.

To act as a guardian of the unborn.

And to trust that the wheel of *Dhamma* turns eternally.

I left his cottage that night, the vast sky above me whispering his words:

"Unobstructed, without hostility or hate."

And though the path ahead may be steep and shrouded in shadows, his teachings remain my guide—a compass pointing toward the boundless heart.

~ Alan Clements

TIMELINE OF KEY EVENTS IN BURMESE HISTORY: 1800–2025

Post-Independence to Present (1948–2025)

1824–1885: **Anglo-Burmese Wars**: Three successive wars (1824–26, 1852, 1885) result in Burma's annexation to British India.

1856: King Mindon's Diplomacy: Burma's King Mindon writes to U.S. President James Buchanan, expressing interest in fostering diplomatic ties with the United States.

1857: U.S. Response: President Buchanan replies to King Mindon, affirming a desire for peace and friendship and pledging respect for Burma's sovereignty.

1937: British Crown Colony: Britain separates Burma from India, establishing it as a crown colony.

December 1941–May 1942: Japanese Occupation: Japanese forces launch ground and air assaults on Burma, beginning with air raids on Rangoon (December 23–25, 1941). By May 1942, Japan fully occupies Burma, granting nominal independence under a puppet regime led by anti-British nationalists, who later resist Japanese rule.

1945: Liberation from Japan: British forces, with support from the Anti-Fascist People's Freedom League (AFPFL) led by General Aung San, liberate Burma from Japanese occupation.

June 19, 1945: Aung San Suu Kyi's Birth: Aung San Suu Kyi is born in Rangoon to Daw Khin Kyi, a nurse and later Burma's ambassador to India and Nepal, and General Aung San, commander of the Burma Independence Army and architect of Burma's independence.

January 1947: Independence Negotiations: General Aung San negotiates Burma's independence, signing an agreement with British Prime Minister Clement Attlee for an interim government to prepare for self-rule.

October 1947: U.S. Recognition: The United States recognizes Burmese independence, establishes an embassy in Rangoon, and appoints its first ambassador.

February 12, 1947: Panglong Conference: General Aung San signs the Panglong Agreement with ethnic leaders, securing their support for a unified Burma.

July 19, 1947: Assassination of Aung San: General Aung San, six cabinet ministers, a cabinet secretary, and a bodyguard are assassinated in Rangoon's Secretariat Building during an Executive Council meeting. The attack, allegedly ordered by rival politician U Saw, who is later executed, disrupts Burma's democratic transition.

January 4, 1948: Independence: The Union of Burma gains independence outside the Commonwealth, adopting a parliamentary democracy. U Nu becomes the first democratically elected prime minister.

Myanmar's Struggle for Democracy: A Timeline (1949–May 2025)
This timeline chronicles Myanmar's turbulent political history, highlighting Aung San Suu Kyi's pivotal role and the nation's ongoing battle for democracy against military rule. It integrates key events from 1949 to May 29, 2025, reflecting the current state of resistance, junta actions, and international responses.

1949–1958: Ethnic and Communist Insurgencies: Ethnic Karen, Kachin, and communist insurgents challenge Rangoon's fragile civilian government, exploiting post-independence instability. General Ne Win's military consolidates power, setting the stage for authoritarian rule. Aung San Suu Kyi, studying abroad, later confronts this legacy through her National League for Democracy (NLD), navigating ethnic divisions under junta repression.

1958–1960: Military Caretaker Government: Ne Win's military assumes temporary control to stabilize U Nu's faltering government, relinquishing power after the 1960 elections. This brief rule foreshadows future coups, a reality Aung San Suu Kyi challenges in 1988 with her nonviolent resistance.

March 2, 1962: Ne Win's Coup: Ne Win overthrows U Nu, establishing the Burma Socialist Programme Party (BSPP) dictatorship. His "Burmanization" policies marginalize ethnic minorities, devastate the economy, and suppress dissent. Aung San Suu Kyi, studying at Oxford, resolves to counter this betrayal of her father's democratic vision.

July 7, 1962: Rangoon University Massacre: Military forces kill approximately 100 students protesting Ne Win's curfew and demolish the Rangoon University student union with explosives. The massacre radicalizes youth, planting seeds for the 1988 uprising. Aung San Suu Kyi, abroad, later draws inspiration from this defiance.

1963: Failed Peace Talks: Ne Win's negotiations with Kachin, Shan, and Karen representatives collapse, deepening ethnic mistrust. His assimilationist policies fuel insurgencies, a challenge Aung San Suu Kyi faces in 2015, her federalism efforts constrained by military dominance.

December 1974: U Thant Funeral Protests: Ne Win's refusal to honor UN Secretary-General U Thant's funeral sparks protests, leading to hundreds of arrests. This public outrage foreshadows the 1988 uprising. Aung San Suu Kyi, in London, recognizes Burma's resilient spirit, preparing for her return.

September 5, 1987: Currency Devaluation Crisis: Ne Win's devaluation of approximately 80% of banknotes wipes out savings, triggering widespread unrest. Condemned by monks, this crisis fuels the 1988 uprising. Aung San Suu Kyi, preparing to return, channels this public anger into her leadership.

March–August 1988: 8888 Uprising: Students and monks lead nationwide protests against BSPP mismanagement, culminating in the August 8, 1988, rallies, known as the 8888 Uprising. Military forces kill approximately 3,000 protesters. Aung San Suu Kyi, in Yangon, delivers her first major speech at Shwedagon Pagoda on August 26 and founds the NLD on September 24, her nonviolent philosophy becoming a moral force.

September 18, 1988: SLORC Coup: General Saw Maung's State Law and Order Restoration Council (SLORC) seizes power, renaming Burma "Myanmar" and killing hundreds in crackdowns. The NLD, led by Aung San Suu Kyi, faces relentless raids, her leadership a beacon amid repression.

July 20, 1989: Aung San Suu Kyi's First House Arrest: SLORC places Aung San Suu Kyi under house arrest in Yangon for "endangering national unity," barring her from the 1990 election campaign. Her six-year confinement, spent meditating and reading, transforms her into a global icon.

May 27, 1990: NLD's Election Victory Annulled: The NLD wins 392 of 492 parliamentary seats, but SLORC annuls the results, imprisoning party leaders. Aung San Suu Kyi, under house arrest, becomes the global symbol of Myanmar's democratic struggle.

October 14, 1991: Nobel Peace Prize: Aung San Suu Kyi is awarded the Nobel Peace Prize for her "non-violent struggle for democracy," receiving $1.3 million, which she allocates to a trust for Burmese health and education. Her sons accept the award in Oslo, her absence amplifying her global influence.

July 10, 1995: Release from House Arrest: SLORC releases Aung San Suu Kyi due to international pressure, though travel restrictions persist. She conducts weekly public talks at her Yangon residence, revitalizing the NLD and challenging junta control.

December 1996: NLD Congress Crackdown: SLORC prevents an NLD congress, arresting approximately 200 members to curb Aung San Suu Kyi's influence. Her resilience in reorganizing despite raids foreshadows further detentions.

September 23, 2000: Second House Arrest: Aung San Suu Kyi's attempt to travel to Mandalay prompts her second house arrest, lasting until May 6, 2002. In isolation, she deepens her Buddhist practice, challenging the State Peace and Development Council (SPDC).

May 30, 2003: Depayin Massacre: A junta-orchestrated mob of approximately 5,000 attacks Aung San Suu Kyi's convoy in Depayin, killing approximately 70 NLD supporters. Suu Kyi escapes but is arrested, marking her third house arrest, sparking global condemnation.

September 2007: Saffron Revolution: Buddhist monks protest fuel price hikes, with demonstrations growing to 100,000 in Yangon. Military forces kill approximately 40 and assault clergy. Aung San Suu Kyi, under house arrest, briefly appears to bless the monks, amplifying global outrage.

May 2–3, 2008: Cyclone Nargis: Cyclone Nargis kills approximately 138,000; the junta's obstruction of aid exacerbates suffering. Aung San Suu Kyi, under house arrest, faces extended detention over an unauthorized visitor, her confinement underscoring her symbolic role.

November 7, 2010: Manipulated Election: The military-backed Union Solidarity and Development Party (USDP) wins a manipulated election boycotted by the NLD. Aung San Suu Kyi's release on November 13 suggests superficial reform while the junta retains dominance.

November 13, 2010: Aung San Suu Kyi Freed: After nearly 15 years of intermittent detention, Aung San Suu Kyi is released, greeted by thousands in Yangon. She revitalizes the NLD, engaging with President Thein Sein's reforms, positioning her for renewed conflict with the military.

October 2011: Myitsone Dam Protests: Public protests lead to the suspension of the Chinese-backed Myitsone Dam, a civilian victory under Thein Sein. Aung San Suu Kyi supports the movement, strengthening her public appeal despite ethnic tensions.

April 1, 2012: Parliamentary Win: Aung San Suu Kyi wins a parliamentary seat, with the NLD securing 43 of 45 by-election seats. Her transition to politics challenges her principles against military vetoes, shaping her State Counsellor tenure.

June 16, 2012: Nobel Speech: Aung San Suu Kyi delivers her 1991 Nobel Peace Prize acceptance speech in Oslo, advocating for "practical peace" and political prisoner releases. Her appeal for unity navigates ethnic conflicts and military dominance.

October 8, 2015: Nationwide Ceasefire Agreement (NCA): Eight ethnic armed organizations sign the NCA, but key groups (Kachin, Wa) decline, hindering peace efforts. Aung San Suu Kyi supports negotiations, but military resistance limits her influence.

November 8, 2015: NLD'S Landslide Victory: The NLD captures 86% of contested seats in Myanmar's most credible election since 1990. Aung San Suu Kyi, constitutionally barred from the presidency, becomes State Counsellor in 2016, constrained by the military's 25% parliamentary allocation.

January 29, 2017: Assassination of Ko Ni: Ko Ni, a Muslim NLD lawyer and Aung San Suu Kyi's advisor, is assassinated at Yangon International Airport by Kyi Lin; driver Nay Win is also killed. Former military officers orchestrated the attack to derail constitutional reforms. Suu Kyi, wary of Buddhist nationalist backlash, mourns privately, calling him a "martyr for democracy."

August–October 2017: **Rohingya Crisis**: Military operations in Rakhine State kill approximately 10,000 Rohingya and displace over 700,000. Aung San Suu Kyi's measured response, including her defense of Myanmar at the International Court of Justice in 2019, shaped by Buddhist nationalist pressures, leads to revoked honors, impacting her international reputation while maintaining domestic support.

November 8, 2020: **NLD'S Second Victory**: The NLD secures 396 parliamentary seats, overcoming military fraud allegations. Aung San Suu Kyi, 75, maintains leadership despite Rohingya criticism, her mandate rejecting the USDP.

February 1, 2021: **Min Aung Hlaing's Coup**: Min Aung Hlaing orchestrates a coup, detaining Aung San Suu Kyi, President Win Myint, and NLD leaders, citing unsubstantiated voter fraud. By May 2025, military forces kill approximately 1,500 protesters and detain over 22,000. Suu Kyi's fabricated charges result in a 27-year sentence, intensifying Myanmar's civil war.

March 2021: **Civil Disobedience Movement (CDM)**: Millions, including doctors and youth, participate in the CDM, staging strikes against the junta. Military forces kill hundreds and arrest thousands. Aung San Suu Kyi, detained in Naypyidaw Prison, remains the movement's moral inspiration.

April 16, 2021: **National Unity Government (NUG)**: Deposed NLD parliamentarians and ethnic leaders form the NUG, establishing the People's Defence Forces (PDF). Aung San Suu Kyi, detained, serves as its moral foundation, her federal democracy vision guiding their governance.

December 6, 2021: **Aung San Suu Kyi's Sentencing**: A junta court sentences Aung San Suu Kyi to four years (reduced to two) for incitement, with additional charges totaling 27 years by 2022. Her politically motivated trials aim to marginalize her, yet her legacy inspires resistance.

July 23, 2022: **Execution of Activists**: The junta executes four pro-democracy activists, including NLD parliamentarian Phyo Zeya Thaw, in Insein Prison, the first judicial executions since 1988. Aung San Suu Kyi, detained, expresses private sorrow, fueling the Spring Revolution.

September 7, 2022: Federal Democracy Charter: The NUG adopts a Federal Democracy Charter, committing to ethnic inclusion. Aung San Suu Kyi's pluralist ideals shape the framework, rallying resistance forces.

October 27, 2023: Operation 1027: The Three Brotherhood Alliance (Arakan Army, Kachin Independence Army, Ta'ang National Liberation Army) launches Operation 1027, capturing strategic towns. Supported by the PDF, the offensive undermines Min Aung Hlaing, fueled by Aung San Suu Kyi's NLD ouster.

April 4, 2024: Naypyidaw Drone Attack: NUG drones target Naypyidaw, damaging military facilities. The attack reflects Aung San Suu Kyi's enduring defiance, her name invoked by fighters.

2024: Civil War Escalates: Resistance forces control approximately 60% of Myanmar's territory, while junta airstrikes kill thousands and displace over 2 million. Aung San Suu Kyi, in solitary confinement at 79, faces declining health, her resilience bolstering PDF resolve.

March 28–29, 2025: Sagaing Earthquake: A 7.7-magnitude earthquake strikes Sagaing, killing approximately 3,100 and damaging Naypyidaw's infrastructure. The junta restricts aid, alienating resistance groups. Aung San Suu Kyi's unreported condition in detention intensifies demands for her release.

May 2025: Resistance Advances, Junta Plans Election: The NUG and PDF maintain control over significant rural areas, while urban centers remain under junta control. Over 22,000 political prisoners, including Aung San Suu Kyi, endure torture; her 27-year sentence persists. At 79, her frail but symbolic presence inspires global campaigns like #FreeAungSanSuuKyi, challenging Min Aung Hlaing's weakening authority.

May 15–26, 2025: Mandalay Resistance Offensive: Mandalay resistance groups claim 50 junta troops killed and seize a Chinese pipeline station in coordinated attacks across four townships, signaling intensified resistance.

Timeline of Key Events in Aung San Suu Kyi's Life

June 19, 1945: A Legacy Begins: Daw Aung San Suu Kyi is born in Yangon, the third child and only daughter of General Aung San, Myanmar's independence hero, and Daw Khin Kyi, a nurse and diplomat. Her father's assassination in 1947, when she is two, leaves a lasting imprint. Raised in a home steeped in national pride, she grows up hearing tales of her father's vision for a free, democratic Myanmar.

1949–1959: Early Education in Yangon: She begins schooling at St. Francis Convent, a Catholic institution in Yangon, before transferring to Methodist English High School (now Basic Education High School No. 1 Dagon). Excelling in literature and history, she develops a curiosity that shapes her intellectual path. Her exposure to diverse cultures in Yangon's cosmopolitan schools lays the foundation for her global perspective.

1960–1964: A Global Education in India: At 15, she moves to New Delhi with her mother, appointed Myanmar's Ambassador to India and Nepal. Enrolled at the Convent of Jesus and Mary, she adapts to India's vibrant post-independence culture while preserving her Burmese identity. Graduating from Lady Shri Ram College in 1964 with a degree in politics, she engages with India's democratic debates, influenced by figures like Jawaharlal Nehru, which later inform her non-violent philosophy.

1964–1969: Oxford Years and Intellectual Growth: At St Hugh's College, Oxford, she earns a BA in Philosophy, Politics, and Economics in 1969. Oxford's liberal ethos sharpens her analytical skills, and she forms friendships with future British leaders. Debating colonialism and self-governance, she hones her vision for Myanmar's future. Post-graduation, she works as an assistant researcher at the School of

Oriental and African Studies in London, deepening her expertise in Asian political systems.

1969–1971: United Nations Service: At 24, she serves as Assistant Secretary for the Advisory Committee on Administrative and Budgetary Questions at the UN Secretariat in New York. Navigating international bureaucracies, she develops diplomatic finesse while embracing New York's cosmopolitan energy. Her time at the UN strengthens her commitment to global cooperation, a theme that recurs in her later advocacy.

January 1, 1972: A Personal Commitment: She marries Dr. Michael Aris, a British scholar of Bhutanese and Tibetan studies, in New York. The couple moves to Bhutan, where Michael tutors the royal family, and she works as a research officer in the Ministry of Foreign Affairs, analyzing regional geopolitics. Their sons, Alexander (born 1973) and Kim (born 1977), are raised in Oxford, UK. Her marriage, grounded in mutual respect, becomes a vital source of strength during her political struggles.

1975–1984: Scholarly Pursuits in Oxford: At Oxford's Bodleian Library, she catalogues Burmese manuscripts, reconnecting with her cultural heritage. Balancing motherhood with intellectual work, she writes essays on Myanmar's colonial history and literary traditions. Her Oxford years are a period of quiet reflection, yet she remains attuned to Myanmar's turmoil under military rule since 1962.

1985–1986: Research in Japan: As a visiting scholar at Kyoto University's Center for Southeast Asian Studies, she researches Myanmar's independence movement, focusing on her father's role in securing freedom from British rule. Her work earns respect among Asian scholars, and Japan's culture of discipline and non-violence, exemplified by figures like Gandhi, deepens her commitment to peaceful resistance.

1987: Doctoral Studies and Fellowship: Enrolled at the School of Oriental and African Studies in London, she pursues a doctoral degree, writing a thesis on the role of media in Myanmar's independence struggle (1910–1945). Her research highlights how Burmese newspapers galvanized anti-colonial sentiment. As a fellow at the Indian Institute of Advanced Studies in Simla, she engages with India's intellectual elite on nationalism and democracy, further shaping her political philosophy.

April 1988: Return to Myanmar: Daw Aung San Suu Kyi returns to Yangon to care for her mother, Daw Khin Kyi, who suffers a stroke. Myanmar is gripped by the 8888 Uprising, with nationwide protests against General Ne Win's regime. Witnessing the junta's brutal crackdown, she is drawn into the pro-democracy movement, a pivotal shift from scholar to activist.

August 26, 1988: A Political Awakening: Addressing over 500,000 people at Shwedagon Pagoda's western gate, she delivers a stirring speech calling for democracy and unity. Her eloquence, invoking her father's legacy and Buddhist principles of compassion, galvanizes the crowd. This moment, during the height of the 8888 Uprising, marks her emergence as Myanmar's moral and political leader.

September 27, 1988: Founding the NLD: She co-founds the National League for Democracy (NLD) with former generals Aung Gyi and Tin Oo, becoming its General Secretary. The NLD rapidly grows into the leading opposition force, uniting intellectuals, students, a nd disillusioned military officers in the fight for free elections and civilian rule.

December 27, 1988: A Personal Loss: Daw Khin Kyi passes away, a profound loss. At her mother's funeral, Daw Aung San Suu Kyi publicly urges military leaders, including Senior General Saw Maung, to honor their pledge for democratic elections. Her defiance amid grief underscores her resolve to challenge the junta.

January 1989: Facing Threats: Campaigning in Irrawaddy Division, she is confronted by soldiers in Danubyu who threaten her at gunpoint. Walking calmly toward the rifles, she displays extraordinary courage, an act that becomes legendary. The incident, widely reported, amplifies her international profile as a fearless leader.

July 20, 1989: First House Arrest: The military places her under house arrest at her family's lakeside villa at 54 University Avenue, Yangon.

Isolated from the public, she relies on books, meditation, and Buddhist teachings to endure confinement. Her resilience during this period solidifies her as a symbol of non-violent resistance.

May 27, 1990: Electoral Triumph Ignored: The NLD wins a landslide victory in the general election, securing 392 of 447 parliamentary seats despite her detention. The State Law and Order Restoration Council (SLORC) refuses to transfer power, nullifying the results and intensifying repression of NLD supporters, cementing her status as a martyr for democracy.

October 14, 1991: Nobel Peace Prize Awarded: Awarded the Nobel Peace Prize for her non-violent struggle, the Norwegian Nobel Committee praises her as "an outstanding example of the power of the powerless." Under house arrest, she is represented by Michael Aris and their sons, Alexander and Kim, at the Oslo ceremony on December 10. Michael delivers her speech, emphasizing peace and reconciliation. The prize, elevating her to a global icon, funds scholarships through Prospect Burma, reflecting her commitment to education.

August 1993: Family Reunion: Michael and their sons visit her in Yangon, their first reunion since her 1989 arrest. The emotional meeting, under strict surveillance, highlights her personal sacrifices. Her family's unwavering support strengthens her resolve during isolation.

February 15, 1994: Diplomatic Visitors: A U.S. delegation led by Congressman Bill Richardson, with UN representative Jehan Raheem and journalist Philip Shenon, visits her at home—the first non-family visitors since 1989. The meeting signals growing international pressure on the junta to engage with her.

September 20, 1994: Talks with the Junta: She meets Senior General Than Shwe and Major General Khin Nyunt of SLORC at a government guesthouse, her first direct engagement with military leaders. The inconclusive talks, prompted by global scrutiny, mark a cautious attempt at dialogue.

July 10, 1995: Release from House Arrest: Freed after six years, she is greeted by thousands outside her home. Resuming NLD activities, she delivers weekly speeches at her gate, drawing crowds despite military intimidation. Her husband and sons join her briefly, reinforcing her determination to lead.

November 22, 1995: Defying the National Convention: The NLD withdraws from the military-led National Convention, citing its undemocratic nature. The convention, meant to draft a new constitution, is suspended indefinitely, underscoring her influence in challenging the junta's agenda.

March 27, 1999: A Heartbreaking Loss: Michael Aris dies of cancer in Oxford, aged 53. Though free to leave Myanmar, she chooses not to visit him, knowing the junta would bar her return. Their final separation, after 27 years of marriage, epitomizes the personal toll of her political commitment.

September 23, 2000: Second House Arrest: Placed under house arrest again after attempting to travel outside Yangon, she faces renewed isolation. She spends her days reading, meditating, and writing, maintaining intellectual rigor despite confinement.

May 6, 2002: Temporary Freedom: Released after 19 months, prompted by UN envoy Razali Ismail's mediation, she resumes nationwide campaigning, drawing massive crowds. Her release reflects the junta's attempt to ease international criticism while retaining control.

May 30, 2003: The Depayin Massacre: Her convoy is ambushed by a junta-backed mob in Sagaing Division's Depayin Township, killing dozens of NLD supporters. Narrowly escaping, she is detained in Insein Prison before being placed under house arrest for the third time. The massacre sparks global outrage, intensifying calls for her release.

September 2007: Saffron Revolution: During a monk-led uprising against military rule, protesters march past her home. Under house arrest, she briefly appears at her gate to greet them, a poignant moment of solidarity captured globally. The junta's violent crackdown further isolates her.

May 3, 2009: **Yettaw Incident**: U.S. citizen John Yettaw swims across Inya Lake to her home, claiming a divine mission. His unauthorized entry, days before her scheduled release, leads to her arrest for violating house arrest terms. Her detention is extended by 18 months, a pretext to keep her sidelined during the 2010 election.

November 13, 2010: **Release and Renewed Activism**: Freed after seven years, she is greeted by thousands at her home. Vowing to continue her democratic struggle, she reconnects with NLD supporters and rebuilds the party, which boycotts the junta's 2010 election.

August 19, 2011: **Engaging the Government**: Meets President U Thein Sein in Naypyidaw, a landmark meeting signaling Myanmar's quasi-civilian government's reformist shift. Their discussions pave the way for the NLD'S re-entry into electoral politics.

April 1, 2012: **Parliamentary Victory**: Contesting a by-election, she wins a seat in the Lower House from Kawhmu Township, her first official government role. The NLD'S success signals Myanmar's cautious democratic opening.

May 2012: **Václav Havel Prize for Creative Dissent**: Awarded the inaugural Václav Havel Prize for Creative Dissent by the Human Rights Foundation at the Oslo Freedom Forum, recognizing her non-violent resistance. In a video message from her Yangon home—filmed at the site of her 15-year house arrest—she dedicates the prize to Myanmar's political prisoners, urging global support. The award, echoing Czech dissident Václav Havel's legacy, underscores her transition to a global advocate.

May–June 2012: **Historic World Tour**: Embarking on her first international tour in 24 years, she visits Thailand, Switzerland, Ireland, the UK, France, and Norway, reasserting her global influence. In Bangkok, she addresses the World Economic Forum and meets Prime Minister Yingluck Shinawatra, advocating economic reforms. In Dublin, she accepts the 1992 Seán MacBride Peace Prize and meets President Michael D. Higgins, joined by U2's Bono. In London, she addresses Parliament, receives an Oxford honorary degree, and confers with Prime Minister David Cameron. In Paris, she meets President François Hollande, accepting the Legion of Honour. Her tour, blending diplomacy with personal reflection, captivates audiences, though some NLD supporters question her time abroad.

June 16, 2012: Nobel Peace Prize Acceptance Speech: In Oslo's City Hall, she delivers her long-delayed Nobel Peace Prize acceptance speech, 21 years after the 1991 award. Before Norwegian royalty and activists, she defines peace as "the courage to pursue justice with compassion," honoring Myanmar's oppressed. Wearing a purple shawl symbolizing her heritage, she stands beside a 1991 portrait, bridging past and present. Watched by her sons, the speech reaffirms her moral authority and vision for inclusive democracy.

September–October 2012: U.S. Tour and Congressional Gold Medal: On a coast-to-coast U.S. tour, she receives the Congressional Gold Medal in Washington, D.C., awarded in 2008 but uncollected due to detention. At a bipartisan Capitol ceremony, she thanks the U.S. for supporting Myanmar's democracy. Meeting President Barack Obama at the White House, she calls the day "most moving." In New York, she addresses the Asia Society, meets UN Secretary-General Ban Ki-moon, and revisits the UN headquarters where she worked in 1969. In San Francisco, she accepts the Global Citizen Award from the Clinton Global Initiative, urging youth empowerment. Visiting Burmese communities in Fort Wayne and Louisville, she inspires the diaspora, though her silence on the Rohingya sparks debate.

November 2012: India Tour: Invited by Prime Minister Manmohan Singh, she visits India, revisiting her alma mater, Lady Shri Ram College, and delivering the Jawaharlal Nehru Memorial Lecture on India's influence on her non-violent philosophy. Meetings with Singh, President Pranab Mukherjee, and Sonia Gandhi strengthen bilateral ties. Exploring technology in Bangalore and rural projects, she informs her Daw Khin Kyi Foundation's mission to uplift Myanmar's underserved. Recalling her youth studying by lantern light, she inspires students with tales of perseverance.

November 19, 2012: Historic U.S. Visit to Myanmar: Hosts President Barack Obama and Secretary of State Hillary Clinton at her Yangon home, the first visit by a U.S. president to Myanmar. Their discussions on democratic reforms and economic cooperation highlight her pivotal role in Myanmar's transition, reinforcing her global stature.

April 2013: Japan Tour: Visiting Tokyo, she meets Prime Minister Shinzo Abe, securing Japan's support for Myanmar's infrastructure. Her speech at Tokyo University, where she studied in 1985, reflects on her intellectual roots, emphasizing education as a pillar of democracy.

November 2013: Australia Tour: In Sydney, she meets Prime Minister Tony Abbott and Governor-General Quentin Bryce, discussing human rights and trade. Her lecture at the Sydney Opera House on democracy captivates audiences, blending optimism with pragmatism, and reinforces Australia's support for Myanmar's reforms.

October 22, 2013: Sakharov Prize Speech: Accepting the 1990 Sakharov Prize for Freedom of Thought in person at the European Parliament in Strasbourg, she urges Europe to invest in Myanmar's youth and institutions. Holding a photo of her father, General Aung San, she connects her personal heritage to her political mission, moving parliamentarians.

June 2015: LennonOno Grant for Peace: In New York, she receives the LennonOno Grant for Peace from Yoko Ono, recognizing her non-violent activism. Her brief speech links her struggle to John Lennon's vision of peace, resonating with younger audiences and highlighting her cultural influence.

June 2015: China Tour: In Beijing, she meets President Xi Jinping, navigating tensions over China's influence in Myanmar. Her diplomatic finesse strengthens economic ties while advocating for equitable partnerships, a theme she revisits at the 2017 Belt and Road Forum.

November 8, 2015: Landslide Victory: The NLD wins a resounding victory in the general election, securing a parliamentary majority. Barred from the presidency by the junta-drafted constitution, she declares herself "above the president," signaling her intent to lead through influence.

March 30, 2016: Ministerial Roles: Appointed head of four ministries—Foreign Affairs, President's Office, Electricity and Energy, and Education—in President Htin Kyaw's cabinet, consolidating her authority within the NLD-led government.

April 6, 2016: State Counselor: The Union Parliament creates the role of State Counselor, formalizing her leadership as Myanmar's de facto head of government. Retaining Foreign Affairs and President's Office portfolios, she navigates complex domestic and international challenges.

August 24, 2016: Rakhine Commission: Establishes an advisory commission on Rakhine State, chaired by Kofi Annan, to address ethnoreligious violence involving the Rohingya. The commission's 2017 recommendations face resistance, and her rejection of a UN fact-finding mission draws criticism, complicating her global image.

August 31, 2016: Panglong Peace Conference: Convenes the 21st Century Panglong Peace Conference in Naypyidaw to address ethnic conflicts. Inspired by her father's 1947 Panglong Agreement, the initiative seeks a federal union but faces challenges from non-signatory armed groups and ongoing violence.

December 10–12, 2019: ICJ Defense: Leads Myanmar's defense at the International Court of Justice in The Hague against Gambia's genocide allegations regarding the Rohingya. Her decision to represent Myanmar, defending her country, not the military's actions, sparks international controversy, alienating some supporters while rallying nationalists at home.

November 8, 2020: Electoral Triumph: The NLD secures 82% of contested seats in the general election, reaffirming public support. International observers, including the Carter Center, deem the election credible, despite military claims of fraud.

February 1, 2021: Military Coup: Detained in a pre-dawn raid with President U Win Myint and NLD leaders, she is ousted in a coup led by Senior General Min Aung Hlaing. Her smuggled handwritten statement urges nationwide protests, igniting a mass resistance movement. The National Unity Government (NUG), formed by elected lawmakers, declares her the legitimate leader.

May 24, 2021: Show Trials Begin: Appears in person for trial in Naypyidaw, facing charges from illegal walkie-talkie possession to corruption. The closed-door proceedings, condemned as politically motivated, aim to discredit her and dismantle the NLD.

July 26, 2021: Election Nullified: The junta's Union Election Commission annuls the 2020 election results, erasing the NLD's victory. The move, lacking evidence of widespread fraud, is condemned by the UN and democratic governments.

June 22, 2022: Prison Transfer: Transferred from house arrest to solitary confinement in Naypyidaw Prison, days after her 77th birthday. Denied access to aides, she faces harsher conditions, prompting concerns about her health.

December 30, 2022: 33-Year Sentence: Convicted on multiple charges, including corruption, she is sentenced to 33 years in prison. The verdicts, delivered in secretive trials, are denounced by human rights groups as a sham to silence her.

March 28, 2023: NLD Dissolved: The junta dissolves the NLD and 39 other parties for refusing to register under new electoral laws, banning Myanmar's largest political force. NLD supporters, many in exile, vow to continue her legacy underground.

July 9, 2023: Rare Diplomatic Visit: Outgoing Thai Foreign Minister Don Pramudwinai meets her in Naypyidaw Prison, the first diplomatic engagement since the coup. The 90-minute meeting, reportedly covering Myanmar's economic crisis, reflects Thailand's ties with the junta, which had denied UN and ASEAN envoys access.

January 25, 2024: Family Home Auction: A Yangon court orders the auction of her historic residence at 54 University Avenue, following a dispute with her estranged brother, U Aung San Oo. Declared a cultural heritage site by the NUG, the villa—where she endured 15 years of house arrest and hosted global leaders—fails to attract bidders in March 2024 and April 2025, symbolizing its untouchable legacy.

March 28, 2025: Earthquake Concerns: A 7.7-magnitude earthquake devastates central Myanmar, killing over 3,700 and damaging Naypyidaw, where she is imprisoned. Amid fears for her safety, unconfirmed reports suggest she is unharmed, with essentials delivered to her cell. The junta's silence fuels global demands for transparency about her condition.

June 19, 2025: The Suu Foundation Renews Urgent Call for the Immediate Release of Daw Aung San Suu Kyi on Her 80th Birthday: On June 19th, as Daw Aung San Suu Kyi quietly marked her 80th birthday in the secrecy of solitary detention, the Suu Foundation has renewed its urgent call for her immediate and unconditional release. The appeal comes amid mounting concern for her health and safety following reports of an injury sustained during the powerful 7.7-magnitude earthquake that struck the prison facility in which she is being held on March 28th.

According to the Foundation's statement, Daw Suu suffered an injury to her left arm during the quake. Disturbingly, she has not been permitted to meet with either her family or her legal team since the day of her arrest in 2021.

"We are deeply concerned about Daw Aung San Suu Kyi's health. The United Nations has made a special appeal for her release," said Jean Todt, President of the Suu Foundation, and Dr. Michael Marett-Crosby, the organization's CEO.

The Foundation emphasized that her continued detention—at her age, under such conditions—is not only inhumane but life-threatening. Her international legal team, François Zimeray and Catalina De La Sota, underscored the urgency of the situation:

"There is real fear that she may die in prison while the world looks the other way. Given her age and the secrecy surrounding her detention since 2021, we are extremely worried about her well-being and the reported injury."

Back in May 2022, the legal team formally submitted her case to the United Nations Working Group on Arbitrary Detention, citing the illegality of her arrest and the conditions of her prolonged isolation as serious violations of international law.

The Suu Foundation's statement further condemned the junta's systemic dismantling of Myanmar's democratic institutions. Since the 2021 military coup, thousands have been imprisoned—including President U Win Myint, members of the National League for Democracy (NLD), civil servants, artists, and journalists. The Foundation cited the regime's escalating violence, mass arrests, and contempt for democratic norms as clear evidence of the nation's collapse into authoritarian rule.

In addition to Daw Suu's case, her legal team and the Foundation highlighted that over 100 civilians have been sentenced to death since the coup—many in secret, without due process.

They called on the international community to intensify diplomatic and economic pressure on the regime, urging world leaders to stand firmly for the restoration of civilian governance and the protection of fundamental human rights.

On this milestone birthday, the Foundation reaffirmed that the release of Daw Aung San Suu Kyi is not only a moral imperative—it is a critical step toward national reconciliation, justice, and the rebirth of peace in Myanmar.

June 2, 2025 | Myanmar Prisons Witness (MPW) Report No. MPW-1 Investigation and Identification of Responsible Persons Regarding the Conditions Arising Inside the Secret Detention Location of Daw Aung San Suu Kyi

Where Is Daw Aung San Suu Kyi Being Held?

According to verified investigations by Myanmar Prisons Witness (MPW), State Counsellor Daw Aung San Suu Kyi is currently being unlawfully detained under high security at the office of a special military task force known as KST (6). This secret facility is located approximately 22.5 kilometers from Naypyidaw Central Prison, or about 14 miles from Myanmar's capital.

She is being denied family visitation rights, in direct violation of both national prison regulations and international standards. In mid-

April 2024, she was silently transferred from Naypyidaw Central Prison to this covert military site—reportedly under the pretext of shielding her from summer heat. The facility lies close to Commander-in-Chief Min Aung Hlaing's office and is under the direct command of a senior lieutenant general.

Psychological Torture and Systematic Abuse

Daw Aung San Suu Kyi, now 79 years old, suffers from dental pain, heart issues, and other age-related health concerns. She is denied adequate medical care, receiving only minimal medication dispensed by military-authorized doctors. Her complete isolation—no family visits, no public contact—constitutes a deliberate form of psychological torture, designed to break her spirit and sever her from the outside world.

Weaponizing the Judiciary

Following the military coup on 1 February 2021, General Min Aung Hlaing and his inner circle orchestrated a series of fabricated criminal charges against Daw Aung San Suu Kyi in an effort to erase her from Myanmar's political landscape.

Complicit judicial figures include:
- **U Maung Maung Lwin (T/2839)**, Zabuthiri Township
- **U Ye Lwin**, Dagon District
- **U Myint Than**, Mandalay Region
- **Chief Justice Daw Khin Thin Wai**, Mandalay Region

These judges presided over cases engineered by the junta, handing down 33 years of imprisonment across multiple charges—often with no credible evidence or due process.

Key Military and Prison Officials Responsible for Her Detention and Conditions
- **Commander-in-Chief:** Min Aung Hlaing
- **Deputy Commander-in-Chief:** Soe Win
- **Former Home Ministers:** Soe Htut (retired), Yar Pyae (now Minister of Border Affairs)
- **Current Home Minister:** Tun Tun Naung
- **Commanders of KST (6):**

- o Lt. Gen. Than Hlaing
- o Lt. Gen. Than Tun Oo
- o Lt. Gen. Tayza Kyaw
- o Lt. Gen. Phone Myat
  - **Prisons Department:**
- o Former Chief Warden: Zaw Win
- o Current Chief Warden: Myo Swe
  - **Naypyidaw Central Prison Authorities:**
- o Prison Owner: U Thein Zaw Maung
- o Deputy Prison Owner: U Kyaw Thu Ya
- o Head Officer: U Aung Than Myint
- o Assistant Supervisor: Kyaw Min Htaik
- o Officer: Thingyi Myint
- o Assistant Supervisor: May Thu Aung

Numerous unnamed collaborators remain complicit in following illegal orders issued by the military leadership.

List of Charges and Sentences Imposed

1. **December 2021 – 2 years**
   Section 505(b): Incitement to cause public distrust in the state
2. **January 2022 – 2 years**
   Sections 67 (Telecommunications), 8 (Customs and Import Law): Possession of walkie-talkies
3. **January 2022 – 2 years**
   Section 25 (Disaster Management Law): COVID-19 regulation violation
4. **April 2022 – 5 years**
   Corruption charges: Linked to gold and cash from ex-Yangon Chief Minister U Phyo Min Thein
5. **August 2022 – 6 years**
   Corruption charges: Related to Daw Khin Kyi Foundation and land projects
6. **September 2022 – 3 years**
   Section 130(a): Misuse of electoral authority
7. **September 2022 – 3 years**
   Official Secrets Act, Section 3(1)(g)

8. **October 2022** – 3 years
   Section 55 (Anti-Terrorism Law): Alleged extortion
9. **December 2022** – 7 years
   Corruption charges: Italian helicopter procurement during NLD
   government
10. **Total Sentence**: 33 years
    Note: In August 2023, the junta announced superficial "pardons"
    for some charges, but Daw Aung San Suu Kyi remains imprisoned
    for 27 years.

Myanmar Prisons Witness Calls on the International Community

The detention of Daw Aung San Suu Kyi under these conditions is not only illegal but an act of systematic cruelty against one of the world's most renowned political prisoners. The Myanmar military is using the penal system as a tool of repression, aiming to destroy opposition through isolation, legal manipulation, and psychological abuse.

MPW Urgently Demands:

- **Immediate release** of Daw Aung San Suu Kyi and all political prisoners.
- **Full restoration of prisoner rights**, including medical care and family visitation.
- **Independent international access**, especially by the International Committee of the Red Cross (**ICRC**) and **UN** human rights observers.
- **International diplomatic sanctions and travel bans** on those responsible.

    This is a call for **urgent global intervention**. The world must not turn a blind eye to the military's deliberate dehumanization of a Nobel Peace Laureate and the thousands of others enduring persecution in Myanmar's prisons.

Myanmar Prisons Witness (MPW)

Documenting truth. Demanding justice.

ACKNOWLEDGMENTS

To Fergus Harlow, my steadfast colleague and co-author—your unwavering support and invaluable collaboration have been indispensable to this work.

To Jeannine Davies, my cherished friend—our profound connection and insightful conversations have enriched every aspect of this book and deeply inspired me.

A special note of heartfelt gratitude to Justine Elliott of Design Lasso in New Zealand, my esteemed book designer—whose remarkable generosity and creative brilliance have elevated this project. It has been a privilege to collaborate with someone of such exceptional artistry and compassion.

In the urgency of this book's creation, I occasionally utilized AI as a tool for research, graphics, and minor editorial support—an imperfect aid that complements, but never supplants, human insight, creativity, or lived experience.

To my supporters and beloved friends worldwide—you know who you are. This book, perhaps the most significant of my career, exists because of your boundless generosity.

With deepest gratitude, from my heart,

Alan Clements

Author's Note

The voice of Daw Aung San Suu Kyi throughout this book is not a literal transcript. It is a devotional reconstruction—woven from decades of conversations with her and those closest to her.

Her presence, her cadence, her moral clarity—these live on in these pages not as direct quotation, but as an act of remembrance.

This book is not reportage. It is a collaboration of memory, empathy, and conscience.

ABOUT THE AUTHOR

Alan Clements is an internationally acclaimed author, investigative journalist, performing artist, and lifelong advocate for democracy. One of the first Westerners to ordain as a Buddhist monk in Myanmar, he was expelled for his outspoken criticism of the military regime. Since then, he has collaborated with resistance leaders, including Aung San Suu Kyi, to document Myanmar's struggle for freedom and explore themes of authoritarianism, nonviolent resistance, and the psychology of totalitarianism.

His work has been featured in Time, Newsweek, Democracy Now, Radio Free Asia, and other global media outlets. Clements is the author of several influential books, including *Burma: The Next Killing Fields?* (foreword by the Dalai Lama), *Voice of Hope* (a landmark dialogue with Aung San Suu Kyi), *A Future to Believe In, Instinct for Freedom, Burma's Voices of Freedom* (co-authored with Fergus Harlow), *A Meditator's Refuge: A Vipassana Insight Reference Guide*, and, most recently, *Conversation with a Dictator: An Illustrated Novel Confronting Myanmar's Tyranny and the Global Rise of Authoritarianism.*

Beyond writing, Clements' creative contributions include films, children's literature, and performance art. A recipient of the Visioneers Hero of Humanity Award, he has spoken at prestigious forums, such as Mikhail Gorbachev's State of the World Forum, and delivered the keynote address at Amnesty International's 30th Anniversary at the John F. Kennedy Center for the Performing Arts.

Clements co-founded UseYourFreedom.org with Fergus Harlow, an international campaign advocating for the release of Aung San Suu Kyi and Myanmar's political prisoners.

For more information, visit www.AlanClements.com. For the campaign, visit www.UseYourFreedom.org.

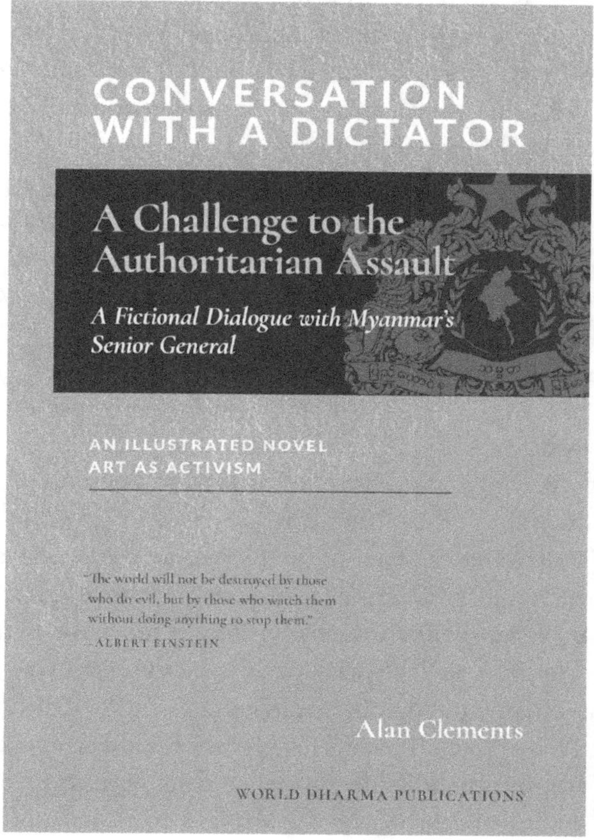

**Conversation with a Dictator: A Literary Reckoning.
A Spiritual Resistance.**

**A Call to Conscience. In an age of silence, this book dares to speak.
In a world of forgetting, it insists on remembrance.**

Part novel, part political indictment, part cinematic descent into the mind of tyranny, *Conversation with a Dictator* is a literary feature film rendered in ink and image. At its core is a fictional yet psychologically exacting dialogue between an exiled journalist and Myanmar's Senior General Min Aung Hlaing—the architect of a military regime that has imprisoned a nation, vanished its elected leaders, and silenced its Nobel Peace Laureate, Aung San Suu Kyi.

ut this is no conventional political drama. It's an act of exorcism—a forensic unmasking of the soul of dictatorship. Told in five acts and accompanied by over 300 haunting, symbolically rich illustrations, the novel becomes an immersive theatre of conscience. It does not describe repression; it embodies it.

The reader is not a bystander—they are a witness, a participant in the unraveling of delusion. What unfolds is a brutal ballet between conscience and power. The dictator speaks, not just to the journalist, but to the ghosts of those he has silenced. The "interviewer" may in fact be his own repressed moral self.

The prose is poetic. The images, arresting. The silences, thunderous.

And hovering over it all is the unspoken presence of Aung San Suu Kyi—absent in voice, but everywhere in spirit, as lotus, as shadow, as luminous defiance. Yet, Burma is only the beginning. This book speaks to a world in crisis—from the algorithmic autocracy of Silicon Valley to the surveillance states of the East; from patriarchal strongmen to soft censorship disguised as civility. It names the global architecture of repression. It makes the invisible visible. It maps the psychology of power's descent into madness. And it does so with language honed as a blade and art charged with moral voltage.

Written by Alan Clements—a former Buddhist monk, frontline journalist, and spiritual dissident expelled from Myanmar for exposing its regime—*Conversation with a Dictator* is a work born of decades of intimate resistance.

This is not just a book. It's a mirror held up to power. A hymn for the 22,000 political prisoners still in chains. A seed of memory planted against the machinery of erasure.

It's the voice of those the world has tried to silence, returning—unbowed, unforgotten, unbroken. Art as activism. Truth as rebellion. Conscience as the last frontier of freedom.

"Freedom and Democracy
Are Dreams You Never Give Up."
—AUNG SAN SUU KYI

"*In the end, we will remember not the words of our enemies,
but the silence of our friends.*"
—MARTIN LUTHER KING JR.